Crime Files

Series Editor
Clive Bloom
Professor Emeritus
Middlesex University
London, United Kingdom

Greenway

Since its invention in the nineteenth century, detective fiction has never been more popular. In novels, short stories, films, radio, television and now in computer games, private detectives and psychopaths, poisoners and overworked cops, tommy gun gangsters and cocaine criminals are the very stuff of modern imagination, and their creators one mainstay of popular consciousness. Crime Files is a ground-breaking series offering scholars, students and discerning readers a comprehensive set of guides to the world of crime and detective fiction. Every aspect of crime writing, detective fiction, gangster movie, true-crime exposé, police procedural and post-colonial investigation is explored through clear and informative texts offering comprehensive coverage and theoretical sophistication.

More information about this series at
http://www.springer.com/series/14927

Mark Aldridge

Agatha Christie on Screen

palgrave
macmillan

Mark Aldridge
Film and Television Studies
Southampton Solent University
Southampton, United Kingdom

Crime Files
ISBN 978-1-349-67695-8   ISBN 978-1-137-37292-5   (eBook)
DOI 10.1057/978-1-137-37292-5

Library of Congress Control Number: 2016955645

Cover illustration: © Zoonar GmbH/Alamy Stock Photo

Printed on acid-free paper

This Palgrave Macmillan imprint is published by Springer Nature
The registered company is Macmillan Publishers Ltd.
The registered company address is: The Campus, 4 Crinan Street, London, N1 9XW, United Kingdom

Dedicated to my late dad, Gary Aldridge

FOREWORD

Up until last October, when I retired as Chairman of Agatha Christie Ltd, I have been immersed in all things Agatha Christie since my grandmother died in 1976. Undoubtedly, the aspect of her work that took most time, and caused the most discussion, was in the adaptations of her work into film and television (not to mention the ones we refused to authorise!). When I heard that Mark Aldridge proposed to write the definitive analysis of this side of Agatha Christie's work, I have to confess that my reactions ranged from fascination to, sometimes, slight apprehension. I need not have worried.

When considering adaptations, my colleagues and I tried to strike a balance between satisfying the large band of passionate Agatha Christie fans, whose primary requirements were a faithful representation of the original story, and the modern television and film viewers, who simply wish to be entertained. The latter, of course, are more numerous, and without their continued support no adaptations would be considered by film moguls, television franchises or the like. When taking this approach, however, one lays oneself open to attack from both sides, sometimes deservedly so. It is to Mark's credit that while continually standing on the side of the consumer, he quite evidently understands and sympathises with the basic dilemma my colleagues and I have always faced.

I have enjoyed reading Mark's book (which is a jolly good read) not only because I am frequently reminded of discussions and negotiations gone by, which resulted in a good number of wry chuckles, but also because in the book there are revelations of correspondence and even relationships of which I was not aware. The book is a mine of information. Perhaps other readers may agree with me that as well as a fascinating insight into the history of Agatha Christie adaptations, the book also throws much light on the whole area of television and adaptation, and its participants on every side of the fence.

Finally, as I write this in early 2016, I am happy to say that many more Agatha Christie adaptations are in the pipeline—demand has never been higher.

This must mean that we have all done something right, and I hope that most of those concerned, viewers and everybody in the industry will sit down and enjoy Mark's book, because it is a fascinating piece of scholarship.

Mathew Prichard
Grandson of Agatha Christie
January 2016

Acknowledgements

Over the course of researching and writing this book, I have come into contact with dozens of people who have helped steer the project in some sense. Inevitably, I will have inadvertently missed out some names from these acknowledgements, but I would like to thank anyone who has taken the time to talk to me about Agatha Christie at any point over the last few years—it has invariably helped me to focus my work on areas that I felt would yield the most interesting discussion.

Firstly, I would like to thank my supportive colleagues at Southampton Solent University, past and present, all of whom have helped in some capacity through general support and interest or specific assistance. I would especially like to thank Darren Kerr, Jacqueline Furby, Donna Peberdy and Karen Randell for their encouragement, while I would also like to thank Terence McSweeney for kindly translating extracts from some of the Russian productions. I am particularly grateful to Claire Hines, not only for her general support of the project, but also her willingness to read almost the entire manuscript so that she could offer constructive and timely comments.

Thanks are also due to those who have provided opportunities for seemingly endless (and enjoyable) discussions about Christie's work in all manner of ways—whether one to one, at an academic conference or on social media. And so, thanks to Rhett Bartlett, Jamie Bernthal, David Brawn, Beverley Button, Mia Dormer, David Fitzgerald, Sophie Hannah and Marjolijn Storm, all of whom have provided interesting and helpful discussions and information about Christie's works.

Researching a topic to the extent required by this study means that I have often relied on others to help me follow up a particular lead, or guide me through unfamiliar archives. From the BBC Written Archives Centre, I would like to thank Jessica Hogg, Louise North and Hannah Ratford, as well as the Corporation's legal and business affairs manager, Lorraine Stiller. Similarly, I would like to thank the helpful staff at the British Film Institute in London, the Margaret Herrick Archive in Los Angeles and the Library of Congress in Washington, DC, all of whom helped me access the material I was looking for.

I have also had valuable assistance from Shauno Butcher, Peter Crocker, Ian Greaves, Toby Hadoke, Andrew Pixley, David Rolinson and Yasmin Wall, all of whom have supplied me with material or information that has helped this project. At my publisher, Palgrave Macmillan, I would particularly like to thank Benjamin Doyle and April James, with whom I have worked over the final few months of writing the manuscript, for their enthusiasm and prompt, helpful assistance.

In my introduction, I outline the special contribution to this book made by John Curran, the leading authority on Agatha Christie, and Mathew Prichard, Agatha Christie's grandson. On a personal level, their help has been instrumental in making the writing of this book such a pleasure. Not only have they offered general support and interest, they have also provided access to materials and information, while also taking part in many hours of discussions about Christie's works. I would especially like to thank John for his invaluable corrections and suggestions, while Mathew's kind agreement to grant permission for the reproduction of much of the archival material in this book has helped make this a distinctive piece of research. I am hugely grateful for the time that both John and Mathew have spent, especially when I know how busy they are. I would also like to thank Mathew's wife Lucy for her kindness and interest in the project, and to thank many of those working either directly or indirectly with the Agatha Christie archives. This includes the staff at the University of Exeter's special collections, as well as Joe Keogh of the family's own archive, and Eva Kelly and Lydia Stone of Agatha Christie Ltd—all have been hugely helpful.

Finally, I would like to thank my close family and friends for their general support, including my friend Sebastian Buckle, who read much of the manuscript and provided valuable feedback as well as proving to be a useful sounding board for ideas and complaints throughout my research. The biggest thanks need to go to my partner James Peel, as well as my family, including my mum Sarah, my late dad Gary and my sister Joanne, for supporting me throughout the long gestation period of this book.

CONTENTS

Introduction

The name Agatha Christie has connotations far beyond her authorship of many
novels, plays and short stories. I am writing this introduction some 125 years
after Christie's birth, and nearly 40 years since her death, and yet there is no
sign of her appeal diminishing, with new attempts to bring her stories to a
general audience continuing to appear. It would be fair to say that there is
something special about Agatha Christie. She is one of a select group of writers
whom many people consider to be genres in their own right, even though the
stories that she wrote encompass mysteries, thrillers, romances, supernatural
stories, historical dramas—and more. The fact that 'an Agatha Christie' can
mean something to the general public shows that there is a constant in her
writing that transcends simple categorisation. To explore the connotations of
her name would be a study in itself, but for this book the important point is
that she creates particular expectations from the audience—some may expect a
mystery, perhaps starring one of her best-known detectives, while others may
look for something light and whimsical, or dark and mysterious—but all will
anticipate a well-plotted story full of incident that commands the attention.

However, many people's first experience of Agatha Christie is not through
her original texts, but through adaptations of her work for film and television. Indeed, while I was writing this book, several acquaintances have declared
themselves to be fans of Christie, only to confess later that they have actually
never read a single one of her published works. While I would always advocate
that any fan of the screen adaptations should at least try some of Christie's
books, I would not be so dismissive as to suggest that they cannot be 'fans'
without having experienced the original, as the world of Agatha Christie is
so much bigger than the published stories. Popular understanding of Christie
now encompasses an indefinable quality that combines not only strong plotting
and characterisation, but also nostalgia and the high production values that
have long been present in the screen adaptations. Although Christie's original
stories remain the definitive canon, and sit at the core of any exploitation of

© The Author(s) 2016
M. Aldridge, *Agatha Christie on Screen*,
DOI 10.1057/978-1-137-37292-5_1

her works, they now combine with adaptations including graphic novels and computer games as well as radio, stage and screen productions and a plethora of merchandise, all of which evoke a sense of what 'Agatha Christie' means to people beyond her original writing.

Given the fact that I knew I was not alone in finding the screen productions of Christie's works fascinating, I have long been puzzled by the fact that they have not received more critical attention. While many general books about Christie will happily use illustrative material from key screen productions, the history of the relationship between Agatha Christie and the screen has generally been brushed over; honourable exceptions include a handful of academic papers tackling the area, including Sarah Street's excellent 'Heritage Crime: The Case of Agatha Christie'. However, although Robert Barnard and Charles Osborne have both written insightful and interesting critical guides to Agatha Christie, their emphasis is understandably on the original texts, while the two books largely dedicated to the screen adaptations (by Peter Haining and Scott Palmer) help to guide the reader through many of the adaptations, and were invaluable when published, but are now decades old and rely little on original archival material.[1] Generally, it is trivia and anecdotes that have served to give some indication of how various adaptations made their way to the screen; however, I knew that there were many more productions that had not even been acknowledged in print, let alone explored in any depth. Having seen so many excellent books covering other areas of Christie's life and works, including John Curran's studies and biographies by Janet Morgan and Laura Thompson (each of which helped to signpost some important information), by 2011 I was tired of waiting for an overarching history of Agatha Christie screen adaptations to be published—and so I decided to write one myself.

My original expectations for this book were small scale—in what was anticipated to be half the length of this volume, I planned to offer a textual analysis of the various screen adaptations of Agatha Christie's stories and look at how each of them approached the source material in a different way. To an extent this is still the case—for academics, this book is designed to work as a case study for how one prominent author's works can be brought to the screen in a variety of fashions. However, this is not a tome that frequently explores adaptation theory and other areas of academic discussion—it is principally aimed at those interested in tracing the story of how Agatha Christie's works made it to film and television. A historian at heart, I could not resist the temptation to use some of my research time to see what new information could be uncovered from various international archives, and I found so much material that I knew I had to use it in order to present an in-depth study and history of these adaptations of Christie's works. I decided to write a book that is a celebration of Christie's impact on film and television, even if much of that impact may have been unwitting. I did not wish to focus on dry academic discussions, but instead to offer a questioning history of events that have brought Christie's works to the screen, looking at attitudes towards adaptations from those involved as well as audiences. I soon discovered that the story behind these productions was a consistently surprising and interesting one. While many of us may be familiar with the broad sequence of events behind some of the best-known adaptations, I found at least as much interest regarding productions that have since faded into obscurity—sometimes fairly, sometimes not. My contribution, I hope, is in the way in which this book looks at the entire canon of Christie on screen and uncovers the rationale behind the individual productions, as well as the hopes for them and their impact. Throughout this study we will see the recurrent themes of the battle between fidelity to the source and perceived popular appeal—but, most tellingly, we will also see that apparently populist choices can often be counterproductive. As it stands, although this book runs to 16 chapters, almost any of these could have been expanded to be an entire book on their own. There is still much to be learned about Agatha Christie on screen, but I hope that this book will satisfy the interest of most people, as it shines a light on areas of her career and legacy that have hitherto been unexplored.

A significant reason this study is able to offer so much new information and previously unpublished correspondence from, and related to, Christie herself is due to the highly valued cooperation of two people. The first is John Curran, a name no doubt familiar to many readers of this book, as he is the world's leading expert on Agatha Christie, having curated her notebooks for publication by HarperCollins and worked extensively with her estate. I made contact with John in the early days of this project and, if I am honest, knowing the general attitude of experts in some fields, I expected to receive a proprietorial response at best, but this could not have been further from the truth. Since our first correspondence, John has been supportive, offering material that I could otherwise not obtain elsewhere, while being so helpful in discussing ideas and individual productions. After a short time, John kindly helped to put me in contact with the second key figure whose support and cooperation have made a significant impact on the information presented in this book—Mathew Prichard, Agatha Christie's grandson. Mathew and his wife Lucy warmly welcomed me into their home and the family archive, run by the ever-helpful Joe Keogh, where a treasure trove of correspondence and scripts helped to frame the story of Agatha Christie screen adaptations within a specific set of contexts. Mathew also graciously gave over a great deal of time to answer my many questions in three separate interview sessions, taking place across the course of more than two years, and gave me permission to consult without restriction the extensive archive material held by the University of Exeter. His assistance has been a great motivating factor for making this as comprehensive a history as I can provide within the publication confines for a book of this nature.

With mention of sources and archives, now may be a good point to explain how this book uses different methodologies, and what this means for different readers. This history employs a variety of approaches to telling the story of Agatha Christie on screen, depending on necessity, which is driven by the availability of source materials. For example, the first two sections of the book deal with a series of adaptations that are not always available to view—most early television productions were not recorded, while a wealth of films from cinema's first half-century have long since disappeared or been destroyed. This means that, when the original production is lost, it is necessary to use any other surviving material to reconstruct the missing adaptation—perhaps through synopses and scripts, or reviews, or production paperwork; whatever is available. This research for this book made use of material housed at archives including the Margaret Herrick Library in Los Angeles, the Library of Congress in Washington, DC, the BBC Written Archives Centre in Caversham and the British Film Institute in London. Combined with contemporary publications and the Agatha Christie archives in Exeter and those held by the family, we can usually (but not always) get a reasonable sense of what a production would have been like. However, this reconstructive approach is almost entirely unnecessary once we reach the 1960s, after which point almost all productions are extant; therefore, the methodology then necessarily changes, as the productions' availability allows for a more textual discussion, still alongside any significant background information. One constant is that critical reaction, original correspondence and production documentation are always used whenever possible, as they assist with giving a sense of context to both production and reception, and help to tell the story of the screen adventures of Agatha Christie's creations.

Because this book is structured in a broadly chronological fashion, more casual readers may be inclined to skip ahead to sections that cover productions with which they are more familiar; these readers should find that the sections are generally easy to follow even out of context, but I would advise starting at the beginning of the book where possible in order to trace the changing attitudes and interesting but lesser-known works. Although I have attempted to cover all productions fairly, regardless of origins, I am a British writer and as such the book is written from that perspective; as a consequence, I have also normally opted for British publication and release dates, unless I state otherwise. Many ostensibly British television productions and films have first been seen elsewhere, while many of Christie's own works were first published in the United States—by keeping to the British dates I hope to offer some consistency.

In terms of spoilers, I have done my best to avoid giving away any significant revelations, but occasionally this has proven impossible—especially when adaptations make radical departures from the source material. As a result, at the beginning of each chapter I have listed the names of any Christie publications whose solution may be inferred from my analysis, even if I do not explicitly state it. I would strongly advise that any readers who have not read the original stories to whose endings I allude should take a break from this book and catch up with the named Christie title before returning and seeing how the screen adaptation 'dunit.

Finally, there is the question of perspective. In telling a story of screen adaptations, whose perspective should be privileged above all others? I decided early on that I would try to look at this journey from the perspective of Christie herself and then, later, her family, principally because they are the only consistent players in this sprawling story. I have not shied away from using critical reaction and my own judgement to assess which productions worked particularly well, and which failed to achieve the desired impact. Similarly, I also try to include material from the producers and adaptors of the productions where possible.[2] What I have always tried to do is be sympathetic towards the original aims of the production. I do find unusual approaches to Christie interesting, and her work has had more than its fair share of fascinating failures alongside the rightly revered jewels in the crown.

For an audience that knows how effectively Christie's works could be transferred to the screen, there may sometimes be a sense of frustration that she was so frequently dismissive of any and all attempts to do so—but I hope that this book will help to justify this approach. Christie was clearly greatly hurt by changes made to her stories, and felt that the poor productions reflected badly on her, while she was also understandably proprietorial. Out of context, it may be frustrating to see that during much of the 1960s and 1970s Christie and her daughter, Rosalind Hicks, would often unilaterally dismiss any discussion of new film or television deals without even provisional discussion; however, when one sees how deeply wounded Christie was by various film projects (most especially the 1964 film *Murder Ahoy* and 1965's *The Alphabet Murders*), the reader may be more sympathetic. I hope that readers will come to understand Christie's approach somewhat better, while also appreciating those involved with the best productions a little more. Nothing could have been easier than Christie signing away various film and television rights to the highest bidder and simply living off the proceeds—and it is testament to her that she refused to do so. Nevertheless, as early as 1923, Christie demonstrated an understanding of the power that film could hold—if not dramatic, then at least financial. Writing to her publishers, she made it clear that cinema, dramatic and foreign rights were not to be casually included in her contract: 'Do your agreements always count 13 as 12?' she asked.[3] While she would never embrace the cinematic (or televisual) form to any significant extent, she understood its impact and potential—and this is precisely what this book will explore.

Notes

1. Specifically *A Talent to Deceive* by Robert Barnard, *The Life and Crimes of Agatha Christie* by Charles Osborne, *Murder in Four Acts* by Peter Haining and *The Films of Agatha Christie* by Scott Palmer.
2. There are practical restrictions at play here, of course—especially of word count. Perhaps one day there will be the opportunity to do this with books dedicated to individual films and series.
3. Janet Morgan, *Agatha Christie: A Biography* (London: HarperCollins, 1997), 110.

PART I

Finding the Agatha Christie Film Form, 1928–37

Chapter 1: The Silent Adventures

Spoilers: 'The Coming of Mr Quin'

It is not difficult to find an opportunity to watch most of the major screen productions of Agatha Christie stories. Even today, decades since the last major English-language film adaptation, many of the movies based on her work are frequently shown around the world on television, while most are readily available to purchase for home viewing. On certain television channels, screen adaptations of Christie's work are a near permanent fixture, shown on what may appear to be a constant loop, losing all sense of original context as high-definition remasters allow for little distinction between any of the major film and television productions from the last half-century. Rather than being seen as a myriad of screen adaptations from various countries, directors, performers and production companies, many Agatha Christie films and television series seem easily separable from any sense of time or place that might have been a crucial stabilising block of the original production. However, the films that turn up with such regularity do not tell the whole story, and may give the impression that the works of Agatha Christie moved to the screen with greater ease than was actually the case. For an indication of the difficulties faced in translating such a popular novelist from the page to the screen, we need look no further than the period covered by this first section, which deals with a lesser-known area of Agatha Christie on cinema screens: namely, the films made prior to the outbreak of war in 1939. Almost all of the movies explored in this section have not been commercially released or shown on television, while several are no longer known to exist, victims of archiving policies designed for short-term distribution rather than long-term preservation. This loss means that the emphasis will sometimes tend towards reconstruction as we build an understanding of how the films operated as adaptations. This forms the basis of our exploration of how Agatha Christie's works have been brought to the screen, often in ways that were highly interesting, if not necessarily faithful.

© The Author(s) 2016
M. Aldridge, *Agatha Christie on Screen*,
DOI 10.1057/978-1-137-37292-5_2

We start in 1928, the year in which Agatha Christie published her eighth novel, *The Mystery of the Blue Train*, a book that she found difficult to complete and that she would later claim was the first time she wrote out of obligation rather than for pleasure—an indication that she now saw her writing as a permanent career rather than a fleeting success. This change of perspective coincided with some of the first appearances of Christie's stories outside of the printed word, most notably the stage production *Alibi*, based on her novel *The Murder of Roger Ackroyd*. However, the year also saw the release of the first film to be based on one of her stories—a production that has posed several mysteries of its own.

THE PASSING OF MR QUINN (1928)

While the most significant films of 1928 included Al Jolson's second 'talkie', *The Singing Fool* (d. Lloyd Bacon), and the landmark French picture *La Passion de Jeanne d'Arc* (d. Carl Theodor Dreyer), the British silent movie *The Passing of Mr Quinn* (d. Leslie S. Hiscott) was produced on a somewhat smaller scale, on a low budget with modest aims for commercial success. The production was ostensibly an adaptation of Christie's short story of the same name that was later renamed 'The Coming of Mr Quin',[1] but the film differs so much from the original mystery that it sits alongside a small selection of screen adaptations that can only be described as 'originally influenced by Agatha Christie', since it is substantially unlike the original tale.[2] In Christie's story, a dinner-party discussion of a suicide that had taken place some years earlier is interrupted by the appearance of the mysterious and charming Mr Quin, whose gentle questioning of the participants results in the revelation that Derek Capel, the man who had taken his own life, had a dark secret from which he was trying to escape. This was Quin's first appearance and he would go on to be a semi-regular figure in Christie's work, but little of the original story was to make it onto screen—an early sign that Christie's works were not always adapted because producers were particularly keen on reproducing the narrative.

Unfortunately, this is one of a handful of Agatha Christie movies for which there is no known copy in existence, meaning that any discussion of it requires the piecing together of information in an archaeological manner. The lack of a known print of the film is undoubtedly the reason it has been relatively little discussed, but this does not mean that the production is either unimportant or uninteresting. In fact, combining the known information about the film presents an exciting puzzle of its own, as it soon becomes clear that this missing film was to play a significant role in the future of Agatha Christie screen adaptations. We are fortunate to have an unusually detailed outline of its plot thanks to a tie-in novelisation that would eventually become the source of some controversy.[3] Credited to G. Roy McRae (likely a pseudonym[4]), *The Passing of Mr. Quinn* was published as a small hardback edition in a series called The Novel Library, alongside such titles as a reprint of John Galsworthy's *Forsyte Saga* and some of the works of H.G. Wells. The novelisation is prefaced with an attempt to create some distance between this story and Christie's own work. Not only do the film and book add an 'n' to the Quinn of the title, but the novelisation's text actually changes the character name further, to Mr Quinny, opening with the curious disclaimer: 'Readers are requested to note that Mr. Quinny of this book is the same person as the Mr. Quinn of the film.'[5] We can have some confidence that this narrative conforms reasonably closely to what was seen on screen, as it correlates with the small number of photographs in existence as well as the contemporary synopses offered in the trade press.

In the film *The Passing of Mr Quinn*, the chemist Professor Appleby (played by experienced film actor Clifford Heatherley) is shown to be abusive to his wife Eleanor (Trilby Clark, an Australian actress who at 25 years old was 15 years younger than the actor playing her husband). Resultantly, Eleanor has sought comfort in a man named Derek Capel (Vivian Baron, in one of only three known film appearances by the actor), who has become her lover. Appleby is then murdered (by an apparently 'untraceable' poison[6]) and Capel disappears. Eleanor is placed on trial, which takes up much of the proceedings, only to be acquitted. So far, the plot has broad similarities to some of the events that are mapped out in Christie's short story; however, what follows is a convoluted and largely unrewarding plot that also fundamentally alters the character of Quinn. Eleanor leaves for Europe in order to become a nun, despite a new love for a doctor called Alec Portal (Stewart Rome, a prolific English film actor with over 150 credits to his name), who tracks her down after two years. Alec manages to convince her to return home, only then to discover a letter that he believes demonstrates that Eleanor killed her husband after all. At this point, the mysterious Mr Quinn also arrives in town. In the film's novelisation, Quinn (or Quinny) is described as a less than attractive character:

> [A] man with bent back, lips that twitched, and eyes that, behind the pince-nez he wore, had a fixed and curious look. His face was yellow, and as he raised his hat he revealed untidily matted hair, heavily streaked with white. [...] Yet his voice was pleasant and musical; it was the only part of him that seemed to have survived the blast of the storm that had struck him and prematurely aged him.[7]

Later, Quinn is shown to be an alcoholic who possesses 'satanic, jeery laughter' and is clearly nearing the end of his life.[8] Given the fact that Mr Quinn appears to possess every theatrically possible anomaly, it is probably unsurprising that this thoroughly unlikeable character is eventually revealed to be a disguise, donned by Derek Capel. Capel confesses to the murder of Professor Appleby and encourages Eleanor and Alec to live their lives together, shortly before he dies.[9] This revelation is nonsensical whether seen through the prism of the film as an adaptation of Christie's story, where this Quinn character bears no resemblance to her ethereal Quin, or as a film plot in its own right, where it serves no real purpose and comes too late in the proceedings to be any real puzzle or revelation. In Christie's story, the charismatic Quin simply encourages those present to work out the solution for themselves, and has no relationship with Derek Capel. The review in *Variety* was particularly dismissive of the film's depiction of its title character, pointing out that 'Everybody save the folk on screen recognized Quinn at once as Capel, so where there was any mystery and what it was still needs figuring out'; an existing photograph of Quinn supports this conclusion.[10]

One reason for the film not closely adhering to the short story's narrative is that the picture did not move into production to capitalise on the ongoing success of Agatha Christie's works, nor due to any particular desire to bring this story to the screen. In later years there would be many ingredients deemed essential to prestigious screen productions, including the emphasis on Britishness and nostalgia, a strong cast and lavish mise-en-scène. However, in this case the sense of national cinema was led by the industrial practices rather than any cultural distinctiveness. The motivating factor for this production was an Act of Parliament that had recently been passed: the Cinematograph Films Act of 1927. This Act was designed to respond to a perceived dominance of Hollywood movies at the British box office, and it introduced a quota for films that had to be produced in Britain by predominantly British crews and based on a scenario or script by a British writer. The result of this was a surge of 'quota quickies': cheaply made pictures that were often of low quality, created only in order to satisfy the government's new regulations. *The Passing of Mr Quinn* was to be one of the first of these, made on behalf of the film distributor Argosy and announced little more than a month after the Act was enacted in April 1928, with no secret made of the fact that it was produced simply in order to balance the foreign features that the company wished to release.[11] It was announced that production would take place at Twickenham Studios[12] under the auspices of producer Julius Hagen.[13]

The sweeping changes made to Christie's carefully structured work would no doubt have dismayed the author. Scholars such as Patricia Maida and Nicholas Spornick have referred to Christie's use of 'the puzzle game', whereby she focuses the reader's attention on the thrill of the chase when it comes to identifying a solution, while distracting them from the emotional reality of murder and serious crime, but it seems that for the audience of this film the distractions confused rather than diverted, especially when it came to the question of dual identity.[14] Quinn's apparently weak disguise throws up a particular problem of an obvious solution to the mystery, but the issue of characters masquerading as others is a common characteristic of Christie's mysteries and was to be a recurrent difficulty when it came to bringing her stories to screen. Christie often used her text to allow the reader to draw inferences that would later be revealed as false, including questions of identity. She does not cheat the reader, but does offer deliberate pieces of misdirection, allowing the dots to be joined to complete the wrong picture.[15] However, if an audience immediately recognises that two characters are played by the same actor—or, indeed, that two actors play the same character—then they will understand this to be a component of the plot. This means that there is a reliance on the effectiveness of any attempts to conceal identity, whether through make-up, costume or camera work—no matter how well plotted.[16] The principle of fair play for the home detective remains on screen as it did for those who read the story originally, but it can result in adaptations having to work hard to ensure that the audience's attention is not drawn to these characters.[17]

Even beyond the issue of an obvious disguise, *Variety*'s review was a strikingly negative one throughout. Calling it a 'poor picture', the reviewer uses his dissatisfaction with the film as a springboard for his further argument that film studios needed to spend more time planning their movies before production. 'Whatever may have been the merits of Mrs Christie's novel [sic], they have almost entirely disappeared in this film. [...] As told on the screen, [the] story is nonsensical.'[18] A sequence where Quinn interrupts a dinner party is described as 'one of the most unconvincing scenes ever watched in any film'.[19] The only positive words are reserved for Clifford Heatherley, who played Appleby, and the presentation of the murder trial, which was a double exposure with the accused on one side of the screen and the witnesses on the other—a stylish innovation at the time. British trade paper *The Stage* was less damning, saying that it 'tells the story of a crime in an effective way, although the action wants tightening up [... the director] Leslie Hiscott is inclined to overemphasise some of the action.'[20]

A review in the film trade periodical *The Bioscope* gives us a further idea of how well, or poorly, the film worked. More positive in tone than *Variety*, it was classified as 'Good for popular halls', citing 'The masterly use of suspense, the professor's death from poison, and the final scene when the murderer confesses' as selling points.[21] *The Bioscope* was most effusive in its praise of the acting, claiming that 'This is excellent in every sense. Stewart Rome plays the doctor [Alec] with much feeling. Ursula Jeans [who was later to have a prolific stage and screen career] is good as the maid. Mary Brough's part [as the cook] is a small one, but cleverly and amusingly played.' Brough had a long and varied film career, and was especially well known for her appearances in farces, so this praise is no surprise, although the reviewer states that 'probably the best performance is that of Trilby Clark as the wife'. Tellingly, Vivian Baron, who played the crucial dual role as Capel and Quinn, is not mentioned, perhaps to lessen his embarrassment given the ridicule of his performance elsewhere and the generally positive dispensation of *Bioscope* reviews. The production overall was said to be 'well staged, a great variety of scenes being introduced. The film is a long one, and a little condensation in the early scenes would be advantageous.'[22] In summary, the reviewer declared that the film was 'A highly sensational mystery of an eccentric professor's death. Gripping interest alternating with feebleness.'

The *Bioscope* review makes no mention of Christie's association with the film, and nor do the brief advertisements. This would likely have been either a relief to, or at the insistence of, Christie herself, given the fact that her biographer Janet Morgan suggests that Christie's disappointment with it was a crucial factor in her decision increasingly to write for performance herself. It is reasonable to conclude further that the film set a precedent for Christie expecting the worst from adaptations of her work. She may have welcomed the fact that *The Passing of Mr Quinn* made little impact, usually being presented as a supporting feature, although there is evidence that the film made it as far as the United States and Australia, where press reports highlighted the starring role for Antipodean Trilby Clark.[23] However, one reviewer, George A. Atkinson of the *Daily Express*, cited the film as one of his 20 favourites from 1928, so it did have its supporters.

Of course, the principle of an original story being adapted for the screen, only for the film itself to bear little or no resemblance to the original text, was not something that exclusively affected Agatha Christie's works, although she may well have found it particularly bothersome. In part, Christie's general dislike of any adaptation of her story by others, whatever the medium, can be traced back to her well-founded belief that having spent considerable time and effort constructing her stories and characters, meddling with the text almost always resulted in the removal of what she could perceive to be a stabilising block of the narrative. By its very nature, this is what adaptations do, but as she was alive and active during a period where her work was reworked for the radio, stage and screen, she was also witness to many early attempts to shoehorn it into unsuitable adaptations, often when the new media were in their infancy. The principle that fidelity to the text should be key to an adaptation has never been universal, and not just when it comes to Christie. For example, there had been all manner of Sherlock Holmes parodies and pastiches—including films merging original stories and chosen elements from Arthur Conan Doyle's own, such as *The Sleeping Cardinal* in 1931 that touched on elements from Conan Doyle's *The Empty House* as part of its original story. In fact, this film was directed by none other than Leslie S. Hiscott, and was released three years after he had adapted and directed *The Passing of Mr Quinn*.

DIE ABENTEUER GMBH [THE SECRET ADVERSARY] (1929)

The second, and final, silent film to be based on a Christie story was 1929's[24] *Die Abenteuer GmbH* (directed by prolific filmmaker Fred Sauer, adapted by German screenwriter Jane Bess) from the German studio Orplid-Film GmbH. Literally translated as *Adventures Inc.*, it was based on Christie's thriller *The Secret Adversary*, which had been published as a novel in 1922; although long thought lost, a print of the film is now known to exist.[25] Although their narratives diverge somewhat, the spirit of the book is broadly present in the film adaptation, even if the details of the plot are often absent or altered. The story follows the adventures of a young couple (the first appearance of Christie stalwarts Tommy and Tuppence, renamed Pierre and Lucienne for the film, played by Italy-born ex-boxer Carlo Aldini and English actress Eve Gray) who set up their own private detective agency. Both plots follow the investigation into one Jane Finn (Janette Finné in the film, played by German actress Elfriede Borodin in what seems to have been her screen debut) who was on board a recently sunken ship, which results in all manner of espionage and counter-espionage, all linked to secret documents in Finn's possession. Both the novel and the film are clear descendants of the serial adventure narrative—it was not unusual for Christie's novels to be serialised in advance of publication as a book, as was the case with *The Secret Adversary* in *The Weekly Times* during 1921, but rarely did a story seem more suited to this format. With many changes of location, an array of cliffhanger moments and a dazzling number of twists, Christie's story owes much to the serial form, which required a strong hook to retain its readership for the next instalment. The film adaptation is no different, as it moves from the action of a sinking ship through to a complex trail of espionage, finishing with a lengthy and visually impressive chase sequence. Such a structure is strongly reminiscent of the *Perils of Pauline* and *Hazards of Helen* schools of serial drama, where our eponymous heroines would find themselves in ever-changing but consistently dangerous situations, with the maximum amount of danger reserved for the end of each part, serving as an encouragement for the audience to visit the cinema whenever the subsequent episode was screened.

Although the serial adventure genre provided the broad thematic and structural inspiration alongside Christie's novel, it was certainly the contemporary rise in complex narratives that accompanied feature films in the late 1920s that allowed this particular plot to make it to the cinema screen. This is immediately obvious at the beginning of the film, as reams of plot and information are relayed in a succession of brief character shots and lengthy intertitles carrying the explanatory text. This opening, on board the doomed ship *Herculania*, is disorientating for the viewer, since for the most part it serves as a prelude for the major events of the following film, but features a cast of characters who will be mostly absent after this point, with the notable exception of Janette Finné. There is evidence that even at the time this caused some confusion, with the audience expecting it to serve some role in the resolution of the film, and the *Bioscope* reviewer saying: 'It is difficult to stifle a hope that [Janette's] brother, last seen when the ship is sinking, will ultimately reappear and influence developments, but he does not.'[26] Such an issue demonstrates the difference between presenting such an opening in terms of a serial, where it can reasonably be expected that the audience will have forgotten or lost interest in the opening scenes by the time of its resolution many weeks or even months later, and when placed together as a single feature, where this opening—while undoubtedly the impetus for the film's narrative—can lead the audience to infer that there will be a reunion or revelation, which ultimately does not arrive.

It is in the final third of the film that the action becomes most difficult to follow, as the audience is swept along by the sheer spectacle of the chases and stunts, including an impressively staged high-wire walk, rather than strictly following whatever the plot may be—a scenario still familiar to those watching many blockbuster films nearly a century later. *Die Abenteuer GmbH* is a good example of the issues that film studios encountered during this crucial transitional period from silent to synchronous sound features, as audiences no longer found the simple appearance of basic scenarios on screen to be a sufficient thrill, but the mechanics and knowhow for presenting a more complex plot that did not purely rely on imagery remained in their infancy. By 1929 silent film was in its final stage as Hollywood abandoned the form in favour of sound films that were financially more advantageous and, in theory, would more readily allow for the complex narratives of thrillers and mysteries that populated the majority of Christie's writing career. However, for a time the arrival of sound also resulted in the visuals of cinema taking something of a back seat, or even a backward step, as the practicalities of recording sound required more static cameras and carefully choreographed movements in order to capture sound correctly. *Die Abenteuer GmbH*, then, made its way into production at just the right time, as it coincided with the combination of greater narrative complexity and audacious visuals present in the dying days of silent cinema. One way in which the film showed its ambition was by filming in Southampton in the UK as well as in Germany in the winter of 1928, continuing into early 1929, marking quite a contrast with the low-budget aspirations of Britain's only Christie adaptation to this point.

Although it made relatively little impact outside of Germany, the film was broadly well received. In the UK, *The Bioscope* recommended it for 'houses where rapid action appeals', saying that the 'picture opens well' while commending the stunt work. However, it does decry the fact that 'soon the plot fails to hold the attention and the story degenerates into a rapid succession of sensational incidents'.[27] *The Stage* drew attention to the film's origins, calling it a 'good example of sensational literature adapted for screen purposes', indicating that the potential problems presented by adaptation were already well understood.[28] For *Variety* in the United States, the reviewer saw the film on its home turf, sending his review from Berlin shortly after the domestic release. After commending strongman Carlo Aldini for his role as Pierre ('he possesses not only strength and agility, but a very sympathetic personality, not without humour'), it summarises the film as 'One of those breathtaking detective stories with innumerable threads to disentangle, tastefully done and entertaining'. In summary, the reviewer declares the picture to be 'A popular success'—in Berlin, at least.[29] Janet Morgan claims that Christie was reasonably satisfied with *Die Abenteuer GmbH*, and it is easy to see why.[30] The film walks a fine tightrope between fidelity to the story and necessary changes to take advantage of the moving image, and with some success, although it is more interested in the latter than the former. While it is not without its problems, it does well as an early attempt to tell an action-orientated story.

The first two attempts to bring Christie's work to the screen had met with mixed results, but there were indications that her stories had strong potential to be suitable for film appearances. However, the next adaptations were to face the toughest challenge yet, as Christie's best-known character was soon to find his way to appearing on film.

NOTES

1. First published in the March 1924 edition of *The Grand Magazine* as 'The Passing of Mr Quin', and later renamed 'The Coming of Mr Quin' when published in the short story collection *The Mysterious Mr Quin* in 1930. The spelling of Quinn/Quin's name has often been the source of confusion and error. Christie's literary character is spelt Quin, while contemporary reviews and advertisements indicate that the film's title spells it Quinn.

2. Later chapters will suggest further additions to this category, but sitting alongside this film must also be 1964's *Murder Ahoy* and 1995's *Innocent Lies*, along with a handful of foreign-language adaptations.

3. No script is known to survive.

4. Certainly, 'he' has no other books or articles to his name that this writer could trace.

5. The rationale for this change appears to be that pressure was put on the author or publishers to ensure that the character is not 'passed off' as Christie's own Harley Quin. As will be seen later in the book, we know that Christie was at pains to insert a clause into later film contracts that forbade the depiction of any original stories featuring her characters in text form, but we do not know if this clause had been present for this particular film. Nevertheless, the fact that the novel's title remains the same while Christie's name is prominently placed on the dustjacket means that any such attempt was negated elsewhere.

6. This is notable since using an untraceable poison breaks one of the rules by which Christie abided: namely, the set of 'fair play' rules that Dorothy L. Sayers and the Detection Club established, adhered to by many of her contemporaries.

7. G. Roy McRae, *The Passing of Mr Quinn* (London: The London Book Company, 1928), 176–177.

8. McRae, *The Passing of Mr Quinn*, 182.

9. In the original story, Quin's 'passing' may be understood to represent his 'passing through' the mystery, leaving no trace. However, for the film Quinn's 'passing' appears to be more literal!

10. *Variety*, 29 August 1928.

11. *The Stage*, 10 May 1928—'Argosy is the latest firm to enter the production business to provide the necessary quota balance for its foreign features. The story chosen is a novel by Agatha Christie, and the title, at least during production, will be The Passing of Mr Quinn.'

12. At the time called Alliance Studios, but it would soon change its name to Twickenham Studios.

13. Hagen would take up residence at the studios for the next decade— Jeffrey Richards, *The Unknown 1930s* (London: I.B. Tauris, 2001), 40.

14. Patricia D. Maida and Nicholas B. Spornick, *Murder She Wrote: A Study of Agatha Christie's Detective Fiction* (Ohio: Bowling Green University Press, 1982), 68.
15. The 1928 short story 'Double Sin' is a particularly good example of this, as readers are introduced to an unusual young man with a pathetic moustache, as well as a woman who also has hair above her lip, raising questions of identity.
16. A rare exception is seen in both the 1934 film of *Lord Edgware Dies* and 1985's TV movie of the same story, using the US title *Thirteen at Dinner*, where the same actress plays the characters of Lady Edgware and Carlotta Adams—however, in the story the resemblance between them is crucial from the beginning and is not presented as a later revelation.
17. As an example, ITV's *Poirot* series (1989–2013) has tackled this issue several times, with varying success.
18. *Variety*, 29 August 1928.
19. *Variety*, 29 August 1928.
20. *The Stage*, 9 August 1928.
21. *The Bioscope*, 1 August 1928.
22. 8259 feet, or almost 92 minutes. This assumes that the film was to be projected at 24 frames per second, which was standard in the latter years of silent film production; 92 minutes was only a little longer than normal for this period, when most standard British films would be 70–90 minutes, although prestige productions often ran longer.
23. *The Advertiser* (Adelaide), 7 August 1929.
24. Often referred to as a 1928 film, which was when much of it was filmed. I usually refer to films by the year in which they were released, and this picture was released in Germany in early 1929, although it was not seen in the UK until later in the year.
25. Translated into English, the film's title is *Adventures Inc*. Some sources indicate that it was released under this title in the United States—when reviewed by *Variety* while it was playing in Berlin the title was translated as Adventure Limited, but in the UK its contemporary *Bioscope* review indicates that it was released under the title of the original novel, *The Secret Adversary*.
26. *The Bioscope*, 2 October 1929.
27. *The Bioscope*, 2 October 1929.
28. *The Stage*, 10 October 1929.
29. *Variety*, 20 March 1929.
30. Morgan, *Agatha Christie: A Biography*, 177.

Chapter 2: Poirot Comes to the Silver Screen

Spoilers: *The Murder of Roger Ackroyd*; 'Philomel Cottage'; *Love from a Stranger*

This chapter looks at the remaining Agatha Christie film adaptations made prior to the Second World War, three of which featured her famous detective Hercule Poirot, while a further production reworked a successful stage adaptation of a Christie short story for the first time—but not the last. However, before the film industry tackled one of Christie's most enduring tales, 1931 saw the first of many attempts to solve one of the toughest problems when it came to bringing her best-known character alive for an audience—how, exactly, can one cast the Belgian detective with his precise demeanour and curiously egg-shaped head? For this first attempt the issue was less complex than it would become, as close adherence to the character as written appeared not to be a concern of producers. Instead, 33-year-old British actor Austin Trevor took on the role of Hercule Poirot in the first of three films.

ALIBI (1931)

In later years Christie would bemoan the difficulties of allowing others to write dialogue for her characters, while she also chastised herself for creating such an impossible character as Poirot in the first place. She flagged up these difficulties to her readers through her fictional creation Ariadne Oliver, a mystery writer who makes similar complaints about dramatised adaptations of mysteries featuring her own detective, Sven Hjerson from Finland. In 1952's *Mrs McGinty's Dead*, Christie has Oliver say to Poirot:

> But you've no idea of the agony of having your characters taken and made to say things that they never would have said, and do things that they never would have done. And if you protest, all they say is that it's 'good theatre'.[1]

Certainly it is easy to believe that Christie had her own experiences in mind here. Writing about the process of working with Michael Morton, who adapted her famed novel *The Murder of Roger Ackroyd* into the play *Alibi*, first staged at

© The Author(s) 2016
M. Aldridge, *Agatha Christie on Screen*,
DOI 10.1057/978-1-137-37292-5_3

the Prince of Wales Theatre in London's West End in May 1928, she expressed dissatisfaction with the changes made, although the broad narrative of the mystery remained unaltered. 'I much disliked his first suggestion, which was to take about twenty years off Poirot's age, call him Beau Poirot and have lots of girls fall in love with him', she writes in her autobiography.[2] In the end this did not happen, but Christie remained dissatisfied with some aspects of the play, especially the replacement of Dr Sheppard's sister Caroline with a much younger woman. Christie's caution about others adapting her work may explain the choice of the first two films to feature Trevor's Poirot, *Alibi* and *Black Coffee*, both released in 1931 and once more directed by Leslie S. Hiscott at Twickenham Film Studios. Hiscott was brave to try his hand at Poirot, given the fact that his previous Christie film had so dissatisfied the author, as well as many critics, two years earlier. The rationale for the choice of these two titles would seem to be eminently practical. Both had ready-made scripts fresh from their theatrical productions (Christie penned the original mystery play *Black Coffee* herself, which was first performed in 1930), which brought with them some public awareness from the attendant publicity, and they no doubt helped with the British film quota now being imposed on distributors.

Alibi was the first of the films to be made and released and, as with the next Poirot film *Black Coffee*, it is now believed to be lost. While the stage production of *Alibi* had not met with Christie's complete approval, she may have consented to its appearance on film because she saw it as a battle already fought, with compromises now made, although some further changes were made by screenwriter H. Fowler Mear, who had experience in quickly writing competent and professional, if unexciting, scripts for the studio. Further, she could not fail to notice that the play had gone on to be something of a success. Perhaps tellingly, four decades later Christie would once more make mention of the changes that Morton made for the stage production but, in the same letter, said that she was unaware of any film version.[3] Clearly, the changes for the stage had made more impression on her than the later film. The picture's lost status does leave us with many tantalising questions of practicality—for example, how did the film distract us from the murderous events in the study (something easily achieved by a closed door on stage)? In all versions of the story the precise timing of the murder is crucial to the final revelation of the killer's identity, so the film would need to tread carefully in order not to signpost the fact that one person's apparent alibi is a fraud. We may also wonder whether the film moved beyond the locations seen in the stage version to show more of the village and the house's surroundings. If it did, then this made little impression, as *Variety* reported that the 'very conventional' film 'cannot be rated as good, or placed as anything but a second feature' while comparing it unfavourably with the stage production, saying that the movie was 'cramped, along stage lines' although 'suspense values are occasionally good'.[4] It dismissed the production as nothing more 'than an attempt to make money with a fast one'.[5]

Beyond its stage origins, the most striking aspect to note about the film is the marked dissimilarity between Austin Trevor's Poirot and the character as written by Christie. While Charles Laughton had played him on stage in *Alibi* as the traditional rotund mustachioed character, on screen Austin Trevor is not only tall and young, but is also blessed with a head that could not be described as 'egg shaped'. However, the greatest sin is not physical but geographical, for it appears that Trevor's Poirot is not Belgian but French, something that had also been alluded to in the original *Alibi* play, but was now in danger of becoming his popularly accepted nationality. *Picturegoer Weekly* flagged up these differences in a brief piece by its editor S. Rossiter Shepherd, under the headline 'Bad Casting', which highlights that such changes did not go unnoticed:

> A number of readers have written me complaining that although Mr Trevor's acting in the part leaves nothing to be desired, he is emphatically nothing like Poirot as described in Mrs Christie's novels. I am a great Poirot 'fan' and the moment I heard that Trevor was going to impersonate him on the films I realised that it was bad casting. The detective is described by the authoress as an elderly man, with an egg-shaped head and bristling moustache. Austin Trevor is a very good-looking young man and clean shaven into the bargain. By a coincidence I happened to run into him in the street this week, and I put the matter to him. Trevor admitted that he was unlike Mrs Christie's conception of Hercule, but blamed the powers-that-be for giving him the part. He thinks it is because some years ago he happened to play a Frenchman in a picture.[6]

The repeated claim that Trevor's Poirot is French in articles concerning his films could be attributed to a lack of attention to detail by the press, but when he is described as such to his face in 1934's *Lord Edgware Dies* (the third, and final, film starring Trevor as Poirot), he does not challenge it; 'You Frenchmen are so cute, I just love your Parisian manners!' says Lady Edgware—perhaps we could convince ourselves that Poirot's politeness prevents him from offering a correction. However, given the extent to which his apparent French nationality is mentioned in secondary material, it seems likely that this is a deliberate intention on the part of the film-makers, and one that echoes his nationality as depicted in the stage production. This may be anathema to fans of Belgium's most famous detective, but it is not the last time this mistake has been made, as we will see. It is easy to dismiss this as a point of pedantry, but to those who have read the Poirot stories, as well as to Christie herself, this should serve as the biggest indication that the rights to film Poirot stories had been purchased as a recognisable and marketable commodity associated with his name and general character, rather than due to any particular keenness to exploit the details of Christie's intricate mysteries. It also demonstrates Christie's lack of involvement with the film once the contract had been signed, as she would never have allowed such an exchange to take place.

Contemporary reviews were divided on the film's merits. The week following its article about Trevor's depiction of Poirot, *Picturegoer Weekly* showed itself to be well disposed towards the film's direction, saying that 'there is plenty of freedom and movement from stage conventions', which indicates that this was more than simply a straightforward filming of the play, which it felt 'took its time getting into its stride', as is often the case with murder mysteries.[7] Later in the picture, however, the reviewer felt that 'Without misleading the audience, the director cleverly represents a series of deductions which lead to an unexpected conclusion'.[8] Although still bemoaning the choice of Trevor, the review calls the film 'a good, well thought out detective story, and one which you will find entertaining'. The one note of real caution among the cast was John Deverell's performance as 'silly ass' Lord Halliford, which, the reviewer felt, 'is completely of the stage and liable to militate against conviction'; this was an early screen appearance for the actor, but he would go on to perform in small roles on film and television for the next 25 years.[9]

The Bioscope similarly took issue with Deverell's 'silly ass' performance and character, even using the same words to describe him, but said that Hiscott had 'made little attempt to break away from the stage play, with the result that this film relies almost entirely upon the super abundance of dialogue for effect'.[10] While it does say that the interior scenes are 'tastefully and impressively mounted', it claims that 'Real action is lacking'.[11] Although 'The ultimate revelation provides a genuine surprise climax', the review expressed displeasure with some of the finer details of that climax's plotting.[12] Declaring the film a 'Good second feature offering', it commended Trevor's acting as well as most of the other cast, with only Harvey Braban as Inspector Davis coming in for any criticism ('rather too heavy and melodramatic' stated the review); Braban's performance in this role echoed his most famous screen role, as the Chief Inspector in the 1929 film *Blackmail*, directed by Alfred Hitchcock.[13] Elsewhere, the *Manchester Guardian* drew comparisons between Trevor and Charles Laughton's[14] depictions of Poirot, calling the former's portrayal 'perky, impish, volatile'.[15] Its indifferent review pointed out, perhaps not unfairly, that 'it cannot be said that in swift cinematic treatment the highly artificial complications of the tale gain in credibility', although any such criticism must also be laid at the door of the play.[16] However, for this reviewer at least, 'By the end the hounds have smelled too many red herrings to be interested in their real quarry'.[17] This was positively ebullient in comparison with the *Daily Express*'s one-word review ('Slow'[18]), while the *Daily Mirror* was almost as concise in its simple commendation of 'a splendid cast'.[19] Overall, the first Poirot film was not an unqualified success, but it certainly showed that there was interest in the potential of seeing the sleuth on screen, even if this particular production had not resulted in much enthusiasm.

BLACK COFFEE (1931)

Alibi was still in cinemas when its follow-up, *Black Coffee*, received its trade screenings in August 1931. H. Fowler Mear once again reworked the play's script for the screen, this time with the assistance of fellow screenwriter Brock Williams. Although this story had been specifically written for performance (albeit on stage), it does not necessarily follow that this resulted in a stronger basis for the film adaptation. Indeed, the fact that this was a mystery always intended for the stage results in a necessarily static story, which on stage takes place entirely in one room, a country house's library. The action follows a top-secret formula that has been stolen from the house of leading physicist Sir Claud Amory, who calls in Poirot and his associate Captain Hastings, only to be fatally poisoned shortly before their arrival. Characters arrive and depart as the plotting dictates in a manner that is natural for the stage, but the locations would have required broadening out in order to make a satisfactory film production. The review in *The Bioscope* does refer to multiple locations, although it points out that they are mostly interior, so there was some attempt to add verisimilitude to the imposed requirements of the stage script.[20]

One area that was singled out for disdain among the critics was the performance of the supporting cast. All seemed to agree that Trevor was ably assisted by Adrianne Allen as Lucia—she had come fresh from originating the role of Sybil in the 1930 West End run of Noël Coward's *Private Lives*—but most of the other cast did not fare so well. 'The film could have been made more convincing had all the actors been equal to the task,' bemoaned *The Bioscope*, 'several of whom certainly overacted'.[21] The *Daily Express* laid the fault not at the door of the actors themselves, however, saying that they 'labour nobly against the banal dialogue and ingenious situations' as it went on to criticise the picture as a whole, calling it 'just a waste of money and good celluloid, for it is a mystery thriller that neither mystifies nor thrills'.[22] *Picturegoer Weekly* flagged up a different issue with the film, criticising it for being 'too slow to grip the attention' as well as being 'hackneyed'.[23] *The Times* was a little more positive, describing the film as 'a reasonable and competent piece of work'.[24] Elsewhere, despite its criticism of some of the cast, *The Bioscope* was generally positive towards the film even given its dismissal of Christie's plot being 'on sternly stereotypical lines', since it described the picture as better than *Alibi* and offered some commendation to Hiscott's direction, especially when it came to the film's conclusion, where it claimed that 'The very best has been made of a thrilling sequence just before the final fade-out' concerning Poirot's apparent poisoning.[25] *The Times of India* simply referred to it as 'an intriguing detective drama [...] capably directed' and 'full of weird mystery',[26] while the *Daily Mirror* called it 'an exciting and unusual murder story with a twist at the end'.[27] Perhaps the reaction to this second Poirot film was best summarised by a brief review in *The New York Times* in September 1931. 'The English critics did their best for it,' wrote Ernest Marshall, 'but their praise was too faint to catch the ears of the multitude.'[28]

Lord Edgware Dies (1934)

Three years would pass before Austin Trevor made his third and final screen appearance as Poirot in 1934's *Lord Edgware Dies*, the only one of the early Poirot films currently known to have survived.[29] This was a long time in the early days of sound pictures, which saw the film industry rapidly adapt to new production techniques, and the audience could reasonably expect that by this stage the direction would be more confident, innovative and fluid as the new sound technology became more flexible. However, the film is clearly still confined by either budget or directorial skill, indicating that the lukewarm response to earlier productions was merited. For example, although its lack of incidental music was not particularly unusual in the early days of sound pictures, the use of a score to complement and underpin the action would soon become the norm, and *Lord Edgware Dies* is ample demonstration of the reason. As a studio-bound, dialogue-heavy and action-light film it makes for dry viewing, a viewpoint shared by some contemporary critics, with *Picturegoer Weekly* summarising that 'Too much dialogue and a tendency to slowness rob the picture of a lot of legitimate suspense'.[30]

The existence of a full print of the film does allow us to see how Christie's creations came across in these early screen adventures. The lack of incidental music also serves to emphasise the performances, which carry more weight when it comes to both the entertainment and attention of the audience. However, the vagaries of sound recording and reproduction during this period mean that dialogue needed to be slow and deliberate so that it could be properly heard, however good or poor the cinema's facilities. This leads to slow and stilted sections of dialogue that lack atmosphere and only serve to distract the audience from the mystery. As some of the press had pointed out, Trevor is clearly miscast for Poirot as envisaged in literature, being tall, young and clean shaven. His performance in its own right is fair, but he seems a little uncomfortable with either the accent or the role and is not a particularly charismatic screen presence here. Faring worse is his companion Captain Hastings, played by mustachioed Richard Cooper (a British actor frequently cast by Hiscott), who is an irritating presence throughout the film. Cooper's Hastings ineffectually offers attempts at comedy at inopportune times, such as walking into a wall when on his way to meet Lord Edgware. This Hastings may have been one of several prototypes for the worst excesses of Nigel Bruce's Watson, who would first appear alongside Basil Rathbone's Holmes five years later. One reviewer succinctly called him 'the usual silly-ass assistant', echoing criticism of John Deverell's performance as Lord Halliford in *Alibi* three years earlier. Praise was reserved for John Turnbull's unremarkable performance as Inspector Japp; both Cooper and Turnbull had played the same roles in *Black Coffee*, and Turnbull was at the peak of his screen career—in his lifetime he would appear in nearly 100 films, of which at least 13 hail from 1934.[31] Some attempts were made to present dialogue-based comedy, no doubt trying to add some levity to what is otherwise a reasonably dark tale, but they did not work particularly well. When Poirot asks 'You believe in heredity, Hastings?', the latter replies 'You bet I do, that's how I got my money!', which is one of Hastings's more amusing moments, but witty repartee is rather misjudged when it comes to the conclusion of the picture. After the murderer is revealed and Poirot points out that the miscreant tried to pull the wool over his eyes, Hastings interjects 'I'm hanged if we can have that!' 'Under the circumstances, that's a very tactless remark' responds the villain of the piece just before the end title card fades in.

The choice of *Lord Edgware Dies* for adaptation was certainly a sensible one. Concentrating on the murder of the title, the story also features a range of interesting characters, not least Edgware's estranged widow who is an early suspect, while a great deal of the plot serves to misdirect the audience in a wholly satisfactory manner. It also relies on questions of potentially deceptive appearances—perfect for the visual opportunities of the cinema. While necessarily simplified, the mystery is largely intact in this adaptation. It was also a recent title, having been published in 1933, and so brought with it a certain amount of residual publicity. However, it was received indifferently by the press and seems to have made less of an impact than the previous two Poirot films. *Picturegoer Weekly* declared it a 'Workmanlike detective yarn [...] It is a conventional affair, with suspicion falling on a number of characters after the murder of a nobleman, but the solution is quite ingenious and the "red herrings" not too obvious.'[32] *Monthly Film Bulletin* simply referred to it as offering 'Quite good entertainment and excellent acting throughout',[33] while *The Observer* called it 'Hearty British entertainment of its type'.[34]

Christie may have been pleased that, as with the other two Austin Trevor Poirot films, her mystery made it onto screen without too many egregious alterations. However, the issue of the film supplying satisfactory characterisation and suitable performances remained. In a 1932 letter to her husband, Max Mallowan, she expressed excitement that she had been approached by a film company that had suggested she might make as much as £200,000 from a deal to adapt her works for the cinema screen.[35] It may be that this film company was Real Art Productions (or Twickenham Film Studios), proposing a deal to adapt Christie's novels rather than her plays, which may have then resulted in *Lord Edgware Dies* making it to the screen. If this is the deal being referred to, then clearly it was not enough of a success for any multi-picture deal to be taken up. Nevertheless, more films were forthcoming.

In fact, more films had been made than Christie, or her agents Hughes Massie, appeared to be aware. In 1936, the agency was perturbed to hear a claim that a French adaption of *Black Coffee* had apparently been produced, and made enquiries to find out if it was true.[36] It was. *Le Coffret de laque* (literally, *The Lacquer Box*, referring to a box containing chemicals that plays a key role in the play) had been released in France in July 1932. The atmospheric posters gave the box of the title a central position, but omitted any mention of Agatha Christie. Produced by Oceanic Studios, directed by Jean Kemm and adapted by Pierre Maudru, the film starred three actors who hailed from one of the most prestigious French theatre troupes, Comédie-Française—namely, René Alexandre (playing 'Préval', this production's name for Poirot), Maxime Desjardins (Claud Amory) and Maurice Varny. *Variety* gave it a mediocre review, writing 'Acting all round is satisfactory', although it bemoaned 'the childish transparency of it all'.[37] The film was publicised as, variously, a thriller, a detective film and a romance, but does not appear to have made much of an impression on the French public. However, French newspaper *Le Matin* referred to it as 'exciting' and commended the performances while highlighting its Christie roots, so there is every chance that she was credited some-where.[38] *Le Figaro*, another French newspaper, was well disposed towards the film, describing it as an 'honest thriller' while commending its sets.[39]

LOVE FROM A STRANGER (1937)

There was to be one more British Christie film adaptation before both the coming of war and Hollywood's first foray into making versions of her stories for the screen. The 1937 *Love from a Stranger* (d. Rowland V. Lee) was to make the biggest impact of any Christie adaptation to date, but the role of Christie in the publicity was markedly small. The film was, in fact, a full generation away from her original tale, since it was an adaptation of the stage play of the same name, which had been written by actor and writer Frank Vosper, adapted from Christie's short story 'Philomel Cottage'.[40] The film concerns a young woman (Carol, played by Ann Harding in the film) who comes into money shortly before the arrival of a charming stranger who sweeps her off her feet (Gerald, played by a pre–Sherlock Holmes Basil Rathbone). The first half of both the film and the play largely covers romance and comedy, but the second half shows a creeping sense of suspicion towards Gerald—has he married Carol for her money and, if so, will he commit murder to get it? The play had been a popular and critical success in the West End when it was first produced in 1936, and the film was keenly anticipated.

Most of the publicity surrounding the film placed the emphasis firmly on two areas. The first was the producer, Hungarian-born Max Schach, who was cultivating a reputation for spearheading lavish British film productions. Meanwhile, the second avenue of publicity focused on the fashionable clothing worn by its star, Ann Harding. This emphasis targeted a secondary market, those who were interested in Harding's star power and her accompanying wardrobe. She was an American actress whose performances in several Hollywood films had been well received, and she was bringing some of the Los Angeles glamour with her. A month before the film's premiere, the *Daily Mirror* told its readers to 'make a note and take a look at the frocks of the crowd girls in Ann Harding's first English film, *Love from a Stranger*'.[41] By the time the film had been seen in January 1937, the juxtaposition between the thrills of the final act and Harding's ever-changing glamorous wardrobe in the picture was flagged up by the *Daily Express*, which referred to the film as 'a most Ritzy thriller. It might be called "The Bride of Frankenstein—Models by Worth," [...] or "Hangman Fashions of 1937!" It is a brides-in-the-bath spine chiller. A bride in a Cecil B DeMille bath.'[42] Quotes purporting to be from Harding also supported several fashion pieces including two in the *Daily Mirror*, one concerning her travelling outfit seen in the film ('Talking of hats, Miss Harding says: "If you have long hair, with a biggish bun at the back, never hide it away"'[43]), while the other claims to be a suggestion for using spare pieces of material ('almost every woman goes to the sales at some time or other and sees remnants of lovely materials which she wants to buy, but doesn't know how to use them afterwards. Well, here's an idea from Ann Harding [...]'[44]).

This extensive publicity was a first for a Christie film, but the author was not the motivating factor behind it. Schach had given the film a generous budget (newspaper reports marvelled at the elaborate costumes supplied for background extras), but did not ignore any avenue for publicity. A *Daily Mirror* report following the premiere discussed his journey

> from being a penniless German [sic] journalist in Paris to the position of a man controlling £2,000,000 in film finance in this country to-day. At one or two early disasters eyebrows may have been raised. They will be raised again at the expense he has lavished on *Love from a Stranger* in:
>
> - Giving Frances Marion, Hollywood scenarist who never works on a picture for less than £5,000 down, the job of adapting the film;—
> - Bringing first-class from Hollywood Ann Harding and Basil Rathbone and employing them for the film at three-figure weekly salaries;—
> - Spending, early last year, £300,000 in rent for three of Denham's ultra-modern studios.

The report concluded that this had been money well spent, as it said of the film that it was 'a study in the macabre—even more spine-tickling than Agatha Christie's original short story or the play of it recently shown in London'.[45]

The publicity press book for the film had happily emphasised the fashions and given the press several suggestions for covering this aspect, but had not entirely overlooked its potential male audience. The tagline for one featured poster was 'The story with a sock that women will love and men will rave about'.[46] Elsewhere, the book contained numerous suggestions for newspaper competitions and features on not only the film's fashions, but also tie-ins with chemists, cosmetics, even typewriter shops. Mention of Agatha Christie is fleeting, but one suggested tagline echoes a later production,[47] imploring 'Please don't tell your friends the climax!'

Such a plea is curious in the context of *Love from a Stranger*, however. To a modern audience the most striking aspect of the plot is its surprising lack of mystery. Gerald arouses suspicions from the beginning of the film, despite (or perhaps because of) his charm, and so his eventual attempt to kill his wife is well signposted. An obvious comparison can be made with Alfred Hitchcock's *Suspicion* (1941), which makes the audience question the motives of a charming husband who may or may not be trying to murder his wife. In Hitchcock's film there is reasonable doubt and a final twist, but *Love from a Stranger* is a more straightforward depiction of Gerald's desperate attempts to make his plan work and Carol's growing suspicions. One sequence halfway through the picture leaves the audience in no doubt, when Gerald's mania grows while developing photographs of his wife to the frenetic tune of *In the Hall of the Mountain King*, which increases in speed and ferocity as his 'madness' (to use Gerald's words) gains control. He also takes the opportunity to explain to his wife the background to his head pains, referring back to the Great War as he remembers that 'standing in cold terror in the trench [...] turned my first ter-ror into ecstasy'. It is an unsophisticated explanation, but it does serve to offer some context for Gerald's actions beyond a purely cynical desire for money.

As a film adaptation of a stage play, *Love from a Stranger* does well to broaden out the action. Although the final half is necessarily, and effectively, claustrophobic, taking place in the new marital home, the film does not feel constrained by its origins. Shots of London help to set the scene early on, before we follow Gerald and Carol to Paris and its locales—courtesy of interior sets and back projection, but effectively done. The cast is uniformly good, including an appearance by Joan Hickson as the ditzy maid; this would not be her last appearance in a Christie adaptation. The transition from comedy and romance in the first half to the tense finale (the film was released as *A Night of Terror* in the United States, after all) is well done and ensures that the audience is not fatigued by the straightforward thriller aspects too early on.

The film was certainly the best-received Christie picture to date, although this transition from comedy did not entirely work for some reviewers. The *Daily Express* referred to the movie as '18 carat', but bemoaned that 'The change from comedy to a study of criminal mentality is abrupt', while commending the final act as 'an unrelieved duet in the macabre'. The reviewer also points out that there was 'at one juncture [...] the loudest scream I have heard in a cinema. That's a tribute.'[48] A later review in the same newspaper claimed that 'when the end comes, you gasp and realise you haven't breathed for an uncom-fortably long time. The two principals probably over-acted madly towards the end. Nothing less would have registered on my shock-dazed senses—and they certainly did register.'[49] *The Times* responded positively to the film, writing that 'suspense is skilfully maintained throughout',[50] while Henry Gibbs, writing in *Action* magazine, put it succinctly: 'Good performances, good story—what more do you want?'[51]

Across the Atlantic, *Variety* reviewed the film twice. It was first declared 'Gorgeously photographed and splendidly cut [...] takes front rank with the long list of gruesome films produced in recent years'.[52] Later, the publication gave a fair assessment that the film contained 'a couple of reels of dramatic dynamite. But the rest is inconsequential.'[53] *Monthly Film Bulletin* and *Sunday News* were less enamoured of the picture, however. The former said that 'The photography is up to standard, the tempo throughout uneven, at times intoler-ably slow while direction seldom gets far from the conventional when dealing with a scenario often overcharged from incidents'.[54] However, it may be seen as a positive that it went on to say that the film 'is sufficiently successful in cre-ating its atmosphere as to be unsuitable for the highly strung or nervous. It is quite unsuitable for children.'[55] Meanwhile, the *Sunday News* gave the film two and a half stars, running with the headline 'Harding movie lets fans down', and criticising it for an 'unexpected lack of conviction'.[56]

Overall the film did well, and was sufficiently successful in creating a thrill-ing and uneasy atmosphere that the usually liberal Danish censors banned the film outright.[57] Despite its success, a year later Max Schach and Capitol Films had nevertheless left London, leaving behind questions of how successful his British producing career had really been.[58]

Never one to take her eye off the ball, Christie had continued to discuss the issue of film rights for her novels with her agent Edmund Cork at the Hughes Massie agency. In March 1936 he wrote to her to say that he thought they would probably sell the rights to her novel *The ABC Murders* to MGM—something that would eventually happen, but the resulting picture was not released until nearly three decades later, as the relatively unsuccessful 1965 comedy-mystery *The Alphabet Murders*.[59] A letter a few weeks later reveals that MGM was also interested in the film rights to *Love from a Stranger* even before the play opened, such was the confidence in the production.[60] In the end, the Broadway run of the play under-performed, so Cork would later point out that Christie did rather well by selling the US rights early.[61] A memo to Edmund Cork from an unnamed colleague indicates exactly what MGM was offering Christie in order to dramatise her works for the cinema.[62] It pointed out that 'The great difficulty is finding a man to play Poirot', before listing the offer. *The ABC Murders* was the title on which MGM was most keen, offering $7500 to buy it outright, with further $7500 options for *The Murder at the Vicarage*, *Murder on the Orient Express* and *The Sittaford Mystery*. It then wanted further options at $6250 each for *Peril at End House*, *Three Act Tragedy*, *The Mysterious Affair at Styles* and *Lord Edgware Dies*, which was then ruled out as the rights were unavailable for the seven years following the 1934 film. The lower price offered for the last four mysteries was because they were felt not to be such strong candidates for the screen, while any deal would tie up the titles for two years for what appeared to be an ungenerous sum.

Cork's colleague points out that these were all titles that had been offered to the movie studios 'many times', while this deal kept newer titles available for separate exploitation, but notes that MGM also wanted the option to pay $7000 to include Poirot in stories of its own creation.[63] Resultantly, Christie insisted on the insertion of a clause in the contract with MGM that 'Poirot shall not be given love affairs in any story they invent'.[64] This indicates that she was still mindful of the battles over the stage production of *Alibi*, but the fact that she did not entirely rule out original stories indicates that she may have considered this scenario to be no less preferable than an unsatisfactory rendering of her own stories. Nevertheless, original films using Christie's characters remain very rare, unlike the plethora of Sherlock Holmes pastiches, for example—only 1964's *Murder Ahoy* starring Margaret Rutherford as Miss Marple can really be considered to be a wholly original use of a Christie character in a licensed film, and it is probably no coincidence that this was also produced by MGM. Another sensible move on Christie's part was to insist that any original stories could not then be published in print form—a further sign that she may have been both aware of, and unhappy with, the appearance of the *Passing of Mr Quinn* novel that accompanied that film.

In the event, these demands were too much for MGM and by May 1936 the deal was cancelled before a contract had been signed.[65] 'I am confident that once one important Poirot film is made we will be able to sell the other Poirot subjects easily at substantial prices', wrote Cork, as he forwarded a letter showing that Christie's demands over the use of the character had been the point of contention.[66] 'I am sure you were right, though, in insisting Poirot should not have absurd love affairs', he wrote. 'He is so frightfully valuable to you that you really can't risk his being destroyed by ridicule.'[67] Cork goes on to mention that negotiations would now take place with an unnamed British film company which was keen to use popular actor George Arliss (who was then 68) to play Poirot.[68]

The correspondence with her agent indicates a wealth of interest in adapting Christie's works for the screen during this time, but equally demonstrates how often this came to nothing. For example, a Czechoslovakian film company expressed interest in adapting Christie's early light-hearted thriller *Why Didn't They Ask Evans?* in 1937, but the film was never made.[69] However, the fact that negotiations were constantly ongoing indicates that interest in Christie's stories among film studios remained consistent, if not growing. Nevertheless, over the course of the next 15 years the majority of screen adaptations of her stories would not appear at the local cinema—instead, they were now available to see in the comfort of the public's own home. Television had arrived.

NOTES

1. Agatha Christie, *Mrs McGinty's Dead* (London: HarperCollins, 2008), 73. All references to Christie's works correlate to the first edition facsimile editions unless otherwise noted.
2. Agatha Christie, *An Autobiography* (London: Harper Collins, 2010), 434.
3. Christie to Lord Mountbatten, 15 November 1972 (Agatha Christie Family Archive).
4. *Variety*, 20 March 1931.
5. *Variety*, 20 March 1931.
6. *Picturegoer Weekly*, 19 September 1931.
7. *Picturegoer Weekly*, 26 September 1931.
8. *Picturegoer Weekly*, 26 September 1931.
9. *Picturegoer Weekly*, 26 September 1931.
10. *The Bioscope*, 29 April 1931.
11. *The Bioscope*, 29 April 1931.
12. *The Bioscope*, 29 April 1931.
13. *The Bioscope*, 29 April 1931.
14. Albeit mis-spelled Charles Lawson.
15. *The Manchester Guardian*, 8 December 1931.
16. *The Manchester Guardian*, 8 December 1931.
17. *The Manchester Guardian*, 8 December 1931.
18. *Daily Express*, 28 September 1931.
19. *Daily Mirror*, 15 June 1931.

20. *The Bioscope*, 26 August 1931.
21. *The Bioscope*, 26 August 1931.
22. *Daily Express*, 24 August 1931.
23. *Picturegoer Weekly*, 12 December 1931.
24. *The Times*, 24 August 1931.
25. *The Bioscope*, 26 August 1931.
26. *The Times of India*, 28 May 1932.
27. *Daily Mirror*, 11 December 1931.
28. *The New York Times*, 27 September 1931.
29. This time the film was produced by Real Art Productions at Twickenham Film Studios and distributed by Radio Pictures.
30. *Picturegoer Weekly*, 2 February 1935.
31. *Picturegoer Weekly*, 2 February 1935.
32. *Picturegoer Weekly*, 2 February 1935.
33. *Monthly Film Bulletin*, August 1934.
34. *The Observer*, 3 February 1935.
35. Morgan, *Agatha Christie: A Biography*, 205.
36. Letter from Hughes Massie & Co to Charlotte Fisher (Christie's secretary), 12 February 1936 (Agatha Christie Family Archive).
37. *Variety*, 2 August 1932.
38. *Le Matin*, 15 July 1932.
39. *Figaro*, 17 July 1932.
40. The story had first been published in *Grand Magazine* in 1924, before forming part of *The Listerdale Mystery* short story collection a decade later.
41. *Daily Mirror*, 14 December 1936.
42. *Daily Express*, 7 January 1937.
43. *Daily Mirror*, 18 January 1937.
44. *Daily Mirror*, 29 January 1937.
45. *Daily Mirror*, 8 January 1937.
46. *Love from a Stranger* Press book.
47. Specifically, the plea at the end of the 1957 film of *Witness for the Prosecution*, as well as a similar request made on stage at the end of *The Mousetrap*.
48. *Daily Express*, 8 January 1937.
49. *Daily Express*, 10 January 1937.
50. *The Times*, 11 January 1937.
51. *Action*, 12 June 1937.
52. *Variety*, 27 January 1937.
53. *Variety*, 21 April 1937.
54. *Monthly Film Bulletin*, January 1937.
55. *Monthly Film Bulletin*, January 1937.
56. *Sunday News*, 18 April 1937.
57. *Daily Express*, 8 July 1937; *Daily Mirror*, 9 July 1937.
58. *Daily Express*, 22 April 1938.

59. Cork to Christie, 3 March 1936 (Agatha Christie Family Archive).
60. Cork to Christie, 25 March 1936 (Agatha Christie Family Archive).
61. Cork to Christie, 2 October 1936 (Agatha Christie Family Archive).
62. An unsigned and undated internal memo to Cork c. March 1936 (Agatha Christie Family Archive).
63. An unsigned and undated internal memo to Cork c. March 1936 (Agatha Christie Family Archive).
64. Cork to Christie, 29 April 1936 (Agatha Christie Family Archive).
65. Harold Ober (Christie's US agent) to Cork, 14 May 1936 (Agatha Christie Family Archive).
66. From Harold Ober.
67. Cork to Christie, 29 May 1936 (Agatha Christie Family Archive).
68. This unnamed company may have been Oxford Films, which is mentioned as expressing strong interest in *The ABC Murders* in a later letter from Cork (14 October 1936, Agatha Christie Family Archive).
69. Cork to Christie, 8 March 1937 (Agatha Christie Family Archive).

PART II

Experiments in Television, 1937–62

Chapter 3: The Early Television Adaptations

Spoilers: 'Wasps' Nest'; 'Philomel Cottage'; *Love from a Stranger*; *And Then There Were None*

Agatha Christie made no secret of the fact that she did not care for television. In 1969, she wrote to her agent Edmund Cork to say:

> I suppose you and I will have to construct something about my 'coming of age'. No television. Definitely. Entirely a personal idiosyncrasy, I have to admit I am not television-minded [...] I find it useful—for watching race meetings, occasional news, misleading weather reports (in common with newspapers)! But not, to me, pleasurable.[1]

When writing to Lord Mountbatten in 1972, she made reference to a television biography of him, but claimed that 'It is one of the few things I have looked at on television, as I am far from being a television fan'.[2] During her lifetime there were no television series based on her work, although some one-off adaptations of her stories did appear on the medium—occasionally in the UK and Europe, but more frequently in the USA. Later chapters will show that following Christie's death in 1976 her daughter, Rosalind Hicks, approached television with similar caution but slowly permitted adaptations of her mother's work, always under her watchful eye. Hicks's son Mathew Prichard has since continued this work, as the number of Christie adaptations across the globe continues to grow. While the sense of suspicion towards television generally may have dissipated somewhat, the Christie estate continues to exert close control over how her work is depicted on screen, no doubt mindful of the importance that such productions can have to her legacy.

CHRISTIE'S EARLY RELATIONSHIP WITH THE BBC

Although the first television adaptation of a Christie story took place in 1937, she had corresponded and worked with the BBC for some time prior to this, mostly in relation to broadcasting some of her work on the radio. In April 1930 Christie had been invited to contribute to a new mystery serial *Behind the*

© The Author(s) 2016
M. Aldridge, *Agatha Christie on Screen*,
DOI 10.1057/978-1-137-37292-5_4

Screen, which was to be written by members of the Detection Club, a group of established mystery writers that included the likes of Dorothy L. Sayers alongside Christie herself.[3] Each of the six linked episodes would be written by a different author, who would also read the story over the air. Later this would be unthinkable for Christie, who did not like such public performances, but on this occasion she was convinced. Following voice tests on 18 June 1930, Talks producer J.R. Ackerley flagged up some areas that Christie was encouraged to remember (including the correct name of one character), but largely commended her performance, writing 'you read it most awfully well, and I am sure it will be the greatest success'.[4] It would seem that relations were off to a good start.

Certainly it was enough of a success that both the format and Christie returned for a longer follow-up, *The Scoop*, early in 1931. This time there were 12 instalments, of which Christie wrote two. She was permitted to read her contribution from Devon, and Ackerley felt brave enough to offer some feedback on her first performance (namely, passages that some listeners had found difficult to follow) in the hope that it would have a positive impact on her next reading.[5] The BBC paid 50 guineas for her work on *The Scoop*, a relatively small sum compared to her potential earnings elsewhere (although no doubt useful to the Detection Club), but it may be that in years to come Christie would regret contributing at all—not because of the perceived quality of the mystery itself, but because it indicated that she was more open to both on-air appearances and cut-price mysteries for the radio than she actually was. The BBC files relating to Christie do not cover all of the correspondence with her, but even that which remains paints a picture of repeated requests, rapidly rebuffed, initially politely and then directly.

One can see Christie's issue with writing for broadcasting, as she lacked any real affinity with it, and her work would be rewarded with a lower fee than an appearance of the same story in her preferred medium of print. By way of demonstration, in 1932 Ackerley wrote to Christie to suggest a radio series along the same lines as *The Thirteen Problems*, a collection of her short stories published the same year, some of which were told under an umbrella theme of characters including Miss Marple recounting mysteries to each other. Christie's secretary Charlotte Fisher responded to the query indicating some interest on her employer's part, saying that she was happy to consider putting Miss Marple into small plays, but it would be dependent on the fee.[6] One hundred guineas for six stories was offered, but declined, as they would be of better value in print.[7] This was a disappointment to Ackerley, who endeavoured to discover what fee would be acceptable to bring Christie to broadcasting. A week later, a new letter from Ackerley had the air of desperation, since it offered an increased fee of 150 guineas. 'Do please be nice and kind and say that this will do for you', he wrote, pointing out that it may enhance her sales elsewhere and that she would only be signing away the rights for one broadcast.[8] This resulted in a personal letter, where Christie, who had already written over 100 short stories, made it clear that she was not keen to write yet more for relatively little gain:

'The truth of the matter is I hate writing short things and they really are not profitable. I don't mind an odd one now and again, but the energy to devise a series is much better employed in writing a couple of books. So there it is!'[9]

Christie's strong and commercially minded attitude towards the worth of her work was the result of her increased understanding of how the publishing process worked, and her growing awareness of how stories needed to pay for themselves, especially when tax demands occupied so much of her accounting. She was keen to avoid exploitation, and even if the BBC were the only domestic broadcasting outlet for her work, she saw no reason to give it any special favours. For its part, the BBC was unacquainted with such a strong desire to protect both her work and her finances—despite the strength of the rejection Christie was asked to reconsider once more in May 1933, a request that Fisher declined on her behalf.[10]

In 1934 Christie's relationship with the BBC showed that she was still valued, but her work was not seen as beyond criticism. In retrospect it seems odd that Christie was largely treated as an in-demand, but jobbing, writer, although she does not seem to have been aggrieved by that, nor did she take criticism of her work personally. It is well known that she wrote the short mystery 'Miss Marple Tells a Story' for the radio, before its later appearance in print, but it is less well known that this was a last-minute replacement for another story that the BBC had found unsuitable.[11] After agreeing to a fee of 30 guineas (less than the £50 she had wanted[12]), Christie sent Ackerley her story 'In a Glass Darkly' in March 1934, possibly with the working or optional title of 'In the Mirror'.[13] Very quickly, Ackerley realised that Christie's supernatural tale of a man who has a prophetic vision of a murder was not what was wanted for the slot, and a replacement was requested. Correspondence from Christie then indicates that she was asked to formulate something along the lines of a Miss Marple mystery, which she duly did, and that may explain the prosaic title of the final story.[14] So last minute was the replacement that the *Daily Mirror* actually (incorrectly) included 'In a Glass Darkly' in its listings for 6 April 1934; in the end, 'Miss Marple Tells a Story' was read out by its author on the Light Programme on 11 May 1934. A couple of weeks after the broadcast, Christie was asked to talk about Poirot in a series called *I Present* (later renamed *Meet the Detective*)—this time, she declined.[15]

In 1935, J.R. Ackerley moved on from the Talks department to take up a new position as Literary Editor for *The Listener* magazine. He remains a figure who commands interest and would go on to write acclaimed pieces of his own, with his works reflecting on his life as an openly gay man in a period when this was rare. In 1938, even though he had left the department, he was asked for his opinion regarding Christie by his BBC colleagues who were looking to commission more work from her. Despite the fact that Christie had clearly found his repeated approaches to her wearisome, Ackerley needed little coaxing to highlight her perceived faults. Had Christie ever seen the private memo, at least she might have been pleased to know that she fared better than one of her esteemed peers. Ackerley acidically recalled:

She was surprisingly good-looking and extremely tiresome. She was always late sending in her stuff, very difficult to pin down to any engagements and invariably late for them. I record these memories with pain, for she is my favourite detective story writer. Her success as a broadcaster has made less impression on me. I believe she was quite adequate but nothing more; a little on the feeble side, if I recollect right, but then anyone in that series would have seemed feeble against the terrific vitality, bullying and bounce of that dreadful woman Dorothy L. Sayers.[16]

Quite why Ackerley had so often begged Christie to return to radio, despite his feeling that her work was 'on the feeble side' (even apart from his take on her personal qualities), is unclear, but demonstrates that either distance had muddled his memories or his understanding of the commercial allure of Christie outweighed his personal feelings about the author.

Christie's participation in both *Behind the Screen* and *The Scoop* had demonstrated that the surest way to encourage her to participate in broadcasting was through offering her a distinctive challenge, rather than simply requesting a standard short story suitable for the radio, and her work with the BBC in 1937 showed that she was attracted to unusual requests. Early in the year, she was asked if she would be interested in writing a mystery that incorporated musical performances in the narrative, something that resulted in her radio play *The Yellow Iris*, which was eventually broadcast on 2 November 1937 and repeated two days later. Alongside Christie's script, it featured music by Michael Sayer and lyrics by Christopher Hassel, arranged by Jack Beaver. The story itself features Poirot (in his first radio appearance, played by Anthony Holles) at a cabaret where there is a reunion of people who had been present at an earlier apparent suicide. The cabaret setting allows the threading of music through the play, making it distinct from a standard radio performance of Christie's mysteries. As well as the short story of the same title, which was first published in July 1937, elements of the mystery were also used in the novel *Sparkling Cyanide*.[17] On the radio it is not one of Christie's stronger works, since it lacks urgency, even in script form (no recording exists), with the musical interruptions rather reducing the story's dramatic effect. The 11-page script is thinly spread across an hour-long broadcast, with the interludes stifling the pace and appearing to be more of an annoyance than an entertaining bonus. Christie also demonstrates that she has not yet fully mastered the craft of writing for audio, as characters tend to announce their feelings and background in a manner that lacks subtlety, although the later reworkings of the plot for publication would be rather more effective.

THE WASP'S NEST (1937)

Mere months after a full television service was launched in November 1936, Agatha Christie was to see a piece of her work premiering on the service for the first time. Broadcast on 18 June 1937, this was an adaptation of her short story 'Wasps' Nest', which had been published in the *Daily Mail* nine years earlier but was not included in a book collection until much later.[18] In fact, many of the viewers may have been forgiven for thinking it an original piece as Christie's one-act adaptation had not previously been performed elsewhere, although it was not specially written for television—nevertheless, the fact that 'televiewers' would be the first to see the play was flagged up in the *Radio Times* listing.[19] Although she did not care for it and it did not form part of her daily habits, we know that Christie did watch some television. Her correspondence indicates that she made use of the medium for more auspicious occasions, such as the televising of key events (including the moon landing) and even BBC2's flagship 1967 drama *The Forsyte Saga*, but while she had access to a set, those who knew her do not recall her being a regular viewer.[20]

The Wasp's Nest was a wise choice for a television production, and in fact this Poirot story saw the character's first broadcast appearance, pre-dating his radio sleuthing in *The Yellow Iris* by five months. The play features only one location and four characters; Francis L. Sullivan played Poirot, having portrayed the character on stage in *Black Coffee* seven years earlier, while D.A. Clarke-Smith, a regular on early British television, played Charles Harborough (the same character as John Harrison in the published story). Antoinette Cellier and Wallace Douglas rounded off the cast as Nina Bellamy and Claude Langdon (the characters known as Molly Deane and Claude Langton in the short story), while the producer was George More O'Ferrall, an institutional figure at the BBC who had played a part in many television firsts.

The plot, which concerns Poirot's intervention in a possible poisoning, is dialogue driven but has a subtlety of characterisation that would benefit from good, expressive actors being seen as well as heard. As was normal for television in this period the play was performed live twice, for afternoon and evening audiences, under the banner of *Theatre Parade*. The day's entertainment was introduced by television stalwarts Jasmine Bligh and Leslie Mitchell, while the choice of music was literal but fitting, as it was the Overture from Ralph Vaughan Williams's incidental music for a performance of Aristophanes' *The Wasps*, from 1909. The script itself demonstrates Christie's strengths and weaknesses when it came to writing for performance—it is very well plotted, especially given the fact that it takes place on one set and runs for only 20 minutes, but the dialogue and some character actions may have struggled to be wholly convincing, although as the play pre-dated systematic recording of television broadcasts we cannot be sure.[21]

Some authors who write for the screen offer lyrical, detailed scripts that outline not only the dialogue, actions and mise-en-scène but express the tone of the piece, offer extended character information and work to create a distinctive and consistent world. Others write on a more technical level, outlining the key requirements and allowing the actors and directors to do the rest; this was the more common way of writing scripts for early television, and Christie's play script was no exception. Live performances, a low budget, a limited running time and the use of just two or three cameras precluded the creation of a convincing new world—instead, the drama was essentially televised theatre, although the one review of the piece indicates that it did the job well, *The Observer* remarking that 'The first performance of Agatha Christie's *The Wasp's Nest* on Friday was excellently done'.[22]

However, it was not merely the technology and the medium that seem to have restricted the visual imagination for this production. Certainly Christie's dialogue for *The Wasp's Nest* is not among her strongest writing for performance, especially when she forces one character into hysteria in order to show her hand in the final minutes, with dialogue that would surely have been very difficult to say convincingly: 'Don't drink it! For God's sake don't drink it. It's poisoned, I tell you, poisoned.' However, this does follow a particularly well-crafted piece of visual business in which Poirot appears to nearly consume an apparently lethal drink, showing that Christie fully appreciated the advantages that a visual performance could bring. A small-scale but effective piece, the mystery is well deserving of its place as a television first, with a denouement that is particularly satisfying.

LOVE FROM A STRANGER (1938)

The following year saw another Christie story make an appearance on television, but this time it was a performance of Frank Vosper's play *Love from a Stranger*, which had already been made into a successful film in 1937 (as outlined in Chap. 2). Starring Bernard Lee (later to find fame as M in several early James Bond films) as Bruce Lovell and stage star Edna Best as Cecily, it was another George More O'Ferrall production, and was first scheduled at 3 p.m. on 23 November 1938.[23] This performance was even listed in the *Radio Times* for that week, although in the end for reasons unknown the production was not performed and was replaced by performances from bandleader Bert Ambrose and various other entertainments, including impressionist Elizabeth Pollock and a screening of the 1932 Mickey Mouse cartoon *Mickey's Nightmare*.[24] In the end the play was performed on Monday, 5 December 1938 instead, heralded by film of Big Ben chiming.

The production appears to have been an effective adaptation of the stage play, and it is likely that its appearance on the schedules would have been welcomed by the watching audience since both the play and the film had been recent successes, and the idea of bringing such attractions into the home had been a key draw of early television. One concession to the fact that this was a television production rather than a stage performance was in the occasional use of film inserts as establishing shots, in this case including views of the Strand and Savoy in London. Critical reaction to the production was positive, particularly from Grace Wyndham Goldie of *The Listener* magazine, who wrote that it was 'beyond all doubt, a winner on the television screen'. Goldie went on to commend both the direction and the performances and ventured that this was a particularly strong example of a stage play being produced for television, writing that 'It must be recognised that television slows up the action of the ordinary stage piece', because the camera tends to focus on only part of the set at a time. Goldie suggested that plays for television need to be chosen carefully, with *Love from a Stranger* cited as a good example of one that works, while in future specially written material may be better—although 'heaven forfend that they should imitate the films'.[25] Elsewhere, *The Times*'s review further indicated that this production had showcased the advantages of television particularly well. It claimed that the production used shots of 'a long flight of steps seen in perspective, the slow ticking of the clock as the appointed hour drew near, and by the actual angles at which the pictures were taken', indicating that a distinctive televisual style was starting to be brought more to the fore in these productions.[26] A combination of this and Christie's mixture of claustrophobic settings and tight plotting would soon be a recurring and successful formula on television in the UK and abroad.

It is unlikely that Christie would have been heavily involved in any negotiations regarding this performance, but she had been asked to contribute to a radio series called *What Happened at 8.20?*[27] The premise of the programme was that, following 20 minutes of music, a pistol was to be fired and that week's writer was to write a 20-minute piece that explained what had happened; Christie declined.[28] Nevertheless, the BBC continued to ask Christie for personal appearances, including a July 1939 request for her to speak to the radio show *Bookshelf*, and a discussion of her work on 'I Am an Expert', a segment of magazine programme *Ack-Ack Beer-Beer* on the BBC Forces Programme radio station in 1942; she participated in neither.[29] Later requests for Christie to appear on a programme for convalescing men overseas[30] and as part of a female quiz team[31] were similarly declined, while it was the BBC's turn to problematise a radio opportunity in July 1943 when an adaptation of Christie's short story 'The Blue Geranium' by Kenneth Betteridge was judged to be 'rather too far-fetched' by the BBC reader Cynthia Pughe (who would check scripts for quality and suggest whether they should be accepted), and it was duly turned down.[32]

The resumption of television after the war saw another appearance of *Love from a Stranger* on the medium alongside a new movie version, which made the short story on which it was based, 'Philomel Cottage', easily the most adapted of all of Christie's work to this point.[33] This performance starred Henry Oscar as Bruce and Joy Harington as Cecily, with an appearance by Arthur Wontner who had played Sherlock Holmes in five films from 1931 to 1937, here playing Dr Gribble. It took place on 25 May 1947 (and was re-performed two days later), running for 75 minutes from 8.45 p.m., indicating some abridgement. This time no film inserts were used, although several sound effects were employed, including a grandfather clock striking nine—perhaps signalling the fateful moment when Bruce plans to murder his wife.[34] Although this was a straightforward appearance of a Christie work on television, her other work with the Corporation the same year was anything but.

THREE BLIND MICE (1947)

At 8 p.m. on 30 May 1947, the BBC Light Programme broadcast Christie's new radio play *Three Blind Mice*, which she had specially written as part of the BBC's celebrations of Queen Mary's 80th birthday. In the lead-up to this, the BBC had supplied Christie with examples of radio scripts at her request, an indication that she still felt she was learning the form and was certainly not complacent.[35] Christie had been a keen participant in the event, attending rehearsals and donating her fee to charity.[36] She could scarcely have imagined that this 30-minute play would eventually lead to one of her most enduring successes, when she went on to adapt the story for the stage under the new title *The Mousetrap*. The play opened in the West End on 25 November 1952 and shows no signs of closing, making it a unique theatrical success.

However, before the mystery made its way to the stage, it had had an immediate impression at the BBC, where its potential was realised. The day after the radio broadcast, BBC producer Barrie Edgar sent a memo to television planner and pioneer Cecil Madden. 'I was listening last night to the sound programme in honour of Queen Mary's birthday,' Edgar wrote, 'and it occurred to me that the Agatha Christie play *Three Blind Mice* would make an ideal television play.'[37] Madden would have preferred an adaptation of Christie's 1939 thriller *And Then There Were None*, but the 1945 film of this story meant that the rights were unavailable at the time.[38] It was felt that *Three Blind Mice* would be an acceptable substitute, with some adaptation for television, since it told a tale of a group of people stranded in a remote location with a murderer in their midst—not unlike Madden's first choice, and perfect for the limited cast and locations possible to show on television at this time. It was deemed to be a 'Slick murder mystery, up to Agatha Christie's usual standard', although it was also perceived not to be the best possible choice.[39]

In the end, the broadcast was scheduled for a 30-minute slot from 8.30 p.m. on 21 October 1947, following a week of rehearsals. The cast featured Lewis Stringer as Detective Sergeant Trotter (the only actor to reprise their role from the radio performance), John Witty as Giles Davis and Jessica Spencer, later to originate the role of Miss Casewell in the West End production, as Molly Davis, while Christie received 50 guineas for the use of her script.[40] The production was performed live using three cameras and not recorded; there were also no film inserts and only four sets, as befitted the claustrophobic setting. The television play opened with a shot of a snowy Culver Street, created in the studio, with a caption showing the play's title and author accompanied by the strains of its nursery rhyme namesake. The performance continued along the same lines as the radio production, with the murderer (whose face is not seen) moving from the street to the victim's bedroom, where she sits at her dressing table listening to dance music. As the murderer approaches, so the music swells up as he grabs her by the throat, strangling her. When he makes his escape through the street he drops a notebook, which features two addresses—Culver Street and Monkswell Manor, to which we then move via a caption card of the house covered in snow. After this dynamic opening, the play becomes a more traditional but no less effective story of characters stranded with a killer. The brave but risky decision to depict this killer in the opening minutes, albeit in disguised form, further indicates that television's ability to focus closely on certain areas allowed for particular strengths—something that would have to be meticulously planned on live television, in case the murderer's identity was accidentally revealed.[41] On stage the events that take place in this opening section are only heard and not seen, prior to the lights coming up fully in Act One.

Changes between the radio and television production were minor. Indeed, an attempt was made to mirror the radio broadcast as much as possible, with production documentation and a recording (which is no longer known to exist) consulted, while Christie was invited to attend either the rehearsal or final performance. Some sections of dialogue were tweaked, while some passages that had been dropped during the live radio performance were reinstated. The minor reworking of the opening sequence is the most notable acknowledgement of the different requirements of a visual medium. On the radio the murderer's disguised voice is highlighted when the victim's landlady asks whether they have a cold, but on television the disguised voice is unexplained, as the emphasis is on not showing their face. For her radio script, Christie offered a prosaic but helpful description of the landlady ('Alcoholic, grumbling voice'), which demonstrates her ability to convey a lot of information in a straightforward manner, and this is euphemistically translated as an 'untidy woman' for the television production description, where her abrupt manner reappears.

The play's appearance on television marked one of the final times that *Three Blind Mice* was not considered an anomaly in the UK, since *The Mousetrap*'s run would soon restrict availability of the work for adaptation or publication. Christie's short story based on the radio play, which predated *The Mousetrap*, remains unpublished in her home country, although it is available elsewhere. Christie herself refused permission for the play to be filmed, and Mathew Prichard has explained why this situation has not changed: 'I made a written promise to my grandmother that I wouldn't [publish *Three Blind Mice* in the UK] whilst the play is running.'[42] Such an exception has ensured that *Three Blind Mice* has maintained a special status in the Christie canon. The long run of the stage play has precluded exploitation of either *The Mousetrap* or *Three Blind Mice* elsewhere, including in film form. Prichard points out that 'Peter Saunders, who was the original producer, sold the film rights early in the run [to British producer John Woolf], and put in the contract that he couldn't make a film while the play was running in the West End. And then Woolf died, and the play went on and went on.'[43] Nevertheless, there have been several attempts to bring the story to screen in some form, including some that pre-date the West End play, such as a proposed deal in 1950 of which Christie appeared to be in favour but which fell through.[44] There were international versions of the play on television, including in Germany in 1954 (as *Die Fuchsjagd*, or *The Fox Hunt*), then in Denmark in 1955, followed by Brazil in 1956. Domestically, ten minutes of the West End production were broadcast live on the new commercial ITV network in the UK in 1955 as part of the *Curtain Call* series, which highlighted current theatrical productions. In 1958 *The New York Times* reported that American film producer Edward Small was to follow up on the success of his 1957 film of Christie's *Witness for the Prosecution* with a film of *The Mousetrap*,[45] but a legitimate film version has never materialised, although there have been unlicensed movie adaptations in India (d. Premendra Mitra, 1960, as *Chupi Chupi Ashey*, or *Silently He Comes*) and Russia (d. Samson Samsonov, 1990), at least.

Although the small-scale nature of proceedings in the story lends itself particularly well to the stage, Prichard is quietly confident that a good film version is possible, pointing out that the characters have backgrounds that are ripe for exploration, possibly as a prologue to the main events: 'If you started with the abuse in the farm which takes place before the play starts [...] I think you could make a wonderful film of *The Mousetrap*. But somehow, I doubt it'll ever be done.'[46] Indeed, the real-life events that had inspired elements of Christie's story (namely, the death of 12-year-old child Dennis O'Neill while in foster care) are so dark that they could only be tackled superficially in the original plays, but they could now be explored more explicitly, lending weight to the motivation of certain characters. 'That was the genius of my grandmother,' says Prichard, 'she read the stories, and then the story carried on. *Orient Express* was the same, of course. Her own version of adaptation.'[47] A bleak snowscape certainly has visual appeal, while the 1960 Indian adaptation shows how effectively the opening murder can be staged, as the killer moves through the pouring rain of a bleak city, homing in on the victim, offering a stark contrast with the cosy environs of Monkswell Manor where later events take place.

Although 1947 had been Christie's most successful year in broadcasting to date, the following year indicated that she still had no particular interest in continuing to contribute to radio and television. She was not opposed to broadcasting in principle, but did not see it as an efficient use of her work or time. However, she was convinced to write a new play for the radio, *Butter in a Lordly Dish*, as her contribution to a series by The Detection Club. The grisly tale followed the repercussions of the prosecution of an apparent murderer some years after the event, and was first broadcast on the Light Programme on 13 January 1948.[48] A few months later, Christie was asked if she would write a special play for the BBC's overseas service as someone who had made a distinctive contribution to broadcasting.[49] She was away and Edmund Cork declined on her behalf, pointing out that her contribution to broadcasting had only been on special occasions, and 'in the light of the large prices she obtains from other markets it is unlikely that the fees which the Corporation could offer her would prove very attractive'.[50]

Christie was also no more convinced by most broadcasting opportunities presented to her, despite not offering any particular objection to the BBC's productions to date. However, when American actor Harold Huber expressed an interest in playing Poirot on television in late 1948, having performed him on US radio since 1945, she refused permission, much to his indignation.[51] She had earlier told Edmund Cork that she was opposed to having Poirot on radio in the UK, writing 'Perish the thought that I should every have a synthetic Poirot on the wireless in this country. It's not easy to bear the thought of it in America.'[52] Her choice of the word 'synthetic' is telling, since it indicates her perception that Poirot could only truly exist as her own literary character—a theory borne out by her decision to remove him from the stories that she then adapted for the stage. This is a marked contrast to modern approaches to literature, where potential castings for any popular literary character are standard discussion for tabloid newspapers. Huber continued to try to gain television rights into the next decade, but was still turned down, although less emphatically than previously; Edmund Cork wished to see how the tax situation was to develop, as at the time Christie would have made very little from any such deal.[53]

On 3 October 1948 an *Observer* profile claimed that Christie was 'violently allergic to the BBC', although it did not offer a quote to back up this assertion. Shortly afterwards, N.G. Luker, the Head of Talks at the BBC, sent Christie a letter that showed remarkable chutzpah. 'I see from *The Observer* that you are violently allergic to the BBC,' he wrote. 'If this report is correct would you like to give a 15 minute talk on the Third Programme saying why you feel so strongly about broadcasting?'[54] Christie took the request in good spirits, calling it 'A most sporting offer!', and succinctly pointed out the truth behind her apparent issue with the Corporation: 'I don't do much at the BBC as I am definitely allergic to its remuneration!'[55]

1949 IN TELEVISION

10 June 1949 saw the BBC televise an adaptation of the short story *Witness for the Prosecution,* four years before Christie's own version of the play opened in the West End. Both the play and the short story rank among Christie's very best work, telling the tale of a man arrested for murder with only his wife in a position to help him. For this production the story was adapted by Sidney Budd and formed part of an occasional BBC series called *Triple Bill,* whereby three one-act plays would be presented to the watching audience. Joining *Witness for the Prosecution* was Irish comedy *A Call to Arms,* which was adapted by John Glyn-Jones from a story by Denis Johnston, alongside *Box for One*, an original piece by Peter Brook about a telephone conversation. Budd wrote the adaptation in late 1948 and the script was well received by his colleagues, who felt that there was perhaps some opportunity for further expansion, believing that television viewers did not really have the same opportunity to process implied information that readers would have—no doubt true, and a demonstration that adaptation required more than simply transferring salient plot points into scripted dialogue.[56]

The production starred John Salew as the solicitor Robert Mayherne, Dale Rogers as the accused Leonard Vole and Mary Kerridge as his wife Romaine— the character later renamed Christine for the 1957 film production and most of the Broadway run of the stage play. Some 36 years later, Kerridge would appear in another Christie adaptation, as Mrs Swettenham in the BBC's 1985 adaptation of *A Murder Is Announced* starring Joan Hickson as Miss Marple. Rehearsals took place for two weeks from 27 May; at 40 minutes, *Witness for the Prosecution* took up the bulk of the production and seems to have been deemed the highlight of the bill. While it only used one exterior film sequence (an establishing shot of the Old Bailey), the production actually appears to have been rather less of a courtroom drama than later adaptations would be. Although no script of the adaptation is known to have survived, we know from production documentation that it opened with a shot of the dead body of murder victim Miss French, and moved on to scenes in Mayherne's office as well as a prison cell, a bedroom, the dock and—perhaps most interestingly—the balcony of a Swiss hotel overlooking a lake. This all implies that the production featured flashbacks that are in line with the later 1957 film, but quite unlike Christie's linear drama that is focused on the contemporary events surrounding the court proceedings, indicating that a more filmic and less static approach was being taken for this television adaptation. The precise use of the Swiss hotel set is unclear (it does not feature in the original story), but it may be a flashback to Leonard's first meeting with Romaine, who hails from Austria, while the presence of Miss French (played by Hilda Terriss) in the list of principal cast indicates that we see more of her than just a corpse—which in itself is more than we are witness to in either the short story or the play, where she is not seen at all given that the story begins after her demise.

This, then, would seem to be rather an ambitious production and one that was not a simple retelling of the basics of the story. The opportunities that television afforded in quickly relating complex relationships were being embraced, perhaps partially embodied by the use of the song 'Quand l'amore est passé' ['When Love Has Passed You By'] from the 1948 British film *Noose* (d. Edmond T. Gréville), which was played during the performance, perhaps in a scene featuring spinster Miss French. Similarly, television allowed the rapid use of multiple locations, even within the confines of Studio A at Alexandra Palace, where British television had been based even before official transmissions started in November 1936. The first regular, high-definition service in the world, the BBC's television broadcasts were a considerable technical achievement, but were also regarded dismissively even within the Corporation, who saw television as a lesser sibling to the more prestigious radio programming. The service was afforded the use of two television studios and almost all original content was transmitted live, often punctuated by newsreels or short films such as cartoons. By modern standards the system was primitive: cameras could not zoom, and scripts needed to be structured in order to allow actors to move from set to set during the broadcast, while there was no opportunity to preserve broadcasts, except through experimental and infrequent means, until the 1950s. The new technology enabled productions that could be less linear than many stage productions, but it required a great deal of skill to transmit the live performances to the audience at home without distracting them with technical hiccups.

The BBC finally got its wish to broadcast a television production of Christie's thriller *And Then There Were None* on 20 August 1949, under its original British title of *Ten Little Niggers*. It was produced by Kevin Sheldon and once more performed in Studio A at Alexandra Palace. As was normally the case, it was an adaptation of Christie's 1943 play rather than the original novel, with the key difference of a more upbeat ending. The production starred John Bentley as Philip Lombard—perhaps now best known as Hugh Mortimer in ITV soap opera *Crossroads* (1968–88)—while Sally Rogers played Vera Claythorne and Bruce Belfrage was Sir Lawrence Wargrave, alongside Arthur Wontner making his second appearance in a television Christie when he took the role of General MacKenzie. The production used one large set, which encompassed a small 'outside' area, and the performance opened by reminding the audience of the origins of the title. Speaking from the adjoining Studio B, the off-screen announcer intoned to the audience 'Now I am sure you must all remember how the rhyme of "Ten Little Nigger Boys" goes', only for the ten characters to appear in vision on set and help with reading the full rhyme out (whether the cast read it all together or take a verse each is unclear—one would hope that each actor was not given their own death verse to read so as not to ruin the specific developments of the play for those who were unaware), before the camera panned down to a collection of the ten ornamental figures. The camera then tracked back to show off the full set, before the announcer informed the audience that 'We begin the evening on a bright August evening on Nigger Island off the coast of Devon'. Hereon in, the script is essentially the same as Christie's play, with some minor changes to dialogue and a few small edits, such as the removal of an early exchange between the servants Mr and Mrs Rogers. The production had a five-minute interval, the first act finishing with Vera holding up a broken china figure, just as in the play, while the pause between the second and third acts was filled with sound effects of stormy weather and a ticking watch as the camera focused on the remaining five china figures.

The action continued as per the play, with the addition of a distinctive curtain call. After a 'The End' caption the announcer spoke: 'And there ends the story of *Ten Little Niggers* as Vera Claythorne, played by Sally Rogers, and Philip Lombard, played by John Bentley wave a thankful goodbye to the house on Nigger Island. But there are seven others who will never leave', before the murderer's victims (with the exception of Blore) reappeared to receive their own credit. Perhaps this staging is an indication that the production was seen as a game for the audience, rather than an outright thriller, since both the introduction and the final speech indicate that everyone involved demonstrates self-awareness of this mystery as a particularly well-renowned and ingenious puzzle. Although Christie did not see the play herself, she was made aware of one unfortunate failing. Using the original name of Arthur Wontner's character from the novel, she wrote: 'Just as well I *didn't* see *Ten Little Niggers* on the television! I hear General MacArthur, after being stabbed, got up and strolled away with his hands in his pockets, quite unaware he was "in view". I should have been *livid*.'[57] Such issues did little to help convince Christie that television was capable of properly depicting her work.

Halloween 1949 saw the first Agatha Christie adaptation on television in the United States, when the anthology series *The Chevrolet Tele-Theatre* broadcast its own version of *Witness for the Prosecution* on NBC; as with the BBC production the same year, this took place some time before Christie's own stage adaptation's 1959 premiere, and it is tempting to believe that the particular interest shown in this story by both UK and US broadcasters helped to convince her that it was one worthy of embellishment. This adaptation saw renowned actor Walter Abel take on the role of Mayherne, with Nicholas Saunders as Leonard Vole and Felicia Montealegre as Romaine. It was to be just the first of many appearances on US television of Agatha Christie adaptations, which reached a peak during the 1950s. The rapid expansion of the medium had resulted in an accompanying rise in anthology shows, where suitable stories could be written or adapted for a wide audience. Television was hungry for drama material, and Christie's accessible and small-scale tales were in demand because they were ideal for a general audience while also being distinctive and well structured.

Asked if he thought that his grandmother was less concerned with television adaptations in other countries, Mathew Prichard thinks probably not, but 'her agents might have been! If they thought that she was adamantly opposed, which she was, to television production in the fairly early days of television [...] It may well have been that her agents thought this was a way to generate some more money and improve the international sales of books.'[58] However, it is notable that these productions did not initially feature her best-known detectives, over whom Christie was understandably protective. 'Particularly, she didn't want to do Poirot or Marple in English as it would have spoiled people's imagination of what the characters looked like,' points out Prichard.[59] The evidence bears this out, as Poirot did not appear on television for a quarter of a century after the 1937 adaptation of *The Wasp's Nest* (with the exception of a 1955 adaptation of *Murder on the Orient Express* for West German television) until he made his 1962 debut on American television, explored in the next chapter. Meanwhile, Miss Marple appeared in just one adaptation prior to the Margaret Rutherford films of the early 1960s, 1956's *A Murder Is Announced* for NBC in the United States—although, as we will see, the star casting for this particular adaptation may have convinced Christie or her agents that this was a prestigious production that should be treated as an exception. Whatever the reason, the 1950s would be a time when television enabled Christie's stories to be enjoyed by more people than ever before.

NOTES

1. Morgan, *Agatha Christie: A Biography*, 347.

2. Probably the Associated-Rediffusion series *Lord Mountbatten: A Man for the Century*, first shown in 12 parts in 1969 and made with Lord Mountbatten's cooperation. Christie to Lord Mountbatten, 15 November 1972 (Agatha Christie Family Archive).

3. Hilda Matheson (Director of Talks) to Agatha Christie, 17 April 1930 (BBC Written Archives Centre: Agatha Christie, Talks, 1930–1958 (RCONT1)).

4. Ackerley to Christie, 19 June 1930 (BBC WAC, Agatha Christie: Talks 1930–1958).

5. Ackerley to Christie, 21 January 1931 (BBC WAC, Agatha Christie: Talks 1930–1958).

6. Fisher to Ackerley, 13 Sept 1932 (BBC WAC, Agatha Christie: Talks 1930–1958).

7. Fisher to Ackerley, 13 Oct 1932 (BBC WAC, Agatha Christie: Talks 1930–1958).

8. Ackerley to Christie, 20 October 1932 (BBC WAC, Agatha Christie: Talks 1930–1958).

9. Christie to Ackerley, 26 October 1932 (BBC WAC, Agatha Christie: Talks 1930–1958).

10. Ackerley to Christie, 4 May 1933 (BBC WAC, Agatha Christie: Talks 1930–1958).

11. As was normally the case, it also appeared in a magazine prior to book publication, as 'Behind Closed Doors' in *Home Journal*'s 25 May 1935 edition. In book form it appeared as part of 1939's *The Regatta Story* in the USA, and within the posthumous 1979 collection *Miss Marple's Final Cases* in the UK.

12. Various correspondence between Christie and J.R. Ackerley, February 1934 (BBC WAC, Agatha Christie: Talks 1930–1958).

13. A 'Talk Fixture' (essentially, a note of planned broadcast) from March 1934 refers to it under this title, but this is then crossed out and replaced with the title 'In A Glass Darkly' (BBC WAC, Agatha Christie: Talks 1930–1958).

14. In the letter from Fisher to Ackerley on 27 March 1934 she writes: 'Mrs Mallowan is extremely sorry that the story she sent to you is not suitable. She has gone to her house in Torquay for the weekend and is going to try to plan out a story while she is there on the lines of a Miss Marple if she can manage it' (BBC WAC, Agatha Christie: Talks 1930–1958).

15. Fisher to Cecil Madden, 26 May 1934 (BBC WAC, Agatha Christie: Talks 1930–1958).

16. Ackerley to 'Talks', 15 August 1938 (BBC WAC, Agatha Christie: Talks 1930–1958).

17. The short story first appeared in the *Strand Magazine*. It is not entirely clear which came first, the story or the play. Christie was asked to con-

sider writing something for broadcast in January 1937, so it is plausible that both were written at approximately the same time.

18. There are several variations in the way this title has been expressed in print—while the original story is 'Wasps' Nest', *The Wasp's Nest* is how it is written in both the script and on the Programme as Broadcast (PasB) document for that day.

19. In the USA it was later published within the 1961 *Double Sin and Other Stories* collection, while the UK had to wait even longer, since it did not appear until 1974's *Poirot's Early Cases*.

20. In an interview with this author, Mathew Prichard recounts that he has no memory of seeing his grandmother watching the television.

21. Although the afternoon performance was granted a 25-minute slot.

22. *The Observer*, 20 June 1937.

23. This was followed by an evening repeat performance on 2 December, with a final chance to see it in the afternoon of 5 December.

24. BBC Television PasB for 23 November 1938.

25. *The Listener*, 5 December 1938.

26. *The Times*, 5 December 1938.

27. BBC Copyright Section to Christie, 11 February 1938 (BBC Written Archive Centre: Agatha Christie, Copyright, 1934–1938 (RCONT1)).

28. Fisher to BBC, 15 February 1938 (BBC WAC, Agatha Christie: Copyright 1934–1938).

29. Fisher to BBC, 15 July 1939 and Programme Contracts Director to Christie, 31 October 1942 (BBC WAC, Agatha Christie: Talks 1930–1958).

30. Jill Allgood to Christie, 24 September 1943 (BBC WAC, Agatha Christie: Talks 1930–1958).

31. Hughes Massie to K.F. Lowe, 20 February 1945 (BBC WAC, Agatha Christie: Talks 1930–1958).

32. Cynthia Pughe, 'The Blue Geranium', 8 July 1943 (BBC WAC, Agatha Christie: Talks 1930–1958).

33. Television was off air in the UK from 1 September 1939 to 7 June 1946. See Chap. 5 for further discussion of the film.

34. BBC Television PasB, 25 May 1947.

35. Martyn C. Webster to Edmund Cork, 28 April 1947 (BBC Written Archive Centre: Agatha Christie, Scriptwriter, 1937–1962 (RCONT1)).

36. Mr Webster's Secretary to Barrie Edgar, 26 Sept 1947 (BBC Written Archive Centre: *Three Blind Mice* television production file (T5/525)).

37. Edgar to Madden, 31 May 1947 (BBC WAC, *Three Blind Mice* production file).

38. Cecil Madden to Cecil McGivern, 27 July 1947 (BBC WAC, *Three Blind Mice* production file). See Chap. 5 for further discussion of the film.

39. Miss Hourd to Madden, 28 July 1947 (BBC WAC, *Three Blind Mice* production file).

40. R.G. Walford to Edgar, 23 September 1947 (BBC WAC, *Three Blind Mice* production file).

41. This sequence was in the first draft of the stage play.

42. Interview with the author, August 2013.

43. Interview with the author, August 2013.

44. A 7 September 1950 letter from Edmund Cork to Christie explains that they are waiting for lawyers to confirm a film deal relating to *Three Blind Mice* (Agatha Christie Archive, Exeter).

45. *The New York Times*, 18 September 1958.

46. Interview with the author, August 2013.

47. Interview with the author, August 2013.

48. The performance was repeated on 16 January 1948, followed by a later broadcast on the Home Service on 8 July 1948 and then on the Light Programme once more on 11 March 1956.

49. Val Gielgud to Christie, 22 April 1948 (BBC WAC, Agatha Christie: Scriptwriter 1937–1962).

50. Cork to Gielgud, 28 April 1948 (BBC WAC, Agatha Christie: Scriptwriter 1937–1962).

51. This is outlined in various pieces of correspondence with Harold Ober Associates in late 1948 in particular, including Ober to Cork 9 November 1948 (Agatha Christie Archive, Exeter).

52. Christie to Cork, 27 January 1947 (Agatha Christie Archive, Exeter).

53. Cork to Ober, 3 February 1950 (Agatha Christie Archive, Exeter).

54. Luker to Christie, 6 October 1948 (BBC WAC, Agatha Christie: Talks 1930–1958).

55. Christie to Luker, 14 October 1948 (BBC WAC, Agatha Christie: Talks 1930–1958).

56. Notes on script from G.A.J. Bevan, 13 October 1948 (BBC Written Archive Centre: Plays—Triple Bill production file (T5/543/1)).

57. Morgan, *Agatha Christie: A Biography*, 272.

58. Interview with the author, August 2013.

59. Interview with the author, August 2013.

Chapter 4: New Prospects and Problems in Television

Spoilers: 'The Case of the Missing Lady'; *And Then There Were None*; 'Philomel Cottage'; *Love from a Stranger*

Just as Agatha Christie's early works had initially coincided with the establishment of more complex narrative cinema, so it was that by the time she was well known as a literary brand in the United States, a new avenue for her stories was becoming increasingly important—television. Unwittingly, Christie had created stories at the right time and in the best format to be exploited by this new medium that had broken into the homes of mainstream America. Her works offered tightly plotted stories of an unusually wide variety, some featuring established characters ideal for series, but she also had a large number of one-off stories—both novels and short stories—that usually covered a small cast of characters in few locations. Such limitations were ideal for early television, which was almost entirely live.

Christie on American Television in the 1950s

In 1950 half a dozen of Christie's stories appeared on television in the United States, an indication of just how quickly her works were embraced as suitable for this method of storytelling—but also a demonstration of just how many new productions were being made for the fledgling medium, and the resultant hunger for easily adaptable narratives. However, one person who was still unsuccessful in his efforts was Harold Huber, star of an American radio series of Poirot stories, due to Christie's decision not to allow such a television series to go ahead. Meanwhile, the suggestion from her American agents that a series could be made from Miss Marple stories was dismissed, although some potential was seen in a possible television series featuring Christie character Parker Pyne, who specialises in helping people out of unhappy situations.[1]

On 17 January, NBC television featured a 15-minute adaptation of 'The Golden Ball', a Christie short story that concerned a young man called George Dundas, who is made unemployed and encouraged to grasp 'the golden ball of opportunity'. What follows is a light thriller, with George (played by George

© The Author(s) 2016
M. Aldridge, *Agatha Christie on Screen*,
DOI 10.1057/978-1-137-37292-5_5

Nader in this adaptation) meeting a headstrong young woman called Mary (Eve Miller), then unwittingly finding himself being held at gunpoint before the young woman's intentions are made clear. It had first been published in the UK's *Daily Mail* newspaper in 1929, but would not be collected in book form in the United States until 1971, in an eponymously titled selection of short stories.[2] Therefore the choice of this little-known story may seem curious, although the lightness of tone and relative paucity of mystery were presumably a key attraction for its appearance in this *Fireside Theatre* anthology series, which had the rare distinction of recording its mysteries on film prior to broadcast, rather than offering a live performance. Unfortunately, no copy of this adaptation is known to exist (as is the case with many productions from this era; exceptions to this norm are noted in this chapter) and resultantly we have little further information about this particular production, but we do know that *Fireside Theatre* was a commercially popular (although critically derided) populist piece of television that ran for a decade, having started in 1949 before finishing in 1958, and so the action elements of this story had natural appeal.

As previously mentioned, *Three Blind Mice* (and later *The Mousetrap*) has a widely acknowledged anomalous status within the canon of Agatha Christie stories, because the long-running play and Christie's own wishes have restricted its appearance. However, the 1950s saw several examples of the story appearing on television prior to its stage success. In the United States, *Three Blind Mice* first appeared as an episode of *The Trap*, a CBS anthology series hosted by Joseph DeSantis. It dealt with people who find themselves in unusual or unexpected situations, and was broadcast live for an hour on Saturday evenings, with *Three Blind Mice* on 17 June 1950 as the eighth of the nine episodes.[3] Although the series was not a success, running for only one season, this particular episode may have had more of an impact, since just four months later the same network broadcast another adaptation of the story as part of the anthology programme *Sure as Fate* on 31 October, this time starring John McQuade. This was the second consecutive year of an Agatha Christie story on US television on Halloween, raising the possibility that her sometimes macabre tales were seen as more suitable for this time of year to this audience than the more comforting advertising of her stories as 'A Christie for Christmas' when she published her later novels in the UK.

The earliest existing television adaptation of an Agatha Christie story is a production of her play *Murder on the Nile*, which was broadcast on NBC on 12 July 1950 and produced by the J. Walter Thomson Company.[4] Christie had written the play as an adaptation of her own novel *Death on the Nile*, and in terms of basic plotting and mystery the stories are broadly similar, with the crucial difference that Poirot appears in the novel but is excised from the stage production. The television adaptation uses Christie's play as its basis, with some minor reworking, which helps to keep the focus on the mystery rather than secondary details, resulting in reduced prominence for several characters, especially the condescending Mrs ffoliot-ffoulkes. The programme was live, with the cast only allowed respite when pausing for commercial breaks. It is a typical early television production, utilising one main set (the deck of a paddle steamer) and essentially operating as a small-scale theatre production. In this adaptation of Christie's tale of betrayal and murder in Egypt, the sleuthing is undertaken by Canon Pennefather, played by Guy Spaull, a regular on early television who seems to struggle a little in the part. Pennefather essentially takes Poirot's role, although he brings with him a personal connection to the ship's passengers. As an adaptation it is reasonably effective in terms of its depiction of the mystery, but it lacks energy and even for live television it has a very high proportion of scenes where characters simply take it in turns to discuss the plot with each other. Nevertheless, the limited resources that such a production utilised help to demonstrate why Christie's claustrophobic settings and clearly outlined set of characters held so much appeal to television producers.

On 7 November 1950, the short story 'Witness for the Prosecution' received another outing on American television; its swift reappearance following the NBC broadcast on Halloween 1949, covered in the previous chapter, is a further indication of how valuable were distinctive, tightly plotted stories suitable for television adaptation. This time it was performed as part of the *Danger* anthology series on CBS and starred Sarah Churchill—British Prime Minister Winston Churchill's second child—as Romaine.[5] Of even more historical interest was the subsequent debut appearance of Christie's partners in crime, Tommy and Tuppence, in a CBS adaptation of the short story 'The Case of the Missing Lady' the following month. This slight tale (in which no crime has been committed) may have had enough mystery to sustain the 30-minute running time of the series in which it appeared (*Nash Airflyte Theatre*), but it is the casting that makes it particularly noteworthy. Oscar-winning actress (and, later, *Dancing with the Stars* contestant) Cloris Leachman played Tuppence, and was partnered by future US President Ronald Reagan as Tommy.[6] Broadcast on 7 December 1950, the fact that no recording is known to survive is felt particularly keenly since, according to a review, the future President played a kazoo in order to aid his concentration; a nod to Sherlock Holmes's violin. *Variety*'s television reviewer called it 'a satire on all great detectives', going on to say that 'while mildly amusing "The Case of the Blessing Lady" [sic] didn't capture the sharp humor that the idea suggests'.[7] It was further described as 'simple and amusing but the possibilities offered by the story weren't captured as sharply as they might have been'. The cast were praised, although Marc Daniels's direction was indifferently received.

Looking at the productions shown on US television in 1950, it is the variety that is perhaps most striking. By this point, the Agatha Christie name is not so overloaded with connotations that any adaptations of her work must either fight against, or conform to, any pre-existing idea of what adaptations of her books must be like. This is a marked contrast to many of the more recent sets of adaptations. Consider, for example, the ITV series of *Agatha Christie: Marple* (2004–13) and the French series *Les petits meurtres d'Agatha Christie* (2009–), where her stories are made to fit within a certain structure and presented as a certain type of mystery, in order to conform to the perceived expectations of the audience. The idea of presenting 'a typical Christie' (or 'a typical Marple') has become so crucial that non–Miss Marple series are reworked to include her, and Christie's own detectives are entirely replaced by other recurring characters in the popular French series. To some extent the economics of television production are to blame here (stories of similar types and duration, with recurring characters, are easier to package for international sales and distribution), but this change also demonstrates that attitudes towards Christie's works have changed over the years, resulting in an impact on the way her stories are now adapted. Her best-known works have become even better known, with the unintended side effect that they threaten to drown out the variety of her other offerings. Since both *Marple* and *Agatha Christie's Poirot* finished their runs, Agatha Christie Ltd has embraced the idea of one-off adaptations of her works, including her standalone mysteries; when the dust settles after these adaptations hit the screen, it will be interesting to see whether the general public's expectation of 'an Agatha Christie story' changes.

By January 1952, it had been more than 12 months since the last appearance of a Christie story on US television, but this was not to say that conversations were at a dead end. Harold Huber continued to push for the rights to show Poirot on television, despite the detective's being considered 'sacrosanct' by Christie and Cork, while negotiations regarding a series based on Parker Pyne to be produced by Robert Emhart continued, although no production was ever made.[8] In the end, the year only saw two productions based on Christie's work, although the chosen stories demonstrated the range of her plots available for suitable television adaptation. The first production of the year was a dramatisation of Christie's supernatural short story 'The Red Signal', written nearly 30 years earlier and published as part of the collection *Witness for the Prosecution and Other Stories* in the United States in 1948, while the second was an adaptation of her thriller adventure novel *They Came to Baghdad*, which had only been published the previous year. With one exception, from this point on recordings of all US television broadcasts of Christie's work are known to exist, and they help to show different approaches to the limited opportunities afforded to these live television productions—never clearer than when comparing these two adaptations.

'The Red Signal' was shown on 22 January 1952 as a 30-minute episode of the anthology show *Suspense*, which ran from 1949 to 1954 on CBS. As the only example of Christie adaptations in this form from the 1950s known to survive, it also offers us our first insight into how her works were treated within the context of these half-hour anthology programmes. The series titles indicate the types of stories told in this particular run of standalone dramas, which are akin to the kinds of stories later popularised in Anglia's *Tales of the Unexpected* series (1979–88). The adaptation was sandwiched between the previous week's tale 'The Spider', which followed a woman who discovers a mysterious doctor undertaking some grisly work in the swamps of Florida, and

'Death Drum', the story of a French mayor whose exposé of Nazi sympathisers has dire consequences.

'The Red Signal' sat well within these often macabre stories, as it covered both the paranormal and associated fears, as well as secrets held by characters and an off-camera murder. The story follows a séance at a London house, where we later learn that one of the guests is wanted for crime. A thriller rather than a whodunit, it offers both atmosphere and incident. For this television performance five of the eight actors were British born, and the English setting was retained. The key character of Dermot was played by London-born actor Tom Helmore, who would later be best known for the role of Gavin Elster, the man who hires James Stewart's character Scottie to investigate his wife in Alfred Hitchcock's *Vertigo* (1958). The performance opens with strained organ music (which permeates and overwhelms much of the production, a standard fixture of the programme's radio incarnation, which had not adapted 'The Red Signal') and the pained cries of the medium who will be conducting the séance, so the scene is immediately set for a somewhat overwrought drama lacking in subtlety. Through an earnest conversation, the audience is immediately told the premise of the story: that this séance is merely a distraction from the real drama of the piece, which follows the attempts of psychiatrist Sir Alington West to study one of his fellow guests. Christie's story is given no context, and she receives a standard nominal credit in the opening titles, indicating that she was being treated like any other supplier of suspenseful tales for the series, with the adapters of her work (husband and wife team Mary Orr and Reginald Denham) receiving equal prominence.

With sponsorship messages removed, the mystery itself runs for only around 22 minutes, and the production works hard to keep the tension as high as possible throughout. 'I suppose you would insist that I was melodramatic if I said there was death in the air tonight?' asks the medium at one point, and while there is indeed 'death in the air', the audience cannot help but conclude that the melodrama she mentions has at least equal prominence. All of the cast give acceptable performances, but the production opens with characters who appear to be at the height of paranoia—and then manages to continue upwards in this vein. This is a common issue with short dramas, and the eight cast members inevitably become indistinguishable from each other at times, while the camera can struggle to keep pace with the action so often prefers to observe statically. There is no slow build of drama; instead, there is a rather frenetic series of discussions about the nature of spiritualism and, later, the psyche of a murderer. By keeping the London location (albeit staged entirely within the confines of the New York studio), the adaptation has an air of exoticism for the domestic audience but also, perhaps more significantly, it evokes the gothic horror of British literature as well as its contemporaries—while this séance may be taking place in what is ostensibly the present day, it carries with it connotations of old dark houses and centuries of ghost stories. Throughout the first act of the adaptation, the audience follows the characters' unease as some dark secret is alluded to, as well as the discomfort from the séance itself. When the commercial break's cliffhanger arrives it signals an immediate shift from para-normal delusions to real contemporary crime, a police inspector arriving to inform us that Dermot is wanted for murder. Helmore immediate changes his voice to a cockney affectation, pretending to be his own servant, which offers a moment of lightness and an indication of a well-thought-through performance that helps to keep the audience's attention as we wonder if he is truly guilty of the crime. When we follow him through the studio's depiction of London's fog-strewn streets, enough intrigue is offered to keep the viewer's attention.[9]

Although the adaptation loses the opening of the short story, it is other-wise a close retelling that may find its overt attempts to induce tension to be counterproductive, but is nevertheless an entertaining diversion. US com-mercial television needed stories with clear and attention-grabbing hooks—the broad strokes of the story were inducements for the audience to switch on and continue watching through the sponsor messages, and 'The Red Signal' ticked enough of these boxes that it was applicable to such a series and further demonstrated the suitability of Christie's stories for the medium. As far as is known, there would only be one further adaptation of Christie's work within these half-hour drama series of the 1950s, a production of 'Witness for the Prosecution' for CBS's *Lux Video Theatre* broadcast on 17 September 1953. No recording is known to exist, which is particularly unfortunate as the adapta-tion featured Edward G. Robinson's debut television appearance in the role of solicitor A.J. Mayherne, alongside Andrea King as Romaine and Tom Drake as Leonard Vole. An associate of Christie's American agent Harold Ober caught the production, which judging by a publicity photograph appears to have been given an Edwardian period setting, and thought it 'really very well done, and quite an interesting performance of an excellent story'.[10] However, this pro-duction was felt to reduce the chances of a Broadway appearance of Christie's own newly written play based on the story, and so the decision was made no longer to license it for television, meaning that this perennial Christie quickly disappeared from the small screen.[11]

Within the canon of Agatha Christie novels, *They Came to Baghdad* is one of a small number never to have received a high-profile adaptation. Published in 1951, it is one of her globetrotting thrillers, with forthright adventuress Victoria Jones at the centre of the novel, uncovering international intrigue and taking the reader through all manner of plot twists, many of which take place in the Iraqi city of the title. Given the scale and scope of the story there is great visual potential for a filmic adaptation of it, as the plot lends itself to elaborate location filming around the world, utilising vast sets and a star cast for its interesting range of characters. Such a production has never come to pass, although there were provisional plans for a television movie from Warner Bros. in the early 1980s.[12] The only time that *They Came to Baghdad* has been adapted for the screen to date was in a scenario that could take advantage of none of the story's most potentially interesting elements—it was a single hour-long adaptation for television, performed live on CBS's *Studio One* (1948–58) strand of dramas on 12 May 1952. Previously, I have suggested the reasons why Christie stories were so often used for early television: tight plotting, small cast of characters and few locations. However, none of these advantages is true of *They Came to Baghdad*. It is certainly not a story that is easily summarised or condensed, as it relies on sudden changes in location and unexpected switches in characterisation. We can only assume that it was adapted because it had been published so recently, and this may be an indication that the interest for broadcasters had started to move towards Agatha Christie as a name known to the general audience, with the hope that viewers would recognise this recent publication and therefore be interested in seeing it on screen, rather than taking advantage of her particular storytelling formulae.

Adapted by Theodore Sturgeon (whose science fiction novel *More Than Human* would make a considerable impact the following year), the production initially implies that this will be a light-hearted adventure story, since its opening credits are superimposed on a cartoon of a person being given a comedy-style bomb. However, the opening scenes indicate a very different type of story. A large amount of background information about character identities is rapidly expressed (including a crucial explanation that we should consider the character Anna Scheele to look almost indistinguishable from Victoria Jones, although they are played by different actresses—Elaine Ellis and June Dayton, respectively), along with details of spy secrets and political speculation, told to the audience through a considerable amount of exposition in a few short minutes, leading to a confused opening that grabs the attention through confusion as much as intrigue. Although the opening is set in London, Jones is played as a New York native and the attempts at verisimilitude fall flat ('Mr Churchill Warns Labor' claims a newspaper headline, using the American spelling), as do some of the accents.

One crucial change in the plotting is that from the beginning the audience knows that Victoria Jones is being ushered to Baghdad for nefarious reasons, even though she herself is unaware. This allows for something of a simplification of the later twists and turns, but has the side effect of making Victoria appear rather stupid when she is induced to take part in what is clearly a manipulated scheme of events; combined with her gung-ho manner the unfortunate result is that our heroine becomes more of an irritant, and one cannot help but side with the villains whenever it seems that she might be disposed of. Nevertheless, the adaptation's ambition is to be commended. A review in *The Billboard* called it a 'delightfully incredible comedy-suspense drama, which fortunately never took itself too seriously'.[13] The review also approved of the casting of different actresses in the roles of Anna and Victoria, pointing out that they were kept separate for the opening acts, so that it was only at the denouement that the audience was sure that we had in fact been watching two performers—an advantage of standard-definition television on small screens—while also calling Dayton's Victoria Jones 'charmingly zany'.[14] We may surmise from this that the production was more effective for its contemporary audience than it may be now.

One of the least-seen adaptations of an Agatha Christie story is also one that has been most frequently referenced, by dint of an oft-repeated trivia question: 'Who was the first person to play Miss Marple on screen?' The answer is Gracie Fields, already famous as a singer and actress before she took on the role in an adaptation of Christie's 1950 novel *A Murder Is Announced*, broadcast live on NBC on 30 December 1956. However, this was not the first attempt to bring Miss Marple to American television screens. Following Christie's dismissal of the prospect, Harold Ober wrote to Edmund Cork to say that he had been in conversation with producer Winston O'Keefe regarding a potential Miss Marple production starring Fay Bainter, who had won the Academy Award for Best Supporting Actress in 1938 for her performance as Aunt Belle in *Jezebel* (d. William Wyler).[15] Ober makes the best case he can, outlining that the production could be sympathetic and dignified, only to concede later that Miss Marple would actually have to become an American from Cape Cod, and that original mysteries would need to be written in order to sustain a weekly series.[16] Surprisingly, Cork does not seem to consider this to be too much of an issue (perhaps swayed by the lure of a $150 weekly fee for the use of Miss Marple, rising to $250 in the second year) and suggests that plans continue while they awaited Christie's return from Iraq.[17] However, Christie was more emphatically against the idea than Cork had imagined.[18] This did not stop negotiations, however, and by 1954 Peggy Wood was in the frame for Miss Marple, having shown an interest in starring in a series to be produced by Carol Irwin, and continued to be interested for the next two years.[19]

It is not clear why there was a four-year gap between Christie adaptations on US television, but we do know that there were sporadic attempts to tie her work into a larger deal with a film studio (often MGM) that could have restricted their availability for adaptation. Certainly, when CBS offered $100,000 to show the Broadway production of *Witness for the Prosecution* in 1955 the amount offered was noted with keen interest, but it was secondary to the attempts to secure a film deal for the play, which could have been negatively affected by any such deal.[20] There is also the further possibility that Christie's ongoing rise in popularity, as well as the high proportion of tax she was paying on her American earnings, resulted in higher fees for using her stories. The timing of this adaptation, between Christmas and New Year, as well as its star cast do indicate that it was designed to be something of a special event, which is a status that television adaptations of her work would largely retain from this point on—it is also an early instance of Christie being credited alongside the title, indicating that she was now a significant draw for the audience. Although not one of her most immediately iconic stories, *A Murder Is Announced* is nevertheless one of her strongest novels, and one that has a particularly striking premise. In the story, a newspaper announcement of a murder is placed—prior to the event occurring. The location of this murder is stated to be the residence of Letitia Blacklock (played by Jessica Tandy in this adaptation, who gets top billing), who claims to know nothing about it—but when the time comes, the lights are extinguished and a murder does indeed occur. Miss Marple (a role for which Gracie Fields receives 'Special Guest Star' status) sets out to unravel the background to these events and unmask the murderer.

Joining Tandy and Fields in this adaptation was Roger Moore—not yet a star name, but still a charismatic presence on screen in the role of Patrick, Letitia's younger cousin. Combined, they represent one of the highest-profile casts for any Christie adaptation, in a production that efficiently tells the story in under an hour. Performances are strong throughout and, although there are one or two minor fluffs, the live nature of the performance does not have a significant impact on its effectiveness. It retains the English setting, although Fields makes the curious decision to play Miss Marple with what appears to be a Scottish accent; this has the unintentional consequence that one now has to wonder quite how long she has been living in the English village of St Mary Mead, and so how well she really knows the community. Nevertheless, the story effectively retains the key plot points of the novel, and showcases some of its most fondly remembered characters, such as the spinsters Hinchcliffe and Murgatroyd (played by Pat Nye and Josephine Brown, respectively), who are clearly coded as lesbians to audience members who are astutely observing the relationships between characters, or who recognise them as a stereotype. Such a relationship was already implicit in the novel, but the sparring between the two actresses makes the affectionate but resigned conversations between them more akin to an old married couple than two friends; in a departure from the novel, it is Hinchcliffe who becomes the final victim of the murderer, leaving the more naïve Murgatroyd to fend for herself in the aftermath. The actresses' performances help to shore up the relatively thin on-screen characterisation in an adaptation that necessarily has to concentrate on plot and atmosphere above all else.[21]

Although this is a perfectly serviceable production with some strong performances, it does not seem to have been well received. The reviewer in *The New York Times* said that the question was 'Not Whodunit—Why', asking 'Why, for example, did Jessica Tandy and Gracie Fields ever get involved in such inferior melodrama?'[22] Further, the reviewer accused the production of using 'a series of stock characters and situations', before declaring that 'it was murder from beginning to end'.[23] If there were ever plans for more appearances of Fields in the role, then such a response seems to have scuppered them. That is not to say that there was a shortage of interest in television productions of Christie's work—there were suggestions of high-profile productions of *The Mousetrap* as well as a number of other Christie stories, including *The Murder of Roger Ackroyd*—but the emphasis was increasingly moving towards protecting stage productions from losing audiences to television, while also ensuring that a television production did not cheapen the prospects for a later movie adaptation. There was also the germ of an idea that all of the film and television rights might be tied together into one overarching deal with a single studio.

At the end of the 1950s, one of the most frequently requested (and best-known) Christie stories finally appeared on American television screens. The 1945 film of *And Then There Were None* (as discussed in the next chapter) appears to have complicated the situation for some time. Although there had been a 1949 BBC production and a claim that the rights were available, the paucity of productions after 1959 may indicate that any contractual loophole was rapidly closed and that the situation was not clear cut. Nevertheless, both an NBC production in the USA and an ITV production in the UK were screened within days of each other in early 1959. The US adaptation aired on 18 January and was broadcast on NBC under the title *Ten Little Indians*. Adapted by Philip H. Reisman, Jr, who had several television credits to his name spanning mysteries and spy thrillers, this live performance condensed the story into an hour (including sponsor messages). Both Reisman and the director Paul Bogart may have regretted that the number of suspects (and potential victims) was so well advertised in the title, since the brief running time means that several guests are despatched with unseemly haste. For example, the character of Mrs Rogers has only a few words of dialogue before her untimely demise, and the actress does not even receive a credit. Nevertheless, despite its brevity the adaptation covers the major plot points of the version of the story told in Christie's stage play, and allows the handful of characters who survive to the last act good opportunities to work together to solve the mystery while maintaining the tension.

The production opens with a rhyme that sets up the locale and the basic premise for the mystery itself. The narrator tells the audience that 'Once upon an island/and once upon a time/off the coast of Devon/according to the rhyme/ten little Indians/though the invitation said for fun/were invited to be murdered/one by one by one [...]' and we see most of the cast in a studio-bound boat, shrouded in fog and with sound effects establishing the journey to the island. As the rhyme indicates, the original location is maintained, including references to nearby Plymouth and Dartmoor, while the characters are predominantly British. Therefore there is little pretence that the audience will not broadly expect what is to follow, another indication that Christie's story had already made a strong impact on the public's consciousness through its iconography if not necessarily the details of the plot. This is reinforced by the choice of the title *Ten Little Indians* for this adaptation, which reflected the name used for the Broadway play rather than the book, but also demonstrates that the whittling down of suspects mirrored by the nursery rhyme was still seen as the most iconic element of the story, echoed by the decision that the opening titles would depict the depletion of ten Indian figures, with one being removed every time a new credit slide was shown. The opening titles also acknowledge that the book was more widely published under the title *And Then There Were None* in the United States, although this adaptation uses the play as its template.[24] Variants of the story have been seen on screen many times over the years, often in circumstances that have expected the audience to make a connection between exotic or unusual stories of isolated strangers disappearing one by one and the Christie original, emphasising the timeless nature of the basic premise.

Although this is one of the strongest early television adaptations of Christie's work, siphoning the core elements of the story down to a 50-minute live television adaptation results in some unfortunate shortcomings. A 15-minute section midway through the performance shows the five remaining characters barely able to move ten feet, or compose themselves for more than a few minutes, before they stumble across yet another body. This changes the tone from a slow-burn mystery to outright horror, as it mirrors the later slasher films more than the understated, unsettling nature of the original story. Indeed, the end of this production features the villain chasing their apparent final victim with the words 'I must have my hanging!', as the noose sits prepared. Instead of a creeping sense of dread, we have a no less effective demonstration of mounting hysteria from early in the proceedings. This shows how production and distribution constraints of adaptations can inadvertently result in a shift of genre; in this case the move towards horror is due to timing, pace and the nature of live production, but other Christie adaptations will see the tone alter radically due to particular casting choices, audience expectations or production issues. Here we have characters immediately jump to the height of emotion at the earliest opportunity. For example, the detective Blore suddenly switches from his usual no-nonsense attitude to absolute terror when he belatedly realises that the killer is still in the house; his rush to escape leads to his being felled by a falling bear statue. In both the book and stage production, Blore leaves because he thinks he spots something outside that can assist them, rather than because he is scared. Nevertheless, despite the incongruity of sudden plot developments and character changes, this is an effective and at times unsettling production that deserves to be made more readily available to a modern audience, despite the issues resulting from its brevity.

CHRISTIE ON BRITISH TELEVISION IN THE 1950s

While there was a steady stream of Christie adaptations on US television during the 1950s, matters were rather different in her home country. When examining correspondence with the author, one is struck by the relentless nature of the ongoing attempts to coax Christie and her work onto radio in particular, sometimes with success, but more often without. For example, in February 1951 she was asked by producer Paul Stephenson to read some original short stories on the radio, an offer that was declined by Nora Blackborow from her agents Hughes Massie the following month, who stated that Christie would be abroad for several months, with no offer made for discussion on her return.[25] The hint was not taken and an identical letter was then sent in May, this time signed by Marguerite Scott of the talks department, only for a more emphatic reply from Blackborow saying that 'Mrs Christie does not regard herself as an accomplished broadcaster, and would not wish therefore to participate in your short-story reading'.[26] Rather than considering this to be a failed attempt, Scott took issue with it in a letter dated 11 June when she wrote to Blackborow that Christie 'underrates her talent as a broadcaster'. The proposed series, *Tellers of Tales*, went ahead, but Christie was not a contributor. Her work did make an appearance on the radio, however, as scenes from her play *The Hollow* were performed on the Light Programme's series *From the London Theatre* on 8 July, although later attempts to broadcast an original radio adaptation of the same story would not come to fruition due to the unavailability of rights—possibly because of this very stage production. Similar difficulties were encountered when the BBC tried to perform *Love from a Stranger* for television once more in 1952, only to discover that the film's rights holders Eagle-Lion had gone into liquidation and there was some difficulty in obtaining the necessary permissions.[27]

The BBC finally had some success in convincing Christie to appear on radio once more at the end of 1952, since she recorded a three-and-a-half-minute interview for a project called *This Is Britain* on 18 December.[28] Nevertheless, this flexibility did not extend to television, because there were attempts throughout 1953 to get Christie on screen, particularly for a proposed interview on documentary series *Panorama*. 'I am afraid Mrs Christie feels she would definitely not like to appear on television, under any circumstances whatever. She is, as I told you, very shy, and she hates publicity of any kind, so I fear there is nothing more we can do', wrote Edmund Cork.[29] This brief interview remained an exception, as she declined similar approaches for *Woman's Hour* in late 1953, although when she was the subject of an edition of *Close Up* (a series profiling contributors to the entertainment industry), she did read a contribution.[30] Nevertheless, requests continued throughout the 1950s, including a proposed interview for radio series *Frankly Speaking* in May 1955, another request to appear on *Woman's Hour* alongside a requested appearance on American Radio Network series *Personal Debt* (both in January 1956), as well as a 'light but profound'(!) talk suggested as part of a religious BBC series in January 1958.[31] All were declined and, given the incomplete nature of the written archives, we can be confident that there were many more requests than this. Christie was in demand, but she was keen to work only on her own terms.

By 1953 Christie's work had found a regular place on the airwaves, with a radio series of *Partners in Crime* starring as Tommy and Tuppence Beresford real-life husband and wife Richard Attenborough and Sheila Sim—both of whom had been part of the original West End cast of *The Mousetrap* the previous year. The idea of adapting the stories for the radio had been floated before, and the impetus for this particular project appears to have been a 5 January letter from the agency Kavanagh Productions, Kevin Kavanagh writing on behalf of character actor Naunton Wayne with the suggestion that Joan Greenwood could star alongside him in the production.[32] In what might seem to be an unfair move, Wayne and Greenwood were never seriously considered, but following the suggestion the project went ahead with Attenborough and Sim in their place. Crucially, this series is an example of how those with important roles in the BBC often had little enthusiasm for Christie's actual works. In this case Andrew Stewart, the Controller of the Home Service, declared the source material to be 'very poor', while recognising that it could be a success.[33]

In 1954 there was the broadcast of *Personal Call*, an original radio play by Christie for the Light Programme, indicating that she was still happy to write for broadcasting when her circumstances allowed.[34] It had been warmly received when first read by the BBC some time earlier, in late 1952, when reader Cynthia Pughe declared it 'very good', saying that 'Miss Christie has made full use of radio techniques and possibilities'.[35] Certainly it is a story that works very well for radio, as it revolves around a mysterious telephone call, a demonstration of Christie's increased sophistication in writing for different media. The positive reaction that it garnered was a marked contrast to Pughe's reaction to a visit to the theatre where she saw Christie's play *Black Coffee*, which she declared 'terribly contrived' shortly before *Personal Call*'s first broadcast.[36] Despite the perceived variable quality of her work, at least when it came to suitability for radio, repeated attempts were made to convince Christie to take part in a proposed 'festival' of her work for BBC radio during 1956.[37] Christie did not express any interest in taking part and the planned season was nearly cancelled, but in the end it did run during February and March 1956, encompassing adaptations of several titles, including the return of Austin Trevor as Poirot (following his appearances as the detective in three films in 1931 and 1934) in an adaptation of the sleuth's debut, *The Mysterious Affair at Styles.*

During this busy time for Christie she had been absent from television, but a nearly forgotten sub-genre of the medium would soon ensure that her contemporary works were being seen by home audiences. One of the original ideas for television was that it would be an opportunity to bring existing entertainments into the home as well as a way to create original artistic and entertainment endeavours; the early emphasis was much more on the former than the latter, and part of this was the live broadcasting of notable theatrical events. The BBC had often shown parts of current West End productions, and in 1955 it was Christie's turn. Described as a 'special performance before an invited audience', on 4 April 1955 several scenes were televised from Christie's play *Spider's Web* starring Margaret Lockwood at the Savoy Theatre.[38] The programme ran for an hour, so we can assume that the excerpt was a substantial one, although such televised productions were often accompanied by interviews and introductions that may have taken up a significant portion of the time allotted.

Given the prolific appearances of Christie's works in the West End during the 1950s, it is unsurprising that another of her plays would get similar treatment later in the year—but this time the appearance was on new rival broadcaster ITV. In August 1955, E.M. Layton of the BBC's copyright department had pointed out to her colleagues that *Three Blind Mice* could not be broadcast while *The Mousetrap* was running in the West End; this would be a recurring query over the next few years. However, while the BBC could not broadcast the original piece on which the theatrical success was based, ITV's weekday London broadcaster Associate-Rediffusion had better luck. It showed ten minutes from the West End production at the Ambassadors Theatre at 11.30 p.m. on Thursday, 1 December 1955 as the second in a series called *Curtain Call*, which featured extracts from current West End hits. This may only have been brief, but it is significant as one of the rare appearances of any part of the story in the UK outside of the stage performances since 1955. Two years later it would be trumped by BBC Television, which showcased an extract of the record-breaking 1998th performance of *The Mousetrap* as part of its occasional trips to the theatre under the banner *Theatre Flash*. Produced for television by Noble Wilson, credit was given to both producer Peter Saunders and Romulus Films, run by John and James Woolf, who had taken out an ill-fated option on moving the play to the big screen whenever it finished its West End run. Part of the performance was introduced by Richard Attenborough, in recognition that the 13 September 1957 performance officially gave the play the record as the longest-running play in West End history. The festivities extended beyond the televised extract, since earlier in the evening BBC Television had even featured the play's wardrobe mistress ('and "mother" to the company') Maisie Wilmer-Brown in its *Tonight* programme, signifying the extent to which this was seen as an event of general interest.[39]

Following its brief transmission of part of *The Mousetrap*, Associated-Rediffusion was more ambitious the next time it sought to televise a Christie stage production. On Monday, 3 September 1956, it offered an extract from Christie's new play *Towards Zero* a day before its official premiere. Coming from the St James Theatre, this took place in front of an invited audience and was introduced by Leslie Mitchell. This was the first time a West End production had been previewed on television in this way, and the risks of such a venture were made clear in the next day's *Daily Mail* review by Philip Purser. 'I must leave judgment of Agatha Christie's *Towards Zero* to the theatre critics', he wrote before going on to give his opinion anyway. 'I can only say that after seeing half an hour of it on TV their most glowing enthusiasm would not get me into the theatre.'[40] It seems unlikely that the underwhelming reception of the extract directly resulted in the play's demise after six months, but it can scarcely have helped. The next time an extract of a Christie play was shown on television was on 13 November 1959, with Associated-Rediffusion's broadcast of a 30-minute extract from the first act of *The Unexpected Guest*. This time the broadcast was supporting an established hit, since the play was celebrating two years in the West End.

The Unexpected Guest had been Associated-Rediffusion's second brush with Christie in 1959: on 13 January, five days before the NBC adaptation, it had produced a 90-minute version of Christie's play *Ten Little Niggers* (using this title). Starring Christine Pollard as Vera, John Stone as Lombard and Felix Aylmer as Sir Lawrence Wargrave, the production was adapted and directed by Robert Tronson, who would go on to direct for many television series, including *Callan* (1967–72), *Public Eye* (1965–75) and *Hetty Wainthropp Investigates* (1996–98). Marketed as the first of a series of revivals of West End successes for television, it was warmly received, the *Times* reviewer calling it 'immaculate'.[41] This reviewer acknowledges that 'It is a commonplace criticism of [Christie's] work to say that the characterization is rudimentary; but the important thing is that it does exactly what she requires. It lures the audience into accepting an illusion which, in the end, will be stripped away to show a grinning death's head.'[42] Unlike the NBC adaptation, it seems that the extra time allocated to this (now missing) television performance allowed for slowly building suspense. Reflecting on the innate differences between the stage and television forms, the *Times* reviewer pointed out:

> Television, in this respect, has an unfair advantage over the theatre, for one is not permitted to view all the characters simultaneously. Perhaps Sir Lawrence is surreptitiously dropping a cyanide capsule into an unguarded whisky; but, as he is off the screen, who can tell? Partly for this reason Mr Robert Tronson's production greatly accumulated in suspense towards the end.[43]

Perhaps unwittingly, the reviewer is highlighting the fact that television offers unique opportunities for Christie's work, which makes it all the more unfortunate that her personal involvement with the medium was so limited. Although there had been a 1958 production of the play *Love from a Stranger* for BBC television, starring Emrys Jones as Bruce and Clare Austin as Cecily, by this point the piece had taken on such a life of its own, detached from the original short story 'Philomel Cottage', that Christie was not even mentioned in the publicity—only Frank Vosper was mentioned in the television listings, although Christie was credited on screen.[44] For this production many minor changes were made, with much of the dialogue condensed and rewritten, although the story kept to the same basic structure as Vosper's play (however, in an attempt at modernisation, this time Cecily has won £30,000 on the football pools). The television performance loses almost all of the first act's second scene, where Cecily's fiancé Nigel returns and their engagement is broken off—instead this occurs over the telephone, and we immediately jump to Bruce and Cecily in residence at their new home, which is pleasingly captioned 'Philomel Cottage' on screen. *The Stage* gave this 'old thriller' a fair review, highlighting a perceived fault with the production that Bruce's 'abnormal reactions' early in the piece surely should have been a red flag for his potential wife.[45] 'More restraint in the earlier scenes would have heightened the tension and the suspense and made the entire play more credible', reads the review—a complaint that is also true of some other adaptations of the story.[46] Despite this small flurry of mostly recycled and familiar productions in the late 1950s, it would be another 20 years before an original adaptation of Christie's work was made for British television, and the next decade saw increasingly restrictive opportunities for her works to appear on the small screen.

Christie on 1960s Television

It was common for Christie to be approached with various film and television proposals over the years, but the majority of these potential projects did not come to fruition and were often quickly and quietly forgotten. However, in the late 1950s there were repeated stories in the trade press regarding more than one proposed television series of her work. One of these was a suggested anthology programme that covered a different Agatha Christie mystery each week, while the other was a fresh attempt to bring Poirot to television. Both suggested series had their origins in the United States, but the intention was for international distribution, and even production, as they would be made as short films suitable for worldwide distribution. On 18 June 1958, *Variety* reported that the American literary agent H.N. Swanson was planning to make a half-hour 'vidfilm' series of Christie's mysteries, alongside adaptations of other work by his clients, including crime writer John Creasey. This project was short-lived, because in April 1960 MGM secured a deal with Christie to adapt her work for the screen. Prior to the finalisation of the agreement, the *Daily Mail* had reported on the plans, quoting her agent Edmund Cork who said, 'We have been asked for years to sell and even now things could go the wrong way.' Asked if the deal was worth the speculated £1,000,000, Cork responded that the amount was 'considerably less'.[47] With some exceptions the deal encompassed the rights to all of Christie's books, although not her stage plays.[48] When this deal was in its early stages, the industry magazine *Broadcasting* indicated that there was an expectation that these stories could appear in a series with the tentative title of *The Agatha Christie Series*, which was now expected to run for an hour with an attempt to find a commitment to make 26 episodes.[49] *Variety* reported the news shortly afterwards, pointing out that hour-long television dramas had been increasingly difficult to sell.[50] A full year was to pass before more news was forthcoming following the signing of the deal with Christie, as reports in November 1960 referred to the preparation of scripts for a series to be filmed at Elstree Studios in the UK, with head of the British MGM division Lawrence P. Bachmann as executive producer.[51] As late as 1961 there were plans for a Miss Marple television series to be made for television in the UK alongside the Margaret Rutherford pictures for cinema.[52]

In the end these Agatha Christie series were not made, but the reports of the signing of the deal had also referred to a potential series of Poirot adaptations, to star José Ferrer.[53] Puerto Rico–born Ferrer's best-known role was his Academy Award–winning turn as Cyrano de Bergerac, and no doubt he was expected to adopt a Gallic accent once more. Although some sources claim that a pilot episode with Ferrer in the role was made (but left unbroadcast), I can find no first-hand evidence of it, and if it ever existed then no copy has been retained by any associated archive.[54] In May 1960 Ferrer was mentioned in correspondence, with the associated hope that he would stay in the role for some time, but there was also an understanding that a decision would need to be made quickly in order to secure his services, perhaps in part due to complications regarding his tax status.[55] When a pilot episode for a potential series called *The Adventures of Hercule Poirot* was finally broadcast on CBS on 1 April 1962, Philadelphia-born actor Martin Gabel was in the lead role and there is nothing in the production files for the series to indicate that it was a second attempt; in fact, Gabel had been attached to the project by 1961.

This pilot episode, which does still exist but has remained unseen since its 1962 transmission, is one of the most intriguing dead ends for Christie's work on television. All of the pre-production material makes it clear that this was intended to be the first of a series of Poirot adaptations for television. The original pitch material for a proposed Poirot series referred to it as 'A one-hour detective series that plays against a world-wide background', although the one episode that was made fitted a 30-minute slot.[56] Several scripts for a potential trailer for the series were put together, all of which emphasised the range of stories available for adaptation and the idiosyncratic character traits of Poirot himself. An outline written in June 1961 claims that Poirot resigned from the Belgian police because their work was too routine, because he takes an interest in more unusual cases.[57] These early attempts to outline the series were reasonably in keeping with the character as depicted by Christie—a meticulous and intelligent man with an occasional mischievous quality. However, he is also referred to as relatively young (a change with which Christie may have sympathised, since she regretted making him so old in her earliest stories given his ongoing success).

Even at this early stage, the outline demonstrates a perception that straightforward adaptations of Poirot stories did not present a sufficient perceived hook for the programme's producers. One of the most bizarre elements of the episode as made is Poirot's mode of travel, which appears to double as his home. It is described in the documentation as 'a limousine which he uses whenever circumstances permit. It is a tribute to his extraordinary personality that he should have had it lavishly equipped with every comfort and convenience. "Where else in the world," he sometimes asks, "is there a man owning a car with a television set, a television, a private bar, and a back seat that turns into a bed!"'[58] This apparent attempt to contemporise Poirot demonstrates how some fundamental changes to the detective of literature were seen as necessary for network television. Not only is this a modern, technologically driven and slightly younger Poirot than in the books, there was inevitably the question of his relationship with women. Initially, it is claimed that he is respectful of and interested in women, who are intrigued by him, and early script notes that he should use his charm to win female characters over.[59] In a trailer for the series, Poirot himself was scripted to say of his creator Christie: 'Her success has been achieved without bloodshed or blackjacks, without sadism and—I admit this reluctantly as a French man—without sex.'[60] As with some earlier depictions of Poirot on screen, his nationality appears to be in doubt here—while there are repeated references to him as Belgian, he is also described as French; in fact, those planning the series appear to have believed that Belgium is a region of France.

Despite some changes in an apparent attempt to make the character more attractive for an American television audience, unlike some earlier adaptations it was not the case that Christie's works were expected simply to be filleted for usable material that happened to have been written by her—instead, the Agatha Christie name was now perceived as a strong selling point. The trailer was scripted to open with an array of Christie books on screen, with her name to be prominent, while Poirot's voiceover called Christie the greatest living mystery writer, also boasting that he himself is a character who stands out above all others.[61] Various versions of this trailer script outline different potential mysteries, some of which are clearly reworked versions of existing mysteries (one outline has a series of murders, listed as names in a guidebook, which sends Poirot to towns and villages in the south of England in an attempt to stop a murderer killing again—a plot that echoes *The ABC Murders*, for example—while *Dead Man's Folly* is transplanted to the United States as a seemingly innocent 'murder hunt' that is the highlight of a California church bazaar's festivities, which suddenly turns into a real hunt by Poirot for a murderer), while others appear to be completely original. For example, while there may be some echoes of the non-Poirot short story 'Swan Song' in a tale described as taking place in an old castle in Spain, where there is a world famous soprano and a stage dagger that turns out to be fatally real in events linked to a strange tale of a dead man's revenge, many of the stories' similarities to Christie mysteries appear to be tenuous at best.[62] Even when specific Christie titles are mentioned, radical changes appear to be anticipated: Poirot claims in *Peril at End House* that a crude rope holds the key to the crime, but the neck it encircles is 'delightfully slim and lovely', an amusingly hyperbolic plot point that is absent from Christie's original.[63]

The distinctiveness of Christie's mysteries is reinforced throughout the planning documents for the proposed series. One memo to the writer of the trailer (and pilot script) Barré Lyndon, a pseudonym for British writer Alfred Edgar, asked that writers emphasise the offbeat aspect rather than stock elements such as a bank robbery, citing a baffling crime that takes place at a bizarre costume ball as one good example.[64] Christie herself is seen as crucial to this perceived 'offbeat' nature, as the same memo suggests that Lyndon mention that Agatha Christie is the most widely known mystery writer, her name synonymous with 'something', which he then explains means unique and outstanding mysteries.[65]

Given the fact that these documents outline that some liberties were expected to be taken with the series, it may be a surprise to learn that the one completed episode is a reasonably faithful adaptation of one of Christie's stronger short stories, 'The Disappearance of Mr Davenheim'. Unlike most previous television adaptations of her work, this pilot was shot on film with high production values, and on this occasion the action was transplanted from Britain to Boston. As with the original story, the plot concerns the titular event, when Mr Davenheim leaves his home one day only to disappear without trace, despite eyewitnesses on the only route that he can reasonably be expected to have taken. By moving the story to contemporary America the emphasis is changed a little—Mrs Davenheim's situation is thrown into focus by the fervent press, including television reporters, when her husband's disappearance makes the news. Poirot is called on by Chief McManus of the police, with whom he had apparently worked on a previous case in Baltimore, while he had also previously met Mrs Davenheim in London. In this case Poirot gets little chance to demonstrate the character traits so meticulously outlined in the pre-production documentation since he elects to approach the case as a puzzle. In the original story Poirot bets Inspector Japp £5 that he can solve the case without leaving his flat; in the adaptation the same bet is made with the Chief, and Poirot is confined to his hotel room with $20 at stake. Although the decision to retain this amusing narrative quirk reinforces the general fidelity of the adaptation, it does result in an unfortunate impression that Poirot—who has been called to this location to help a distressed woman—is almost cruel in his decision to approach the case as a game. This is less of an issue in the original story where the case is not brought to Poirot directly, while the decision to remain in one's home is rather less of an affectation than travelling to a hotel only to refuse to leave it to help solve what might be a murder case. Poirot's reasoning does little to make him seem any more empathetic when he claims: 'I am not staying in this hotel bedroom just to prove how clever I am—only to show that what I do is an extension, a development beyond ordinary police work.'

Within this episode Poirot is also said to be a criminology lecturer, which may help to justify his stance in some way, but in this context the wager feels like a cruel game undertaken with the full knowledge that it would cause emotional damage to Mrs Davenheim despite the eventual successful conclusion of the case. Poirot is even less sympathetic when he ruminates on the likely outcome of the case just before the first commercial break. 'When I take you to your husband, as in the end I'm sure I shall, he may be dead,' he says to Mrs Davenheim, 'but if he's not you'll wish that he were.' On the whole, the production is more impressive than the documentation surrounding it may have indicated. Although some elements are nonsensical to the point of ridiculousness (particularly Poirot's apparently magic car, which seems to have been designed for Batman's middle age), there are some stylish moments, including a dissolve from Poirot's monocle into a flashback of events, while Martin Gabel offers a reasonably faithful portrayal of the Belgian detective. It is clearly an inexpensive production, however—perhaps explaining why Poirot is scripted to spend the whole time in his hotel room—and it is bizarre that, even when seen in flashbacks and the eventual denouement, Mr Davenheim is not given a single line. Judging by some of the plans in place any resulting series may not have paid close attention to the Poirot canon, but it is easy to believe that it could have been a diverting and entertaining collection of unusual mysteries. At the end of the episode Poirot is called to Palm Beach to investigate the discovery of three bodies there, and it would be an interesting exercise to see how this portrayal of a different location and mystery each week would have worked alongside Christie's stories. It is unfortunate that the pilot episode remains out of circulation at the time of writing, since it is an interesting contribution to the world of Agatha Christie on screen, and was to be the last adaptation of its type for two decades.

In the end, the disappearance of Christie's work from British and American television productions was a quiet withdrawal rather than an announced intention. Following another attempt to broadcast a new radio version of *Three*

Blind Mice as well as an adaptation of *A Murder Is Announced*, the rights situation was made clear by Heather Dean of the BBC Copyright Department on
24 January 1961. 'No broadcasting rights of any material by this author are
available following an agreement MGM made some months ago', she wrote.[66]
There was a rare exception on 9 February 1963 when there was a televising
of the light comedy/mystery *Afternoon at the Seaside* on BBC Television (part
of Christie's *Rule of Three* set of one-act plays), but this was a simple outside
broadcast of the performance then running at the Duchess Theatre, with an
audience in residence. Critically it was not well received, with Derek Hill of
Contrast magazine wondering why the BBC had chosen to broadcast a play
of apparent low merit, asking if it was 'part of some Machiavellian scheme to
convince viewers that theatre standards are infinitely lower than those of even
the worst television drama', while *The Listener* deemed it a 'timid choice'.[67]
However, audience research was more positive, the broadcast gaining a score
of 72 on the Reaction Index scale against an average of 66 for stage show
excerpts, with 67 % of respondents grading it A or A+ and none giving it lower
than a C. Some respondents were not keen on the staging, which they felt was
not convincingly seaside-like, and the cameras missed some portions of the
action. Those less keen on the production felt that it was rather old-fashioned.
However, on the whole reaction was positive, with the Christie name being
enough for some to tune in, and most responding that they found it witty and
entertaining.[68] Nevertheless, there was no subsequent lift at the box office for
the production.[69]

Following its failed attempts to make television series of her works, it seems
that MGM decided that the cinema was the way forward for Christie adaptations. Throughout most of the 1960s and 1970s televised depictions of her
stories were reserved for broadcasts of films such as MGM's own Margaret
Rutherford pictures, and the occasional discussion of her work, such as when
Poirot himself paid tribute to Christie on her 80th birthday during an edition
of BBC2's *Review* on 18 September 1970. In 1972 actor Ronald Fraser took
part in the documentary series *Having a Lovely Time*, which followed the rec-
reational pursuits of Britons, in which he observed a Hastings amateur dramat-
ics group tackle *The Hollow*; Christie received a fee of £150 for an extract of
rehearsals running to up to 15 minutes. Viewers and BBC personnel alike may
have mulled over the fairness of only being able to watch these local machina-
tions, rather than see an adaptation proper, but at the time Christie's works
were starting to find more success than ever on the cinema screen.

NOTES

1. Ober to Cork, 19 July 1950 and Cork to Ober, 14 August 1950 (Agatha
   Christie Archive, Exeter).
2. In the UK it formed part of 1934's *The Listerdale Mystery* collection.
3. A recording was made but is not known to have survived. We know
   from the television listings that John Newland, Augusta Dabney and

Bertha Belmore performed three of the roles, although it is not clear who took which part. Readers may wish to make some educated guesses given their ages at the time (32, 31 and 67, respectively).

4. An earlier agreement had been put in place to broadcast *And Then There Were None* but, for whatever reason, such a production did not appear, even though the film contract was checked to ensure that such a production was permissible. Ober to Cork, 16 March 1950 (Agatha Christie Archive, Exeter).

5. Some sources imply that the *Danger* episode 'Appointment with Death', which aired on 16 January 1951, was an adaptation of the Christie story of the same name. There are few details available about the production, but while this is possible, on the evidence we have it seems likely that this 30-minute production was a different story that happened to share the same title.

6. According to a review the couple adopts the surname Blunt rather than Beresford for this adaptation—in the original story, this is a pseudonym that they adopt because it is the name of the detective agency that they take over.

7. *Variety*, 13 December 1950.

8. Ober to Cork, 25 January 1952 (Agatha Christie Archive, Exeter).

9. This use of fog was particularly timely, given London's 'Great Smog' of 1952.

10. Ober to Cork, 30 September 1953 (Agatha Christie Archive, Exeter).

11. Cork to Ober, 25 September 1953 (Agatha Christie Archive, Exeter) More specifically, Francis L. Sullivan had written to Christie regarding the television production, and Cork reports her to be upset that it may have affected the play's chances—which was not to be the case.

12. As covered in Chap. 10.

13. *The Billboard*, 24 May 1952.

14. *The Billboard*, 24 May 1952.

15. Ober to Cork, 20 October 1950 (Agatha Christie Archive, Exeter).

16. Ober to Cork, 6 March 1951 (Agatha Christie Archive, Exeter).

17. Cork to Ober, 16 March 1951 (Agatha Christie Archive, Exeter).

18. Cork to Ober, 31 January 1952 (Agatha Christie Archive, Exeter).

19. Ober to Cork, 17 February 1954 (Agatha Christie Archive, Exeter).

20. Cork to Ober, 22 July 1955 (Agatha Christie Archive, Exeter).

21. In this adaptation Hinchcliffe is murdered, rather than Murgatroyd, although for the same reason—that she had worked out the identity of the killer. This does the character of Murgatroyd rather a disservice, since she does not have a moment of intellectual redemption from being an apparent simpleton.

22. *The New York Times*, December 31 1956.

23. *The New York Times*, December 31 1956.

24. Indeed, although *Ten Little Indians* was occasionally used as a title for US editions of the book, none of these appears to pre-date this 1959 adaptation.

25. Correspondence in BBC WAC, Agatha Christie: Talks 1930–1958. Paul Stephenson to Christie, 28 February 1951 and Nora Blackborow to Stephenson, 6 March 1951.

26. Correspondence in BBC WAC, Agatha Christie: Talks 1930–1958. Marguerite Scott to Christie, 21 May 1951 and Nora Blackborow to Scott, 25 May 1951.

27. As outlined in correspondence in the *Love from a Stranger* production file (BBC WAC T5/301).

28. Jill Cork to 'Talks Booking', 24 December 1952 (BBC WAC, Agatha Christie: Talks 1930–1958).

29. Morgan, *Agatha Christie: A Biography*, 304.

30. Other big names with a Christie connection listed as contributors include Richard Attenborough, Margaret Lockwood and Francis L. Sullivan. It was broadcast on the Light Programme on 13 February 1955.

31. As per correspondence in BBC WAC, Agatha Christie: Talks 1930–1958.

32. Probably best known as cricket-loving Caldicott in Hitchock's 1938 film *The Lady Vanishes*.

33. Stewart to Audrey Cameron, 27 January 1953 (BBC WAC, Agatha Christie: Scriptwriter 1937–1962).

34. Broadcast on 31 May 1954.

35. Cynthia Pughe, Drama Script Reader's Report 16 October 1952 (BBC WAC, Agatha Christie: Scriptwriter 1937–1962).

36. Cynthia Pughe, Drama Script Reader's Report 14 May 1954 (BBC WAC, Agatha Christie: Scriptwriter 1937–1962).

37. See, for example, letter from H. Rooney Pelletier (Controller of the Light Programme) to Christie, 25 January 1956 (BBC WAC, Agatha Christie: Scriptwriter 1937–1962).

38. *Radio Times*, 4 April 1955.

39. *The Stage*, 19 September 1957.

40. *Daily Mail*, 4 September 1956.

41. *The Times*, 14 January 1959.

42. *The Times*, 14 January 1959.

43. *The Times*, 14 January 1959.

44. Transmitted on 26 December 1958—a Christie for Christmas, even on television, and the camera script shows that she was given a credit on the opening captions. It followed 'Ericson the Viking', a new episode of the hugely popular sitcom *Hancock's Half Hour* that—in part—saw its eponymous star suffering a miserable Christmas Day.

45. *The Stage*, 1 January 1959.

46. *The Stage*, 1 December 1959.

47. *Daily Mail,* 12 March 1960.
48. *The Stage and Television Today,* 21 April 1960.
49. *Broadcasting,* 26 October 1959.
50. *Variety,* 4 November 1959.
51. *The Stage and Television Today,* 10 November 1960.
52. Edmund Cork to Anthony Hicks, 6 October 1961 (Agatha Christie Archive, Exeter).
53. *The Stage and Television Today,* 10 November 1960.
54. For example, its apparent existence is noted in *The Encyclopedia of Television Pilots* by Vincent Terrace (Jefferson, North Carolina: McFarland & Company), 122.
55. K. Ewart to Cork, 4 May 1960 (Agatha Christie Archive, Exeter).
56. Barré Lyndon Collection (Folder 28), The Margaret Herrick Archive (Los Angeles).
57. Series and character outline, 21 June 1961. Barré Lyndon Collection (Folder 28), The Margaret Herrick Archive (Los Angeles).
58. Series and character outline, 21 June 1961. Barré Lyndon Collection (Folder 28), The Margaret Herrick Archive (Los Angeles).
59. Undated notes on script, c.22 June 1961. Series and character outline. Barré Lyndon Collection (Folder 28), The Margaret Herrick Archive (Los Angeles).
60. Undated trailer script, c.22 June 1961. Barré Lyndon Collection (Folder 28), The Margaret Herrick Archive (Los Angeles).
61. Undated trailer script, c.22 June 1961. Barré Lyndon Collection (Folder 28), The Margaret Herrick Archive (Los Angeles).
62. A short story collected in 1934's *The Listerdale Mystery.*
63. Undated trailer script, c.22 June 1961. Barré Lyndon Collection (Folder 28), The Margaret Herrick Archive (Los Angeles).
64. Anonymous production memo to Barré Lyndon, c. June 1961. Barré Lyndon Collection (Folder 28), The Margaret Herrick Archive (Los Angeles). Perhaps the writer of the memo is recalling the Poirot short story 'The Affair at the Victory Ball'.
65. Anonymous production memo to Barré Lyndon, c. June 1961. Barré Lyndon Collection (Folder 28), The Margaret Herrick Archive (Los Angeles).
66. Heather Dean memo 'Three Blind Mice/A Murder is Announced' (BBC WAC, Agatha Christie: Scriptwriter 1937–1962).
67. *Contrast,* 1 July 1963; *The Listener,* 14 February 1963.
68. Audience Research Report (BBC WAC VR/63/87).
69. Cork to Max Mallowan, 11 February 1963 (Agatha Christie Archive, Exeter).

PART III

Agatha Christie Films, 1945–65

Chapter 5: Christie Films Make an Impact

Spoilers: *And Then There Were None*; 'Philomel Cottage'; *Love from a Stranger*; *Witness for the Prosecution*

This chapter covers the four British and American films based on Agatha Christie's work made between 1945 and 1960. These pictures bridge a gap between the early attempts to find a way to bring Christie's stories to the cinema, which resulted in either sweeping changes or alterations of key elements (although in some cases such changes had already been made for stage adaptations), and the commercial success found by MGM's decision to cast Margaret Rutherford as Miss Marple in a series of comical mysteries for the big screen. The years covered in this chapter saw no end of discussion regarding rights to exploit Christie's works on screen, and many adaptations for the fledgling medium of television, with varying results. However, these four films demonstrate that closely following the source material could result in impact and longevity, despite the fact that there was no singular approach that guaranteed commercial or critical success.

Two of the films, *And Then There Were None* (d. René Clair, 1945) and *Witness for the Prosecution* (d. Billy Wilder, 1957), have gone on to become regarded as some of the best adaptations of Agatha Christie stories and are frequently shown on television and readily available for purchase for home viewing.[1] By contrast, the two other films, a new version of *Love from a Stranger* (d. Richard Whorf, 1947) and an adaptation of Christie's play *The Spider's Web* (d. Godfrey Grayson, 1960), have largely disappeared from view.[2] The 1947 version of *Love from a Stranger* has rarely been seen on television, although poor-quality versions can be purchased for home viewing in some countries, while *The Spider's Web* is particularly difficult to track down.

AND THEN THERE WERE NONE (1945)

We might regard the 1945 film version of *And Then There Were None* as a straightforward adaptation, one that holds few surprises as a relatively simple reworking for a new format of Christie's story, in which ten strangers are

© The Author(s) 2016
M. Aldridge, *Agatha Christie on Screen*,
DOI 10.1057/978-1-137-37292-5_6

brought to an island only to be murdered one by one. Yet to do so would ignore the context of the production. To this point, adaptations of Christie's works had imposed the format strengths of the chosen form of adaptation on the production and so stories were remodelled to work better on stage, radio or screen. However, *And Then There Were None* eschews the temptation to primarily exploit many of the clear advantages of film—its ability to expand the scope of stories, the flexibility of filming and the available star names—and, for this version at least, concentrates instead on the core strengths of Christie's novel and play, using the source material to the best advantage of the mystery, rather than the artistry of film. In any adaptation, there is always a struggle between the demands of the original story and the general expectations and demands of the medium for which it has been adapted—for the cinema, this film may be classed as the first time that Christie's original work won this battle, even if she had little direct influence on the making of the picture.

As with almost every other adaptation of this Christie story, this film uses her stage play as its basis, which allows two people to survive the events on the island; the original novel featured the death of all ten characters, with the murderer among them revealed in an epilogue. It is to the film's advantage that Christie had already created an ending that might work better for a general audience than the format offered in the book. Having the murderer engage with his final two potential victims means that most of the story's loose ends can be easily tied up, while it also creates a real sense of a denouement. The original novel relied on a conclusion that incorporated surprise deaths, shocking the reader, but leaving the remaining pieces of the puzzle to be put together as a postscript. The change for the stage production results in a tautly structured thriller that can more easily satisfy audiences unfamiliar with the original novel as well as those who know the story well or, more commonly, had some knowledge of the story's iconography and basic premise.

Although based on the play, the film does not reuse Christie's script. Instead, it is adapted by Dudley Nichols, who had written the screenplays for such esteemed films such as *Bringing Up Baby* (d. Howard Hawks, 1938) and *Stagecoach* (d. John Ford, 1939), while it was directed by René Clair, who had cultivated a strong reputation in his native France before moving to Hollywood in the early 1930s. The film had a difficult background, since the rights were initially purchased by producer Samuel Bronston, although according to contemporary reports there were then issues regarding the use of the *Ten Little Indians* title and changes that had been made for the stage version, which resulted in Christie threatening legal action. In the event Bronston was ousted from the picture, and it was instead produced by Harry Popkin and Edward J. Peskay, distributed by 20th Century Fox.

Tonally, the film mixes light moments with brief sequences that are rendered horrific by dint of the frequency of the murders, making the killer seem inescapable; the deaths themselves are often gruesome in their description if not depiction. There are some moments of physical comedy, especially in the opening boat sequence, as well as more droll comments on the priorities and social standing of those present on the island. For example, when the wife of butler Rogers is murdered, there is murmured assent to his decision that he should only put on a cold meat selection for dinner, with no suggestion that the guests could fend for themselves—indeed, there is uproar when, once accused, Rogers decides not to serve the meal at all. Given the attitude of those present, the audience is sympathetic to his subsequent decision to find companionship at the bottom of a bottle.

Although the film mirrors the book by taking place on an island off the coast of Devon, it does boast an international cast, which ensures that the action is not too parochial, and is presumably a deliberate attempt to help the film appeal to an international audience. In common with most adaptations of murder mysteries, the characters almost immediately accept the scenario in which they have been placed and, on the whole, end up playing the game and accepting the story's structure. The emphasis on mystery is made clear when a large question mark is displayed to the audience during the film's opening credits, which also depict the model Indians of the rhyme. Once the story starts there is little in the way of genuinely empathetic material for the audience to latch onto, the emphasis being placed firmly on the nature and motive of the murders rather than the repercussions of such events. This is most clearly seen not only when the characters tend to continue to function as normal following a murder, or reacting with a comedic slant (as with Rogers), but also at the end of the film. As is usual with adaptations of this story, the movie presents a happy ending, including a simmering romance between two of the characters; while there are benefits to this in terms of a satisfactory stand-off between the murderer and two of his potential victims, it also means that there is a remarkable and rather inappropriate shift into a lighter tone. At the end of the film, two characters are rescued only to laugh and cheerily walk out the door, leaving their rescuer standing in the lobby of a house filled with corpses. Censorship concerns no doubt influenced such a decision, as we will later see.

And Then There Were None has often been cited as one of the more successful Christie film adaptations. Certainly, Clair uses his cast to their best advantage and presents a sense of claustrophobia and danger throughout. Given the amount of material that needs to be established during its hour and a half, it is generally restrained in the amount of time spent watching characters outline the plot to each other, with several directorial flourishes only adding to the successful sense of paranoia. At one point we witness a selection of characters spying on each other, two through keyholes, indicated by the camera moving from within the spied-on character's room, through the keyhole, and then showing us who is watching. This sequence takes place while discussions between characters continue, ensuring that it does not deviate from the plotting or pace but does complement the sense of unease. It is also a sequence that can only really work on film, where the camera can be manipulated in such a way. Similarly, establishing shots of the island and scenes shot on the beach help to open out the mystery and make it feel less like a stage adaptation, while still demonstrating the sense of claustrophobia—we may be outside of the house, but we are still a long way from the mainland. As characters are killed off, so the relationships alter, veering between suspicion and attraction, but the film makes such changes in characterisation a success by ensuring that the audience is similarly unsure who to trust and who to root for—especially significant when we are left with two sympathetic victims in the final act, one of whom must surely be the murderer.

One significant change was made for the British audience. For several decades after its first publication the novel was still known as *Ten Little Niggers* in the UK, despite concerns over the offensive word resulting in a name change to *And Then There Were None* in the USA, and the original title was also adopted for the British stage production and the release of this film. Consequently, different opening titles were produced for the British audience, although the *Ten Little Indians* rhyme remains intact throughout the film.[3] At least one British newspaper commended the production for substituting 'Niggers' with 'Indians' within the film, implying that the reviewer wished that the international title had been used when it was shown in the UK.[4] However, the title was an area of relatively little concern during production. In fact, several elements of the film proved to be problematic with the censors in the USA, to the extent that it ran the risk of not being made at all.

In the final act it appears that we are left with two characters, Vera Claythorne and Philip Lombard, played by June Duprez and Louis Hayward. When Vera fails to shoot Lombard, it is made clear to the audience in advance that this is a ruse—she does not really want to wound him, for this is an attempt to bring the real murderer, a mysterious third person, into the open. Later adaptations would make Vera appearing to have shot Lombard a point of high drama, but the fact that this version made it clear that this was not a real shooting is a good indicator of the sorts of precautions needed in order to satisfy the censorship regulations of the time. As was common during this period, the film's script was sent to the Production Code Administration, headed by Joseph Breen, who had been responsible for ensuring that films adhered to the new set of rules required for wide distribution in the United States. Unfortunately for the producers, when he read the script in November 1944 Breen saw the resolution of the film (where the villain commits suicide) as fundamentally unacceptable.[5] He raised further issues with the script, including 'appropriate' costuming of Vera, the deletion of mentions of cyanide, the use of the phrase 'before God', the possibility of a character appearing to retch in the opening sequence (albeit for comedic reasons) and Lombard's scripted use of the word 'darling' (this was because it appeared in the script shortly after a fade-out and so, to Breen's mind, could imply a sexual relationship between him and Vera). To the relief of the film's producers, by early 1945 Breen had decided to consent to the inclusion of the crucial suicide, since he had been convinced that the character killed himself in order to frame another character for his apparent murder, not in order to evade justice.[6] In the end, a certificate for the film was granted on 17 May 1945, although in Canada it was initially rejected for exhibition in British Columbia, before the province relented in March 1946, while Ohio removed some of the dialogue relating to the Bible.[7] The strictures imposed on film distribution in North America during this period resulted in films that had to be precise in the way they conformed to all manner of rules—and even the less than realistic world of Christie's mysteries had to comply.

When the film was released in both the USA and UK in late 1945, the posters and publicity emphasised the darker aspects of the story. Disembodied heads of the lead characters floating on a black background drew focus towards the island's house, giving off an impression akin to Edgar Allan Poe adaptations, with connotations of old dark mansions and associated horror elements. The film was received positively by audiences and critics alike, although given the esteem in which it was later held it may be surprising to learn that the critical praise was not particularly effusive. *Time* magazine offered a considered take on the film, identifying it as 'sultry [rather] than chilling', as the reviewer goes on to point out that the power of the story lies not in the number of corpses but the relationship between the remaining characters once the picture starts to reach its climax—the early deaths kill off ciphers, single-characteristic personalities whose presence makes this seem like a mass killing spree even though, in fact, the audience is only really invested in the survival of two characters.[8]

Elsewhere, the *Daily Mail* called the film 'ingenious and exciting' as well as 'lightly macabre', giving Clair first credit for the mystery, above Christie.[9] Most reviews demonstrated disinterest or dismissiveness; *The Observer* even asked why Clair had taken on such an assignment.[10] It is possible that such deprecation was the result of familiarity with the material, given the prominence of the stage production and the success of the novel. The film fared better among the general public, most of whom would only have had the opportunity to read the novel, rather than London-based reviewers who would have easily been able to see the West End production. Christie is not unique in having her work re-evaluated over time, receiving some of her warmest notices in the 1960s, when even well-received previous novels were often rerated upwards. With the passing of 70 years, claims such as those in the *Variety* review that the story is a 'dull whodunit' seem curious given its longevity, but only help to emphasise that history has given Christie more credit for her work than some contemporary critics did.[11]

LOVE FROM A STRANGER (1947)

The second film adaptation of *Love from a Stranger* occurred in 1947, this time directed by Richard Whorf, a man who had tackled small-scale romance and mystery pictures over the previous few years. Once more based on Frank Vosper's reworking of Christie's short story 'Philomel Cottage', this time it was adapted for the screen by the successful crime novelist Philip MacDonald, who had also worked on the adaptation of Daphne du Maurier's novel *Rebecca* for Alfred Hitchcock's 1940 movie version. Although only a decade had passed since the first screen adaptation of *Love from a Stranger*, it was not unusual for movies to be remade so quickly, usually in order to capitalise on a new star or trend. In this instance it seems likely that the success of the 1944 film *Gaslight* (which followed a 1938 play and 1940 British film of the same story[12]) resulted in studios looking to produce similar pictures that could be easily and inexpensively made. Christie was offered £5000[13] for her portion of the rights to a story that may have pre-dated all versions of *Gaslight*, but now happened to be a perfect choice to capitalise on this suddenly popular sub-genre of the thriller concerning women who marry dangerous men.[14] The film of *Gaslight* is set in Victorian London (the stage play stipulates 1880) and concerns a woman whose husband tries to convince her that she is going mad, only for it to be revealed that her apparently imagined dimming of the gas light is in fact a cover for her husband's plot to steal a stash of jewels hidden in their building.

The 1944 film of *Gaslight* had been a commercial and critical success, and there are clear direct influences on the 1947 version of *Love from a Stranger*. Most notably, the action is transplanted to 1901, rather than being contemporary with the production. Not only does this make it the first Christie film to be a period adaptation, it also brings the picture more explicitly in line with the Victorian psychological melodrama of *Gaslight*.[15] Certainly, this type of psychological thriller had become more common since the original 1937 film, especially those thematically based on the French folk story of serial wife murderer Bluebeard, who is even explicitly mentioned in the 1947 film as well as the original short story. Aside from the relocation to the Victorian era, this version of *Love from a Stranger* offers the audience few surprises. Sylvia Sidney gives a spirited performance as Cecily (reverting to the character name used in Vosper's original play), who is portrayed as a much stronger and more forthright character than in earlier versions of the story, while the character of Bruce is reworked as South American Manuel Cortez, played by John Hodiak. He gives a muted, almost downbeat performance, but at least in part this may be due to the film's increased emphasis on the thriller and horror aspects from the beginning, making his character less of a mystery. In this version we are witness to the shadowy depiction of a murder taking place in Liverpool during the film's opening, thus the genre is set out more directly than had happened in previous versions of the story. Resultantly, the audience is more suspicious from the very beginning and, given the frequency with which *Love from a Stranger* and similar stories had been seen over the previous decade, the requirement for mystery was more overtly replaced with the suspenseful question of when and how Manuel's deeds would be uncovered—and would it be too late for Cecily?

As the film progresses, so we reach its inevitable conclusion as Manuel and Cecily face off against each other in their isolated cottage, with only occasional moments of interest for the contemporary viewer. Some limited location filming, a cartoonesque set and a matte shot depict the couple's Devon cottage, which is rather more akin to California (and Disneyland) than South West England, with muddled Yorkshire-leaning accents of the locals to match. Running to just 81 minutes, there is little opportunity for the audience to be bored with the production, although it is a surprise that the denouement is rushed through so quickly. Manuel meets his demise in an atmospheric and well-shot (albeit clichéd) sequence where he rushes from the cottage during a rain storm, only to be trampled underfoot by a horse; such 'act of God' resolutions were a common solution to censorship requirements of the time. More surprising is that this brief finale does not even allow for a proper reconciliation between Cecily and her former fiancé Nigel, played by John Howard. In this remake Cecily had clearly outlined her desire to end the engagement, and perhaps this is a further indication of her emancipation, demonstrating that attitudes towards female characters had developed in the previous decade.

The critical response to the film was lukewarm at best. *Variety* summarised the issues well when it pointed out that the key elements were so well worn that it 'never seems plausible or particularly interesting and, of course, it never causes any spinal shivers'.[16] By the time the film finally made it to the UK in 1949 (released under the title *A Stranger Walked In*), a decade had passed since the first *Gaslight* production had found domestic success—enough time for the picture to seem old hat, and several reviewers were more mystified than intrigued by the picture, especially its Hollywood take on rural England. The *Monthly Film Bulletin* called the setting 'rather peculiar', with which most other reviews agreed. When reviewers were not distracted by the lamentable attempts at cultivating a British atmosphere, they largely decried it as a poorly put together film—more than one critic punned that while *A Stranger Walked In*, they very nearly walked out.[17] '*Love from a Stranger* is such a good story that it is difficult to spoil. But this film spoils it' declared *The Times*, a thought echoed elsewhere, with *The People* terming it a 'Hollywood howler' and several critics calling it unintentionally hilarious.[18] For the Christie scholar, *Love from a Stranger* is so far removed from her original work that it sits slightly awkwardly alongside other adaptations, since so much was added by Frank Vosper, but the stage and film adaptations proved that with judicious additions and alterations Christie's stories could be reworked to great success—as well as ignominious failure. It was not the case that fidelity to the original source was an essential ingredient of success or failure; the alchemy of a successful adaptation has proven to be more complex than such a set of rules. One thing that is never successful is a lazy adaptation of a Christie story: her work must be treated with care in order to be an effective translation to the screen or stage. A great deal of effort was expended, and talent utilised, the next time that a Christie story made it to the cinema screen—and the result spoke for itself.

WITNESS FOR THE PROSECUTION (1957)

There had been several films proposed to Christie in the 1940s and 1950s, including a request to make a Cuban movie of *Witness for the Prosecution* (which she dismissed as 'silly!').[19] Other enquiries from the likes of RKO covered titles including *Three Blind Mice* (the short story rather than the play), *Spider's Web* and *Towards Zero*. However, for *Witness for the Prosecution*, it had been immediately clear that the play was such a success that it needed to be capitalised on, and there was no shortage of offers. The story's impact was such that it had already received a great deal of positive critical and commercial attention prior to its appearance on film. The original short story had appeared in collections of Christie's work in both the UK and USA after its initial publication in a 1925 magazine under the title 'Traitor Hands', followed by four different television adaptations, but it was the 1953 transition to the stage that had made it a hot property in Hollywood, where three film studios fought over the rights to the play.[20] Christie had adapted her short story into the play herself, and it had had a successful run on both sides of the Atlantic (468 performances in London, 645 in New York), as well as winning the New York Drama Critics Circle award for best foreign play, alongside Tony awards for Francis L. Sullivan and Patricia Jessel, who had played Sir Wilfrid and Romaine (whose character name was soon altered to Christine), respectively. Christie made £116,000 from the rights to the film, which she then gifted to her daughter Rosalind; this was more than 20 times the amount offered for *Love from a Stranger* a decade earlier.[21]

It is difficult to imagine a better fit for a film production of *Witness for the Prosecution* than Billy Wilder, a legendary figure in Hollywood who had already written and produced such classics as *Double Indemnity* (1944), *Sunset Boulevard* (1950) and *The Seven Year Itch* (1955), while his next project would be *Some Like It Hot* (1959). His production of *Witness for the Prosecution* was nominated for six Academy Awards, including best picture, and has remained one of the most readily accessible adaptations of Christie's work through repeated screenings on television and home video releases. However, there is an intriguing dead end that was briefly explored when the play had first come to the attention of Hollywood. On 6 December 1954, Finlay McDermid, a story editor at Warner Bros., wrote to Alfred Hitchcock regarding the positive reaction that *Witness for the Prosecution* had received during its try-out performances off-Broadway. McDermid enclosed a synopsis of the play, but pointed out that two issues would need to be tackled before any film could be made: firstly, ensuring that the film adhered to the production code, and secondly, dealing with Christie herself, as it was already well known that she was generally not interested in selling the film rights to her stories.[22] There is no record of Hitchcock's reply, although cuttings of the positive press reaction were sent to him the next month, alongside similar extracts from reviews of his film *Dial M for Murder*, indicating that he had expressed at least some interest. These plans did not come to anything, perhaps because Warner Bros. failed to secure the rights to the play, while a second and final brush with the Master of Suspense briefly occurred elsewhere: in 1957 interest was expressed in adapting Christie's short story 'Accident' for an episode of *Alfred Hitchcock Presents*—however, this too went no further.[23]

In the event, producers Edward Small and Arthur Hornblow purchased the rights to the play, to be released through United Artists, a distributor for smaller production companies. By April 1956 a script had been drafted and Billy Wilder was brought on to the production as director, working with Harry Kurnitz and Larry Marcus to continue work on the screenplay. At this point

Small and Hornblow sent the current version of the script to Joseph Breen's successor Geoffrey Shurlock, who was now the gatekeeper for the industry's production code. This script does not appear to have survived, but judging by the notes there are several differences from the final film, including more sexually charged scenes in the cabaret, more time spent at the police station (featuring young women who are implied to be prostitutes) and even a sequence at a house that could be a brothel—given its placement late in the script (page 114), it seems likely that this is where Sir Wilfrid was to meet the woman who owned the letters that would be crucial to the film's conclusion; in the final version this meeting takes place at a railway station, but the original location is echoed in the 1982 TV movie adaptation of the story.[24]

Hollywood had increasingly relied on adapting existing stories for its films, and *Witness for the Prosecution* was heralded by *The New York Times* as one example of the studios' dwindling interest in original screenplays, apparently because films based on existing novels or plays were perceived to be a lower risk.[25] That is not to say that adaptations were always faithful, although in this case the screenwriters' main changes simply added more humour and character moments, including scenes concerning Sir Wilfrid and his nurse, written with the knowledge that Wilder hoped to cast real-life husband and wife Charles Laughton and Elsa Lanchester in the parts. Such a decision would lighten the tone at certain points while never distracting from the central mystery, and allow secondary characters to remain engaging to the audience; this also helped to distract the audience from the fact that even though the film is superficially a murder mystery, albeit courtroom based, it has an extraordinarily small pool of suspects. The choice of Hollywood star Tyrone Power as Leonard Vole also added a new dimension to the film's chief suspect.[26] Christie had not described the character as an American, but this proved to be a master stroke, as not only does Power deliver a strong performance in a complex role, his nationality also makes the character even more of a mystery to the audience, who are aware that he is a fish out of water and may be seen as unusual by his British contemporaries. Are Vole's forthrightness and friendly nature with the victim deemed suspicious because he was simply doing the 'done thing' in London of the 1950s, or indicative of a Machiavellian nature? Meanwhile, Wilder's distraction techniques encompassing comedy, flashbacks, witty dialogue and strong performances prevent most of the audience from spending too long on the key question: if Leonard did not commit the crime, then who did?[27]

A similar scripting decision was made when it came to accommodating the casting of Marlene Dietrich in the key role of Christine. Hollywood legend (and publicity) has it that a $90,000 scene was inserted merely in order to show off Dietrich's legs (or, some claim, singing performance). This does the scene a disservice—it opens out the picture, although it also robs it of some of the mystery. The unknowable relationship between Christine and Leonard is now explicit, although this does little to affect first-time viewings of the film, where the audience is less likely to scrutinise the relationship's background until the resolution. Some critics have dismissed the scene entirely, seeing it as an example of Hollywood's propensity to meddle with an already successful small-scale drama in order to added glamour and scale. However, this flash-back to Christine and Leonard's war days does more than just offer Dietrich a chance to do a cabaret turn. We learn more about Leonard—a lucky chancer, a man who manages to dodge a bar fight and return in time to find his drink sitting where he had left it, undisturbed. It is a small joke, but indicative of his character. Crucially, the scene also allows a glimpse of Leonard and Christine together, away from the murder, emphasising that a human drama underpins the mystery. Outside this flashback, Leonard and Christine only interact to any significant extent after the final verdict has been given. The filmic qualities of the cabaret flashback were played up in the publicity for the film, the couple's embrace in this sequence featuring prominently in most posters.

At this time Dietrich was not at the peak of her career, so the principle that a film would be written around her is verging on the preposterous, but that is not to say that her well-known background did not affect the character of Christine. She is now a Berliner, and much is made of what the audience could read as either her stoicism or her cold nature. In the event, writing Christine as a German performer only helps to sell the film's final revelations. Similarly, moments that were referred to only anecdotally in the initial play (such as the first meeting between Leonard and the murdered woman) are charmingly and effectively presented in the film version, allowing it to have the lighter touch typical of Billy Wilder pictures. We may be grateful that a decision was made to abandon a song that had been written for the film by Sammy Cahn and Matty Malneck, since its lyrics hardly complemented the action on screen, with their reference to the moon acting as a witness to romance.[28] Several reviewers mentioned that the film did more than merely present the court scenes as seen on stage, and the response to this was genuinely favourable—as the reviewer in *The Times* put it, 'a compact and stimulating thriller, skilfully expanded for the medium of the screen to include a number of pertinent sequences outside the court room, but yet retaining all the forensic crossfire of the original play, and if anything improving on the final, sensational denouement'.[29]

Perhaps the main reason the film is such a success is because Wilder and Christie complemented each other so well; Christie's plotting is stronger than ever, while the story demands that the characterisation be complex if the audi-ence is to be truly unsure of who to trust. In the event, Wilder's sparkling dialogue and humorous asides help to make the film much more than a simple adaptation, even if it does stick closely to the original play in terms of its basic plotting. Sir Wilfrid's scathing remarks to his staff on his return from hospital demonstrate vicious wit and character that keep the audience's interest from the beginning ('He wasn't really discharged you know, he was expelled', says his nurse). By the time Sir Wilfrid meets with Leonard Vole, we might be dis-tracted by his comedic efforts to procure a cigar and lighter, but it is Vole's diligent thinking that allows them to escape censure for the rule breaking; the moment is not dwelled on, but neatly establishes Vole's capabilities when it comes to deceit. Such sequences further indicate that successful Christie screen adaptations need an accomplished and confident guiding hand who is respect-ful of the original work but also understands the appeal and strengths of film and television—something in which Christie herself failed to express an inter-est. In the event, Christie would later indicate that she liked the film. In 1972 she wrote: 'It is the only movie made from one of my plays or books which has really satisfied me. It was very well done.'[30] In another letter written two months later, she noted: 'Plays are, I think, easier to adapt than books are, since stories do not have so many pitfalls in them.'[31]

Christie may also have been grateful that the film managed to avoid the censor's knife, although the frequent cries of 'Lord', 'Damn' and 'God' were trimmed as far as possible—enough that one wonders whether such experi-enced writers may have deliberately included them so as to distract the produc-tion code office from scrutinising other elements more closely, especially the final scene of the film and the ever-crucial question of motivation and retribu-tion. On a point of censorship, audiences who have watched the film closely may have noted the apparently abrupt removal of the word 'murder' from a line that Christine speaks in the final scene; according to the existing paper-work, such a removal was not at the behest of the production code office, so the rationale for it remains a mystery.

The film was very well received by the critics, who tended to concentrate on the lead performances. Charles MacLaren of *Time and Tide* recounts a meet-ing he had with Tyrone Power prior to the filming, where Power referred to the film as 'a pet scheme of Charles [Laughton]'s', which leads to the reviewer recounting that with this in mind, the film 'has so arranged affairs that the whole thing becomes, in effect, a Laughton family joke [...] There were times when I could hardly restrain the feeling that the Laughtons were making up business and dialogue as they went along, and because the Laughtons are amusing people *Witness for the Prosecution* is often very funny too. But it isn't quite the sharp, dry melodrama that Mrs Christie fashioned for the stage.'[32] Elsewhere, Dietrich's commanding turn was the focus—'Grandma Dietrich springs a surprise [...] Aunt Agatha should send her a case of champagne', said one newspaper.[33]

When it came to the transition to film, many of the critics had already seen the production on stage and most commended Wilder's influence on the pic-ture. Not all agreed, however. Arthur Knight of the *Saturday Review* wrote that 'In a way it's too bad that Agatha Christie, that master of the logical surprise, did not write *Witness for the Prosecution* directly for the screen. No matter how effective it was as a theatre piece, it makes an even better movie', for which he credited Christie's original story, adding that 'much of the new material added by Billy Wilder and Harry Kurnitz in adapting her play for the big screen proves quite unnecessary'.[34] Whatever Wilder's influence, the core components of the original play were still widely praised. Milton Shulman of the *Sunday Express* considered that the combination of Christie, Wilder and Kurnitz had been effective, saying that 'Christie vindicates her reputation as the Thriller Queen by blazing a trail of circumstantial non sequiturs, logical cul-de-sacs, and flaming red herrings that should keep cinema audiences purring for months. But what makes *Witness for the Prosecution* much more entertaining than a mere murder conundrum is the witty screen play written by Billy Wilder and Harry Kurmitz [sic].'[35]

Nevertheless, this increased emphasis on the characters was not enough for some ('The audience's chief interest is academic rather than emotional', said the *Times Educational Supplement*[36]), although overall the reviews were filled with superlatives—'Verdict: A wow of a whodunit!', claimed the *Daily Herald*,[37] the *Financial Times* called the film a 'Dazzling Whodunit',[38] while the *Daily Mail* simply labelled it 'Christie's best'.[39]

THE SPIDER'S WEB (1960)

Given the high profile of *Witness for the Prosecution*, it is perhaps surprising that the next film to be based on a Christie story was on a somewhat smaller scale and has remained one of the lesser-known adaptations. Although Christie was negotiating with MGM to sell the rights to most of her major properties at the turn of the 1960s, this excluded her plays, which explains why several titles after this point turn up from different distributors and producers.[40] Although she had secured a lucrative deal for the sale of *Witness for the Prosecution*, she was to make rather less from *Spider's Web*. Christie had written the play especially for actress Margaret Lockwood and in London it had been even more successful than *Witness*, running for 774 performances from its opening in December 1954. It is lighter in tone than many of her plays, and offers several farcical elements, since it concerns the appearance—and disappearance—of a dead body at the home of Clarissa and Henry Hailsham-Brown; each character suspects that another is guilty of the murder and endeavours to cover it up.

It seems that Christie felt the play had good potential for the cinema, as shown by the existence of a typed and unsigned 1958 document that appears to be her own outline of how the play could be structured as a film.[41] If the outline was indeed penned by Christie, then the two pages of notes demonstrate how she felt the early action (prior to the events of the first scene in the play) could be transferred to the screen—an indication that the success of *Witness for the Prosecution* had led to her being more open-minded when it came to film productions of her plays in particular. In this outline, the film opens with a shot of a giant spider's web dissolving into a scene set in Clarissa's garden, where a similar web is to be seen, before the 'what a tangled web we weave' phrase is flagged up by her aunt.[42] The proposed structure then opens out the action even further from the stage play (which takes place entirely inside the house on a single evening), showing Clarissa meeting her husband Henry at a dance while he is still married to his first wife, whose death soon follows. Clarissa then adopts the difficult role of stepmother to Henry's daughter Pippa, which includes a trip to the zoo. Some comical scenes are added in line with the lighter tone of the play, before the writer ponders whether the emphasis should be on the robbery of an antiques shop (a prior event that is instrumental to the mystery) or Clarissa herself. The former is decided to be preferable if the 'sinister' aspects are most important, whereas an emphasis on Clarissa makes sense if the romantic elements are to be the focus; a preference for the latter is expressed.

Unfortunately, these well-thought-out additions did not reach the final film, which made the economical decision to adhere closely to the stage action. The reason for this lies in the motivation of the producers, since although *Spider's Web* had been a considerable success on stage, for reasons unknown the rights to the film version were secured by Edward J. and Harry Lee Danziger, American brothers who had made a name for themselves with cheap films and television programmes designed for international distribution, often as supporting features. Operating from a base in Elstree, the films and television programmes made by the Danzigers from the early 1950s would permeate the late-night schedules of television stations across the globe for decades, but by the mid-1960s the production company had disappeared. The commercial potential of the title is clear, but they must have paid an uncharacteristically high price for the material, even if it was rather less than had been paid for *Witness for the Prosecution*; alternatively, perhaps Christie had been advised that no major studio was interested in the rather low-key story and she took the best offer available. Although it had a high budget when compared to other Danziger productions (unusually for them the film was made in colour, with a cast of known actors, headed by Glynis Johns as Clarissa), as a feature film it is still small scale.

The Spider's Web keeps closely to Christie's original play, using a script adapted by Albert G. Miller and Eldon Howard. Miller had worked on such films as the infamous sex/horror movie *Horrors of Spider Island* (d. Fritz Böttger, 1960), which was refused a certificate for British film exhibition, while Eldon Howard was the mother-in-law of Edward Danziger. Director Godfrey Grayson was hardly more auspicious, having previously worked on such titles as Hammer's *What the Butler Saw* (1950). The picture is remarkably static for one produced in 1960, with the cameras simply observing the action throughout, offering little in the way of dynamism and showing an approach to Christie films unseen since the Austin Trevor films three decades earlier. In such circumstances the strong cast are forced to work extra hard in order to keep the audience's attention. Combined with the fact that the whole film is shot on a studio set, this means that it feels more like a stage play than ever, with the performances and Christie's story having to do their best to maintain interest, with scant assistance from the director.

Released to British cinemas in 1960, the film made little impact. The poster implied that the movie was more of a thriller, or even horror film, than the light mystery it actually was. 'Who conked and killed the intruder?' one advertisement asked, pointing out that Christie had 'razzled and dazzled you with *Witness for the Prosecution*', while the near traditional request that audiences refrained from revealing the ending was also made—'They won't believe you' was the tagline, a bold but unlikely claim. An accompanying statement echoed

Hitchcock's *Psycho* (1960) by saying that no one would be seated during the last five minutes. There were relatively few reviews, an indication of the spotty distribution for the picture. *Monthly Film Bulletin* wrote that the film 'does not really come off [...] The attempt at light relief falls flat [...] far from being one of Agatha Christie's better whodunits'.

Although *Variety* claimed that *The Spider's Web* would be released in the United States in November 1960, if it was then it was little seen; the television broadcast of an edited version of the movie the following year was the first opportunity for most in the country to watch it.[43] It was then shown on British television in a few ITV regions at different points in the late 1960s and early 1970s, with the final screening in the Yorkshire region on the afternoon of 30 December 1971.[44] After this point the film simply disappears, having apparently been removed from circulation. Many of the Danzigers' films have suffered a similar fate since the company was wound up, leaving dozens of titles in limbo. It seems that once the deals to show or release the movies expired, there was simply no way to license a rerelease, even if there had been interest. At the time of writing the film has never been made available for purchase in its original form, although a dubbed version is available in Italy (where it appears the title was bought by local distributors in perpetuity) and it has been screened at the British Film Institute, which owns a print of the movie. It is not one of the great Christie adaptations, but as a depiction of the basic elements of the play supplemented by strong performances it is of interest, and will hopefully be seen by more Christie fans one day.

Up to this point, pictures based on Christie's stories had followed no particular trajectory, being made by a variety of studios, with many different attitudes towards the original text and a resultant variety in quality. However, soon there would be a consistent and popular series of films that would keep one of Christie's best-known characters in the limelight—although that is not to say that Christie would be happy with the results, and nor would many of her readers.

NOTES

1. Mathew Prichard regards *Witness for the Prosecution* as probably his favourite film adaptation of his grandmother's work—as does the author of this book.
2. Christie's original play is simply called *Spider's Web*; the film adds the definite article to the title.
3. Charles Osborne has pointed out that the original *Ten Little Niggers* and *Ten Little Indians* rhymes are actually different, but that in Christie adaptations and some editions of her story it is simply a case that the offensive word is substituted with 'Indian', with a version of the former rhyme used.
4. *Newcastle Chronicle*, 28 September 1945.

5. Joseph Breen to Samuel Bronston, 21 November 1944 (Production File held at the Margaret Herrick Library, Los Angeles).
6. Popkin to Breen, 9 January 1945 (Production File held at the Margaret Herrick Library, Los Angeles).
7. PCA notes (Production File held at the Margaret Herrick Library, Los Angeles).
8. *Time*, 15 October 1945.
9. *Daily Mail*, 21 September 1945.
10. *The Observer*, 22 September 1945.
11. *Variety*, 11 July 1945.
12. The play presents the title as two words, *Gas Light*.
13. Morgan, *Agatha Christie: A Biography*, 260.
14. The story has its origins as the play *Gas Light* by Patrick Hamilton, originally staged in 1938 and first adapted for the screen for a 1940 British film. Angela Lansbury won an Oscar for her role in the 1944 Hollywood film, decades before she took on the role of Miss Marple (and then Jessica Fletcher on the popular detective series *Murder, She Wrote*).
15. Although technically the events in *Die Abenteuer GmbH* probably take place about a decade prior to the film's release.
16. *Variety*, 11 May 1947.
17. For example, *The People* (11 December 1949) and *Daily Mirror* (9 December 1949).
18. *The Times*, 12 December 1949 and *The People* 11 December 1949.
19. Ramon Peon to Christie's representatives via *Ellery Queen* magazine, 12 June 1947 (Agatha Christie Archive, Exeter). Peon was an accomplished Cuban-born director and screenwriter.
20. Warner Bros, MGM and United Artists (Morgan, *Agatha Christie: A Biography*, 298).
21. Laura Thompson, *Agatha Christie: An English Mystery* (London: Headline Review, 2008), 357.
22. McDdermid to Hitchcock, 6 December 1954 (Agatha Christie Archive, Exeter).
23. Harold Ober Associates to Edmund Cork, 2 August 1957 (Agatha Christie Archive, Exeter).
24. See Chap. 10.
25. *The New York Times*, 11 August 1957.
26. Power was to receive top billing for the film, followed by Dietrich and then Laughton, while the title was prefaced by the caption 'Agatha Christie's international stage success', giving her a prominent credit of her own.
27. For example, it takes nearly an hour for the possibility of a botched burglary to be raised, and little attention is paid to it.
28. Sammy Cahn Papers (Margaret Herrick Library, Los Angeles).
29. *The Times*, 29 January 1958.

30. Christie to Mr David G. Kamm, 29 September 1972 (Agatha Christie Family Archive).
31. Christie to Lord Mountbatten, 15 November 1972 (Agatha Christie Family Archive).
32. *Time and Tide*, 8 February 1958.
33. *Daily Sketch*, 29 January 1958.
34. *Saturday Review*, 15 February 1958.
35. Milton Shulman in *Sunday Express*, 2 February 1958.
36. *Times Educational Supplement*, 7 February 1958.
37. *Daily Herald*, 31 January 1958.
38. *Financial Times*, 3 February 1958.
39. *Daily Mail*, 1 February 1958.
40. The various versions of *And Then There Were None* are a good example of this.
41. The precise provenance of the document is impossible to verify—although it has been catalogued as having been written by Christie herself, this is not certain. I think it likely that it is a summary document typed up by someone else, following a discussion with Christie and (perhaps) an unknown other person.
42. Held by the Agatha Christie Archive, Exeter (item is dated 1958 but catalogued as 1956).
43. 'Danziger Dickers on TV Cheaters' in *Variety*, 10 August 1960.
44. As far as this author could see, at least—last-minute changes and occasionally inaccurate or incomplete listings make it possible that it has been seen elsewhere.

Chapter 6: Margaret Rutherford as Miss Marple

It is not necessarily the case that Agatha Christie adaptations exist in order to please, or even appeal to, fans of her writing. While few authors have commanded such a large and devoted readership, by the very nature of adaptation it is normally the case that when any writer's work is produced for a different medium, this is done in order to widen the appeal of the original piece. In many instances, this has resulted in versions that nevertheless satisfy many fans of the original work—when it comes to Christie, most of the ITV *Poirot* (1989–2013) and BBC *Miss Marple* (1984–92) series would fall under this banner. Yet occasionally, adaptations will appeal to people who are not strong admirers of the primary work more than to its fans. The four Miss Marple films starring Margaret Rutherford, produced between 1961 and 1964, are a good example of how adaptations that achieve popular success can have a divisive reception among fans of the original works.

Murder She Said (1961)

By the time a deal between MGM and Agatha Christie was secured in 1960, negotiations had been ongoing for many years, having been initiated nearly 25 years earlier before being curtailed due to disagreements over the treatment of her works.[1] When discussions resumed in the late 1950s, Christie's career writing for the stage was rivalling the success of her novels, demonstrating her ability to find popular and critical success away from the publishing industry. Having waited so long, MGM was keen to exploit her works as quickly as possible. With its television division working on bringing Poirot to the small screen, the choice of Miss Marple as a leading character for the film adaptations was a natural one. The first story to be adapted was Christie's 1957 novel *4.50 from Paddington*, in which Miss Marple investigates a murder witnessed by her friend while aboard said train. The screenplay initially used the title *Meet Miss Marple*, but was soon changed to *Murder She Said*.[2] The story took many

© The Author(s) 2016
M. Aldridge, *Agatha Christie on Screen*,
DOI 10.1057/978-1-137-37292-5_7

key elements from Christie's novel and retained them, while weaving some different characterisation and plot points around the basic mystery. In many respects the script was not the difficult part—that would be finding the correct characterisation for Miss Marple and, similarly, the best actress for the part.

Margaret Rutherford was a popular actress, particularly well known for her comedy parts, and had made her name as Madame Arcati in the stage and screen productions of Noël Coward's supernatural comedy *Blithe Spirit*. No doubt her performance as the quirky medium was firmly lodged in the minds of those at MGM when they approached her to take on the part of Miss Marple. Rutherford's biographer Gwen Robyns has indicated that some convincing was needed: 'She thought that she wouldn't be in a film with crime, and they had to explain to her that Miss Marple was a very good woman, and then she decided to do it. There was a childlike comprehension of life, which was of course her great charm.'[3] Nevertheless, she signed up to the series for a fee of £16,000 per picture.[4] Described as refined, self-confident and intrepid in the scripts and synopses for the film, Rutherford certainly brought some of this to the role, but her background in comedy added a further dimension and the script was written to emphasise this part—as well as to include the new character of Mr Stringer, played by Rutherford's husband Stringer Davies.

Agatha Christie liked Margaret Rutherford and respected her as an actress. When her name was first proposed, she was seen as eminently preferable to the 'sophisticated American minxes' who had otherwise been suggested.[5] However, when Rutherford took on the role of Miss Marple, Christie was not satisfied with what she saw, although she was careful to be diplomatically silent in public while Rutherford was alive. They were on friendly terms, and Christie went so far as to dedicate her 1962 Miss Marple novel *The Mirror Crack'd from Side to Side* to Rutherford, sending her a specially inscribed copy of the book. In this personal copy, Christie praised Rutherford's 'superb performance' in *Murder She Said*, while in return Rutherford wrote to Christie that this was one of the proudest moments of her life.[6]

Privately, Christie was less keen. She had noticed that a test screening of the film was taking place at the Regal cinema in Torquay, which she then visited having already had a preview in London. Calling it 'pretty poor', she found the movie unexciting, with a disappointing script and sub-standard photography. She compared it unfavourably to *Witness for the Prosecution*, and considered the new film to be more akin to a television production.[7] Writing to an admirer of her work in 1972, a few months after Rutherford had died, Christie was able to be more honest—perhaps also because she had seen how each subsequent film had moved further and further from her original work. 'Margaret Rutherford was a very fine actress, but was never in the least like Miss Marple', she wrote— a view with which many fans would agree.[8]

However, the Miss Marple films starring Margaret Rutherford are also some of the adaptations that have lasted longest in the public consciousness, and many people hold them in great affection. They were enough of a success that four films were made, as well as an accompanying Poirot feature—no mean feat. There appear to have been multiple factors for the success of the series of films, not least the fact that Rutherford was a popular actress, while Christie was more successful than ever. The relative paucity of film adaptations of Christie's work no doubt added to the appeal of this first attempt to bring Miss Marple to the big screen. However, although three of the films are recognisable reworkings of her original plots, by the time of the fourth film the producers had made the decision to put Miss Marple into an original mystery. This tells us a great deal about the apparent appeal of these films: the specifics of Christie's carefully crafted novels were not seen to be crucial. Instead, the movies capitalised on the 'sense' of what people thought was Agatha Christie, and this is what was put onto the cinema screen. The details of the mystery were seemingly unimportant to the producers; it was the overall effect that was key. And so we have Miss Marple, mystery and a take on the light thriller than manifests itself as comedy in this instance.

It is telling that humour was seen as instrumental to the character of these films. It is difficult to tell from the scripting and production notes whether this was a genuine misunderstanding of the tone of Christie's stories, or an attempt to reinvent them. By the 1960s, many of her mysteries may have seemed increasingly dated to those making the films—not enough time had passed for them to be seen as wholly nostalgic, and although Christie made attempts to keep her references, situations and characters up to date, the overall style and structure of the stories were generally the same as she had written 40 years earlier. Such an approach brought great success for her literary career, but when transplanted to a contemporary film series a whole new audience had to be considered. The choice would seem to be simple: the stories could be treated as classic pieces of literature with film adaptations closely following the originals, or the films could be ironic takes on the original mysteries (to a greater or lesser extent), whereby the script pastiches the original and likely acknowledges or emphasises any apparently old-fashioned elements. For some reason, the Rutherford films pursued a third option where the mystery itself is presented in a reasonably straightforward manner, but there is considerable comical window dressing. However, the humour is not self-reflexive—there is no real parody here, unless we are supposed to chortle at the fact that Miss Marple is now a keen reader of detective fiction who even brandishes a copy of Christie's novel *Murder Is Easy* at one point. Instead, the comedy is of the sort that is more old-fashioned than the mystery presented, often centred on Miss Marple's physicality, especially her age as well as her body. This overt attempt to make Miss Marple a source of amusement creates an unfortunate situation where she is sometimes one of the few people who appears not to take the murders seriously, a most unfortunate miscalculation of character. This indicates that the producers had little confidence or interest in the merits of the original work, apparently believing that the mystery had the best chance of keeping the attention if the audience was frequently distracted by the heavy-handed comical asides that were seen as Rutherford's forte. Nevertheless, the films did strike a balance that appealed to many audiences, especially those who were less familiar with the original works. They are good-natured and well-paced pictures that feature many strong performances and perfectly adequate mystery content; they may not be a definitive depiction of Christie's stories, but nor were they designed to be. *Murder She Said* is often entertaining, but it also lacks tonal consistency. There are awkward sections where drama and mystery alternate with light sparring dialogue, clumsy innuendo and broad physical comedy. Characters are either given a comical angle or are wholly one-dimensional, reduced to squabbling between each other in order to further the plot and provide sufficient motivation for murder. This is an incongruous contrast—one wonders why the bristling, short-fused and strong-minded character of Ackenthorpe, played by James Robertson Justice, is the head of a family of such bores, although the film does boast some strong character actors in smaller roles, including Peter Butterworth, Richard Briers and even one Joan Hickson, in her second of four brushes with screen adaptations of Agatha Christie.[9]

One possible reason for the strange mixture of styles is down to the writers who worked on the film. The adaptation was undertaken by David Osborn, whose career covered many genres, including crime, while the final screenplay was by David Pursall and Jack Seddon, who would later work on television comedies such as *The Liver Birds* (BBC, 1969–79) as well as co-writing the penultimate film of the original run of Carry On movies, *Carry On England* (d. Gerald Thomas, 1976). For the devoted readers of Christie who were looking for a film that simply presented her Miss Marple mystery on screen, there was much to disappoint. Rutherford's boisterous Miss Marple was quite unlike the refined and thoughtful figure of Christie's stories. She was now an adventurer, a go-getter who was proactive rather than reactive. Scenes of Miss Marple in disguise as a railway workman, as well as the bulk of the film where she works undercover as a maid, are quite unlike the demure character on the page of Christie's stories. The publicity for the film played up Rutherford's robust personality when she directly addresses the audience in the trailer, asking 'Now, you saw that, didn't you? Didn't you? Do you think anyone will believe us?', before a selection of moments of the film that demonstrate both mystery and humour, including Miss Marple climbing over the estate wall ('Mr Stringer, will you kindly give me a leg up?') as well as Ackenthorpe's reaction to her: 'A plainer Jane I've never seen in my life'. 'This is the 4.50 from Paddington', points out one caption, perhaps in order to reassure the audience that this really is based on an Agatha Christie work, while they were also asked to 'Take a personal part in this murderously funny thriller!' If such extracts from the film were not enough to convince any Christie fans that the film was not a faithful reproduction of her work, then the unlikely claim that 'Only Agatha Christie can mix murder and mirth with such hilarious abandon!' would certainly have ensured it.

The film certainly gets its money's worth from Margaret Rutherford, since Miss Marple also takes the part of two other key characters from the novel, entirely absent here—her friend Elspeth McGillicuddy, who saw the initial murder, and Lucy Eyelesbarrow, a young friend who carries out the undercover work. This certainly puts Miss Marple at the centre of the action from beginning to end, rather than her sitting in her cottage in Milchester (as St Mary Mead is renamed in the Rutherford films); an understandable change, but one that has ramifications for the rest of the story. Given that it is concluded early on that the murderer must be a man, this means that a good array of male suspects must be present in the film—and with the merging of three key female roles, this means that the movie is somewhat imbalanced towards the men. However, Miss Marple does get plenty of opportunity to be on screen, and her relationship with the child Alexander has some nicely pointed dialogue that enlivens much of her investigation.[10] The direction by George Pollock, who would also direct the other three films in the series, is adequate but underplays certain plot points, such as the crucial moment when the murderer is effectively revealed through a reflection of their image.

When first released in late 1961, the reception of *Murder She Said* was broadly kind, with near universal praise for Rutherford's performance and a general sense that the mystery was gentle, but satisfactory. Derek Prouse of *The Sunday Times* summarised the critical response when he wrote that Rutherford 'lends distinction to an unpretentious but likeable little film'.[11] Watched now, the movie works as a light mystery, although it does feel unsure of itself as it searches for the right direction in which to take Miss Marple. As the series of films progressed they became more confident, but moved even further from Christie's original stories.

MURDER AT THE GALLOP (1963)

While Christie had felt uneasy about much of *Murder She Said*, it had performed well at the box office, so she agreed with Edmund Cork to allow MGM to continue with a follow-up picture. In the meantime she was turning her attention to a film script of her own for a proposed screen adaptation of Charles Dickens's *Bleak House*. Although the production was never made the script survives, and it demonstrates that even with the increased scope of film technology and budgets of the era that brought the world the likes of the gargantuan production of *Cleopatra* (d. Joseph L. Mankiewicz, 1963), Christie's emphasis remained on dialogue and structure rather than cinematic visuals. Detailed descriptions and tonal indicators are few and far between in her *Bleak House* script, perhaps an unconscious indicator that Christie's strengths when it came to writing for performance lay in plotting rather than poetics. However, it is pleasing to see her obvious keenness for the source material and her attempts to bring it to the big screen. She sent the overlong script to MGM executive Lawrence P. Bachmann in May 1962 with an acknowledgement that she knew it would need to be shortened, and asking for guidance. The script did not make it into production, and it may be that this dismissal helped to feed Christie's dislike of the later MGM films—although she was not short of material about which to be disdainful.

To much of the audience it must have appeared to be business as usual when Margaret Rutherford reappeared in the role of Miss Marple for the second of the MGM films, *Murder at the Gallop*. The opening credits point out that the film is once more based on an Agatha Christie story—but readers of her works would have immediately recognised that the story on which it was based, *After the Funeral*, was a novel featuring Poirot rather than Miss Marple, concerning an investigation into the murder of a woman, Cora Lansquenet, who has suggested that the death of her wealthy brother, Richard Abernethie, may have been the result of murder rather than natural causes. The choice of this novel serves as an indication that MGM was using Christie's works in any manner it chose and that there was no particular desire to bring her original stories to the screen. The first draft of the script was finished on 7 July 1962, using the title *Funerals Are Fatal*, the name given to Christie's original novel when it was published in the United States. The final film features many similarities to the original story, but is also quite different to any depiction of Miss Marple as written by Agatha Christie.

The film operated broadly along the same lines as *Murder She Said*. Miss Marple was back at her Milchester cottage (once more filmed in Denham, Buckinghamshire), with key plot points of Christie's original mystery retained, interspersed with comedy characters and moments. Stringer Davies reprised his role, as did Charles 'Bud' Tingwell as Inspector Craddock. Alongside the retention of Ron Goodwin's jaunty theme music, this meant that *Murder at the Gallop* feels less like a standalone sequel and more like the latest instalment in an ongoing series, which is what it proved to be, as all of these elements were retained for the following two films. The film itself is a reasonably effective melodramatic mystery, which offers Rutherford more opportunities to demonstrate her comedy skills when poor Miss Marple is shown to do the twist at a party—a decision that, indirectly, helps her to solve the crime. Credulity is often stretched thin: Marple and Stringer are purely coincidental witnesses to the murder in the opening reel, in which the wealthy Mr Enderby tumbles to his death after being deliberately scared by a cat. Following another death, Miss Marple elects to stay at Enderby's hotel and stables while she investigates. *After the Funeral* contains a key revelation in its closing act that Christie often used in her stories, and it is something that is particularly difficult to depict visually—here, director George Pollock does a good job preserving the surprise. As with *Murder She Said*, the film ends with the hint of wedding bells for Miss Marple—this time, both parties may consider themselves to have had a lucky escape when the proposal is declined.

One of the most curious aspects of the Rutherford film is that the publicity is so keen to make connections with Agatha Christie's original stories, far beyond the amount needed to capitalise on any commercial value of the name association, to the extent of implying that the films were a faithful reproduction of the original character. Even the milder hints of romantic interest in Miss Marple go beyond the contented spinster of the original stories, and the ostentatiousness of Rutherford's portrayal really has no similarity to the character on the page.

In *Murder at the Gallop*, Miss Marple mentions a book called *The Ninth Life* by Agatha Christie (no such title exists in the world outside of Milchester), which might be considered to be a hint to the audience that if Agatha Christie exists in the world of these films, then we should view the whole thing as a self-aware pastiche. However, the publicity is rather more insistent that the audience should consider these films to be close to the original story, which is particularly curious when it is obvious to any reader that they are not, and that the dissimilarity appeared to have benefited the earlier picture, where Rutherford's performance was the most highly praised aspect of the film. Nevertheless, the trailer for *Murder at the Gallop* opens with a selection of Agatha Christie books: we are told that these were written by 'the inimitable Agatha Christie', with references to 'a murderous sense of humour!' over footage of Rutherford's dancing. Then there is the claim that 'Agatha Christie must have had Margaret Rutherford in mind when she wrote her fascinating murder series around that lovable busybody Miss Marple'. That this is clearly not true in any sense is obvious, but it does show us that the Agatha Christie name was still important to publicity, and that perhaps all that was needed was for the films to give the impression of being a fair reproduction of a well-known series of books—that they actually were not appears to have been a secondary consideration.

While Christie had not liked the first Rutherford film, she had accepted that liberties were going to be made with her story and that 'Whether I liked it or not was my headache!'[12] When it came to *Murder at the Gallop*, however, she felt that the film 'went too far'. She wrote that 'Miss Marple gallivanting around on horses was ludicrously unlike the original [...] But worst of all she was never in that book at all. I do not think that you should allow yourself to distort a book to that extent.'[13] Nevertheless, some reviewers felt that Rutherford was indeed the perfect fit. She 'plays the eccentric lady detective Miss Marple as if the character had been created for her', said the *Daily Mail*, calling the movie 'unbelievably enjoyable'.[14] Several reviews also mentioned the world within the film as being 'typically Christie' or even 'never-neverland', indicating once more that not only were her stories seen to be a little old-fashioned, there was also an acceptance that the world they summoned up had never really existed. The 1960s would appear to be the turning point at which Christie's books tended to be seen as more nostalgic than contemporary thrillers. There was 'enough comedy and interest to keep you intrigued', wrote Nina Hibbin of the *Daily Worker*, which neatly summarised the general critical reaction to the film.[15] The fact that the mystery elements were usually glossed over, while Rutherford's performance was praised, raises the strong possibility that it was the latter rather than the former that had made the films a commercial hit. 'Margaret Rutherford is bound to become a regular in the role of Miss Marple', said *The Times*—which she was to be, for two more films at least.[16]

MURDER MOST FOUL (1963)

In her short story 'Mr Eastwood's Adventure', Agatha Christie's titular character is a writer struggling to pick a title for a new story. He considers his editor, and realises that 'ten to one, he'll alter the title and call it something rotten, like *Murder Most Foul*.[17] One can only imagine Christie's reaction when MGM's third Miss Marple film, based on the Poirot novel *Mrs McGinty's Dead*, adopted the title that she had ridiculed four decades earlier.[18] 'I've been dreading having to see *Murder Most Foul*', she wrote to Lawrence P. Bachmann. 'Your practice seems to be to invite me to see a film after it is made. And what, I may ask, would be the use of protesting then?'[19]

The decision to place Miss Marple into a Poirot story for the second time demonstrates that *Murder at the Gallop* was not a one-off, and that MGM's attitude towards using the extensive back catalogue of Christie's work was not a desire to bring her mysteries to the screen, but rather to fillet them for the most commercially advantageous elements—and in this case, it was the character of Miss Marple as portrayed by Rutherford that was the most popular element. The changes made in the transition from page to screen were rarely commented on in contemporary reports and reviews, and we can surmise that most of the audience were similarly unaware—or uninterested. The fact that the first three Rutherford films use a Christie story as their basis simply indicates that either these tales were seen as particularly suitable, or that the producers soon believed that they were not the main attraction for much of the audience. As one review put it, 'Marple's fans may have reservations, but Rutherford fans will have none.'[20] It was not just her fans who would have been dissatisfied, but also her creator. Christie wrote later that the MGM films were

> a thoroughly bad bit of work—so much so that I was recommended by my literary agent not to go and see them when they appeared. They left out characters, added others of their own and moved characters from one book to another, and ended up with the film being absolutely nothing like the book or story of which it bore the title.[21]

As it moves away from the source material, which had followed Poirot's investigation into the apparent murder of Mrs McGinty by her lodger, so *Murder Most Foul* places an even greater emphasis on Rutherford's comedy talents when Miss Marple goes undercover once more to investigate the crime. This time our sleuth has been on the jury of a murder trial and is the only person to declare the suspect not guilty, which she then sets out to prove. Following some not entirely convincing deductions, she declares that the murderer must be a member of a repertory performance company, which she promptly joins. Given the theatrical basis there is little call for Rutherford to underplay any moments. There is no doubt that she is a compelling presence on screen—many reviews make cruel mention of her 'blood hound' or even 'gargoyle' features while acknowledging that nevertheless, she is a commanding and charismatic actress. Once more, she is the centrepiece of a strong cast including Ron Moody, James Bolam, Francesca Annis, Terry Scott, Windsor Davies and Annette Kerr.

Perhaps *Murder Most Foul* requires a stronger suspension of disbelief than the previous two films, but it offers some enjoyable moments, even if the changes from the novel are more marked than before. It is curious that, having selected a village-based mystery of the type in which Miss Marple usually featured, the changes for the screen only serve to move her further away from such domestic comforts, since she lodges with the group of actors for most of the duration. Such a change feels uncomfortable, as Miss Marple is fully placed in a scenario that seems wrong for the character, a point made by some contemporary reviews. In fact, on the whole, the critical reception was poorer than the previous two films had enjoyed. Although Rutherford was still well received, there was a sense that critics were already tiring of the series's charms. Indifference was a recurring theme; as a muted review in the *Daily Mail* put it, the comedy thriller was 'neither side-splittingly funny nor breathtakingly thrilling'.[22]

MURDER AHOY (1964)

When Agatha Christie's novel *A Caribbean Mystery* was first published in November 1964, the title page included an additional piece of information that had not been present in earlier books. It read: 'Featuring Miss Marple, The Original Character as created by Agatha Christie'. In the context of Christie's dissatisfaction with the films, it is hard not to see this as a sideswipe aimed at the Rutherford pictures; they may feature *a* Miss Marple, but *the* Miss Marple was still residing in St Mary Mead, ready to be given a new lease of life by Christie whenever her services were required.[23] Certainly *the* Miss Marple surely would not have been a party to events in the final film in the series, *Murder Ahoy*. Later, Christie would painfully recall the picture that featured 'poor Miss Marple dressed up in an admiral's uniform'.[24]

By this point the Miss Marple films had taken on such a life of their own that it is difficult to discuss them in relation to Agatha Christie. However, even the strengths of Rutherford as a character actor do not compensate for the mediocre offerings in this, the last of the four Miss Marple films in which she starred. MGM had long negotiated for the option to include Christie's characters in original mysteries, but this was the first (and only) time that it exercised this right.[25] In *Murder Ahoy*, Miss Marple is revealed to be the grand-daughter of a respected admiral and is consequently embroiled in a series of nautical mysteries including multiple murders. Much of the action takes place on board an old battleship, where young criminals are being rehabilitated. During the course of her investigation the audience must endure a tedious running joke from returning writers Pursall and Seddon, where Miss Marple is shown to be unbelievably gifted in areas that other characters do not expect. As a result we discover that she is everything from an expert chemist to the women's fencing champion of 1931.

Although it once more attracted a strong cast, including Lionel Jeffries as Captain Rhumstone, *Murder Ahoy* is a tired entry in the Miss Marple series. The comedy is less sophisticated than ever, with accompanying broad attempts to portray a particular sense of 'Englishness'; the opening shot features a fox hunt making its way through the village and there are repeated uses of Rule Britannia throughout the film. The script asks for a 'very olde-English' village, featuring a 'tea shoppe', indicating an attempt to attract an international or nostalgic audience who would be less interested in realism than in an idealised version of Britain—albeit one that features a disproportionately high murder rate. In the future, such sentimental views would often be seen in adaptations of Christie's stories, as the time of adaptation moved further from the period in which the original mystery was written, perhaps reaching an apex with ITV's series of Miss Marple adaptations, which took place in an arch, soft-focus version of the 1950s that appears to have been put together from a collection of vague memories of previous depictions of the era.

When Christie read the script for the film, she was greatly distressed. Calling it a 'farrago of nonsense', she wondered why MGM was subjecting her Miss Marple to such a scenario, asking why it could not just make films with its own character.[26] 'I don't suppose there can be any greater misery for an author than to see their characters completely distorted', she wrote. She continued:

> I really feel sick and ashamed of what I did when I signed up with MGM. It was my fault. One does things for money and one is wrong to do so—since one parts with one's literary integrity. Once one is in the trap one cannot get out. [...] I held out until seventy but I fell in the end. If they can write limitless scripts of their own, we've really had it. But I still hope that isn't true.[27]

Christie was apparently unaware that MGM had the right to make films of its own invention featuring her characters, but the contract permitted this. Clearly her attention had not been drawn to this section of the agreement; she had previously allowed such a clause in an earlier deal that had fallen through, but this was more than a quarter of a century earlier.[28] In the event, the later films did not even provide anything in the way of profit share because they failed to perform well in the international market, although an advance had been paid for the rights, ensuring that they were of some economic worth to Christie.[29]

Christie was so upset by the script that an investigation into the matter was launched, with some thought given to whether the production as a whole could be cancelled. Following the dispute, she insisted on a rewritten credit in the opening titles.[30] As a result, Pursall and Seddon are credited for the screenplay, with an additional note that it is 'Based on their interpretation of Agatha Christie's Miss Marple', a brief but explicit acknowledgement that what we are seeing is a different character to Christie's creation. To the credit of producer Lawrence P. Bachmann, he sympathised with Christie and apologised for the situation, promising that it would not happen again. She wrote that the whole situation 'horrified and upset me more than I can say'.[31]

The publicity for the film centred on Rutherford and the comedic elements, with a cartoon of Miss Marple water-skiing above miniature depictions of three sailors and an embracing couple sitting below her. She was also seen to be clutching an Academy Award, recognition that Rutherford had recently won Best Supporting Actress following her performance in *The V.I.P.s* (d. Anthony Asquith, 1963). The trailer had a similar emphasis, proclaiming: 'Now hear this—you hearty laughers—Here comes Academy Award winner Margaret Rutherford'. It went on to promise that 'Excitement storms the high seas on a wacky wild voyage of homicide and hilarity as only Agatha Christie can mix with such riotous abandon'. Christie, then, still gets a credit, but not for work that she would recognise, nor for a genre towards which she had any positive inclination, whatever was implied.

The distance of the film from Christie's original creation was noted in reviews at the time. Claiming that Rutherford seemed to be sent a script when the producers had 'nothing better to do', *Time*'s negative review pointed out that this was Miss Marple 'in name only, buoying up a nonsensical plot [...] on these shallow comedy seas'.[32] The *Monthly Film Bulletin* was even more hostile, calling it 'Elementary and lethargic in the extreme; this is rock bottom Miss Marple'.

It would have surprised few, then, that this was to be the final major outing for Rutherford's Miss Marple. The series had done well in attracting an audience, but the patchy distribution of *Murder Ahoy*, as well as the combination of the actress's elevated status and advancing age, would have made any future entries even more difficult to coordinate. It is entirely credit to Margaret Rutherford that the films are so well remembered; it says much that MGM's next Christie film, in which she made only a brief, and final, appearance as Miss Marple, is rather forgotten by comparison.

THE ALPHABET MURDERS (1965)

'It's really no mystery how this girl can be murder', proclaimed the posters for 1965's *The Alphabet Murders* (d. Frank Tashlin), accompanied by a drawing of actress Anita Ekberg as key suspect Amanda, wearing a short skirt beneath a tight T-shirt emblazoned with 'ABC'. However, the real mystery of *The Alphabet Murders* is how the film came to be made at all, especially considering the fact that it was in the wake of Christie's emotional and emphatic criticism of the MGM pictures in general and, more specifically, *Murder Ahoy*. The film features Tony Randall as Poirot, later to be best known for his starring role in the TV series of *The Odd Couple* (ABC, 1970–75), and uses a script that actually replaced an original, even more problematic attempt to make the novel into an MGM film. Nevertheless, Christie would later write: '*The ABC Murders* I was not allowed to see. My friends and publishers told me the agony would be too great [...] these movies added insult to injury.'[33]

The Alphabet Murders brought Poirot back to the cinema screen after a break of more than three decades, in a film based on a novel that had interested MGM for nearly as long. However, it was only with the success of the Margaret Rutherford Miss Marple films, and the failure of the Poirot television pilot, that it finally made its way into production. Once more, producer Lawrence P. Bachmann oversaw the movie, with a script by Pursall and Seddon. Although based on *The ABC Murders* (with a title change to avoid confusion with the ABC cinema chain), the final film in fact only retains the idea of murders occurring in alphabetical order of the victims' names, and the motive for this. Beyond these basic details it is a complete deviation from the source, not only in plot but also in tone. It is clear to see the genesis of the project as an attempt to integrate Poirot into a 'sexy' comedy, with many elements removed and replaced by similarly broad physical humour, such as a sequence where the character of Hastings, played by Robert Morley, is forced to run down a busy street in nothing more than a towel, only to be confronted by a marching parade. The story as a whole lurches between disparate events, concerning everything from hypnotism to a murdered clown falling from a diving board, in an apparent attempt to emulate the type of surrealism that had proven so popular on television's *The Avengers*. In the film, Hastings is a member of the secret service whose role it is both to protect Poirot and enlist him to work on their behalf as they investigate these murders, each of which is accompanied by a copy of the ABC railway guide. At the beginning, the picture offers self-reflexivity as Tony Randall appears and introduces himself as Poirot—recognition that both the character and the actor were the film's star names. Randall's Poirot is squeamish and prone to comedy in a manner similar to Rutherford, but at least he is a refined figure for the most part and is generally portrayed as the most intelligent person in the film. This was the result of Bachmann's attempt to appease Christie's concerns that the character would not deviate too substantially from Poirot as written. Although there are many differences, other characters are even more buffoonish, making him the touchstone for common sense during much of the film, even during lighter sequences.

Throughout the discussions about *Murder Ahoy* between Christie, her agent Edmund Cork and Bachmann, it was clear that there was some confusion about exactly how free MGM was to do as it saw fit with Christie's characters. Whatever its contractual rights, Bachmann was keen to keep Christie on side and so reined the film back from the initial plans, which would have emphasised the sex element much more, as well as changing Poirot in a way that would have horrified Christie. In the film as it stands, Poirot often acts out of character in order to reflect fashions of the 1960s (he dons a polo-necked jumper to play a game at a bowling alley, for example), but this was nothing compared to the earlier intention. Initially, Tony Award–winning actor Zero Mostel was supposed to write the script as well as star. His draft featured several fantasy and sexual sequences that Christie and Cork met with hostility. A copy of this script, which was completed in early 1964, is not known to exist, but the notes from the Motion Picture Association of America (MPAA) regarding its adherence or otherwise to the United States' Production Code give us some idea of its contents.[34]

The MPAA cleared the four Rutherford films without issue, but Mostel's *The Alphabet Murders* was to meet a different fate. The script was deemed unacceptable due to 'excessively' sexually suggestive scenarios. It was criticised for introducing sexual content for no reason other than titillation, with the notes indicating that in this draft the story opens with Poirot in the midst of a sexual act with an unidentified woman, something apparently suggested by sound effects.[35] Following this, an erotic dance sequence would include Poirot being buffeted back and forth by female bottoms, which was considered unacceptable by the MPAA, as was a scene where a short man is called into bed by an Amazon. The man's line 'I gotta fix a leak' was then ruled out due to its perceived erotic significance. Further issues with the script included implied or actual female nudity, a sequence where Poirot and a female character slap each other and masochistically cry out for more, as well as a scene in which Poirot searches a woman for a concealed weapon that included her reaction to visible evidence of his sexual excitement.

In the event, it would be more than a year until a certificate for the final film, with its different script and star, was granted, a longer lead time than the earlier pictures, no doubt due to the rewriting. A fortnight after MGM had been informed about the production code difficulties, Cork was relaying to Christie the news that the script was being completely rewritten following the protests, and by May 1964 Mostel was off the picture and had already left for New York.[36] The final film was more in line with the later Rutherford features, and even included a brief cameo by Miss Marple and Mr Stringer accompanied by her familiar theme tune. 'I cannot see why they're having such difficulty. The solution is ABC, to anyone with half a brain cell', says Miss Marple, before pointedly looking at Poirot. Meanwhile, the film also acknowledged the last appearance of Poirot on film with Austin Trevor appearing in the role of Judson—Trevor would retain the record for most appearances as Poirot on film or television until Peter Ustinov surpassed him some two decades later, more than half a century after the former's final performance as the Belgian detective.

By this stage Christie's daughter and son-in-law, Rosalind and Anthony Hicks, were taking a more central role in discussions about her work, and Rosalind wrote to Cork to say that the *Murder Ahoy* dispute had so upset her mother that she did not expect her to read any future screenplays. Such was her dislike of the films that even tie-in editions of her novels were downplayed as much as possible. As Edmund Cork pointed out to Rosalind, 'I think it is very important to us that we should preserve the literary image [of Miss Marple and Poirot].'[37] This correspondence sowed the seeds for Rosalind's later dealings with film and television producers following Christie's death, as she sought to maintain her mother's legacy and not go through the same issues that all had experienced under MGM. In the end a new agreement was drawn up that clarified matters for all parties, but the experience had soured Christie's view of adaptations of her work even more. It is little wonder that when Christie struck up a correspondence with Billy Wilder in 1963, she apparently expressed a wish that he would return to make a film of her work instead. 'I would be ecstatic to be working on a Christie again,' he wrote to her. 'How about a great big eight million dollar all-conclusive mystery to end all mysteries? Got anything up your sleeve?'[38]

When it was finally released in 1965, *The Alphabet Murders* made little impact. Reviews were mostly indifferent, although some were positive. However, several questioned the casting of Tony Randall and some unfairly criticised Christie for nonsensical or uninteresting plot revelations that had been introduced to the script. By the time of release it was clear that MGM and Christie wanted very different things and neither party was particularly inclined to continue the relationship. The MGM pictures remain anomalies, loved and despised by pockets of the general audience and Christie fans alike. They took no more liberties with original Christie stories than many other adaptations, from the earliest days of 1928's *The Passing of Mr Quinn* to ITV's twenty-first-century *Agatha Christie: Marple* series. In Rutherford MGM had discovered a formula that worked for many people. However, what it did not do was find a way to present Christie's original work while simultaneously preserving its ethos, characterisation and plotting, as *Witness for the Prosecution* had done. Only the second truly successful adaptation to do that would come nearly a decade later, when EMI Films tackled one of Christie's best-known, and most popular, novels to great success.

Notes

1. See Chap. 2.
2. Although the original title still featured as an invitation on some promotional material that bore the final name of the film, including the trailer.
3. *Truly Miss Marple: The Curious Case of Margaret Rutherford* (d. Rieke Brendel, Andrew Davies, 2012).
4. *Truly Miss Marple: The Curious Case of Margaret Rutherford* (d. Rieke Brendel, Andrew Davies, 2012).
5. Edmund Cork to Rosalind Hicks, 11 January 1961 (Agatha Christie Archive, Exeter).
6. Rutherford to Christie 3 November 1962 (Agatha Christie Family Archive).
7. Christie to Cork, 17 September 1961 (Agatha Christie Archive, Exeter).
8. Christie to Mr David G. Kann, 29 September 1972 (Agatha Christie Family Archive).
9. Ackenthorpe is renamed from the Crackenthorpe of the novel.
10. Alexander is played by Ronnie Raymond, although his voice is rather eerily dubbed by Martin Stephens, who had appeared as one of the sinister children in the 1960 MGM film *Village of the Damned*.
11. *Sunday Times*, 1 October 1961.
12. Christie to Bachmann, 11 April 1964 (Agatha Christie Archive, Exeter).
13. Christie to Bachmann, 11 April 1964 (Agatha Christie Archive, Exeter).

14. *Daily Mail*, 11 May 1963.
15. *Daily Worker*, 11 May 1963.
16. *The Times*, 9 May 1963.
17. 'Mr Eastwood's Adventure' in *The Listerdale Mystery* (London: HarperCollins, 2010), 177.
18. The story first appeared in *The Novel Magazine* in 1924.
19. Christie to Bachmann, 11 April 1964 (Agatha Christie Archive, Exeter).
20. *The Times*, 22 October 1964.
21. Christie to Kann, 29 September 1972 (Agatha Christie Family Archive).
22. *Daily Mail*, 24 October 1964.
23. The notice is also reminiscent of the issues regarding the novelisation of *The Passing of Mr Quinn* when it comes to ownership of the 'original' characters (see Chap. 1).
24. Christie to Kann, 29 September 1972 (Agatha Christie Family Archive).
25. Some commentators have noted superficial similarities to *They Do It with Mirrors*, notably the group of young miscreants undergoing rehabilitation while actually undertaking nefarious acts, as well as an embezzling criminal.
26. Christie to Patricia Cork, 18 March 1964 (Agatha Christie Archive, Exeter).
27. Christie to Patricia Cork, 18 March 1964 (Agatha Christie Archive, Exeter).
28. See Chap. 2 for further details on this abandoned deal.
29. This is according to a 5 July 1967 letter to Rosalind Hicks from Edmund Cork (Agatha Christie Archive, Exeter), where he pointed out that *Murder She Said* was the only one of the films for which a profit-share cheque had been issued. He also cites apparently higher budgets as a reason for the lack of residuals.
30. Bachmann to Christie, 7 April 1964 (Agatha Christie Archive, Exeter).
31. Christie to Edmund Cork, 25 March 1964 (Agatha Christie Archive, Exeter).
32. *Time*, 2 October 1964.
33. Christie to Mr David G. Kann, 29 September 1972 (Agatha Christie Family Archive).
34. The Production Code was in its dying days, but had been in place as a form of self-regulation for over three decades by this point—scripts would be vetted to 'help' producers whose films might otherwise be completed only to be found to be in breach of the code, which would mean that most cinemas would not show the picture.
35. Shurlock to Vogel, 10 April 1964 (The Alphabet Murders file, Margaret Herrick Library, Los Angeles).
36. Cork to Christie, 24 April and 4 May 1964 (Agatha Christie Archive, Exeter).
37. Cork to Rosalind Hicks, 14 January 1964 (Agatha Christie Archive, Exeter).
38. Wilder to Christie, 20 December 1963 (Agatha Christie Family Archive).

PART IV

Prestige Films and Beyond, 1965–87

Chapter 7: A New Era on Screen

Spoilers: *And Then There Were None; Endless Night; The Murder of Roger Ackroyd*

Given that this chapter looks at a period bookended by two broadly similar film adaptations of *And Then There Were None*, an expectation may be that this decade signified a period in which little changed for Christie screen adaptations. Both of these pictures were produced by Harry Alan Towers, a British film producer who specialised in immediately commercially attractive properties, and they take similar approaches to the source material since they are once more based on Christie's play, rather than her original novel.[1] The first of the two films, released in 1965, sets the action atop a snowy mountain, while the 1974 adaptation relocates the murders to a desert hotel; despite the change in locale, both versions use largely the same script. However, these films are anomalies in the development of Agatha Christie screen adaptations, functioning as two of the last 'unthinking' English-language versions—that is to say, films that have used the basis of Christie's stories without close consultation with either the author, her agents or her estate, and simply formulated a screen adaptation that works as a piece of entertainment in its own right, rather than as a contribution to the Christie legacy. With their source material tied up in a separate deal to the bulk of Christie's works, these two films stand alone as adaptations of a well-known story rather than a reflection of any particular desire or willingness to authorise adaptations of a certain type by either Christie and her family or her agent, Edmund Cork. However, their existence partially conceals the fact that this period also sparked two of the most interesting Christie films, one of which would become the new template for adapting her mysteries to the screen.

The 1965 adaptation of *And Then There Were None*, which has been most commonly released under the title *Ten Little Indians*, forges an uneasy alliance between 1960s sensibilities and the traditional elements established in the original play and film.[2] On the one hand, director George Pollock appears to have been considered a safe pair of hands, from a commercial perspective at least, with the production following on from his work on the Margaret

© The Author(s) 2016
M. Aldridge, *Agatha Christie on Screen*,
DOI 10.1057/978-1-137-37292-5_8

Rutherford Miss Marple pictures earlier in the decade. He is given a script that deviates little from the basic structure of the by now well-known Christie original, once more following the stage play closer than the novel, no doubt as a result of both practical dramatic concerns as well as licensing issues. However, the film also demonstrates attempts to offer a production grounded in the 1960s, rather than a vague placement in a 'Christie era'.

Perhaps the most overt attempt to appeal to contemporary audiences was in the casting. Appearing in the two key roles of Lombard and Ann Clyde are Hugh O'Brian and Shirley Eaton, with O'Brian even lending his first name to Lombard, now named Hugh, while the more fashionable name of Ann replaced Vera.[3] Hugh O'Brian had made a name for himself as the star of popular television series *The Life and Legend of Wyatt Earp* (ABC, 1955–61), in which he had asserted himself as a strong masculine lead upholding the law, with a more complex approach to characterisation than had usually typified the Western genre. Eaton had recently been the focus of one of the most iconic moments in cinema, when she appeared covered in gold in the James Bond film *Goldfinger* (d. Guy Hamilton, 1964). Therefore, both actors had inbuilt appeal to audiences who had been taking any notice of popular culture. While O'Brian and Eaton would be the focus of much of the picture, perhaps the most overt attempt to situate the film as a new and modern take on the story was in the casting of pop singer Fabian as the unlikeable Mike Raven, a man who shows no remorse for the deaths he has caused and is the murderer's first victim. It perhaps says something about the producers' confidence in Fabian's acting skills that his character departs so swiftly, but in truth he acquits himself well. In fact, his straightforward obnoxiousness does all that is required of him, and the actor performs rather better than some of those cast as other victims, such as Daliah Lavi's awkward turn as actress Ilona Bergen. Israeli-born Lavi had made a name for herself as a model prior to her acting career, and certainly her striking modern hairstyle allows the film to have at least one foot in the world of 1960s fashion (as well as a hat tip to exoticism and glamour), but the film grinds to a halt whenever the person sporting it is required to carry a scene.[4]

The film itself is functional but unexceptional, offering few fully engaging or exciting moments for the audience. However, it is well paced and keeps the core components of Christie's story intact, albeit with changes to specific characters and their backgrounds. The decision to set the action in a snowbound mansion at the top of a mountain (filmed in County Dublin, Ireland), accessible only by cable car, initially seems rather unnecessary as it provides no more opportunities for plotting than the island of Christie's original story, but it does offer a visually interesting opening and unwittingly sidesteps one of the bigger leaps of faith required by the reader of Christie's original novel—the murderer's good fortune that the weather is so bad that any attempt to leave the island would be immediately disastrous. The change of location also helps to differentiate this film clearly from previous movie and television versions of the story. While the casting of younger actors engrained in 1960s cultural fashions has mixed results, another attempt to contemporise the film falls flatter still, with Malcolm Lockyer's inappropriate jazz score undermining any tension that manages to make it on screen.[5] The decision to integrate some characters with links to contemporary youth culture has the interesting, but probably unintended, result that the house is now clearly divided between the 'old guard'—characters and actors who would have been at home in René Clair's 1945 take on the story— and the more modern group. With the emphasis on the relatively youthful pairing of Lombard and Ann, this means that many characters are swiftly relegated to the background, wandering around waiting for their turn to be murdered. One unintentionally amusing result of this culture clash takes place when one of the older characters, William Blore (Stanley Holloway), investigates one of his fellow 'Indians' by spying on a shirtless Lombard through the keyhole of the latter's bedroom door; to a sexually liberated audience this may imply more about Blore's character than was intended.

In terms of role and plot function, Shirley Eaton's Ann is little different from Christie's original independent and strong-willed Vera, showing how modern Christie's characterisations often were, but as a 'sixties woman' she is presented as a character who embraces her own sexuality. Indeed, there is a clear implication that she and Lombard make love, albeit couched in a rather reactionary approach to sex on screen, since when we rejoin the post-coital lovers Eaton is wearing more clothes than she was before. Occasionally Ann is a little more emancipated than Vera had been in the play and 1945 film, and this time she gets to carry the resolution of the film independently, since the audience momentarily believes that she has actually shot and killed Lombard. These developments are no longer framed by the original conclusion of Christie's play, which implies that apparent feminine failings have saved the day ('Thank God, women can't shoot straight!' she scripted Lombard as saying); this time her gender is perceived as a strength ('Never trust a woman!' complains Judge Cannon in the film, played by Wilfred Hyde-White, as he dies). In yet another apparent Bond reference, a white cat is the focus when our unseen villain comes face to face with Ann in the final scene. Such is the strength of Ann's character as she appears to be the sole remaining victim that we might even consider her to be a prototype 'final girl', often seen in horror movies of the 1970s and beyond.[6]

One area of which the film-makers were acutely aware was the fact that to many viewers, the basic premise of the movie may have seemed over-familiar. We have seen that *And Then There Were None* was adapted several times for television alongside its considerable success on stage, while all the time the original novel remained in print. It has also been the subject of many pastiches on film, television and radio, meaning that even those who had not seen or read the story before were likely to be familiar with the basics of the plot. This implicit expectation of foreknowledge is manifest in the film itself, where there is no attempt to hide the fact that most of those on the mountain will be fatally injured by the final reel. Instead, this expectation is embraced, starting with particular emphasis on the reading of the full *Ten Little Indians* rhyme aloud during an early scene, effectively laying out the structure for the audience who may now wonder how, precisely, one person may be shown to die at the hands of a bee, for example ('Six little Indians playing with a hive; A bumble bee stung one and then there were five'). In terms of publicity, the promotional material for the film made the premise quite clear, stating: 'Seven Arts Productions presents Agatha Christie's Classic Mystery *Ten Little Indians.* Ten people trapped in a house of death and one determined to kill them... one by one by one...'. Accompanying this was a cardboard wheel affixed to a promotional flyer. This could be spun to show a different face of a suspect in a portion of a stopwatch. The more astute may have noticed that only eight of the characters were afforded this privilege, since Marianne Hoppe and Mario Ardorf were missing (the actors played analogues of Mr and Mrs Rogers, the butler and cook); a clue that these characters were not to be major players in the mystery.

However, the biggest portion of the publicity was reserved for a non-diegetic portion of the film. Just as William Castle and other B-movie producers of the 1950s had used cinema-based gimmicks to entice an audience to their picture, so *Ten Little Indians* offered what it claimed was a first for motion pictures. While Castle had floated skeletons above the audience (advertised as 'Emergo!'), and even given some patrons small electric shocks as the action unfolded on screen ('Percepto!'), *Ten Little Indians'* device was a little more demure—this film offered a 'Whodunit Break'. As the promotional literature sent to cinema owners put it:

> STOP! for the most unique exploitation device to ever play your theatre. Just before the gripping climax of the film, your patrons will have a chance to discuss among themselves who they think the killer is, while on the screen they will see the 'whodunit' clock ticking away for 60-seconds while each of the murders is replayed to help them decide the killer's identity. We doubt they will be able to guess; or, for that matter, if you will either!

In practice, this simply means that when Ann holds Lombard at gunpoint towards the end of the film, the action freezes and an announcer implores the audience to discuss with their neighbour who they think 'dunit', while a reprise of the murders appears on screen. Given the nature of the mystery's structure, where from the beginning the audience is asked simply to pick out which single character they think the killer is (and, perhaps, who they think might survive), this is a rather effective idea.

On the whole, though, 1965's *Ten Little Indians* fails to capitalise fully on the possibilities of utilising the 1960s culture that it so tentatively acknowledges; nor does it explore the opportunities afforded by increasingly liberal censorship and renewed viewer expectations for horror and thriller films. While the movie does show many of the murders, unlike its 1945 predecessor, it is no more explicit than standard popular films of the previous two decades. As a result, it feels particularly dated considering that it comes five years after the release of both *Psycho* (d. Alfred Hitchcock, 1960) and *Peeping Tom* (d. Michael Powell, 1960), two movies that had helped to redefine how horror, murder and sexuality could be portrayed on screen.[7] Both of these films had emphasised psychology and enabled complex characterisation to sit at their core. Both were also the tales of men motivated to kill because of sexual desire in some form, an approach to character psychology that went beyond Christie's murderer's interesting but straightforward stated motivation during this particular story (although psychology—in this case, personal takes on 'justice'—still plays some part, and is more prominent in some of her other mysteries, such as her 1938 novel *Appointment with Death*). The incident-based motivation for murder (by this point seen as archetypal, whereby the crime is the result of specific triggers) meant that the picture could never move beyond its 1930s origins for the audience, even if framed within some 1960s window dressing. While this might be unhelpful to the producers of this particular film, it does demonstrate how Christie had helped to set the template for murder mysteries, in terms of how the general public understood them—it could hardly be her fault that the scenarios were so well received and widely imitated that they would eventually be deemed 'old hat'. This widespread recognition of the archetypal Christie factors meant that the makers of Christie adaptations soon would have to decide whether to overhaul the stories for modern audiences, or present them as heritage pieces. A middle-ground approach was becoming increasingly unsatisfactory.

The sense that what the film offered had all been seen before pervaded the reviews. Most noted the change in title (the previous film and play having both used the original *Ten Little Niggers* in the UK, a title that editions of the novel there still used well into the 1980s), although none bemoaned the loss of the offensive word, merely seeing it as indicative of changing sensibilities.[8] *The Times* declared the film 'a pretty straightforward rendering of Agatha Christie's classic conundrum. Too straightforward, really, for if one happens to remember who the villain is there is absolutely nothing else to hold the attention', a pretty damning indictment of the attempts to modernise the mystery.[9] In *The Sun* Ann Pacey made the same point, while she also called Pollock's direction 'cosily competent'.[10] More forceful criticism was found in *Time* magazine, which declared it 'an anaemic copy of the 1945 film [...] nothing has been added but tired blood. [...] Properly done, this old fashioned brand of carnage can hardly miss. The remakers of *Indians* fail in every possible way.'[11] In the *Daily Mail*, Cecil Wilson felt that the film was 'played with the tongue so firmly in the cheek that you wonder how the characters can get their words out, let alone keep a straight face', presumably referring to the more experienced actors, although their performances are not as arch as suggested—more likely, they are simply in keeping with performances as seen on stage, where the occasional absurd elements of Christie's stories have tended to be celebrated rather than glossed over.[12] The 'Whodunit Break' was viewed as effective, although not necessarily to the film's advantage. While Patrick Gibbs of the *Daily Telegraph* saw it as a way to lift an otherwise old-fashioned piece of cinema,[13] Alexander Walker of the *Evening Standard* highlighted an unintended consequence when he recounts a conversation that took place during the break: 'I remarked to my neighbour: "Do you remember how much better René Clair did it all in 1945?"'[14]

This film of *Ten Little Indians* sits awkwardly within the canon of Christie film and 1960s cinema more generally, wanting to find a fresh audience and be perceived as contemporary, yet unwilling to make anything other than superficial changes to a well-worn narrative. This was one of the first attempts to modernise Christie (after all, 26 years had passed since the novel's publication), but the uneasy meddling set the mould for such attempts to be largely unsuccessful. The next film to be made of Agatha Christie's works would have no such concerns, enabling one of her most recent and darkest novels to make its way to the screen.

ENDLESS NIGHT (1972)

Although the rights to many of Christie's stories had been sold or assigned by the mid-1960s, this did not stop interest from other parties who wished to bring her work to the screen, as she repeatedly received enquiries from individuals and businesses interested in particular titles. These included Joseph Furst—an Austrian actor who appeared in many films and television programmes including *Diamonds Are Forever* (d. Guy Hamilton, 1971) and a memorable turn as villainous Professor Zaroff in *Doctor Who* (BBC, 1967)—who wished to adapt Christie's 1930 short story collection *The Mysterious Mr Quin* as a series for television.[15] This approach was turned down, as were all the offers and requests from members of the public to adapt her works that had been received over the years, rebuffed with a simple explanation that rights were either unavailable or that Christie herself had no interest in film or television adaptations. In addition, there was repeated correspondence regarding the film rights for Christie's play *The Unexpected Guest*, including a dispute with its producer Peter Saunders, which further muddied discussions of exploiting her stories for the screen.[16] General discussions of film rights were linked to Christie's own professed dislike of screen adaptations of her work, as her agent Edmund Cork explained in a letter to her daughter, Rosalind Hicks, in May 1967.[17] Cork clarified:

> Perhaps I should say that the stiffening up of our attitude has been influenced by the fact that your mother seems to be so strongly opposed to films at this time. I told her about the possibility of selling the film rights to [her 1951 thriller] *They Came to Baghdad*, and she said—"Don't talk to me about film rights!! It always makes my blood boil. If they belong to the Company they will do as they please. My own feeling remains the same—I have suffered enough!"

He pointed out that the relevant rights were held by the Christie Copyrights Trust and that selling them would be to the trustees' advantage, but 'I would be against doing anything now that would cause your mother more distress'.

This attempt to make a film of *They Came to Baghdad* stemmed from American film producer Elliott Kastner, but he had been unable to find substantial studio backing for the project, and by July 1967 it was clear that the adaptation was not going to happen; Kastner would go on to be at the helm of such pictures as the popular 1968 war film *Where Eagles Dare* (d. Brian G. Hutton), starring Richard Burton and Clint Eastwood. However, the apparent intention to make a film out of one of Christie's stories as a prestige picture with a high budget and strong cast may be an early indication of the shifting attitudes towards her, from talented mystery novelist to author of classic stories.[18] In the meantime, there was to be a rare opportunity for a Christie film adaptation to be made shortly after the publication of the novel on which it was based.

In 1967 *Endless Night* appeared, a Christie novel that has often been cited by readers of her work as a highlight of the later years of her career, and many consider it to be one of her very best pieces of work from any period. A standalone thriller, it is narrated by the charming but directionless Michael Rogers, a young man who documents his meeting with millionaire heiress Ellie Guteman and the subsequent hurdles that they overcome in pursuit of a happy life together, living in a dream house built on an apparently cursed piece of land called Gypsy's Acre. The novel recalled elements from some of Christie's most successful work, including both 'Philomel Cottage' (and Frank Vosper's play *Love from a Stranger*, based on that story) as well as *The Murder of Roger Ackroyd*. The novel was well received critically, and by 1968 discussions were already taking place regarding purchase of the film rights to the book.[19] Although 78-year-old Christie was not dealing with business affairs as much as she had been, she was sent the contract and so we know that she personally assented to the deal, perhaps because she realised that the nature of the story made it a particularly strong candidate for a British film of this period.[20] Christie had—wittingly or unwittingly—written a drama well suited to the style of many successful films of the late 1960s, and offered up a strong psychological thriller.

Since the publication of *Endless Night* post-dated previous film contracts, it was available for adaptation to interested parties, should they secure Christie's agreement. The rights to the film were sold to production company British Lion and when it was finally filmed in summer 1971, in the Home Counties and on the Isle of Wight, contact with the author was maintained through her daughter Rosalind, with an offer to visit the film set extended to them by its director Sidney Gilliat, who had also written the screenplay and had been working in the British film industry in various roles since the dying days of the silent era. The letter containing this offer outlined the strong cast, which included rising star Hywel Bennett as Michael along with Hayley Mills as Ellie and Britt Ekland as her companion Greta.[21] When released in 1972, the film immediately identified itself as a contemporary picture: Michael narrates the opening in dialogue with an unknown other person while we see flashes of sur-real Pop Art imagery, including heavily tinted crash zooms on Ellie standing in Gypsy's Acre, in which she is revealed to have no face.[22] Accompanied by

Michael's cry of 'No, not that!', it is therefore made unequivocally clear to the audience that this is a film that will contain its fair share of high drama. This is an effective opening given later events, as one of *Endless Night*'s great strengths is that it does take quite some time to reveal exactly what type of story it is telling. Indeed, the question of genre is the biggest mystery of the piece and hiding it helps to ensure that the author can stay one step ahead, because the audience members do not know if they are watching a murder mystery, a simple romance or (as is eventually revealed to be the case) a thriller littered with red herrings until the final half hour.

Aside from the occasional overtly contemporary style, not only in the early surreal imagery but also the mise-en-scène of the film, including the modern design of Michael and Ellie's dream house on Gypsy's Acre by architect friend Santonix (Per Oscarsson), the principal influence on the film would appear to be Alfred Hitchcock. Potentially devious relationships often form the back-bone of Hitchcock's films, just as they do in Christie's stories, while mysteries layered within other mysteries are similar tropes of both. Given the fact that producer, writer and director Sidney Gilliat had co-written the screenplay for Hitchcock's *The Lady Vanishes* (1938), perhaps this should not be a surprise, while his choice of Bernard Herrman to write the score only cements the links. Herrman's music is effectively biased towards strings and evokes memories of his work on *Psycho* and *North by Northwest* (d. Alfred Hitchcock, 1959) in particular. While following the story of Michael and his attempts to get hold of Gypsy's Acre, the film-literate audience is reminded of suspicious characters in several Hitchcock films, whose true motivation similarly takes time to be revealed. This suspicion is only made more overt by the fact that, through flashbacks, the audience is aware that Michael is at best capable of deception, and at worst is an unreliable narrator, since we see him attempt to explain being dismissed from jobs and his own mother's suspicion of his motives in a man-ner that is not wholly convincing. Such moments are passed over quickly and we soon return to him as a charming contemporary figure, but this sows the seeds of suspicion, while the audience is witness to his determination to do as he wishes and get what he wants.

One area that is more overtly explored in the film than in the novel is the role of Michael's sexuality in the mystery, in all senses. Christie was unhappy with the inclusion of a sex scene in the closing act, as well as the death of a character in one of the final scenes, which she called 'very unpleasant' and 'very unnecessary'.[23] The sex scene in question is actually brief and not explicit by 1970s standards, but it is interesting that it takes place shortly after Michael's friend Santonix has died, having apparently worked out the true motivation behind Michael's actions. Michael becomes more aggressive following this death, including his forceful initiation of sex with his wife, implying a high level of emotional connection with Santonix that may extend beyond that of sim-ply a friend. Sex and passion do not seem to underpin Michael's motivations; the real source of his excitement is his work with Santonix to put his dream house together—his relationship with Ellie simply enables this. When we see

Michael chauffeuring an obnoxious passenger during one of his brief spells of employment, we may detect a mild bristle in his demeanour after a reference to a 'mean looking fairy in a jockstrap', while the passenger's subsequent offer to take Michael to the red-light district is flatly declined. This then provides the impetus for Michael becoming more abrasive in his character and failing to pick his passengers up—an over-reaction that may indicate that his client touched on a sensitive area of his character, which in turn leads to his dismissal from the job. Michael's sexuality is a complex one, but we are never in any doubt that he will use any means to get what he wants, regardless of any romantic attraction.

Although Christie had been aware of the film from its earliest stages of production, this did not translate to her being keen to see it, given her distress over MGM's films during the 1960s. 'There has been a film made from my book *Endless Night*, but I have not yet had the courage to go and have a clandestine look at it', she wrote about a month after its release.[24] While we know that once Christie saw the film she was less than satisfied with it, overall it is an effective reworking of the novel in line with the contemporary film style for British thrillers. In itself this can have been of little surprise to Christie, who had been to the cinema to watch films including *Rosemary's Baby* (d. Roman Polanski, 1968) and so was fully aware of how modern thrillers operated.[25] Resultantly, it is curious but perhaps telling that many of the reviews of *Endless Night* decided to focus on elements perceived as traditionally Christie-esque rather than the more strikingly contemporary elements, which are usually mentioned only in order to highlight their apparently anomalous status. David McGillivray of the *Monthly Film Bulletin* wrote that '*Twisted Nerve* may not have been, as British Lion claimed, "enough to make Hitchcock jump" [referring to a 1968 psychological thriller that also starred Mills and Bennett, as well as having a score by Herrman], but their latest vehicle for Hayley Mills and Hywel Bennett may well be sufficient to give the master a start of surprise'. Despite this positive opening the review went on to bemoan the apparent locating of the film in 'Christie Country' while also criticising the 'lean' material and praising Gilliat for apparently improving on the original novel's dialogue. David Robinson of the *Financial Times* betrayed the fact that he went to the film with certain preconceptions when he says it is 'comfortably set in that rural imagination which exists only in the imagination of Agatha Christie, where there is always a vicar, a philosophical doctor, a rose-tending bobby', characters that appear minimally if at all, while his claim that Bennett and Mills 'still look a bit too modern in this between-the-wars world [...] It must take real confidence to go on resurrecting such wheezy old stuff' shows how little attention he was paying to this contemporarily set film.[26]

Modern concerns did occasionally appear in reviews, for instance Ken Eastaugh in *The Sun* giving the film short shrift, complaining 'If you want to understand what's wrong with the British film industry take a look at *Endless Night*'.[27] Dilys Powell in the *Sunday Times* was a rare critic who enjoyed the picture, although she was hardly rapturous in praise,[28] but Alexander Walker of the *Evening Standard* was one of many who felt that the film did not play fair.[29] Linked to this was a recurring complaint from critics that the denouement, where it is revealed that Michael had orchestrated the mysterious events and murder, was confusing or, some claimed, illogical. Tom Hutchinson of the *Sunday Telegraph* recounts how, having previously read the book, he was besieged by other critics asking for clarification of plot details—most curious, considering that the film is not shy of emphasising plot points and, come the final act, the motivation, including the use of flashbacks, but perhaps indicative of how much attention the critics had been paying to what they assumed was a standard thriller. Examples include Ronald Hayman in *The Times* calling it 'rotten with the stink of red herrings',[30] while Ian Christie of the *Daily Express* called the denouement 'irritating and unsatisfactory'[31] and Richard Barkley in the *Sunday Express* simply called the ending 'a bit of a con trick'.[32]

The film was not a box-office success and did not receive a wide release in the United States, despite high interest in Christie's novels and short story collections. However, this was a brief lull in the fortunes of Agatha Christie adaptations on screen, since even while the film was on release plans were forming for the biggest and most successful Christie film of them all.

MURDER ON THE ORIENT EXPRESS (1974)

Critically, and popularly, the 1974 film of *Murder on the Orient Express* is widely seen as the centre of the Agatha Christie screen universe. It was not the first to use big names for an adaptation, nor to receive a healthy budget, nor even to receive warm critical notices—both René Clair's original film of *And Then There Were None* and Billy Wilder's *Witness for the Prosecution* had accomplished some or all of these feats. Nevertheless, those films did not establish the type of screen legacy that *Murder on the Orient Express* was to have. Christie's mystery about a murder aboard a stranded train, with the resultant claustrophobic realisation that the killer must surely be among those travelling on board in the first-class carriage, was a well-known and widely respected novel, but it had not been seen on cinema screens before. Crucially for the understandably wary Christie family, the rights to make the picture would only be sold if it were treated as a one-off event that was not immediately tied to further films, unlike the MGM deal that had repeatedly produced disappointing efforts, prolonging the family's misery. This film saw the transition of Christie from an author whose popular appeal and plotting allowed her works to be deconstructed and reformatted for (normally) low-budget films of middling success to being treated as an author of repute, whose earlier books in particular were now being considered outright classics, rather than entertaining but disposable pieces of popular fiction. No doubt this was at least partly due to the passage of time, whereby not only had she been able to be reassessed by readers old and new, but her earlier works had the added cachet of representing a nostalgic view of the past—even if close readers of her books would be well aware that her stories were rarely situated in the cosy environment that some commentators would have us believe. Such was Christie's repeatedly asserted hostility towards filmed versions of her stories that it may be a surprise that such a project was to take place less than a decade after the low point of the MGM contract with the 1965 release of *Murder Ahoy* and *The Alphabet Murders*, but it was a firm yet personal approach that was to result in Christie assenting to a big-screen adaptation of one of her most famous works.

Christie's representatives at the Hughes Massie literary agency had been as busy as ever fending off proposals for her to appear on screen in some form, whether for an interview with *60 Minutes* (1968–) on the CBS network in America or a German documentary film about *The Mysterious Affair at Styles*.[33] One particularly insistent, but consistently rebuffed, request came from David Schine, a controversial character who had inherited great wealth as the son of a New York hotel magnate.[34] Schine expressed keen interest in making a film of Christie's globetrotting thriller *Passenger to Frankfurt*, which had been published in 1970, even going so far as to write to her at her home address in spring 1972, enclosing a list of Academy Awards won by *The French Connection* (d. William Friedkin, 1972), of which he was one of two executive producers.[35] Writing to Lord Mountbatten on 15 November 1972, Christie outlined the letters she had received from Schine with frustration:

> I have been engaged in a battle for some time now with Mr David Schine of New York who has, apparently, a terrible yearning to make a film from my *Passenger to Frankfurt*. From what I have heard and seen of the extremely successful films he has apparently made, I have refused with the utmost firmness to meet him and discuss the matter, and my literary agent backs up this refusal about twice a month, as far as I can make out. I have pointed out that seeing films adapted from my books has given me so much agony that I now wish to have no more films of any kind made from my writings.[36]

For Christie readers, Schine's choice of story to adapt might seem curious, since *Passenger to Frankfurt* is generally regarded as one of the very weakest Christie novels, described as an 'incomprehensible muddle' by Robert Barnard in his critical appreciation of Christie's works, a sentiment echoed by many readers.[37] However, the rationale for the choice appears to lie in Schine's background, rather than the literary merit of this particular adventure. One of the controversies in which he had been involved was his assistance of US Senator Joseph McCarthy in the anti-communist hearings of the 1950s, so we may infer that questions of international conspiracies, the relative merits of nationalism and the threat of political extremism—all explored in *Passenger to Frankfurt*'s tale of a secret Nazi cabal—were of particular personal interest. It seems possible that the intention was to make a piece designed to provoke public interest in apparent enemies of the United States, especially as, despite his credit on *The French Connection*, Schine would not go on to forge a career in the film industry, indicating that celluloid was not his artistic calling.[38] While Schine's approaches were rebuffed, some interest had been taken in an enquiry about a possible film of Christie's unproduced 1937 play set in ancient Egypt, *Akhnaton*.[39] The interested party was Kevin Scott of Scott-Kyffin Productions, who had recently made a film called *A Story of Tutankhamun* (d. Kevin Scott,

1973). An Egyptologist, Scott was keen to produce the play in Egypt with a talented local director, but after Edmund Cork saw his previous work it was felt that the director would not be suitable for *Akhnaton*.[40]

It was in this environment that *Murder on the Orient Express* slowly started to take shape and steal the focus of film dealings. The impetus behind the big-screen adaptation largely came from one man, Lord (John) Brabourne, following a suggestion from Nat Cohen of EMI Films.[41] Brabourne had two advantages on his side, the first of which was his strong grounding as a producer of high-quality, well-cast productions, including Franco Zeffirelli's *Romeo and Juliet* (1968) and Lewis Gilbert's *Sink the Bismarck!* (1960), as well as the ballet *Tales of Beatrix Potter* (1971), a distinguished production that cast him in a particularly good light for Christie. However, probably even more advantageous was the fact that he was the son-in-law of Lord Mountbatten, who was a friend of Christie's. Mathew Prichard tells the story of how his grandmother came to approve of Brabourne's plans, which 'sounds apocryphal but it's not', demonstrating how Brabourne determinedly sought out this particular project. He started by calling Christie's agent, Edmund Cork:

> Edmund Cork said 'I think it would be quite a good idea if you made an Agatha Christie film, but you can't really expect, first out of the traps, to pick up *Orient Express*, to do the best story'; 'I want to do *Orient Express*', [Brabourne] said, and Edmund Cork said 'Well, I don't think that has a cat's chance in hell of being accepted by Agatha Christie herself or anything, so just go away and think of another book and we'll do our best for you'. So John Brabourne went away in a sulk. About a week later my grandmother was at Wallingford, where she spent most of the year, and the phone rang, and it was John Brabourne. He said, 'oh, is that Lady Mallowan?',[42] she said yes, and he said 'My name's John Brabourne and I want to make a film of *Orient Express*'. I think her agent had told her that someone had been sniffing around. She said 'Why do you want to make a film of *Orient Express*?'; 'Oh,' he said, 'your agent didn't ask me that, but I'll tell you—because I like trains!' She said, 'Well, I think we'd better have a little chat about it then.' He said, 'I'd like that very much, when would be convenient?' She said, well, we live forty miles from London [...] we could have lunch one day. He said, 'Well, what about now?' She said, 'but we're forty miles from London, and you're in London'; 'No I'm not,' he said, 'I'm in the telephone box at the bottom of your garden!'[43]

A proposed film of *Murder on the Orient Express* presented difficulties for the Christie family and her agents, since it was perceived as one of the crown jewels of the Christie canon and also featured a character who had never been cast to their satisfaction in previous films—Hercule Poirot himself. On 2 February 1973, Rosalind Hicks wrote to Patricia Cork at Hughes Massie to say that the family were seriously considering Brabourne's offer but they were conscious of the casting difficulties, and worried about giving away a degree of artistic freedom that would be inevitable in any film of this scale, while they also wanted clarification that the MGM deal was now at an end (which it was, excluding residual rights for the films already made).[44] Brabourne had clearly impressed the family to get this far, and by some accounts Lord Mountbatten had personally intervened to help convince Christie. The same month Mathew Prichard had met with Brabourne and it was felt that he could make an 'acceptable' film of the novel, but it would be subject to a modified agreement regarding profit share as well as Christie formally agreeing to the production.[45]

By March 1973 a verbal agreement was in place that gave Christie a more favourable share of the profits and also ensured that Poirot had only been licensed for this one appearance, while there was to be no merchandise—no doubt a hangover from the difficulties encountered with 'passing off' works as affiliated to Christie, something that had been an issue as early as 1928 with *The Passing of Mr Quinn*, a problem that had been revisited with the MGM deals.[46] Shortly afterwards Paul Dehn, screenwriter of films such as *Goldfinger* and *The Spy Who Came in from the Cold* (d. Martin Ritt, 1965), was brought on board to write the script, with production scheduled to start on 25 March 1974. In January of that year Christie noted the list of actors attached to the picture with polite interest,[47] but protested elsewhere that she remained 'allergic' to films of her works.[48] The publicity surrounding the forthcoming film was starting to grow, and with it disgruntlement from those who had previously been turned down when enquiring about film rights. This included David Schine, who once more wrote to Christie about his proposed film of *Passenger to Frankfurt*, only for her to be more forceful than ever, writing to Edmund Cork that she 'will in no way consent [...] I am absolutely sick of these eternal requests from him'.[49]

Soon director Sidney Lumet, best known for his 1957 film of the courtroom drama *12 Angry Men*, was attached to direct, with a budget reported at anything from £1.25 m[50] to £2 m.[51] It was clear from the beginning that Lumet and Brabourne, along with second producer Richard Goodwin, intended to make this a star-studded picture, filling it with as many high-profile and well-regarded actors as possible. Sean Connery and Anthony Perkins were the first to show serious interest in participating, in the roles of Arbuthnot and McQueen, respectively, and this was used as leverage in discussions with other potential cast members. One of the toughest roles to cast was the elderly Princess Dragomiroff, with reports suggesting that Marlene Dietrich had been Lumet's first choice, only for producers to disagree with her suitability for this particular film. Lumet's own correspondence indicates another early choice for the role, however, as he wrote to Katharine Hepburn in early 1974 asking if she would consider the role of either the Princess or Mrs Hubbard. He stated that Hepburn could enjoy playing either role, and that performances were expected to be very theatrical, while reassuring her that there would be other stars of her calibre.[52] For reasons that are not recorded Hepburn did not take Lumet up on his offer, and in the end the roles of Princess Dragomiroff and Mrs Hubbard were played by Wendy Hiller (who was made a Dame the following year) and Lauren Bacall (in her first film since 1966), respectively.

Other cast members were indeed of a high calibre, including Sir John Gielgud as the valet Beddoes, Vanessa Redgrave as Mary Debenham and Ingrid

Bergman, who had turned down the part of Princess Dragomiroff in favour of playing Swedish missionary Greta—a performance for which she would then win an Academy Award.[53] However, the biggest task was in casting the Belgian detective himself. A choice between Alec Guinness, Paul Scofield and Albert Finney was first proposed, before the latter was dismissed as being too young for a Poirot of his mid-1950s, given that he was just 38. When Guinness and Scofield both proved unavailable thoughts nevertheless returned to Finney and the decision was made that he could be made up to resemble a Poirot of the desired age, adding two decades to the actor. Finney had found great success both on screen and on stage and, despite his relative youth, was well regarded enough that he would more than hold his own even in a crowd of Hollywood stars.

With casting finalised, production could commence. After a subdued start with stage and screen actors working in apparent awe of each other, the rehearsal period on which Lumet had insisted became a useful bonding exercise.[54] Filming for the location shots of the boarding of the train and its journey largely took place in France, with some sequences also shot in Turkey. However, this did not include Istanbul station where the train starts its journey, as it had changed too much in the previous decades to still pass as a 1930s station and so had to be recreated near Paris instead. Production then dominated EMI's Elstree Studios in Borehamwood, just north of London, where the film's sets occupied stages 1, 3 and 4. The train's interior had been recreated from the remaining vintage Orient Express carriages held in various museums, while an impressive system of back projection allowed the illusion of movement to be maintained throughout while the train was surrounded with dry salt to portray snow. The film's production also had to work around the theatrical commitments of five of the key performers, including Finney himself, who would be brought to the studio by ambulance so that work could commence on his make-up while he dozed. As production continued, so those dealing with Christie's affairs started to become more optimistic that this might be the film to break an unfortunate run of unsatisfying productions based on her work. When the film neared completion, Christie readied herself to see the final product. 'I hope I shall like it,' she wrote, 'but anyway I certainly have got to go and see it as soon as I have the opportunity even if my feelings should not be as favourable as I would like them to be. But after all, nothing could be worse than Metro-Goldwyn-Mayer, could it? All results of which were loathsome and I usually try to distract at any rate friends of mine going to see any of them.'[55]

In the end, Christie was satisfied with the film overall. Mathew Prichard has said that 'all these famous, or infamous, MGM films [...] they put her off good and proper. And then Paul Dehn did *Orient Express* and everything was lovely again. The amazing thing is, if you've actually read the script of *Orient Express*, large parts of it are virtually verbatim. The best ones often are.'[56] Christie had earlier stated an interest in dramatising *Murder on the Orient Express* herself, which explains why such a popular story did not make it to the stage and may indicate why a film took so long to be made.[57] Indeed, in a process that would be repeated a few years later for television adaptations, the form that *Murder on the Orient Express* takes is calculating in its decision to stick so closely to the original novel, with the producers no doubt mindful of the fact that only a single film adaptation was permitted under the contract, with no automatic rights to further Christie novels should it prove a success—they would need to play their cards right in order to gain permission to make any more. While no adaptation can cover every nuance of the original, or even follow an identical structure, *Murder on the Orient Express* only reaches beyond the novel in any significant way when fleshing out background details; this occurs most overtly at the beginning of the film.

The opening 20 minutes, depicting the kidnapping and murder that are the impetus for the events on the train, followed by the boarding of the Orient Express itself, set the tone for this as something rather more ambitious than most previous movies made from Christie mysteries. Lumet acknowledged that it was perfectly possible to make a motion picture of the novel as a small-scale domestic production, but that he had consciously chosen to eschew that in order to make the film feel more of an event. This sequence demonstrates that even though the film was largely a faithful adaptation, this does not mean that it failed to assert its own artistry. It is comfortably one of the most stylish Agatha Christie adaptations to reach the screen. This is not only down to the mise-en-scène of the piece, with lavish sets and costumes (the costume designer was asked to ensure that the characters were dressed in *costumes* rather than *clothes*, contributing to the sense of glamour and larger-than-life individuals), but also cinematographic and post-production decisions.

From the beginning it is clear to the audience that this is a film that has taken extra steps to create a production that embraced cinematic stylings as well as the mystery element. The opening titles are strongly evocative of 1930s Hollywood, with the Art Deco–style credits superimposed on a satin background. In doing so the film immediately indicates that it will be a lavish motion picture that creates a sense of period through nostalgia, before it sidesteps these expectations and destabilises any sense of a cosy past by provoking memories of one of the more brutal moments of this period that was the inspiration for the original novel, the kidnapping and murder of Charles Lindbergh's baby.[58] This is achieved by the film immediately broadening out the story, moving from the reassuring glamour of the credits into a stylishly arranged and edited flashback sequence of the kidnap and murder of a famed aviator's child (the Armstrong family), setting up the background for events that follow with filmed sequences then transformed into newspaper reports, all accompanied by memorable and chilling musical cues from composer Richard Rodney Bennett rather than any dialogue. This dark and attention-grabbing sequence means that the audience is given a clear sense of place and time, but is also made aware that there is a hard-edged and brutal story underpinning the apparent glamour of the train and its passengers, which does not allow it to assume that this is a glib whodunit where actions do not have consequences.

The film is undoubtedly successful in portraying Christie's story and, given the fact that Christie had so frequently battled with radical changes being made to her work, it might seem perverse to suggest that the adaptation may be a little too faithful. As with the book it is a methodical piece, Finney's Poirot working his way through the list of 12 suspects before arriving at a solution. Indeed, the methodology is crucial to the original book's success, since Christie lays out every single bit of evidence and the full conversations with each suspect before she almost dares the reader to make sense of it—something that is probably best suited to reading the evidence at one's own pace. In a film, this does mean that after the opening act's dizzying visuals the drama steps down a gear for perhaps a little too long until the denouement. Certainly several critics considered the movie to be a strong accomplishment somewhat hindered by a slow pace, but more than any of the Christie screen productions this is the easiest to pardon when it comes to such quibbles. The adaptation cements the fact that Christie's stories can be effectively transferred to the screen without making major changes, while for a general audience the sheer quality and range of stars mean that there is little chance for attention to wander before another A-lister takes centre stage, even though there is very little in the way of actual incident after the murder itself. The entertainment value of Finney's Poirot should also not be understated—although he has divided opinion among many viewers the performance was broadly well received, and he is never less than a captivating presence, since his blustery demeanour attracts attention and his almost childlike response to the mystery in front of him helps to build momentum. When Finney exclaims 'There are too many clues in this room!' he almost sings the line, making it clear that Poirot may not be young in body but still has fully active 'little grey cells', waiting to work everything out. Given later developments, it is also clear that this conscientious appropriation of all the key elements from the original novel was a deliberate decision in order to build confidence in any future projects based on Christie's works.

The film was immediately marked out as a production of interest when it was selected for a series of royal premieres to help raise money for charitable organisations, with the highest-profile occasion taking place in London on 21 November 1974, with Queen Elizabeth II in attendance alongside Prince Philip and Princess Anne, as well as Dame Agatha herself in what was to be one of her final public appearances.[59] This followed visits to the set by Princes Charles, Andrew and Edward, the first taking the chance to bring along King Constantine of Greece.[60] Critical reception of the film was warm, although not ecstatic, with the sense that the best praise that could be given would be it being a good example of its 'type'. Typical of the reviews was David Robinson's write-up in *The Times* where he wrote that the film was 'a deliberate period pastiche [...] it is touchingly loyal to Mrs Christie (Paul Dehn's scenario hardly alters a word) and to the period. No more nor less than the book itself, it is a perfectly pleasant entertainment, a couple of hours of nostalgic escape, if you're prepared to go easily with it.'[61]

Richard Barkley of the *Sunday Express* enjoyed the whole production, writing that there was 'something to relish every step of the way', while the *Financial Times* wondered whether the film might do enough to reinvigorate the fortunes of the British film industry—something to which it would indeed contribute.[62] Most critics were positive towards Finney's Poirot, although some were less keen, Patrick Gibbs in the *Daily Telegraph* calling the performance 'distressingly theatrical' and claiming that it was unlikely to change Dame Agatha's attitude towards film adaptations of her work.[63] Tom Hutchinson of the *Sunday Telegraph* agreed, writing that Finney 'never seems to have the measure of the Belgian detective [...] He shifts between lurching like Richard III and sounding like Sydney Greenstreet.'[64] Elsewhere, *Esquire* magazine called it 'that unusual thing: an inflated trifle that actually works',[65] while the star cast was the focus of Barry Norman's review on the BBC's *Film '74* programme, where he noted that the film 'looks like *That's Entertainment!* [a 1974 film compiling the best song-and-dance moments of classical Hollywood]—with a plot', although he bizarrely claimed that the film's main weakness was that the audience was presented with a list of suspects who could have committed the murder. Perhaps the best summary was from *Variety*, which called the film 'Delightfully old-fashioned, marvellously old-fashioned, gloriously old-fashioned'.[66]

Critically, the movie's reputation was to grow almost as soon as it was released and it was warmly received by audiences and international markets. It was nominated for six Academy Awards and several BAFTAs, including Best Film, while Bergman added a BAFTA to her Oscar, this time joined by Finney who won Best Actor. In fact, the film made appearances on nearly every film award list for 1974 and was an undoubted critical and commercial success that has become a perennial favourite, repeatedly playing on television and frequently referenced in popular culture.[67] The film was a success around the world, with the *Evening Standard* reporting that it was 'breaking box office records' in London and New York, as it went on to gross nearly $30 m at the US box office alone on a budget no more than a tenth of that.[68] Meanwhile, it was reported that the film had been such a success with families that more pictures of a similar type were planned. Some reports even claimed that Albert Finney had already signed on for another film as Poirot, this time appearing in an adaptation of the 1941 novel *Evil Under the Sun*.[69] This was not to be, but a successful formula had been found and it was one that would be repeated several times in the next decade as the works of Agatha Christie finally found success with both a general audience and those who cared for the original stories.

TEN LITTLE INDIANS (1974)

The success of *Murder on the Orient Express* had naturally led to a discussion within the Christie camp about a potential follow-up. Even before the lavish production had been released to cinemas another Christie film was imminent, but this time it was one over which Christie and her agents had very little control. While work was continuing to build a stronger big-screen legacy of her works, a ghost from the past was re-emerging, with producer Harry Alan Towers presenting his second film adaptation of *And Then There Were None*.[70] Following the contract with RKO to make the 1945 picture based on the play, the rights had never reverted to Christie, making it an entity entirely independent of her. Indeed, although Christie's name was put above the title in most promotional literature and on screen, no attempt was made to involve the author, her family or her agents. Instead, this was simply a case of a producer's savvy exploitation of the rights available to him, no doubt hopeful that the high-profile adaptation of *Orient Express* would have a residual effect on the box-office returns of his own similar picture. However, such a context was probably secondary to the enduring appeal of the mystery itself, which had become a standard with broad appeal that was always likely to be a low-risk venture.

It was only when Christie's agents started to field queries about the film adaptation in July 1974 that they were aware of it at all, and by this point filming had finished. The British Film Institute had first spotted mention of it in a European publication, while Christie's American agents had heard that a new adaptation was planned to be released in the United States the following year, and so were thinking about a reprint to tie in with the new movie. In the event, the manner of the film's production would also be instrumental in the general lack of impact that it would make in the primary markets of the UK and USA, as it was made as a European co-production. As a result, the distribution of the film was patchy, and while it was very well received in some countries, elsewhere it often sneaked in and out of cinemas without causing much of a ripple.

For this, Towers's second of three films based on the story (the third would follow in 1989), the action shifts to an abandoned desert hotel in Iran, which might be a contrast with the snowy 1965 version in terms of temperature but fulfils the same purpose of retooling a familiar story to offer distinctive visuals in a hazardous terrain. Despite this striking difference, the most notable aspect of the 1974 film is how closely it follows Towers's previous version, to the extent that the script (itself largely written by Towers, using the pseudonym Peter Welbeck) is essentially unaltered for the majority of the film.[71] This is perhaps the strongest indication that he was adopting a pragmatic and commercially sensible approach to the film, concentrating on ensuring that it made the maximum financial return. This is quite a contrast to *Murder on the Orient Express*'s focus on fidelity to the original source and elevating the production out of the sub-standard rut in which many previous adaptations had found themselves, but was of course eminently sensible in terms of economics and profit; the goal here was short-term gain, rather than a long-term plan to bring other stories to the screen. The pragmatism extended to the casting, where three star names of Oliver Reed, Elke Sommer and Richard Attenborough played the key roles of Hugh Lombard, Vera Clyde (in a reversion from 'Ann' of the 1965 version) and Judge Arthur Cannon, performers who brought prestige and publicity with them.[72] Elsewhere, the cast reflected the international co-production by bringing in performers from a range of European countries, including the famous French/Algerian entertainer Charles Aznavour as Michel Raven. Joining him were the likes of Czech-born actor Herbert Lom, who had appeared in many British films including *The Ladykillers* (d. Alexander Mackendrick, 1955), playing Dr Armstrong, while Blore was played by Gert Fröbe, a German actor best known for his appearance as the titular character in *Goldfinger*.[73] In fact, Reed and Attenborough were the only British actors to be featured, giving the film a heightened international flavour and, perhaps, a resultant increased appeal to markets outside of North America and the UK.[74]

The film itself is reasonably effective in parts and, as one would expect, largely evokes memories of the 1965 adaptation. Some concessions are made for the modern audience, nevertheless, as the film was released at a time when New Hollywood was riding high, and realism and mature themes were more regularly and explicitly reflected on screen, while audiences had grown to expect increased naturalism from both directors and performers. This means that it feels less like a game and, even though the trailer is structured as if it is a horror film, with piercing sound effects and a countdown to murder, the movie itself is rather more subdued. It would perhaps be over-complimentary to say that this is a thoughtful picture, but it is certainly not afraid to take a step back and allow the audience to dwell on pauses in the action. Director Peter Collinson, who was best known for 1969's *The Italian Job*, allows the camera to take on a largely detached, observational role. The audience is often witness to long takes and wide shots, while the director certainly has no fear of pauses between the action since some sequences continue in silence for some time, while both characters and the audience adapt to the new surroundings and growing danger. This approach is quite unlike the high-drama approach of both the 1965 film and the 1959 television adaptation. Instead, the film gives a sense of creeping horror, although such suspense is so slow to build that the first half of the film in particular is markedly lacking in atmosphere, falling rather flat. That is not to say that this technique is always ineffective—the opening sequence shows the silent arrival of most of the suspects and victims by helicopter, with Collinson appearing to echo *Lawrence of Arabia*'s famous shot heralding the arrival of Omar Sharif's Ali, emerging from the desert mirage. It is an unsettling and unexpected start that is an effective way to set out the isolation of the hotel, and this is a film that will take some advantage of the impressive visuals afforded by filming at the Abbasi Hotel in Isfahan, Iran, which adds exoticism and glamour to the proceedings while maintaining a sense of unease and mystery.

Once the guests and staff are installed in the hotel matters continue as expected, with singer Aznavour taking over from Fabian as the musical star who barely lasts beyond his performance at the piano—although in this instance at least Aznavour is permitted to perform his signature song 'The Old Fashioned Way', which somehow manages to gain the accompaniment of an unseen orchestra. Oliver Reed's Hugh Lombard is played as a more gruff and dangerous version of the character than we have previously seen, and is therefore rather more plausible as a potential threat than the traditional hero character played by Hugh O'Brian in the 1965 picture. This characterisation is hardly sophisticated, but is less straightforward than before and denies the audience the sense of safety instilled by the 1965 casting of an actor well known for a character that upholds the law; Reed's complex private life meant that he was not an obvious hero for the audience, although he was a captivating personality. There are a few more concessions to the modern audience: the attraction between Lombard and Vera grows naturally over the course of the film, and is less overtly linear than in previous adaptations, with Reed and Sommer allowing body language to show their growing trust and attraction, including holding hands in a key dialogue scene, making this feel more like characters finding love and, perhaps surprisingly, offering less of a sexual kick than the previous adaptation.

The naturalism is reinforced by a musical score by Bruno Nicolai that lacks bombast, but occasionally veers into easy-listening music and does little to heighten the impact of most scenes, although there are some effective musical stabs when we are witness to some of the murders; this is a little surprising given that Nicolai often scored rather more extreme Italian *giallo* (horror and exploitation) pictures. Because the film embraces some of the nuances of 1970s film-making, it is somewhat disorientating for the audience when it harks back to its 1930s roots in its discussion of gender. When it is pointed out to Vera that the villain need not be a man, the apparent surprise of those present is several steps behind the audience, who had seen corrupt women and even demonic children acting out their villainous roles in Hollywood box-office hits of the past decade; a female serial murderer was positively tame by comparison, and a natural possibility. However, by the end of the picture the strength of Vera's character is clear once more, especially when the villain encourages her to place her head in a ready-made noose that hangs next to her. The time spent on this part of the finale may mean that the audience has more time to mull over the ludicrousness of the offer (is consenting to the hanging really the best option for Vera?), but it seems more stark and realistic than before because the option is visually presented with such clarity.

The film's co-production origins had a significant impact on its release. It was never anticipated that it would be met with great fanfare as a prestige picture in the way that *Murder on the Orient Express* had, but its spontaneous appearance in various markets, with no overarching release pattern, showed the extent to which it was not seen as a priority by most distributors, as it was released in various countries at any point between 1974 and 1976. However, a more radical impact on the release was the fact that the version seen in the Spanish and Italian markets was somewhat different to the one elsewhere. In these markets extra scenes were added starring local actors in order to satisfy quotas for domestic film-making. This version of the movie opens not with the guests arriving at the hotel by helicopter, but rather with their arrival at an airport, where they board said helicopter. Throughout the film scenes starring Italian actor Rik Battaglia and Spanish actress Teresa Gimpera are then interspersed with the main action, as they engage in their own sub-plot where they try to find out more about the origins of the Indian figures. This entails much discussion in bars as well as in the Iranian street markets, and even encompasses a trip to see a belly dancer's performance. Some sequences from the main body of the film are trimmed to accommodate these unnecessary and disruptive extra scenes for moviegoers, although this version includes some brief additional footage of the main action. The inclusion of an extra shot showing a helicopter arriving shortly before the denouement rather dissipates the tension, and English-language audiences should be grateful that their version of the film does not include these unnecessary sequences.

Critically, the film was received with a degree of bafflement due to its international origins and a perception that the mystery was rather old-fashioned and had received more than its fair share of translations to the screen already. In the UK this was not helped by the fact that the movie did not receive a wide release, and instead showed up as and when convenient for local cinemas. Resultantly, both reviews and publicity were thinner on the ground than normal—when Felix Barker of the *Evening News* finally managed to see the film in London in January 1976, he noted that it was already a year old.[75] John Pym of the *Monthly Film Bulletin* was unhappy with the transplantation to a new location as well as the cast and the 'happy ending'—indicating that he had read Christie's book, but presumably forgotten or missed the previous films, showing that it was starting to become difficult to imagine a definitive version of the story that satisfied expectations of both the novel as well as the stage and screen versions. When this version showed up on television a decade later, *Sunday Express* critic Hilary Doling could not hide her disdain for the 'worst film of the week', writing that if she had been present during the events of the film 'I'd probably have committed suicide just to speed things up'![76] However, *Variety* took a more pragmatic approach and pointed out that while it may be less distinguished than other versions (although it is arguably stronger than the 1965 film in many respects), it could nevertheless be expected to find moderate success. Indeed, it has gone on to be seen on television reasonably often, and performed well in some European countries, but was unable to shake off the sense of being somewhat old-fashioned and 'more of the same'. Nevertheless, for the producers it served its purpose—it made money, it presented the mystery in a serviceable manner, and it had been relatively easy to make. It was also the only Christie story available to the producers, and so another decade or more needed to pass before it could be dusted off again. For those looking to see more of Agatha Christie's works on screen there was one obvious way forward—and that was to capitalise on the success of *Murder on the Orient Express* and see if the formula could work again.

Notes

1. As the 1945 film had, see Chap. 5 for further details.
2. As with most of the films of this story, it also adopted alternative titles—in this case, *And Then There Were None* for some countries and television screenings.

3. Ann's surname also changed, from Claythorne.

4. Lavi was to become a star of a Bond picture herself—albeit the 1967 comedy version of *Casino Royale* that is not part of the main series of Bond films.

5. In fact, Lockyer's score bears more than a passing resemblance to another film for which he composed the music in 1965—*Dr Who and the Daleks*, hardly a movie from the same mould.

6. As famously written about by Carol Clover.

7. Although, admittedly, both pushed boundaries to their limits in this regard—*Peeping Tom* in particular was met with hyperbolic revulsion from much of the press.

8. Specifically, *The Times*, *The Sun*, the *Evening Standard*, *The Daily Telegraph*, *The Sunday Times*, *The Daily Worker* and the *Daily Mail* all mentioned the change without complaint—although Alexander Walker of the *Evening Standard* asked 'but won't redskins feel hurt?'

9. *The Times*, 3 February 1966.

10. *The Sun*, 1 Feb 1966.

11. *Time*, 11 February 1966.

12. *Daily Mail*, 1 February 1966.

13. *Daily Telegraph*, 4 February 1966.

14. *Evening Standard*, 3 February 1966.

15. Furst to publishers William Collins, 29 June 1965 (Agatha Christie Archive, Exeter).

16. Letter from 'Claire' at Harold Ober Associates to Patricia Cork at Hughes Massie Ltd. 22 April 1965 (Agatha Christie Archive, Exeter).

17. Edmund Cork to Rosalind Hicks, 3 May 1967 (Agatha Christie Archive, Exeter).

18. This might also be reflected in the increasingly generous reviews of her work during the 1960s and beyond, even when some of the titles are generally considered to be rather weaker than her earlier work.

19. Nora Blackborow to 'Claire' at Harold Ober, 9 August 1968 (Agatha Christie Archive, Exeter).

20. On 15 August 1968.

21. This letter included a reference to Basil Dignam playing an unspecified role—he does not appear in the final film and so presumably proved unavailable at the last minute, unless the part his was playing was deleted during editing. It is possible that he was replaced by David Bauer in the role of Ellie's Uncle Frank.

22. Film fans may notice here possible influences from both *The Cabinet of Dr Caligari* (d. Robert Wiene, 1920) and *Blowup* (d. Michaelangelo Antonioni, 1967).

23. Thompson, *An English Mystery*, 476.

24. Christie to Lord Mountbatten, 15 November 1972 (Agatha Christie Archive, Exeter).

25. Morgan, *Agatha Christie: A Biography*, 324.

26. *Financial Times*, 6 October 1972.
27. *The Sun*, 6 October 1972.
28. *Sunday Times*, 8 October 1972.
29. *Evening Standard*, 6 October 1972.
30. *The Times*, 6 October 1972.
31. *Daily Express*, 3 October 1972.
32. *Sunday Express*, 8 October 1972.
33. CBS' John Tiffin to Hughes Massie, 15 February 1973 among other correspondence (Agatha Christie Archive, Exeter); Wolfgang Löhde of Zweites Deutsches Fernsehen to Hughes Massie 22 March 1973 (Agatha Christie Archive, Exeter).
34. Sometimes known as G. David Schine.
35. Schine to Christie, April 28 1972 (Agatha Christie Family Archive).
36. Agatha Christie Family Archive.
37. Robert Barnard, *A Talent to Deceive: An Appreciation of Agatha Christie* (New York: Dodd, Mead and Company, 1980), 202.
38. Schine's only other credit of note was as executive producer on a 1977 compilation film *That's Action*, reminiscent of 1974's musical collection *That's Entertainment!* (d. Jack Haley, Jr) and its 1976 sequel. The role of executive producer usually has minimal artistic input in any case. Via Twitter, I asked William Friedkin (director of *The French Connection*) what influence Schine had on the film—his response was simple: 'Zero. None whatsoever.'
39. Hughes Massie Limited—Agatha Christie Report, February 1973 (Agatha Christie Archive, Exeter).
40. Hughes Massie Limited—Agatha Christie Report, May 1973 (Agatha Christie Archive, Exeter). As it has not been possible to track down the film, it is difficult to know precisely what the objection to Scott's approach was.
41. John Coleman, 'Murder Unlimited' in *The Observer Magazine*, 17 November 1974.
42. The name Christie went under following her marriage to Max Mallowan in 1930.
43. Interview with the author, August 2013.
44. Rosalind Hicks to Patricia Cork, 2 February 1973 (Agatha Christie Archive, Exeter).
45. Hughes Massie Limited—Agatha Christie Report, February 1973 (Agatha Christie Archive, Exeter).
46. Hughes Massie Limited—Agatha Christie Report, March 1973 (Agatha Christie Archive, Exeter). See Chap. 1 for further discussion of *The Passing of Mr Quinn*.
47. Christie to Edmund Cork, 25 January 1974 (Agatha Christie Archive, Exeter).
48. Christie to Edmund Cork, 21 January 1974 (Agatha Christie Archive, Exeter).

49. Christie to Edmund Cork, 19 February 1974 (Agatha Christie Archive, Exeter).
50. *Daily Mail*, 3 April 1974.
51. *The Sun*, 22 November 1974.
52. Letter from Sidney Lumet in the Katharine Hepburn Papers (Margaret Herrick Library, Los Angeles); undated but likely January 1974.
53. Best Supporting Actress, 1974.
54. Most films do not have such extensive rehearsal periods, beyond basic read-throughs of the material. Scenes are usually rehearsed separately from each other, often on set shortly prior to shooting.
55. Christie to Cork, 20 June 1974 (Agatha Christie Archive, Exeter).
56. Interview with author, August 2013.
57. Unknown (Probably Edmund Cork) to Harold Ober, 8 October 1948 (Agatha Christie Archive, Exeter).
58. The famous aviator's child was kidnapped in March 1932, apparently for a ransom, and was later murdered. The story was a press sensation at the time and pressure on the family and staff resulted in the suicide of one of the servants—an incident repeated in *Murder on the Orient Express*.
59. Christie passed away a little over a year later, on 12 January 1976, aged 85.
60. *Evening Standard*, 5 August 1974.
61. *The Times*, 22 November 1974.
62. *Sunday Express*, 24 November 1974.
63. *Daily Telegraph*, 22 November 1974.
64. *Sunday Telegraph*, 24 November 1974.
65. *Esquire*, February 1975.
66. *Variety*, 20 November 1974.
67. One of the more entertaining examples of this is in NBC comedy *30 Rock* (2006–13), when Liz Lemon (Tina Fey) starts the 'Big Print' edition of the book only to end up watching the 1974 adaptation. She then realises that all of her friends have been involved in a similar conspiracy—albeit involving Liz's love life rather than murder. Liz outlines her conclusions in typical Christie fashion, as a revelatory monologue in front of the suspects, in the episode 'It's Never Too Late for Now' (2011).
68. *Evening Standard*, 27 November 1975.
69. *Daily Mail*, 9 July 1975.
70. Once more, the title used has often changed depending on the distributor—it is most commonly seen with the title *Ten Little Indians* although, in the case of the UK DVD, the cover nevertheless presents it as *And Then There Were None*, despite a different title appearing on screen. *And Then There Were None* is the title under which it was originally released in the UK.

71. There are additional screenwriter credits for Erich Kröhnke from Germany and Spanish writer Enrique Llovet, despite that fact that any changes are minimal. Perhaps this internationalism helped to secure funding, or satisfy production quotas.
72. Note how even the first name of Hugh for Lombard is retained from the 1965 picture, despite the change having been made in order to reflect the casting of Hugh O'Brian in the role.
73. A film that, along with the rest of the James Bond franchise, is repeatedly linked to the screen adaptations of Agatha Christie.
74. Attenborough had actually replaced James Mason, who was originally cast as the judge but proved unavailable following his move to Switzerland.
75. *Evening News*, 22 January 1976.
76. *Sunday Express*, 8 July 1984.

Chapter 8: Peter Ustinov as Hercule Poirot

Spoilers: *The Mirror Crack'd from Side to Side*; *Lord Edgware Dies*; *Three Act Tragedy*; *Appointment with Death*

The success of *Murder on the Orient Express* had helped to increase the already substantial interest in the back catalogue of Agatha Christie. Although Christie's age and poor health meant that she was no longer writing new stories for publication, there were opportunities to repurpose older stories into new volumes, while some unpublished work would soon see the light of day. When a number of Poirot short stories were collected into book form as *Poirot's Early Cases* in September 1974, it was a commercial success and, with the film of *Orient Express* looming, Judith A. Coppage, Director of Development at Paramount, wrote to enquire about the possibility of adapting it.[1] The approach was dismissed but it demonstrated that major studios recognised the potential of Christie's stories even prior to the commercial and critical success of this one film. Meanwhile, requests for interviews continued apace, as did interest from smaller production companies and members of the public—all were held at bay, with the explanation that *Orient Express*'s journey to the screen had been an exceptional one, while the general dismissal of television remained the same as ever.

It was clear that the future of screen adaptations was now anticipated to be via pictures that replicated *Orient Express*'s most successful features as much as possible. It was envisaged that there could be a series of similar films featuring Poirot, but one immediate difficulty needed to be flagged up. After a great deal of discussion it had been decided that 1975 would see the publication of *Curtain*, the final Poirot novel. Christie had written the book many years previously, having originally intended for it to be published after her death; in the end, the novel made it to bookshops in September 1975, mere months before she died, creating a new literary sensation—with news of Poirot's demise even reaching the front page of *The New York Times*. Such success was welcome, but the juxtaposition of Poirot's final story with a potential new series of films was noted. Interest had been expressed in adapting *Curtain* as a film, but Christie's agents and family, including her daughter Rosalind Hicks, felt that this was not

© The Author(s) 2016
M. Aldridge, *Agatha Christie on Screen*,
DOI 10.1057/978-1-137-37292-5_9

a desirable move.² As a result, it was suggested that Agatha Christie Ltd, the family company that had controlled most of Christie's works since the 1950s, could buy the film rights itself from Hicks, to whom Christie had gifted the rights to her final novel, in order to ensure that they were not made available in any separate deal (although the likelihood of Hicks doing such a thing was not high). Clearly, any such film would not only have the standard artistic issues to confront, but would probably put Poirot on film to bed for many years. Rather than capitalising directly on the commercial and critical success of *Curtain*, it was decided to continue Poirot's appearances on screen in a manner that would be rather less final.

EMI Films and John Brabourne had always been clear about the next film that they wished to make—the 1937 Poirot mystery *Death on the Nile*. However, this particular title presented difficulties, as Mathew Prichard recalls:

> John Brabourne and EMI always knew that *Death on the Nile* was part of a group of books which my grandmother had reserved to herself and not put into the various family trusts, for the reason that they obviously had dramatic potential of one sort or another. Therefore if any of those was used for something like a major film it might have had a really serious effect on the tax situation, if and when my grandmother died. Now even I remember Edmund Cork telling John Brabourne this time after time after time and EMI spent an absolute fortune on lawyers, because they always wanted to do *Death on the Nile*, trying to find ways, but they failed. Second on the list was always [the 1941 Poirot novel] *Evil Under the Sun*, so Edmund Cork said, well, you'll have to do *Evil Under the Sun* next. They wouldn't accept it, they went to even more lawyers and spent an absolute fortune trying to convince us it could be done, which it couldn't.³

Christie's sense that *Death on the Nile* was a strong candidate for dramatisation had resulted in her writing *Murder on the Nile*, a stage production of the story that completely removed Poirot, and had been screened on American television in 1950; she had even sent Brabourne a copy of the script.⁴ However, as the title was not being made available, it was decided that *Evil Under the Sun* would indeed be the next title to go into production, with filming in 1976 anticipated. Several press reports indicated that Albert Finney had already signed up to appear in a film of this book, but in the end he declined the opportunity to continue with the role (according to reports, because he did not relish the idea of revisiting his prosthetics in extreme heat). In truth, any second film was far from a done deal, as even though John Brabourne retained the option to adapt *Evil Under the Sun*, any developments were always under the watchful editorial eye of Agatha Christie Ltd. The company's board of directors was unhappy to see that this apparent news had been reported far in advance of any agreement, seemingly as a result of an interview with Brabourne himself. However, in the end real life intervened, changing the expected course of events.

DEATH ON THE NILE (1978)

On 12 January 1976, Agatha Christie passed away at the age of 85. Tributes were paid around the world, and affection towards both her and her works had never been higher. In terms of the impact on the development of the films based on her books, this resulted in an about-turn when it came to the next planned production. The tax issue relating to *Death on the Nile* no longer applied after Christie's death, so work could continue on adapting Brabourne's preferred title; *Evil Under the Sun* would have to wait a few years for its opportunity to reach the big screen. However, Brabourne and fellow producer Richard Goodwin were not without their competitors—for example, Columbia Pictures had been rather literal-minded in its attempt to mirror the success of *Murder on the Orient Express* when it enquired about adapting another of Christie's railway-based mysteries, the 1928 Poirot novel *The Mystery of the Blue Train*; the approach came to nothing.[5] In the event, Brabourne's option for a further adaptation was exercised with the proviso that no other Poirot films would be authorised within 18 months, giving him a head start on any competitors.

We might instinctively see *Death on the Nile* as a direct continuation of *Murder on the Orient Express*, since it features an all-star cast travelling through an exotic locale with a murderer in their midst. Hailing from the golden age of both Christie's work and detective fiction more generally, the story centres on the murder of wealthy heiress Linnet Ridgeway (Lois Chiles), who is honeymooning in Egypt with her new husband Simon Doyle (Simon MacCorkindale), only for them to be stalked by former friend, and Simon's former fiancée, Jacqueline De Bellefort (Mia Farrow). Frustration between the couple and Jacqueline reaches a peak on board their cruise down the Nile on a paddle steamer, but when other passengers appear to have their own motivation for Linnet's death, suspicion is cast in many directions. In part, these other passengers perform the same function as the cast in *Murder on the Orient Express*. The star names involved evoke memories of classical Hollywood movies and give the film a sense of importance and grandeur, while the decision to have such a cast also makes individual characters immediately identifiable as well as entertaining. This time, the passengers included the iconic Bette Davis as the elderly kleptomaniac Marie Van Schuyler, with the role of her companion Miss Bowers played by the esteemed Maggie Smith, rubbing shoulders with Broadway and film legend Angela Lansbury as the entertaining drunk Salome Otterbourne. Among the three of them, these actresses increase the camp value of the film by quite a margin when compared with *Murder on the Orient Express*, in which director Sidney Lumet had expressly tried to avoid such a tone. Here, however, we are presented with a puzzle that is framed between what at times feels like the actors' best party tricks—Bette Davis as the mischievous old woman, and Maggie Smith in masculine clothes evocative of lesbian style of the period while talking disparagingly (but amusingly) of the 'body massage' with which she provides her employer. These performances are almost demure by comparison with Lansbury's hilarious and full-bodied turn as the apparent comic relief, who actually ends up playing a pivotal role in the whole mystery. While *Murder on the Orient Express* had worked hard to make Christie's story feel more palpably real than most previous adaptations, presenting serious actors playing complex characters (with Finney's rather over-the-top Poirot being the exception), *Death on the Nile* happily acknowledges the increased kudos that such decisions brought Christie's work on screen while heading in a somewhat different direction. One of the biggest reasons for this shift was down to the casting of Poirot.

Peter Ustinov was a well-known actor who also had an excellent reputation as a raconteur, often being invited to speak on television and radio about his experiences on any given point of discussion. A popular presence on screen, his casting as Poirot immediately signalled the emergence of a warmer, more audience-friendly approach to the part. This Poirot is more charming, less extreme and more real than Finney's had been, albeit more detached from the text. 'I don't think we were particularly enthusiastic', recalls Mathew Prichard of Ustinov's casting. 'It stood out a mile that Peter Ustinov would never play Poirot, he would play Peter Ustinov. They needed somebody who did have a profile, perhaps particularly in America, and I'm not sure they ever thought Albert Finney would do it again.'[6] In the original stories Poirot was almost removed from the real world—he saw events and people in a different way to his contemporaries, and this would often hold the key to his investigation. Here, Ustinov's Poirot may be rather supercilious on occasion, but he feels like a character that actually comfortably co-exists in the world that we see on screen. It might seem that Ustinov's demeanour and public reputation meant that a more jovial, softer Poirot was a natural result of the casting decision, but it appears that this is not how the process worked. According to Brabourne and Ustinov, it was actually decided that a different type of Poirot would be needed for this film so as to stave off any accusations that the actor was merely mimicking Finney, and Ustinov's softer personality was felt to be a better fit with this particular story. The decision to cast famed British actor David Niven as Colonel Race helped to cement this slightly more cosy vision of murder, as the character accompanies Poirot throughout much of the investigation and brings with him a certain cool demeanour that the audience would instinctively recognise from his earlier pictures, such as *A Matter of Life and Death* (d. Powell and Pressburger, 1946).

The film itself is an effective and reasonably close retelling of the original story, following a script written by Anthony Shaffer, whose 1970 play *Sleuth*, and the subsequent 1972 film (d. Joseph L. Mankiewicz), had been considerable successes. Director John Guillerman filmed much of the action in the Egyptian heat for seven weeks under less than ideal conditions, including difficulties securing accommodation, a lack of telephone service and no opportunity to watch the daily rushes of the film that he had shot. Guillerman generally uses the scenery to its best advantage, staging many key dialogue scenes in the sometimes striking Egyptian locale, but the film does feel more old-fashioned and less stylistically contemporary than *Murder on the Orient Express*. This is particularly curious when we consider that Guillerman's previous two films had been action-orientated blockbusters, namely *The Towering Inferno* (1974) and a remake of *King Kong* (1976). It naturally follows that this sense of spectacle, pace and action would be expected to continue here, and there is indeed an impression of large-scale drama when we see reams of servants in grand locations early on. However, attempts to make the picture visually distinct do not last; for example, we are witness to several flashbacks showing potential scenarios in which various villainous deeds played out, but the scenes do not differentiate themselves from the material that surrounds them, employing standard shots and framing. This is despite that fact that we are explicitly told that they are speculative, and indeed we later learn that most of them are false, resulting in lost potential for them to be depicted in a less realistic and more stylistically interesting manner; this type of decision makes the film seem more straightforward than its predecessor, and also less exciting.

Since the movie relies rather heavily on conversation rather than incident for much of the time, more significant visual diversity would have helped to maintain audience interest. Instead, it sometimes feels like the picture has been shot in a deliberately slow and old-fashioned style in order to make it fit with the period. This is in contrast with the directorial style of the previous film, which had successfully centred on a contrast, with cosy, nostalgic expectations set up on one hand by the mise-en-scène, only to be countered on the other by the harsh truth of the murder and the striking visual accompaniment. This would be less of an issue if it were not for the fact that at 140 minutes, *Death on the Nile* is rather over-long and so has some inevitable lulls; indeed, the main criticism of the film from the press concerned its running time. However, this is not to say that it is unsuccessful—it is one of the most fondly remembered and well-played Christie stories on screen, and when it reaches its surprising and gruesome resolution the audience may be left shocked, but satisfied.

Critical response to the film was divided, although in recent years it has been more well received than its contemporary reviews may indicate. Several critics who had not cared for *Murder on the Orient Express* declared this new picture to be rather better, while some who had lauded *Orient Express* felt that this was an inferior attempt to replicate its predecessor's success. Critical response was particularly underwhelming in the USA, where the film was released prior to the UK so as to coincide with an exhibition of Egyptian artefacts. Joseph Gelmis echoed the thoughts of many when he wrote in New York's *Newsday* that it was a 'dismal follow up to an earlier, superior movie adaptation of an Agatha Christie whodunit'.[7] However, Richard Freeman in *The Star Ledger* was rather more positive, calling it 'even more successful' than *Orient Express*, going on to say that 'Until fairly recently the movies never knew quite how to cope with the classic English murder mysteries of the 1920s and 1930s because they were more cerebral and less cinematic than the contemporary American tough-guy thrillers. It's very hard to film pure thought processes.'[8] Several reviews praised Ustinov and, more particularly, Lansbury's scene-stealing turn. However, although many reviews were positive, the film's pace was a recurring issue, with David Ansen of *Newsweek* going as far as to headline his review 'Snoring down the Nile'.[9]

In the UK the film mimicked its predecessor by receiving another royal premiere, with both Queen Elizabeth II and Prince Philip in attendance—although, to their bemusement, the event was so large that they were forced to watch the film on separate screens showing it simultaneously at the ABC cinema on Shaftesbury Avenue, London on 23 October 1978, just prior to its wider release. The press once more highlighted pacing issues but were generally kind; David Hughes of the *Western Mail* was one of the critics who preferred it to *Orient Express*, calling it 'entertaining, witty and generally most agreeable'.[10] Similarly, David Castell of the *Sunday Telegraph* expressed the surprise repeated in many reviews from critics apparently expecting to dislike the picture, calling it 'unexpectedly more than the sum of its parts'.[11] Some reviewers were happy to accept the slow pace in exchange for the scenery and performances, but most identified it as a problem. In the *Daily Telegraph*, Eric Shorter summed this issue up by writing that while a highlight of the film was the 'presence of so many self assertive personalities [...] it is hard to believe that they needed to be there for so long'.[12]

AGATHA (1979)

Overall, *Death on the Nile* was a success, comfortably turning a profit and demonstrating sustained interest in the appearance of the Agatha Christie 'brand' on film, perhaps something that was more important now that the author had passed away, meaning that interest in her would need to be cultivated from outside her published works. It was, then, more important than ever that a clear Agatha Christie identity was established on screen, and one that placed boundaries beyond the world of Poirot. It was decided that the time was right to broach a new Miss Marple adaptation at the cinema—but before this was to happen, a more controversial appearance of Christie on cinema screens was looming.

In 1979 there was the release of *Agatha*, a production not affiliated to or authorised by the Christie estate—technically the film falls outside this book's remit, but its existence should be acknowledged. Rather than covering any of Christie's mysteries, the movie looks at the author herself, dealing with her brief disappearance in 1926 following the breakdown of her marriage with Archie Christie. The opening credits call the film an 'imaginary solution to an authentic mystery', and the story follows a mostly fictitious series of events where Christie (Vanessa Redgrave) disappears in order to ruminate on life and revenge—all the time being observed by an American journalist, Wally Stanton, played by Dustin Hoffman. Since its inception the production had been heavily opposed by the Christie family, to the extent that legal action was launched in an attempt to prevent it from being made. In the end, the film is rather idiosyncratic, but presents a highly sympathetic impression of Christie herself; however, one can understand that as she had been such a private person who did not even cover her disappearance in her own posthumously published autobiography, she would likely have been mortified by the appearance of a fictionalised take on a sensitive part of her life. Speaking to the press at the time, Rosalind Hicks and Mathew Prichard expressed the family's unhappiness that the film was being made so shortly after her death and without consultation. Prichard pointed out that Christie had entertained millions with her books and plays, and that 'We as a family think she should be remembered for all the things she wrote rather than for one unhappy incident in her life'.[13]

The film's origins lay with a proposed documentary researched by journalist and writer Kathleen Tynan, who then turned it into a film with a script co-written with British scriptwriter Arthur Hopcraft (who had helped bring *Tinker Tailor Soldier Spy* to the small screen) and directed by Michael Apted. At the time, Apted was best known for his work on the *Up* series for Granada television, a project that revisited a group of children at seven-year intervals from 1964, which has continued to the present day. In terms of film direction, Apted was near the beginning of his career, although he would go on to make films such as *Gorillas in the Mist* (1988) and the James Bond movie *The World Is Not Enough* (1998). Together, the creative team present a low-key film that only occasionally gives itself over to cinematic scale, such as in the torch-wielding search party covering the moors. *Agatha* was largely well received, even though its difficult genesis had been widely reported, including Hoffman's unhappiness throughout the filming. Nevertheless, the actor wielded a great deal of power as he also co-owned the company producing the film, First Artists. He insisted on rewrites to increase the role of his character, and when he was denied the opportunity to film what he felt was a crucial extra scene, he even looked to sue his own company; his intervention led to producer David Puttnam removing his own name from the credits.[14] Once made, the film's rough ride continued when the Christie family tried, unsuccessfully, to ban it from being shown, while the BBC insisted that as it had contributed to the cost of producing the script it should be allowed to show the film after three years, rather than the usual five. In the event, legal action from the BBC was to delay the film's release and temporarily ban it from British cinemas; eventually, an agreement was reached and the film was screened in cinemas from March 1979, while it turned up on BBC television on 5 December 1982. Reviews commended the direction and performances, but also noted that it sometimes veered towards the dull.

In terms of its role within the pantheon of Agatha Christie productions, it is most interesting because of not its content, but its existence. As is so often the case with well-known figures, Christie's death had served to remind many people how much affection they had towards her, and it was now clear that the stories she created would ensure that she remained fondly remembered for a long time to come, with her name a major draw. Although her stories were readily available, Christie's name was also a brand that was increasingly recognisable beyond the simple publication of her written word—she had established a legacy and, arguably, a genre all of her own. The name Agatha Christie had the potential to be a bigger attraction than any of her individual creative scenarios or characters, something only cemented by the later decision to incorporate her signature on most licensed merchandise.

THE MIRROR CRACK'D (1980)

When it came to Christie's actual mysteries, the next appearance on the big screen was once more produced by John Brabourne and Richard Goodwin, but for their third film based on her works they headed in a different direction, with Miss Marple returning to film in an adaptation of a novel that, coincidentally, Christie had dedicated to the last actress to play her in an English-language movie, Margaret Rutherford. This was the 1962 murder mystery *The Mirror Crack'd from Side to Side*, which features the fatal poisoning of a woman during a fête held by a Hollywood movie star, Marina Gregg, who has bought Gossington Hall in St Mary Mead from Miss Marple's friend Dolly Bantry. The novel is one of Christie's strongest stories for Miss Marple and especially suitable for screen adaptation given the fact that it offers several moments that lend themselves to visual depiction, such as the colourful fête that helps to set up proceedings and the sub-plot following the filming of a new movie with its accompanying egocentric stars. The story also features good character motives and a background that some have claimed was based on true events that happened to actress Gene Tierney—however, Christie's agents denied that she knew of any connection.[15] With a shortened title of *The Mirror Crack'd* the story was brought to the screen by writers Jonathan Hales and Barry Sandler; Hales is probably best known for later co-writing *Star Wars Episode II: Attack of the Clones* with director and creator George Lucas (2002), while Sandler would soon write the script for *Making Love* (d. Arthur Hiller, 1982), one of the first Hollywood films to deal with a married man coming out of the closet.

Angela Lansbury was the actress selected to play Miss Marple; no doubt the producers were mindful of her well-received turn in *Death on the Nile*, as well as her acclaimed screen heritage. Lansbury had been highly respected in the industry since her debut in the 1944 film of *Gaslight* (d. George Cukor) when she was just 18—her performance as Nancy the maid earned her an Academy Award nomination for Best Supporting Actress, and was the beginning of a successful career on stage and screen. The decision to cast her in the role of Miss Marple met with the approval of the Christie family. Lansbury's involvement was announced in April 1979, but it would be nearly a year before further details were forthcoming, as an event elsewhere in the world had understandable repercussions. On 27 August 1979 the Irish Republican Army (IRA) detonated a bomb on Lord Mountbatten's boat in Ireland while he was on board with his family—including his daughter and son-in-law, Patricia and John Brabourne, as well as their two children and John Brabourne's mother, along with a young local crew member. The blast killed four of those on board, with the three survivors—John and Patricia Brabourne, and one of their sons—seriously injured. In the face of such a traumatic experience it is only to be expected that work on the film would no longer be a priority, but Mathew Prichard remembers Brabourne's dogged insistence on continuing work as soon as he could. 'Being John he was adamant he was going to go on', he recalls. 'John was actually very fussy about what he did, those films were not the only ones he could have done, but they were the only ones he wanted to do.'[16]

It was not until March 1980 that the production was in a position to confirm the remaining cast members, and such was their calibre that it was soon clear that while Lansbury may have secured the leading role, she was not the biggest star name in the picture. Accompanying her were Hollywood legends including Rock Hudson, Kim Novak and—biggest of all—Elizabeth Taylor in the role of Hollywood actress Marina (with the new surname of Gregg-Rudd), replacing Natalie Wood who had first been cast. The fact that this was the first major film to star either Taylor or Novak in some time gave the production some publicity, as did the fact that Taylor's private and professional life had been intensely scrutinised by the media for some years, although it was envisaged that this could be an easily executed return to form for her. Many of the press reports focused on the glamour offered by both actresses, often accompanied by a picture of a busty Novak in her Mary Queen of Scots outfit, which she donned in the film because her character, Lola Brewster, was making a movie about the ill-fated monarch. The *Sunday People* dubbed the picture 'Battle of the Bitches' when it reported on the put-downs uttered by each actress on set—while in character, of course.[17]

Given the talent both behind and in front of the camera, it is difficult to pinpoint the precise reason this adaptation falls flat. It lacks flair, a difficult feat for an adaptation with such a good heritage, including director Guy Hamilton, whose work on several James Bond films had been so successful. The lack of an exotic background means that there is little distraction for the audience from the somewhat leaden dialogue, filled with well-worn jokes and cursory exposition. Perhaps there was the expectation that the star cast would be enough to elevate an unexciting script that offers much Hollywood snark, but little in the way of terribly interesting or original dialogue or narrative devices. Added to its woes is the fact that the film struggles to know what it wants to say about the period it depicts. For her original novel Christie located the story firmly in the 1960s, since it includes Miss Marple musing on the new council estate that has been built near to the village—and, in a move that may surprise critics who wrongly assume Christie to be a reactionary, Miss Marple points out that people must live somewhere, and that progress is inevitable. This commentary on the dying days of old village life runs though the novel, but is dispensed with in the film, which moves the action back to 1953. This change of period results in a safe, toothless and rather dull depiction of St Mary Mead, with the production appearing to have nothing to say about Britain at the time, nor any real justification for the choice of year aside, perhaps, from a hope that the audience has some remaining nostalgia for the early 1950s.[18] Elsewhere, the film is happy to poke fun at Hollywood stars of the period (and beyond), but never has the gumption to move into a clear commentary on the politics of film-making, meaning that it is unsatisfying on both counts—as a reflection, or discussion, of the era. These issues are not helped by questionable choices for Miss Marple's appearance and some added character traits—including her smoking cigarettes. Although Lansbury was a perfectly good choice to play the character, she is given some exceptionally poor make-up (including a terrible grey wig) that leads her to be something of a distraction whenever she appears on screen—she is quite clearly an actress made up to look like an elderly lady, dressed in clothes that never feel like they would be worn by a real older woman of the period; a similar issue would be encountered with Geraldine McEwan's portrayal of the part in the 2004 ITV series of *Agatha Christie: Marple*. What we have in this film is a caricature, not a character, and without either the sense that this is a real woman, or conversely the innate charm and bustling arrogance that the audience had seen in Ustinov's Poirot, it is difficult to take any great pleasure from her appearance. Resultantly, the audience struggles to buy into this world, or at least be entertained by it, in the way that they had been able to for previous films. Lansbury would later say that she thoroughly enjoyed making the film but did not care for the final product, and this may be the key to its shortcomings—everyone on screen seems to be having much more fun than the audience.

Despite these issues, *The Mirror Crack'd* is not a bad film, although it is certainly a missed opportunity. It features an excellent opening scene, where Miss Marple happily reveals the solution to a murder mystery movie after the projector fails, while it is better paced than *Death on the Nile* had been (and over half an hour shorter). It also uses the smaller but well-cast selection of Hollywood stars to good effect, especially as the story moves towards its emotional resolution. The press received it reasonably warmly, although some claimed that this was the least of the three Brabourne films to this point. The *Sunday People* called it 'cracking good fun', while the *Daily Mirror* felt it was one of the stronger Christie pictures and was 'glossy, enjoyable entertainment', and the *Daily Mail* found it 'irresistible'.[19] Meanwhile the *Sunday Express* deemed the film 'shamelessly escapist, wildly improbable, and delightfully entertaining', although writing in its daily sister paper, Ian Christie declared it 'a waste of time and talent'.[20] However, by this point it seemed that critical reviews of Christie films served little function, and the critics themselves understood this—audiences knew what to expect, and the producers were happy to supply it. Perhaps it was this realisation that resulted in notices that were actually better than *Death on the Nile* had seen.

When the film had been officially announced in April 1979 it was claimed that the plan was to alternate Miss Marple pictures with Poirot movies. In the end, however, there was no direct follow-up. This was not due to the film being particularly unsuccessful; in the United States it made $11 m, which was less than *Death on the Nile*'s $14 m and under half *Orient Express*'s exceptional $27 m haul, but this was not a dismal failure. However, Agatha Christie films were experiencing diminishing returns that would only continue, since the next Poirot picture would gross even less, despite its later enduring popularity on television. The reason we never saw another Lansbury picture would appear to be more to do with a gradual tiring of the audience regarding this series of films, rather than due to any inherent failing of this particular movie.

EVIL UNDER THE SUN (1982)

When the plans to alternate Poirot and Miss Marple pictures was announced, it was claimed that *The Mirror Crack'd* would be followed by an adaptation of Christie's 1938 Poirot novel *Appointment with Death*.[21] However, when production started two years later it was the 1941 murder mystery *Evil Under the Sun* that was finally being brought to the screen; *Appointment with Death*'s time would come. As outlined earlier, *Evil Under the Sun* had been fêted as a follow-up to *Murder on the Orient Express* as far back as that film's 1974 release; with the story moved from Devon to the sun-drenched Adriatic, it was now its turn to be the latest glamorous prestige picture based on Christie's works.

Evil Under the Sun saw the return of producers Brabourne and Goodwin, while Guy Hamilton continued on from his work on *The Mirror Crack'd* to tackle this picture, directing another star cast headed by Ustinov's Poirot, albeit one less steeped in the classical period of Hollywood than the previous three pictures. The story follows the murder of actress Arlena Marshall, who is holidaying at an island resort along with many guests and staff who have good reason to see her dead. Arlena is played by Diana Rigg, a highly respected actress who had found fame for her iconic role as Emma Peel in British action-adventure series *The Avengers* between 1965 and 1968. Playing her nemesis, and owner of the hotel, Daphne Castle, is darling of the British film and theatre industries, and co-star of 1978's *Death on the Nile*, Maggie Smith—both actresses were later to become Dames and have backgrounds in classical performances, but they are clearly having a ball with the somewhat lighter but highly entertaining material they are given here.[22] The animosity starts early, when they meet for the first time in many years. Smith's Daphne reminisces that Arlena 'could always throw her legs higher in the air than any of us [...] and wider', while Rigg's Arlena soon gets her own back, with a scene-stealing turn singing Cole Porter's 'You're the Top', which Daphne does her best to both sabotage and upstage. The relationship between these two characters helps to set the tone of the picture, which is rather lighter than the previous three Brabourne films, as if the franchise had now found the confidence to have fun with the story rather than have to worry too much about presenting a studiously close adaptation of the original novel.

That is not to say that the film eschews the mystery in favour of farce. Although some changes are made to the original story, they are not to the movie's detriment and are sometimes to its advantage—such as the removal of a red-herring sub-plot about potential witchcraft, which helps to focus the action for a two-hour movie.[23] Occasionally the humour might stray a little too far—Poirot's comedic turn when trying to swim in the sea in his oversized bathers is rather more Peter Ustinov than it is Belgian detective, but it is brief, and the detective himself is never less than in control and is treated with respect by the other characters, rather than as a figure of fun. Joining Ustinov, Rigg and Smith are several performers who would have been familiar faces to the audience, including Jane Birkin in the role of apparently unhappy tourist Christine Redfern—Birkin had become well known when the 1969 song 'Je t'aime... moi non plus', on which she shared lead vocals, was banned by the BBC for its suggestive lyrics. Playing her husband Patrick is Nicholas Clay, fresh from his appearance in the 1981 film of *Lady Chatterley's Lover* (d. Just Jaeckin), who would go on to appear regularly in film and television, including a lead role in fondly remembered BBC series *Virtual Murder* (1992). British actors James Mason and Roddy McDowell, well known for many Hollywood films and television series, including *A Star is Born* (d. George Cukor, 1954) and *Planet of the Apes* (d. Franklin J. Schaffner, 1968), respectively, lend weight to the proceedings in the roles of tourist Odell Gardener and gossipy biographer Rex Brewster.

It was decided to film much of the movie on the Mediterranean island of Majorca, which perhaps not coincidentally was also where director Guy Hamilton lived. Although the original novel had followed the geography of the real Devon location Burgh Island very closely, the action was easily transferred, with the impression of a smaller resort conveyed through cheated geography. Shifting the story to a more exotic locale makes sense, and helps to reintroduce the more interesting environment that had been missing from *The Mirror Crack'd*. However, the film also effectively establishes from the very beginning that it is not simply a glamorous travelogue, since the opening scenes show the discovery of a murder on a bleak English moor. Although it is easy to forget this opening once the more exotic action commences, it will later pay a key role in the resolution and clearly establishes the genre early on while the audience awaits the inevitable contemporary murder.

Following the opening scene, Poirot is introduced by a secretary as 'Hercules Parrot', establishing the humour of this particular adaptation, which is also even more overtly camp than the three previous pictures; perhaps it is also the first that gives itself over almost fully to pure entertainment. However, because these factors accompany the key twists and turns of the original story, it is the case that for the first time since 1957's *Witness for the Prosecution*, here was a film that established its own distinctive personality that effortlessly complemented Christie's own story. Advertisements for the film evoked the Art Deco style of the 1930s, emphasising that it is a period piece, with one poster rather cheekily quoting a reviewer for *The Observer* who called the mystery the best Agatha Christie since *And Then There Were None*—what was not made clear was the fact that the review in question dated from the novel's original publication in 1941 and did not refer to this new film.

Many reviewers saw this picture as a stronger adaptation than *The Mirror Crack'd* and found it to be entertaining, although notably lacking in any innovation. Once more it was given a royal premiere, after which most critics indicated that audiences who had enjoyed the previous films should expect more of the same. Most reviewers saw the performances of Ustinov, Rigg and Smith as highlights, although some felt the film was a little over-long and veered close to outright parody. Ian Christie of the *Daily Express* was once more one of the more vociferous critics, claiming that 'It's a crime to murder Agatha in this way [...] Personally I didn't care who did it.'[24] The exact opposite senti-ment was expressed by *Daily Mail* reviewer Margaret Hinxman, who felt that the producers and cast had added to the success of the production, going so far as to claim that the film 'only verges on the tedious when it stays true to Agatha', highlighting Poirot's final explanation of the crime in front of all the suspects.[25] These films had established their own characteristics and identity, and it was this on which they were generally judged, rather than Christie's role in the proceedings. Many press reports also covered the glamorous cos-tumes worn by Diana Rigg in particular, and reported on the snappy dialogue between Daphne and Arlena with glee, with the *News of the World* borrowing the *Sunday People*'s headline from two years earlier when it deemed this to be the 'Battle of the Bitches'.[26]

Although the film received the warmest notices since *Murder on the Orient Express*, this was to be the final Christie picture produced by the winning team of John Brabourne and Richard Goodwin, who would go on to work together on two more heritage movies, *A Passage to India* (d. David Lean, 1984) and *Little Dorrit* (d. Christine Edzard, 1987). However, the box-office perfor-mance of *Evil Under the Sun* had further indicated the ongoing decline of the fortunes of Christie films, this time falling to little more than $6 m in the United States, just over half the takings of *The Mirror Crack'd*. That is not to say that the general public appetite in Christie was rapidly diminishing, never-theless, and although Ustinov indicated to one reporter that he was not sure how much longer he could continue to play Poirot ('If they decide to make more of these stories I will be so old they'll need to wheel me on', said the 60-year-old—in truth, the right age for the character), he would remain in the role for four more mysteries.[27] Instead, while interest in cinema adaptations was on the wane, other avenues for Christie's mysteries were starting to see greater success, most especially the one medium to which she had always taken particular exception—television.

USTINOV'S POIROT MOVES TO TELEVISION

The performance of *Evil Under the Sun* at the box office meant that it was looking increasingly unlikely that there would be a big-screen follow-up. When asked about the possibility of the company producing further adapta-tions of Agatha Christie works, the incoming director of EMI's film produc-tion, renowned film and television producer Verity Lambert, stated that she felt they had 'done enough' and that, as of January 1983, 'there's just no life there at the moment'.[28] However, while interest was certainly on the wane in the cinemas, Christie had continued to attract an audience on television. As the next section of this book details, the late 1970s saw the emergence of the first deals for decades that allowed television adaptations of Christie stories—and the early 1980s saw several of these productions reach the screen in both the USA and the UK. One of the keenest producers of Christie's works had been Warner Bros., which had made several television movies for the CBS network in the USA, with international sales allowing them also to be seen across the globe, including in the UK.

The original deal between CBS/Warner Bros. and the Agatha Christie estate had allowed for five television films of her novels, and given the success of Ustinov's portrayal it is unsurprising that the producers tried to enlist his services for at least one more appearance, this time on the small screen. Although Ustinov had started to express his doubts about his longevity in the role during the making of the previous film, in contemporary interviews he confessed that he was feeling more proprietorial over the character. It may well be that the thought of another person playing Poirot was a bigger motivation for Ustinov than the prospect of a rather lower-budget picture than his previous escapades had been. The title selected for adaptation was the 1933 novel *Lord Edgware Dies*, in which the title murder takes place at the same time as a dinner party at which one key suspect, his estranged wife Jane Wilkinson, is in attendance. As is often the case with Christie, the mystery can be solved by unravelling the truth regarding questions of appearance, especially concerning the impressionist Carlotta Adams, who plays a key role in the plot.

Filming began in February 1985 in London, with the movie using the title under which it had been published in the United States, *Thirteen at Dinner*. The schedule was tight, just four weeks, compared to the months required for theatrical features. The budget was in the region of $2 m; reasonably, but not especially, generous.[29] The choice of London for filming was not a purely aesthetic one—although it was a natural fit with Christie's story, there were also financial incentives due to the strong dollar at the time, which had encouraged many companies to use England as their filming base. Explaining the choice to film yet another Christie adaptation, trade magazine *Screen International* highlighted 'insatiable' demand for her works. Producer Neil Hartley was quoted as saying that there were millions of people who wanted to see Christie mysteries but that many 'are not the kind of people who necessarily go out to the theatre to see a show, but would love to see it in their own homes'.[30] Adopting a model that would be followed by the following two television movies, the film eschewed the expense of an all-star cast in favour of a single piece of big-name casting—in this case, Faye Dunaway in the dual role of Jane Wilkinson and Carlotta Adams. Dunaway was a coup for the production, probably best known for her performance as gun-wielding Bonnie Parker in *Bonnie and Clyde* (d. Arthur Penn, 1967), while she won an Academy Award for Best Actress for her appearance in 1976 film *Network*, which had been directed by *Murder on the Orient Express*'s Sidney Lumet.

One point that had been decided during the film's commissioning and production was that while it might seem to be a continuation of the Ustinov cinema films, there was to be one key difference—all of the Warner Bros. television movies bring the mysteries into the present day.[31] However, unlike the other movies, which were effectively brand new offerings to the audience, this clearly goes against the previous depictions of Ustinov's Poirot. Such a move was not without precedent, however—for example, Basil Rathbone's Sherlock Holmes similarly made two high-budget in-period appearances on film before moving to the present day in rather less expensive movies for the rest of the run. For Poirot, as with Sherlock Holmes, one key reason for this change was financial—setting films in the present day is less expensive than hiring costumes and creating sets to evoke the past. However, as later chapters will show, this was also the beginning of a period where the Christie estate was happy to explore attempts to modernise the stories for screen adaptations.[32] Of course there is the sense that this was a move designed to appeal to new audiences, a not unreasonable motivation, and such decisions tend to go with the fashion—the popularity of close literary adaptations versus modernising appears to ebb and flow according to networks' and producers' whims and comparable successes. From the opening moments the audience is immediately made aware that this film is situated in the present day, when Poirot is a guest on a television talk show hosted by David Frost. This version of Poirot appears to be much calmer and gentler than we have seen before—indeed, in this scenario he is so relaxed that this is the clearest indication that Ustinov is playing Poirot as an Ustinovesque character, since he was famed for his entertaining talk show appearances. No doubt this is an in joke in part, but it also demonstrates how comfortable Ustinov is in the role, although having rounded off some of the eccentricities he does move the character further from Poirot as written.

Joining Ustinov and Dunaway are Jonathan Cecil as Poirot's companion Hastings (now ex-Military Intelligence) and David Suchet as Inspector Japp. Cecil was in the midst of a busy career playing supporting roles in many British productions, including Stanley Kubrick's 1975 picture *Barry Lyndon*, while Suchet needs no introduction, as he would later don the moustache of Poirot himself for the acclaimed ITV series from 1989. In later years Suchet has expressed regret about his performance in this film, where he plays a spiky, cockney Japp who particularly riles Hastings (as in the novel). He helps to enliven the somewhat leaden pace and flat tone of the film and he should consider reappraising the strength of his contribution. By contrast, Cecil's Hastings feels like a definite backward step towards the clichéd, dim-witted companion of the detective so frequently seen in screen mysteries.

Overall, the film updates the story reasonably well, with a script by actor and writer Rod Browning whose biggest success had been a Chevy Chase film, *Oh Heavenly Dog*, concerning a crime-solving canine (d. Joe Camp, 1980). However, *Thirteen at Dinner* struggles to maintain the attention of the audience while it moves through developments in a disinterested, workmanlike manner, with director Lou Antonio rarely offering moments of high visual interest as the plot shifts between incident and deductions. A veteran of television movies (this was his tenth since 1980), Antonio's direction appears to exert the minimum of effort in order to ensure that the plot comes across;

everyone involved seems a little tired and to be wishing that the unveiling of the murderer could happen a little sooner than after the required 90 minutes. There are some moments of charm, such as when Poirot interviews Jane Wilkinson while she is on her daily run (sporting a jumper festooned with the US flag); he keeps pace by commandeering a boat that can follow her along the river path. Meanwhile there are also some clear attempts to appeal to a modern audience, with several scenes tracking stunt sequences being filmed for a picture being made by some of the key characters, thus allowing for some action to be presented without it actually affecting the original plot. Although such attempts to make the film feel more contemporary largely fall flat, they do demonstrate that Christie was seen as a strong brand for screen adaptation above and beyond any apparent nostalgia for the original stories. Here, we see an adaptation that uses the key elements from the original mystery and simply transplants them to the modern day.

The drop in quality from the big-screen Ustinov pictures was noted by several reviewers, many of whom had enjoyed much of the mystery anyway. The review in trade paper *Variety* demonstrated the general confusion that a film with so many 'big' actors involved could be so lacking in character. Drawing particular attention to characterisation, the review pointed out that 'Poirot's maddening manners and precise timing have been supplanted by a softening approach, maddening in its own way—maybe more so, since Poirot has become a warm, soothing man [...] the Christie style has been sabotaged— the characters aren't interesting, the murders unsurprising'.[33] When the film debuted on CBS in October 1985 it was the 52nd most-watched programme of the week, sandwiched between contemporary action series *Knight Rider* (NBC, 1982–86) at 51 and *Airwolf* (CBS/USA, 1984–87) at 53. While it was not reaching the upper echelons of the television ratings, it was reaching a reasonable-sized audience and—more crucially for Warner Bros.—the film had sold well abroad.

Indeed, the film had sold so well that production returned to London's Bray Studios in September 1985, a month prior to *Thirteen at Dinner*'s television premiere. Although *Thirteen at Dinner* relies on a visual puzzle as its centrepiece, much of the rest concentrates on interviews and deduction, often through inference, which made for a story that did not always lend itself particularly well to a one-off screen adaptation. However, the next choice of work was a more natural fit, bringing *Dead Man's Folly* to the screen. Christie's 1956 novel features a 'murder hunt' game at a summer fête that leads to a real killing, and covers so many elements that are popularly recognised as Christie-esque that it almost feels like a pastiche, with the colourful village events taking place in the grounds of a house owned by Sir George Stubbs and his wife, Lady Hattie Stubbs, along with questions of identity, betrayal for love and money, and the dire warnings of locals. Although the victim is an innocent girl, the setting is at Christie's most cosily nostalgic, certainly for the period. Given all of this it is a strong choice for adaptation as an immediately recognisable piece of Agatha Christie, while not being one of the more familiar mysteries.

For this adaptation, the film-makers could have their cake and eat it in terms of nostalgia—such a fête is timeless, and only the fashions and occasional flashes of technology betray the 1980s setting. It is an archetypal Christie in many senses, including both subject matter and iconography, while the satisfying resolution follows on from a rather more linear structure with an entertaining cast of characters that is well suited to 90 minutes. Unlike the plans to include the story in an aborted Poirot series in the 1960s, this version does not transplant the mystery to the United States—instead, it is both filmed and based in England, a further example of how the apparent 'Britishness' of Christie's mysteries was now a draw in itself, even with the addition of American actors and a present-day setting. Ustinov is once more teamed with Cecil's Hastings, despite the fact that the latter has no real function in the story, but this may be because the production team had hoped to cultivate a strong double act for future adaptations; on the strength of the three TV movies featuring the pair, such hopes were overly optimistic. Rather more interesting is the appearance of Ariadne Oliver, the mystery writer who featured in Christie's original book (among others), played by Jean Stapleton, who was best known as Edith Bunker on the hugely successful CBS sitcom *All in the Family* (1971–79). Although Stapleton portrays Oliver as an American, at odds with Christie's intent, this actually helps to make the character an immediate contrast to Poirot—she is vivacious, energetic and an enthusiastic talker; the accent only marks her out as rather more ebullient than Poirot and the mostly British guest cast. Although Stapleton is the star casting for this film, Shakespearian actor Tim Piggott-Smith lends the movie some gravitas in his portrayal of Sir George Stubbs, while future *Desperate Housewives* star Nicollette Sheridan provides glamour as his wife, although much of her dialogue appears to have been dubbed later for reasons unknown. The performances maintain interest throughout, while the direction from Clive Donner—another recurring figure in TV movies of the era, working to another script from Rod Browning—signposts the clues well, while using the waterside locations to good effect.

When the film was broadcast in January 1986, this time *Variety* was kinder than towards its predecessor. 'The solution doesn't matter,' the review read, 'since the diversion is beyond far-fetched and credible. But getting there [...] makes the puzzle entertaining.'[34] However, the *Chicago Tribune* flagged up an important contextual point that would soon move attention away from movies of this type. Calling it 'a rushed waste of talent', Clifford Terry found the production to be markedly weaker than the BBC *Miss Marple* adaptations that were now screening on PBS.[35] Soon enough, a Poirot series following a similar template would indeed displace any American adaptations.[36]

By the time Ustinov returned for his third, and final, television outing as Poirot, interest in the productions was on the wane. Several press previews referred to 'yet another' outing for the Belgian sleuth, who was this time accompanied by Hollywood star Tony Curtis. The story chosen was Christie's 1934 novel *Three Act Tragedy*, filmed under its American title of *Murder in Three Acts*. Curtis plays the role of Charles Cartwright, a wealthy American

actor whose dinner party is interrupted by the seemingly unmotivated poisoning of one of his guests. When a second dinner party held elsewhere sees
another death, Poirot tries to find the link between them and unmask the
murderer. As is often the case for filmed adaptations of murder mysteries, the
audience would do well to inspect the cast list before making their deductions;
frequently the star name is the guilty suspect, and this story is no exception.
Nevertheless, despite his presence removing some of the mystery, Curtis is a
welcome addition to the film, as is the location in which much of the action
takes place—a stunning house on the coast of Acapulco. The film is entertaining and, although modernised, preserves the key twists and turns of the
original novel—or, more precisely, the twists and turns of its American edition.
Murder in Three Acts is a rare occasion where there are substantial differences
between the UK and US publications. In the British edition, Cartwright murders his friend Dr Strange because the doctor knows that Cartwright's apparently deceased wife is, in fact, still alive and in a mental institution—since she
is unable to grant him a divorce, her existence would prevent Cartwright from
marrying his real love. In the version printed in the United States and used for
this movie, the motivation is rather more prosaic—Cartwright himself is mad,
and knows that Dr Strange has recognised his symptoms. Fear of this being
public knowledge, or resulting in his incarceration, leads him to murder Dr
Strange. It is at this revelation that the strength of casting Curtis is shown,
because the sudden and difficult transition between charming and maniacal for
the final revelation is well handled. At the end, Cartwright promises to give the
performance of his life when he is carted off to jail.

The film is directed by Gary Nelson, probably best known for his work
heading the Disney pictures *The Black Hole* (1979) and *Freaky Friday* (1976),
working from a script by Scott Swanton who had previously written a partial
pastiche of *And Then There Were None*, *The Calendar Girls Murders*, starring
Sharon Stone (d. William A. Graham, 1984). Production took place in June
1986, finishing just in time for Ustinov to head back to Britain to join the
crowd at his beloved Wimbledon. It made little impact when shown, but was
no disaster—of the 330 television movies screened on major American networks in the 1986–87 season it ranked at number 115, actually performing a
little better than the highly publicised *Thirteen at Dinner* had done a year earlier, demonstrating sustained interest in Christie and Ustinov.[37] Nevertheless,
after a glut of appearances on American television, it seemed that the Christie
films had started to run their course, especially in light of the success of the
BBC's *Miss Marple* series, which had debuted in 1984.[38] *Murder in Three Acts*
was the penultimate TV movie made under the Warner Bros. deal, followed
only by 1989's *The Man in the Brown Suit*, but their appearances would rumble
on in repeats around the world as well as home video releases. In the UK
they were the subject of less welcome attention, since British acting union
Equity claimed that Warner Bros. had resold the transmission rights in such a
way that performers were not being compensated for out-of-contract screenings.[39] Nevertheless, the films still turn up on daytime television in Britain and

continue to be widely seen elsewhere, helping to cement the public's generally fond memory of Ustinov's appearances in the part—of which there was to be one more before he hung up his Poirot moustache for good.

APPOINTMENT WITH DEATH (1988)

In May 1986, in the midst of Ustinov's performances as Poirot on television, the trade press noted that plans were afoot to get him back to the big screen. Cannon Films, a rapidly growing production company that had previously made the 1985 Christie adaptation *Ordeal by Innocence*, was reported to be bringing Christie's 1938 novel *Appointment with Death* to cinemas, with Ustinov returning as Poirot and—most intriguingly—with Brabourne and Goodwin coming back as producers following their four big-screen successes starting with 1974's *Murder on the Orient Express*.[40] Anthony Shaffer was also announced as taking on scripting duties once more, following his work on *Death on the Nile* and *Evil Under the Sun*.[41] Brabourne and Goodwin's involvement with an *Appointment with Death* film had first been mentioned in the press release for *The Mirror Crack'd* back in 1979, but whatever their connection with this production turned out to be, it was brief. Perhaps it is a coincidence that once an announcement was made that strong-willed director Michael Winner was attached to the picture, Brabourne and Goodwin were no longer mentioned—but perhaps not. Instead, the pair worked with Cannon on the aforementioned 1988 adaptation of Charles Dickens's *Little Dorrit*.

However, *Appointment with Death* was not the only potential Poirot film in the works. In 1986 Julian Bond, a writer on many British television dramas, completed two drafts of a screenplay for a film adaptation of Christie's 1936 Poirot novel *Murder in Mesopotamia*. It is difficult to envisage this as designed for Ustinov's Poirot from the script, although this was the novel reported to be in pre-production in 1989 with Ustinov on board and Christopher Miles as director; the film never materialised.[42] Although Poirot's entrance on an RAF plane, sporting flying goggles and fur-lined boots, echoes some of Ustinov's more outlandish moments, he is then described as a 'small, slight man'—hardly a description of the incumbent actor. As with the original story, this script does not feature Poirot for quite some time—in this case, page 63 of a 122-page script (he makes his first appearance in the 13th of 29 chapters in the book). Considering the emphasis on Ustinov when it came to his later Poirot films in particular, this delayed appearance is unlikely to have satisfied the actor, producers or audience. Christie's novel is narrated by a nurse, Amy Leatheran, who had cared for the woman who was to become the murder victim. The central role of Amy is maintained in Bond's script, where she narrates the action and is effectively the lead character, who we are told has an 'almost telepathic' bond with Poirot. The adaptation keeps the story in period and expands the action, adding detail to Amy's journey to Mesopotamia, including her leaving on a ship from Southampton—although a second draft dispenses with much of this prelude. As a story that offers such an overtly outsider's view of Poirot (Amy's voiceover recounts how she struggles to understand the detective to begin with, before his actions start to make more sense to her), it might have been a title suitable to open a new series of Poirot productions, but it was not to be, perhaps because of the surfeit of Poirots in the late 1980s. Ustinov's Poirot was on both the big and small screens, while London Weekend Television would soon ready its own series of adaptations, with filming commencing in 1988; there simply was not room for another.

Cannon's chosen mystery, *Appointment with Death*, is a story that fans have often cited as one of Christie's stronger novels, since it features a particularly psychologically complex character at its centre. Mrs Boynton, the murder victim, is a domineering and cruel matriarch and so when she is found dead while apparently relaxing in the sun during a trip to the Middle East, suspicion falls on the rest of her family. Piper Laurie, who had just received her third Academy Award nomination, was cast as Mrs Boynton, and other characters are mostly played by well-known actors, including John Gielgud, Carrie Fisher, Hayley Mills, David Soul and—in a starring role—Hollywood legend Lauren Bacall. Production of the film took place in Jerusalem during summer 1987, and Winner seems to have lived up to his reputation as a forceful and difficult personality on set, while his contribution even extended to the script itself as he was credited alongside Shaffer and television writer Peter Buckman. Reporting from the set, Andrew Duncan of *The Times* described Winner's film-making as 'aggressive', perhaps no surprise given the fact that his biggest successes, the Charles Bronson action film *Death Wish* (1974) and its two sequels, were so steeped in machismo—but the report also revealed a miserable cast.[43] Duncan quoted Soul as being particularly bothered by Winner's propensity to raise his voice, while an interview with Gielgud revealed this to be an unhappy experience for him, as he found his character, Colonel Carbury, to be 'one of the least rewarding I have ever played [...] I wish the character had fun, or stupidity, something I could hang on to'. Bacall, making her first film since 1980, was also not keen on her character Lady Westholme ('a bit Margaret Thatcherish'), but had even fewer positive things to say about the filming process or Winner himself. 'He doesn't do anything for actors, except make you nervous', she said, 'I hate screaming and tension.' Although Gielgud wondered about the apparently high budget (stated to be $10 m), he also said that 'Presumably because it's Agatha Christie it will be a success'; however, the days of Agatha Christie pictures being a guaranteed popular hit had passed.

Although the finished film is considerably lacking when compared with the stronger films made by Brabourne and Goodwin, its poor critical reputation reflects general boredom with pictures of this type, as well as the shortcomings of this particular film. It is simply an exceedingly dull adaptation of the core elements of the novel. The greatest problem is its reduction of the intricate and fascinating family dynamics of the original down to a bland selection of characters whom it is difficult either to care about or take much notice of, which has rather an impact on the equivalent fun to be had when guessing whodunit. The performances throughout are unexceptional, even among the more esteemed members of the cast, not helped by a lack of sophistication in the script. Nevertheless, there are some nice touches, such as the way in which when each character explains their alibi it is accompanied by a flashback using disorientating camera angles; this reminds the audience that this is not necessarily the truth, as well as adding visual variety and helping in the piecing together of the puzzle, as we can work out which stories may not be compatible with the others. It is in these more ostentatious moments that the film works best, although any hope for similarly effective subtleties are vanquished when the opening scene features the reading of a will during a thunder storm, a particularly tiresome screen cliché. The picture follows the original novel, rather than Christie's later stage adaptation that not only removed Poirot but included a solution that would have forced the film-makers to spend more time thinking about the characters, which are reduced to ciphers or (in the case of the victim) an outright pantomime villain. For the play, Christie revealed that Mrs Boynton was not murdered, but had in fact committed suicide, in the desire that the act would put several family members under suspicion and thus create unrest for the rest of their lives—a final malicious act.

Cannon had a poor reputation in the film industry, and with the additional baggage brought by Winner it is unsurprising that the press reaction to the film when it was released in May 1988 was particularly vociferous in its negativity. More than one critic called it an 'appointment with boredom', with several labelling it 'dated'[44] and claiming that it was one of Christie's lesser mysteries anyway.[45] *The Times* felt that it 'cannot be counted even a moderate success', while the *Daily Telegraph* echoed one of the actors' own thoughts when it stated that 'It is a grim script indeed that can defeat John Gielgud'.[46] So unpopular was the film that several critics seemed to revise down their opinion of previous productions in its wake, claiming all-star adaptations to be lazy and even examples of bad film-making. *Sky* magazine decided to use its review to shame who it perceived to be the film's villain: 'We name the guilty party,' it read, 'he's producer-director Michael Winner, who has made a limp thriller with the same appeal as an appointment with the dentist—no fun while you are there but a great relief when it's all over.'[47]

While filming his final appearance as Poirot, Ustinov mulled over the way in which he had made the character his own. Speaking to Andrew Duncan, he said: 'Much as I admire Albert Finney I think he was too conscientious in trying to be what the book said the man was.'[48] Indeed, the Poirot that Ustinov played may not always have been close to the depiction in Christie's books, but it has remained a popular portrayal—an indication that what works on the page is not necessarily the same as what resonates with screen audiences, and as a result there was room for more than one version of such a character. By the time of *Appointment with Death*'s release, production was already well underway on the next Poirot project, this time without Ustinov—and the next person to take on the role would stay in the part for a quarter of a century.

NOTES

1. Coppage to Dodd Mead, 19 September 1974 (Agatha Christie Archive, Exeter).
2. Various correspondence in late 1975 covers these issues, mostly summarised in November 1975's 'Aide Memoire RE Poirot Film Rights' (Anon.) (Agatha Christie Archive, Exeter).
3. Interview with the author, August 2015.
4. See Chap. 4 regarding this earlier production.
5. Cork to Hicks, 19 December 1975 (Agatha Christie Archive, Exeter).
6. Interview with the author, August 2015.
7. *Newsday*, 29 September 1978.
8. *The Star Ledger*, 29 September 1978.
9. *Newsweek*, 2 October 1978.
10. *Western Mail*, 21 October 1978.
11. *Sunday Telegraph*, 24 October 1978.
12. *Daily Telegraph*, 27 October 1978.
13. *Evening Standard*, 16 December 1977.
14. *Evening Standard*, 6 April 1978.
15. As her American agents wrote to an enquiring reader, 'This may sound incredible to you, but it is a fact, and it was not until after the book was published that she learned of this coincidence.' Hughes Massie Ltd to Sarajane Beal, 9 June 1964 (Agatha Christie Archive, Exeter).
16. Interview with the author, August 2015.
17. *Sunday People*, 14 September 1980.
18. It may be that the choice of period was simply so that it could be retained for later Miss Marple pictures, in which case a book that more overtly deals with juxtaposing the 'safe' old village with the reality of crime and murder might have been a better choice for the first picture—perhaps *The Body in the Library* or Miss Marple's actual debut novel appearance, *The Murder at the Vicarage*.
19. *Sunday People*, 1 March 1981; *Daily Mirror*, 27 February 1981; *Daily Mail*, 27 February 1981.
20. *Sunday Express*, 1 March 1981; *Daily Express*, 28 February 1981.
21. Some sources have claimed that the publicity for *The Mirror Crack'd* actually announced a film called *Appointment with Murder* [sic] as the next Miss Marple picture. However, this was not correct and seems to have been the result of some garbled misreporting of the press release.
22. A conflation of two characters from the novel: Mrs Castle, owner of the hotel, and dressmaker Rosamund Darnley.
23. Changes include the island's relocation, the conflation of two characters into one for Daphne Castle and the changing of one character's gender.
24. *Daily Express*, 26 March 1982.
25. *Daily Mail*, 26 March 1982.

26. *News of the World*, 21 March 1982.
27. *Sunday Mirror*, 31 May 1981.
28. *Variety*, 23 January 1983.
29. *Screen International*, 27 April 1985.
30. *Screen International*, 27 April 1985.
31. Throughout this book I use the term 'present day' to mean 'the time of production'—of course, the 'present day' here is more than three decades ago.
32. This reached an apex with the 2001 television adaptation of *Murder on the Orient Express*, explored in Chap. 15.
33. *Variety*, 23 October 1985.
34. *Variety*, 15 January 1986.
35. Covered in Chap. 11.
36. *Chicago Tribune*, 8 January 1986.
37. *Murder in Three Acts* had a 15.4 rating and 25 share (meaning that 15.4 % of all monitored households watched the film; 25 % of those actually watching television were tuned in to this particular programme) versus *Thirteen at Dinner*'s 12.8/21.
38. See Chap. 10 for more examples of American television appearances, and Chap. 11 for coverage of the BBC *Miss Marple* series.
39. *The Stage and Television Today*, 13 October 1994.
40. See Chap. 10 for coverage of the *Ordeal by Innocence* film.
41. Reported by *Variety*, 14 May 1986 and *Screen International*, 17 May 1986.
42. *Screen International*, 11 June 1988.
43. *The Times*, 20 July 1987.
44. For example, *The Guardian*, 26 May 1988 and *Western Mail*, 21 May 1988.
45. For example, *Today*, 27 May 1988 and *Evening Standard*, 26 May 1988.
46. *The Times* and *Daily Telegraph*, both 26 May 1988.
47. *Sky*, June 1988.
48. *The Times*, 20 July 1987.

PART V

Rethinking Agatha Christie Adaptations, 1979–95

Chapter 9: Christie Comes Back to Television

Spoilers: 'The Case of the Missing Lady'; 'The Unbreakable Alibi'; 'The House of Lurking Death'

While the early 1970s had seen a blanket dismissal of any approach made to Christie regarding small-screen adaptations, by the end of the decade the medium found itself in a position where it was finally permitted to prove itself to Agatha Christie Ltd. However, the journey to television's most acclaimed adaptations of Christie's works required a great deal of negotiation and, initially at least, an important proviso.

It was London Weekend Television (LWT), the capital's weekend commercial television franchise, which initially got furthest in its negotiations with Agatha Christie Ltd regarding plans to bring Christie's works to television. Such progress had been facilitated by the arrival of Brian Stone as Agatha Christie Ltd's literary agent, who worked to convince Christie's daughter Rosalind Hicks that television could be a positive venture for the estate. Hicks's son, Mathew Prichard, remembers Stone being the motivating factor for this change of attitude. 'Brian was very interested in television and in exploring Agatha Christie on television', he recalls. 'He and my mother actually had a few stand up disagreements but they actually got on very well. I think Brian introduced a different atmosphere into the whole question of adaptation.'[1] Stone brought with him not only a keenness to establish Christie on television, but also industry contacts, including television mogul Michael Grade, then Director of Programmes for LWT. Yet although Hicks would eventually be convinced to allow some of her mother's works to be transferred to the small screen, she was adamant on one point—Agatha Christie's two best-known characters were not available for television. Mathew Prichard explains how this led to the choice of a standalone mystery to relaunch Christie on British television:

> My mother was determined that we weren't going to use Poirot and Miss Marple for television, and therefore it was almost the case that [they had to look for] anything else. My mother was a very shrewd person and I suspect that *Why Didn't They Ask Evans?* was her choice, and she chose them a rattling good story,

© The Author(s) 2016
M. Aldridge, *Agatha Christie on Screen*,
DOI 10.1057/978-1-137-37292-5_10

although it didn't have a major character in it and it was, therefore, as far as my mother could see, risk free.[2]

Why Didn't They Ask Evans? is a light mystery thriller hailing from 1934 that follows an investigation into the death of a man whose final words are the titular question. The novel is filled with strong characters who are perhaps more archetypal than many of those in Christie's other stories, but nevertheless provide the reader with an entertaining journey. In fact, the book is very much in the vein of the type of story that some might identify with Christie but is actually only present in the early era of her work, where we sometimes meet jolly young adults dashing round the countryside solving mysteries while waiting for the family inheritance. Along with novels such as *The Secret of Chimneys* (1925), *The Seven Dials Mystery* (1929) and some of the Tommy and Tuppence stories, the tone of the novel is easier to compare with the likes of P.G. Wodehouse than it is with the majority of Christie's work. There is a sense that the author is having a lot of fun with a complex but energetic story of this type and it is easy to get swept along by her enthusiasm, even if, by Christie's own admission, such characters were increasingly rare in the real world. It is an understandable choice for a television production as it takes in multiple locations in the English countryside, making it visually appealing but not laboured with expensive international filming, and encompasses many twists, even if it is not in the very highest echelon of Christie stories.

The choice of this particular novel as the story to be adapted appears to have been pre-ordained, since *Evans* had actually made a brief appearance on television the year before production started on LWT's adaptation. On 12 November 1978, BBC One showed an episode of its documentary series *Crime Writers*, called 'Puzzles: Pure and Complex', based on the factual book *Bloody Murder* by Julian Symons. This episode concentrated on Christie and her peer Dorothy L. Sayers, and featured a newly dramatised scene from *Why Didn't They Ask Evans?*, starring Patricia Hodge as Moira Nicholson and Christopher Scoular as Bobby Jones, covering the characters' meeting at the inn at the beginning of Chapter Eighteen where Moira outlines her fears that she is going to be murdered. In a sign of how tight the restrictions seem to have been, the dialogue is taken from the story almost verbatim, with only very light abridgement and minor rewording. It is possible that a senior member of the LWT crew had seen the excerpt and deemed the story particularly suitable for their aims, but given the lengthy lead time of production, this seems unlikely. More likely is the scenario that Rosalind Hicks had decided that this was a strong story that had no linking elements with other Christie mysteries and so was a safe choice as a title to offer television producers when discussing possible adaptations— the BBC simply got there first, and LWT must have hoped that few viewers had seen or remembered the BBC documentary, since it gives away a significant part of the story's resolution. In the programme, no rationale is offered for the choice to adapt a section of this particular mystery, other than an implication that it is a typical Christie. *Murder on the Orient Express* is represented by clips from the 1974 film, while the documentary also dramatises the inauguration of a female member of the Detection Club—unnamed, but we may believe it to be Christie, played by Avril Cookson. This episode's brief, dramatised excerpt from a Christie story was the first original British television production of her works for nearly two decades, and might seem to indicate a thawing of the estate's attitude when it came to them appearing on the small screen. However, it is also clear from the rights agreement that the BBC emphasised that it saw the programme as a 'further education' series rather than a general documentary; Christie and her agents had always been better disposed towards extracts in this context. Nevertheless, the fact that the approach was not dismissed out of hand is significant, especially as the family will not have got rich from the £26 that the BBC paid to license the scene.[3]

Production of LWT's adaptation was announced to the press in May 1979, and there was very much the sense that this was seen as an experiment that could result in more valuable properties making it to the small screen. 'I'm sure there was a lot of discussion about Poirot and Marple,' says Mathew Prichard, 'but Brian said [to LWT] "Look, you're never going to get Poirot and Marple, so you might as well [...]"' *Variety* quoted Prichard as saying that only an English company could bring such a script to the screen, while the article also claimed that the Brabourne films were the reason behind the non-appearance of Poirot or Miss Marple.[4] The adaptation was expected to take place across three episodes, possibly with broadcasts over a weekend on a Friday, Saturday and Sunday (the three nights on which LWT had control of the London commercial television franchise).[5] One report also indicated that there had been something of a battle between up to five different broadcasters to bring Christie to television, and that at least one 'was a little miffed that LWT managed to pull it off'.[6] As with Brabourne, it seems the personal relationships and—more importantly—the trust that goes with them were the biggest motivating factors where Christie adaptations were concerned. The early publicity also referred to the adaptation as one of LWT's two forthcoming prestige productions, along with a new deal to make six television films with esteemed television writer Dennis Potter, which was to prove short-lived.[7] However, the focus was mainly on the cast, including the famed John Gielgud alongside Eric Porter, best known for his performance as Soames in the 1967 BBC Two adaptation of *The Forsyte Saga*, as well as Francesca Annis as jovial protagonist Frankie Derwent and James Warwick as bored vicar's son Bobby Jones, who finds the dying man—two faces who would soon turn up together for a longer stint as Agatha Christie characters.

Originally the programme was due to be seen in the final quarter of 1979, but August of that year had seen a strike across the ITV network that lasted some ten weeks and had not only resulted in delayed transmissions of many programmes, but had also interrupted their production. When the network came back on air it took time to return to full service and the programming schedules needed to be reworked. So it was that ten months passed between publicity photographs in the press showing Annis trying out her golfing skills and the final transmission on Saturday 29 March 1980, with the whole adaptation being shown on one evening.[8] With the insertion of commercials and a 15-minute break for the news, this meant that this single production dominated the country's most popular television channel for the whole evening, running from 7.45 p.m. to 11.30 p.m. Such a lengthy production at a time when home video recorders were rare was a gamble, but it is one that paid off, as the scheduling served to further the impression of the production as a prestigious television event rather than just another literary adaptation. On the day of transmission, *The Times* offered its readers the following advice:

> Cancel all unnecessary engagements, take the telephone off the hook and most important—tell any fellow viewers there might be that your lips will be sealed for the duration of the film and that the least they can do is seal theirs, too. That done, you can look forward with confidence, I think, to an Agatha Christie yarn of exceptional quality and exceptional length.[9]

This 'exceptional length' was a result of a production that—at over three hours long, even excluding commercials—must surely rank as one of the adaptations that follows the source material the closest. That is not to say that it is ineffective, since it is highly entertaining and well performed, with a more satisfying pace than the running time might indicate, but nevertheless, it does feel like rather a long time to spend on one of Christie's lighter stories. Adapted by Pat Sandys, who would go on to produce *The Agatha Christie Hour*, the producer was Jack Williams, who had previously worked on period drama *Lillie* (1978), another LWT production starring Francesca Annis. *Lillie* had also featured James Warwick as Annis's character's husband for three episodes; their performances in that series had resulted in them being approached for these roles. *Why Didn't They Ask Evans?* was directed by John Davies and Tony Wharmby, both of whom had worked on prestigious and popular television series in the past, including *War and Peace* (BBC 1972–73) and *Bouquet of Barbed Wire* (LWT, 1976), respectively. Davies would later direct the BBC's adaptation of *Sleeping Murder* (1987), while Wharmby (who also served as Executive Producer) would go on to be better known for his work directing episodes of several US television shows, including *The X Files* (Fox, 1993–2002) and *NCIS* (CBS, 2003–).

In this adaptation, changes from the novel are infrequent, and when they do occur they are for practical reasons or even offer an improvement on the original plotting—for example, in the novel one character is recognised as an imposter because of the shape of his earlobes; in the television adaptation this is changed to the more straightforward absence of scratches on his face. The extent to which the production stuck to the original story can be ascribed to two factors. The first is the clear keenness on the part of LWT that this adaptation could be a springboard to utilising more commercially recognisable parts of the Agatha Christie library, including her recurring characters. In order to build up trust, an adaptation that adhered closely to the original material would be needed. Fortunately, it was the fashion of the time to produce works that did adapt material in a faithful manner. As Mathew Prichard puts it, 'I think television people, beginning with *Why Didn't They Ask Evans?*, began to introduce some people who were serious television professionals who were interested in the science of adaptation. Whereas, to use the obvious opposite, people like MGM simply took the stories and tore them to pieces.'[10]

The second factor that will have influenced the production taking rather longer than might later be the case is simply due to the style of television production at the time. ITV's attempts to bring Christie to the screen between 1979 and 1984 fall in a period that saw huge upheaval in the way television drama was produced and presented. Prior to this point, most British television dramas were produced in a particular manner—the majority of scenes would be performed in a multi-camera television studio and recorded onto videotape. Any scenes that needed to take place outside or required particular visual effects would be shot on film and inserted into the recording. This resulted in a disjointed look that was nevertheless accepted as the grammar of television; internal scenes would be akin to a theatrical performance, while exteriors appeared on grainy 16 mm film. *Why Didn't They Ask Evans?* utilised this method of production, since usually only programmes that were designed to be sold widely internationally or, more specifically, to American networks were made entirely on film. However, the early 1980s saw many of television's more prestigious productions adopt the latter production method, with some television series made in a manner akin to movies. Adaptations of such literary titles and figures as *Brideshead Revisited* (ITV, 1981), *Sherlock Holmes* (ITV, 1984–94), *The Jewel in the Crown* (ITV, 1985) and even the BBC's own *Miss Marple* series (1984–92) meant that productions shot mostly in the studio on videotape were starting to look old-fashioned. Indeed, when ITV had returned from the 1979 strike its biggest production was the highly publicised miniseries *Quatermass* (d. Piers Haggard), a four-hour return of the eponymous professor whose adventures had been a hit on BBC television when first seen in the 1950s. This time the professor moved on from his live television origins to a serial shot entirely on 35 mm film in an adventure structured in such a way that there was also an edited version that could be released to cinemas, highlighting the cinematic nature of the serial. Although *Why Didn't They Ask Evans?* had a healthy budget of nearly £1 m, it has aged rather less well than such all film productions. However, as a first step towards gaining Christie a permanent place on television, it served its function extremely well, and presented the audience with a well-received version of the novel.

Reviews of the film drew attention to the star-studded cast, and while one or two felt it was a little too long, most welcomed the allocation of so much airtime to a prestigious production. Pat Sandys's script, which had to keep many plates spinning while all the time concealing various twists until the time was right, was widely praised. *Variety* also drew attention to the 'stunning cameo' of Joan Hickson as an elderly socialite, now in her third of four appearances in

Christie adaptations—her final, and most famous, role would soon beckon.[11] However, Michael Ratcliffe of *The Times* called the film 'as crisp and riveting as an old lettuce leaf', while Hillary Kingsley of the *Daily Mirror* was also not impressed, terming it 'terrible tedium', although a letter from a member of the public on the same page found it to be 'a perfect period piece'.[12] Writing in *The Guardian*, Nancy Banks-Smith (a keen reader of Christie) immediately deduced that this story would hardly have been LWT's first choice, but that it had done its best to make it a worthwhile adaptation.[13] With 15.55 m people tuning in, making it the ninth most watched programme that week, it was clear that there was a strong appetite for Christie's work on television.[14]

Given the success of *Why Didn't They Ask Evans?*, it was probably inevitable that the follow-up would be along the same lines. Not only had the programme rated well, it had attracted a high proportion of ABC1 viewers, those deemed to be in the most skilled professions and, resultantly, the most wealthy and attractive to advertisers—52 % of the audience for Evans had fallen into this bracket, compared to 29 % for top-rating soap opera *Coronation Street* (ITV, 1960–).[15] This time, LWT secured the rights for Christie's 1929 novel *The Seven Dials Mystery*. The story's premise is one of Christie's most intriguing, concerning a dead body found in a room with multiple alarm clocks. However, as the tale progresses it becomes increasingly similar to LWT's previously adapted story, including high-spirited wealthy youngsters uncovering the crime, spurred on by a second dying man's mysterious last words ('Seven Dials… Tell Jimmy Thesiger').

Most of the key production personnel from *Evans* returned, including producer Jack Williams, adaptor Pat Sandys and director Tony Wharmby, who was also executive producer once more. Location filming started on 20 August 1980, while the interior scenes were videotaped in the studio later in the year, during November and December.[16] One concession to the critics—or perhaps the schedulers—was the fact that this production ran a full hour shorter than *Why Didn't They Ask Evans?*, with the resultant quicker pace and higher suitability for broadcast across a single evening. However, on the whole this close adaptation felt like a retread of the previous production (a feeling helped by the appearance of some of the same cast members, including James Warwick and John Gielgud), although given the paucity of television Christie in the years up to this point two similar productions can hardly be considered to be overkill. As with *Evans*, it was a highly publicised affair, with Michael Watts of the *Sunday Express* calling it a 'rare old publicity blitz', saying that he had sworn not to watch *Evans* due to the incessant publicity for it, but had ended up tuning in anyway—just as he was sure he would do this time round.[17]

Broadcast on Sunday 8 March 1981 between 7.45 p.m. and 10.30 p.m. with a 15-minute break for the news at 9 p.m., *The Seven Dials Mystery* proved to be a popular hit, seen by 17.6 m viewers, surpassing the viewers for *Evans* and making it the fourth highest rated programme of the week. Critical response was often framed by disappointment that the production was of what some called a 'minor Christie', when the reviewers knew that there were many stronger and certainly more iconic productions untouched by television; despite the production's success, LWT certainly agreed. In *The Listener*, Andrew Sinclair deemed it 'trivial and dated',[18] while Michael Church of *The Times* enjoyed the production against his expectations of 'an obscure confection by Agatha Christie', praising the script and the direction, and referencing the realities of television production when he wrote that 'The millions around the world on whom television co-productions are regularly foisted will in this case get their vicariously-spent money's worth'.[19] This reference to co-production acknowledges the realities of Christie's appeal to television producers at the time, who were not just looking at the home market. As the Agatha Christie brand grew, overshadowing even her own fictional creations, so too did the appeal for international broadcasters that were willing to collaborate or purchase productions. Here, thanks to more than half a century of publications and the well-received films of the prior decade, Christie had an inbuilt advantage. In part this explains the proliferation of her works on television from this point on, while the identity of the author was continually emphasised by the way that all licensed adaptations of Agatha Christie works now featured her name as part of the title; in later years this was stylised as her own signature in graphics and logos for each series or film.[20] The next production would only help to cement the positioning of Christie herself as a popular brand.

THE AGATHA CHRISTIE HOUR (1982)

The 'anything else' approach to procuring the rights to show any Agatha Christie adaptations on television at all continued with the next project for ITV viewers, *The Agatha Christie Hour*. This ten-part series was produced by Thames, which had no doubt seen the success of sister franchisee LWT's work and wanted to find a way to create a recurring series out of stories that had nothing in common other than their author.[21] Although John Brabourne was chairman of Thames at the time, he does not appear to have had any influence in this production, but Pat Sandys was brought on board from her work on the LWT adaptations to be the producer for the new show. This series may mark the point at which Agatha Christie as a brand emerged most fully, as Christie herself is the only linking element between these ten adaptations that cover some of the lesser-known areas in her catalogue of works. As far back as the late 1950s, MGM had expressed interest in using Christie herself as the centrepiece for a range of adaptations of her work that encompassed different characters and genres, but this time the emphasis steered away from the familiar types of mysteries for which Christie was so well known. Sandys referred to the series as ranging 'from the comedy thriller to romantic thriller', and while these two examples do not exactly run the gamut of genres, they do give a fair indication of what the show was all about: it covers some of the lighter or more character-based short stories from Christie, which—with two exceptions—do not feature any of her recurring characters. Sandys went on to say that 'They show a side of her that people just don't know. The stories illustrate that she was very wise, knew a lot about human beings, and could write with wit and compassion.'[22] As had previously been the case, months of negotiations took place before the series was agreed between the broadcaster and Agatha Christie Ltd, although no doubt Sandys herself was a positive influence on the agreement.

The ten episodes encompass a range of short stories, including two featuring Christie's 'love detective' Parker Pyne ('The Case of the Middle Aged Wife' and 'The Case of the Discontented Soldier'), which meant that this was the first time that an Agatha Christie character had appeared in more than one television production played by the same actor.[23] Joining Parker Pyne were three adventure stories from the 1934 collection *The Listerdale Mystery* ('The Girl in the Train', 'Jane in Search of a Job' and 'The Manhood of Edward Robinson'), and three stories that have implied or apparent supernatural elements from 1933's *The Hound of Death* ('The Red Signal', 'The Fourth Man' and 'The Mystery of the Blue Jar'). The ninth episode is 'Magnolia Blossom', a story of love in a difficult marriage that would form part of a published collection for the first time when a book accompanying the series was released, despite being one of Christie's earliest pieces of professional writing. The final story, 'In a Glass Darkly', had first been written for, but rejected by, the BBC in 1934 (see Chap. 3) and was later published in the posthumously released collection *Miss Marple's Final Cases and Two Other Stories*—the titular character does not appear, making this one of the 'others'.[24] With the exception of 'The Red Signal', which had been adapted for American television in 1952 as part of the *Suspense* anthology series, this was the first time that any of these stories had made it to the screen.[25] Most of the episodes were made entirely on videotape, including location scenes, and while the stories were often expanded somewhat in order to make an hour of television (with commercials), changes were minor and occasionally made for more satisfying resolutions. One such example of this is in 'The Mystery of the Blue Jar', where the eponymous object has one final secret that allows the charming lead character to finish the story on a more positive note. This episode was written by T.R. (Trevor) Bowen, who also adapted 'The Case of the Discontented Soldier'. To this point Bowen had mostly worked as an actor, with few writing credits to his name, but he would go on to write for some of the most esteemed dramas of the next decade, including Granada's *Sherlock Holmes* series and, more significantly, the BBC's *Miss Marple*, for which he adapted eight of the twelve novels, as well as a single episode of *Agatha Christie's Poirot* ('The Mystery of Hunter's Lodge' in 1992).

Had they been divorced from the Agatha Christie name there is little doubt that these stories would not have been considered strong candidates for television adaptation. That is not to say that they are poor or uninteresting pieces of fiction—in fact, they encompass some of the most endearing elements of Christie and, as Sandys indicated, they do emphasise a side to the author that had been little explored in previous adaptations. While the gentle nature of many of the stories seemed positively old-fashioned by 1982, audiences and critics alike reacted warmly to the series and welcomed the chance to watch dramas that may be lower on incident than either Christie's usual works or television drama of the period, but nevertheless present thought-provoking and interesting scenarios that concentrate more on what might be termed the human condition than high drama. The series was broadcast on Tuesdays at 9 p.m. and reactions to the first episode, 'The Case of the Middle-Aged Wife', showed that viewers were well aware that this was not what might be considered a traditional Christie, but welcomed a different type of series, such as in *Broadcast*'s review, which rather understated the subtlety of characterisation in some of Christie's more well-known works when it stated: 'Unlike the mystery stories which made her fame and fortune, [Christie's] characters in "The Case of the Middle Aged Wife" had dimension, insight and a life of their own. And we had time to absorb them [...] A delight.'[26] Similarly, the *Daily Express* welcomed the emphasis on characters, calling it a 'charmingly 1930s flirtation that every woman and every sympathetic man will enjoy'.[27] The series debuted on 7 September 1982, and the first two episodes were the fifth highest rating programmes of their weeks, beating everything shown on either of the BBC television channels, with 11.6 m tuning in for the first edition and 11.5 m for the second.

As well as the tie-in book of the same title, which republished stories adapted in the series, the programme had longevity beyond British television screens. It joined most of the ITV productions of the 1980s in being screened on PBS in America, as part of a Mobil-sponsored slot dedicated to drama, while the episode 'The Girl in the Train' was also awarded a gold medal at the 1983 International Film and TV Festival of New York. Although it is accessible through repeats and DVD releases, *The Agatha Christie Hour* tends to be rather overlooked, perhaps because of its general basis away from crime, as well as production values that would soon look outdated. However, its emergence as a popular and critical success should remind us that the strengths of Christie's work do not always lie in her well-plotted mysteries—her other works, such as her character-led non-crime stories written under the pseudonym Mary Westmacott, may also be strong candidates for adaptation. Over the years, Agatha Christie Ltd has been approached by some parties interested in adapting these very titles, and there is every chance that any resulting production could be a success.

TOMMY AND TUPPENCE ON TELEVISION

By the summer of 1982 it would have been fair for the teams behind the LWT and Thames productions to believe that they had now proven their worth to Agatha Christie Ltd. Certainly, LWT was starting to feel that it needed a recurring character so as to develop a series of Agatha Christie adventures, rather than a set of costly one-off films based on less marketable individual books. Mathew Prichard points out that, despite the success of the ventures to date, Christie's two biggest characters were not available: 'I think [Brian Stone] was softening us up a bit so he could then move on to Miss Marple and Poirot. But

I think he knew that, especially my mother, was never going to allow him to go straight into the Miss Marple and Poirot [stories].' Although negotiations with the BBC regarding a series of Miss Marple mysteries were in the earliest stages, Poirot was firmly off the table and it took some difficulty to convince Rosalind Hicks to allow the third best-known names in the Christie canon to come to television—Tommy and Tuppence Beresford. The couple had made their debut in Christie's second novel, 1922's *The Secret Adversary*, where they are reunited several years after having first been friends, and end up falling in love. Their married life as private detectives was chronicled in the short story collection *Partners in Crime*, published in 1929, which was then followed by three more novels, including the final one written by Christie, 1973's *Postern of Fate*. While clearly secondary to Poirot and Miss Marple in terms of cultural impact, the characters are nevertheless very popular among her fans and depict a particular type of Christie that had been successfully adapted in the previous LWT productions—1920s fashionable characters moving in interesting social circles who tend to treat mysteries like a game to pass the time.

Interest in the series was motivated not only by LWT but also the oil giant Mobil, which had shown interest in purchasing more Christie titles for its sponsored drama slot on public television in the United States. Having proven their success playing similar roles in the previous two LWT productions, Francesca Annis and James Warwick were brought on board to play the crime-solving team, with Warwick telling the press that Mobil had particular aims in mind, referencing another series that concentrated on a crime-fighting married couple: 'They wanted something like *Hart to Hart*,' he said, 'but with a 1920s flavour.'[28] A comparison to the contemporary ABC series (1979–84) starring Robert Wagner and Stefanie Powers might seem surprising, but is perhaps indicative of just how broad the stated aims of any given co-producer could be.

It was soon decided that the series would constitute ten hour-long episodes drawn from the *Partners in Crime* collection (stories dealing with an overarching villain, as well as those covering the setting up of the agency, were dispensed with), which would follow on from a two-hour television film of the novel *The Secret Adversary*. Production would be headed by Jack Williams once more, with Pat Sandys and Tony Wharmby on duty to write the script for the opening film of *The Secret Adversary*, although more writers and directors were brought on board for the *Partners in Crime* series itself. Filming began on the series in early 1982, with production on seven episodes, which were largely shot in studio on videotape in the same way that interior scenes for the previous two LWT adaptations had been, with location filming carried out when needed. After seven episodes completed production, a pause took place so that filming could take place on *The Secret Adversary*.[29] Here, the production methods changed, and for the first time British television elected to produce an entire Christie story on film, with shooting taking place around the Home Counties and London for five weeks beginning in late July 1982. Once the opening film had been completed, the crew and key cast members returned to the studio to make the three final episodes in production, 'The Unbreakable Alibi', 'The Case of the Missing Lady' and 'The Crackler'.

The production history for this series is significant, since it signalled how Christie adaptations of this era were caught between the old and new ways of producing prestigious television dramas. Just as the series entered pre-production, so Granada also announced its intention to make a series of Sir Arthur Conan Doyle's *Sherlock Holmes* stories, this time shot entirely on film with an eye on international sales and longevity, as well as marking out the programme as a high-class production. As a result of this forethought *Sherlock Holmes* is still regularly sold and shown around the world and is now available in high definition, in which it has been broadcast and released, meaning that the show has barely dated since its first transmission. Conversely, *Partners in Crime* was produced in such a way that it failed to reap the advantages of either the old system for high-profile literary adaptations (simple, relatively inexpensive productions) nor the new (filmic) way.

Speaking at the time, Vic Gardiner, head of LWT International, claimed: 'Particularly on the drama side we are now moving very emphatically towards film [...] For example, we made the Christie film *The Secret Adversary*, but when it came to the follow up series *Partners in Crime* it would have been too great a speculation to do the whole thing on film.'[30] It is difficult to reconcile this thinking with the facts, since Gardiner also acknowledges that high-end videotaped dramas like *Partners in Crime* actually cost nearly the same as all-film productions. Although he cited the series as an example of something unlikely to sell to the USA, the pre-sale to Mobil for PBS broadcast demonstrates that this simply was not true.[31] Instead, the issue was actually tied to LWT's lack of resources when it came to producing series on film—an unfortunate situation that would soon leave *Partners in Crime* with limited attraction for international markets. Had it been made a few years later it seems likely that the whole series would have been shot on film, and it could have had the same lasting appeal to broadcasters as the later Miss Marple and Poirot adaptations, which hardly show their age. By comparison, with its studio-based episodes it stands out as a style of drama that simply does not exist any more, outside of soap operas. Although the series has been repeated many times and is commercially available, it is very much a distant third to those dealing with Christie's two better-known creations.

The television film of *The Secret Adversary* certainly sets high expectations for Tommy and Tuppence, since a dynamic script by Pat Sandys manages to preserve the often baffling rollercoaster of events that Christie depicted, as her two lead characters endeavour to find out the truth about a mysterious 'Jane Finn'. Tony Wharmby's direction features several striking moments, not least the sepia-tinted flashbacks showing the sinking of the *Lusitania* that motivates much of the plot, while an excellent guest cast is headed by *Avengers* and James Bond star Honor Blackman. However, the series of *Partners in Crime* that follows it struggles to maintain this carefully tuned balance between plot, characterisation and humour. There are positives, such as Reece Dinsdale's perfectly cast appearance as film-obsessed bellboy (and, later, assistant) Albert, while costume and set design are exemplary. However, there is no avoiding the limitations of multi-camera studio production, and this method means that the performances of the cast are over-relied on to induce atmosphere or indicate tone. Warwick and Annis acquit themselves extremely well, but are given a near impossible task to keep up the jovial atmosphere at all times without irritating the audience—given the thin nature of many of the original stories (a deliberate choice by Christie, who had hardly envisaged them being stretched out to nearly an hour), the series is crying out for visual flair beyond Annis's impressively elaborate costumes, as well as stylishness that surpasses what can be achieved in a videotape studio. This is exactly the sort of production where style is sometimes needed in order to make up for the lack of substance. For example, as previously pointed out, in the story 'The Case of the Missing Lady' a crime has not even been committed, while 'The Unbreakable Alibi' relies on a twist so obvious to the viewer that it makes the crime-fighting duo seem complete dullards—a blow that would have been cushioned by lavish production values. For the 1989 *Agatha Christie's Poirot* series, the lighter or shorter stories featured additional characters and sub-plots (often of a humorous type) that helped to maintain the attention, but here existing material is often stretched beyond breaking point. However, there is much to like about the series, not least the excellent performances, and excessive criticism seems cruel given its apparent intentions to be lighter than the darker crime and adventure dramas that populated television at the time; it is well placed as a piece of Sunday-night entertainment. Perhaps if the programme could have been more confident in its generic boundaries, and decided on a clearer balance between humour and drama, it would have been more effective, since sometimes the outright comedy works well, as do some of the more dramatic moments—when the villain dies of shock after having their bed set alight in 'The House of Lurking Death', there is a real sense of surprise that such viciousness can rear its head in this series.

From beginning to end, *Partners in Crime* found itself in conflict. In March 1982, tabloid newspaper *The Sun* reported that this new LWT series was a potential rival to Thames's *The Agatha Christie Hour*, which was nearing the end of its production, with spokespeople from both companies saying that they were aware of each other's projects. LWT pointed out that it did not intend to broadcast *Partners in Crime* until 1983—the possibility of a clash may explain why the series sat on the shelf for so long before broadcasts finally began almost a year after production had ended.[32] Held over until the peak of the television year, in October 1983, it then faced serious opposition from the BBC when *The Secret Adversary* was first broadcast opposite only the second British television screening of the classic 1939 film *Gone with the Wind* (d. Victor Fleming). Warren Breach, controller of programme planning for LWT, claimed that the scheduling was an attempt 'to try to kill the undoubted success of our Agatha Christie movies', although the BBC denied this and pointed out that the corporation did not 'cry foul every time ITV puts on a James Bond film'.[33]

Although *The Secret Adversary* followed the formula of the two success-ful previous productions, critical response was negative. Herbert Krezmer's review in the *Daily Mail* was headlined 'What a Tupenny dreadful!', while the review itself called the film a 'rubbishy tale' with an 'indigestible script [that] relied almost entirely on coincidences'—although such reliance on chance was a fault of the original novel.[34] Hilary Kingsley in the *Daily Mirror* was equally unimpressed, writing that 'some of us chaps rather think two hours was about an hour and a half more than these upperclass twits with their overdressed, over-mannered nonsense deserved [...] I can't care tuppence for this.'[35] Nancy Banks-Smith for *The Guardian* found it over-complicated and pointed out that Christie was 'a unique social historian. *The Secret Adversary* tells you a good deal about the attitudes, slang, assumptions and trivia of the 1920s. The dramatization less so.'[36] Almost all reviews commended the lavish production standards, including Francesca Annis's ever-changing wardrobe, but bemoaned that they had apparently been wasted on a story that was not deemed worth all the effort. Gethyn Stoodley Thomas of the *Western Mail* wrote that 'No matter how you dress up rubbish, rubbish it remains'.[37] Julie Davidson of the *Glasgow Herald* was more positive, saying that 'Shorter adaptations will suit them better'.[38]

Unfortunately, if such a claim were true then it was not reflected in the critical notices received by the series proper. Reviewing 'The House of Lurking Death', Richard Last in the *Daily Telegraph* wrote that 'The only serious whodunit question it poses is: who killed off LWT's once flourishing drama department?',[39] while Maureen Paton of the *Daily Express* liked the lightness of tone, claiming that 'the incidental comedy's the thing', perhaps uninten-tionally highlighting its uneasy straddling of genres.[40] By the end of the series it seems to have been widely accepted as unsuccessful. Ratings had opened at over 10 m (seeing off the BBC's transmission of *Gone with the Wind* after all), peaking at over 12 m for 'The House of Lurking Death', but by the time it returned after Christmas, interest at LWT seems to have waned: its transmis-sion time was moved from the peak slot of 7.45 p.m. on a Sunday, which it had occupied for its first eight episodes, to directly opposite popular BBC produc-tion *Bergerac* on a Saturday evening for its final episode, which was watched by fewer than 6 m people.[41] Even the reception of the series in the United States was frostier than usual; John J. O'Connor in his *New York Times* review wrote that 'Its efforts to be lighthearted will leave you either slightly giddy or mildly irritated', claiming that it was for serious Anglophiles only.[42] 'So why is Agatha Christie's *Partners in Crime* not working, coming over with the heady flavour of a wet blanket?' asked Stanley Eveling of *The Scotsman* at the conclusion of the series.[43] Eveling put the blame at Christie's door, writing that 'the dim-mest crossworder can solve the problems this series has on offer'. Even before transmission it is unlikely that more Tommy and Tuppence adventures would have been filmed, since shortly after the series premiered James Warwick was quoted as saying 'I shan't be doing any more Agatha Christie [...] The scripts are fun but I want to do something stronger.'[44] Such comments reinforced the fact that although Christie may have found some of her recent popular success as a result of television, engrained snobbery against her continued.

Such reactions highlight the problem of making light and comedic mysteries into fully fledged dramas—the expectations of the audience may not match the intentions of the source material, an increasingly difficult problem once a particular 'brand' for Agatha Christie had been established as complex whodunits. When this collection was published it would have been clear to readers that the stories were all pastiches of different fictional detectives, a point that has been lost on most readers in later years, and the removal of this element for the series forces the mysteries to operate independently. However, among Christie fans the series has a stronger reputation, since it does feature close adaptations of some of Christie's more overlooked adventures, with a cast that was warmly received and many entertaining episodes on offer. As for the rivalry between Thames and LWT, while Thames bowed out from any future Christie adaptations, it did secure the upper hand in commercial and critical terms—*The Secret Adversary* took bronze for entertainment drama programming at the 1983 International Film and TV Festival of New York, at the same ceremony that saw *The Agatha Christie Hour*'s 'The Girl in the Train' awarded gold. *Partners in Crime* did win an Emmy for outstanding graphic and title design at the 1985 ceremony. The series saw a temporary end to the relationship between Agatha Christie Ltd and LWT; Prichard recalls thinking that they 'rather gave up on us because we were obviously not going to do Poirot at that stage'. The Belgian detective's time in the sun would soon come, nevertheless, and LWT would play a key role in his successful appearance on the small screen.

MURDER BY THE BOOK AND THE LAST SEANCE (1986)

While hardly an outright failure, the treatment of, and reaction to, *Partners in Crime* indicated that interest in Christie's works on television may have been waning. The next two chapters demonstrate that the Warner Bros. television movies and the BBC's rapturously received adaptations of Miss Marple were plenty for the casual viewer. Without a key character such as Poirot there was no way for ITV to compete—and it would take until 1989 for a series starring the Belgian sleuth to make it to television screens. In the meantime, ITV made only two original productions related to Christie for the rest of the decade—and both were unusual, albeit in different ways.

The first, *Murder by the Book*, is undoubtedly the odder of the two, but has a charm all of its own. The hour-long drama may have starred Hercule Poirot, but it was not an adaptation of any of Christie's stories—instead, it featured the detective (played by Ian Holm) meeting Christie herself (Dame Peggy Ashcroft) just as the author mulls over killing off her creation by publishing his final novel, *Curtain*. The one-off drama could hardly have been more prestigious: both cast members had been highly acclaimed members of the acting profession for many years, with Ashcroft taking on the project so that they could work together, while the programme itself was shot on 35 mm film, rather than the 16 mm usually afforded to television productions (including the BBC *Miss Marple* and ITV *Poirot* series). *Murder by the Book*, which had an alternative working title of *Murder by Writing*, was made by TVS, the company that held the ITV franchise for parts of the South of England, which was keen to use it as a way of emphasising its commitment to quality productions, since it was a relatively new part of ITV (having started broadcasting in 1982) and had been best known for children's and light entertainment programming. Publicising it in the trade press as a 'razor sharp comedy thriller', TVS used the production as part of an advertising campaign asserting that it would be able to compete with the bigger and better-established franchisees, such as LWT and Thames. The following year TVS would make its most successful step into drama when it launched *The Ruth Rendell Mysteries* (1987–92).

The film was the brainchild of Nick Evans, who wrote and directed the piece having previously worked on arts documentary programme *The South Bank Show* (ITV/Sky 1978–). He set the film in 1975 and laced the dialogue between Christie and Poirot with many points of discussion based on the truth of Christie's decision to write the novel during the war, with publication designed to be delayed until after her death (although, in the event, it was published shortly before she passed away). The dialogue between the two is often humorous, especially during a discussion of the actors who had taken on the role—Poirot is genuinely hurt when the prospect of David Niven is dismissed because he is deemed too good looking, while the often-repeated claim that Christie only disliked Finney's moustache is reiterated here. For his part, Poirot is particularly aggrieved that he was replaced in two films of his work by the 'untrained senile spinster'(!) Miss Marple, which had happened in two of the Margaret Rutherford pictures, revealing how well the writer knew his subject. When Poirot retires to the privacy of the bathroom to read his own demise, having stolen the manuscript, it is a genuinely affecting scene, while we can also feel Christie's frustration with both the situation and the character. The film may be rather idiosyncratic in its form but in terms of the human story behind it, the situation is well depicted in an affectionate and highly engaging manner. As Christie says in defence of her decision during the film, she would not want Poirot 'stranded in limbo, or worse still, a prey to writers who would exploit you—not look after you properly—like they did to poor James Bond. That would be so humiliating to you.'

Production took place in Hertfordshire during early winter 1985, with transmission scheduled for the following year in order to mark a decade since Christie's death (in the United States it was finally seen in 1990 to mark a century since her birth). Broadcast across most of the ITV network on 28 August 1986, *Murder by the Book* was well received. In *The Times*, Peter Davelle pointed out that both Poirot and Christie felt real, with no dialogue or actions that seemed alien to them.[45] Critics praised the performances, with Nancy Banks-Smith calling it a 'brilliant little psychological thriller', while she betrayed her allegiance to Poirot when she wrote that she could never forgive Christie for 'making him the murderer' in *Curtain*.[46]

The second of ITV's curios followed the next month, with the broadcast of an adaptation of Christie's short story 'The Last Seance', which had been published as part of *The Hound of Death* collection in 1933. In common with several others in the book, 'The Last Seance' is an example of a Christie story that offers only a supernatural explanation of events, something more common early in her career, before her work was dominated by murder-mystery novels. This adaptation formed part of the second series of the anthology show *Shades of Darkness*, made by the ITV franchise for North West England, Granada Television. Planned to be one of three mysteries made for the second run of the show, as it turned out it was one of only two broadcast under the series title. Adapted by Alfred Shaughnessy, best known for his work writing and script editing *Upstairs Downstairs* (ITV, 1971–75) for LWT, 'The Last Seance' was produced and directed by June Wyndham-Davies, who would also produce Granada's *Sherlock Holmes* series from 1986 until the final episode in 1994.

This adaptation of the story of French medium Simone's contact with a dead child of the mysterious Madame Exe is a lavish production, shot entirely on film in specially constructed sets during October 1984. The production has much in common with the BBC's run of ghost stories for Christmas, which were produced during the 1970s. As with 'The Last Seance', these productions had concentrated on period adaptations of eerie stories rather than visceral horror—titles had included Charles Dickens's *The Signalman* and M.R. James's *A Warning to the Curious*. Certainly 'The Last Seance' effectively construes a sense of creeping unease throughout, with exemplary art direction and production design giving a disquieting depiction of 1933 Paris. The adaptation follows the original story reasonably closely, although it extends it beyond Christie's finale, and cultivates a strongly unsettling atmosphere through special effects (including effective lighting) as well as sound design that appreciates the strength of using silence. The key cast is made up of British actor Anthony Higgins as Simone's lover Raoul, while Simone herself is played by Norma West, who would also appear in episodes of *Partners in Crime*, *Miss Marple* and *Poirot*, with renowned French film actress Jeanne Moreau joining them as Madame Exe.

In the event, the production was not broadcast until nearly two years after it was made, finally being shown late in the evening on Saturday, 27 September 1986, months after the previous episode of the series, indicating that it was a programme in which the network had lost interest.[47] This is a great shame, as it is a production that has an excellent pedigree and effectively achieves what it sets out to do. It is especially unfortunate that neither 'The Last Seance' nor *Murder by the Book* has ever received a commercial release or a national repeat in the UK, since both have aged well and deserve to be seen.[48] A DVD release of *Shades of Darkness* omitted the Christie adaptation, indicating rights issues, while TVS's archive is in legal limbo following its acquisition by Disney several years ago. By contrast, Chap. 12 will show that the next time ITV tackled Agatha Christie, it created a series whose longevity has kept it in the public eye for over a quarter of a century. However, in the meantime, Christie stories faced a resurgence of attention in one of the most difficult markets of all—American television.

NOTES

1. Interview with the author, August 2013.
2. Interview with the author, August 2013.
3. £6.50 a minute for a maximum of four minutes; costings attached to memo from Jenny Walker to Ben Travers, 8 February 1978 (BBC Written Archive Centre: Agatha Christie, Copyright, 1975—(RCONT21)).
4. *Variety*, 23 May 1979.
5. *The Stage and Television Today*, 24 May 1979.
6. *The Stage and Television Today*, 24 May 1979.
7. *The Stage and Television Today*, 19 July 1979. In the event only three of the Potter films were produced.
8. Although it was originally felt that it would probably be transmitted in three parts, early reports are quite clear that this is only an option—and so this should not necessarily be considered to be a decision forced by circumstance.
9. *The Times*, 29 March 1980.
10. Interview with the author, August 2013.
11. *Variety*, 9 April 1980.
12. *The Times*, 31 March 1980; *Daily Mirror*, 5 April 1980.
13. *The Guardian*, 31 March 1980.
14. *Screen International*, 12 April 1980.
15. *The Stage and Television Today*, 15 September 1983.
16. The gap between location filming and the studio recording may simply be because August weather would be more amenable to exterior scenes than the winter; alternatively, it may have been due to actor availability, which was often a factor in the scheduling of prestige productions with high-profile (and therefore busy) cast members.
17. *Sunday Express*, 15 February 1981.
18. *The Listener*, 12 March 1981.
19. *The Times*, 9 March 1981.
20. For reasons of both brevity and readability I have generally omitted *Agatha Christie's...* from the names of productions beyond the first mention in each chapter. Although such a credit had not been unusual prior to this point, the use of Christie's name in the title was now a permanent fixture.
21. Thames operated the commercial television franchise between Mondays and Fridays, handing over to LWT on Friday evening.
22. *Broadcast*, 16 August 1982.
23. Parker Pyne is played by Maurice Denham, joined for both episodes by Angela Easterling as Miss Lemon, as well as Lally Bowers as Ariadne

Oliver in 'The Case of the Discontented Soldier'. These latter two characters are perhaps most familiar to readers and viewers of Agatha Christie as friends and colleagues of Poirot.

24. As was normal with Christie, all of these short stories were published in periodicals prior to being collected in book form.
25. See Chap. 4 for more on the earlier adaptation.
26. *Broadcast*, 20 September 1982.
27. *Daily Express*, 7 September 1982.
28. *Daily Mirror*, 26 June 1982.
29. It is not that case, as some have speculated, that the film was effectively a pilot for the series—instead, it was always envisaged as a one-off, prestige production to introduce the characters prior to the full series.
30. *Screen International*, 23 April 1983.
31. Gardiner was surely not thinking about sales to a US network, which was nearly unheard of for British drama at this time.
32. *The Sun*, 13 March 1982.
33. *Evening Standard*, 7 October 1983.
34. *Daily Mail*, 10 October 1983.
35. *Daily Mirror*, 10 October 1983.
36. *The Guardian*, 10 October 1983.
37. *Western Mail*, 15 October 1983.
38. *Glasgow Herald*, 15 October 1983.
39. *Daily Telegraph*, 24 October 1983.
40. *Daily Express*, 24 October 1983.
41. Perhaps tellingly, the popular *Bergerac* was a series shot all on film.
42. *The New York Times*, 29 November 1984.
43. *The Scotsman*, 21 January 1984.
44. *Daily Mirror*, 29 October 1983.
45. *The Times*, 28 August 1986.
46. *The Guardian*, 29 August 1986. In truth, the reality is a little more complex than that, but he does indeed commit murder.
47. Shown at different times, between 10 p.m. and 11 p.m., depending on region.
48. The DVD release of *Shades of Darkness* in the United States pointedly removes this episode.

Chapter 10: New Approaches

Spoilers: *Murder Is Easy; Witness for the Prosecution; They Do It with Mirrors; And Then There Were None*

This chapter looks at the movies made for American television during the 1980s, as well as the handful of standalone English-language theatrical films from both the 1980s and 1990s that do not comfortably sit within the categories explored in previous chapters. These films are reflective of attempts to make adaptations of Christie's work find a new permanent place on the big or small screen—either through updated thrillers for television, or artistically driven adaptations for the cinema that do not adopt the by now traditional approach of a star-studded murder mystery that had been popularised by the Brabourne pictures since 1974's *Murder on the Orient Express*. Some of these approaches bore fruit and were returned to, while others were dead-ends in terms of critical or commercial impact, but almost all demonstrate an attempt to reinvigorate and refresh the idea of what an Agatha Christie adaptation could be like.

The television movies covered in this chapter have achieved a degree of infamy among both armchair and professional critics, who have often dismissed them as characterless and dull, even before considering the impact of the decision to rework them in order to give them a contemporary setting. Certainly, they are usually seen as poor relations to their British counterparts—something that is repeatedly drawn attention to when they are reshown on television. However, although they generally perform poorly as adaptations, they did have a purpose to serve beyond satisfying Christie fans, and their very existence tells us a great deal about how the Christie brand continued to rise even as the success of cinema adaptations of her work was on the wane. 'Not every British property gets the offer to make TV films for a network in America', points out Mathew Prichard, referring to the origins of the CBS/Warner Bros. deal in the late 1970s. 'I think I'm right in saying not any more common then than it is now.'[1] This is one of the key issues with a literary legacy such as Agatha Christie—in order for it to survive it needs not only to satisfy current fans, but to find ways to appeal to new audiences who might not usually take an interest in the heri-

© The Author(s) 2016
M. Aldridge, *Agatha Christie on Screen*,
DOI 10.1057/978-1-137-37292-5_11

tage or nostalgic form of Christie stories that was usually depicted. There is also the fact that Agatha Christie Ltd is a business that serves more than just the family—by this point 64 % of the company was owned by Booker-McConnell, a division of the food wholesalers which had first bought a stake in 1968 (this stake in the company would later be sold to the production company Chorion, and then Acorn Media). As Prichard further points out: 'The money was quite attractive so I have a feeling that our partners, Booker, would have been really quite upset if we'd refused.'[2] As a result, a deal was struck for at least five television movies to be made from Christie properties by Warner Bros. Television, subsidiary of the famous film studio, to be shown on the American television network CBS, with sales of each film to broadcasters around the world.

MURDER IS EASY (1982), SPARKLING CYANIDE (1983) AND WITNESS FOR THE PROSECUTION (1982)

When the deal with Warner Bros. Television was publicly announced in August 1979, it was accompanied by a list of five Christie titles that the studio had acquired for adaptation. These were all standalone mysteries that did not star any of her big-name detectives; the titles cited were *Murder Is Easy, The Man in the Brown Suit, They Came to Baghdad, Destination Unknown* and *The Secret of Chimneys*.[3] In the event, although the studio made more than five Agatha Christie television movies across the next decade, only the first two of these novels ended up being adapted. The presence of *The Secret of Chimneys* in the deal no doubt explains why the title was never seriously considered by London Weekend Television (as it shares so many similarities with its successful television productions of *Why Didn't They Ask Evans?* and *The Seven Dials Mystery* that it might have been a natural continuation), but neither it nor *Destination Unknown* appears to have made it as far as serious pre-production. The reports of the deal also claimed that it granted exclusivity of the works of Christie's titles while the films were in production or airing, although this must have had exceptions and conditions—nevertheless, the later decision of Warner Bros. to make two Miss Marple films in place of two of its originally optioned titles was to have an impact on the BBC series starring Joan Hickson that launched in 1984, as the next chapter will show.

Executive producer on these new films was Stan Margulies, who had previously had the same position on the acclaimed series *Roots* (ABC, 1977), while the deal was brokered by the president of Warner Bros. Television's programming, Alan Shayne. Shayne was to be instrumental in the negotiations with Agatha Christie Ltd and, most especially, Christie's daughter Rosalind Hicks. When conversation turns to these television films, Mathew Prichard always recalls one thing above all others—the charm of Shayne himself. 'He became a friend,' he remembers, 'he stayed at Greenway, he stayed in Wales [where Prichard lives], he was hospitable to us in Los Angeles. My mother hated his films but he was a really nice and persuasive man.'[4] In his autobiography, where his memories are intertwined with those of his husband, Norman Sunshine,

Shayne remembers the culture shock of visiting the family. When Rosalind offered to show him Greenway's garden on a rainy day, he was baffled by the extensive woodland: 'I kept feeling like a gauche American,' he wrote, 'but I was so unprepared for English country living.'[5]

Shayne was the latest in a short line of people working high up in the film and television industry who discovered that the personal touch was the best way to encourage successful negotiations with the Christie family. There has never been any shortage of speculative attempts to secure rights to Christie properties that happen to pique the interest of any given producer or studio (or, particularly vaguely, interest in securing 'an Agatha Christie'); often these follow on from Christie adaptations that have been a particular success for a different producer or studio, and the residual interest tends to be a simple attempt to reproduce this. Such approaches have usually been viewed with caution or summarily dismissed, particularly when Christie was alive. However, when a specific proposal that is better thought through is brought to the table, more interest is shown. In this case, one can see that it would be difficult to dismiss the option of reaching a wide and fresh audience for Agatha Christie through these television films. There was also a particular vision for these features, which would be updated to the present day, as seen in Chap. 8, where Peter Ustinov's Poirot made a three-film detour to the 1980s, before falling back into period for his final appearance at the cinema. Also, although the films featured many American cast members, they often offered a heavy dose of Britishness, in terms of both location and cast. Not all were a success, but in the sense of using the essence of Christie while competing with contemporary action series on television, they strike a better balance than could have been the case.

By late 1980 pre-production had commenced on the first two of the five films, which were expected to be made in mid-1981 for transmission the following year. First up was *Murder Is Easy*, an adaptation of the 1939 novel that has much in common with the style of some of Christie's Miss Marple mysteries, as a string of apparently accidental and natural deaths in a country village may be something more sinister. The film stars Bill Bixby, best known for playing Bruce Banner in *The Incredible Hulk* (CBS, 1978–82), in the lead role of Professor Luke Williams, a computer scientist from America who heads the investigation. Naturally, this had not been the profession of the character from the novel, Luke Fitzwilliam, who is a retired policeman returning from India—British director of the film Claude Whatham explained the change at the time, saying that 'by making him a computer expert, it certainly puts it into 1981, as well as giving him the kind of logical, orderly mind which is accustomed to problem solving'.[6] Inevitably, these overt attempts at updating the story are now the most dated elements of the whole picture, far beyond anything conceived by Christie. In particular, a red-herring situation where a list of facts and suspects is fed into a huge computer in order to 'solve' the case is now unintentionally hilarious. However, this type of character is in keeping with the style of American television at the time, and the creation of a production that slotted into popular audience tastes in the United States was the main reason for bringing the stories to the small screen at all. Stan Margulies explained that moving the plot to the modern day not only allowed a quicker pace for proceedings, but made it feel more like other shows on television, finishing his outline with a typically blunt request for characterisation for the films he produced:

> While I knew we couldn't have the pace of an American cops and robbers show, I wanted it to have at least a little of that excitement [...] Also, I was very worried about period acting—the thin border line between camp and arch, and being correct. So I wanted the whole storyline brought up to date—including the suggestion that a love affair is more than platonic. Obviously we're not going for an R-rating [...] it wouldn't be in keeping with the spirit of the stories. But as I said to my writers, even though this is an Agatha Christie, could we at least have the feeling that someone gets laid?[7]

Murder Is Easy cost $2.1 m, at the higher end of TV movie budgets, and was mostly filmed in England across four weeks in July 1981, using Pinewood Studios for interiors and the village of Hambledon in Hampshire for many of the location scenes. The cast and crew worked from a script by Carmen Culver, using the original British title rather than *Easy to Kill*, under which it had been published in the United States; Culver specialised in melodrama and would soon adapt novel *The Thorn Birds* for a popular 1983 miniseries on the ABC network. Joining Bixby in the cast is *Upstairs Downstairs* star Leslie-Anne Down, playing Bridget Conway, a fellow investigator into the crimes, with whom Williams strikes up a romantic relationship. However, the most prestigious cast member is undoubtedly Olivia de Havilland, winner of two Academy Awards for Best Actress, in the role of Honoria Waynflete, an old lady in the village, while her ill-fated friend Lavinia Fullerton is played by Helen Hayes, whose brief but important performance no doubt put her at the top of the list when producers were soon looking to cast Miss Marple for two TV movies of her own.

Whatever the deficiencies of the Warner Bros. television movies, Christie's plots remained largely intact despite the 'window dressing' changes to period, location or character. The producers recognised that Christie had supplied them with excellent source material that in many ways lent itself well to the contemporary expectations of action and adventure series. Director Whatham pointed out that 'There are many things about the Agatha Christie novels which remain valid. A typical example is her heroines, who are incredible. You don't have to do much with them because they're spunky, fast on their feet, resourceful—young ladies ahead of their time.'[8] The real issue with *Murder Is Easy,* and several of the Warner Bros. television movies that followed it, is the lack of directorial flair or energy in the proceedings. Whatham seems less interested in the central mystery than he is in both the romance and, more particularly, the computer science gimmicks, at which point the editing and camera work become rather more innovative and interesting.[9] This interest in the present day is firmly established by opening with Luke using a (then) modern calculator, later followed by his persistent mocking of the local policeman's apparently archaic bicycle, and a resolution that involves rather more physical action than Christie had used—but akin to other series on television. Nevertheless, the opening section where Lavinia explains that she thinks she has identified a murderer, and ends up being killed in a road traffic accident, is well presented and nicely shocking, while overall the film is generally enjoyable, doing well to preserve the identity of the murderer—at least, until one remembers that the relative fame of those on the cast list often signals the identity of the villain. Mathew Prichard recalls that, initially at least, the Warner Bros. TV movies served their function perfectly well:

> I would even say that the early Warner Brothers adaptations—*Murder Is Easy* and *Sparkling Cyanide*—are actually not too bad. But we did them for an American audience. I think what people don't realise is we have always been a family company. We're not making films to watch in our own living rooms. We're making films for other people to enjoy wherever they live, whether that's in America, or China, or wherever. So it stands to reason that you make films for the market in which they intend to operate, and they won't always look the same. We try to ensure that everything we authorise [is] recognisable as something she might have written.[10]

By any measure, the deal's first television movie was a success. First broadcast on CBS on 2 January 1982, it was the 34th highest ranking TV movie for the entire 1981–82 season (in a field of well over 100 titles), while it was also the 19th highest rated programme for the week—no mean feat—even beating programmes such as the hugely popular *Magnum PI* (NBC, 1980–88). When it debuted in the UK, on Monday, 3 May on ITV, it did even better, attracting 14.2 m viewers, putting it second for the week (behind an episode of *Coronation Street*) and sixth highest rated of the whole month (behind five episodes of the soap opera). It was indifferently received by the critics, however—John J. O'Connor of *The New York Times* rightly surmised that 'the whole of *Murder is Easy* is not equal to the sum of its parts. Carmen Culver's script keeps sputtering and backtracking just when everything should be running smoothly and unobtrusively.'[11]

As the cameras rolled on *Murder Is Easy*, plans were afoot for the follow-up film—although they were soon to change. Up to this point, it had been envisaged that the next film would be Christie's international espionage thriller *They Came to Baghdad*. The story had only been brought to the screen once before, as a live television production in 1952, but this time it was to be given a budget surpassing even the $2.1 m allocated to *Murder Is Easy*.[12] A script had been written by William Hanley, who wrote the screenplays for several prestigious television productions including NBC's star-studded *Little Gloria… Happy at Last* from 1982, which told the story of the famous

Vanderbilt custody case, but his adaptation was never produced. The precise reason for this is not clear, but the likelihood is that the story simply was not filmable on the budget available. Later in this chapter we will see that when a similar thriller, *The Man in the Brown Suit*, was adapted in 1989, it included careful scripting to allow much of the action to take place in locations that could be recreated close to Los Angeles or during a limited shoot in Spain. As with this later adaptation, the *Baghdad* story was contemporised, but the old-fashioned themes of globe-trotting adventure and spying mean that while the proposed production may have been set in the then 'present day', it also feels nostalgic and old-fashioned in tone. As with the 1952 production, the script establishes that the film is a mystery of sorts from early on, rather than the travelogue-cum-adventure story of the early portion of Christie's novel. Characters and situations are quickly established—we learn that Victoria Jones (an American in the script) is bored with her job, from which she is then fired anyway. After a chance meeting with a charming man called Edward, she decides to follow him to Baghdad. In the book this is seen to be a spur-of-the-moment decision, and Victoria spends quite some time looking for Edward once she arrives in the city. However, the script establishes early on that Edward has contrived to bring Victoria to Iraq, having noted her physical similarity to another character called Anna Scheele, and they immediately meet up once she has arrived.

The audience might not be aware precisely what these events mean for our heroine, but it does mean that those watching know from the very beginning that Victoria is in the middle of manipulated events—a revelation that comes later in the novel. This helps to establish genre early on, and simplifies the narrative somewhat, but as with the 1952 production it means that our lead character knows less than the audience for quite some time, making her seem naïve at best. The script retains the novel's reliance on coincidence, but lavish location filming and high production standards would help to paper over the cracks and divert attention from some of the less believable plot developments, such as the ramifications of Victoria's almost randomly chosen pseudonym. Such reliance on style over clear narrative may be the reason this project was not pursued beyond pre-production—the budget needed would be considerably higher than the more straightforward likes of *Murder Is Easy*. The script is breezy, with some nice moments (such as when Edward cannot properly hear when someone mentions Victoria due to the sound of a helicopter and so, in typically British fashion, just smiles as if he had heard and moves on), and condenses the story into a manageable but inconsistent 90 minutes, but the tone veers wildly between drama and comedy, while there is a somewhat perfunctory resolution to events when the lead villains are arrested off screen and just seen being escorted in handcuffs.

In the event, the next two films into production from this deal were not titles that had been part of the original contract—one was *A Caribbean Mystery* (which will soon be discussed alongside its follow-up, 1985's *Murder with Mirrors*) and the other the 1945 mystery *Sparkling Cyanide*. This is a story that allows producers to be more flexible with their budget, and consequently their storytelling, as the focus of the mystery is a poisoning at a dinner party, which can be recreated as lavishly or economically as they wish. Once more updated, this production moved the action to Pasadena, California and is more overt in its attempts to ape contemporary trends in action-orientated television; when the action pauses for a water-skiing action sequence in the final act, this is more of hat tip to the likes of *Knight Rider* (NBC, 1982–86) than homage to Christie's penchant for surfing. Similarly, the refinement of the novel's dinner party is replaced by the amusing brashness of *Dynasty*-era glamour (ABC, 1981–89). The awkward mix of styles, and uneven pace, across the film might in part be credited to the presence of the three screenplay writers with unexceptional professional histories who worked on the script (Robert M. Young, Steve Humphrey and bestselling crime writer Sue Grafton), while the film was directed by Robert Michael Lewis, whose career mostly covered television movies—this was one of over 20 that he headed during the 1980s alone. Such inauspicious names, and a less stellar cast than usual (with a few exceptions, such as *Brideshead Revisited*'s Anthony Andrews), betray the fact that this is a lesser Christie adaptation, lacking excitement or intrigue. Broadcast on 5 November 1983, it performed less well than *Murder Is Easy*, ranking 37th of the week (out of 68 programmes), although this is still a respectable figure. This time John J. O'Connor of *The New York Times* felt it was 'sometimes too exquisitely constructed for believability' and pointed out that no one really asks why Andrews's character Tony is investigating until the final reel—although he accepted this as an apparently typical Christie-ism.[13] When the film debuted in the UK in April 1984, Julie Davidson, reviewer for the *Glasgow Herald*, was rather more forthright: 'what on earth are the Americans doing to Agatha Christie?' she asked in her negative review.[14]

Between these two standalone television films two other new productions had been seen on American network television. One, the first of the Warner Bros. Television Miss Marple pictures, we will come to shortly. The other, however, was a film with different origins to the pictures sewn up in the deal brokered by Alan Shayne. For many years greetings card manufacturer Hallmark had sponsored dramas under the *Hallmark Hall of Fame* banner. By 1982 almost 150 dramas had gone out under this title, and although only two a year were being made at this point, they tended to be productions with more prestige than standard television movies. For a time there had been some consideration that one of these productions could be a remake of Billy Wilder's 1957 film of *Witness for the Prosecution*, with production planned for 1983. Summer 1982 saw the readying of a Hallmark film about American War of Independence general Benedict Arnold—an ambitious project needing complicated battle scenes, so requiring a great deal of pre-production. Then at short notice Hallmark indicated that it needed a film to be ready for early December, in order for its sponsorship to catch the all-important Christmas market so crucial to its business. As Wilder's script was effectively ready to go (with relatively few alterations made), incorporating more easily achievable production requirements, *Witness for the Prosecution* was moved up to be next in production, despite the extremely tight deadline.

The production history of this film is an incredible one by comparative standards, and it is to the credit of the producers, cast and crew that the final product is such an accomplished one. Pre-production took only a few weeks, and given the brief window for casting it is impressive that such a fine range of actors was brought on board. Heading the cast was the great Shakespearian actor Ralph Richardson as Sir Wilfred,[15] while Diana Rigg made her second Christie appearance of the year following her role in *Evil Under the Sun* when she took on the crucial part of Christine Vole, with Hollywood actor Beau Bridges cast as the accused, Leonard Vole. Joining them for filming was an array of well-known faces who had found considerable success on British stages and screens as well as beyond, including Donald Pleasence, Michael Gough, Deborah Kerr, Wendy Hiller and Peter Sallis. Apart from the lure of an appearance on American television, one other factor may explain why so many well-known faces were able to appear at such short notice: they did not need to be available for long, as filming for the whole production took place across only three weeks, an unbelievably short period. This all-film production mixed location work with lavish sets including a reconstruction of the Old Bailey set up at Twickenham Studios and was directed by Alan Gibson, who had come to the producer's attention following his work on British television production *Churchill and the Generals* (BBC, 1979). This all took place at a time when London Weekend Television's mostly studio-based adaptations of *Partners in Crime* took two weeks to make productions of rather less visual appeal, and only half the running time; it is easy to see why British television drama became almost entirely film-like by the end of the decade.

Although the film's producer, Norman Rosemont, claimed that it 'opened the story up infinitely more than the [1957] film and we do a number of things that aren't in either the film or the play', the script actually sticks closely to the original film's screenplay, although television writer John Gay is credited as adapting it for the medium; it is kept in period (which is required in order to maintain the threat of the accused being hanged).[16] The small changes work to make the film darker and perhaps more atmospheric than its predecessor, helped by the fact that much of the humour—still present in the script—is a little lost in the new performances. One interesting and worthwhile addition is an effective and atmospheric opening showing the night-time journey home of Janet Mackenzie (Wendy Hiller); on arriving back at the house she briefly sees her employer conversing with an unseen person, only soon to find her dead. Aside from this opening, there are few differences from the 1957 film of any note, although there is one welcome change back to the script's original intention—when Sir Wilfred meets the mysterious owner of Christine's love letters, this takes place in what appears to be a brothel; originally, censors had demanded this be changed to somewhere more wholesome, so the meeting in the previous film takes place in a train station.[17] This version of the film also reinstates the previously muted word 'murder' in the final scene. Although some may feel that no remake of this type can be worthwhile, that does not make them any less popular, and in this case there are sufficient changes in tone to make it an interesting exercise at the very least—and a laudable adaptation in its own right, even if it cannot hope to match the success of the original. Unfortunately, one of its biggest weaknesses is something that one would expect to be a great strength—Sir Ralph Richardson is not at his best here, appearing to struggle with some of his lines and offering a performance surprisingly lacking in nuance. He often seems to be unwell, although he is more effective in the smaller scenes with other distinguished actors; he died the next year. Elsewhere, performances are strong throughout, although Rigg is not given all the help that she could have received from the director and make-up team when it comes to her dual role.

Despite the tight production schedule, filming finished in October, leaving just enough time for post-production work to be carried out in order for the film to be screened on CBS on 4 December 1982. The adaptation was popular, beating out opposition from perennials *The Love Boat* (ABC, 1977–87) and *Fantasy Island* (ABC, 1977–84) to be the top-rating show of the night. *The New York Times* called the film 'lively' and said it 'still works wondrously well', although *Variety* was less keen, terming it a 'pointless remake' while praising Rigg.[18] Seen less often than many of the other television productions of the period, there is much to be admired in this film, and if it falls flat on occasion then this is only in comparison with arguably the greatest Christie adaptation of them all—Wilder's 1957 film.

HELEN HAYES AS MISS MARPLE

Agatha Christie's family had continued to keep a tight rein on her two best-known characters, Hercule Poirot and Miss Marple, during the years following the author's death. However, it was no longer the case that any new proposal to bring the characters to the screen would be dismissed out of hand—and, as Mathew Prichard points out, there was a balance to be achieved between protecting the characters and also trying to eradicate memories of some of their previous depictions: 'you could argue that such was the "in your face" nature of the MGM films then the sooner we did a proper Miss Marple the better', he points out.[19] Even by the 1980s, Margaret Rutherford was still closely associated with the character, and her films were affectionately remembered by many (as they still are). In the event, a cautious agreement was made, with the rights to one of the Miss Marple novels, *A Caribbean Mystery*, granted to Alan Shayne at Warner Bros. Television. Shayne had already earmarked Helen Hayes to play the elderly detective, following her short but crucial appearance in the opening act of *Murder Is Easy*. She was one of America's most acclaimed actresses, one of only a handful of people to achieve an EGOT (that is, an Emmy award, a Grammy, an Oscar and a Tony—in fact, she received two Academy Awards and three Tonys). Then in her early eighties, she was still active in the industry, and would seem to be a natural choice for the producers given the focus on American audiences. However, Hayes's nationality does create some problems when watching her in the role—she casually mentions her home village of St Mary Mead in England with no explanation of how she has then come to adopt a curious accent that is mostly American, with apparent flashes of Scottish.

Despite the titular setting, the opportunity to show off Caribbean scenery was not embraced by the production since the film was shot in California instead, with rather dreary-looking inland locations that give little sense of atmosphere and squander one of the biggest opportunities in bringing this particular novel to the screen—the exoticism of the locale. *Sparkling Cyanide*'s director Michael Robert Lewis once more worked from a script adapted by Sue Grafton and Steve Humphrey, while Helen Hayes is joined by prolific and esteemed film and television actor Barnard Hughes playing Mr Rafiel. The action was again updated to the present day, although the basic plot of the novel remained unchanged, and the film is not a particularly dynamic production. The pace is slow and it lacks tension, while performances are rarely better than serviceable, with great variance in tone, some actors cruising along with apparently minimal effort or thought while others decide to ham up their performances. The direction does not help, lurching between perfunctorily covering the action and more bizarre moments—most notably in a sequence where the actors are forced to stand still as if in a freeze frame while the characters are discussed. There is no excitement, no charisma on display and no fun—a reminder that Christie adaptations always work best when there is true passion behind the project, notably lacking here.

Rosalind Hicks offered similar views on the film. 'I have to admit that I was most disappointed with this production', she wrote in a letter to Alan Shayne, having seen it prior to transmission, continuing:

> I'm afraid the biggest disappointment—this I think goes for all of us—was the performance of Helen Hayes as Miss Marple. I know she is a bit old but she is a good actress. I felt she could have put a bit more sparkle into the character. She was quite frankly dull and also very American. You promised me that you would take some note of my criticisms of the American phrasings in your script like [...] mailing as letter (we post it), things like that, but nothing was done at all. I do believe that Miss Marple should be English! I don't think enough was made of the Caribbean scenery and the beach and the direction seemed rather slow—all on the same level—the characters aren't sharp enough—It was a good story and the plot was all there but I'm afraid it seemed dull.[20]

Hicks was seemingly unaware that the film had not been made in the Caribbean at all, but her point still stands—there is no real sense that this is taking place anywhere interesting, as the characters circle each other within an uninteresting hotel complex for most of the time, despite some heavily accented performances and steel drum music trying to convince the audience that they are in the Caribbean. On the crucial question of casting Miss Marple,

Alan Shayne disagreed with the Christie family. 'I had loved Helen Hayes as Miss Marple,' he wrote in his memoirs, 'but Rosalind and Mathew always felt that Dame Agatha had intended Miss Marple to be an old, rather fey, maiden aunt rather than a feisty, strong, capable woman like Helen. They got their way in a long series that was done in England. The production values there were much better than we could do in America (after all, the stories do take place in England), but I found Joan Hickson not as interesting playing Miss Marple as Helen was.'[21]

Whatever reservations the family may have had about the film, its broadcast on CBS on 22 October 1983 was met with a much more positive reception than had been anticipated. *A Caribbean Mystery* attracted approximately the same size of audience as its big opposition *The Love Boat* (which slightly outperformed Miss Marple's detective work) and *Fantasy Island* (which rated a little lower than the film), finishing as the 29th most watched programme on American television that week. More significantly, it was a marked improvement on the programme that had previously held this time slot on CBS, *Cutter to Houston* (1983), and it gave an above-average performance for the network. A screening of the film received a guarded reception from John J. O'Connor of *The New York Times*, who called the red herrings 'occasionally irritating' but concluded that 'Under Robert Lewis's direction, the collection of actors proves understandably diverting'.[22] British transmission followed a repeat run of the Margaret Rutherford films, and Margaret Paton of the *Daily Express* said that the film was 'Not bad—but Margaret dunnit better [...] there were any number of ludicrous red herrings to spin out the long-winded thing [... but Helen Hayes] managed to portray a substantial character all the same'.[23]

From the perspective of both Alan Shayne and CBS the film had been a real hit, as the television premiere of *The Mirror Crack'd* had also been—and in network television, success is always looked to be repeated. Mathew Prichard remembers the difficult conversations that followed:

> Two or three weeks after it was shown Alan Shayne rang up and said—'We're in the money, Mathew, CBS want to sign up for sixty one hour versions of Miss Marple on American network television!' He was in Los Angeles but I could practically see the saliva on the telephone! So I said to him, 'Hang on Alan, there aren't sixty Miss Marple stories.' He said, 'Oh, don't worry about that, we'll invent our own!' And I said look, we don't do that. He said, 'You're not serious?' and I said yes, I am. And he said 'well, can I come over and talk to you about it?' [...] Anyway he did come over, and we did talk and he presented his case. All of us actually, not only my mother, were adamant that this was not the way we wished to go.[24]

In fact, not only were the Christie family adamant that new Miss Marple stories could not be written for a television series, Rosalind Hicks in particular was not keen on the idea of allowing even one more Miss Marple film to be made.

However, for CBS this was not the end of the story. The success of the Agatha Christie pictures had convinced it that murder mysteries of this ilk had inbuilt appeal to much of its audience, as Prichard recalls:

> Literally, within a few months, *Murder, She Wrote* appeared [...] with Angela Lansbury who had, by a strange coincidence, just appeared in *The Mirror Crack'd* [...] I went to see [Shayne] after we heard [about it] and we sat in his office. He said 'I feel like suing them, but I've talked to my business department, and the question will be asked, what damage are these doing to the reputation of Agatha Christie and the answer is none.' And for all the years they were on television, I think people did think they were by Agatha Christie [...] People probably bought thousands of Agatha Christie books thinking they were *Murder, She Wrote*, so they were probably quite beneficial.[25]

Murder, She Wrote (1984–96) ran for 12 seasons on CBS, produced by Paramount and running for over 250 episodes, including four later TV movies. The programme offered a variety of murders in the Agatha Christie vein, albeit often simplistically and, as the years progressed, in an increasingly formulaic manner. However, as Prichard says, the establishment of murder mysteries as a mainstream success can hardly have done much damage to the Christie brand, since interest on the genre rose, whatever the frustrations of those involved. In the final regular episode of *Murder, She Wrote*, 'Death by Demographics', Jessica Fletcher is referred to as 'The first lady of mystery writing'—her response is: 'Careful... Agatha Christie's ghost may strike you dead!'

Although Rosalind Hicks had not been keen on *A Caribbean Mystery* and was little inclined to grant access to further Miss Marple works to Warner Bros. Television, there was a way around the difficult situation because of the way in which Christie had gifted a handful of her works to others, including relatives. 'My mother got quite angry with me because I owned *They Do It with Mirrors* and I sold that to Alan', says Mathew Prichard. 'As far as I remember I wanted to buy quite an expensive sculpture at the time!'[26] While Hicks may not have approved, one can see the reason for it—the adaptation of *A Caribbean Mystery* may have been unexceptional and on the dull side, but it had been popular in a large and important market, the United States, and its mediocrity when compared to the best adaptations hardly reflected badly on Christie herself. *They Do It with Mirrors* is a Miss Marple mystery, first published in 1952, in which Miss Marple visits friends now running a home for juvenile delinquent boys. One night, while everyone is distracted by an argument taking place in another room, a murder takes place. Miss Marple then endeavours to discover the method and motive behind it, as well as the culprit. The film was readied for production in the UK during 1984, with a script by television producer and writer George Eckstein, who had a long history in the industry having written episodes of shows such as *The Fugitive* (ABC, 1963–67) and *Gunsmoke* (CBS, 1955–75). The script followed the core plot of the original novel, although it adopted the book's American title, *Murder with Mirrors*.[27] In keeping with what would be his usual formula for productions of Christie stories, Shayne was keen to cast at least one big Hollywood name, perhaps in the twilight of their career. He chose to explore the possibility of casting Bette Davis as Miss Marple's friend Carrie Serrocold. Davis's career had had its ups and downs (a relatively recent highlight having been an appearance in 1978's *Death on the Nile*), as had her health, and she was known to be difficult on occasion, but she was also a star name with some drawing power.

In his memoirs, Shayne recalls that the casting of Davis was problematic from the beginning. When he visited her to discuss the possibility of her taking the part, the actress was clearly still ill, having had a stroke that affected her speech as well as her appearance. Nevertheless, she discussed the project as if she had already been offered the role, stipulating that she must see her costumes in advance and that her character should not be ill, as the script had indicated. When Shayne pointed out that Davis's character is the victim of poisoning, so they could not accede to her second demand, he thought he had escaped. However, the quiet word of an assistant changed Davis's mind. The network insisted that Davis was kept on, even when dailies showed her looking 'like a cadaver'—in the end, much of the film was edited around her appearance, and some of her lines were given to co-stars Leo McKern (best known for playing Rumpole of the Bailey) and Helen Hayes, much to Davis's resentment.[28] Alan Shayne later wrote that Davis's behaviour on set was no better than her appearance in the film rushes. As well as ignoring Hayes throughout a joint interview, Shayne recalled what happened after Hayes had greeted Davis on set on the first day, saying 'How are you Bette? I'm so glad we are working together':

> 'Look,' Bette said, 'We're going to be here for days, and there's no point wasting our breath saying "Hello" and "How are you?" every time we see each other. Let's just do our work.' To my knowledge, the two ladies never spoke again.[29]

The production difficulties caused by Davis may partially explain why the final film is so uninspired, as the cast and crew scrambled to make a watchable piece of television. To its great advantage is the cast of actors—although Davis's poor health makes her performance an uncomfortable one to watch, she is supported not only by the likes of Hayes and McKern, but also Sir John Mills, along with several accomplished British actors who were familiar faces on television, such as Frances de la Tour and John Woodvine. Some changes made to the film are sensible and help to make the solution more plausible, such as in the use of a tape recorder to explain how voices could be heard in one room while the person speaking was committing the murder, which is rather more convincing than one character simply imitating another, as the book had had it. There are also the familiar additions for American network television expectations—when a car crashes into a gate only to be engulfed in a huge fireball, it is amusing in its ridiculousness. And the ending does benefit from the 'show, don't tell' method of these productions: we see a villain of the piece get his comeuppance in a well-realised sequence in the house's lake, when he drowns—in the original book, this event is simply described in a letter after the fact.

Murder with Mirrors did less well than its Miss Marple predecessor, but nevertheless performed respectably, with a 26 % share of all television watching at that time. Critically, interest was waning. John J. O'Connor of *The New York Times* wondered if repeated broadcasts of Christie's work might 'call undue attention to Miss Christie's flaws—the conservative archness, the snobbery, the plethora of red-herring contrivances—but the better moments can be diverting, especially if, as in [*Murder with Mirrors*], they are produced with style'.[30] After praising the cast and direction, he went on to say that the film 'adds up to more than the sum of its fairly ordinary parts [...] In some instances, at least, style will out.'[31] By contrast, London's *Evening Standard* felt that the cast seemed lost in the proceedings, saying that 'They all looked mighty bewildered as the body count rose but the biggest puzzle of all was what the sadly frail Bette Davis was doing in this farrago [...] A case here for Joan Hickson.'[32] This last sentence was to be crucial to the fortunes of Miss Marple on American television—the BBC series, covered in the next chapter, had been rapturously well received since its debut the previous year, becoming a critical and commercial hit of a type unseen since 1974's *Murder on the Orient Express*. The memory of Margaret Rutherford had not been wiped from the collective consciousness, but few people could deny that Joan Hickson was very much the Miss Marple that Agatha Christie had envisaged.

ORDEAL BY INNOCENCE (1985)

While the 1980s had seen several television producers frustrated by the Christie estate's refusal to grant easy access to Poirot or Miss Marple stories for adaptation, and certainly no opportunity to be given free rein with the characters, this had the helpful side effect of reminding the public that there was much more to Christie than her two most famous detectives. With producers forced to concentrate on other areas of the canon, what might first have been seen as a defensive act on the part of her family—to protect the 'crown jewels' of the author's legacy—coincided with Christie's reputation climbing to higher levels than ever, now that the public and critics had the chance to digest her entire catalogue with a little distance. They could now appreciate not only its immediate entertainment value but also its longevity, making this sometimes seem like a targeted offensive in order to show how much of value Christie had written. With consistently high interest in bringing Christie to the screen, British television had seen recurring depictions of her lighter, earlier period of adventure mysteries, while American television had concentrated on her international thrillers as well as more traditional mysteries. The general success of these projects perhaps showed that Christie's name had appeal beyond the obvious titles, but also demonstrated that her stories worked even when detached from the best-known iconography.

In these circumstances, it was fortuitous that the next person to put together a film based on a Christie story had aims that coincided with those of the Christie family. Producer Jenny Craven worked to secure the rights to a Christie novel that had been one of the author's personal favourites. 'I decided from the beginning I didn't want to do a Poirot or a Miss Marple', Craven said at the time. 'I read about 35 of her books and settled on this one. The characters in the book are much younger and much tougher than in many of the other novels, and the book has a good plot.'[33] The book in question is *Ordeal by Innocence*, a 1958 mystery that sees scientist Dr Arthur Calgary return from an Arctic expedition, only to find that he is a witness who could have cleared the name of an innocent man now convicted of murder, who has since died. Calgary sets out to find out the identity of the real killer, but is surprised to learn that the family seem happy to believe that Jacko, the convicted man, had committed the crime—and are not keen to see old wounds reopened.

This was Jenny Craven's second, and to date final, film as producer, but she had previously met Donald Sutherland while he was working on the 1981 movie *Eye of the Needle* (d. Richard Marquand) and managed to convince him to sign up for the lead role of Calgary. Having the star in place helped to convince the Christie estate to license the film, and Mathew Prichard recalls that during filming Sutherland got on well with Rosalind and her husband Anthony Hicks:

> He was brilliant with my parents and used to take them out for dinner almost every night at a brilliant restaurant in Dartmouth called the Carved Angel, and Donald said to my stepfather, who loved his wine—'right, Anthony, you can organise the wine and I'll organise the food'. By the time he left there was no wine left in the Carved Angel! And at the end my stepfather said, 'don't you mind how much this is costing [...]?'; 'Oh forget it', he said 'It'll just go on the budget!' They had a marvellous time, he was really charming to them and had no reason to be really.[34]

Finance for the film was secured from Cannon Films, which specialised in low- to medium-budget productions that had a strong commercial hook to make them attractive to audiences—in this case, we may presume that both Christie and Sutherland were seen as sufficient draws to protect its investment. The company was formed in the late 1960s and its business model operated at its peak during the 1980s, with a film released most months—often action, horror and adventure, such as *Death Wish 3* (d. Michael Winner, 1985), *The Texas Chainsaw Massacre 2* (d. Tobe Hooper, 1987) and the infamously under-budgeted *Superman IV: The Quest for Peace* (d. Sidney J. Furie, 1987). *Ordeal by Innocence* was the first of three Agatha Christie films produced by the company, followed by 1988's *Appointment with Death* and 1989's *Ten Little Indians*.[35] Desmond Davis was appointed its director, having previously directed *Clash of the Titans*, the 1981 adaptation of the Perseus myth. Aside from this he had mostly worked on television, including an episode of *The*

Agatha Christie Hour ('In a Glass Darkly') as well as the dynamic first episode of *The New Avengers* (ITV, 1976–77), 'The Eagle's Nest'. The film's screenplay was written by journalist and novelist Alexander Stuart—to date Stuart has only written one other screenplay for a feature film, an adaptation of his own novel *The War Zone*, which was made into an acclaimed film directed by Tim Roth in 1999.

Although the production team behind the film lacked experience, they were keen to bring a faithful version of the novel to screen and had no intention of following Warner Bros. Television's direction by bringing the action up to the present day. 'I wanted to make a story that was set in the 1950s, because that's a period which I love', said Craven. 'Even if I'd wanted to, it would have been wrong to update it, because Christie's characters just don't work if you do that. Their conversation rings true for the period in which they exist. I think she's a brilliant craftswoman, but I don't think she's a timeless writer.'[36] This choice is clearly shown in the atmosphere of the film, which shows intent to make a serious, visually striking, contemporary and thoughtful picture, based on a book that has complex human psychology at its centre. The film also offers a further plot development that firmly placed it in period: in the novel, Christie has the convicted man, Jacko, die in prison of natural causes, whereas in the film he has been hanged for the crime—an impossibility had the film been set even a decade later.

The movie was shot in February and March 1984, with much of the filming taking place where Christie had set the story—Dartmouth in Devon, near to her holiday home Greenway. The beautiful scenery effectively operates as a character in the final film, as Sutherland's Calgary navigates the boats running along the river Dart to uncover the truth about the crime—other locations include Christie's own local cinema, Torbay Picture House, barely changed from when she had been a visitor decades earlier. Joining Sutherland in the cast is a host of names, familiar from both Hollywood and British television and films, most of whom appear on screen for little more than ten minutes, such was the structure of the piece as Calgary moves from person to person during the mere 90 minutes of drama; these names include Christopher Plummer, Faye Dunaway, Michael Elphick, Annette Crosbie, Ian McShane, Sarah Miles and Diana Quick. The key part of Jacko (played by Billy McColl) is barely present in the finished film, since flashbacks to the events surrounding the murder were reduced in scope in order to keep the budget down. As the victim, Dunaway is only present in these atmospheric monochrome flashbacks—and it is a shame that they are not better expanded on, because they are some of the most interesting and evocative parts of the film.

In May 1984 a work-in-progress print of the film was screened at the Cannes film festival. *Variety* reviewed this version, calling it 'set-bound' and reminiscent of television productions, and it was deemed to be less accomplished than some of the small-screen Christie adaptations.[37] Following the review, an additional week's filming was undertaken with scenes featuring Sutherland along with Annette Crosbie, Michael Elphick and Cassie Stuart, shot at the original Devon locations—this time, direction was undertaken by Alan Birkinshaw (who would later head up Cannon's *Ten Little Indians*), as Desmond Davis was apparently unavailable, although displeasure with the film as it stood may have meant that either he or the producers were keen for him to leave the project.[38] Christopher Plummer was also required to shoot further material, but could not return to England because of his tax status—as a result, his additional scene (where he is visited by Sutherland's character while shooting in the woods) was shot in New Jersey. Apart from Plummer's scene, it is not clear precisely what material was added or changed at this stage, but given *Variety*'s criticisms of the film's visuals it seems likely that some scenes were transplanted to more interesting exterior locations; since the film runs for a relatively slight 90 minutes we can imagine that most of it was replacement rather than additional material.

By September 1984 the picture had been further screened to test audiences, who had not reacted positively. This panicked the studio, and the decision was made that a fundamental change was needed. At this point the film had been fully scored by Italian composer Pino Dinaggio, whose previous work included the evocative and acclaimed music in Sutherland's 1973 thriller *Don't Look Now* (d. Nicholas Roeg). Dinaggio's score still exists; it uses strings and woodwind instruments, with occasional electronic sounds, to create an atmosphere reminiscent of a ghost story and the associated creeping, under-stated unease— particularly suitable for a film about characters haunted by the past. Although it is common for film fans to consider drastic post-production changes to be mistakes, regardless of how much they may have actually helped a production achieve its aims, in this case there can be little doubt that Dinaggio's music was eminently preferable to the questionable decision to turn instead to jazz musician Dave Brubeck. Whatever the skills of the composer, a jazz score is simply inappropriate and distracting when matched with the long takes and brooding atmosphere of the film. Brubeck was not able to write a new score, so instead improvised mostly pre-existing material while watching the film at a studio in San Francisco, under the supervision of producer Jenny Craven as well as Sutherland.[39] The intention was that this fast turnaround on the new score would enable the film to be released in December 1984—however, in the end it was not put on general release until March the following year. In keeping with many Christie pictures, it received a special royal charity premiere when Queen Elizabeth II and Prince Philip viewed the film at the Classic Haymarket cinema in London on 14 February 1985.

The final result is a disappointing treatment of a strong novel, especially considering the cast and striking atmosphere of the locations. In its favour, the film effectively tries to evoke the style of 1940s detective thrillers. 'It's reflected in the look we've gone for—rainwashed streets, and so on', said director Davis during filming. 'In a way, I've tried to set the story in "movieland" rather than Dartmouth.'[40] Such comments reinforce the fact that some film-makers do not feel that Christie's stories can take place in the 'real world', which perhaps over-emphasises the difficulty in reworking period dialogue. Nevertheless, the problem here is not genre, but that the entire picture lacks urgency and pace, something that is not made up for by its meditation on complex characterisation and situation. It meanders in a frustrating manner, with no charm and little excitement or interest for the audience, despite the exceptional cast and location. It is difficult not to put the blame at the door of the director, who seems keener on making each scene have its own distinctive visual look, rather than thinking about how the film as a whole hangs together. Jimmy Summers of *Boxoffice* magazine wrote a damning review:

> *Ordeal by Innocence* is a serious treatment of Agatha Christie. For the past two decades Christie's whodunits have been given tongue-in-cheek or campy treatments which, as this bodge-job proves, may be the only way to do them today. [...] As if an illogical story, uneven acting, awkward dialogue, clumsy moralizing and opening titles that seem hand-lettered weren't enough, someone had the twisted idea of using old Dave Brubeck songs for background music. There's nothing wrong with Brubeck, of course, but as background for a downbeat mystery set in a foggy, English village? Actually, background isn't even accurate. This is foreground music, with drum solos and rim shots used to accent dialogue [...] It makes the actors sound like stand-up comics.[41]

Gilbert Adair in *Monthly Film Bulletin* stated that 'plotting has never been Desmond Davis' forte and, when not agonisingly slow and explicative, the film's narrative seems skewed to the point of incomprehensibility [...] Many transitional scenes between relevant exchanges are mere time-wasting exercises in postcard pictorialism.'[42] Adair goes on to call Brubeck's score 'grotesquely mismatched' with the visuals. However, *Screen International* gave the film a positive review, calling it 'a serious drama worthy of more than superficial attention' and commending both the direction and the score.[43] Newspaper reviewers were sharply divided between those who felt that the film evidenced that Christie was near impossible to bring to screen effectively (neatly forgetting the many successes) and those who welcomed a film that tried to depict her story in a very different way—more hard-boiled and focused on psychology; even the score had its fans. It is difficult to judge the finished product as anything other than a frustrating near miss.

Ordeal by Innocence was one of several proposed feature films about which Agatha Christie Ltd had been approached during the 1980s, most of which went little further than vague propositions. However, one title piqued the interest of several parties, despite the difficulties it presented. The novel *Death Comes as the End* was published in 1945 and, in terms of structure, is almost a typical Christie, with a patriarch's new lover the murder victim, leaving an array of suspects within his family. However, the book takes place 4000 years in the past and is set in Thebes, Egypt. The prospect of recreating Ancient Egypt on film might be attractive in terms of visual potential, but it also requires a considerable financial commitment, one that has scared off many investors.

Mathew Prichard thinks it is particularly unfortunate that none of the proposals to make a film of this novel has ever succeeded, as it is one of his favourite
works by his grandmother, and he understandably believes that there is the
potential for a striking picture. 'We had a fellow who was keen on doing *Death
Comes as the End*', he recalls. 'He was a friend of Brian Stone's and he even
got to the stage where he had these wonderful designs of Egyptian costumes
and it would have made a wonderful film, but I think his finances were a bit
shaky [...] while I'm still working, I'd love for someone to make a film of
that.'[44] Two scripts for potential film productions of the story still exist in the
possession of the Agatha Christie family archive. One, dated 1984, was written
by Dutch screenwriter Gerard Soeteman, and may have formed the basis of a
proposed film from *RoboCop* director Paul Verhoeven mentioned in the press
at the time. Soeteman's script is the more engaging of the two, liberal in its
use of colloquialisms in the dialogue from certain characters, while it portrays a
rougher, more real and more dangerous Egypt than might usually be depicted
in fiction. The characters speak in a mostly modern manner, rather than as if
lifted from Victorian fiction (as often happens with stories set in the distant
past), and the abrasive nature of some of the relationships is well portrayed.
Soeteman uses descriptions of actions and motivations extensively throughout
his script, and sensibly broadens out the action to make it suited to the cinema
screen, including a sequence where the murderer falls to their death in the final
act, rather than simply being slain by an arrow.

The other script was written by Laird Koenig, who had been awarded
the Golden Raspberry for Worst Script for the co-written picture *Inchon* (d.
Terence Young), a film about the Korean War that was a box-office disaster in
1982, although he is best known as author of 1974 thriller novel *The Little Girl
Who Lives Down the Lane*. In this screenplay, which renames the story *Murder
in Ancient Egypt*, the importance of the visuals is immediately apparent given
that the first page of the document includes a drawing of the area by the Nile
where the action is to take place—it would require the construction of a boat
landing, villa, tombs, a temple and outbuildings. Realistically, this is a script
for a film that would need backing from a major studio. Koenig's script largely
follows the plot of Christie's novel, but it exposes a key problem with bringing the story to the screen: the tone of the dialogue to be used. While Christie
portrays the family unit in a modern way, her dialogue is largely formal, in the
same way that many stories set in the past tend to be—this creates a distancing
effect for some readers, and on screen would make it difficult for audiences to
identify with the characters. Unlike Soeteman, Koenig also largely adopts this
approach, although he occasionally slips into less formal dialogue (one slave is
called a 'lazy cow' early in proceedings), which, although more contemporary
in tone, inevitably jars. However, advances in technology mean that the novel
is no longer quite such a difficult prospect to bring to the screen, as evidenced
by the 2016 announcement that the BBC plans to make a television adaptation
of the mystery.

THE MAN IN THE BROWN SUIT (1989)

The late 1980s was a time for spectres of Christie screen adaptations past to rear their heads once more: while Peter Ustinov's Poirot returned to the big screen for *Appointment with Death*, so Alan Shayne presented his final television film based on the author's works, as a familiar title was being readied for cinema release. Shayne's efforts to secure more Miss Marple or Poirot titles had been blocked by the Christie family following his earlier pictures, but he hoped to gain the goodwill to secure more titles of his choice by making a different Christie adaptation. However, the only available title that Shayne deemed even partially suitable for his plans was 1924's *The Man in the Brown Suit*, another international thriller that he had optioned back in 1979, despite being a novel that he actively disliked. Pre-production on the film started as early as 1986, intended for broadcast in the 1987–88 television season. Nevertheless, work on it was difficult from the beginning.

Shayne's first difficulty was finding someone to write the screenplay. He claimed that 'No one liked [the book], and no one would do it', before finding a new writer by the name of Bruce Singer who agreed to take on the task.[45] Although the first script Shayne received 'made as little sense as the book', with an ending that showed the protagonist couple embracing below a pair of curtains made out of the brown suit ('We would have needed a voice over to explain that one'), he felt that the final one, by new screenwriter Carla Jean Wagner and once more updated to the present day, was little better.[46] Shayne had similar issues in finding a director, with British television director Alan Grint eventually taking on the role. Cast in the role of adventurer Anne Beddingfeld (now an American rather than British) was *Remington Steele* star Stephanie Zimbalist, joined by British actor Edward Woodward, best known to American audiences for his lead role in *The Equalizer* (CBS, 1985–89), alongside Rue McClanahan of *The Golden Girls* (NBC, 1985–92) and Tony Randall, ex-Poirot from 1965's *The Alphabet Murders* (see Chap. 6). With a director and cast now on board, filming in Spain took place during the summer of 1988, mostly in the cities of Madrid and Cadiz, but the relationship between director and producer was not a good one. Disagreements reached a peak when Grint decided to present band members playing at a costume party in black face, as an apparent homage to old movies, much to Shayne's understandable incredulity; the make-up was removed before filming recommenced.[47] The relationship between the two almost entirely disintegrated after this point and Shayne seems to have despaired of the project. To add to the producer's woes, filming over-ran and although Shayne felt that the final product was 'respectable, if not good', he was unhappy with the experience.

The finished film is a very strange production that selects some of the key developments and twists of the original novel and reworks them into a movie that takes little notice of the particular requirements of a visual medium. For example, several wealthy characters are stranded aboard what feels like a run-down tug boat for a large stretch of the action, offering no glamour but at least the chance to enjoy the company of some fine actors. However, the audience can only react in disbelief when a stewardess appears on the scene—with the camera making no attempt to hide the fact that the character is clearly played by Tony Randall, who is also playing a strange vicar. The script continues as if Anne has not noticed this, leaving the audience baffled and confused even before the twist (that there is no stewardess on board) is revealed as a pre–commercial break cliffhanger. This sequence must rank as one of the oddest scenes ever committed to film, and such moments bemuse the audience even more than the plot developments of the original novel; when Randall's character is revealed to have donned multiple disguises, those watching can only wonder how he got so lucky as to take a trip on a boat apparently entirely made up of short-sighted guests. The film may not work, but it does occasionally—unwittingly—creep into the 'so bad it's good' collection, helped by arch performances from Woodward and McClanahan. Shayne was seemingly unsurprised by the reaction of Rosalind and Mathew Prichard when he showed it to them: 'they hated it'.[48] Although the film performed well, posting CBS's best ratings on a Wednesday night that year, ranking 125th of the 753 shows broadcast on primetime network television in the 1988–89 season, the difficulties it posed meant that Shayne elected to cease his work on adapting further Christie stories.

TEN LITTLE INDIANS (1989)

While Shayne was having difficulties making his film for television, more familiar ground was being trodden in the cinemas. For the final time, producer Harry Alan Towers resurrected *And Then There Were None* after his 1965 and 1974 films of the play, using the title *Ten Little Indians*. Having previously put the story atop a snowy mountain and in the middle of the desert, this Cannon-funded picture elected to set the action on an African safari, albeit a visually uninteresting one. This time Towers indulged in a new script, once more based on Christie's stage play with its more upbeat ending.[49] The screenplay was by Gerry O'Hara who had written for several British television programmes, such as *The Professionals* (ITV, 1977–83), while he had also been a director for television programmes including *The Avengers* (ITV, 1961–69); also credited was Jackson Hunsicker, for whom this was only his second (of four) screenplays to be produced. Director Alan Birkinshaw returned to Cannon after his work on the pick-up material for *Ordeal by Innocence*, making the film back to back with his 1989 movie *The House of Usher*, an adaptation of the Edgar Allan Poe short story.[50] Starring in both *The House of Usher* and *Ten Little Indians* was Donald Pleasence, perhaps best known to general audiences for his appearances in the Halloween film franchise since 1978. Pleasence had been a highly regarded actor on British stage and screen, including appearances in the BBC's seminal 1954 production of *Nineteen Eighty-Four* (d. Rudolph Cartier), but by this point in his career was happy to accept almost any cinema role that offered a fee and schedule that suited him. He took on the role of Sir

Justice Wargrave and, uniquely for this production, also provided the barely disguised voice of U.N. Owen, the mysterious host whose speech is played from a gramophone record. Joining Pleasence for filming was Herbert Lom, who had been Dr Armstrong in the 1974 version of the film, and was now playing the frequently renamed General (Macarthur in the book, MacKenzie in the stage production and Romensky for this film), while the key roles of Vera and Lombard went to relative unknowns. Vera is British actress Sarah Maur Thorp, whose entire filmography consists of three movies released in 1989 (including this one), followed by guest appearances in two television shows; despite this short screen career, she acquits herself perfectly well. Faring less well is Frank Stallone, younger brother of Sylvester, who had largely forged a career in the music industry; his self-satisfied performance as perpetually smirking Lombard is one-note at best.

The movie was filmed on location in September and October 1988 under the title *Death on Safari*, which it kept until February 1989 when it reverted to the name under which it was best known internationally, *Ten Little Indians*, although not before the trade press had printed a poster for the film featuring the working title. The script largely adopted the structure of the original and also keeps the action in the 1930s, despite the changed location. Little use is made of the new locale, either narratively or artistically—clichéd 'natives' are depicted early in the picture, but offered straight-faced without comment or context. This is a film that has nothing to say and no artistry to explore; it is no more than a financial investment. The script offers relatively minor amendments to the plot, such as the changing of Mr Rodgers's role from butler to bodyguard and occasional attempts to modernise the picture (despite its retained period setting), such as one character's allusion to a lesbian affair, which serves no real function.[51] Aside from the use of his voice on the record early on, the film does its best to preserve the final surprise, as when Wargrave falls dead at the feet of Vera, with an apparently realistic bullet wound on his forehead—we are later told that the surrounding blood was, in fact, tomato ketchup, in true *Scooby Doo* fashion. With a running time of only 98 minutes there is plenty of opportunity for the story to keep up the pace, but it languishes for a dreary 35 minutes before the first victim is slain. The lack of chemistry between any of the actors means that the only real point of interest is the question of how grisly the next murder will be, since this adaptation particularly relishes the dead bodies on display in keeping with contemporary interest in slasher films. With flat direction and dull performances retreading a well-worn story, it is difficult to sum up any enthusiasm for the picture.

This lack of enthusiasm was felt not only by the audience, but also film distributors. *Ten Little Indians* was first screened at 1989's Cannes Film Festival in an attempt to drive up interest from distributors, only for it to be largely ignored. Perhaps *Variety*'s review from the festival served as sufficient warning to any potential investors, calling it 'a dud' that 'ranks near the bottom of all Christie adaptations'.[52] The reviewer did praise Sarah Maur Thorp, but made it clear that the film could not expect commercial or critical success. In

the event, the movie opened in only 17 screens in a handful of American cities during November 1989, including Philadelphia and New York; it was not
screened for critics, and its financial performance was abysmal for a project that
was such a cynically commercial venture. Those who indulge in schadenfreude
may wish to know that in the first week the picture raked in only $18,000 at
the US box office, putting it 43rd for the week. While this might be automatically attributed to the fact that it only opened in five cities, the low $1058
per-screen gross tells a different story—people simply were not interested in
seeing it.[53] After an even more dismal second week (when it earned a minuscule
$546 from three screens in Philadelphia), cinemas pulled the film.[54] Cannon
immediately cut its losses and readied the movie for a speedy VHS release in
February 1990; although the film had been part of a package sold to international distributors, it was not released in many key territories, including the
UK. In fact, Britain only saw a limited home video release, and nor was it reis-
sued in the United States after its first VHS appearance. The net effect of this
is that the film remains largely out of circulation, with no DVD release in any
country at the time of writing. Fans should not be too upset—there are worse
Christie adaptations, but few are as uninteresting as this lazy effort—while it
should serve as a warning to other film-makers that using Christie's name and
the basics of one of her plots is no guarantee of success on any level.

INNOCENT LIES (1995)

The next film to make it into production benefitted from interesting origins.
For many years Claude Chabrol, one of the pioneering directors of the French
New Wave in the early 1960s, had been interested in bringing Christie's 1944
mystery novel *Towards Zero* to the screen. By the early 1990s he was still interested, as was the Christie estate, which saw the potential in an artistically motivated retelling of one of Christie's darkest stories, in which the reunion of a
dysfunctional family leads to murder. 'What I don't remember is how we got
from there to where we eventually did get to', admits Mathew Prichard, as
by the time plans for the Anglo/French co-production gained momentum,
Chabrol was nowhere to be seen. 'Suddenly, I remember being sent the odd
script written by someone who wasn't Claude Chabrol and they got further
and further away from the story', Prichard recalls. The first script was rejected
due to the omission of key characters, but later drafts made an even more
problematic change, as he remembers: 'Incest appeared. And we said to them
look, if you want to do this, we'll give you your money back and you can go
and make your film.'[55]

In fact, the termination of the relationship between the film's producers
and Agatha Christie Ltd took some time, as it seems that Polygram, which was
making the film, would have preferred to retain the Christie name and so discussions rumbled along until close to the release date. With a budget of £8 m,
filming took place in Twickenham Studios as well as on location in Morbihan,
France, from May to July 1994. The cast included Adrian Dunbar, Stephen

Dorff and Joanna Lumley, working under French director Patrick Dewolf, who had co-written the script with a producer of British daytime legal drama *Crown Court* (ITV, 1972–85), Kerry Crabbe. As a concession to the Christie estate, while in production the film was renamed *Halcyon Days* ('sounds like a shop' said Agatha Christie Ltd's agent, Brian Stone) so as to distance it from the original novel.[56]

When the film was near to release the tabloid press started to take note of the dispute. The *Mail on Sunday* headlined its article 'Agatha Risque', distastefully calling the addition of incest a 'sexy new twist' while highlighting the Christie estate's dissatisfaction with the script.[57] Julia Short of Polygram was quoted as saying: 'We wanted the incest to give the film a bit more of a bite. The estate vetoed the title because we misrepresented the book, but the storyline's exactly the same.'[58] By this point filming had been completed for eight months, with the title then changed to *Innocent Lies* by May 1995, while by the time the film was released in June 1995 the only allusion to Christie is at the end of the credits:

> The producers gratefully acknowledge the inspiration provided by Agatha Christie for the making of this film, which does not purport to be a faithful adaptation of any of her work.

Although the plot of *Innocent Lies* does have broad similarities to *Towards Zero* it is far from a close adaptation, and is not generally considered to be an Agatha Christie film, despite its origins. Both novel and film feature a family haunted by a past death, with reignited tensions leading to more murders. However, the film seems actively to work to make the audience dislike it, littered as it is with cryptic dialogue by unlikeable characters. Even for those who persevere there is no payoff—no revelatory performance, no well-crafted plot developments, nor any fascinating psychology. It is a loose collection of unfinished ideas that does not seem to know what to do with itself, beyond hoping that brooding exchanged glances and unorthodox familial relationships will somehow concoct a captivating atmosphere that will intrigue its audience. It does not, and it received very poor notices from critics—Christopher Tookey of the *Daily Mail* stated that 'Space does not permit a lengthy catalogue of the film's defects', while Geoff Brown in *The Times* called it 'a frigid exercise in style', with other critics terming it 'inept' and 'confusing'.[59] Slightly more kindly, *Variety* deemed it an 'interesting failure'.[60] The film was not a commercial success, making only £65,000 at the UK box office. As the latest in a string of disappointing films it seemed that cinema was not the best outlet for Agatha Christie adaptations at this time—something made even more obvious by the clear contrast between the big-screen failures and the exceptional success of the small-screen adventures of Joan Hickson's Miss Marple and David Suchet's Poirot since 1984 and 1989 respectively. The next section will show that Christie's works had found a near permanent, and acclaimed, home on television, thanks to two exceptional series that helped to remind the public quite how good the Queen of Crime's mysteries actually were.

Notes

1. Interview with the author, August 2015.
2. Interview with the author, August 2015.
3. *Screen International*, 25 August 1979.
4. Interview with the author, August 2013.
5. Alan Shayne and Norman Sunshine, *Double Life* (New York: Magnus Books, 2011), 287.
6. *Screen International*, 15 August 1981.
7. *Screen International*, 15 August 1981.
8. *Screen International*, 15 August 1981.
9. The romance is present in the original novel.
10. Interview with the author, August 2013.
11. *The New York Times*, 21 December 1981.
12. See Chap. 4 regarding the earlier production.
13. *The New York Times*, 4 November 1986.
14. *Glasgow Herald*, 28 April 1984.
15. A change of spelling from the Sir Wilfrid of the original film.
16. *Screen International*, 9 October 1982. Britain's final executions took place in 1964.
17. See Chap. 5.
18. *The New York Times*, 3 December 1982; *Variety*, 8 December 1982.
19. Interview with the author, August 2013.
20. Rosalind Hicks to Alan Shayne, 20 August 1983 (Agatha Christie Family Archive).
21. Shayne and Sunshine, *Double Life*, 289.
22. *New York Times*, 6 May 1984.
23. *Daily Express*, 26 March 1984.
24. Interview with the author, August 2013.
25. Interview with the author, August 2013.
26. Interview with the author, August 2015. Prichard sold limited screen rights, not the full ownership of the novel.
27. This title may have been considered more eye-catching for the American readership, but it makes little sense in context—the point of *They Do It with Mirrors* is that it is a phrase evocative of stage effects and misdirection. Mirrors do not feature in the actual murder!
28. Shayne and Sunshine, *Double Life*, 291–2.
29. Shayne and Sunshine, *Double Life*, 292.
30. *New York Times*, 20 February 1985.
31. *New York Times*, 20 February 1985.
32. *Evening Standard*, 2 September 1986.
33. *Screen International*, 27 March 1984.
34. Interview with the author, August 2014.
35. See Chap. 8 for discussion of *Appointment with Death*.
36. *Screen International*, 27 March 1984.
37. *Variety*, 23 May 1984.

38. *Screen International*, 30 June 1984.
39. *Billboard*, 22 September 1984.
40. *Screen International*, 17 March 1984.
41. *Boxoffice*, 1 December 1985.
42. *Monthly Film Bulletin*, 1985.
43. *Screen International*, 9 February 1985.
44. Interview with the author, August 2013.
45. Shayne does not name the young writer, but a *Variety* report has Singer attached to the picture on 15 April 1987. I can find no record of a writer with that name being credited with work on the screenplay for any film or television productions, so he does not appear to have continued his work in this area of the industry.
46. Shayne and Sunshine, *Double Life*, 288.
47. Shayne and Sunshine, *Double Life*, 288–9.
48. Shayne and Sunshine, *Double Life*, 289.
49. Some sources claim that Towers originally intended to use the novel's ending for this film version—the reason for his change of mind is not clear, but quite apart from any dramatic reasons for it, Towers would not have been permitted to use elements unique to the novel, as he only had the rights to the play through a quirk of its original licensing.
50. More accurately, the Poe short story is called 'The Fall of the House of Usher'.
51. The spelling of Rodgers's name also changes from Rogers.
52. *Variety*, 31 May 1989.
53. *Variety*, 22 November 1989. By comparison, the top picture of the week, *Look Who's Talking*, was making over $13,000 per screen. $1058 put Ten Little Indians below all but one other film in the top 50 for per-screen gross.
54. *Variety*, 6 December 1989.
55. Interview with the author, August 2013.
56. *Mail on Sunday*, 6 March 1995.
57. *Mail on Sunday*, 6 March 1995.
58. *Mail on Sunday*, 6 March 1995.
59. *Daily Mail*, 30 June 1995; *The Times*, 29 June 1995.
60. *Variety*, 17 July 1995.

Televising the Canon, 1984–2013

Chapter 11: Agatha Christie's Miss Marple

Spoilers: *Crooked House; The Murder of Roger Ackroyd; Nemesis*

Earlier in this book, we followed the sometimes fractious relationship between Agatha Christie and the BBC, which had resulted in a handful of radio productions, including one with a distinctive legacy (*Three Blind Mice*, in 1947, which later formed the basis for *The Mousetrap*). However, forays into television were even rarer, and it took until the 1980s for the BBC to really strike gold when it came to portraying Christie's works on screen: it broadcast a series of Miss Marple adaptations starring Joan Hickson from 1984 to 1992, covering all 12 of the novels featuring the character. This chapter focuses on this series, but its background is really a story of the relationship between Christie's family (including Dame Agatha herself) and television generally, as well as the BBC more specifically. In order to understand the history and significance of the series, we need to go further back than 1984, and instead pick up the story in 1970, when Christie made her position abundantly clear.

As previously outlined, a 1960 deal between Christie and MGM had meant that most of her works were unavailable to the BBC for any use, even if Christie could be convinced—exceptions included publications that post-dated the deal and several of her plays. This meant that the decade was a quiet one for relations between the author and the BBC, but by 1970 the MGM deal had reached an end and the Corporation investigated bringing her mysteries to television once more. This was instigated by Gerald Savory, Head of Plays at the BBC, who stipulated that he wanted to look into adapting Christie's novels ('not interested in her plays') and would be happy to make any series a co-production, should the rights be held by an American film company which was happy to work together.[1] Such BBC co-productions were rare at the time, although not unheard of, and showed that the series was hoped to be high profile; this approach indicates more respect being shown towards the author and her work than earlier communications. The suggestion was that an anthology series could be made, consisting of 13 episodes. Nora Blackborow at Hughes Massie was contacted to investigate the possibility of using her client's

© The Author(s) 2016
M. Aldridge, *Agatha Christie on Screen*,
DOI 10.1057/978-1-137-37292-5_12

work, which she duly did, understanding that the BBC was not necessarily looking to restrict the stories to Miss Marple, Poirot or any other recurring characters. The prompt response was clear—while Blackborow admitted that rights to televise most of Christie's novels were 'probably' available (the imprecision giving some indication of how unimportant their contractual status was while Christie still wielded a veto in practice), according to the anonymous note-taker Christie then stated that she 'does not wish her work to be used for television' and that she was 'anti-TV and not interested in our purpose'.[2]

Christie's specific issues with broadcasting tended to evolve over time. Generally, she had no objection to the reading of her stories on the radio, but was rather less likely to agree to any dramatised performance. We can trace the origins of her issue with adaptations back to her problems with alterations made by those reworking her stories for some stage productions, including her dislike of some of Michael Morton's original changes when he adapted *The Murder of Roger Ackroyd* as *Alibi* in 1928. Her unhappiness with adaptations was only magnified by her distress relating to the MGM films of the 1960s, which had made her novels into thinly plotted comedic versions of the original stories. Understandably, Christie wanted to retain control over her creations, so she generally did not allow the slightest opportunity for such alterations to take place. Thus, when she was asked if actor Leslie French, best known for his stage work, could portray Poirot in a five-minute piece celebrating her 80th birthday on the *Review* television programme, she declined, even though French was only to quote from her work.[3] Instead, it was agreed that French would be permitted to read an excerpt from *Murder on the Orient Express* only as himself, not in character as the Belgian detective. Similarly, requests to read out stories using more than one voice were refused—only one actor was permitted, so as to curtail any temptation to add drama beyond Christie's original words. In June 1971 permission was granted to repeat a Polish translation of a reading of 1963 Poirot novel *The Clocks* on an international station, but the BBC was advised that 'as the position of Christie rights changes from day to day almost, it will be a good thing if you clear such rights in time for something else to be substituted if the rights you want are no longer available'.[4] Indeed, just three months later, permission to read an extract from *The Murder of Roger Ackroyd* was refused, with no explanation offered for the apparent change of heart.[5]

The copyright position was complicated, in part due to Christie's control over the treatment of her works, but most especially because those works had proved so successful that at any given time rights to any of them could be tied up in any number of pre-existing deals, making it near impossible to predict whether the rights could be granted. For example, in June 1973 Christie's agents at Hughes Massie were asked if Christie's one-act play *The Rats* could be broadcast on a Spanish-language service. Permission was refused. The BBC then asked if it could have *The Patient* instead and permission was granted— despite the fact that both plays had similar backgrounds and had been publicly performed together as two of the three plays making up *Rule of Three* in the 1960s. Consequently, the BBC simply had to try its luck with titles that appealed.

When Christie died in January 1976, BBC radio felt that the best tribute would be to repeat what had been her greatest broadcasting success—her original 1947 play *Three Blind Mice*. An agreement was drawn up to repeat a recording of the original performance, for a fee of £180, before it was realised that the rights were unavailable due to *The Mousetrap*'s continuing run in the West End. The plans for this repeat are interesting because, although we know that the original play was recorded (since it was consulted for the later television production), it is no longer known to survive. As the contract is quite specific about this being a repeat of the original performance, and the necessary paperwork had been carried out, we may infer that the archives had been checked and its existence confirmed. During the writing of this book the BBC archive checked its holdings once more in light of this information, but *Three Blind Mice* remains missing—although Christie fans may be cautiously optimistic that a recording may come to light one day, as has been the case for some of her other radio plays. Meanwhile, the mystery of its disappearance would soon be joined by an altogether different one concerning one of Christie's favourite books.

THE MYSTERY OF *CROOKED HOUSE*

'Well, well, well…' says Mathew Prichard when shown a piece of BBC paperwork dated 28 August 1979.[6] This annotated letter is a copy of one sent to Brian Stone, who was by now handling Christie's works for Hughes Massie. It details a request to broadcast an abridged reading of her 1949 mystery *Crooked House* on the radio. Underneath the letter, discussions with Rosalind Hicks are noted—following her mother's death, Hicks was instrumental in agreeing to or vetoing any new Christie projects. According to the notes, which appear to record a telephone call with Stone, Hicks stated that there was a 'family jinx on the book and won't allow any use', further saying that an attempt would be made to persuade her to give permission at the trustee board.[7] However, by 10 October it was noted that permission would not be forthcoming.

The 'jinx' claim is an intriguing one—on the one hand, we might dismiss it as a case of Hicks simply hoping that such an outlandish claim would lead to no further pestering, but this letter was hardly an unusual request, and neither Hughes Massie nor Christie and her family had ever been averse to flatly refusing projects that they could not permit without any explanation. However, if it were the case that *Crooked House* was deemed to be a title that Christie and her family did not wish to be adapted for personal reasons, this would help to explain why one of her best mysteries has taken so long to make it to the screen; it even took until 2008 for BBC radio to adapt it for broadcast. It is also the case that if one were to pick a story to associate with a family jinx then *Crooked House* would be it: its portrayal of twisted family relations, including the revelation that the murderer is a child, helps to classify it as one of Christie's darkest works.

However, there are two sticking points in the 'jinx' story—the first, and most important, is the fact that Mathew Prichard has never heard of it. 'I mean *Crooked House* was certainly one of my grandmother's favourite books', he says. 'I think my mother had a vague feeling that because of the subject matter and the nature of the criminal it perhaps wasn't the most suitable one to adapt. I've always had a suspicion, actually, that my mother refused a few things without even asking—I mean, I was chairman of the company then!'[8] It would not be unreasonable for the family, and perhaps even Christie herself, to feel that real-life events that followed *Crooked House* had created the potential for the story to seem tasteless if adapted badly. In particular, the 1968 case of Mary Bell, a 10-year-old murderer who, like 12-year-old Josephine in *Crooked House*, revealed details of the crime in her own childish writings, may have felt too close for comfort. One other issue that the letter raised is that the reading would be abridged, although not considerably. 'My grandmother always loathed *Readers Digest*', says Prichard, reinforcing how unhappy she would be with edited and reworked versions of her stories—but it seems clear that this was not the reason it was declined, as permission for an abridged reading of the 1948 Poirot novel *Taken at the Flood* was granted only three months later.[9]

The second sticking factor in the 'jinx' story is that there have been several attempts to bring the story to the screen in the last 30 years. Scripts for two of these proposed adaptations reside at the Agatha Christie family archive, while another attempt is still ongoing—although it is possible that the wariness of any 'jinx' simply pre-dated this. The first script is from 1990 and appears to have been sent on spec since its California-based writers, Jillian Palethorpe and Sparky Greene, hardly had the reputation to be independently approached, as their only credits of any note are a 1984 film *The Oasis*, directed by Greene from his own story about survivors of a plane crash in Mexico, and a single co-written episode of TV series *The Hitchhiker*, which followed the wanderings of the mysterious eponymous character, for the USA Network in 1989. Their script opens with a description of Josephine floating in mid-air before she starts to narrate the film, unlike Christie's novel where the events are narrated by the character Charles Hayward. Changing the narrator causes two substantial alterations to the story overall. The first is that the advantage of Charles's narration is that he is an outsider. His writing details how he falls in love with Sophia Leonides, but she refuses to consider marriage until the identity of her grandfather's murderer is discovered. As the cast of suspects is made up of the family of Aristide Leonides, the murdered man, Charles can offer an outsider's take on their unusual family dynamics—as a member of this family, Josephine's narration is necessarily an insider's one. Secondly, and more significantly, Josephine is the killer, and making her the narrator gives the character undue prominence throughout the screenplay, offering an unsubtle echo of *The Murder of Roger Ackroyd*'s central device. The script also characterises Josephine as an outright psychopath, with trips to the bathroom to dab on tears and an unrelenting obsession with drawing attention to herself.

This proposed adaptation translates the action to the modern day, perhaps an indication that the writers had paid attention to the American TV movies of the 1980s that did the same, although the dialogue remains old-fashioned despite occasional mentions of computers and other contemporary devices. Characterisation is thin and sometimes baffling—Josephine's brother Eustace is described as a 16-year-old, but he drives around in his own car and otherwise acts like an adult.[10] The broad developments of the novel are mostly present, albeit with an additional murder—that of young Detective Inspector Glover, who is killed by poisonous mushrooms (likely a coincidental echo of the Miss Marple short story 'The Thumb Mark of St Peter', where mushrooms are a red herring for the cause of death). At the end, Josephine dies in a deliberately orchestrated car crash, just as in the novel, with her final movements echoing the opening of the film as she moves through space—through the windscreen of the car.

The second script is a two-part television adaptation dating from 1993, written by Robin Chapman, who had adapted many novels for the screen, including *Jane Eyre* for the BBC in 1973 and 1985's ITV version of P.D. James's *Cover Her Face*. It is highly reminiscent of some of ITV's attempts to bring standalone Christie mysteries to the screen later in the decade, especially 1997's *The Pale Horse* (covered in the next chapter), in the way that it rather melodramatically tells its story with an emphasis on a strong, young, male lead with 1990s sensibilities despite the period setting. This script is set in approximately 1957 and the male lead is called Mike, who performs the function of the narrator Charles from the original book. Mike is from northern England and often speaks colloquially; he also rides a motorbike and is characterised as an 'Angry Young Man', in line with the frequent contemporaneous cultural references to such a group. The plotting of the scripts works perfectly well for a typical two-part commercial TV adaptation, with mini cliffhangers at each commercial break, but the screenplay struggles more when it comes to dialogue, which tends to be rather on the nose, lacking subtlety—for example, Mike asks characters questions that both know the answer to, just for the audience's apparent benefit. Given the action-led perfunctory manner of many ITV dramas of the time, this lack of subtlety may well be a deliberate choice—this is mass-appeal, heavy-handed drama. Other changes in the script include the decision to have Eustace lose the use of his legs due to a failed bet with his grandfather, who wagered £1000 that the child could not climb the chimney of the house—when he fell, Aristide gave him £2000. The culprit and resolution remain broadly the same, although perhaps inevitably Mike is now on hand to chase the car containing Josephine on his motorbike, but does not do enough to prevent the fatal crash. It is not clear why this adaptation was not made, but 1993 saw the conviction of two 10-year-old boys for the murder of 4-year-old James Bulger in a case that had a very high profile in Britain, and parallels would inevitably have been drawn had the script made it to the screen.

In 2011, there was a widely publicised deal that saw Neil LaBute brought on board to direct a script by Julian Fellowes and Tim Rose Price, which would have starred Julie Andrews, Gabriel Byrne, and Matthew Goode. By the time filming began in September 2016, the cast had changed to include Gillian Anderson, Glenn Close, Christina Hendricks and Max Irons in a project directed by Gilles Paquet-Brenner, who also contributed to a reworked version of the script. '*Crooked House* came close to being my grandmother's favourite book, and as we trust her judgement in so many things, I think we can trust her on this', pointed out Mathew Prichard some time before filming finally began on the production. 'But I would love to do it. We'll have to do it really properly if we do.'

SPIDER'S WEB (1982)

The next BBC television adaption followed ITV's successful productions of *Why Didn't They Ask Evans?*, *The Seven Dials Mystery* and *The Agatha Christie Hour*, but unlike these it was not a lavish, high-profile affair. Instead, this 1982 adaptation of *Spider's Web* simply brought Christie's successful 1954 light-hearted murder mystery to the television studio, with very few changes from the original, which shows farcical attempts to cover up a murder following the discovery of a body in a country house. The play had previously been filmed in 1960 (see Chap. 5), but it had made little impact and has rarely been seen since. Like the earlier film, this adaptation makes no real attempt to broaden out the story from its theatrical origins—outside action is restricted to an establishing shot of the house where we see the character Mildred gardening, while music punctuates only a few non-dialogue scenes—and for the most part a lightly abridged version of Christie's script is left to speak for itself. One significant coup for the production was in its casting, not only for the renowned Elizabeth Spriggs as the aforementioned Mildred (Spriggs had already won an Olivier award in 1978, and would go on to be nominated for a BAFTA for her performance as Mrs Jennings in 1995's film of *Sense and Sensibility*, directed by Ang Lee), but also Penelope Keith in the lead role of Clarissa Hailsham-Brown, whose attempts to protect the person she presumes to be the murderer become an entertaining farce. Keith was at the height of her popularity at this point, off the back of two highly popular sitcom characters, the snobbish Margo Leadbetter in *The Good Life* (BBC, 1975–78) followed by deposed Lady of the Manor—and opposer of the nouveau riche—Audrey fforbes-Hamilton in *To the Manor Born* (BBC 1979–81), which had attracted over 23 million viewers at its peak.[11]

Keith is perfectly cast, and her presence no doubt helped bring attention to the production, which was transmitted on BBC2 on 26 December 1982. Its showing on the BBC's second channel, designed for items of niche interest, helps to explain why this was effectively televised theatre rather than a production specifically designed for the small screen. However, its placement in the Christmas schedules indicates that it was envisaged as a special treat for the audience, bolstered by its prominence in publicity for the channel's festive offerings, including a large *Radio Times* photograph on the TV listings of the day—such a transmission date recalled the old 'A Christie for Christmas' slogan that would accompany publication of her novels in the later years of her writing career. There is no indication that there is a direct link between this adaptation and the 1984 Miss Marple series, especially as it had always been easier to license Christie's plays for screen adaptations than her other stories, but the background of the director and producer did indicate that Christie was not being treated as a throwaway piece of entertainment, but rather someone of more reputable standing. This perspective would continue in the BBC's later series and offer a marked contrast to most attitudes towards Christie's works at the Corporation during her lifetime. The producer, Cedric Messina, had been at the helm of 80 episodes of the BBC's *Play of the Month* since 1965, before spearheading the Corporation's project to broadcast television productions of all of Shakespeare's plays, which ran from 1978 to 1985, with Messina producing the first two seasons. The production was Basil Coleman's final work as a director, after forging a long professional career with composer Benjamin Britten while working on such heavyweight productions as the BBC's 1977 adaptation of Tolstoy's *Anna Karenina*.

The production of *Spider's Web* was well received, with the BBC's management commending it. David Reid, Head of Series and Serials, called it 'hokum beautifully done' (perhaps an indication that for some, appreciation and enjoyment of Christie still needed qualification), although one of his colleagues found it less effective than the rather higher-budgeted ITV adaptations had been.[12] It had 5.4 m viewers, making it the second most watched programme of the week on BBC2, only behind the light entertainment of *Des O'Connor Tonight*. However, *Guardian* critic Nancy Banks-Smith was not enamoured of the play, despite her usual appreciation of the author, calling it 'one of those bits of Christie so dreadful that the rights haven't been bought for films'.[13] Certainly it is a piece that does not instinctively lend itself to the screen. However, a rather more extravagant series of adaptations of some of Christie's most well-loved mysteries was soon to appear for BBC viewers—and Banks-Smith was one of those who would be most impressed by these near faultless productions depicting one of Christie's most iconic characters, making a long overdue appearance on the medium after a period of gestation lasting almost a decade.

The Beginnings of *Agatha Christie's Miss Marple* (1984–92)

We can trace the specific attempts by the BBC to create a series from Christie's Miss Marple stories to a decade prior to its 1984 launch. When enquiries were made on 15 November 1974 Agatha Christie was still alive, and there was a little more than a week to go until the long-awaited film adaptation of *Murder on the Orient Express* was released in British cinemas. There can be little doubt that the attendant publicity of this Poirot screen adventure had inspired senior BBC producer Pieter Rogers to seek out permission to make a series concentrating on Christie's other well-known character, elderly sleuth Miss Marple. Once more, Nora Blackborow was the point of contact, and Rogers acknowledged in his letter to her that he knew that Dame Agatha was not well disposed towards such a possibility, but it was felt that this was the most opportune time to make an enquiry.[14] Rogers had even gone as far as to approach the agent of the actress who he wished to take on the lead part—Barbara Mullen, who had first appeared as Miss Marple on stage in 1949 where, at 35, she had been rather too young for the part. As Rogers points out in his letter, Mullen had successfully reprised the role in a more recent revival of the play, which he had seen and enjoyed. 'I do understand Dame Agatha's reluctance to bring her work to the small screen in the light of difficulties from the past,' Rogers wrote, 'but were she to consider this suggestion, the whole project would have all the care the BBC could bestow upon the production.'[15] The BBC copyright department was not optimistic, given its previous dealings with Christie's works, but nevertheless outlined which Miss Marple novels and short stories had been published.[16] However, the plans progressed no further, and it took considerable changes in the landscape of Agatha Christie adaptations for such a proposed series to be investigated more seriously.

As is so often the case, a personal relationship underpinned negotiations over the Miss Marple series that would eventually launch on BBC One at the end of 1984. Mathew Prichard points out that the existence of ITV adaptations of various novels and short stories, which had started in 1980, helped to establish the groundwork for conversations about how Christie's work should be adapted for television. Meanwhile, Christie's death had meant that her daughter, Rosalind Hicks, was now in charge of negotiating and vetoing any potential adaptations—and it was to the advantage and credit of BBC producer Guy Slater that she came to like and trust him while he negotiated to make a lavish and faithful series of adaptations of the Miss Marple novels. Prichard recalls Slater as 'just brilliant. I remember him coming down to Greenway and talking my mother round, and he had this brilliant idea about Joan Hickson, who was not well known at the time [...] quite apart from exchanging letters, they had long discussions at Greenway, much earlier on than I'm sure the BBC usually accorded to most people. My mother got on very well with Joan too. It was a good partnership.'[17] The casting of Hickson is a rare instance of such a decision meeting with near universal acclaim (just as David Suchet's performance as Poirot would later do); she had given a stand-out cameo performance in LWT's 1980 adaptation of Christie's *Why Didn't They Ask Evans?* and had a lengthy career on stage and film, even if she had never quite progressed to becoming a household name—something that this new series would change.

By August 1983 discussions had reached an advanced stage, although the BBC did fear that clauses in LWT's contract may have allowed it to scupper any planned Christie productions; in the event, this was not an issue. Slater wrote to Hicks in order to reassure her formally of his plans. In a letter where he first outlined his hopes of casting Hickson, he also wrote:

> I do, I think, have some idea how important Miss Marple is to you and I would only say that when/if we get the go ahead I can promise you two things. Firstly, I will aim for perfection, and secondly, I will consult you all along the line. I cannot promise that everything you want can be done but will give my word that it will be taken very seriously and that I will make every effort to accommodate you.[18]

In the event, Hickson would need some convincing to take on the role, but Guy Slater's approach worked, and he had managed to do the almost impossible by convincing the Christie family that they should allow a series of adaptations on the BBC. Nevertheless, there were still many details that needed to be agreed on, not least the titles that would be adapted. Prichard recalls that his 'conservative' mother was still keen to keep the Corporation in check. He explains:

> The story there is that the BBC needed three stories to make it worth their while assembling all the people and, indeed, Joan Hickson. They did television very differently in those days and they said they needed at least three, and my mother categorically refused to give them more than two [*The Body in the Library* and *A Murder is Announced*]. If you ask me why, I have absolutely no idea, but she said 'I am not prepared to risk the reputation of Miss Marple on television. What happens if we don't like the first one and then we have to grin and bear it through the other two?' In the end, what happened was that we sold them two stories, and the Cork family,[19] who owned an institution called the Copyright Trading Company, they owned *A Pocket Full of Rye*, so they sold [it] to the BBC at the same time we sold our two. Everybody dug their heels in [...] but once it was done we started to speak a common language.[20]

In fact, by the time negotiations were over, the BBC had the rights to four of Agatha Christie's novels, with the 1942 Miss Marple novel *The Moving Finger* completing the set. Although the *Daily Mirror* had broken the news of both the series and the casting back on 17 December 1983, it was formally announced in the 1 March 1984 edition of *The Stage and Television Today*, accompanied by a picture of Hickson in smart, modern attire standing alongside a beaming Guy Slater, whose white tie and tinted glasses are a contemporary fashion statement—a reminder of how well crafted the series is when we know that just off camera were such highly contrasting appearances.

The ten-part series was to be an expensive one, shot on 16 mm film with extensive location work and a budget of approximately £350,000 per episode, something counterbalanced by co-production agreements with the A&E Network in the United States, whose contribution covered the costs of approximately two episodes, while Australia's Seven Network paid nearly £250,000. Production on the series commenced on 8 April 1984 with *The Body in the*

Library, which was to be produced in three parts, each running to approximately 50 minutes. The script was written by T.R. Bowen, who had written one episode of *The Agatha Christie Hour* and would go on to adapt all but four of the stories tackled by the BBC Miss Marple series. Director for the story was Silvio Narizzano, probably best known for the 1966 film *Georgy Girl*, while Hickson was joined by esteemed actors including Valentine Dyall and Andrew Cruickshank, as well as Gwen Watford and Moray Watson as entertaining Miss Marple allies Dolly and Colonel Bantry, in whose library the titular corpse had mysteriously appeared overnight. Joining them for filming was David Horovitch as Detective Inspector Slack, the first of the character's five appearances in the series, whose irritation with, and begrudging respect for, Miss Marple contributes some of the lighter moments; for each appearance Slack is accompanied by his younger, less austere colleague Detective Constable Lake, played by Ian Brimble.[21]

It is immediately obvious that this production, first broadcast between 26 and 28 December 1984, has been made with care, and an absolute desire to follow the source material as much as possible. It comes as no surprise that Rosalind Hicks had been closely involved in the whole production process, including commenting on scripts at every stage. Changes from the original novel are so minor that they do not warrant discussion, while the casting and production standards are exemplary. Like *Agatha Christie's Poirot* five years later, this is a confident series that is almost fully formed from the very first episode—something that is unusual for television. Hickson is immediately settled in the part, and although her role in the first episode is limited, her opening scenes where she discusses with her maid how best to light a fire set out the character straightaway as a woman who notices the smallest details with a penchant for firmly but kindly pointing out the truth. There are very few elements that might have been changed had the story been adapted later in the run; one unusual occurrence is on the soundtrack, where the lush orchestral score is occasionally embellished by ill-considered stabs of electronic music. This is dropped for later adaptations, and is a rare instance of the style of the series betraying its 1980s origins.

However, the production is not an old-fashioned one. It unashamedly shows off the best and worst of the past beyond any assumption of cosy nostalgia, especially when it comes to highlighting the darker side of human nature present whatever the period and location. This is a complicated and nuanced world, not simply a pretty blank canvas populated by suspects like an edition of *Murder, She Wrote* or *Midsomer Murders*, while the series's penchant for lingering close-ups and long shots shows a confidence in allowing the audience to gather their own conclusions from character moments without having their hands held. Assuming intelligence and maturity on behalf of those watching may explain why the adaptation dispenses with one convention of film and television murder mysteries—the visual flashback. Indeed, the only concern that senior BBC management raised was its feeling that such a depiction of the key events seemed to be missing from the production. The fifth story to be adapted, *The Murder at the Vicarage*, is the only one of the BBC Miss Marples to feature a fully dramatised flashback portraying events leading up to the crime, and this was the first to begin production after the management comments were made. Nevertheless, this element was not retained for future adaptations.

The production was keenly anticipated and well publicised, with a last-minute decision made to move it away from the broadcast of popular comedy drama *Minder* on ITV in order to give it the best chance. The press paid much attention to Hickson herself, whose personal links with the character were often emphasised in interviews and previews. One of these links was with Margaret Rutherford, who had portrayed the same character in the 1960s MGM films; Hickson was happy to recall that she featured in the first of these films, but only spoke about Rutherford as a friend (and godmother to her son), perhaps kindly claiming that she had not really seen her performance as Miss Marple. The other link was a letter from Christie herself, which had been rediscovered by Hickson's daughter; the note commends Hickson's performance in a play (often said to be Christie's own *Appointment with Death*, but likely the 1946 production of Warren Chetham-Strode's play *The Guinea Pig*, according to Slater's private recounting of the story to Rosalind Hicks) and Christie writes that 'I hope one day you will play my dear Miss Marple'. When she did come to take on the role, Hickson had the spinster's persona in mind. 'I see her as multi-faceted,' she told the *Radio Times*, 'shrewd, unobtrusive, extremely determined, and full of surprises.'[22] Hickson also observed that this characterisation was not one that was also true of herself. 'I'm terribly woolly minded', she confessed to Maureen Paton of the *Daily Express*. 'I'm not a sleuth at all. I'm just an old character actress, dear.'[23]

Critical reaction to the first adaptation was almost wholly positive. John Naughton of *The Listener* called it 'preposterously, impossibly enjoyable',[24] although his colleague Phil Hardy felt that it had played too safe, rather unfairly claiming this to be the result of influence from international co-producers. The *Daily Express* called the adaptation 'a delight',[25] while Nancy Banks-Smith of *The Guardian* declared it 'top drawer',[26] and the *Glasgow Herald* said that it was 'one of the most successful of the many variable adaptations of Christie classics, and has at last presented us with the perfect Miss Marple'.[27] Within the BBC the reaction was just as positive, since the series was discussed in positive terms at the Corporation's review board, where senior management considered programmes that had been broadcast the previous week. The production was described as 'marvellous' with Hickson and Bowen singled out for praise, as was Christie's original novel.[28] Viewing figures peaked at nearly 13 m, while audience feedback was highly positive, the summary report noting that the panel found it 'reasonably exciting' and 'most entertaining'.[29] Only 8 % of viewers felt it was too slow, even though it ran to two-and-a-half hours in total, while the acting was the most praised element, especially Joan Hickson, who was compared positively with Margaret Rutherford. In her preview of this first production, Mary Cadogan had written for the *Radio Times* that Hickson was 'likely to emerge as the definitive Miss Marple'; she was to be proven correct even quicker than anyone could have imagined.[30]

One person who was particularly thrilled by the completion of the first story was Rosalind Hicks herself, whose notes to Guy Slater following a viewing of *The Body in the Library* indicate both relief and pleasure with the final production. So happy was Hicks that she made a move that would have been unthinkable during previous negotiations, as she wrote: 'I thought I might just mention that if you did want to do any more the time might be right to make a suggestion to Brian Stone.'[31] Slater had achieved the near impossible—creating a popular hit that was also a critical success, which had so impressed Christie's family that they were actively courting him for more.

As soon as the production wrapped on *The Body in the Library*, the team spent much of summer 1984 working on their next adaptation, although unseasonable bad weather meant that they had only a handful of sunny days during the Norfolk and Sussex filming of Christie's 1942 tale of poison pen letters and murder, *The Moving Finger*. The plan had always been to broadcast each story's episodes in close succession, on consecutive nights, rather than across ten weeks, as both the BBC and Guy Slater felt that this helped to keep audience attention on the story and meant that audiences would know that each week brought a new story. Although Hicks would have preferred the series to have a fixed weekly time slot, she was happy to defer to the broadcaster and producer, which indicated the trust that they had earned. Having taken a short break after the series's Christmas premiere, the programme returned on 21 and 22 February with a two-part adaptation of the story.

Although Christie rated *The Moving Finger* highly, citing it as one of her ten favourites when asked in 1972, Guy Slater considered it the weakest of the four mysteries adapted in this first wave, partially explaining the decision to spread the story across two episodes rather than three. He brought Julia Jones on board to script the adaptation, a writer who had worked on series such as *The Duchess of Duke Street* (BBC, 1976–77) and *Anne of Green Gables* (BBC, 1972). Slater found it particularly difficult to translate the story to a screen adaptation, something not helped by the fact that Miss Marple plays a very small part in the original novel. Hicks agreed that although it had been one of her mother's favourites, that did not necessarily mean that it was an easy story to bring to television. Both Slater and Hicks picked up on the fact that the novel requires some suspension of disbelief when it comes to the envelopes that contain the poison pen letters—the story has it that they were typed up some ten months previously, even though some of those who receive them have not been in the village that long. Slater's solution was a simple one: the actors playing the characters involved were directed not to look at the envelopes too closely. Hicks visited the location filming in Nether Wallop ('Miss Marple land' as she called it, since it doubled for the sleuth's village of St Mary Mead) in early June 1984 and enjoyed the experience. Her letters to Slater at around this point broadly show how she was feeling more comfortable with the production, especially Hickson and the rest of the cast, although she was unhappy that the character of Aimee was renamed Eryl in order to give the sense that the village was situated close to the Welsh border. By now comments were minor—Miss Marple's cottage seemed a little dull on the inside, Hicks felt, while another location was deemed to be over-decorated—and a strong working relationship seems to have been forged, due in no small part to the extent to which Slater kept Hicks abreast of developments, an approach that she valued.

Hicks was happy with the final result, writing to Slater that 'I thought the script was good and it had a lot of humour, and although I know Joan Hickson thought she looked untidy she was <u>very</u> good'.[32] The humour of which she speaks may well be a direct influence of the director, Roy Boulting, who along with his twin brother John had built a career producing and directing tightly plotted British film thrillers as well as lighter pictures, ranging from the hard-edged *Brighton Rock* (d. John Boulting, 1947) to the comedy *Lucky Jim* (d. John Boulting, 1957). This was to be his first foray into directing for television and would be his final directorial credit, but it did allow him to revisit an old acquaintance by working once more with Joan Hickson, whom he had directed in the film of *The Guinea Pig* in 1948. When both brothers were interviewed by the *Radio Times* about the production, John Boulting did not try to hide his disdain of the source material that his brother had just directed, despite the fact that their older brother, Peter Cotes, had been the inaugural director of *The Mousetrap* in 1952. While Roy pointed out Christie's popularity in Russia, John remarked that it was 'a measure of their literary incompetence'. 'John is a snob', riposted Roy. 'I enjoyed this as a challenge—either to divine the depths to which television can sink, or to scale the slopes on which one may ascend to greater glory.'[33]

While *The Moving Finger* is not one of the most well-known Christies, the programme continued in the mould of *The Body in the Library* to produce an adaptation that is sharp and funny, and perhaps better paced than its predecessor due to the shorter running time. The adaptation does not entirely eschew nostalgia, but exposes the less palatable aspects of village life. Such a sense is effectively set up by the hand-drawn images that make up the programme's opening sequence, where superficially pleasant and old-fashioned images conceal more sinister details—a body at the edge of a cricket pitch, sharp-eyed villagers gossiping in the street and a mysterious figure observing the outside world from behind flowing curtains. This title sequence follows Slater's original idea of 'a film montage of an idyllic English village bathed in sunshine—a cloud goes across the sun and the village suddenly appears malevolent, frightening, etc'.[34] Because the novel did not feature Miss Marple with the prominence that one might expect from a series bearing her name, the character's role was increased in this adaptation, bringing her into the heart of the mystery much earlier. Such a change also made for a welcome, small alteration to Miss Marple's character—by being on the scene earlier she is not forced to rely on solving the mystery in the abstract (she attributes her working out of the crime to her understanding of 'human nature' in the novel); instead, her powers of observation are just as important. Reception was positive although not ecstatic, with the *Observer* preview calling it 'prettily made' and 'unpretentious', while Lucy Hughes-Hallett of the *Evening Standard* wrote that 'although the tale it told was a nasty one of repressed sexual passion bursting out in poison pen letters and finally murder, it was somehow as reassuring as hot buttered toast', an indication of just how difficult it was for any Christie adaptation to shake off the 'cosy' label.[35] As for the Corporation itself, the BBC's Review Board deemed the episode 'beautifully produced' and 'in no sense seemed old-fashioned'.[36] Indeed, the series seemed to be at pains to ensure that it was not making lazily produced programmes fixated on scenery: stylish touches include a sepia-tinted montage of images depicting a trip to London, a choice that helps to keep the audience on their toes; the scene itself had been removed from earlier drafts but was reinstated at Slater's suggestion.

Plans for the third story to be adapted, *A Murder Is Announced*, began in September 1983, with playwright Alan Plater contacted to see if he would undertake scripting duties, something that he was happy to do, later citing the strength of Christie's female characters as one of the joys of the material. However, production was at such an early stage that he had no model from which to work and needed to seek basic details from Slater—for example, would the stories be set in the 1950s or in the 1980s (the former, although some production documentation indicates 'late 1940s' as a period), and what sort of village would the series be filmed in? Initially Plater was keen to avoid the 'traditional' ending of an Agatha Christie mystery, where all the suspects are assembled in order for the solution to be revealed, but he eventually decided that it was the most suitable way to end the story. He found the process of retaining the mystery's logic intact exhausting, and implored Slater to ensure that he had not created any illogical deductions. As with the novel, Plater kept Miss Marple's role to a minimum in the first portion of the story, something that worried Hicks more than the BBC—indicating that she understood the expectations of a television audience whose happiness was as important as keeping strictly to the novel. After all, *The Moving Finger* had successfully increased Miss Marple's role, but as *A Murder Is Announced* was to be shown in three parts, a light first episode for the elderly sleuth still gave her plenty of screen time. Neither Plater nor Slater felt that the novel's remarkable depiction of Miss Marple's voice-throwing skills could be convincingly depicted on screen, and it was happily removed.

Although Rosalind Hicks was becoming more comfortable with the production and more amenable to necessary changes, the script for this adaptation caused an unexpected flare-up in relations between her and the production team. Plater's adaptation had been widely considered to be the strongest of the four, and Slater had been enthusiastic when he sent the draft material on to Hicks, only to be disappointed by her reaction. When Hicks first had sight of the scripts in February 1984, she declared them to be 'very readable and amusing', although she was concerned that more action might be needed for the length of the piece.[37] As well as her concern that Miss Marple did not come into the action early enough (indicating that absolute fidelity to the novel was not necessarily her over-riding concern), she also felt that some good character moments had been lost in this first draft. These included Miss Marple's reminiscences about people she knew in St Mary Mead, while Hicks was most annoyed at some of the 'trite' pieces of dialogue given to her, including 'I find it impossible to resist a juicy murder' (which was then removed) and 'I've never seen a real bullet hole' (which was not).[38] Further, both she and her husband Anthony Hicks had felt that the characters' responses to the murder were altogether too flippant. Slater replied by saying that he shared concerns about some of the dialogue, which had been duly changed, but reassured her that 'We have no intention of being facetious and by playing it seriously I hope it will be funny rather than flippant and silly'.[39] Hicks replied that 'I think *A Murder is Announced* is good and will be a success. I only said I didn't like it as much as I feel it is too full of facetious remarks and jokes that are easy enough to play but can be distracting.' Referring to the novel's character of Mitzi, whose name was changed for the adaptation, Hicks then asked: 'Why [is she called] Hannah? What country does she come from? Perhaps Mitzi could be overdone and become too funny?! [...] It isn't muddling for me—it is other people who read the books I am worried about.'[40]

A Murder Is Announced was rehearsed during the latter half of July 1984, before filming took place throughout August and September, with locations ranging from Dorset, to Wales, to Scotland—variety that only a healthy budget would allow. When production moved to the village of Powerstock in Dorset, which doubled as Chipping Cleghorn where the story is set, it caused a flurry of excitement in the local community, with the village's primary school putting together an exhibition based on the production, including their own 20-minute film and correspondence with both Hickson and star of stage and screen Sylvia Syms, who played Mrs Easterbrook. Production progressed smoothly, except for a dispute with the owner of Manor Farm, which doubled for Letitia Blacklock's residence Little Paddocks (and is now a bed and breakfast), due to the house not being left in the state that had been agreed at the end of filming.[41] Another issue emerged when the red setter hired to discover Murgatroyd's body refused to perform any task—the trainer's response that the dog was simply being as stupid as requested did not go down well, not least with Joan Sims, who had to lie on the damp ground covered in chicken liver paste in an attempt to coax it in her direction.[42]

The adaptation's director was David Giles, who specialised in popular depictions of the past and literary adaptations, with success ranging from *The Forsyte Saga* (BBC, 1967) to *Vanity Fair* (BBC, 1967) and *The Darling Buds of May* (ITV, 1991–93). Hickson was joined in the cast for this production by Ursula Howells, playing Letitia Blacklock, in whose house the murder takes place. Howells was a striking and in-demand actress whose television credits included *Upstairs Downstairs* and *The Forsyte Saga*, and it was the latter series that had also starred the original choice for the role, Margaret Tyzack, who had also made a considerable impression in her exceptional performance as Antonia in

I, Claudius (BBC, 1976), the eponymous character's mother. Making his first of two appearances is John Castle as Detective Inspector Craddock; by the time we meet him again in *The Mirror Crack'd from Side to Side* in 1992, he has mysteriously become Miss Marple's nephew, although there is no evidence of this here. Kevin Whately accompanies him as Detective Sergeant Fletcher; he would soon become the sidekick to John Thaw's *Inspector Morse* (ITV, 1987–2000) as Detective Sergeant Lewis, before progressing to his own eponymous series in 2007. Having visited the set with her husband, Rosalind Hicks started to feel more confident about the production. 'If I was a little sceptical about the script I feel that David Giles will sort it out as I cannot think he will stand for any cheap laughs', she later wrote to Slater.[43]

The first episode of the production was shown to the press at the Preview One Cinema in London, along with the whole of *The Moving Finger*—key cast members were also invited, and must have been pleased to see the final results of their work, which ranks among the very finest Christie adaptations. An exemplary cast perform one of her best mysteries, all with clearly defined characters who resist any temptation to send up the material (as had been Hicks's concern), while accompanying events result in a story that grows increasingly dark and gripping as it progresses. Although there are instances where we seem to be set up for cosy nostalgia, including shots of cows being walked through the village, this is soon turned on its head by sequences such as the murder of Murgatroyd, where the creeping killer's attack is filmed like a horror movie. As Hinchcliffe and Murgatroyd have been clearly established as joint protagonists with Miss Marple (in fact they do at least as much deducing), and are clearly a happy if bickering couple, the death of one of them is a shock for the audience, while its viciousness also helps to misdirect armchair detectives away from the actual culprit.

Jonathan Powell was among the members of the Weekly Review Board at the BBC who highly commended this adaptation in particular, marking it out as even stronger than *The Body in the Library*, while other members of the Corporation's management wondered if more Agatha Christie titles could be made available for broadcast. Alan Plater's script was commended, along with Hickson and Slater, with the latter particularly complimented for his work with the Christie family.[44] Broadcast between 28 February and 2 March 1985, all three of the episodes featured in the top ten BBC programmes for the week, beaten only by perennial comedy *Last of the Summer Wine*, with viewing figures ranging from 13.75 m to 15.35 m. For the final episode the BBC commissioned an audience research report, which indicated that it had achieved an audience appreciation score of 87 out of 100—the highest of the week for drama, and substantially above the average of 74. 'The great majority of those responding had nothing but praise for this serial', the report read, before outlining spontaneous remarks from the panel that had praised just about every aspect of the production; fewer than one in twenty participants had any negative comments to make at all. The BBC could be satisfied that it had a success on its hands.[45]

The success of the productions had been apparent even before broadcast, however, and as production moved towards the final novel to be adapted, *A Pocket Full of Rye*, thoughts turned to how the relationship could be continued. Two areas were considered and flagged up—the first was with the rights of Warner Bros. to some of the Miss Marple stories, which, it seemed, could not be stopped as easily as had been expected; in the end, these television films would indeed have an impact on the BBC series, as we will later see. However, even by November 1984 Rosalind Hicks was bringing up the possibility of a second run of Miss Marple stories with the BBC, which it was happy to discuss with her, although she was sad to hear that Slater would not stay on for any subsequent set of adaptations—in the end he did remain as executive producer, while George Gallaccio took on the role of producer, having been associate producer for the first batch.

The final adaptation to be made in this first series was once more scripted by T.R. Bowen, while Guy Slater decided that he would direct this adaptation himself, resulting in George Gallaccio filling his shoes as producer prior to his permanent move to the role. One small but immediate change was in the title, amended from Christie's *A Pocket Full of Rye* to the more commonly written *A Pocketful of Rye*. The mystery involves the death of Rex Fortescue, a wealthy but unpopular man, whose dead body is found to include a pocket filled with rye; his murder is the first of several in a particularly cynical and vicious Miss Marple tale. The two-part script met with the approval of Rosalind Hicks, who wrote: 'I really thought [the script] was quite good. I know you were worried about it. Miss Marple comes out particularly well I think. I like two episodes rather than three. I have a number of minor points to make about it but I'm sure it could be a lot worse!'[46] These small points included 'Why is breakfast so early?', referring to Rex's final meal, and the observation that 'Miss Marple would never have sat doing nothing for over an hour', as she was scripted to do in the second episode. 'She would have made much more fuss.' Hicks also drew attention to the ending of the script, where the most radical departure from the novel occurs when the villain of the piece makes a high-speed departure from the scene, resulting in a car chase. In the final production this does feel rather over the top, and a little silly, but Hicks was more concerned with the characterisation, writing: 'While the ending is quite dramatic, I don't believe that [the culprit] would have acted in this way.'[47]

A Pocketful of Rye is the only *Miss Marple* production for which the full list of auditionees for the main cast survives in the BBC production file. Usually looking through such a list may present some interesting moments of trivia, but in this case it is an insight into how good an eye the production team had for talent, since the names feature many actors and actresses who would go on to greater success, as well as several who had been or would soon become well known by association with particular characters or series. First through the doors of the audition room was one Kathy Burke, reading the part of ill-fated maid Gladys, eventually played by the exceptional Annette Badland. Burke would later find fame in comedic roles, as well as critical acclaim in dramas such as *Nil by Mouth* (d. Gary Oldman, 1997), before becoming a highly respected theatre director. Actresses auditioning for the role of cook Mrs Crump included Maggie Jones, best known for her iconic role as Blanche Hunt, mother to Deirdre, in long-running soap opera *Coronation Street*—the part went to Merelina Kendall—while instantly recognisable television actor Norman Bird turned down the role of Mr Crump, despite enjoying the script, because he was disappointed by the character's lack of prominence in the second part in particular. Other well-known faces included Celia Imrie and Jan Harvey, star of *Howards' Way* (BBC, 1985–90), who both auditioned for the part of housekeeper Mary Dove, a role that went to Selina Caddell; while interviews for unspecified parts were undertaken with both Bill Nighy and Julian Fellowes, whose later move behind the camera would lead to him penning a Christie script of his own (*Crooked House*, discussed earlier) alongside his *Downton Abbey* duties nearly three decades later. The only actor considered for the part of Dr Foster was Louis Mahoney, which was a relatively rare instance of the series casting a black actor in a role, although it did demonstrate that unlike some period dramas the producers made some attempts to show the real make-up of Britain in the post-war period, not an entirely fictionalised one devoid of non-white faces. Mahoney wrote to Slater to say that he was sad that he had joined so late in production, since the 'family' was already well established, but gently reiterated how keen he was to establish opportunity for 'Afro-Asian' actors, a reflection of his standing on Equity's Afro-Asian Committee.[48]

Filming took place between 8 October and 11 November 1984, much of it in Norfolk, while Nether Wallop in Hampshire once more stood in for Miss Marple's home village of St Mary Mead. This was not without its own problems, as the owner of the house had been upset by the disruption and damage caused during the first set of filming and was not keen to have the production back inside, although exteriors were filmed without a hitch.[49] The cast already listed was joined by Timothy West in the small but important role of the murdered man; Slater thanked him for his strong performance that cast such a long shadow over the production despite his early death, and considered acceptance of the offer of the role by such an in-demand and esteemed actor to be a personal favour, especially as this was the first time Slater had directed a film production.[50] Clive Merrison was cast as Pervical Fortescue, eldest son of the deceased, while Peter Davison played second son Lance, adding to the myriad roles that barely kept him off television in the 1980s.

Any adaptation of *A Pocket Full of Rye* has two issues to contend with. The first is that the book is an example of where Christie's decision to replicate the nursery rhyme of the title tends to distract rather than embellish, even if the final explanation is reasonably convincing. The second issue is that the whole premise of the book relies on the fact that the characters are inherently unlikeable, and this is successfully transferred to the screen; there are moments when one can only hope that the murderer will not be caught and eventually the whole family will be picked off sooner rather than later. This makes it more difficult than usual to engage with the story, although Slater uses his best techniques to keep the audience on board, not by shying away from the nasty undertone of the characters in the book but by embellishing it. When maid Gladys is found dead with a clothes hook on her nose it is a cruel and shocking image, almost distressing given what we know of her character—the death is presented much more forcefully than in the book, and helps to keep the audience keen to see the murderer exposed, as they surely will be.

The BBC Review Board was once more pleased with the production following its broadcast on 7 and 8 March 1985, although one member felt that it was probably the least satisfying of the four stories to date. Slater's direction was commended, as was Hickson's performance again, with the feeling that 'there were many more series in her yet'.[51] Maureen Paton of the *Daily Express* was particularly happy to see a story that she felt reflected a less 'cosy' vision of the past with its 'detestable' group of suspects.[52] The first run of *Miss Marple* had left an exhausted and poorly Guy Slater at the end of it (in letters he apologises for the 'lurgy' he has inevitably caught as soon as production finished). He was in need of a well-deserved break, but could feel confident that he had created a lasting success and established a template that the talented producer George Gallaccio could continue with. Nevertheless, there were to be a few bumps in the road yet before all 12 Miss Marple novels could be brought to the small screen.

Miss Marple Goes Back to the Beginning

Even before broadcast it was clear that the *Miss Marple* series was likely to be a successful venture, and the high ratings and critical acclaim that the programme received only cemented this. So it was that the production could barely catch its breath before work needed to begin on the next batch of four stories to be adapted. The first of these was to be broadcast at Christmas and, for the first time, was to be a self-contained film, rather than a two- or three-part serial; the mystery selected was *The Murder at the Vicarage*, the first novel to star Miss Marple, published in 1930. Since the first series had launched, *Miss Marple* had proven not only to be a domestic success, but had also fared well in international markets as one of the BBC's top exports, with purchasing countries including China, while the series was cited as a co-production success story, blazing the trail for a new way to make BBC programmes.

Although Slater had stepped aside as producer, to be replaced by Gallaccio, he stayed on as executive producer—likely at the behest of either the BBC or Rosalind Hicks, who had written to him to say she understood his keenness to move on to new ventures, but would be sad to see him leave; both parties had been extremely pleased with the way in which his personal qualities helped to make relations so cordial and effective. Nevertheless, beyond a newly coloured title sequence, little had changed from the first run of stories. The filming of T.R. Bowen's script began in March 1987, with the series covering many locations including Dorset, Devon, Oxfordshire, Norfolk and, of course, Nether Wallop in Hampshire, which once more doubled for St Mary Mead. Julian

Amyes was brought on board to direct *The Murder at the Vicarage*, having worked on several literary adaptations including BBC productions of *The Old Curiosity Shop* (1979), *Great Expectations* (1981) and *Jane Eyre* (1983), while his later ventures into crime included four episodes of ITV's *Rumpole of the Bailey*. Joining Hickson for filming was Paul Eddington, cast in the role of Reverend Clement; Eddington was a well-known name and face following a long and successful television career, including programmes such as *The Good Life* and *Yes Minister*, and his exasperation in the role helps to elevate the production, especially when he is treated as a potential suspect after the despicable Colonel Protheroe is found shot in the vicar's study, rather than his being above suspicion, as had seemed to be the case in the novel.

The Murder at the Vicarage concerns a curious case of two confessions for the titular crime, which confuses the police, only for the local busybody Miss Marple to work out the solution. Later novels would rein back on some of the harder edges of Miss Marple's character—she is more overtly nosy and even interfering in this story, although the character takes a back seat to proceedings, initially appearing simply to be a witness to events linked to the crime. The TV adaptation puts her more in line with later characterisations, a simple observer who quietly works everything out without fuss, but understandably makes her more prominent. This Miss Marple is not a gossip and speaks no more than she needs to, but is clearly depicted as a figure who knows more than she is saying, while an expectant audience awaits her final deductions—unlike in the novel, where her late prominence is designed to be something of a surprise. This 'grey haired cobra', as Detective Inspector Slack calls her, now operates in the foreground of the mystery rather than the background, but the main spirit of the novel is faithfully reproduced. This includes depictions of awkward relationships between staff and their employers—a consistent theme in Christie's stories, which capture a changing world in this respect. A significant alteration occurs at the end when a villainous character commits suicide rather than be taken to trial; something that is more dramatically satisfying in an adaptation of this type, which requires all loose threads to be tied up promptly. In fact, this event is symptomatic of a slight change of tone from the book, which is one of Christie's lighter murder mysteries, now presented with a darker edge, even if it still has the initial appearance of a safe, timeless past with thatched cottages and quiet village ways of life.

Such was the esteem with which the production was held that it was given the prime slot in the evening on BBC One's 1986 Christmas Day schedules, sandwiched between hugely successful shows *Only Fools and Horses* and *EastEnders*. It was very well received, the BBC's Review Board calling it 'a Rolls-Royce of a programme',[53] while Wendy Cope of *The Spectator* found it 'quite delicious'[54] and Richard Cast of the *Daily Telegraph* cited it as his pick of the Christmas television fare, writing that 'one can hardly imagine it being better done'.[55]

Production continued with an adaptation of *Sleeping Murder*, a novel that had been posthumously published in late 1976 with the suffix 'Miss Marple's

Last Case', since it was the final novel featuring the sleuth to make it to print. However, there was nothing particularly 'final' about the story, other than that it had been written by Christie decades earlier and reserved as a gift to her husband Max Mallowan to be published after her death, as had also been the plan for the final Poirot book, *Curtain* (ownership of which rested with Rosalind Hicks). Indeed, the Miss Marple of the story is as sprightly as she ever appears to be, and so there is no problem with presenting the story at this point in the series. Rights issues and practicalities had meant that the series never intended to adapt the stories in chronological order, and this presented no issues—with one notable exception, as we will later see.

Ken Taylor, who had adapted *Jewel in the Crown* for the lavish Granada series in 1984, was the person chosen to adapt *Sleeping Murder* for the screen, and his script sticks faithfully to the novel, which perhaps requires something of a suspension of disbelief when it comes to the central conceit that a young woman unconsciously buys a house in which she had lived many years earlier, which reawakens memories of a murder in the distant past. At times the adaptation implies that the truth behind this unlikely sequence of events will be a crucial part of the actual mystery, as memories of boarded-over doors and old wallpaper cause confusion and distress—might it be the case that these events are being manipulated by an unknown hand? In the event, no, but reawakened memories of a murder do lead to another death, which only brings the investigation closer to the villain, who is then caught by a weedkiller-wielding Miss Marple.

Viewers did not detect any slip in quality from the exceptional highs of previous productions when this adaptation was broadcast on 11 and 18 January 1987, although some critics felt it had been a little slow, and although generally well directed by John Davies, there were moments where subtlety was uncharacteristically lacking, such as in the rather over-the-top music that accompanies some of the more tense moments. Coincidentally, Davies had headed the aforementioned ITV adaptation of P.D. James's *Cover Her Face* in 1985—this had been Christie's first choice of title for *Sleeping Murder*, but the publication of James's novel forced a rethink. The BBC Review Board praised the adaptation again, citing the characterisation and story as particular strengths alongside the perennially popular performance by Hickson.[56]

Summer 1986 saw filming continue, coinciding with a landmark birthday for Joan Hickson, who turned 80 on 5 August; at this point she was showing no signs of slowing down as she worked through her second arduous run of filming for the series. The final two stories to be adapted in this run are perhaps the least famous of the Miss Marple novels—they were also the final two to be written, with *At Bertram's Hotel* published in 1965 and *Nemesis* in 1971. In *At Bertram's Hotel* nostalgia underpins the whole story, with Miss Marple revisiting the London hotel of the title, in which she had first stayed as a child—she is pleased to see that things have changed little, unlike the rest of the capital. However, there is a criminal undercurrent to events at the hotel, and it is one that leads to murder. The adaptation feels like as much of a culture shock to the viewer as modern London had once been to Miss Marple—we are suddenly put into surroundings that seem far more contemporary, with rock music and Miss Marple visiting a coffee bar, not to mention appearances of television in the hotel ('the Americans like it but it's well tucked away'). However, once more Miss Marple is not an opponent to the march of time, although that does not mean that she cannot wistfully recall the past.

Writer Jill Hyem, whose previous work included several episodes of *Tenko* (BBC, 1981–84), provides a script that does its best to misdirect the audience and keep the whole story more engaging than had perhaps even been the case with the original novel. However, her two-part adaptation cannot escape the fact that this is not a vintage Miss Marple story. Unfortunately, it also cannot rely on attractive visuals, as it feels rather claustrophobic and downbeat with its emphasis on hotel interiors, even though director Mary McMurray works hard to broaden out the action.[57] Some parts of the mystery seem bolted on and extraneous to the action, while few are wholly engaging in their own right. By the time the script reaches its conclusion, with the villain shimmying up a drain pipe and, once more, falling victim to a high-speed car chase instigated by themselves, it feels like this is an adaptation that has struggled to do its best with weaker than usual source material. After broadcast of the first episode on 25 January 1987, the BBC Review Board was unsure about the series for the first time; although it had enjoyed the episode, both the direction and Joan Greenwood (who played Miss Marple's friend Selina Hazy) came in for criticism.[58] Once the concluding half had been broadcast the following week, these doubts had been dispelled and the board was much happier with the production, making this just a small blip in the reception of the series.[59] Certainly it is still a high-quality production, even if it does not quite reach the highs of some earlier entries in the series.

The issue that any adaptation of *Nemesis* needs to face is that even Miss Marple does not know quite what is going on for some time. The reader, or audience, understands that Miss Marple has been asked to solve an unspecified mystery on behalf of her late friend, Mr Rafiel. As Christie readers will know, Mr Rafiel is a memorable character from her 1964 novel *A Caribbean Mystery*, and so the portrayal of his death (filmed on Burgh Island in Devon, inspiration for *Evil Under the Sun* and possibly *And Then There Were None*), prior to our meeting him, seems odd. It is unlikely that the casual audience would remember his name by the time the adaptation of the earlier story arrived in 1989, but the change of order may seem puzzling for Christie fans. The reason for this switch in the order of the mysteries is simple—along with two other Miss Marple novels, the rights to *A Caribbean Mystery* were not available to the BBC due to previous film adaptations.[60] So it was that *Nemesis* had to come first.

Given the obscure nature of the story early on, where Miss Marple is invited on a coach tour and expected to await a mystery that requires her skills, the production is especially fortunate that Joan Hickson dazzles once again, because her satisfaction with the situation assures us that we are in safe hands and not on a wild goose chase. Characterisation is a particular strength in this adaptation, with individuals being given a chance to breathe as Miss Marple scrutinises their actions in a manner that, for once, has been overtly requested. She is accompanied on this tour by her nephew, Lionel Peel, played by Peter Tilbury, who has been forced to leave his family home after a dispute with his wife—Lionel is not present in any Miss Marple novel, but is a welcome addition here since he gives Miss Marple someone to talk to who we can trust is not a suspect. After an unsuccessful attempt to cast Margaret Tyzack in *A Murder Is Announced*, she is finally brought on board to play the complex character Clotilde Bradbury-Scott, one of three spinster sisters who live in a house close to one of the coach's locations.

Miss Marple soon learns of the death of a young woman, Verity, and sets out to discover if she had actually been murdered by Mr Rafiel's son, Michael, as many had thought. Along the way another murder occurs, and Miss Marple soon works out exactly who was responsible and why. The story's conclusion is one of the most chilling of the series, and shows Miss Marple at her strongest. Having avoided a poisoned drink offered by the murderer, she calmly listens as they explain how the murder occurred out of love and its resulting jealousy. Miss Marple will not tolerate their excuses, or any misguided sense that the murderer had done their best for the victim: 'She's safe now, from any unsuitable princes? Sleeping beauty lies in the ruins, and flowers grow round her? No... She's a rotted corpse and there is no-one to kiss her awake.' The source material may be at the weaker end of the Miss Marple stories, but the performances, script and direction elevate it so that the ending in particular is one of the best of the series. This is not a nostalgic murder mystery, this is not a 'safe' murder or murderer—Miss Marple will not tolerate such an argument—this is the senseless death of a young woman that has an impact on those around her, and is an unforgivable act.

Writing about *Nemesis* after its broadcast on 8 and 15 February 1987, Benny Green of the *Today* newspaper said 'I love every tinkling minute',[61] while it also garnered a very positive review from John J. O'Connor of *The New York Times*, who wrote that 'This is the Christie detective to the very letter [...] Ms Hickson is giving a performance to be savoured by mystery buffs and just about everybody else'.[62] The BBC Review Board felt the production was 'marvellous', with Jonathan Powell citing it as his favourite, the direction from David Tucker resulting in particular praise.[63] However, the press that accompanied the series alluded to a considerable problem on the horizon. In an interview with Joan Hickson, the *Daily Mail* claimed that 'There are plans for one more BBC Christmas special and then [Miss Marple's] latest incarnation will be laid to rest because America owns the rights to all the remaining [novels]'.[64] The newspaper was correct—only one title was still available for adaptation, but no one at the BBC or among Christie's family was keen to see the end of the series. A solution would need to be found, but another problem was also coming into view—one concerning Joan Hickson herself.

COMPLETING THE CANON

It had always been the expectation that the second run of Miss Marple mysteries would be followed by an additional Christmas special, shot after the others and ready for the 1987 festivities. The novel *4.50 from Paddington* was the title selected for this prime slot, the same story that had heralded Margaret Rutherford's stint in the role back in 1961 in the loose adaptation *Murder She Said*. The plot is instigated by a friend of Miss Marple's, who has seen a murder take place on a train; when a body is nowhere to be found, further investigation is needed, which Miss Marple helps to mastermind. Filming for the production took place between 8 August and 25 September 1987, with Martyn Friend directing Bowen's script, having previously worked on successful Jersey-based detective series *Bergerac* (BBC, 1981–91). Various small changes were made to the story, including the deletion of a sub-plot concerning the poisoning of the Crackenthorpe family (the body having been found in the grounds of their home), but the basic mystery remains the same. It is to the credit of the script and Friend's direction that the denouement is wholly satisfying, since on the page Miss Marple's method for capturing the murderer is a little difficult to believe, especially as there is little overt deduction, with Miss Marple seeming to piece together the solution through instinct more than facts and clues. Nevertheless, it is a wholly enjoyable adaptation, with Miss Marple displaying a sharper tongue than usual in the presence of Detective Inspector Slack, who is not happy that his superior forces cooperation with the elderly amateur sleuth.

For some, a *Miss Marple* at Christmas was becoming an annual expectation, and interest was piqued when Joan Hickson was invited to lunch with Queen Elizabeth II on 9 December—whereupon the monarch revealed herself to be a keen watcher of the series. Broadcast on Christmas Day, following on from popular comedy show *Christmas Night with the Two Ronnies*, the BBC Review Board praised it as 'a joy', while Hilary Kingsley of the *Daily Mirror* felt that it was 'the best yet'.[65] However, few viewers had realised that despite the ongoing success of the series, this was expected to be the final production. 'Miss Hickson has completed all the novels available to us', a BBC spokesperson was quoted as saying in the *Daily Mirror* nearly a year after transmission, while Hickson herself was happy to move on, having been quoted as saying that although she had enjoyed herself she 'would like to do something quite different'.[66] While there were still three novels left to film, the cupboard was bare as far as the BBC was concerned, as the rights remained tied up following the 1980 film *The Mirror Crack'd* and the Helen Hayes adaptations of *A Caribbean Mystery* and *They Do It with Mirrors*. While Hickson did not feel that she would continue no matter what, neither the BBC nor the Christie family wished to leave the run of novel adaptations unfinished.

One possibility for keeping the series alive was discussed with Joan Hickson—that of adapting some of the Miss Marple short stories, with the likely first choice of 'Greenshaw's Folly'. Even so, discussions did not progress far (in fact, Mathew Prichard does not recall the idea ever being seriously entertained) because Hickson declined to start tackling the short stories. All was not lost, though, and after a break of two years, 1989 saw one of the remaining three novels become available to be made into a BBC film, 1964's *A Caribbean Mystery*. The adaptation had been announced early in the year to coincide with plans to celebrate the 100th anniversary of Christie's birth in 1990, although the programme would eventually be broadcast at the end of 1989 in a Christmas Day slot once more. As the series had been out of production for so long, it was quite a coup that the core cast and crew were able to regroup—of course Hickson's availability was crucial, but similarly important were screenwriter T.R. Bowen and George Gallaccio, who was now busy producing *Bergerac*. Perhaps it was a sign of how happy the experience had been that all three were able to reconvene on what was, once more, expected to be the final *Miss Marple* production; not only were the rights to the remaining two novels still unavailable, but Hickson had signalled her wish to finish on a high.

Filming took place on Barbados at the very hotel that had formed the basis for the original novel's location, the Coral Reef, at which Christie had stayed three decades earlier and had renamed the Golden Palm for the story; co-star Donald Pleasence stayed in the cottage that had once been Christie's. Christopher Petit was chosen to direct this production, another new face (to this point, each *Miss Marple* had been directed by a different person in an attempt to keep the series fresh) probably best known for the 1982 adaptation of P.D. James's *An Unsuitable Job for a Woman*. As might be expected for September, the temperature was high, leading to the discomfort of some crew and cast, including Hickson, who later said that 'it was murder'; however, the discomfort was nothing compared to the dangers of Hurricane Hugo, which shut down production for three days.[67] Once more Bowen's script shines, dispensing with a couple of minor characters but otherwise keeping tightly to the original story. On occasion, perhaps the expectations of a modern television audience are not quite met as the script sticks so closely to the novel—little is made of a death that occurs late in the book, and the final reveal of the murderer is also under-played, but no more than had been the case in the original. Some charming character moments are emphasised, such as Miss Marple's closeness to a maid who ends up murdered, while Donald Pleasence's turn as the obnoxious but entertaining Mr Rafiel nearly does the impossible in stealing the focus from Hickson on occasion; their repartee is a joy to watch.

While many people were excited to see Hickson back in the role, there was one party that was not happy to see the return of a series that had near guaranteed popular and critical success—rival broadcaster ITV. In an attempt to tempt audiences away from BBC One on the biggest broadcasting day of the year, ITV dusted off its copy of the American 1984 adaptation of the story starring Helen Hayes, and broadcast it in a prime time slot on a Sunday night two weeks before Christmas, in the hope that it would result in casual viewers declining to watch the Hickson version; the move was also retaliation for the BBC showing the film of *The Day of the Jackal* (d. Fred Zinnemann, 1973) opposite ITV's own new Frederick Forsyth drama. In the event, ratings were down a little, although still above 10 m (beaten by both *Coronation Street* and sitcom *After Henry* on the commercial channel); to what extent this was the result of ITV's decision is impossible to judge. Critical reaction was positive, and audiences gave the programme a rating of 77 out of 100 in the latest polling conducted on behalf of the BBC.[68] This was seven points above the average for drama at the time, with 94 % of those asked praising Joan Hickson's performance, and 80 % deeming it to be a 'high quality programme', while the BBC Review Board praised it as highly as ever.[69] Certainly ITV's move showed how the Christie brand was seen to be such a big hitter—something of which the commercial channel was now acutely aware, as its own *Poirot* series had launched to much success earlier in the year. 'Next year I think I should meet Poirot and have a long chat', Hickson told the *Radio Times*. 'I don't think they'd get on, do you?'[70]

Two years were to pass once more until the rights for the remaining two Miss Marple stories were freed up, and this time it really was the end of the line for the series. Despite the length of time between adaptations, Hickson's Miss Marple had remained a recurring fixture on TV screens, with regular repeats continuing to rate well, often in the BBC's top 20 for the week. However, no one involved with the production appears to have been particularly enthusiastic about the eleventh of the twelve novels to be adapted, the 1952 mystery *They Do It with Mirrors*, which deals with a murder at the home of an old friend of Miss Marple's that has become part of a centre for juvenile delinquents. 'We had a lot of trouble with this book. It doesn't make sense', said producer George Gallaccio to the *Daily Mail*, while Joan Hickson also claimed that this was not one of her favourites—before quickly clarifying that, of course, she *had* no favourites.[71] Christie's original story creates difficulties for adaptation, since it requires drastic contrasts in tone between the young offenders (who may, or may not, be a crucial part of the mystery) and the more traditional country house elements, as the murder takes place in rather more archetypal Christie circumstances. Seeing Miss Marple alongside ruffians who would not have looked out of place in some contemporary dramas feels wrong for the audience, and makes it difficult to buy in to this world, where characters can apparently run private rehabilitation institutions in the grounds of their home.

Nevertheless, a suspension of disbelief is crucial to all dramas, period ones even more so. As the *Daily Mail* noted after its reporter visited the set, 'The crew has to pander to viewers' perceptions of the past, not to the past itself'.[72] By this point, the dating of the films could no longer conform to the approximate chronology of the original novels, so Gallaccio simply moved the period on slightly for each production. Resultantly, this mystery takes place in 1956, some four years after the book was published, and a year after the date stated on the scripts for *Sleeping Murder*. Joining the production was Norman Stone as director, whose past films included two Screen Two productions, and most of the filming took place in Derbyshire during summer 1991, although the house and its lake were several miles away from each other—the illusion of the water at the bottom of the lawn was created by plastic sheeting. Speaking to Lynda Lee-Potter after filming had finished, Hickson reiterated how keen she was to find new challenges in her acting career: 'She plans to work till she drops, saying "I'm 85 but you've got to go on. When you stop working your brain goes, then your body goes."'[73] Hickson then went on to say: 'We start the new Miss Marple at the end of April but I think that ought to be the last, or people will start to say "Oh, not that again." We're at its peak and that is the moment to finish.' This time, the next adaptation really would be the end.

Those making the film were right to be unsure about the merits of this particular novel, although there is much to like, including some classic Christie misdirection (helped by the script's decision to have the characters watch a film at a crucial point in proceedings, thus making it easier to distract them from what is actually going on). The production feels more modern than the earlier Miss Marple adaptations, including avant-garde dancing, working-class boys and a spruced-up Savoy hotel, which perhaps leaves the audience a little disorientated. Nostalgia is evident once more when old home movies are watched, thus going even further than normal and creating nostalgia within a nostalgic product, while the decision to spare the life of one character is perfectly sensible as the death adds nothing to the proceedings—it is the murderous attempt that is crucial.

The adaptation pulled in more viewers than *A Caribbean Mystery* had, with over 13 m watching this time, despite the fact that ITV tried to counter with an example of its own Christie success, bizarrely deciding to show a repeat of the *Poirot* episode 'The Theft of the Royal Ruby' at the same time. However, critical reception was the poorest to date. The *Mail on Sunday* called the production 'a pudding very severely over-egged',[74] while Peter Paterson in its sister paper made some baffling and unsubstantiated claims when he wrote that 'I somehow doubt if there was anything of Miss Christie in the plot, which was credited to T.R. Bowen, except the personality of Miss Marple herself. And I suspect the way that Joan Hickson has made the character her own owes very little to the original creation, or to the long line of actresses who preceded her.' Paterson would have done well to realise that there was a simple way to alleviate his ill-founded suspicions—by reading the novel that had been readily available for nearly 40 years.[75] The *Sunday Times*'s critic offered a fair explanation for why this story had seemed uninvolving to much of the audience: 'To keep one interested for the full two hours, even with the mesmerising Joan Hickson as Miss Marple, an Agatha Christie must have an exotic location or a rapid turnover of corpses, or preferably both. This one had neither, and suffered badly.'[76] Lynne Truss in *The Times* highlighted an important point that dogs many visual adaptations of mystery novels and thrillers, saying that while this was 'not a classic story, by any means', there were issues with Miss Marple identifying facial similarities that the audience cannot share because actors are, of course, not related—and so, at best, the audience is forced to second guess the casting decisions.[77] Even the BBC Review Board expressed its disappointment with the film, although it acknowledged that 'Within the boundaries of the material, the production had worked well. This was the penultimate story, and there were probably good reasons why it had not been made earlier.'[78] Meanwhile, A.N. Wilson in the *Sunday Telegraph* repeated a widely held conspiracy theory, asking:

> Isn't it time that Slack put on his thinking-cap and realised that Miss Marple is one of the most dangerous serial killers since Jack the Ripper? Not content to shoot, strangle and poison her way through England, this dangerous person, simpering modestly over the teacups, always manages to frame somebody else. Apart from the people she has killed with her own bare hands, she must have sent dozens to the gallows.[79]

Filming for the twelfth, and final, BBC Miss Marple adaptation, *The Mirror Crack'd from Side to Side*, began in late April 1992; this mystery follows movie star Marina Gregg (played by Claire Bloom) who moves into the Bantrys' old house near to St Mary Mead, only for a local woman to be poisoned while a fête is being held in the grounds of the film actress's house. It had previously been adapted for the 1980 film starring Angela Lansbury, but this production seems more down to earth, with characters more fully developed as individuals, rather than pawns moving within the game of the mystery. The BBC version might be a little less fun as a piece of general entertainment, because it misses the star power and amusing asides of the Lansbury film, but it is a better adaptation and more satisfying production overall.

By this point Joan Hickson was starting to feel the strain of filming, so she was assisted by cue cards held out of shot in case she struggled with her memory. Mathew Prichard recalls:

> By then I think she was too old. I remember Geraldine McEwan [who played Miss Marple for ITV between 2004 and 2009] was moaning for the world about how old she was and how she couldn't do it—she was at least ten years younger than when Joan was doing it! You never heard from Joan, she never complained. I remember going to the filming and they had some policeman who forgot his line six times running and Joan, who is word perfect, eventually said "Come along my dear! This won't do, I'm getting old and I can't be doing with all these takes just because you can't remember your lines!"[80]

For the first time a director was brought back to the production, with Norman Stone now given one of the stronger Miss Marple stories. He does an accomplished job, especially in a crucial sequence where Marina Gregg is distracted by something while looking at the stairs during the party—Stone does well to play fairly without over-emphasising an element that will later become a key revelation. Rejoining Miss Marple for this final adventure was not only Superintendent Slack (the detective having received a promotion) but also Detective Inspector Craddock, who, as mentioned, is now mysteriously cast as Miss Marple's nephew. Since his previous appearance, in *A Murder Is Announced*, was one of the occasions where T.R. Bowen did not write the screenplay, this unusual slip of characterisation may be a remnant of an abandoned plan. Perhaps the writers and producers considered giving Craddock a more personal, and stronger, reason to trust Miss Marple's instincts by making him her nephew, which Bowen had forgotten did not make it to the final adaptation.

After the relative disappointment of the previous production, *The Mirror Crack'd from Side to Side* is a welcome return to form, and an excellent way to finish the run of Miss Marple adaptations. Joan Hickson was allowed to retain Miss Marple's handbag and her straw hat. 'I shall miss her, oh, I certainly shall', she told the *Daily Mirror*. 'I really do like Miss M. The more I have played her, the more I have grown to like her. I do so admire her. She is a good egg. And I have so much enjoyed making the series.'[81] In the final scene we may be happy to see the production rely on cliché for once, as Miss Marple intones her last line of the series, which so neatly sums up many people's instinctive expectations of her mysteries: 'More tea vicar?'

Despite the series having begun more than 30 years ago, it says much about the quality of the productions that they are still repeated, remastered and released throughout the world—and, despite pretenders to the throne, Joan Hickson remains the quintessential Miss Marple in most people's eyes. 'I'm really sorry that my grandmother never saw it', says Mathew Prichard, something that was also echoed by his late mother during the programme's run, when she wrote: 'I am sure she would have loved her in the part. The BBC television series of the Miss Marple stories is one of the best things done with my mother's work.'[82]

NOTES

1. Untitled notes, 22–28 July 1970 (BBC Written Archive Centre: Agatha Christie, Copyright, 1970–1974 (RCONT20)).
2. Untitled notes, 22–28 July 1970 (BBC WAC, Agatha Christie: Copyright, 1970–1974).
3. Assistant to Gavin Millar to Sandra Coombs, 17 September 1970 (BBC WAC, Agatha Christie: Copyright, 1970–1974).
4. Mrs H. Ryder of Hughes Massie to Miss K.S. Dyson, 16 June 1971 (BBC WAC, Agatha Christie: Copyright, 1970–1974).
5. It may be that this second title was simply unavailable, of course, but there are consistent indications that Christie's personal views were the barrier to many of these proposed productions, with no clear rationale beyond that.
6. Interview with the author, August 2013.
7. Marian E. Tregear to Brian Stone, 28 August 1979 (BBC Written Archive Centre: Agatha Christie, Copyright, 1975–(RCONT21)).
8. Interview with the author, August 2013.
9. Interview with the author, August 2013.
10. The minimum age to obtain a driving licence in the UK is 17.
11. This figure was boosted by the same ITV strike that had delayed transmission of *Why Didn't They Ask Evans?*, but the programme peaked at over 21 million in the next series even without this help.
12. BBC Review Board Minutes covering 26 December 1982 (BBC Written Archives Centre).

13. *The Guardian*, 28 December 1982.
14. Pieter Rogers to Nora Blackborow, 15 November 1974 (BBC WAC, Agatha Christie: Copyright 1970–1974).
15. Pieter Rogers to Nora Blackborow, 15 November 1974 (BBC WAC, Agatha Christie: Copyright 1970–1974).
16. Of course, at this point this did not include *Sleeping Murder*, which had not yet been published.
17. Interview with the author, August 2013.
18. Slater to Hicks, 31 August 1983 (Agatha Christie Family Archive).
19. Edmund Cork had been Christie's agent for most of her writing career.
20. Interview with the author, August 2013.
21. By the time we last meet them in *The Mirror Crack'd from Side to Side* the characters have been promoted to Superintendent and Sergeant respectively.
22. *Radio Times*, 22 December 1984.
23. *Daily Express*, 24 December 1984.
24. *The Listener*, 3 January 1985.
25. *Daily Express*, 28 December 1984.
26. *The Guardian*, 28 December 1984.
27. *Glasgow Herald*, 29 December 1984.
28. BBC Review Board Minutes, 2 January 1985 (BBC Written Archives Centre).
29. BBC Written Archives Centre, 'Television Audience Reaction Report' [TV/84/168].
30. *Radio Times*, 22 December 1984.
31. Hicks to Stone, 10 November 1984 (BBC Written Archives Centre: *A Pocketful of Rye* production File (T65/118/1))*.
32. Hicks to Slater, 9 February 1985 (BBC Written Archives Centre: *A Murder is Announced* production File (T65/117/1)).
33. *Radio Times*, 16–22 February 1985.
34. Slater to Plater, 23 November 1983 (BBC WAC: *A Murder is Announced* production file).
35. *Evening Standard*, 22 February 1985; *The Observer*, 17 February 1985.
36. BBC Review Board Minutes, 27 February 1985 (BBC Written Archives Centre).
37. Hicks to Slater, 26 February 1984 (BBC WAC: *A Murder is Announced* production file).
38. Hicks to Slater, 26 February 1984 (BBC WAC: *A Murder is Announced* production file).
39. Slater to Hicks, 25 June 1984 (BBC WAC: *A Murder is Announced* production file).
40. Hicks to Slater, 28 June 1984 (BBC WAC: *A Murder is Announced* production file).
41. The correspondence about this is tortuous: it includes a dispute between departments regarding an agreement to allow the owner to purchase

the summer house that had been erected. Such problems were important to resolve, as the producers relied on the cooperation of residents
to be able to film in the best possible locations, and they could not risk
having a bad reputation.

42. Similarly, the production file for the adaptation features frustrated correspondence on this issue.

43. Hicks to Slater, 27 August 1984 (BBC WAC: *A Murder is Announced*
production file).

44. BBC Review Board Minutes, 6 March 1985 (BBC Written Archives
Centre).

45. BBC Written Archives Centre, 'Television Audience Reaction Report'
[TV/85/22].

46. Hicks to Slater, 6 August 1984 (BBC WAC: *A Murder is Announced*
production file).

47. Undated notes from Rosalind Hicks (BBC WAC: *A Pocketful of Rye*
production file).

48. The response to this letter is held in the BBC WAC: *A Pocketful of Rye*
production file.

49. It is not clear from the correspondence whether an agreement was
reached or whether an expensive contingency plan was instigated—the
rebuilding of the downstairs interior in studio. It may be significant that
the interior scenes in *A Pocketful of Rye* are shot in such a way that we
never see out of Miss Marple's front door.

50. Guy Slater to Timothy West, 21 November 1984 (BBC WAC: *A
Pocketful of Rye* production file).

51. BBC Review Board Minutes, 13 March 1985 (BBC Written Archives
Centre).

52. *Daily Express*, 8 March 1985.

53. BBC Review Board Minutes, 31 December 1986 (BBC Written
Archives Centre).

54. *The Spectator*, 3 January 1987.

55. *Daily Telegraph*, 27 December 1986.

56. BBC Review Board Minutes, 21 January 1987 (BBC Written Archives
Centre).

57. McMurray would go on to direct several episodes of the *Ruth Rendell
Mysteries*, which starred George Baker, who features as Chief Inspector
Fred Davy here.

58. BBC Review Board Minutes, 28 January 1987 (BBC Written Archives
Centre).

59. BBC Review Board Minutes, 4 February 1987 (BBC Written Archives
Centre).

60. Namely adaptations of *A Caribbean Mystery* and *They Do it with Mirrors*
starring Helen Hayes, and *The Mirror Crack'd* film with Angela
Lansbury.

61. *Today*, 15 February 1987.

62. *The New York Times*, 12 December 1987.
63. BBC Review Board Minutes, 11 February 1987 (BBC Written Archives Centre).
64. *Daily Mail*, 14 February 1987.
65. BBC Review Board Minutes, 6 January 1988 (BBC Written Archives Centre); *Daily Mirror*, 26 December 1987.
66. *Daily Mirror*, 19 October 1988 and 11 November 1987.
67. *Daily Mail*, 23 December 1991.
68. BBC Written Archives Centre, 'Television Audience Reaction Report' [TV/89/M203].
69. BBC Review Board Minutes, 3 January 1990 (BBC Written Archives Centre).
70. *Radio Times*, 23 December 1989.
71. *Daily Mail*, 23 December 1991.
72. *Daily Mail*, 23 December 1991.
73. *Daily Mail*, 23 December 1991.
74. *Mail on Sunday*, 5 January 1992.
75. *Daily Mail*, 30 December 1991.
76. *Sunday Times*, 5 January 1992.
77. *The Times*, 30 December 1991.
78. BBC Review Board Minutes, 8 January 1992 (BBC Written Archives Centre).
79. *Sunday Telegraph*, 5 January 1992.
80. Interview with the author, August 2015.
81. *Daily Mirror*, 21 December 1992.
82. Interview with the author, August 2013; *The Times*, 8 September 1990.

Chapter 12: Agatha Christie's Poirot

Spoilers: 'The Adventure of the Western Star'; 'The Adventure of the Italian Nobleman'; *The Murder of Roger Ackroyd; Murder on the Orient Express; The Big Four; Curtain: Poirot's Last Case*

We saw in the previous chapter that the BBC's series of Miss Marple adaptations were almost universally considered a success, including by the Christie estate, which had previously continued the author's own attitude towards the medium by treating it with suspicion at best. One notable change that occurred as the series progressed was in the attitude of Christie's daughter, Rosalind Hicks, as she saw the care and attention that the BBC had lavished upon the productions as well as their respectful consultation with the Christie estate on a personal and professional level. So pleased was she that the possibility of the same team bringing Poirot to the screen was floated just as the first batch of four Miss Marple adaptations neared completion. Writing to *Miss Marple* producer Guy Slater in November 1984, Hicks wondered if the BBC could create a series featuring the Belgian detective, produced 'in a different way'.[1] Despite the popularity of the character and the repeated wishes of many producers and broadcasters to bring Poirot to the small screen, including the BBC in the past, this tentative invitation was not followed up on. 'I haven't read [the Poirot stories] since I was at school,' wrote Guy Slater to Jonathan Powell, then Head of Drama Series and Serials at the BBC, 'but my impression is he's too cold a fish as a character to sustain a series.'[2] Soon, Slater would be proven wrong.

While London Weekend Television had been frustrated in their attempts to create a long running series based around one of Christie's 'big two' characters in the first half of the 1980s, having been forced to create an indifferently received run of *Partners in Crime* starring Tommy and Tuppence instead, by the latter part of the decade the writer's estate and agents were willing to consider the possibility more seriously. It helped that the BBC's *Miss Marple* series demonstrated a standard to aspire to for the series, and the increasing power of international sales for prestige programmes had become an increasingly important factor, as it helped to justify higher budgets. Following discussions with LWT's head of drama Nick Elliot, the Christie estate agreed to work with

© The Author(s) 2016
M. Aldridge, *Agatha Christie on Screen*,
DOI 10.1057/978-1-137-37292-5_13

producer Brian Eastman who would make the series through his own company Carnival Films on behalf of the ITV franchise. The series would form part of LWT's £38 m investment in drama for 1989 alone, perhaps in a move designed to showcase the company's strengths in the face of the forthcoming bid to renew the channel's franchise agreement to broadcast in the capital beyond 1992, a bid that LWT was to win, unlike its sister channel Thames, which went off air at the end of 1992, replaced by Carlton Television from 1 January 1993.

However, in many respects, *Miss Marple* was not the template for this new programme. While its production standards and generally close adherence to the original books formed part of the model to be embraced for this new series featuring Poirot, they also operated in a rather different way. *Miss Marple* was a collection of individual adaptations, not a series designed to flow from story to story, nor to work from an established template of characters and action; most television series adhere to at least one of these two methods. Even the scheduling showcased each story as an individual event, often stripped over consecutive nights or, later in the series' run, shown as a single movie at a peak time of the television year, such as Christmas. Some characters did reappear but the different directors and the solitary nature of Miss Marple's investigations meant that she did not have close family or friends who could be convincingly shoehorned into every production. By contrast, from the very beginning *Agatha Christie's Poirot* sets itself out to be much more in the mould of Granada television's similarly lavish set of Sherlock Holmes productions that had premiered in April 1984, just as *Miss Marple* was starting production. As with *Poirot*, this series had launched with hour long adaptations of the Sherlock Holmes short stories, with the recurring characters of Watson, Inspector Lestrade and Mrs Hudson providing a permanent familial structure to the proceedings, as did the famous residence of 221b Baker Street.[3] As with *Poirot*, the adaptations generally kept closely to the story, embellishing and adding subplots when necessary in the slighter stories, while using the additional characters to add warmth to the programme that could be lacking if the fastidious lead were left to his own devices.[4]

One area that had the potential to be the most significant problem was, in fact, handled with little fuss—the casting of Poirot himself. The precise timeline of events changes according to the person telling the story, but it seems that Rosalind Hicks herself suggested David Suchet as a likely candidate for the role, something that Brian Eastman readily agreed with. However, this suggestion did not make his casting a foregone conclusion, not least because the favoured actor wasn't sure himself. Even at this point David Suchet was a renowned and frequently seen character actor on television, one whose work on the stage and screen had been consistently well received even though he never quite broke into the realm of being a household name. He had already had a brush with Christie, playing Japp in the 1985 TV movie of *Thirteen at Dinner* starring Peter Ustinov, but it was his performance as Blott in the BBC's 1985 adaptation of Tom Sharpe's novel *Blott on the Landscape* that brought him to the attention of both Hicks and producer Brian Eastman, who had also executive produced *Blott*. In Autumn 1987 Eastman took Suchet to dinner and asked if he would be interested in taking on the role of Poirot—Suchet was initially unsure, not helped by the opinion of his older brother, news broad-caster John Suchet, who said 'I wouldn't touch it with a barge pole'.[5] Hicks wished to ensure that Suchet would take the role seriously and not make Poirot a figure of fun—she wanted him to be a character who the audience could laugh with, rather than at.[6] Mathew Prichard recalls Suchet meeting his mother at Greenway, identifying it as a crucial part of her approving of both the series and the actor:

> I think it was David who convinced her. David will tell you, even to this day, how he was summoned to Greenway to be interviewed, and even in those days he was not accustomed to that. David convinced my mother that if he was going to do this he was going to do it in a properly authentic way, read all the Poirot books, read how he walked and talked etc., and constantly be there to protect the origi-nal image of Poirot on screen. And he convinced her.[7]

By early 1988 Suchet had been cast in the role, but there was still a sense of unease on all sides as no-one was under any illusions that it would be anything other than a difficult part to get right. This may explain why, although Suchet's casting was briefly mentioned in the trade press in March 1988, it took until June for it to be properly announced and reported in the newspapers. This was the same month that saw Suchet undertake several test shots as he worked out the character, the accent, the costuming and—most especially—Poirot's walk. Once Suchet was satisfied, production could progress more smoothly. There had been no doubts that Suchet would treat the role with anything but the utmost seriousness, but this was only reinforced when his attention to detail was made clear—not least in the list of characteristics that he made when read-ing the books and kept to hand throughout the production.[8]

It had been decided that Poirot was to be accompanied by a group of charac-ters who would help to provide a regular structure for the programme and also assist in subplots and deviations necessary to bring some of the slighter short stories to the small screen. Two of the characters were obvious choices—the first, Captain Arthur Hastings, had narrated several of the early Poirot books and many of the short stories, as well as the final Poirot mystery, *Curtain: Poirot's Last Case*. As with Watson in the Sherlock Holmes stories, his character may be a little undefined on the page but is much clearer on screen with the casting of Hugh Fraser in the role. Along with the writers, Fraser creates a surprisingly complex and highly likeable character—he may be rather gullible, but is always good natured, on the side of right, and keen for adventure—with a love for cars and travel (as well as beautiful women), at odds with Poirot, a key juxtaposition in many of the series' stories. Joining Hugh Fraser is Philip Jackson as Chief Inspector Japp, a recurring character in the stories who is made the near permanent link with Scotland Yard in the television series, which dispenses with most of the other police inspectors who make appearances, putting Japp in their place. Initially, the plan had been to round off the regular characters with the addition of Poirot's valet George, but Eastman convinced the Christie estate to allow the inclusion of Miss Lemon, who had been occasional secretary to both Poirot and Parker Pyne, another recurring Christie character.[9] Eastman's main reason for the inclusion of Miss Lemon was that he felt that George's presence would make the series feel too much like *Jeeves and Wooster*, which he was also producing an ITV adaptation of (1990–1993)— an understandable concern, especially as Hastings has his fair share of Bertie Wooster qualities. However, at least as important in the end was the way that the character not only helps to redress the gender imbalance of the leads, but is also perhaps the most down to earth of all the characters, helped by Pauline Moran's performance as a woman who wearily but amusingly brings real world insight into proceedings. Viewers may be grateful that although Miss Lemon's fastidious filing system moves from page to screen, her rather brusque nature and disinterest in her employer does not, and nor can she be described as 'unbelievably ugly', as Poirot claims in one of Christie's stories.[10]

The series was formally announced to the press in June 1988, with accompanying details clarifying the ten episodes were to cost some £5 m in total. At this point the series was called *Hercule Poirot's Casebook*, a title that it retained until very shortly before transmission—at least one review of the opening episode uses this title. There are two likely reasons for the title change; the first is the grammatical difficulty of adding Agatha Christie's name to the beginning of it, as was now standard for adaptations of her work. However, producers may also have been aware that Granada's Sherlock Holmes series had used the title *The Adventures of Sherlock Holmes* for its first two series, followed by *The Return of Sherlock Holmes* for the adaptations shown between 1986 and 1988. It followed therefore that there was a strong likelihood that the series would eventually move on to one of the other titles given to published collections of Conan Doyle's short stories—*The Case-Book of Sherlock Holmes*, which it was indeed to do in 1991; neither series would have benefited from sharing half of their title.

Filming on the first episode, 'The Adventure of the Clapham Cook', began on 11 July 1988, taking place around London and at Twickenham Film Studios, where Austin Trevor had made his own Poirot adaptations over half a century earlier. Throughout his time in the role Suchet found that staying in character required concentration, and so retained the mannerisms and voice of Poirot whenever he was in character—an approach that fellow actors were warned about, should they find it disconcerting. For this first story, the script was written by Clive Exton, who was head writer for the series and guided those who worked on other scripts so as to help appropriate a house style. Exton's background as a screenwriter included the chilling *10 Rillington Place* (d. Richard Fleischer, 1971) as well as episodes of *Ruth Rendell Mysteries* (ITV, 1987–2000), and so his pedigree was strong, especially as he was a fan of Christie's work. Initially, the decision to open with a mystery with such a slight premise may seem odd—it is instigated by events surrounding the titular servant, who has disappeared, much to the irritation of her employer—but in fact the episode sets out everything that the series was to be. This episode shows us that *Agatha Christie's Poirot* is to be faster paced than most of the Sherlock Holmes and Miss Marple adaptations, achieved through frequent use of sub plots and lighter moments that keep the momentum going and never make the programme feel like a dry translation of the mysteries to the screen. Instead, it is a series with its own style and atmosphere that retools a Christie story within its own parameters every week, thereby generally being able to keep closely to the original mystery and story, while still exploiting the recurring elements (especially the cast) with whom the audience can form an attachment.

This is not a series that relies on individual episodes providing attention-seeking publicity—such as the casting of big names in key roles (which was actively avoided, so as not to distract the audience), high octane stunts or the introduction of a romantic sub plot. This is a series that has a variety of strengths at its disposal—the actors, the characters, the scripts, the stories and the location setting—which it uses in different ways each week; some episodes see an emphasis on character interplay, often with a comedic slant, while others offer sumptuous visual reconstructions of period events, and some simply bring the original story to screen with the minimum of fuss. All the elements are well established from this first episode, but the way they are used reduces the potential for stagnation. In this first episode we not only establish the relationship between characters but also show the scale of the production, with vintage cars crossing what are usually busy London bridges, well populated city parks, excursions from town to country, as well as a climactic sequence set at Southampton docks. We also have our first glimpse of Whitehaven Mansions, where Poirot resides—in reality, Florin Court in London, which had just been refurbished. The production crew had two days in which to film as many establishing shots of the apartment block as possible, before the new tenants moved in and inevitably dressed their windows in styles more appropriate for 1988 than 1936—many of the shots recorded on these two days would turn up throughout the rest of the series. When watched many years later, aficionados of the series may note some elements that were to be refined, such as Suchet's make-up and styling, as well as accent, all of which evolve over the course of this first series. However, it is a fully fledged and confident opener. The production was completed by the addition of two key elements—Christopher Gunning's memorable score, which after some tweaking reflected both the lighter and darker edges of the series, and the acclaimed opening title sequence, which mixed live action and both traditional and computer animation and techniques—cutting edge for the time, at a cost of £50,000.

One decision necessarily made early in proceedings was that of period. On the page, we meet Poirot in a reasonably linear fashion from 1917 (and even earlier in reminiscences and flashbacks) through to at least 1972, an impossibly long period, but the golden age of both his stories and detective fiction more broadly must be from the 1930s, and this is when the series would be based. Exton and Eastman mutually decided on 1936 as the specific year for *Agatha*

Christie's Poirot, as it was felt that the series should be comfortably pre-war while still on the cusp of modern life as we know it—with technology ingrained into society, but a visual appearance that is striking and distinctive. Similarly, this is a year in which families could still live off inherited wealth in large houses with the requisite servants and guests so crucial to many of Christie's stories. The fixed year is understandable, but the series has attracted criticism from some fans when it became clear that the programme would not be progressing to a later era (at least, not until much later productions). Mathew Prichard is familiar with the debate, which often comes up. 'I think we had to,' he says of sticking to 1936. 'You can't expect the audience to move at will. If my mother had had her way I think we would have tried to do the books in the period as written, but you can't really. How do you keep the public up with you? The public don't care a damn when the books were written.'[11] In fact, the programme does not keep rigidly to 1936 as events from other years are sometimes referenced; instead, it feels like it is set at some indeterminate pre-war age in most episodes—even if 1936 is the year given when necessary. In the first decade or so of the programme this created relatively few problems, as most of the stories adapted hailed from the pre-war era, but as it progressed more overt changes were needed to make sense of the context to some of the mysteries, which were sometimes rooted in later decades.[12]

When the series debuted on 8 January 1989 critical response was positive, with many reviewers making the point that they had enjoyed the portrayals of both Peter Ustinov and Albert Finney in the role, but that Suchet was already shaping up to offer the definitive portrayal of Poirot. 'It took all of fifteen minutes to convince me,' wrote Ann Mann of *Television Today*, while Peter Lennon in *The Listener* called Suchet's performance 'the most pleasing and "authentic" piece of fabrication … Suchet's Poirot is almost as meticulously thought out as Jeremy Brett's [Sherlock] Holmes. There is a touch of provinciality about Suchet's Belgian detective which is more accurate than Peter Ustinov's fruity Parisian version.'[13] Hilary Kingsley of the *Daily Mirror* dubbed the opener 'Perfect Poirot' and went on to say that 'If every episode is as neat, it will be a crime to miss it.'[14] However, Nancy Banks-Smith of *The Guardian* had one significant reservation—Poirot's moustache, which she believed to be 'laughably small', although she enjoyed the programme and felt that Suchet's performance was 'magnificent'.[15]

As the series progressed, so the audience continued to enjoy it, with ratings ranging from 9.65 to 12.88 million viewers—comfortably keeping the detective in ITV's top 20 programmes, and often in the top ten. Following the first episode was 'Murder in the Mews', which like the opener was written by Exton and directed by Edward Bennett, who would continue to work on many episodes for several years before going on to work on programmes such as *Waking the Dead* and *Silent Witness*. Bennett's strength is in not allowing the scale of the action to overwhelm the people at its centre—those working in modern day television may be amazed to see how often expensive period setting elements such as authentically dressed extras or redressed streets and parks are peripheral to the main action, but this makes the programme feel all the more authentic as attention is not overtly drawn to such scene setting. 'Murder in the Mews' continues the template set out by the first episode, with only a few moments reminding the audience how early in the run this is, such as the lack of familiarity between Japp and Hastings, as well as a street scene where Suchet's accent is markedly different to the rest of the series.

The third story, 'The Adventure of Johnnie Waverly', faced one recurring adaptation issue head-on—the simple fact that many of Christie's short stories are very short indeed; in this case, a mere thirteen pages. In this instance, this is tackled by an increased concentration on the relationship between an unusually genial Poirot and particularly Wooster-ish Hastings, and more time spent assessing the grounds and suspects surrounding little Johnnie, who is expected to go missing. On screen, as on the page, the audience may be rightly incredulous that even with forewarning the crime occurs with relative ease—although Poirot is one step ahead. This episode was the first to be directed by Renny Rye, who shared duties with Bennett for this first set of ten stories—Rye would later be a regular director for *Midsomer Murders.* Following this, 'Four and Twenty Blackbirds' was the fourth episode to be shown, this time written by Russell Murray, with Clive Exton as script consultant. This mystery is assisted by a Poirot who is more light-hearted than would later be the case, despite his fear of the dentist running as a necessary sub plot. This episode neatly demonstrates how the series refused to rest on its laurels—a sequence with a comedy theatre act is largely unnecessary but adds colour to the production, while Murray and Rye cleverly decide to place the key revelation that one character was in disguise earlier in the proceedings than the short story had revealed it. The issue of character disguises is certainly one of the most difficult elements of Christie to convincingly depict on screen, and both director and writer were right to second guess that much of the audience would be likely to recognise the visual deception, no matter how well the make-up is done. For those who do, there are more twists to come.

By the time the series reaches its fifth episode, 'The Third Floor Flat' adapted by Michael Baker, the core team of Poirot, Japp, Hastings and Miss Lemon are well established—and so when a crime occurs in Poirot's own apartment building, this is a chance to not only cement Poirot's domestic arrangements but also concentrate on a small scale but highly satisfying mystery. As would often be the case, contemporary culture and technology are often mentioned by this point, with a key character singing along to 'Life Is Just a Bowl of Cherries', which is playing on a gramophone. Radio, music, travel, fashion and cinema would all frequently feature throughout the series, to help remind us of the period and also supply a quick way to make a particular point about either history or the nature of society at the time—in this instance, when Poirot pays a trip to the theatre to see a play reminiscent of Christie's own *Black Coffee*, we may note his disdain for it. At the end of the episode, the story's small scale is opened out somewhat, as we witness one of the first of many car chases that often resolve Poirot episodes—largely unnecessary in plot terms, but lavish and entertaining for the audience, especially as it dovetails neatly with Hasting's restoration of his car. It seems curious that this episode is followed by the only two of this first series to include filming abroad, and stranger still when we consider that both were filmed on the same island, Rhodes, which was intended to pass for a different locale in the second story. The first, 'Triangle at Rhodes' adapted by Stephen Wakelam, uses several elements that would later be used by Christie in other stories, especially a relationship reminiscent of *Evil under the Sun*. For this episode, the final chase sequence is transplanted from the road to the sea—for the first time we see Poirot without any of his recurring acquaintances, which helps to cement Suchet in the role as the series' lead. Exton's adaptation of 'Problem at Sea' follows, where the question of disguise rears its head once more—this time, the audience may be right to feel a little cheated as, when the flashback apparently reveals all, a key part of the sequence has been changed from our first viewing. Given the nature of the mystery it is difficult to see how else this could have been achieved, and few viewers in 1989 would have been able to go back and check that they had missed a significant clue the first time around. Any disappointment surrounding this is more than countered by the pleasure of Suchet's visibly increased confidence in the role, as he interacts with other guests and recounts the solution in a manner that is both momentarily chilling and endearing.

'The Incredible Theft', adapted by David Reid, opens with another of the programme's preoccupations—air travel, specifically the fictional fighting aircraft the Mayfield Kestrel, the plans of which are stolen by an unknown perpetrator. The series' ongoing attempts to broaden out the action and avoid the repetition of characters meeting in nondescript rooms is tackled here by Poirot meeting his anonymous client at the penguin enclosure at the zoo, as his colleagues get some character embellishment after even Poirot suggests that Miss Lemon is overly fixated on her filing, while we learn of Japp's bizarre blancmange based dream before we career into the near-obligatory car chase sequence. For the penultimate episode, 'The King of Clubs', the technological emphasis is placed on the cinema, as we join characters on a film set early in proceedings, helping to draw attention to the industrial and cultural context of these mysteries. This is the result of a change from the original story's casting of a character as a dancer, with the murdered man a theatrical impresario—they are now an actress and head of the film studio respectively. These roles may be less timeless than Christie's choice, but are more easily reflective of this particular era, as is the house of one key character, which showcases the 1930s modernist style. Exton's decision to draw attention to a nearby gypsy camp in his script helps to make this story a more traditional murder mystery, as it brings with it a cast of suspects. The final episode opens with a newsreel, an oft-repeated trait of the series as a way to quickly establish character and context, in 'The Dream', adapted by Clive Exton—a story that once more relies on disguise, although the attempts to distract the audience from the truth of the characters' identities are less convincing. However, Christie supplies further twists for the pleasure of the audience, and Exton wisely discards others—such as an unconvincingly utilised stuffed cat. In its use of Perivale's famous Hoover building the programme retains its striking visuals and shows once more that the programme is capable of variety in all forms as it moves from the domestic arena to the workplace to good effect.

The first series had done well in commercial terms, while as it progressed the critical reception grew increasingly warm; there was also the all-important interest from international broadcasters. LWT had found a formula that worked and wished to keep it, and so more of the same was ordered—an option on Suchet's contract was taken up, and filming was set to begin on another ten episodes. *Agatha Christie's Poirot* was a success, and there seemed to be no shortage of mysteries available to continue the run.

THE RETURN OF POIROT

When filming on the series resumed on 3 July 1989, it was not quite business as usual. While familiar faces had returned both in front of and behind the camera, the first story tackled was to be a novel rather than a short story for the first time. The adaptation was of *Peril at End House*, a 1932 mystery about repeated attempts on the life of a young woman, this time stretching across two broadcast hours of television. Once more the script was penned by Clive Exton, with Renny Rye on directing duties, which included extensive filming in the seaside town of Salcombe, South Devon. No chance is missed to film a scene in these beautiful surroundings, with standard dialogue sequences shot outside whenever possible. The episode opens with a reminder of the series' fixation on 1930s modernity and the comedic play made on the differences between the lead characters, as Poirot and Hastings fly over the countryside on the way to their holiday—much to the delight of Hastings, and horror of Poirot. Japp and Miss Lemon also make appearances but add little in terms of the story, a sign of the extent to which the programme presented itself as an ensemble piece in these early years, in contrast to later adaptations that used the other regulars only when required by plot.[16] One striking element is the way the production uses music, as the episode demonstrates both a nostalgic, generalised vision of the past with its orchestral score, alongside the more contemporary trends as heard when the fashionable friends of the threatened woman listen to their own records. Two versions of the production were prepared, one running for two hours, with the other splitting the story into two hour-long episodes. It was the first version that was transmitted on ITV on 7 January 1990, reaching 11.36 million viewers and ranking 19th for the week amongst ITV's programmes during the busy new year period—a return dubbed 'marvellous' and 'very welcome' by the *Daily Mirror*.[17,18]

Filming on the series then continued all the way up until 23 December, just as publicity for this second run was gearing up. Interviews with the cast, including Suchet and Moran, frequently appeared in the press, while opinion pieces on the characters cropped up from several columnists, who seemed particularly obsessed with Poirot's moustache, his fastidiousness, and his apparent lack of interest in women—something refuted by Suchet. Another area of interest in both the popular and trade press was the lengths to which the series went to accurately present the 1930s on screen; the answer was simple—money and hard work. The first mystery to follow the series' bumper opener was 'The Veiled Lady', in which Poirot endeavours to return a missing object to the woman of the title. In a contrast to the intricate plotting and red herrings of *Peril at End House*, this story has more than its fair share of added material inconsequential to the plot in order to make an engaging and enjoyable hour of television, but is no weaker for it. Like Billy Wilder's *Witness for the Prosecution* in 1957, the best Christie adaptations are often those that leave her original stories largely untouched, but add their own charm to it, and this is a good example. When Poirot dresses up as a workman in order to gain entry to a house, the housekeeper's baffled and generally xenophobic response to a person of (to her) indiscriminate heritage is an amusing statement on the generalised suspicion of 'foreigners' witnessed by many members of society, offence only multiplied when Poirot is referred to as 'one of your un-naturals' with 'shifty little eyes'. Beyond this part of the plot, there is no shortage of colour and amusement to keep the audience entertained, including Hasting's adventures with a miniature sailing boat, Poirot's brief imprisonment and a climactic chase through the Natural History Museum; at this stage, there was no such thing as a small scale episode of *Poirot*.

For the next episode, 'The Lost Mine', the writing team was joined by David Renwick, who is best known for creating and writing *One Foot in the Grave* (BBC, 1990–2000) and *Jonathan Creek* (BBC, 1997–2014). Renwick co-wrote this story of criminality in Chinatown with Michael Baker, but although it portrays a vivid recreation of the area it is difficult to enjoy not only because it is one of the weaker mysteries, but also its uncomfortable reliance on outdated attitudes (no doubt historically accurate, but unchallenged), including Japp's description of the residents as 'vermin'. The episode is enlivened a little by a highly serious game of Monopoly between Poirot and Hastings (the former wins second prize in a beauty contest) and the pride shown in the police's technologically advanced special operations room. This episode is followed by more traditional fare, with 'The Cornish Mystery', filmed in Dunster, Somerset, rather than the county of the title. The story concerns a woman who fears she is being poisoned by her husband, and the decision to film this episode in November resulted in an atmospherically rain-drenched location that breaks away from the series' traditional bright and sunny view of the past, while the extensive location filming makes this feel almost as exotic as the series' trips abroad.

The next episode to be transmitted is arguably one of Christie's best Poirot short stories, 'The Disappearance of Mr Davenheim', although readers of Conan Doyle may have an advantage in working out the solution, which it partially shares with the Sherlock Holmes story 'The Man with the Twisted Lip'. The story of a man who simply disappears while walking down a country lane is effectively a twist on the classic locked room mystery, and allows for plenty of investigation based around Davenheim's stunning art deco house. This was the first episode directed by Andrew Grieve, who would go on to film several *Hornblower* television movies, while it was also David Renwick's first solo effort. When Renwick came to write the next series of *One Foot in the Grave* (its second, transmitting in late 1990), *Poirot* reared its head once more, as Victor and Margaret Meldrew are forced to try to work out the solution to a (fictional) episode of the series because their video recorder has missed the ending. They end up convinced that one character's decision to clutch a basil leaf is key to the mystery, an action that bears some similarities to 'How Does Your Garden Grow', which would appear in the third series of *Poirot*, and was written by Andrew Marshall, Renwick's previous writing partner. Renwick also supplies the programme with one of its best and funniest moments, as Poirot is confronted with a parrot, only for their names to become confused.[19] Motor racing supplies the clear link to contemporary culture and technology this week, while an early visit to a magic show where fire is transformed into a dove may provide a clue to the nature of this mystery. The question of appearances underpin the mystery once more when we reach the next episode, 'Double Sin', one of the toughest of all Christie mysteries to adapt as it relies on characters' visual perceptions and a marvellous double bluff, when the reader is encouraged to wonder if there is a link between an old lady and a young man who both sport budding moustaches. This element of the story is removed from the adaptation for the most part, making it a more traditional mystery, bolstered by Miss Lemon's amusing terror when she loses her keys to Poirot's flat, and a bizarre sequence where she tries to think like her employer.

'The Adventure of the Cheap Flat', the seventh mystery of this second series, was directed by Richard Spence, who had also worked on the previous episode and would later direct for programmes including *Lewis* (ITV, 2006–2015). This episode features an unusually prominent homage to the film noir and gangster film genres, resulting in a very odd sequence where Poirot explains the back story in a style that is clearly meant to be reminiscent of the genre but comes across as awkward and stagy, a rare example of the programme failing to convince. A question of convincing the audience would be key to the next episode, 'The Kidnapped Prime Minister', which has problems when being dramatized as some of the characters are not telling the truth about the circumstances that led to the titular crime. As a result key events must happen off screen, immediately arousing the suspicion of a television literate audience who will recognise that this is an unconventional approach, likely undertaken for specific reasons. It is probably a coincidence that the episode continues the Noir-ish theme, with the filmic scenes at the train station and criminal activity lurking in the shadows. The final episode, 'The Adventure of the Western Star', follows one of Christie's less baffling mysteries and is rightly hidden towards the end of the run as it features tropes already familiar to even the most casual viewer of the series, as the Western Star diamond is stolen from its owner under cover of darkness—she is the only person to have seen the villain, a man of rather clichéd Chinese appearance. Christie readers and viewers alike will know that foreign characters are usually used fulfil the role of red herring, not the villain, and so this mystery does not take much unravelling.

For this second series, the audience continued to grow, never falling below 11 million and sometimes getting almost two million more than this. At this time, the first series episode 'Triangle at Rhodes' also won first prize at New York's International Film and television Festival, while the series was lauded in newspapers and trade journals including *Variety* and continued to sell well to international broadcasters, including to Christie-loving Russia.[20] Suchet had established himself as the definitive portrayal of the part to almost all commentators, and so it was only natural that he should take part in 1990's celebrations of the 100th anniversary of Christie's birth. Two special events marked the occasion—one was a charming, brief, meeting between Suchet and Joan Hickson in Torquay during centenary events in September, which was captured by local photographers and news programmes and became the only occasion when the public could see the two definitive portrayals together. The second was the decision to open production of the third season with the story that was not only Poirot's first case, but the first novel to be published by Agatha Christie—*The Mysterious Affair at Styles*, which began production in May 1990. Despite the success of the series, Suchet's services had not been promptly secured for further episodes, leading him to believe that the series was not expected to continue—at least, not any time soon.[21] As a result, he had less time to acclimatise himself to the demands of Poirot after his performances on stage in the Royal Shakespeare Company's production of *Timon of Athens* that ran at the Young Vic during April and May of that year.

Any discomfort that Suchet may have felt because of the requirement for him to launch straight into the production does not manifest itself on screen, despite the particular demands of a feature-length episode that requires him to play the Belgian detective some two decades younger than earlier in the run. *The Mysterious Affair at Styles* effectively sets itself up as not only the origins of Poirot the detective as we know him, but a prequel to the series so far. The film opens without the usual opening titles, with the series' theme music waiting until later proceedings for it to start to creep into the score, before a fuller variant arrives for the closing credits. As with the book, the emphasis is initially on Hastings, who has been invalided away from the warfront and is recuperating at a military hospital, where films remind him and the viewer of the fighting going on across the channel in 1917, the year in which the story is set. Highlighting the story as a special event and emphasising in publicity that this was Christie's first novel is a wise move as, although it is an exceptional debut, many of the elements contained within would later be refined by the author and used to better effect elsewhere. In particular, the peculiar decision to hide rather than destroy an incriminating letter is suspicious at best, if not completely unbeliev- able, and the unavoidable attention given to it on screen only helps to remind the audience of this. Nevertheless, the production itself is an accomplished one that tackles a difficult task with aplomb and has a highly satisfying congratula- tory feel that could hardly be better placed than at this point in proceedings, with the programme already established while the cast remain young enough to convincingly play younger versions of their characters. When screened in September 1990 it was very well received critically, except by the *Daily Mail*'s Peter Paterson who repeatedly reviewed the series in order to tell his readers how much he hated the character of Poirot. Although ratings were lower than they had been at 9.92 m this was reflective of smaller audiences generally, and was enough to put the programme in ITV's top ten for the week.

Following *Styles* was another run of ten stories, with production stretching all the way to Christmas once more. Several early newspaper reports had mentioned a proposed initial run of thirty episodes over three years, but David Suchet remained in the dark regarding the ongoing plans for the series. At this point, there was no expectation that this series was designed to be a definitive chronicle of all the Poirot stories; such a possibility would only be raised much later, as Mathew Prichard recalls: 'I don't think Brian [Eastman] had any conception that David would do them all. He may have paid lip service to it, but I don't think they were ever going to happen [at this stage]'.[22] As it was, the programme continued with the same formula as before, including the recurring characters of Japp, Hastings and Miss Lemon. First up was the summery tale of 'How Does Your Garden Grow?', which deals with the tale of an old lady being poisoned while under the care of a suspicious young Russian woman; Christie fans will know to look elsewhere, although the decision to open the episode with an unsubtitled Russian language sequence preserves the suspense for a while. Here, we first learn of Poirot's desire to retire and grow marrows, which he eventually achieves in *The Murder of Roger Ackroyd* four seasons later, with limited success. As is often the case, subplots concerning the regulars provide the key to the solution, in this case Miss Lemon's furious reaction to Hastings settling a bill by cash. Most supporting characters have their chance to act suspiciously, and when the murderer screams 'You've condemned me to the gallows!' at the story's denouement we are reminded that, despite the context of a beautiful and timeless garden we are visiting an unforgiving past where not only the victim but also the miscreant will usually end up dead whenever there is a murder to solve. With its balance of humour, strong characterisation and a solid mystery this episode is one of the best examples of the hour long Poirot stories, with a script from newcomer Andrew Marshall, who created and wrote the under-rated sitcom *2point4 Children*, and director Brian Farnham who also worked on other Brian Eastman productions such as *BUGS* (BBC, 1995–1999) and *Crime Traveller* (BBC, 1997).

The second episode, 'The Million Dollar Bond Robbery', is the first to be scripted by Anthony Horowitz, whose success reaches far beyond his work on this series, including his series of Alex Rider novels and licensed continuation novels for both Sherlock Holmes and James Bond. In the original story, much of the tale of a robbery aboard a cross-Atlantic ship is told in retrospect, but here Poirot is informed in advance allowing him to remain on board—and a gung-ho Hastings to be struck down with seasickness. Perhaps strangely, the adaptation also adds an instance of a character in disguise, although it is effectively done as part of a rather more convoluted story than had been presented on the page. The next mystery, 'The Plymouth Express', was adapted by actor and writer Rod Beacham who had penned several episodes of *Bergerac* since 1983, and is a curio in the context of adapting the stories to the screen. There are a handful of instances where Christie later expands some of her short stories into either reworked (usually longer) short stories or, as in this instance, a fully-fledged novel, as *The Mystery of the Blue Train* reworks the basics of this short story into a novel. Usually, the series only adapts the most substantial form of any story; for example, 'The Market Basing Mystery' was later expanded and reworked as 'Murder in the Mews', and it was the latter that was adapted for television. Perhaps the reason for tackling this story was a perceived paucity of suitable short stories or, more likely, the sense that it was unlikely the series would reach a point where the full novel would need to be adapted. Under director Andrew Piddington this is a colourful and engaging version of the mystery, which expands the story and has an unusual but welcome emphasis on the real impact of murder, with a sympathetic depiction of the victim's grieving father contrasted with the brutality of her stabbing.

'Wasps' Nest' had been the first Poirot story to be shown on television, in a 1937 BBC production, but the version seen in this series expanded the story beyond the simple staging of Poirot's intervention in a possible poisoning. The script from David Renwick embellishes the mystery with events taking place at a local fête, which also adds stylised visual appeal. In effect, the original story forms the final act of the programme, which is aided by the choice of a beautiful riverside house for the final key sequence. Renwick's next script follows immediately afterwards, with 'Tragedy at Marsdon Manor', which allows him to demonstrate his skill at dovetailing comedy and mystery, as Poirot visits an inn run by a fan who hopes that the Belgian sleuth will be able to provide the solution to a story he's writing. The story does require one of the series' occasional forays into the ghoulish, partly exemplified by a comedy visit to the local wax museum, but also events such as an apparently mystical curse, causing apparent manifestations at a 'haunted' house. As the paranormal is not 'real' in the world of Poirot, identifying the mischief maker takes less detection by the viewer than normal. One of the apparently disturbing events, the claimed appearance of a face in the branches of a tree, may have provided the inspiration of a similar device in his next series of *One Foot in the Grave*, where Victor Meldrew can see a laughing face in a neighbour's television aerial—a demonstration of how easily horror can turn to comedy.

The next episode, 'The Double Clue', allows Poirot to meditate on love and life as he discusses marriage with Hastings, pointing out how often spouses turn to murder. Viewers may take pleasure in seeing Poirot courting the Countess Vera Rossakoff in this tale of stolen jewels taking place in the world of the nobility amidst grand locations. Most viewers will probably spot the villain, but how they will be dealt with remains a lingering question throughout. A rather bloodier tale was to follow, with 'The Mystery of the Spanish Chest', in which a corpse is found in the object of the title the day after a party took place in the room. The audience is taken through the clever and memorable central mystery via events such as a trip to the opera and black and white flashbacks to a fencing duel, while the method of the murder is more effective and disturbing than Christie's original story, and retains the graphic outpouring of blood that identifies the location of the corpse.

Given the fact that the series debuted in early January 1991, it is a surprise that the next story, 'The Theft of the Royal Ruby', was shown in late February rather than at the beginning of the series as it is set at Christmas, when perhaps the alternative title 'The Adventure of the Christmas Pudding' might have been a better option. The episode allows Poirot to witness the idiosyncrasies of English family traditions as he tries to solve the mystery of a missing gem through careful scrutiny of those taking part in the festivities. The episode provides Suchet with the chance to show the characters (and audience) how to de-stone a mango, as had been taught to him by Prince Philip, but sadly missing is the moment from the story where the Belgian receives a kiss under the mistletoe. The adaptation's final sequence includes an impressive chase at an airfield incorporating a plane, but the production is more satisfying if viewed during the Christmas period.

Poirot makes a short diversion to the BBC for the penultimate mystery of the series, as a radio play performed at Broadcasting House provides the key to 'The Affair at the Victory Ball', our latest allusion to contemporary culture and technology; 'He's with the BBC, but quite a decent chap!' says Hastings at one point, a friendly jab at the rival broadcaster. The mystery itself utilises a voiceover from Poirot where he ruminates about the 'mystery' and 'beauty' of the Commedia dell'arte depicted as porcelain figures and, later, as costumes at a party. Special emphasis is given to the harlequin, always Christie's favourite, and while the mystery once more relies on disguises, and here the use is overt. Following this, the final episode of the third series is also the only one to have been adapted by T.R. Bowen, who wrote the scripts for the majority of the BBC's *Miss Marple* series. In Christie's 'The Mystery of Hunter's Lodge', Poirot is indisposed from the beginning due to illness, but here he joins a hunting party so as to have a chance to taste a bird he particularly wishes to try. He is unimpressed with the cold, but his presence allows the story to be broadened out more than it is on the page. It is unfortunate that one character's disguise is particularly weak, but their real identity remains a mystery for most viewers. However, there was perhaps a sense that this story was retreading areas of Christie's writing that had been more than satisfactorily covered in earlier stories, and so the time was right to consider a different approach when production recommenced.

This third series debuted on 6 January 1991, with each episode following on successive Sunday evenings. The first episode received the series' highest ratings to that point, at 13.32 m, staying above 10 m for the whole run, while critics warmly received the detective's return like an old friend. Poirot was now an established figure on television, but when he returned the following year it set a new pattern for the series.

A CHANGE OF PACE FOR *POIROT*

The decision to change the format for *Poirot* for its fourth season, into a hand-ful of two hour adaptations of novels rather than hour long episodes, is likely to have been partially informed by how busy the cast and production team were, including Suchet himself as well as producer Brian Eastman. To get the key personnel back together for another six months or more, as had been the case for the previous two years, would have been no easy task, especially as an option had not been taken out on Suchet's services and he was keen to fur-ther explore his stage work.[23] Meanwhile, Eastman was busy producing no less than six film and television projects during the 1992–1993 period, including the Anthony Hopkins movie *Shadowlands*, directed by Richard Attenborough. However, probably of more importance was the recognition that two hour movies were now particularly commercially appealing; the series' previous for-ays into novel adaptations had worked well, and the international buyers' mar-ket were keen to buy more, as they were considered to be more financially viable in terms of selling advertising space. 'Because of a feature's long format, its ad breaks are of a value as audiences are perceived to be more attentive,' claimed a 1992 article in *Screen International*, 'It's no coincidence that ITV's *Inspector Morse* and *Poirot* are now running to two hours.'[24] For *Poirot*, three novels were selected for adaptation for this shortened run of episodes set to be broadcast in January 1992. Production began in May 1991, running until August, and the first title to be tackled was one of Christie's cleverest myster-ies, *The ABC Murders*, in which a serial killer appears to be killing their vic-tims in alphabetical order, with no further apparent link between them. The production, directed by Andrew Grieve from a script by Clive Exton, is one of the jewels of the series overall, as it skilfully juxtaposes the comedic stories of Poirot's home life (where he struggles with Hastings' present of a stuffed, pungent, crocodile) with a dark and chilling story that follows not only the vicious murders, but also a man called Cust who appears to be carrying them out. Playing Cust is Donald Sumpter, in an exceptional performance of a man tormented by the evidence of his own apparent misdeeds, lending an affect-ing and effective air of torment to the proceedings. The whole production is a particularly atmospheric one, especially during sequences where attempts are made to apprehend the murderer at Doncaster race course as well as the stab-bing of a man during a viewing of a hard edged crime film at the cinema. The displays of blood and bodies were enough to garner a complaint from a viewer that some scenes were unacceptably graphic, but it was not upheld.[25] Poirot is allowed to show off his most sympathetic side, while also offering a first class series of deductions that solves the case.

The next film to be shown adapts another well-known Christie classic, *Death in the Clouds*, in which a person is murdered on a plane through an unknown method—unknown, that is, until Poirot cuts through the red herrings to reach a conclusion that stays just on the right side of plausible. This adaptation was the only contribution to the Poirot series from both screenwriter William

Humble, who had written for programmes including *Flambards* (ITV, 1979) and *All Creatures Great and Small* (BBC, 1978–1990), and director Stephen Whittaker, who would direct an episode of *Inspector Morse* (ITV, 1987–2000) the following year. In a sign of how casually the series treated the precise period setting, this episode features a Fred Perry tennis match that places it in 1935, a year earlier than the explicitly August 1936 setting of *The ABC Murders*. The tennis match, and the surrounding material shot in Paris, is a lavishly executed affair, offering little in the way of actual plot but allowing for some background to some key characters to be established—such characterisation could not doubt have been achieved in lower budget surroundings, but the series always emphasised its prestigious nature. The film offers an entertaining take on the intriguing mystery, largely continuing the high quality set up by its predecessor.

A little more problematic is the final film of the three, which adapts *One, Two, Buckle My Shoe*, a good but not especially filmic Poirot novel that is more heavily situated in the 'real world' than normal, with the background of Black Shirts and political uprisings. The story of a murdered dentist offers its fair share of surprises, although it may be that the solution comes across rather better on the page than it does on screen. The mystery is also an example of where Christie's obsession with nursery rhyme themed novels can be a bit of a curse for the adapter, forced to either largely ignore it so as to avoid cliché or, here, build it into the story in a stylised way—an early sequence shows young girls playing hopscotch in the street, singing the rhyme, and at least in this instance we learn that the story's title does have direct relevance to the solution. Where the adaptation works particularly well is in its broadening out of the central characters, allowing the audience to see them in different contexts, including an occasion where Poirot visits Japp at home.

When shown on consecutive Sunday evenings from 5 January 1992 it was clear that the decision to make the films was a good one, as *The ABC Murders* garnered the series' highest ratings to this point, at 14.67 m viewers, with the next two episodes following this with 11.86 m and 12.84 m, still high figures that showed that interest in Poirot was far from waning, and may have helped to convince ITV that *Poirot* worked better as individual pieces of event television rather than as a standard ongoing series. Nevertheless, before the programme adopted feature length novel adaptations as its permanent structure, there was one further series of hour-long adaptations of short stories to come. Filming began on 10 May 1992, covering eight of the stories, leaving two linked collections (*The Sign of Four* and *The Labours of Hercules*) outstanding, along with the 'The Lemesurier Inheritance', a short story that some have claimed is unfilmable—but, as the series would prove, apparently unfilmable works can be altered so as to be suitable for the screen, sometimes to good effect, sometimes less so.[26] The particular problem with the story is that the antagonist's motivation is simply that he has been driven mad, apparently due to a family curse, something that is hardly a satisfactory revelation for an episode of the series.

This fifth series tends to provide the audience with the sense of 'more of the same', as some of the weaker Poirot stories are brought to the fore, and several that use elements better expressed in other stories are given their own hour of television. 'The Adventure of the Egyptian Tomb' takes viewers to an archaeological dig, in an episode directed by newcomer to the series Peter Barber-Fleming, who had just filmed two episodes of *Lovejoy*. We open with a favourite device of the series, as a newsreel gives the audience the background to events that will lead to the murder of one member of the archaeological party. Mysticism and superstition play their own role, bolstered by Miss Lemon's sudden infatuation with tarot cards and a Ouija board. The Egyptian locale also gives Poirot plenty to complain about, but reviewers of the series noted that while it was accomplished and comfortable viewing, the episode also felt like more of the same. In *Television Today,* reviewer Harry Venning complained that a vital piece of evidence had been obscured from the audience, making it impossible to make the same deductions as Poirot, although he enjoyed it overall calling it 'mass murder for the whole family to enjoy'.[27] Following this was an adaptation of 'The Under Dog', which perhaps only cemented the sense that the series was starting to get a little repetitive, and even dull.[28] A fairly typical country house murder, it requires Poirot and the police to initially take highly suspicious witness statements at face value in order to preserve the mystery until the final act, and while director John Bruce (who had previously worked on *The Adventures of Sherlock Holmes*) provides some impressive depictions of central London in period, the performances feel wrongly pitched with a sense of archness, perhaps as a result of the thinner than usual material in a script from Bill Craig, whose previous credits included *Callan* (ITV, 1967–1972) and *The Duchess of Duke Street* (BBC, 1976–1977), in his only contribution to the series.

That the mystery 'The Yellow Iris' would help to bring the series back to the level of its earlier episodes is not too surprising when we consider its origins as a radio play (so therefore suitable for broadcast) and short story, before the central premise was reworked into a Poirot-less novel, *Sparkling Cyanide*, which retained the clever and mysterious method of the murder. Such re-use of the story shows how strong Christie felt the premise and resolution was, although many British viewers would have been unfamiliar with it in this form as the story was not collected into book form in the UK until 1992, as part of the *Problem at Pollensa Bay* collection. It is unfortunate that the episode follows so closely on from *Death in the Clouds* as the murder is committed in a similar manner, but it is unlikely any viewers will make the connection until all is revealed. There is plenty of entertainment to be had from a story told partially in flashback, as Poirot fails to solve the case of a poisoning at a restaurant in the Argentine, followed by a reunion of the characters two years later where the murderer may strike again. While this episode almost had a surplus of material with which to work, the same cannot be said of the next instalment, which ostensibly adapted the story 'The Case of the Missing Will', but in fact presented an episode that was almost entirely a new creation. The script, by

Douglas Watkinson, creates its own mystery out of the same premise of the original story, where Poirot is begged to help discover the location of the crucial legal document, but while this is a simple and brief mystery on the page, the series' almost entirely new story bears no real resemblance to the original. It has some entertainment value, but sets an uncomfortable precedent for the series to attempt to 'improve' upon Christie's original works, which it would later embrace more fulsomely and frequently.

In 'The Adventure of the Italian Nobleman' the viewer may be forgiven for automatically being suspicious of the motivations of one Mr Graves, who has been having tea dates with Miss Lemon, as the series adamantly refuses to create recurring roles for the characters' spouses, meaning that we never meet Mrs Japp and even when Hastings gets married his wife stays in Argentina whenever he makes a trip back to assist Poirot in the latest mystery. The mystery is an interesting one, satisfyingly solved through deduction, although Hastings may be rather put out that his car once more comes out the worst off in the finale's car chase. This episode is followed by Poirot's reminiscences of a case that took place much earlier in his professional career, in 'The Chocolate Box', the first of two episodes from established television director Ken Grieve. In the original story the mystery is recounted by Poirot as an explicit acknowledgment of his own apparent failure at the time, but on screen it is rather more gently described as a demonstration of the mistakes made by several of those involved. Benefitting from lavish location filming, including at Antwerp station, this interesting but simple poisoning mystery is one of the highlights of the season and the series as a whole.

In his book *Poirot and Me*, David Suchet cites the final two episodes of the season as ones that he felt unhappy with, partially because of events in his private life but also due to (unfounded) doubts over his performance. There is certainly the recurrence of the sense of tiredness that had crept into several of the earlier episodes from this production block. The penultimate episode of the series adapts 'Dead Man's Mirror', a locked room mystery that, in typical Christie manner, hinges on a seemingly small detail—the striking of the dinner gong. The episode is a perfectly pleasant adaptation, but shows the beginnings of a lack of confidence in the source material, as a 'spooky' atmosphere is emphasised throughout, including billowing white curtains and a score clearly designed to evoke a sense of near-paranormal unease in the viewer. When the final shot features the superimposition of a hangman's noose on a close up of a thoughtful Poirot the audience might sense a movement towards style over substance. The season's finale, 'Jewel Robbery at the Grand Metropolitan', is based on a small scale and rather dialogue heavy short story, and uses by-now standard methods to open out the story, including the programme's latest example of a newsreel in order to set the action. The line 'If it isn't just like a play!' from the original story may have provided the inspiration for an additional element in this screen version, where an expensive necklace is used as the centrepiece for a stage production, only to be stolen from under the noses of the owners while stored at a local hotel. The basics of the short story are preserved, albeit with its fair share of window dressing and red herrings, and although the mystery relies on very specific geography of the hotel room which is easier to show on screen than express in print, it should be said that by seeing it the audience may struggle to believe that the method by which the jewels are stolen could plausibly take place.

The fifth run of Poirot stories continued to be largely satisfying as adaptations of the original stories, but it is certainly the weakest of the series to this point, especially when operating in the shadow of the stronger two-hour adaptations that it had followed. Launching on 17 January 1993, the programme drew 12.44 m viewers for its opening episode, although this only just placed it within ITV's top 20 at number 19. By the second episode the programme had dropped to 26th position on ITV's chart, with 10.58 m viewers, making it the 42nd most watched programme across all channels that week, a small but significant drop. It stayed at the lower end of the top 30 until the final episode of the series, which was watched by 9.5 m viewers and put the programme just outside of ITV's top 30, the programme's worst comparative performance to this point. There had clearly been an appetite for Poirot, but it seemed that the programme struggled to grow its audience week by week, although one-off events and series premieres performed better. That the series was now effectively forced to make individual two-hour films rather than an hour long series, as the well of short stories was nearly dry, seemed to be fortuitous. One suggestion relating to the short stories went unexplored, however. 'I think it was an absolute tragedy that Brian [Eastman] never did *The Labours of Hercules*,' recalls Mathew Prichard, referring to the linked collection of short stories that showed Poirot solving cases that he considers to be reminiscent of the twelve trials of Hercules. 'I did try but perhaps I should have tried harder. What I wanted them to do was to do them properly, perhaps you'd do ten over Christmas, and maybe you could have done it as a special. But I think ITV wouldn't buy that, but then you couldn't persuade them what a jewel this was. You could only persuade them in terms of television scheduling. And when they finally did *Labours* [as the programme's penultimate episode, broadcast in 2013] it was a travesty, actually—it wasn't a bad film but it didn't even have a flavour of what the original was.'[29]

The fifth series of the programme was to be the final time that it was a regular fixture on television, in the sense that new episodes were afforded a regular weekly slot. After this point Poirot was usually transmitted at whichever point of the year ITV wished to show them, something that resulted in lengthy gaps between transmissions no doubt bolstered by the fact that ITV's accounting system meant that the broadcaster had not 'paid' for a programme until it had actually been broadcast; in this context, an expensive edition of Poirot was easy to put off. Due to a delay in securing Suchet's services, the original plan to film the next set of adaptations in summer 1993 was scrapped, as he instead performed on stage in his award winning turn as college professor John in David Mamet's play *Oleanna*. Filming on four new two-hour productions commenced in March 1994, continuing until July, starting with *Hercule*

Poirot's Christmas, which would eventually be broadcast on New Year's Day, a decision that was to shape the future of the series.

Hercule Poirot's Christmas follows an investigation into the death of Simeon Lee, a millionaire whose death would seem to benefit several members of his family. One of the core plot points of the novel was a horrific scream apparently let out by Simeon as he died, although the truth is rather less prosaic and, in this adaptation, the audience is in no doubt that there is something unusual about the specific nature of the scream; Poirot's early trip to a local joke shop might make the solution seem less strange than it is on the page. The film itself feels very much like an archetypal Christie with its country house mystery, making it a seemingly ideal candidate for the festive season as it does not ask too much of its audience while still providing a satisfying mystery. There is some evidence that the decision to brand the film as an episode of the ongoing series, with the use of the usual opening titles, was a late one as it results in David Suchet being credited twice at the beginning—an indication that the programme makers may not have felt fully comfortable with establishing *Poirot* as a collection of individual films rather than an ongoing series.

Perhaps the decision to show the mystery on New Year's Day 1995 was less than ideal given the festive focus of the programme, which some viewers may have been bored of by this point, but placing Christmas specials at New Year is not an unusual occurrence in television scheduling. More problematic was the fact that the programme found itself scheduled against the third highest rated programme of the week, as 16.34 m viewers tuned in to see the latest episode of *One Foot in the Grave*, while 9.91 m stayed on to watch the all-star adaptation of *Cold Comfort Farm*, against a mere 7.98 m viewers for the Belgian sleuth's latest outing on ITV, easily the programme's lowest ratings to this point. Provisional schedules for the following week showed Poirot retaining the series' Sunday slot—only for ITV to quickly take remedial action, and substitute it for the new series of *A Touch of Frost* (ITV, 1992–2010). The remaining three films were rescheduled for an unspecified 'later date'. Almost overnight, ITV had lost confidence in the series.

Nevertheless, when the next instalment was transmitted on 12 February 1995 the ratings bounced back to 11.2 m, beating the BBC One opposition of *Pie in the Sky* (1994–1997), which had 9.59 m viewers. Trailed by the broadcaster as an 'Agatha Christie Film', the situating of the series as one-off specials had been cemented. It is unfortunate that *Hickory Dickory Dock* was lined up to be broadcast in a slot where support for the programme needed to be rallied, as it is not one a particularly strong film, nor is it one of Christie's best mysteries. The story is the first of the series to hail from the post-war period, having been published in 1955, but keeps its close links to the pre-war 'family' of the series as it follows a mystery centring on Miss Lemon's sister, who runs a boarding house for students where a series of small thefts have taken place, which act as a prelude to murder. The novel itself had an awkward expression of contemporary youth, and broad and stereotypical characterisations of the non-Caucasian lodgers, all of whom are removed from this adaptation, which at best feels like a rather drastic solution to the problem, and at worst creates an impression that only white characters are seen as suitable for this world of *Poirot*. The novel and adaptation exhibit some of the most tiresome shoehorning in of the titular nursery rhyme, with repeated strains of the song as well as relentless and distracting close ups of mice. Even the humour seems broader than ever, with Japp mistaking Poirot's bidet for a device with which to cool his face. The film ends with the apparent death of the murderer in an effective chase in the London Underground, although the tension is dissipated a little as the villain's identity is revealed to keen eyed viewers in a poorly judged shot rather earlier in proceedings than was presumably the intention.

By the spring of 1995 there had been some reports that ITV was not looking to make any more editions of the series, although their spokesperson refused to confirm the claims. However, it was clear to even a casual observer that *Poirot* was not a programme in which ITV had confidence. Summer and autumn 1995 came and went without any news on new productions, nor on the intended transmission dates of the remaining two films, adaptations of the novels *Murder on the Links* and *Dumb Witness*. Provisional Christmas schedules featured 'Murder on the Links' on ITV's schedule for New Year's Eve, but this was eventually substituted with a repeat of *Death in the Clouds*, allowing ITV to defer internal payment for the new film until a later date. Eventually, *Murder on the Links* was shown on 11 February 1996, almost precisely a year since the last new edition of *Poirot*. This film of one of Christie's earlier Poirot mysteries retained the lavish French setting, which was further embellished with an extravagantly staged bicycle race. The mystery is well expressed, although as with the original it is perhaps a little too convoluted for its own good at times. The comedy is represented by Poirot's rivalry with local detective Giraud, played by Bill Moody; oddly, all of the character's lines have been dubbed later—perhaps the original intention had been for him to have a French accent, which he does not have in the final version, despite his nationality. Once more the series was scheduled at an unfortunate time as it was broadcast opposite the opening episode of what was to become one of the BBC's biggest popular successes of the next few years, Irish drama *Ballykissangel* (1996–2001), which debuted with a good rating of 14.11 m viewers. Nevertheless, *Murder on the Links* rated well with a little over 11 m people tuning in.

Viewers had to wait over a year once more to see the last of the four films made for the sixth run of Poirot, with *Dumb Witness* transmitted on 16 March 1997.[30] The film establishes a sense of scale, as well as technology and period, with attempts to break the water speed record forming the backdrop to this where a dying woman appears to emit a mysterious spirit.[31] This means that this is another Christie story that emphasises the supernatural possibilities behind events, before offering a rational explanation at the end. Poirot is made a more prominent part of the plot from early in proceedings as he meets all the key characters, and his charming relationship with the dog Bob (the dumb witness of the title) does well to stay on the right side of schmaltz, while Poirot indignantly responds to the way that so many people he meets treat non-British characters with suspicion. The film is a good one, but with so many Poirot nov-els left to choose from the audience could legitimately feel short changed by ITV's apparent decision to not produce more episodes at this time, especially as the film was the 13th most watched programme of the week, beaten only by the soap operas, the National Lottery draw and an episode of ITV drama *Reckless* (1997–1998); in reality, the ratings blip had been a brief one. It was only in February 1997 that official confirmation was given to the enquiring press that LWT had no plans to make any more, something that was reported on the same day that David Suchet received the London Theatre Critics' Award for best actor.[32] After such a strong start and near universal acclaim, it seemed that this was the end for *Poirot*.

POIROT'S HIATUS AND RETURN

The late 1990s were not a stellar time for British television drama in general, as commercial realities meant that ITV went for safe and cheap drama produc-tions, a long way from their prestige dramas of the 1980s. The cosy nostalgia of programmes such as rural period drama *Heartbeat* (ITV, 1992–2010) had proven successful, and with a relatively low budget, as they generally used fixed locations and recurring characters, which allowed them to be shot in a man-ner more akin to a soap opera than *Poirot*. Certainly we can make connections between programmes of this ilk and the only new Agatha Christie adaptation to appear on ITV during the hiatus in *Poirot* films between 1997 and 2000, a production of her standalone cod-supernatural mystery *The Pale Horse*, which aired on 23 December 1997. Made by Anglia Television, whose production of *Tales of the Unexpected* (ITV, 1979–1988) was probably their best known drama series, the film was written by Alma Cullen, an alumnus of *Inspector Morse* and *A Touch of Frost*, and directed by Charles Beeson who would later work on major US TV series including *Supernatural* (WB/CW, 2005–) and *Fringe* (FOX, 2008–2013). Starring as Mark Easterbrook, a sculptor accused of murder and determined to prove his innocence, is Colin Buchanan. A star name at the time following his lead roles in popular crime drama *Dalziel and Pascoe* (BBC, 1996–2007), he injects some grit into the part that is perhaps more in keeping with then-contemporary trends in television drama than the original novel. The story removes the character of Ariadne Oliver, in her only novel appearance away from Poirot (and in a film that would predate the adap-tation of novels featuring her), but does present an excellent cast of known names and faces, including Leslie Phillips, Jean Marsh, Hermione Norris, Louise Jameson, Ruth Madoc and Andy Serkis. The film revels in *Macbeth* alle-gories, showing the witches early in proceedings, but veers towards the dull on too many occasions, while the attempts to situate it more keenly in the 1960s, through Easterbrook's character and pop culture references (including a *Lolita* poster) fall flat and detract from, rather than add to, the entertainment value of what is one of Christie's more intriguing later mysteries. Reviewers questioned the wisdom of so clearly taking influences from other ITV dramas, while the final rating of 6.78 m viewers only helped to show how well *Poirot* had done, especially as it was only scheduled against the BBC news and a screening of the 1994 Harrison Ford film *Clear and Present Danger* (d. Phillip Noyce), which drew in two million more viewers than *The Pale Horse*.

While *Poirot* was out of production, Brian Eastman had hardly been resting on his laurels, as he was busy with projects including the miniseries *Oktober* (ITV, 1998) as well as the high profile flop *Crime Traveller*, penned by Anthony Horowitz. However, *Poirot* had refused to stay dead, as the programme remained popular in repeats and continued to sell well around the world. It was this international success that led to the revival of the series, as the American Arts and Entertainment (A&E) network came on board as the principal financial backer of the series, rather than LWT. Despite this change, many of the original cast and crew returned, including Brian Eastman as producer, but the seventh season of *Poirot* mysteries was to be made up of a paltry two films. However, at least they were to adapt two of the best novels in the Christie canon, the first of which was the novel often called her masterpiece— *The Murder of Roger Ackroyd*, first published in 1926.

In *The Murder of Roger Ackroyd*, we follow Poirot's retirement to a village, and subsequent involvement in the murder of the wealthy businessman of the title. The novel is narrated by Dr Sheppard, a neighbour and confidante of Poirot. At the end, Christie reveals what is probably her best twist—Sheppard, our narrator, is also the murderer. The story had previously been adapted by Michael Morton for the stage play *Alibi* in 1928, which in turn was filmed as the first Poirot movie in 1931, and Morton's estate even receives a credit on the television adaptation despite the passage of more than 70 years.[33] While Morton had made his own changes to the story, including the removal of Sheppard's sister, this television production fails to do any better and despite the experienced and successful team of writer Clive Exton and director Andrew Grieve, the film can only be classified as a disappointment at best. The removal of the central premise (Poirot narrates the story by reading from the journal of an unknown murderer) shows an uncharacteristic lack of faith in the source material, while the film overall feels like a generic and broad murder mystery rather than a faithful adaptation of what is widely considered to be a classic piece of literature. The character of Ackroyd is now a snarling and unpopular figure, whose business is (unconvincingly) said to have been initially funded by Poirot himself. Sheppard also demonstrates clear sociopathic tendencies, including an additional murder where he viciously runs down a key witness in his car. Some of Grieve's touches are effective, including the emphasis on the importance of time, partially achieved by a huge modern clock in the entrance hall of Ackroyd's house, but the production feels less lavish than previous adaptations and certainly less subtle and thoughtful, a perspective only cemented when the film ends with Sheppard shooting his way through the factory before committing suicide. 'Nobody, including David Suchet, ever thought the television film made of *Roger Ackroyd* was very satisfactory,' Mathew Prichard points out.[34] For Christie fans, it remains one of the most disappointing *Poirot* episodes, but it rated reasonably well with 9.31 m viewers when it transmitted on 2 January 2000, putting it 32nd for the week across all channels.

The general dissatisfaction with *The Murder of Roger Ackroyd* was not repeated when it came to the series' adaptation of *Lord Edgware Dies*, transmitted a few weeks later on 20 February 2000. This tale of doppelgangers and apparently unbreakable alibis reunites Poirot with Hastings and Miss Lemon, as well as Japp who had also featured in the previous mystery. There is a congratulatory sense to proceedings, as Japp claims that the only thing missing from their reunion dinner is a dead body, while Miss Lemon highlights that Poirot's role is to find the solution and when Poirot does solve the case it is with the help of one of his old friends. The production largely follows the original story, albeit with a strengthening of the killer's motive and a cinematic embellishment of some of the sequences set at the theatre. The series seemed to be back on track, with positive reviews (sometimes begrudgingly phrased, as ever, indicating that several critics felt they shouldn't enjoy the show quite as much as they did), including one from Robert Banks of the *Independent* who wondered why the series was so happy to closely recreate plot and period, but not Christie's casual anti-semitism that appears in the original novel, writing that 'it's all right to give the viewers a bit of harmless killing, but we're too delicate to be exposed to old-fashioned bigotry.'[35] In terms of ratings, the programme slipped to slightly below 9 m but this was enough for it to be ranked 24th most watched programme across all channels that week, at a time when almost no programmes other than soap operas were receiving ratings of more than 10 m.

Although these two episodes of Poirot could fairly be considered a success in terms of ratings, there was no sign of the pace being picked up for the next run of episodes. Gaps between editions of *Poirot* had long since frustrated the Christie estate, and this was only confounded by disappointment with *Ackroyd* and a perception that the series was no longer as prestigious as it once had been. 'We never really understood why sometimes there were big gaps and why sometimes not,' Mathew Prichard explains, 'I think those decisions had far more to do with Brian Eastman than they did with us or even LWT ... There was quite a bit of coming and going, ill-feeling even, between us and Brian Eastman. We felt very strongly that Brian was not being fair to us and he was simply doing them when he felt like it and was not spending enough money on the productions.'[36] From Eastman's perspective, he might have felt the same of ITV, who had failed to commit to more productions a few years earlier, but there was certainly a sense from several involved that even with the gap in production the series was starting to feel tired after more than a decade on air.

By June 2000 pre-production had started on the eighth series of Poirot mysteries, which was once more to be only two episodes. First up, on 2 June 2002, was *Murder in Mesopotamia*, a locked room mystery set at an archaeological dig that has a particularly clever method of murder. There is much to like about the mystery, although it is not one of the more dynamic tales on screen, feeling as it does rather like a retread of several earlier adaptations.

Reviews demonstrated a tiredness with the production, some highlighting it as the latest example of a formulaic and cliché driven series.

The second adaptation, *Evil Under the Sun*, was the last *Poirot* to feature all three supporting characters of Japp, Hastings and Miss Lemon until the final series of the show more than a decade later. The mystery had already been effectively filmed in 1982 with Peter Ustinov, in a version that was often repeated, and so it is understandable that this new production elected for a strikingly different visual look by filming much of the action on Burgh Island off the coast of south Devon, which had been the inspiration for the original novel.[37] The island and its striking period hotel had often featured on television, including in the BBC *Miss Marple* adaptation of *Nemesis*, but this is the story that best required its services. In this adaptation Poirot is sent to the hotel in order to lose weight, allowing for the inevitable moments of comedy. For the most part, the production works well, but some of the changes are unnecessary and arbitrary (teenager Linda is changed to Lionel, with the character's witch-craft obsession changing to one of poisons), and it struggles a little to assert its own identity at times, feeling rather less stylish than some other editions of the series despite the exceptional location. There is no doubting the genius of Christie's original story, however. When broadcast on 15 December 2002 it made perhaps less impression than usual, with gentle but kind reviews simply referring to it as 'comfort food', indicating that even when adapting one of the more iconic mysteries the programme was struggling to make an impact.[38,39] A situation affecting more than just this series would see prompt action that would move it away from the formula it had adopted since the beginning.

A CHANGE OF STYLE FOR *POIROT*

The idea of changing the direction of the *Poirot* series had been fomenting ever since the series had gone on hiatus, as Mathew Prichard remembers:

> We thought, in the late 90s, they'd got rather tired and formulaic. It took some little while to convince ITV of this because, television by and large, dog doesn't eat dog and they were quite reluctant to bypass Brian Eastman … The reason we changed producers also had something to do with that's when Chorion bought shares in Agatha Christie Limited and they had this guy, Phil Clymer, he felt very strongly we should try and start again.[40]

As Prichard points out, the 1998 purchase of shares in Agatha Christie Ltd. by Chorion (who bought them from the Booker group) had led to a substantial rethink of how Christie was handled. Some of the results of this are explored in Chap. 15, but as Poirot remained one of the company's biggest successes there was no chance that they were going to let him disappear without a fight. In a timely coincidence, Granada Television (which would soon merge with other commercial television franchises to simply become ITV) had noticed that, whatever the domestic impact, the international sales for the series were only continuing to grow. In the wake of ITV's disastrous attempt to launch its own subscription television service OnDigital (later ITV Digital), which had ceased broadcasting in June 2002 with massive losses, ITV bosses were keenly eyeing up the £20 m in revenue generated by *Poirot*. 'Ailing Granada calls in *Poirot*', as *The Times* put it, reporting that an adaptation of *Death on the Nile* was set to be the highlight of a new run of adaptations.[41] However, this new lease of life for the series was not without its casualties.

Mathew Prichard candidly recalls that the series had not always been plain sailing, pointing out that 'in those days, we the family and even Booker, we weren't very close to what went on'. Recalling the relationship between Brian Stone, the estate's literary agent, and Brian Eastman, Prichard says that:

> [They] fenced around each other quite a bit and I don't think they really got on very well together ... The whole of the Brian Eastman reign was a history of minor disputes between David and Brian about the character of Poirot, and all sorts of things, like Brian was a firm believer that Poirot was a character who worked better for television if he had Miss Lemon and Japp and Hastings, and Brian wanted to insert at least one, preferably two, characters into everyone he did. My mother was implacably opposed to that. But the later the stories got, the more difficult it became. And, of course, when Michele Buck and Damian [Timmer] took over, luckily they decided that Poirot worked much better on his own—maybe they decided that as a matter of convenience, I don't know.[42]

The decision to appoint Michele Buck and Damian Timmer to the roles of Executive Producers of the series required consultation with not only the Christie estate, Chorion and the production partners of A&E and ITV, but also Suchet himself. Both potential producers had backgrounds in successful television dramas, having worked on series including *Wycliffe* (ITV, 1994–1998) and *Peak Practice* (ITV, 1993–2002), but this did not mean that any transition was a done deal. 'The difficulty, of course, was in persuading David to change as well because actors are very loyal to producers who have given them a lot of work in the past and David was very, very reluctant to change,' recalls Prichard. 'In the end, we had a bit of a beauty parade, and Damian and Michelle convinced both us and David, they were going to spend more on these productions, be more comparable perhaps to what the BBC had spent on *Miss Marple*.' Eastman's reaction to this was perhaps understandable. 'He was pretty cross. At the wrap party [for the whole series, in 2013] we clinked glasses and he said "I wasn't very happy at the time!"'[43]

The decision to change producer had been spurred on not only by a sense that the series had become rather formulaic and needed invigorating, but also through an interest in tackling stories that had previous been overlooked in a series that had concentrated on the pre-war Poirot mysteries. Prichard feels that without a change of producer it would have been highly unlikely that all of the Poirot novels would have been brought to the screen. One explicit acknowledgment of a new approach was immediately obvious to regular viewers—the removal of Hastings, Japp and Miss Lemon as regulars on the programme.

'When we employed Michele Buck and Damien Timmer, they preferred David working on his own,' Prichard says, 'I even think that David rather fancied the idea of being on his own.' Such a decision was no slight against the actors involved, but indicative of an understanding that most of the remaining stories simply didn't feature these characters. Although they had been inserted into stories that did not feature them throughout the run to this point, often this was a way to shore up the slighter stories, something that was less of an issue when tackling full novels. So it was that a decision was made that *Poirot* would escape even more of the trappings of an ongoing series, as it was now without a regular cast beyond Suchet, while it even dispensed with the opening titles and the original version of the theme tune.[44]

Poirot was now a programme that credited no less than eight producers, including Suchet himself as an associate producer, as well as representatives from all the interested production companies—this variety of influence may explain why some of these later episodes can feel muddled and confused, although others have a clearer focus, to their benefit. Certainly, few episodes of *Poirot* are of a higher quality than the first of these new style films, an adaptation of *Five Little Pigs*, shown on 14 December 2003. The adaptation, directed by Paul Unwin, stakes its claim as a modern piece of television from the beginning, with extensive use of handheld camerawork used to show subjective memories, alongside the past coloured with alternately sepia tones and bright colours, contrasted with the grey of the present. The opening dream-like sequence sets up the external appearance of the characters before, as in Christie's novel, the rest of the mystery takes us closer and gives a psychological perspective of the murder of a philandering young painter, whose wife was convicted of his murder. Unlike the novel, the film brutally depicts her hanging; she dies of natural causes in the original Christie story. Told mostly in flashback, the film is a sombre and complex one that mulls over the relationship that each of the 'little pigs' had with the murdered man. Retrospective investigations tend to work better on the page than on screen, but this adaptation by Kevin Elyot (in his first of three excellent scripts contributed to the series) is an exception, and its striking new style even caught the eye of the critics. 'But wait,' wrote Gareth McLean of the *Guardian*, 'There's a twist in the plot. A sting in the tale. The camerawork was jittery, the direction terribly modern, the palette washed out … Instead of picture-postcard vistas we had painful, lingering close-ups. Jaunty out, gritty in. *Poirot* has gone all *NYPD Blue*. Christie's come over all *Cops*. It was all the better for it.'[45] In addition to the modern direction, the film also boasted a star cast of known names including *Queer as Folk*'s Aiden Gillen and *Tipping the Velvet*'s Rachael Stirling, who is also an acclaimed stage actress and daughter of Dame Diana Rigg—it was even able to employ the talents of Annette Badland for the relatively meagre role of housekeeper Mrs Briggs.[46] The result is a film that establishes itself as a special event, rather than simply 'another Poirot', as the previous adaptations had deliberately avoided name actors. '*Five Little Pigs*, I think, is almost the best thing David ever did,' says

Mathew Prichard, calling it 'one of the best adaptations of anything,' a sentiment echoed by many Christie fans.[47]

The next novel to be adapted once more covered an imprisoned woman who Poirot believes to be innocent of murder—only this time, he may be able to intervene before she reaches the gallows. *Sad Cypress* covers the murder of a wealthy woman, and a mysterious letter that alerts her relatives to an unknown person who allegedly had been 'sucking up' to her. Regular viewers of the programme may be immediately suspicious of Poirot's sidekick, Dr Peter Lord, given memories of *The Murder of Roger Ackroyd*—although they may also wonder if he is little more than a red herring. Certainly the solution is one of Christie's more surprising but it is still convincing. While the novel had the solution revealed in court, here the series retains its more personal touch, as Poirot takes tea with the murderer. Once more, the direction is more modern, with sequences including Poirot imagining a skull in place of one character's face. While it is not one of the best remembered stories, and perhaps lacks the secondary incidents key to Christie's very best novels, the extent to which *Sad Cypress* tends to be overlooked is not deserved.

In contrast, *Death on the Nile*, the third adaptation of the ninth series of Poirot and Kevin Elyot's second, could hardly be said to have been overlooked over the years, having been adapted for an all-star 1978 film that still receives regular screenings on television today. If the previous film had seemed a formidable backdrop against which the new adaptation could be made, then the final production does not betray any lack of confidence. With the advantage of a leaner running time than the film, and no need to indulge the famous faces on board, this tale of a couple being stalked on their honeymoon by the groom's aggrieved ex-fiancée is able to concentrate on the final mystery, the murder of one of the newlyweds. Suchet's Poirot almost fades into the background here and observes the early action, unlike the attention seeking antics of Ustinov's portrayal in the film, while the stylish production is bookmarked with evocative and atmospheric aerial shots showing two of the characters embracing, dancing and—in a *Poirot* first—making love. Some of the characterisation does feels surprisingly arch in contrast to the previous two more sombre *Poirot* films, especially the character of Timothy Allerton, who is established as gay even if there is a hint that his relationship with his mother may be more than platonic. When Poirot apprehends the murderer at the end, the villain's tears hold no sway and Poirot even—oddly—gloats about the efficiency of the hangman's noose. The character's take on the nature of justice would later become an even more prominent part of the series. By this point, the character of Poirot is being increasingly well established as a solitary figure, something that only continues, as he fails to have his companions on hand in order to keep his idiosyncrasies in check and provide a more stable home life. While this is all true of the novel it can sometimes be sad for an audience who cares so much about the fussy Belgian to see him travelling without companionship, and even moving house, without any particular ties.

Poirot's next change of location, to another country cottage within easy walking distance of a larger country house, inevitably leads to a murder investigation. *The Hollow*, the name of the mystery as well as the larger house, provides a perfect murder scenario with the victim shot on the edge of the house's swimming pool; by the time Poirot arrives all the suspects are gathered around. To Poirot's eyes, this might almost be too perfect, and one can see why the stage managed nature of proceedings led to Christie's decision to adapt the mystery for the theatre, where she also removed Poirot. This was a good decision, as this is a story that has to twist and turn to convince that Poirot would not only be around for all of the important action, but also see so little that he doesn't solve the mystery almost instantly; a dimmer detective would have been more convincing in plot terms. However, it is still a good mystery, with a good script from Nick Dear, who would write five more screenplays for the series, with some excellent visual elements, including Poirot's discovery of the murder weapon within a clay sculpture, which rounds off an excellent run of adaptations.

With the ninth series having been broadcast sporadically between December 2003 and April 2004, it was soon time for *Poirot* to pause between production blocks once more. Elsewhere, the lion's share of attention in the world of Agatha Christie was devoted to the premiere of ITV's new series of Miss Marple adaptations, simply called *Agatha Christie: Marple*, which debuted in 2004. To many, this series appeared to actively work against everything that *Poirot* had done well, and so it was with some relief that the Britain's favourite Belgian returned to television at the beginning of 2006. Viewers of *The Mystery of the Blue Train*, never one of Christie's favourite novels, may have had a sense of déjà vu following the adaptation of the similar story 'The Plymouth Express' fifteen years earlier. This adaptation, the first of four from Guy Andrews, boasts an excellent cast including Elliott Gould and Lindsay Duncan, as it contributes a surfeit of red herrings to the original mystery of the murder of a woman on a train. Understandably, characters are allowed to interact more, and a mysterious Count is made more prominent, as in the novel he is referred to more than he is seen. However, so many extraneous events are added that at times it lacks focus, although this does maintain the energy of the mystery. From the beginning the film makes it clear that the story's emphasis is on class and money, which is interesting and allows Poirot to display his most sympathetic side to a young woman elevated to a world unknown to her, although the final revelation that the culprits were aroused by their murder feels awkward and unconvincing. Some critics had lost interest before this: 'As if the build-up to the murder hadn't taken long enough, we then had to follow Poirot up a series of blind alleys,' wrote Fiona Sturges of the *Independent*, 'Poirot's final epiphany didn't come a moment too soon.'[48]

Cards on the Table, the next novel to be adapted, could hardly have been a less cinematic choice. A tale of a murder that takes place during a game of bridge, Christie assured readers of her novel that there were to be no tricks—it was simply the case that one of the other players had murdered the victim.

The result is a clever exercise in the architecture of murderous practices, as the reader puts together the clues to work out who could have performed the deed, and when—something made infinitely easier to anyone who also knows how to play the card game. The production is not one of the more accomplished *Poirot* films due to the restricted necessary emphasis on a single set of conversations and routines, although it should be said that even the original novel divides Christie fans between those who find it a particularly tedious mystery and those who enjoy the intricate and precise nature of the clues, which require pure logical deduction. Some attempts are made to broaden out the action, with conversations taking place outside so as not to make the adaptation too claustrophobic or visually uninteresting, but it is a difficult task—not helped by some exceptionally poorly realised backdrop effects supposedly depicting Switzerland and Egypt. One highlight is the inclusion of the character Ariadne Oliver, a writer of mystery novels who makes her series debut in a highly entertaining performance from Zoë Wanamaker, one that she would later reprise. However, the final revelation that a gay relationship formed the motivation for a murder (something that is not the case in the novel) demonstrates a worrying movement of the series towards *Marple*'s oddly juvenile obsession with homosexuality as either red herring or motivation. This decision also grated with Rupert Smith of the *Guardian*, who also wrote that the production was full of 'pointless deviation and exaggeration … I can't stop wondering why they felt the need to meddle.'[49]

However, almost the opposite occurred during the adaptation of the next mystery to be tackled, *After the Funeral*. In the novel a reading of a will leads to the deceased man's sister, Cora, to express her opinion that he had been murdered—only for her to later be found murdered. The novel alluded to a lesbian relationship between Cora and her companion Miss Gilchrist, something dispensed with in this adaptation so as to promote a more simplistic relationship where Miss Gilchrist simply hated the victim. There are some character moments between Miss Gilchrist and Poirot as a result, but there is a more subtle and interesting story to be told here than manifests on screen. Subtlety is also not a strength of the final film of the tenth series, an adaptation of *Taken at the Flood*, which presented its own particular difficulties. Originally published in 1948 the story firmly establishes itself as taking place in an England still recovering from the war, during which an apparent bomb blast has consequences that appear to motivate someone to commit murder. With the Poirot television series still firmly set pre-war—although now a little later than 1936—changes had to be made, including the replacing of the bombing with an apparent gas explosion. The change of period robs the story of much of its interest to the modern day reader, as it depicts Christie's take on a country rebuilding after devastating conflict, and forces the emphasis on to one of her less interesting Poirot mysteries, which struggles to find enough incident to fill out the running time. Perhaps in an attempt to shore up interest, the cast almost uniformly give arch and ostentatious performances more at home in *Marple* than *Poirot*, while allusions to homosexuality crop up once more—a tic that Christie adaptations of this period struggle to shake off. The film is a disappointing resolution to a series that, on the whole, failed to follow through on the promise shown by the first four adaptations from this new production team.

The next, eleventh, series of *Poirot* debuted in September 2008 with an adaptation of *Mrs McGinty's Dead*, a well-publicised return for the detective that reaches the zenith of the series' later style with a surfeit of soft focus shots that steer the programme away from the more modern and dynamic style of the likes of *Five Little Pigs*, and towards a more generalised sense of hazy nostalgia, although that is not to say the direction lacks style, including an impressive crane shot when Poirot arrives. In an interview to promote the series Suchet was keen to make it clear that, despite the occasional veering into *Marple* territory in terms of tone and changes to the source material seen in some recent adaptations, Poirot would not go for what James Walton of the *Daily Telegraph* called 'embarrassingly ill-advised modernity' of its sister series. 'That's not going to happen in *Poirot*,' Suchet was quoted as saying, 'No way. He will not become gay.'[50] Returning for this film was not only Ariadne Oliver but also George, Poirot's valet played by David Yelland, who had first appeared in the previous adaptation, *Taken at the Flood*, and would make occasional appearances for the rest of the series' run. The adaptation is a pleasant one that slightly simplifies the plot, and perhaps feels like a generic Christie mystery thanks to its country village trappings, but is no less enjoyable for it.

The next two novels to be tackled for the series both presented their own particular difficulties. *Cat Among the Pigeons*, the first of the *Poirot* series to be adapted by Mark Gatiss, is an example of what we might consider to be the begrudging Poirot mystery. Mindful that Poirot was seen as a particular draw by her publisher and readers alike, but keen to work without him, Christie sometimes reduced his appearance in later novels down to the bare minimum. In this case, Poirot makes his first appearance on page 182 of the 255 page novel, something remedied in this adaptation where Poirot is invited to visit a girls' school to award a prize, only for there to inevitably be a murder within the bullying atmosphere of the educational establishment. Writer Gatiss (co-creator of *Sherlock* (BBC, 2010–) among many other things) makes under-standable changes to the source material, given its particular difficulties—not least the fact that, despite some intriguing characterisation, it is hardly one of the better Christie novels, while it also needed to be moved from 1959, the year of its publication, to the pre-war period. The decision to change a mur-der weapon from revolver to javelin is a good, pleasingly visual choice while Christie's own subplots are altered in ways that make them no less effective in terms of overall impact.

The next adaptation, *Third Girl*, is another Poirot novel that is from the weaker end of the canon but in this case moving the story from the year of publication, 1966. Very much set in the 1960s, the original novel opens with a young woman, Norma, who visits Poirot because she fears she may have mur-dered someone, only to flee when she sees how old he is. She is the 'third girl' of the title, a phrase applied to her as the final person to join a flatshare with two other young women, all participants in swinging sixties culture. Bringing this back to the rather more staid and culturally conservative pre-war society removes much of the potential interest and colour of the novel, which in itself had some intriguing elements even if interest is not always maintained throughout the mystery. The most surprising change by screenwriter Dan Reed is one that alters the explanation for Norma's belief that she may be a murderer, changing it from drug-induced manipulation by a third party to simple coercion while she was in a vulnerable state following her mother's death, an event which in itself is an addition from the novel. This approach to psychological effects as a simple exercise in contextual manipulation is a rather more old fashioned approach to mental health and perception than the novel had presented over forty years earlier. The adaptation does offer a lot of peripheral moments to maintain interest, including some particularly grisly scenes and even a moment when Ariadne Oliver is revealed to be the author of a source of Tony Hancock's frustration, the novel *Lady Don't Fall Backwards*. However, Poirot's decision to have Nancy to stay at his apartment seems bizarre at this point, alluding to a more sensitive side that does not develop beyond this; it seems that this is an example of where a Poirot adaptation appears to exist in order to complete the canon rather than because of any particular interest in the source material.

While *Third Girl* is a middling adaptation of a relatively weak book, the final film of the eleventh series performs far worse, offering an abysmal take on one of Christie's outright classics. The novel *Appointment with Death* is one of Christie's most psychologically-focused mysteries, with the murder of a family's bullying matriarch in the Middle East offering no shortage of suspects. The psychological focus applies not only to the relationships between characters, but also plays a key role in the provision of an alibi that is later proven to be false. This adaptation, scripted by Guy Andrews and directed by Ashley Pearce in his second contribution to the series after *Mrs McGinty's Dead*, can only be regarded as a disappointment on almost every level. In technical terms, Poirot has never looked poorer than during the sequence showing the journey to the archaeological dig, with particularly unconvincing green screen work. In terms of the plot, any subtlety of the original novel is replaced by brash and bombastic alternatives, such as when the crucial clue of a servant being sent to fetch the dead woman, as well as the intriguing perspective on psychological influence that provides a key alibi, is replaced with a peculiar placement of a waxed ball of blood that drenches the victim under the hot sun. When it comes to the performances, the normally excellent actors in the cast, including the likes of Tim Curry, generally play their roles as if this were a spoof, with an arch OTT-ness that sits uncomfortably with the tone of the rest of the series.[51] Any of the psychological interest from the novel is dispensed with or overlooked, while the nadir of both the adaptation and the series as a whole must be the superfluous introduction of a new character in the form of a nun who is actually a white slave trader. It is no surprise that the result was left on ITV's shelf for over a year, after the previous three films had aired on consecutive weeks, finally being broadcast over a year after it had been released on DVD.

Thankfully, the twelfth run of mysteries went some way towards redressing some of the weaknesses of the previous series, and none even come close to the poor standard of *Appointment with Death*. Opening the run was *Three Act Tragedy*, an excellent Christie novel that perhaps suffers from being adapted at this stage in proceedings as some of its best surprises have already been seen in other adaptations.[52] Broadcast in January 2010, Nick Dear's adaptation faithfully reproduces the twists and turns of the original novel, which follow an apparently motiveless murder at a dinner party, which is then replicated when many of the guests regroup for another party at a later date. Unlike the 1986 adaptation of the story starring Peter Ustinov, this version uses the motivation for murder as presented in the British edition of the novel, although Poirot's accusation that the murderer is 'deranged' perhaps alludes to the alternative explanation for murder. As the novel had opened with credits for the characters along the same lines as those seen in a theatre programme, so this adaptation also opens like a play, as the stage curtain of a theatre rises to show the opening titles. Ashley Pearce's direction is particularly strong here, with an effective dream-like quality throughout, and an emotionally satisfying resolution.

The next novel to be adapted, *Hallowe'en Party*, is perhaps one of the most underrated Poirot mysteries, possibly because it was published in 1969, and so during Christie's later period, where her novels were generally weaker than they had been in her heyday. Mark Gatiss is a highly suitable screenwriter for this production, being an avowed lover of the macabre, and he makes the good decision to overplay rather than underplay the horror elements, making for an enjoyably sinister film of one of Christie's darkest mysteries, where the victim is a thirteen year old girl who is drowned in a bowl of bobbing apples. Gatiss sensibly ignores the fact that Hallowe'en parties of the type described in the book were practically unknown in the UK in the pre-war period, and continues with the mystery regardless. Ariadne Oliver makes another appearance here, taking part in the party in the midst of a classic horror film thunderstorm, while Poirot listens to a horror story on the radio, and when he solves the case the denouement speech opens with 'It was a dark and stormy night …'. The film does have some problems with the way it has to depict flashbacks, as we know that some of these must be false, but this is handled by handheld camerawork making them seem more explicitly subjective than the rest of the production. While Gatiss makes several changes, including a well-handled gay subplot (in contrast to earlier adaptations), the spirit of the novel is left intact and he even improves on tying up or removing loose threads that the elderly Christie had left in her original novel.

In the UK, the series' long awaited adaptation of *Murder on the Orient Express* was saved for Christmas, broadcast on 25 December 2010. Had the series handled this mystery earlier in its run then we may have anticipated a standard adaptation of the novel. However, on screen this adaptation provides a springboard to the final era of Poirot, as the stage is set for his considerations of faith and justice that will become a crucial part of his final case. Unusually, this adaptation by Stewart Harcourt appears to almost expect the audience to know the basic elements of the mystery, and understands that they are likely to have seen the 1974 film. Resultantly, it emphasises the personal effect on Poirot above and beyond the events surrounding the murder itself. At its denouement, Suchet gives a chilling performance as a furious Poirot rages at the culprits, frustrated by the moral quandary they have placed on him. This is a sad and world-weary detective, haunted by a gruesome suicide that opens the film, and the audience may note that he appears to have worked out the solution early in proceedings as he quickly dismisses red-herrings laid for him as he spends longer searching for the solution to what he is going to do about the murder, rather than exposing the murderers. Nevertheless, some of the themes are explored in a heavy handed manner, such as when Poirot witnesses the stoning of a woman, an example of vigilante justice, while casual viewers may be surprised by his sudden embrace of Catholicism, little alluded to in the series prior to this (although occasionally present in the novels). His anger can only have real resonance when the audience have not only followed Suchet's Poirot through more than two decades of mysteries, both light-hearted and hard-edged, but know that we are moving into the final era of the show.[53] The result has divided fans—those looking for a simple, faithful adaptation of the novel have come away bitterly disappointed. Those who enjoy the theatre of Suchet's performance and the setting out of themes that will only become more prominent have found rather more to like.

A year would pass before the twelfth run finished with the broadcast of *The Clocks* on 26 December 2011, coming shortly after the long awaited announcement that Suchet was to complete the canon with a final run of five films, welcome news to those who had heard the oft-repeated rumours that, once more, *Poirot* was to be rested indefinitely.[54] Published in 1963, the novel starts with an intriguing premise, with a body found in a room where multiple clocks are all stopped at the same time, but soon meanders into less interesting areas involving cold war spying. Stewart Harcourt's adaptation is necessarily reframed as a pre-Second World War thriller instead but struggles with the basic constraints of the relatively unengaging novel. Nevertheless the script does its best and the performances help to elevate the material, including appearances from Frances Barber, Geoffrey Palmer and a charismatic performance from Phil Daniels.

POIROT'S FINAL CURTAIN

Nobody was under any illusion that finishing the run of Poirot adaptations would be an easy ride, least of all Mathew Prichard and David Suchet himself. 'I wish I could remember exactly when David's eye lit up and he thought—do you know, I really might make all these!' says Prichard. 'Then he sort of looked at me and he said, "but that would mean we would have to do *Elephants...*".'[55] Published in 1972, *Elephants Can Remember* was the final Poirot mystery to be written by Christie, and is generally derided as a wandering, meandering story with little in the way of incident but a plethora of dead ends; many feel that it shouldn't have been published at all as it shows clear signs of Christie struggling to put together basic material, something that a team of researchers have recently attributed to possible Alzheimer's.[56] Nevertheless, this story was to be the first adaptation broadcast for this final run of five films, with Nick Dear given the near-thankless task of bringing to the screen the mystery of a married couple found dead, each with bullet wounds—events that had occurred several years before Poirot begins his investigation. Rather than simply following the book's unengaging structure of lengthy and repetitive interviews with each of the major characters, Dear injects a substantial subplot into proceedings, where a grisly murder in the present day keeps Poirot occupied while Ariadne Oliver helps with the investigation into the older crime. Unlike some adaptations in this final run, the issue Dear faced was not having enough material to work with, and he does very well to preserve much of the original mystery with highly satisfactory embellishments. His work is complemented by highly stylised direction from John Strickland, which makes extensive use of green screen work, that while not always completely effective helps to give the production a distinctive un-real quality of its own that keeps the plot engaging for the audience. Performances are also strong, while the transplanting of the action from 1972 to just prior to the Second World War is mostly effectively done, although references to chemotherapy as a possible reason for a character wearing wigs are unfortunately anachronistic. The film is hardly in the top tier of *Poirot* episodes but it has the rare distinction of actually improving upon the source material.

Following the broadcast of *Elephants Can Remember* in June 2013, the final four Poirot films aired in consecutive weeks from 23 October 2013, opening with a particularly difficult story to adapt, 1927's *The Big Four*. The novel had been published out of expediency, as it was an unhappy time in Christie's personal life as her marriage to Archie Christie had broken down, and so in order to have something to publish she reworked a set of previously published short stories that see Poirot working to unmask and depose a 'Big Four' group of villains intent on world domination. The mysteries owe more to the spy genre than the mystery, and are generally quite unlike any other Poirot title. Mark Gatiss's adaptation, written with his husband Ian Hallard, dispenses with some of the more incredible moments, including an exploding mountain filled with spies, as well as the appearance of a man who may (or may not) be Poirot's twin brother. Instead, this film takes only vague inspiration from the original story, reworking some of the events so as to make them coherent for a single film. As a result of these difficulties it is not one of the greater successes of the series, but satisfies the audience in one particular way as it reintroduces Miss Lemon, Captain Hastings and (promoted) Assistant Commissioner Japp, for one final outing together, as with the exception of Miss Lemon they had all appeared in the original book. Gatiss and Hallard also provide a resolution to the plot more in keeping with the general ethos of the television series (as it is revealed that actually there is no 'Big Four') and, although purists may dislike an adaptation so detached from the original, realists can find plenty to enjoy from the performances and witty script, while details of the plot take a back seat to our final goodbye to a quarter-century of these four actors working together.

The third story to be shown from this final run was also the final one to be filmed, an adaptation of *Dead Man's Folly*, a straightforward murder mystery that is almost an overtly archetypal example of Christie, making it something of a pleasant surprise that it had been left so long, enabling the audience to see Poirot playing his traditional role one final time as the series neared its end. The original book, which centres on a murder themed treasure hunt at a fête leading to the real thing, had been set at a house and grounds clearly based on Greenway, Christie's holiday house in Dartmouth, South Devon, which by the time of production had been given over to the National Trust to great success. The producers of the series were highly aware that both the estate and fans were keen for the production to be filmed at Greenway, and so it was.[57] Nick Dear once more wrote the script, which keeps close to the original novel and provides a thoroughly entertaining, well-paced and traditional Poirot perfect for this final run of stories. Whether by accident or design, it is good to see Poirot at the peak of his powers while still in good health at one point during this final run.

Less satisfying, however, is the penultimate adaptation, which is a disappointment in several respects. Bringing *The Labours of Hercules* to the screen as a ninety minute film was simply an impossible exercise, as the original book is a collection of short stories rather than one single mystery; many fans had not expected the series to ever tackle it, once it had moved on from hour long adaptations of the short stories. Understandably, some of the stories are removed, which results in some of the more amusing and small-scale mysteries making no appearance at all (including what may be Poirot's slightest mystery, as he investigates the kidnapping of a Pekingese dog). This balance between giving some impression of the range of the collection's mysteries, and making a coherent overall plot, is clearly a difficult one, and it is a surprise that this task was handed to Guy Andrews, who had scripted many of the weakest Poirots to this point. Andrews presents a film that touches on aspects in many of the stories, especially 'The Erymanthian Boar', but essentially creates a new mystery from them—this makes the film less confusing than it may have been, but it is also curiously unengaging, not helped by the lack of colour in the hotel scenes, while the depiction of its location (atop a Swiss mountain) is also less than convincing. It boasts a good cast, including Orla Brady as the Countess Rossakoff (previously played by Kika Markham in the third series' 'The Double Clue') and Simon Callow, whose presences help to maintain some interest, but not enough.

Thankfully, the long-awaited final adaptation of the whole series was not to disappoint. When the programme began filming in 1988, only 12 years had passed since Christie's death, which occurred shortly after publication of the novel that killed off the Belgian sleuth once and for all—*Curtain: Poirot's Last Case*. By the time filming on the story began it had been some 37 years since Poirot had solved this last mystery and, understandably, it had never been adapted for the screen before. As is well known, Christie had originally written the novel in the 1940s, meaning that this final case hails from a period where she was still at the peak of her powers, and it does not disappoint as either a mystery or a finale for the dying detective. The decision was made to film this adaptation at the beginning of the thirteenth run of production, largely in order to lessen the emotional and physical impact on Suchet, whose performance as the frail detective is truly exceptional, having lost a significant amount of weight for this final story. In an interview with Elizabeth Grice of the *Daily Telegraph*, Suchet expressed mixed emotions about the end of the series, likening it to climbing Everest. Discussing the last day of filming, he said that 'I cannot deny it was the hardest day filming of my whole career. Poirot has been my best friend, part of my family, part of my life. I've lived with this man. He's allowed me the career I don't think I would have had without him. He's given me stability in a profession that is insecure.'[58] Writing for the *Daily Mail*, Suchet said that filming Poirot's death was 'one of the hardest things I have ever had to do.'[59]

The mystery sees the return of both Captain Hastings (as well as, briefly, Poirot's valet George) and the house of Styles, the location of Christie's first book, now a guest house where Poirot is resident—and on the trail of a killer. Kevin Elyot's script is exceptional, closely keeping the dialogue and incidents from the original novel while structuring the mystery for the screen.[60] Surprises abound, not only in the mystery itself, but also Poirot's role, and although the fact that the detective dies in the novel has never been kept a secret, many audiences were still surprised and shocked to see his lifeless body discovered before the final act.[61] The production garnered excellent reviews, and was keenly anticipated by the audience, having been trailed for some time, including the release of photos showing the wheelchair-bound detective, now almost unrecognisable from his earlier self. The *Daily Telegraph* gave it a five-star review, with James Walton calling the series 'one of the great TV achievements—and great TV performances—of the past 30 years … Only now that he's gone, perhaps, are we beginning to realise how much there is to be said for a show that's content to concentrate simply on being reliably good. Or, as the owner of Styles said to Poirot in last night's programme, "We'll all miss you, old chap—but you won't be forgotten."'[62]

Indeed, the atmosphere may be maudlin during much of the film, but the audience leaves upbeat, happy with their memories of Poirot the character, and the series, both exceptional examples of their type. It would be near impossible for a series that ran for so long to create consistently faultless productions, but even if some individual episodes may have disappointed, there is no doubting the overall quality of the programme. It is for the very best episodes that the programme will be most well remembered, while the whole run can easily be revisited by casual audiences and fans alike through repeats on various channels. Those working on the series may have felt both sadness and joy when it came to completing the final collection of stories, but the audience shared these conflicted emotions, and such was the impact that it made, and regard that it was held in, that the series show no sign of disappearing from the nation's television sets any time soon.

NOTES

1. Rosalind Hicks to Guy Slater, 10 November 1984 (BBC WAC: *A Pocketful of Rye* production file).
2. Slater to Jonathan Powell, 16 November 1984 (BBC WAC: *A Pocketful of Rye* production file).
3. Unlike Poirot, there are only four 'long stories' in Arthur Conan Doyle's Sherlock Holmes canon, so the decision to work from the short stories initially was almost an inevitable one.
4. There are exceptions to this general fidelity, of course—*The Last Vampyre* is a particularly poor extensive reworking of a Conan Doyle short story. Unfortunately Granada's Sherlock Holmes adaptations did not complete the canon, principally due to the ill health and subsequent death of Jeremy Brett, who played Holmes. Most of the strongest stories were covered, although some highlights remained sadly unfilmed, such as 'The Five Orange Pips'.
5. David Suchet and Geoffrey Wansell, *Poirot and Me* (London: Headline, 2013), 18.
6. In reality, there are several instances in the series where the audience is invited to chuckle at Poirot's idiosyncrasies but Hicks' meaning was likely more subtle—she did not want an overtly comic character, as Ustinov's portrayal had sometimes been.
7. Interview with the author, August 2015.
8. This list is reproduced in *Poirot and Me*.
9. Peter Haining, *Poirot: A Celebration of the Great Detective* (London: Boxtree, 1995), 82.
10. In *The Labours of Hercules* story 'The Capture of Cerberus', published in 1947.
11. Interview with the author, August 2015.
12. There is also a possible financial incentive here—international broadcasters are usually keen on productions that do not clearly change period or cast as they can be shown in any order without confusing the audience.
13. *Television Today*, 19 January 1989 and *The Listener*, 9 February 1989.
14. *Daily Mirror*, 14 January 1989.
15. *The Guardian*, 16 January 1989.
16. In between seasons Pauline Moran had starred as the terrifying *Woman in Black* for a Christmas Eve production on ITV—a far cry from Miss Lemon!
17. *Daily Mirror*, 6 January 1990.

18. Internationally, it is usually the two-part version that has been broadcast. This version does not simply split the story in two, it adds a new scene between Poirot and Hastings at the beginning of the second episode where the plot so far is outlined. The scene takes place on the hotel set, which is lit and shot less sympathetically than elsewhere in the episode, so may well have been filmed later or rather quickly.

19. A version of this joke also appears in a 1992 episode of *2point4 Children*, by Andrew Marshall.

20. See Chap. 14 for more on Russia's on takes on Agatha Christie on screen.

21. Suchet and Wansell, *Poirot and Me*, 108. Suchet recalls making *Styles* at the end of the second series, but the trade press notes the '100 anniversary special' going into production in May 1990, five months after the second series finished production, immediately followed by filming of the third run of episodes.

22. Interview with the author, August 2015.

23. Suchet and Wansell, *Poirot and Me*, 121.

24. *Screen International*, 28 February 1992.

25. *Broadcasting Complaints Bulletin*, February 1992.

26. There is also 'The Regatta Mystery', which originally featured Poirot but was later expanded into a story featuring Parker Pyne instead, as well as the play *Black Coffee* and some stories either later expanded into longer versions of the mystery or discovered and published posthumously.

27. *Television Today*, 28 January 1993.

28. The television episode condenses the title into 'The Underdog'.

29. Interview with the author, August 2015.

30. As with many of the transmission dates for the Poirot series in particular, at the time of writing the claimed date on IMDB and Wikipedia is incorrect—both placing the film a full year earlier than its actual transmission.

31. The remastered version of this film, as released on Blu-ray, has not properly graded the sequences that are supposed to take place at night time but were shot during the day—this rather dulls the effect of the escaping spirit, and makes a later sequence, where a break in at the house now takes place in broad daylight while the residents sleep, a complete nonsense.

32. *The Independent*, 21 February 1997.

33. As Morton died in 1931 his estate presumably retained copyright in his portion of the play for the standard period (in British copyright law) of seventy years from his death, which would have expired in 2001.

34. Interview with the author, August 2013.

35. *Independent*, 21 February 2000.

36. Interview with the author, August 2015.

37. Albeit with some cheated geography, no doubt due to inaccessibility of some of the island's coves.
38. *The Times*, 16 December 2002.
39. Once more, the airdate widely reproduced online (of 20 April 2001) is incorrect, at least in the UK, where it premiered on 15 December 2002.
40. Interview with the author, August 2013.
41. *The Times*, 24 July 2002.
42. Interview with the author, August 2015.
43. Interview with the author, August 2015.
44. That is not to say that there were no longer recurring characters after this point, of course.
45. *The Guardian*, 15 December 2003.
46. Badland made an especially memorable appearance on the BBC adaptation of *A Pocket Full of Rye* as the unfortunate housemaid Gladys.
47. Interview with the author, August 2015.
48. *The Independent*, 2 January 2006.
49. *The Guardian*, 20 March 2006.
50. *Daily Telegraph*, 10 September 2008.
51. In terms of tone, this adaptation is more reminiscent of *Marple* than *Poirot* at times.
52. In some countries the adaptation of *Murder on the Orient Express* opened this series, but I am working to the UK broadcast order.
53. I have made this point before, in more detail, in 'Love, Crime and Agatha Christie', published within *Screening the Dark Side of Love* (eds. Karen Randell and Karen Ritzenhoff. Basingstoke: Palgrave Macmillan, 2012).
54. Or, at least, complete it as far as was practicable at this point.
55. Interview with the author, August 2015.
56. Alison Flood, 'Study Claims Agatha Christie had Alzheimer's,' *The Guardian*, 3 April 2009, accessed 15 March 2015, http://www.theguardian.com/books/2009/apr/03/agatha-christie-alzheimers-research.
57. Although not to the extent that the publicity may have indicated. Those who have visited Greenway will notice that scenes showing the fête and what is depicted as the rear of the house take place elsewhere, at a location that has a large flat lawn (unlike the steep slope behind Greenway) and, more tellingly, a two storey house, rather than the three that Greenway has.
58. Elizabeth Grice, 'David Suchet interview,' *Daily Telegraph*, 30 October 2013, accessed 5 January 2014, http://www.telegraph.co.uk/culture/tvandradio/10374111/David-Suchet-interview-Poirot-has-been-my-best-friend.html.
59. David Suchet, 'My Agony as Poirot Drew his Last Breath,' *Daily Mail*, 13 November 2013, accessed 5 January 2014, http://www.dailymail.co.uk/tvshowbiz/article-2506890/Poirot-finale-My-agony-Poirot-drew-breath-David-Suchet.html.

60. A minor niggle is that Poirot's fake moustache now seems superfluous, as he no longer attempts to pass for the real killer.
61. Most memorably in an edition of *Gogglebox* shown shortly after the episodes.
62. James Walton, 'Poirot's Last Case review,' *Daily Telegraph*, 13 November 2013, accessed 13 November 2013: http://www.telegraph.co.uk/culture/tvandradio/tv-and-radio-reviews/10447645/Poirots-Last-Case-ITV-review.html.

International Adaptations

Chapter 13: European Adaptations

In the Introduction, I remarked that almost every chapter in this book could justify an entire book of its own. This is particularly true of the two chapters in this section, which cover the non-English-language adaptations of Christie's stories. In discussions and analysis of Agatha Christie screen adaptations, those that were produced outside of the UK and USA tend to be either ignored, or treated as little more than footnotes. However, before we move on to the final section of this book, which looks at the most recent era of adaptations, I wanted to dedicate some space to these lesser-known film and television productions. Although this section cannot fully redress the balance in their favour (a dedicated team of multilingual international researchers would be needed in order to do so), I do hope to shine a light on some Christie adaptations that have often been overlooked, but offer some interesting takes on the canon.

GERMANY

Germany was one of the first countries to create a screen adaptation of an Agatha Christie story, with the silent film adaptation of *The Secret Adversary* in 1929.[1] On television the nation was another relatively early adapter of Christie stories, as public service broadcaster ARD screened a 50-minute version of *The Mousetrap* (as *Die Fuchsjagd*, or *The Fox Hunt*) on 13 April 1954. This live broadcast was performed by members of Berlin's 'Theaterclub Berlin im British Centre', which, as the name implies, specialised in British plays. The script was adapted by Kurt Nachmann, whose colourful later career would include scripts for several sex-based films, boasting titles such as *Sexy Susan Sins Again* (d. Franz Antel, 1968) and *The Viking Who Became a Bigamist* (d. Franz Antel, 1969). Judging by the extant information, *Die Fuchsjagd* appears to have been an abridged version of the West End production that had been running for over a year by this point, rather than a reworking of either the original radio script or Christie's subsequent short story based on it.[2] The pro-

© The Author(s) 2016
M. Aldridge, *Agatha Christie on Screen*,
DOI 10.1057/978-1-137-37292-5_14

duction was director Werner Simon's only credit, perhaps implying that he was a member of the theatrical troupe who did not work in television. With the exception of Wolfgang Spier (playing Mr Paravichine) and Helmut Ahner (Christopher Wren), who would forge a long and successful career acting on German television, the cast members would not go on to be frequent performers on screen; this includes Rudi Geske who played the lead role of Detective Trotter, for whom this was one of only a handful of screen credits.[3] As with many of the non-English-language adaptations, the fact that this production was permitted at a time when a screen version of the story was strictly verboten indicates either a more relaxed attitude towards adaptations away from the UK (something that is possible, given the number of American television adaptations, and that Christie only objected to broadcasts of Harold Huber's Poirot radio stories in Europe if they could be heard by British audiences or expatriates), or that the local broadcasters were not as stringent in their licensing arrangements as they should have been. Germany was not the only country to transmit an adaptation of the play, however, as Denmark showed its own version of *The Mousetrap* on 27 August 1955 (as *Musefælden*), directed by Svend Aage Lorentz, who would later establish himself as a documentary film maker.

The next German television adaptation featured one element that had previously been met with a firm dismissal from Christie—the appearance of Hercule Poirot himself, in his most famous mystery, no less. The 1955 series *Die Galerie der großen Detektive* was an anthology programme that each week dramatised a story featuring a famous detective. The series opened with an adaptation of the Sherlock Holmes story 'The Dying Detective', starring Ernst Fritz Fürbringer; its fixed location and small cast made it ideal for the programme's live broadcasts, although it is not one of Conan Doyle's more dynamic or convincing tales. The series then worked through other famous sleuths before finishing its run with a 50-minute adaptation of *Murder on the Orient Express*, starring famous German actor Heini Göbel as a cigar-smoking Poirot. Broadcast on 24 August 1955, it was written and adapted by Peter A. Horn, who regularly worked on German television productions of the 1950s.[4]

The next two Christie adaptations to appear on German television were once more reworked versions of stage plays. The first, *Das Spinnennetz*, was an opportunity for German audiences to see another of Christie's more recent West End successes, *Spider's Web*. Translated by Gerhard Metzner, its director Fritz Umgelter headed several television productions every year, including an adaptation of *The Hound of the Baskervilles* in 1955. This adaptation starred Marlies Schönau as Clarissa and was broadcast on 19 August 1956. Following it was an adaptation of *Love from a Stranger*, which was the nearest that Christie had come to a screen perennial by this point, with several film and television adaptations already made. Translated from the stage play script by Frank Vosper, it was broadcast on 26 June 1957. The production was adapted and directed by the prolific Wilm ten Haaf, who appeared to specialise in crime thrillers and mysteries at this point, and starred Elfriede Kuzmany as Cecily, with Fritz Tillmann as Bruce, actors who would go on to have long careers on German television.

A decade would pass before another Christie mystery was made in Germany, likely a result of the 1960 MGM deal that had also prevented adaptations appearing elsewhere in the world. Between 1967 and 1973 German television would show four Agatha Christie productions, all of which still exist, and each of which was a reasonably straightforward performance of one of her stage productions—her plays had always been easier to license, and were largely exempt from the agreement that excluded the availability of most of her novels and short stories. The first to be made was an adaptation of *Love from a Stranger*, shown on 5 December 1967, and although in German (as with all of these productions), it used the English-language title and retained the British setting, even down to using an English title for the book that proves to incriminate Bruce at the story's resolution (*The Offenders*). Credited to Agatha Christie and Frank Vosper, it is a black-and-white multi-camera television production that in many ways feels like a live relay of a theatre presentation. The script is a reasonably straightforward translation and adaptation of the original, directed by Kurt Früh. The main changes occur in the first act, which is condensed (to its benefit), while the role of Cecily's fiancé Nigel is greatly reduced, to the extent that he does not even reappear at the story's resolution; our final shot is of a clearly traumatised Cecily running out of the door in search for him, before silent credits roll. Unusually for a Christie adaptation of this period, the story is treated with the utmost seriousness—the almost complete lack of music and subtle (but effective) performances result in an adaptation that is unusually downbeat and makes more of the psychological trauma than some of its predecessors, which tended to emphasise the physical threat posed by Bruce.

Two years later it was the turn of *And Then There Were None* to appear on German television, with a production highly similar in style to *Love from a Stranger*, with the serious performances and largely music-less drama highlighting the tension and character psychology, but making it a little less enjoyable as a piece of entertainment. The production uses a translation of the original English title (*Zehn kleine Negerlein*) and prominently features the dolls that formed the foundation of Christie's original story, including on the title screen where they are boldly illustrated. Director and actor Hans Quest directed the play, before he moved on to head up an ongoing series of German adaptations of G.K. Chesterton's well-known amateur sleuth *Father Brown* the following year. Broadcast on 5 July 1969, the cast of *Zehn kleine Negerlein* included Rolf Boysen as Lombard and Ingrid Capelle as Vera. At 49 years old, Boysen was older than Lombard had generally appeared to be on screen, although his donning of sunglasses throughout may indicate some attempt to give him a youthful edge. At the end, the story may imply some relief that these two characters survive, but the actors barely show it—preferring to prolong the nihilistic edge to proceedings.

Germany's adaptation of *Murder at the Vicarage* (*Mord im Pfarrhaus*), broadcast on 21 November 1970, immediately showed one innovation—it moved into colour. However, if anything, the visuals were even more stage-like than before, with a basic camera-facing set providing the bulk of the action. By contrast, the previous two adaptations had showcased sets that offered rather more visual interest and seemed to be attempts to make the productions feel at home on television rather than at the theatre. Although the production broadly conforms to the 1949 play (which had been adapted by Moie Charles and Barbara Toy from Christie's original novel), some changes are made, including various pieces of abridgement, while a handful of plot details are modified as well—for example, the character of the curate Hawes now lives at the house, rather than elsewhere. The decision to show the passage of time through the use of on-screen captions helps to emphasise to the audience that much of the build-up to the murder goes unseen, and so prioritises the puzzle element of the story, as we have to try to put the pieces of evidence together. This comple-ments the play's economical decision not to show the victim prior to his death, making it less about the characters and more about the overall mystery. Once again, the story is played very straight and is rather lacking in atmosphere, as if the emphasis should be wholly on the puzzle—or, indeed, as if the source material needed to be handled with the sort of reverence that Christie rarely received in her own country at this point. Once more directed by Hans Quest, the role of Miss Marple is played by Inge Langen who, at 46, is rather too young for the part—just as Barbara Mullen had been when she took the role in the play's first run (when she was aged 35). Langen's Miss Marple is not the kindly, softer version seen in most later adaptations. Instead, her performance is more in line with the original novel, with Miss Marple shown as an outright busybody—something of an irritant whom most characters are happy to see the back of. She is perhaps too strong and forthright to be wholly likeable, but is certainly portrayed as a character that should not be under-estimated.

Black Coffee, the last of these four adaptations, was first broadcast on 3 August 1973 and is a more radical departure from the straightforward stage adaptations seen previously. This time the play was adapted as a film, includ-ing some limited location work and more ambitious sets, which use the full 360 degrees, rather than positioning characters towards a fourth wall as multi-camera productions and stage plays usually require, while in an overt nod to the story's creator, the set also includes a portrait of Christie above the fire-place. It feels little different to any other low-budget theatrical movie of the time, but the decision to shoot it on film for television indicates that it was seen as a prestigious production. This version also appears to put the story even further in the past than the play, which was first performed in 1930, indicating that Christie adaptations were generally starting to feel like period pieces. The opening sequence deals with a horse-drawn carriage rather than the play's car, and the mise-en-scène generally alludes to the Edwardian period rather than the 1930s. However, in the face of this the play also emphasises the inventions of physicist Sir Claud Amory (who is the murder victim), such as a door-closing device, which were previously only vaguely alluded to in the play and give an indefinite sense of period.

The production overall works very well, successfully broadening out the action, including the addition of other sets (impractical to accommodate on stage) and some brief but effective outside filming, including a sequence where a group of British policemen arrive and, in a quaint touch, have to spend time putting blocks behind the wheels of their car in order to keep it in place. Playing Poirot is Horst Bollmann, who provides the screen with probably the first completely satisfying portrayal of the character. Bollmann performs his greying (and short) detective as a spry and jaunty character, often with a smirk and a great deal of charisma. The portrayal offers more energy than usual, something that can only benefit one of Christie's duller plays. Meanwhile, the Poirot of the books would surely be pleased that on screen his companion Captain Hastings (played by Ernst Fritz Fürbringer) wears the moustache that he had implored him to grow.

After this brief surge in interest in Christie, German television moved away from creating its own adaptations, no doubt in part due to the difficulty of obtaining the relevant rights that affected all markets during the 1970s. However, there was a tentative attempt to model a series on some of the iconography of Christie's works with the 2005–07 series *Agathe kann's nicht lassen* (roughly translated as *Agatha Can't Leave It Alone*), which not only borrowed the author's name, but also the personality and appearance of Miss Marple. The Austrian co-production was a success, but the 2009 death of its star, Ruth Drexel, meant the end for the programme. Even if it was skirting round the edges of Christie's own work, it does demonstrate that interest in her remains strong in Germany, as shown by the local broadcasts of the British television productions.

FRANCE

Since the turn of the twenty-first century, France has been one of the most prolific adapters of Christie's works for the screen, second only to the UK. Previous decades had not shown such a high level of interest in her mysteries, even though France had produced one of the first Agatha Christie films, with a 1933 adaptation of her play *Black Coffee*.[5] It took until the end of the 1960s for Christie's work finally to make an appearance in a French-language television programme, but it was hardly an adaptation at all. Instead, it was a simple televising of a translation of her play as part of an ongoing series, *Au théâtre ce soir* (*In the Theatre Tonight*), which had started in 1966, bringing the theatre to the living rooms of the watching audience. Unlike Germany's televising of her plays, which transplanted the action to the television studio, this was a simple relay of a live theatrical performance, complete with audience. In 1969 the series televised a production of *Spider's Web* (*La toile d'araignée*), starring Italian actress Gaby Silvia as Patricia Brown-Gibson, the French production's name for Clarissa Hailsham-Brown. The next year it was the turn of *And Then There Were None* on 1 October 1970, translating its original English title (as *Dix petits nègres*) and starring prolific film actor Henri Garcin as Lombard alongside Juliette Villard as Vera, only a few months before her untimely death at the age of 28. The series maintained the full theatrical experience, with the cameras operating as simple observers of the on-stage action, usually set well back rather than integrated into the performance. The viewers at home were shown the audience at the theatre settling into their seats, before the play commences with no acknowledgement of the television transmission in the theatre. The intermission is preserved, as is the curtain call, before the credits play out over the audience exiting. Even for the period this simple live relay was an old-fashioned use of television, but the fact that the programme continued for 20 years indicates that it was popular, and certainly allowed a wider audience to see the productions.

It took until 2005 for there to finally be another fully fledged French film adaptation, when Pascal Thomas directed a production of *By the Pricking of My Thumbs* (*Mon petit doigt m'a dit...*), a 1968 Tommy and Tuppence novel that involves strange goings-on at a retirement home, which may be linked to murder. The film stars Catherine Frot and André Dussollier as new versions of Tommy and Tuppence, Prudence and Colonel Bélisaire Bereford. Both actors are highly lauded in France, with Frot finding particular plaudits for her work in comedy as well as classical texts, while Dussollier is probably best known to non-French audiences as the narrator in *Amélie* (d. Jean-Pierre Jeunet, 2001). This first film, adapted by Pascal Thomas with Nathalie Lafaurie and François Caviglioli, sets the template for many of the French adaptations of Agatha Christie that would follow by taking some of the key points of the original mystery but reworking them within a film that is as much a comedy as it is a mystery. Although ostensibly set in the present day, Thomas's production is really set in the vague 'Christie time' that has often been alluded to by critics, since despite the presence of modern-day innovations such as mobile phones it offers a vaguely situated, nostalgic view of the world, supplemented by an old-fashioned country setting. The comedy of the piece comes from its parachuting of the absurd into otherwise very traditional mysteries, although at this stage at least this rarely overshadows the plot. The film benefits from exceptional performances from the lead cast and a biting edge that makes them anything but cosy productions, since we see versions of the lead characters who are bored with the idea of semi-retirement, especially in Prudence's case, desperate to escape the tedium of their own extended family. As with many of the later French adaptations, the film has a strong sense of its own personality, despite using Christie as a springboard into its vision of the world. In fact, to think of these as adaptations is perhaps not helpful—it may be better to consider them to be influenced by her works. What the film and its sequels do show is that it is possible to take core elements of Christie's books and rework them for an audience that had not been specifically catered to before, unlike the British/American Christie viewers at whom most previous adaptations had been aimed. The French audience can (and did) embrace this Gallic version, which spawned many imitators, although Grant Rosenberg of *Screen Daily* felt that Christie fans should also be pleased with the final product, which he even considered owed more to the British sense of comedy than the French one: 'Agatha Christie fans everywhere should find it a winning adaptation, particularly in the UK', he wrote. 'After all, the story may have been translated into another language and country, but its humour and tone remain decidedly more British than French.'[6] Among Christie fans there are many who would prefer pure Christie or nothing, but given the fact that there is no shortage of traditional adaptations, it is hard to begrudge a format that has found so much success and, on its own terms, is highly entertaining.

After the success of *By the Pricking of My Thumbs*, Pascal Thomas moved on to tackle another Christie title, this time handled in a more traditional manner. For the 2007 adaptation of *Towards Zero* (*L'heure zéro*), Thomas does not receive a writing credit although he directs once more, which may explain why the tone is so different: the production offers up a more portentous take on a story that had previously formed the basis for an ill-fated French film production, which eventually appeared as 1995's *Innocent Lies*.[7] This tale of murder within a dysfunctional family, investigated by Superintendent Battle (or Commissaire Martin Bataille, played by François Morel), is more realist, and occasionally more downbeat, than Thomas's other Christie adaptations, although sometimes it drifts into more ethereal directions with an almost dream-like atmosphere and has flashes of comedy. Once more set in the present day, but with old-fashioned sensibilities and tone, it tackles the mystery with a detached air that is difficult for the audience to engage with, making this one of the less entertaining French adaptations of Christie's works, even if it is one of the more faithful, sticking relatively closely to the original novel.

By the Pricking of My Thumbs' core team of Thomas, Frot and Dussollier reconvened once more in 2008 for another mystery starring Colonel and Prudence Beresford, in *Crime Is Our Business* (*Le crime est notre affaire*).[8] Although the film claims to be adapted from Christie's short story collection *Partners in Crime*, which starred Tommy and Tuppence, in fact it takes its principal influence from the 1957 Miss Marple novel *4.50 from Paddington*. In the film it is Prudence's aunt who, like Mrs McGillicuddy in the original, witnesses a murder only to find that she is not believed—and no body can be found. The adaptation broadly follows the style of the earlier film starring the two sleuths, perhaps pushing the comedy even further, including a well-worn joke involving an updraft from a drain when the Colonel is wearing a kilt. When Prudence takes on the role of a maid (just as Miss Marple had in the 1961 adaptation starring Margaret Rutherford, *Murder, She Said*) there is plenty of opportunity for comedy in her investigations, but the film is also atmospheric (helped by the presence of snow) and uses wit as much as farce, especially in scenes where the Beresfords verbally spar with each other. Away from the sleuthing couple, the same year saw another French film adaptation, this time of the Hercule Poirot mystery *The Hollow*, filmed under the title *Le grand alibi* (*The Great Alibi*) and directed by Pascal Bonitzer, who had predominantly forged a career writing a string of screenplays since the 1970s—here, he co-writes the script with Jérôme Beaujour. A disappointing and dull picture, which removes the character of Poirot (just as Christie had for her own stage adaptation), it retains the basic features of the original mystery but eventually twists in a different, less satisfying direction. The most interesting element of the film was possibly its poster, which merged the worlds of Agatha Christie and Cluedo in its iconography.

The third and final film to feature the Beresfords was released in 2012 under the title *Partners in Crime* (*Associés contre le crime*), and this time the mystery did actually use one of the collection's short stories as an influence.[9] In Christie's story 'The Case of the Missing Lady', Tommy and Tuppence investigate a mysterious disappearance—only to discover eventually that the missing woman had simply taken time out to visit a health farm, following a rather problematic desire to satisfy her fiancé's personal taste in slimmer women. This very light premise is extended in an unexpected direction in this film, which is subtitled 'The Ambroise Egg, or the Secret of Eternal Youth' ('L'oeuf d'Ambroise, ou la recherche de l'éternelle jeunesse'), in which a precious egg-shaped object has fantastical properties. This results in a film that is a rare attempt to mix Christie's work with science fiction, as the egg provides a link with a local 'space-time fault', which can revitalise those who are able to harness its power(!). This leads to a conclusion where Colonel Beresford is transformed back into a baby, who now must be cared for by his wife. If this description sounds bizarre, then it is no less so on screen. However, the performances are so strong, especially in lighter moments, that it is difficult not to be swept along by the action and enjoy the film on its own merits, even if it bears very little resemblance to the original Christie story. The characters are as well drawn as ever, benefitting the film's more comedic scenes in particular, particularly when Prudence sets up her own detective agency in a fit of pique because she is fed up with Tommy taking credit for her work, in a partial echo of the relationship between the two in the original stories. The three films starring France's own Beresford couple may propel the stories in directions quite unlike the originals, but they do show a confident and entertaining handling of the material that never claims to be a faithful reproduction of the written word. Such an approach is arguably more satisfactory than a version that makes wholesale changes to the detriment of the mystery, but purports to be a straightforward adaptation—at least the French films have the gumption and honesty to say that they are their own takes on the material.

In 2006 Agatha Christie adaptations emerged on French television, using a template similar to the Pascal Thomas film, where humour was injected into loose adaptations of Christie stories using newly established characters. The first adaptation was a standalone production of *Hercule Poirot's Christmas*, running for some six hours across four episodes. Missing from the story is Poirot himself, replaced by two detectives—the experienced Captain Larosière, played by Antoine Duléry, and his younger protégé Emile Lampion, played by Marius Colucci. Although on paper the relationship between the detectives may seem like something of a cliché, with the grumpy older partner exasperated by the up-and-coming investigator's lack of experience and fresh-faced naïvety, in practice it is a charming and amusing double act. The story itself takes some of the elements of Christie's novel, renamed *A Family Murder Party* (*Petits meurtres en famille*), but twists and turns in different directions before reaching its conclusion, although unlike the Pascal Thomas films the production is set in period, in this case in 1939 Brittany. One element that is established here and expanded on in the later series that it spawned is that the detectives are not simply present in order to observe the action and provide the solution. Instead, they play active parts in the drama, including falling victim to assaults and attempted murder, while—as set out in this first production—we are also witness to Lampion's sexual awakening when he nervously begins to act on his feelings for other men.

The first production was a popular success, and in 2009 Larosière and Lampion returned for four more adaptations under the new series title *The Little Murders of Agatha Christie* (*Les petits meurtres d'Agatha Christie*), premiering with its own take on *The ABC Murders*, which re-established the template once more, as the programme makes no claims that it is portraying faithful adaptations of the original stories. Instead, it overtly reworks novels that originally featured any of the original detectives—including Miss Marple and Poirot as well as one-off characters—into its own format, starring its original detective team. This is an unusually honest approach to adaptation: whereas episodes of Poirot and Marple that have eschewed much of the original story still purport to be adaptations, here there can be no doubt for the audience that we are seeing a hybrid of ideas, as each episode not only features lead characters not created by Christie, but the stories themselves are clearly situated in France's past, rather than Christie's own Britain. They may not work as great Christie adaptations, but they are popular and distinctive television programmes that utilise the strengths of the production team (principally the casting, humour and mise-en-scène) alongside the undoubted staying power of the bare bones of Christie's own mysteries.

The ABC Murders sees the first use of the stylish animated titles that establish the programme as mysterious but also comedic and light on occasion, with Christie prominently credited. The adaptation juxtaposes darker moments with comedy—one victim is a tramp who has been burned alive, while a sequence where Lampion confuses the name of a woman with her dog is classic farce. Lampion's sexuality is also re-established, since he spends the night with another man, and despite the changes to many details of the story it still manages to have the feel of an Agatha Christie mystery, which is no mean feat. The principle of keeping the detectives' characters at the forefront while investigating mysteries broadly based on Christie originals is maintained throughout the series, with *The ABC Murders* followed by adaptations of *Ordeal by Innocence*, *The Moving Finger* and *Peril at End House* in this first season. Both *Ordeal by Innocence* and *The Moving Finger* have their fair share of dark and atmospheric moments to set up the danger (the former featuring the murder of the accused person by stabbing a fork into his throat, while the latter sees ravens delivering the poison pen letters), before finding time for comic interludes. *Peril at End House* allows Larosière to take much of the spotlight, as his infatuation with a woman whose life has been threatened motivates his actions. At the end, when the murderer is sent to the guillotine, he is genuinely upset, while the adaptation also shows some historical context in featuring Jewish refugees desperate not to be sent back to Germany.

After the success of these first five mysteries, Larosière and Lampion headed up seven more cases, across two more seasons, which met with further popular success among French audiences. The series seemed to be keener than ever to emphasise the grisly nature of murder, the second run opening with a particularly bloody murder in the woods heralding a new adaptation of *Cat Among the Pigeons*, soon followed by Lampion nearly vomiting after seeing a corpse on a mortuary slab. The next adaptation, *Sad Cypress*, focuses more on contemporary issues and politics, with discussions of women's rights (accompanied by suffragettes) as well as homosexuality, with the result that Larosière spends some time dressed as a woman. *Five Little Pigs* is then more downbeat than usual for the series, as befits a reasonably close adaptation of one of Christie's most unhappy tales. Following the next adaptation, of *Taken at the Flood*, was *The Body in the Library*, in which the audience is presented with a cliché of detective fiction, although not of Christie, when Larosière wakes up next to the murdered body and is immediately suspected of her murder—in an attention-grabbing move, the resulting mystery is translated from Gossington Hall to a brothel. This is followed by adaptations of *Sleeping Murder* and then, in a final outing for the two detectives, *Lord Edgware Dies*, which uses the fact that the story also concerns the production of a stage murder mystery to its advantage, as it both utilises and rejects clichés of detective dramas. This adaptation is particularly dissimilar to the original novel beyond its theatrical setting, especially in its understandable removal of the aristocratic relationships that underpin the original mystery, which would not have the same resonance relocated to France. Although elements of the puzzle remain the same, here it is placed within a highly different plot that includes the inspection of a disembodied foot, two of our heroes being buried alive, and one of the detectives taking a role on stage while the other fantasises about one of the lead actors.

Fans of the series were disappointed when both actors decided to leave the production after three successful seasons, but this was not the end of the programme. Instead, it has a new investigating duo, encompassing police commisaire Swan Laurence, played by Samuel Labarthe, and journalist Alice Avril, played by Blandine Bellavoir. The series now has a more 1950s flavour, with an emphasis on Hollywood glamour and fashions, and the first adaptation with this new team (of *They Do It with Mirrors*) sets the tone with its highly sexualised opening of women in bikini tops dancing, soon to be contrasted with a bloody death. Avril is often wooed by the male characters but asserts herself strongly, even if she does have to undertake the role of a maid in order to continue her undercover investigation. This new incarnation was very much in the same spirit as the earlier adaptations in the series, and at the time of writing these characters continue to star in new productions of Christie stories, showing that close fidelity to the source is not necessarily instrumental to creating a popular success.

OTHER EUROPEAN COUNTRIES

The process of cataloguing the entire output for every country's television service and cross-referencing them with Christie's back catalogue would be a near impossible task, and therefore we can be confident that there are likely to have been more productions in various countries than are currently known about—indeed, it is likely that Agatha Christie Ltd was similarly kept in the dark in many cases.[10] However, we do know about the existence of some interesting adaptations, many of which have been little seen since their first transmission. One particularly intriguing set of examples comes from Italian television in 1980, which produced at least five adaptations of Agatha Christie plays. The country's film industry had previously skirted around the edges of Christie's works with the 1970 horror film *Five Dolls for an August Moon* (d. Mario Bava), which is one of the many pastiches of *And Then There Were None*, but the 1980 adaptations were rather more straightforward iterations of several of her plays. The titles adapted were *Go Back for Murder* (Christie's stage adaptation of *Five Little Pigs*, removing Poirot), *Towards Zero*, *Spider's Web*, *The Unexpected Guest* and *The Hollow*. All are transplanted to the television studio and are creditable productions, albeit generally rather downbeat in tone, but include sound effects and some interesting visuals in order to make them seem like more than just televised theatre—*Go Back for Murder* has a particularly effective opening, where a picture of one character is depicted as a jigsaw puzzle.

In 1980 Agatha Christie made an appearance in a Hungarian film—quite literally, as she was cast as a character in a movie called *Kojak Budapesten* (d. Sándor Szalkay), a murder mystery that takes place at a crime writer's conference; we can be reasonably confident that neither the rights owners to Kojak nor the Christie estate were any the wiser about the existence of the film, in which Christie was played by local actress Hilda Gobbi. Two years later the Netherlands produced an effective 42-minute adaptation of Christie's one-act play *The Patient*. The viewing audience may have been grateful that the programme dispensed with Christie's original choice of an ending, where the murderer remained concealed behind a curtain while a recording of the author's voice told the audience that all the information they needed to solve the case had been supplied—so they should be able to identify the culprit themselves. Thankfully, as with most performances of the play, the villain is clearly identified at the end of this production and even tries to escape, before being apprehended just before the credits roll under some light jazz music.[11]

Notes

1. See Chap. 1.
2. Nor does it appear to have been based on the BBC television production, which modified Christie's radio script.
3. However, Ottaker Runze (who played Giles Ralston) became successful behind the camera, as a film and television producer.
4. Unfortunately, no more details about this intriguing production have been forthcoming.
5. See Chap. 2
6. Grant Rosenberg, 'By the Pricking of My Thumbs,' *Screen Daily*, 11 May 2005, accessed 1 July 2015. http://www.screendaily.com/by-the-pricking-of-my-thumbs-mon-petit-doigt-ma-dit/4023009.article.
7. Clémence de Biéville and Roland Duval have both been credited in addition to the previous writers, instead of Thomas, with Nathalie Lafaurie's name being shown above the title. See Chap. 10.
8. This film's script is credited to Clémence de Biéville and François Caviglioli alongside Thomas and Christie.
9. This film's script is credited to Clémence de Biéville and Nathalie Lafaurie alongside Thomas and Christie.
10. There are some titles of which I have found some evidence but have not included here as I have not been able to independently verify their existence.
11. Quite why light jazz is so often used to score Christie adaptations is a mystery.

Chapter 14: Adaptations in the Rest of the World

Spoilers: *And Then There Were None*; *The Murder of Roger Ackroyd*; *Murder on the Orient Express*

Throughout the rest of the world, there have been all manner of films and television productions either overtly or implicitly based on Agatha Christie stories. Many, if not most, of these productions were not properly licensed and, resultantly, it is impossible to catalogue them all. For every official screen adaptation there has been of an Agatha Christie story, there is probably another one that is an illicit take on one of her mysteries. This is particularly the case with versions of *And Then There Were None*, which has been adapted many times in numerous guises, sometimes as a clear homage, and often simply as a straight adaptation with some changes made for the local audience. There are reports of adaptations in countries including Cuba and Lebanon, while Brazilian television broadcast versions of the mystery in both 1957 and 1963, as well as an earlier production of *The Mousetrap* in 1956. Although the legal issues surrounding the latter play made legitimate productions of it near impossible, this did not stop producers in some countries filming their own version of a story based on Christie's mystery, often to good effect.

INDIA

India is one of the more interesting producers of Agatha Christie films because, unlike many regions, its productions transplant the basics of Christie's mysteries to its own society, location and characters. While productions in countries including Russia and Japan usually try to preserve the essence of Christie's British settings, either by keeping the mysteries based there or by transplanting features of that society to a new environment, the Indian adaptations put the domestic audience first. This is a refreshing take on the normal principles of Christie adaptations, where the heritage features are so often part of the substance and appeal—here, the central puzzle and mystery elements of her stories are able to have precedence.

© The Author(s) 2016
M. Aldridge, *Agatha Christie on Screen*,
DOI 10.1057/978-1-137-37292-5_15

India's first film of a Christie story was a 1960 Bengali adaptation of *The Mousetrap* called *Silently He Comes* (*Chupi Chupi Ashey*,[1] d. Premendra Mitra), a black-and-white production that often uses striking visuals to good effect, although the lengthy dialogue scenes are rather less visually interesting. The film opens with credits showing the outline of a figure with a question mark superimposed over it, immediately setting out the story as a mystery, although the brash accompanying music owes more to the horror genre. The first sequence then builds the suspense when it depicts the events that opened Christie's radio play, with a disguised figure walking through the street (this time through atmospheric heavy rain, rather than snow) until he reaches the building where his victim lives. The whistling, physically disguised figure gets past the irritated landlady, conversing with a croaky voice in order to preserve the surprise of their identity for later, just as had been the case in Christie's original mystery. Moving upstairs, the victim then appears to recognise the mysterious intruder and is clearly terrified—the film cuts away before the murder itself. After this prologue, the rest mirrors the claustrophobic suspense of Christie's isolated country house, even though it is set in contemporary India. Several sequences are the most nerve-wracking of any Christie screen production to this point, with atmospheric music underpinning explorations of the house (surrounded by water rather than snow) and a general sense of distrust between characters helping to fuel the tension. The film is hindered by the fact that Indian censorship requirements mean that some sequences do not show viewers as much of the crime or threat as they might hope, but it does support the suggestion that any official film of *The Mousetrap* has the potential to be a highly effective production.

In 1965 there was the next Indian film adaptation of an Agatha Christie story, this time a colour production of *And Then There Were None* in Hindi. Released under the title *Gumnaam* (which translates as *Unknown*, d. Raja Nawathe), it is a particularly hard-edged take on the story, featuring two murders before the opening titles (one run over by a car, another shot with a gun), which also features references to rape and suicide as well as the expected murders. However, alongside some of these more brutal moments, there is a typical Bollywood soundtrack. The Hindi songs are sometimes used diegetically (such as in a song and dance sequence that the main characters view just prior to their introduction), while at other points they are played over the action, usually in relation to the plot (the words 'someone is anonymous' are sung while the characters make their way to the isolated mansion where most of the action will be based, having been abandoned by the plane that brought them to the small island).[2] The central premise of the original story is preserved for this adaptation, where each of the core cast members is apparently responsible for some past misdemeanour for which they will be punished by an unknown perpetrator. However, the details differ, including the identity of the murderer, who is revealed to be a disguised escaped convict (echoing a theme of *The Mousetrap*). While the film lacks the simplicity of Christie's carefully structured tale, it still works well as a take on the same basic concept, with some entertaining lighter moments mixed with darker, more sinister sequences. It proved to be a commercial success when released in India, and is certainly more interesting than Harry Alan Towers's English-language remake that was released the same year.[3]

The Unexpected Guest may be one of Christie's less iconic plays, but there has been no shortage of countries that have made their own versions of it for the screen, and India is no exception. Between 1973 and 1990 there were at least three Indian films based on Christie's play, in which the victim of a car accident seeks help at a local house, only to find a woman standing over the dead body of her husband, holding a gun. The unexpected guest of the title suspects that there is more to the situation than meets the eye, and the audience eventually discovers that all is not as it seems. The first adaptation, from 1973, intriguingly used Christie's working title, *Fog* (*Dhund*, d. B.R. Chopra), and initially it follows the premise and structure of Christie's play closely, with an atmospheric fog-bound opening, while it also includes a handful of musical numbers that comment on the action.[4] However, the last act moves the action to the courtroom, where the truth about the night of the murder is revealed. In a legally suspect move, the murderer is allowed to go free because it is felt that restorative justice has been served. The next adaptation, 1989's *Tarka* (*Logic*, d. Sunil Kumar), was made in the Kannada language, unlike *Dhund*'s Hindi, and situated itself more as a clear-cut thriller and mystery film by not including song and dance sequences. The film structures the story differently, opening with the 'unexpected guest' escaping from the police, giving the audience reason to be suspicious of him from the beginning. Various details are then changed, but the premise and character developments stay the same, before the same conclusion is reached as in the original story. Although it is a rather over-long slice of melodrama, the film was a success in its domestic market, and spawned two direct remakes. The first, the Tamil-language *Puriyaadha Pudhir* (d. K.S. Ravikumar, 1990), is a more contemporary take on *Tarka*'s reworked version of Christie's story, and once more includes musical numbers, including one that appears to be a pastiche of Michael Jackson's videos for 'Beat It' and 'Thriller'. The film uses these dances alongside action sequences and slow-motion shots to emphasise its visual appeal above the mystery itself. In doing so it aims squarely at the teenage film audience and shows an attempt to bring the action in line with light thrillers such as Hollywood's *Beverly Hills Cop* (d. Martin Brest, 1984). Reportedly, there was a second attempt to remake *Tarka* in 1990, with a Malayalam-language version called *Chodhyam*, directed by G.S. Vijayan; however, the film was not released.

Another Bengali take on Agatha Christie occurred in 2003, with *Shubho Muharat* (*The First Shoot*, d. Rituparno Ghosh), a loose adaptation of the 1962 Miss Marple novel *The Mirror Crack'd from Side to Side*. The film retains some of the basics of the plot, such as the motivation for murder and the key characters' involvement with the film industry, but transplants the action to Indian society, including a change in the nature of the lead sleuth. It opens with a message that indicates how the film's placement within Indian culture now leads to an emphasis on familial relationships and, most especially, the role of matriarchs. The text reads:

> To those Miss Marples who have guessed what's wrong when their sons skip school feigning an upset stomach, but have remained silent [...] To those Miss Marples who have guessed what's wrong when their daughters return from their in-laws with blotchy eyes, but have remained silent [...]

Playing Ranga Pishima, the film's equivalent of Miss Marple, is the popular and critically lauded actress Raakhee Gulzar. Her character is the aunt of a journalist who is involved with the case—as with Miss Marple, her intuition plays an important part in solving the mystery—although here her emotions are another influence. The role is reworked as a motherly character rather than a detached spinster, one who should command respect due to her matriarchal role. The film does not overtly credit Christie, although it is rather more than a homage, and the final result is an interesting and well performed (if over-long) take on the basic story.

Later Indian productions include 2004's *Khara Sangayach Tar*, a simply filmed version of the stage play of *Witness for the Prosecution* directed by Vijay Kenkre. The mise-en-scène does not rise above the level expected for amateur or community performances, while the use of hyperbolic music makes the movie feel like a soap opera, but it is interesting to see such a straightforward version of Christie's story set halfway around the world from the original's location. There is no sign of India losing interest in Christie's works, with a 2012 film *Grandmaster* (d. B. Unnikrishnan) using the principle from *The ABC Murders* of a killer working through their victims in alphabetical order, while in July 2015 director Subhrajit Mitra claimed he was about to commence production on a film based on the Poirot novel *Cards on the Table*, which he hoped would lead to more productions.[5]

RUSSIA

Russia has a long history of producing its own distinctive and high-quality screen adaptations of classic literary texts, although many are not officially licensed and are rarely given mainstream distribution elsewhere in the world. One particularly effective series of adaptations was of Sherlock Holmes stories, which were filmed between 1979 and 1986, directed by Igor Maslennikov and starring Vasily Livanov as Holmes. In several respects these productions set the template for the later Christie adaptations, as they faithfully follow the original text, including the (normally) British setting, while using locations distinctive to the Soviet Union that could in no way pass for the location they purport to be—the architectural style of Riga being rather different to that of London. The result is a set of adaptations that may sometimes distract the audience through its unusual meshing of two very different cultures, but often serves as faithful and interesting takes on the original stories.

The first of these Russian adaptations of Agatha Christie came in 1983, with *Tayna chyornykh drozdov* (*The Blackbirds Mystery*, or *Secret of the Blackbirds*, d. Vadim Derbenyov), an adaptation of the 1953 Miss Marple novel *A Pocket Full of Rye*. Here we have what looks like a Soviet castle standing in for an English country house, but in terms of narrative, for the most part the story of a murdered patriarch sticks reasonably closely to Christie's original novel. One notable change is that the action is transplanted to the modern day and includes specially shot footage in London—although it appears to have been a surreptitious shoot since most of the action is captured from inside a moving car, including footage of the Houses of Parliament.[6] Easily the best actor in the variable cast is Ita Ever as Miss Marple; she gives a restrained and effective performance, playing a Marple who is charmingly confident and amusingly self-satisfied. As was common in Christie's own books, Miss Marple is not the focus of the action but pops up in order to reassure the audience that someone is piecing together the clues. In a moment that emphasises the 1980s setting even more than the synthesised soundtrack, at one point Miss Marple even solves a Rubik's cube while mulling over events. Sometimes the production tries a little too hard either to convince the audience about the British setting (such as one background character dressed in union flag–emblazoned attire) or to place it in the action-adventure bracket (when a bomb is placed in Miss Marple's handbag), but it is a pleasant and interesting approach to the mystery that puts some home-grown productions to shame.

Things took a darker turn the next time Russia produced a screen version of an Agatha Christie mystery, with a new version of *And Then There Were None* (*Desyat negrityat*, d. Stanislav Govorukhin), a 1987 film that is probably the best known of all the Russian adaptations because it opts for the book's downbeat ending rather than Christie's stage version, which allowed two of the victims to survive. To call it bleak would be something of an under-statement, and it is no surprise that Christie fans have embraced the adaptation so whole-heartedly, as it offers a close retelling of the original novel. For a general audience there is perhaps a little less to enjoy—certainly among those who expect their Christie adaptations to balance lighter moments with the undoubtedly strong central mystery, while the pace in the early portion of the film is slower than it could be. However, for an audience that has been starved of adaptations that preserve the resolution of one of Christie's best novels (at least until the 2015 BBC miniseries), there is much to enjoy here. The film opens with our group of suspects and victims travelling to an island by boat, a place depicted by matte painting with a decidedly Soviet-style mansion nestling at its peak. The orchestral score immediate sets the downbeat tone, before later becoming a little ostentatious and melodramatic at some of the more dramatic moments. Where the film works best is in depicting each character's unease with their own life (this is a collection of particularly world-weary individuals), as well as with the situation and their fellow suspects. This is especially well dramatised in sections such as a monochrome flashback to Vera's life prior to the events on the island, while the resolution is depicted through a combination of flashbacks and contemporary moments, with stylised close-ups and use of both colour and black and white. The murderer has the chance to explain all to the audience in a voiceover, revealing events that are likely to surprise any previously unaware viewers. The film is quite unlike any of the previous screen adaptations, a point made particularly clear when the almost inevitable sex scene between Lombard and Vera actually depicts him raping her, an unnecessary addition. Unashamedly bleak and sometimes hard going, this version has long been enjoyed by fans of dark-edged mysteries because of the harshness that had previously been deemed so unpalatable for wider audiences.

The next Russian adaptation has received less attention, but is arguably at least as strong as its predecessor. The director of the 1983 adaptation of *A Pocket Full of Rye*, Vadim Derbenyov, returned to Christie's mysteries in 1989 with a version of the 1932 Poirot novel *Peril at End House*. This is once more set in present-day Britain, although entirely shot in the Soviet Union. The score evokes memories of Vangelis's music for films such as *Blade Runner* (d. Ridley Scott, 1982) and is surprisingly effective, emphasising some of the eerier moments of the story, which concerns repeated attempts on the life of heiress Nick. In what may be a sly dig at capitalism, an English-language newspaper is emblazoned with the headline 'Unity Does It!'—perhaps a typo for a United-suffixed football team, or a comment on Britain's workforce hierarchy. The part of Poirot is well performed by Anatoliy Ravikovich, who sports an impressive moustache, although the Belgian of Christie's books would have been unhappy to see Hastings with a beard as he has here, played by Dmitri Krylov. In a typical change of tone, one of the superficially lighter and sunnier Poirot mysteries is made darker, both in terms of cinematography and characterisation. The happy-go-lucky Nick of the novel has a rather more negative disposition, but the biggest change is in Poirot himself. The character is now emotionally attached to events, and is visibly upset following the death of Maggie at a fireworks display. This whole sequence is vivid and effective, with dramatic lighting emphasises the fireworks going off at the same time, while the camera tightly focuses on Poirot's face as he surveys each of his suspects one by one.

Both Poirot and Hastings find their own ways to contemplate the details of the case—Poirot by playing with cards, as in the novel, and Hastings preferring to seek solace by making notes in front of the television while he watches the James Bond film *Moonraker* (d. Lewis Gilbert, 1979).[7] As with many of the Russian adaptations, the film's finale is a particular strength, when Poirot discovers the truth behind the events that he has been investigating. Ravikovich gives a strong, measured and emotional performance as Poirot, while the suspects all appear to be visibly upset by the revelations concerning the attempts on Nick's life. This is not depicted as a gentle mystery, and characters do not react like they know they are in an Agatha Christie story—the events are devastatingly portrayed, with the murderer committing suicide after attacking Poirot while in some emotional distress, and the whole production is one of the most memorable and affecting of any Christie adaptations. It was followed in 1990 by a version of *The Mousetrap* (d. Samson Samsonov), once more a downbeat take on the original story, which has often been staged in a more light-hearted manner in recent decades. This bleak approach may emphasise the danger of the scenario, but it is hard for the audience to engage with such a gloomy dramatisation. It includes nudity and what appears to be an attempted rape (both of which seem to be common prerequisites of Russian adaptations), but otherwise progresses along the play's normal lines.

In 2002 Russia embarked on its most ambitious adaptation, a five-hour version of *The Murder of Roger Ackroyd* (d. Sergey Ursulyak).[8] This five-part screen version is barely even an adaptation; instead it is more a simple and systematic transplantation of action from page to screen. Non-Russian speakers do not require subtitles in order to follow the action—instead, one can simply read the book alongside it and see the events that take place on the page play out on the screen. The final result would not work for many of Christie's stories (nor, indeed, for most novels by any author), but the meticulous plotting and well-placed red herrings of this particular story mean that the extended form is extremely suitable.[9] As with the novel, the series is narrated by Dr Sheppard, played by the highly regarded actor Sergei Makovetsky. The opening monologue sets the scene and tone:

> A true classical detective story usually starts in bad weather. It is of utmost importance to begin a novel well and also to finish it correctly. As for the ending, it is hard for me to judge how well I've managed it. And the beginning [...] I could possibly open with rain, which we often have in our small town.
>
> It is five o'clock in the morning already and I still don't have the beginning. Maybe I should start by saying that I like looking through the window when it rains? Our house is right on the precipice of a cliff, so when you look through the window while it is raining it feels as if the house is floating [...] like a ship in the ocean. A ship like the one I have dreamt all my life of taking a voyage in.[10]

Each episode opens with a collection of period newsreel footage, mostly concentrating on shipping in a literal depiction of Sheppard's metaphor. Strangely, this is then followed by a pertinent extract from the 1939 American radio adaptation of the story, which starred Orson Welles as both Poirot and Dr Sheppard. The overall effect is an odd culture clash, since we have a British setting and story, anonymous stock footage, a mismatched synthesised score, Russian dialogue and locations, while each episode closes with a popular period song. Nevertheless, somehow this manages to be less disorientating than it might seem as we follow the basic threads of the mystery through to its denouement, with the emphasis always on the puzzle. The adaptation is not perfect, however: Konstantin Raykin's Poirot is perhaps a little cartoonish in appearance and demeanour, while the recording of the production onto videotape gives it a flat appearance that nevertheless removes the darkest excesses of the earlier Russian films. Indeed, this is the first of the Russian productions to balance humour and lighter moments satisfactorily with the central crime. Visually it still offers some effective sections, including the opening storm alluded to in the dialogue quoted, although the music is thin and ineffective.

Because the adaptation is not part of a Poirot series, it has the advantage that there is no need to foreground the 'star', allowing the production to retain the structure of the novel, with the resultant emphasis being on Dr Sheppard rather than the Belgian detective. This means that Poirot makes very few appearances in the first two hours of the mystery, enabling Sheppard to be the star and some of Poirot's quirkier moments to be emphasised, such as when he dances with Dr Sheppard's sister, Caroline, in the fourth episode. However, the title is translated as *Poirot's Failure*, giving the character top billing—even if it is something of a bluff, given that this is the title that Sheppard would like to call his book, but cannot do so in the end.

JAPAN

Japan's adaptations of Agatha Christie stories have provided some of the most interesting, idiosyncratic and yet—usually—faithful adaptations produced anywhere in the world. Many of the Japanese productions have disappeared after initial television airings, making it difficult to construct an in-depth history of them, but enough have been made available for consultation that we can piece together a strong impression of their approach to bringing the stories to the screen.

In 1980 Japan became the latest country to tackle *The Unexpected Guest* (d. Ogino Yoshito), a Christie play that has yet to see an English-language screen adaptation but has made many appearances in translated productions.[11] The curious popularity of this particular mystery was cemented further by another adaptation in 2001 (d. Toshihiro Itô), but in the meantime Japanese cinema had tackled Christie's 1946 novel *The Hollow*. As with Christie's own stage adaptation, this film discarded Poirot from the proceedings, although on this occasion he is replaced by another mustachioed detective. The 1985 film renames the mystery *Dangerous Women* (d. Yoshitarô Nomura) and transplants the action to contemporary Japan. Rather than the murder occurring around the pool, this version takes place in a modern house atop a rocky outcrop, where a glamorous and wealthy family have reunited. Here, the victim is murdered by the sea, in apparently clear sight of several witnesses. The adaptation has its fair share of lighter moments derived from strong characterisation (as in Christie's original story), but maintains the focus on the plot. The use of coloured filters over the opening titles sets the tone for a movie that is not a typical heritage production, but has characters living at the high end of modern society, including in the pop music and technology businesses. The result is a highly watchable take on the original story, and the audience may be a little sad that the ending is such a melancholy one, as we have come to enjoy our time with these characters.

It should be no surprise that the 2004–05 series *Agatha Christie's Great Detectives Poirot and Marple* (shown by broadcaster NHK) is the set of adaptations that feels most distinctively Japanese, since these 39 episodes are in anime form. The distinctive look of Japanese animation has often been seen on Western screens through programmes including *Pokemon* (TV Tokyo, 1997–) and *Belle and Sebastian* (NHK, 1981–82), but there are relatively few instances of anime programmes aimed at adults receiving mainstream distribution, which is a shame as the form is well deserving of an audience in both Europe and North America. The basic premise of the series is that young girl Maybelle is Miss Marple's niece, as well as junior assistant to Hercule Poirot, allowing her to take up residence with either detective in order to watch them solve their latest case. Maybelle is accompanied by her pet duck Oliver—a partially anthropomorphic character typical of anime series—and together they experience many Christie mysteries, ranging from short stories to novels. At a running time of 25 minutes per episode, the series is the perfect outlet for short, uncomplicated stories that have never been adapted for the screen elsewhere (such as 'The Tape-Measure Murder', 'Motive vs Opportunity' and 'Ingots of Gold'). Similarly, the mysteries can also be spread out over multiple parts if they are longer or more complex—for example, 'The Adventure of the Christmas Pudding' encompasses two episodes, while *Peril at End House* is in three parts, with *The ABC Murders* taking up four.

The series manages to achieve something that seems ridiculous on paper—animated versions of Christie adaptations, entirely in Japanese, all featuring the additional characters of a girl and a duck—and yet incredibly, these are some of the most charming and faithful adaptations to reach the screen. Perhaps it is best for the cynical viewer to consider that Maybelle and Oliver are essentially narrators rather than participants: there to observe the actions of Miss Marple and Poirot and to relay background information and off-screen events. Their participation in the stories themselves is minimal, relegated to reaching conclusions near simultaneously with the leads, or making a small deduction or discovery on which the final conclusion hinges. That is not to say that the programme does not occasionally become unintentionally amusing for non-Japanese audiences, especially in its choice of an up-tempo love song as its theme music ('I notice the presence of summer, your eyes sparkle [...]'), accompanied by visuals that appear to imply that Miss Marple and Poirot are lovers (something that is not the case in the series—each character rarely cameos in episodes starring the other, and they never appear together). Despite this unusual use of the two leads, the adaptations themselves are methodically close to the original text, including character names and setting. As with many Japanese productions, character and actor names are put on screen, allowing the audience to focus on the plot itself rather than working out who is who. Few changes are made, the most notable being the renaming of Inspector Japp to Inspector Sharpe, no doubt due to the connotations of the original name in a Japanese context. Most characters are animated as Western European Caucasian, unless the story dictates differently—Maybelle is an exception, being animated as traditionally

Japanese in appearance. There is a great deal of attention to detail in each episode, including a strong evocation of 1930s Britain in terms of architecture and background detail, including English-language signs and newspaper headlines. The series may be a heavily stylised take on the original mysteries, but as adaptations it is difficult to find fault once one accepts the culture clash at their centre, and they also function well as pieces of entertainment, making them a highly entertaining foray into the world of Agatha Christie outside of the best-known markets.

Further Japanese adaptations of Christie stories have been in the more traditional live-action mould, including two 2005 productions set in pre-war Tokyo, which adapted *The ABC Murders* and *Murder on the Links* under the banner title of *Great Detective Akafuji Takashi* (d. Yoshikawa Kunio)—the name of the character replacing Poirot, although with his moustache we are surely being encouraged to draw comparisons. Following these were adaptations of *4.50 from Paddington* (d. Ryûichi Inomata), *A Murder Is Announced* and *The Mirror Crack'd from Side to Side* (both d. Kusuda Yasunobu), broadcast in 2006 and 2007.[12] After a short break, 2015 then saw one of the most intriguing and well received of all of Japan's adaptations when the Fuji TV network tackled *Murder on the Orient Express* as part of its 55th anniversary celebrations, in an original screen version that runs for nearly five hours.

This version of the mystery stars 48-year-old Mansai Nomura as Poirot on the 'Special Orient Express', travelling between Shimonoseki and Tokyo in 1933. Despite the change in locale, the story itself stays faithful to the original novel for the rest of its duration. Nomura's performance as the detective moves between eccentric and entertaining to rather over the top in the less effective comedic moments; however, because he is clearly enjoying himself in the role, the audience finds itself being swept along by his energy. One striking element of the production is that the high-definition picture is interlaced—essentially, that means that the picture has an immediacy that most audiences would associate with news and light entertainment, and it does not have the cinematic look for which drama productions in most of the rest of the world aim. This decision makes it more difficult to cultivate an effective filmic atmosphere, but is presumably part of the accepted grammar of television drama in Japan. The first part of the two-episode adaptation follows the structure and detail of the original story closely, but some audiences may have been confused when it appears to be reaching its conclusion even though there is a second part yet to come. The reason for this is that, after Poirot starts to outline his findings to those present in the railway carriage, the second part then takes an unusual but effective turn and spends more than two hours dramatising the background to the case—namely, the kidnapping and murder of a young child—before following the suspects as they make the decision to commit murder as a form of retribution. The flashback is still framed by Poirot going through the details of the mystery on the train, but it is now that we see the whole story from the murderers' perspectives. This is an excellent and original idea, and the dramatisation clearly draws on the original parallels with the Lindbergh case that had inspired Christie, with the use of a ladder against the window as a strong piece of evidence. It is surprising that this flashback section is not more atmospheric—the kidnapping occurs in the middle of the day in natural lighting, for example—but as the story is so complex it serves a good function. Nevertheless, one has to wonder whether the idea really justifies more than two hours of screen time; for Christie fans there is much to be interested in, but for more casual viewers it perhaps over-eggs the pudding somewhat. Nevertheless, the adaptation is a clear success, despite some shortcomings (including some less than impressive special effects), and it was a popular and critical success, being viewed by over 16 % of the audience, a very good rating for Japanese television.[13]

Each of the countries covered in this section of the book has demonstrated a willingness to adapt Christie's stories with fondness rather than cynicism— the adaptations generally show respect for the original mysteries, and when changes are made they are usually in order to allow the original story to have resonance in a different marketplace. Given their frequent success, they also demonstrate the resilience of the core components of these stories, which shine through even the most extreme reworking into a new production for a new audience. In the final section of this book, we will see that some of the attempts to update Christie that took place closer to home have been rather more problematic, while others rank among the very finest Agatha Christie screen productions.

NOTES

1. There are many spellings of this title—this is the one that appears on the Indian film censors' certificate.
2. The film also features a duet between its version of the characters of Lombard and Vera; Bollywood's own version of a love scene.
3. See Chap. 7.
4. The working title is outlined in Julius Green, *Curtain Up: Agatha Christie—A Life in Theatre* (London: HarperCollins, 2015), 470.
5. Anindita Acharya, 'Subhrajit Mitra working on films based on Agatha Christie's works,' *Hindustan Times*, 30 July 2015, accessed on 1 September 2015, http://www.hindustantimes.com/regional-movies/subhrajit-mitra-working-on-films-based-on-agatha-christie-s-works/story-4bFoZDt8C6517MNdASbmdL.html.
6. This footage shows scaffolding around Elizabeth Tower, which houses Big Ben, dating it to some point after March 1983 when restoration work began, which lasted until 1985.
7. In the novel Poirot actually makes a house of cards, sadly missing here as he prefers to play a version of solitaire.
8. Some sources claim that there is a 2002 Russian version of *Witness for the Prosecution*, but attempts to verify its existence have drawn a blank so far.

9. That is not to say that there are no changes at all—for example, some extraneous characters are removed, such as Colonel Carter and Miss Gannett at the Mahjong game with Dr Sheppard and his sister, which is resultantly changed to a card game suitable for two characters instead.
10. I am very grateful to Terence McSweeney for kindly translating this section of the adaptation for me.
11. I am indebted to the website *Delicious Death* for making me aware of this and some of the other Japanese adaptations: http://www.deliciousdeath.com/index.html.
12. Despite my best efforts, as well as the kind cooperation of Agatha Christie Ltd and several Christie fans from around the world, I have not been able to track down copies of these particular adaptations and so can only apologise for their brief treatment.
13. *Netease Arts*, 'Oriental flavor *Murder on the Orient Express* not just a cosplay,' 26 February 2015, accessed 1 November 2015, http://www.iduobo.com/2015/02/26/oriental-flavor-murder-on-the-orient-express-not-just-a-cosplay-22666.html.

PART VIII

Remaking and Reworking, 1999–

Chapter 15: Christie with a Twist

Spoilers: *Murder on the Orient Express*; *Witness for the Prosecution*; *The Body in the Library*; *By the Pricking of My Thumbs*; *Murder is Easy*; 'Greenshaw's Folly'; *Endless Night*

Agatha Christie: Marple originated with developments that took place several years prior to the series's 2004 debut, with the 1998 purchase of shares in Agatha Christie Ltd by the media company Chorion, which resulted in a change of direction and priorities when it came to screen adaptations of her work. Although *Agatha Christie's Poirot* would return from its hiatus at this time, albeit with an eventual change in style, there were no other long-running or distinctive Christie projects contemporaneously appearing on film or television, so Chorion could work from a relatively blank canvas. Instrumental in the company's decision to reinvigorate the brand on screen was the 1999 arrival of Phil Clymer as Chorion's Director of Film & TV.

Clymer immediately made his mark with the instigation of a proposed adaptation of *The Secret Adversary*, the debut story for Tommy and Tuppence, for which a full script was written before the project was abandoned. 'When Chorion bought the shares they were a public company so needed to make a clear expression of what they were doing', points out Mathew Prichard when recalling the early plans for the literary property.[1] *The Secret Adversary* certainly marks itself out as distinctive from the very beginning, with a script by Jeremy Front, Clymer's brother-in-law, which cites *The Thin Man* (d. W.S. Van Dyke, 1934), *The 39 Steps* (d. Alfred Hitchcock, 1935) and *The Lady Vanishes* (d. Alfred Hitchcock, 1938) as stylistic filmic influences. The Tommy and Tuppence of this adaptation have had their childish excesses removed, and we see a slightly more sedate, older, married couple. This version of Tommy has been guided by his experiences in the Great War, and Tuppence gently teases him while asserting her independence and spirit of adventure; indeed, the script for the 90-minute film asserts Tuppence's modern credentials early, with her opening line—'Bugger!' The action is moved from the 1920s to the eve of the Second World War, and the script notes make it clear that the reason for this move is that it allows a closer link to the next planned adaptation, the

© The Author(s) 2016
M. Aldridge, *Agatha Christie on Screen*,
DOI 10.1057/978-1-137-37292-5_16

1941 thriller *N or M?*, which explicitly references the war period. Otherwise the change of period is relatively straightforward, with Bolshevik conspiracies replaced by Nazi sympathisers, but similarly executed twists and turns.

This attempt to bring Tommy and Tuppence's adventures to the screen was more than a passing suggestion; the treatment was delivered in early 1999, while by the second half of 2000 the script was still being redrafted. However, in the end Chorion would make its mark with a new version of the biggest Agatha Christie story of all, when *Murder on the Orient Express* was brought to the screen for the first time since the 1974 film. This time it was in the form of a television movie for the American network CBS, which was broadcast on 22 April 2001 and starred Alfred Molina as Poirot. To the film's credit, it is clearly trying to do something very different to the traditional heritage-based adaptations of Agatha Christie stories, offering up a production that is much more akin to the earlier American television movies of the 1980s, which presented Christie stories to an audience that might not otherwise seek out her work. In line with these movies, *Murder on the Orient Express* also transplants the action to the then-present day—however, this is where the film really starts to unravel. There is a great deal of potential in reworking Christie's stories to locations or periods where they were not originally set; the Indian adaptations of her work are testament to how this can result in an interesting take on the same central mystery. However, the manner in which this movie firmly establishes itself in 2001 soon becomes a bore, as it ham-fistedly inserts modern references in a way that seems ridiculous and can only inspire mirth in the audience—we may tolerate the clunkily emphasised addition of a laptop to gather evidence, but when the appearance of a hand-held computer's stylus becomes a clue, the screenplay seems to have gone rather too far in trying to prove its modern credentials. The film would be much better off making an impact as a modern Christie adaptation by using distinctive, stylish direction and a sparkling, witty, well-paced script; unfortunately, director Carl Schenkel and writer Stephen Harrigan provide none of this. Neither Schenkel nor Harrigan had an illustrious film history, with Harrigan's credits consisting of other television movies such as 1995's *The O.J. Simpson Story* (d. Jerrold Freedman), while this would be Schenkel's final film, following productions such as *Tarzan and the Lost City* (1998).

The film's plot is a slimmed-down version of the original novel, and although it is understandable that a production running for only 100 minutes needs to reduce the number of characters, this does mean that the underlying principle of the 12 suspects acting as a jury is unfortunately removed. Tellingly, the opening caption states that the film is 'From Agatha Christie', acknowledging that it has moved away from its origins somewhat, something reinforced when we join Poirot investigating the death of a belly dancer. The Poirot of this adaptation feels like a person who could exist in the real world in 2001. Molina's performance is less mannered than most of his predecessors, as presumably he surmised that there was the potential for the character to look ridiculous in contemporary surroundings—he may have been right, but it is another example of how the production removes the character of the story while keeping only the bare bones. In this adaptation Poirot also encounters Vera Rossakoff, the Russian jewel thief seen in other Poirot stories by Christie (but not this one), and it is heavily implied that they may join forces in the future, although the poor reception of this production put paid to the chance of a follow-up movie. The film is also an example of Christie featuring as a real person in the fictional screen universe, with the audience being informed that one character ends up performing in Agatha Christie's *The Mousetrap*. It is difficult to see what pleasure this blurring of boundaries between fictional and real worlds is supposed to supply, but clearly someone was amused by the idea. The production was not deemed a success by Christie's family at the very least; 'We'll draw a line under that one!' says Mathew Prichard when asked about it.[2]

The next attempt to update Christie's works for the modern age saw another of her mysteries moved to the present day (in this case 2003), in what would be the second attempt to rework the 1945 novel *Sparkling Cyanide* for a contemporary audience.[3] This production was made for ITV in the UK, and moved the story of a mysterious poisoning at a dinner party into the world of football, with the murder of a club manager's wife. Such a change of setting owed more debt to the channel's then popular high-camp drama series *Footballers' Wives* (ITV, 2002–06) than anything in Christie's original story, but the basic plot remained relatively unchanged, as did several characters. A notable strength of the production was the casting of Pauline Collins as Dr Catherine Kendall, who investigates the crime with her husband, Colonel Geoffrey Reece, played by Oliver Ford Davies. As a team they are reminiscent of Tommy and Tuppence with their background in spying as well as their convincing and interesting relationship with each other.[4] However, they are hampered by a script by Laura Lamson that rather heavy-handedly tries to put a modern spin on proceedings, with excessive and unconvincing utilisation of technology (the use of CCTV and facial recognition extends far beyond the contemporary possibilities, which allows unforgivable cheating in order to reach conclusions). Broadcast on 5 October 2003, the reaction to the production seemed more bemused than hostile, with *The Guardian* preview wondering what it was all about, while claiming that 'the script's a bit *Scooby Doo*'.[5] *The Times* was even less keen, highlighting the parallels with *Footballers' Wives*, before saying that 'Despite a wonderful cast it is still two hours of lifeless tedium'.[6]

Prior to the broadcast of *Sparkling Cyanide* a handful of newspaper reports quoted Rosalind Hicks and Mathew Prichard regarding their opposing views on updating Christie's works for the present day. Hicks was unequivocal about her preferred treatment of her mother's works, telling *The Times* that 'I'm not in favour of setting things in the modern era [...] If people want to write stories in the modern era why do they need them to be Agatha Christie?'[7] Certainly on the evidence of productions such as *Sparkling Cyanide* one can sympathise with Hicks's barely disguised disgust with the changes, but then one also has to consider the practical realities of keeping a long-established figure such as Christie relevant to modern audiences. Not all adaptations can be suitable for all viewers, and there is a case to be made that compromises can be worthwhile in order to bring in new viewers and, eventually, new readers—and the adaptations covered in this chapter show more compromises than many in order to achieve this aim. This central struggle between fidelity to the source and satisfying general audiences with slightly different tastes goes back to the earliest film adaptations, and is an argument that is more prominent than ever today— the apparent dichotomy demonstrates the central struggle between finding a new audience and satisfying the old. Speaking to *The Times* in 2003, Mathew Prichard said: 'To me, this is not traducing the original in any way. It's translating my grandmother for a modern audience and if she was writing today maybe it's what she would have done herself, because as far as work was concerned she was not at all old fashioned.'[8]

This period saw several more attempts to reinvigorate Christie's work for the screen, although they were generally ill-fated. In *Sparkling Cyanide* there are heavy hints that the programme was intended as a pilot for further investigations by the lead characters, but this came to nothing, while other projects did not even get beyond pre-production. Discussions of Agatha Christie Ltd's future plans during this period often referred to a proposed new Hollywood film version of *Witness for the Prosecution*, set in the present day. The script was written by venerable producer and writer David E. Kelley, whose work on *L.A. Law* (NBC, 1986–94) had been highly acclaimed in the 1980s, before he went on to create critical and popular hits including *Ally McBeal* (Fox, 1997–2002), *Chicago Hope* (CBS, 1994–2000) and *Boston Public* (Fox, 2000–04). Kelley wrote his version with a particular actress in mind for the crucial role of Christine Vole—his wife, Michelle Pfeiffer. It is difficult to see how his script would have worked on screen, and yet with such a fine pedigree behind him it is only fair to have a degree of confidence in his vision.

Such is the power of the 1957 Billy Wilder film of the play (arguably an even stronger version of the mystery than either the original short story or Christie's stage version) that it is difficult to shake off the vision of Charles Laughton's take on Wilfrid Robarts, making it extra surprising when we meet the Wilfred (sic) of Kelley's version. Set in contemporary Philadelphia, we see that this Robarts teaches law as well as practises it, while he also attends a party with half-naked women, habitually checks his BlackBerry phone and eats Cheerios. This version also retains some of the elements from the Wilder version, including the prickly relationship between Robarts and Nurse Plimsoll, while Christine (now a dance teacher) revels in some incongruous innuendo that we can only hope would not have made it to screen—on pointing out that the police had already searched her husband's drawers, Christine asks Robarts if he would like to have a peek at hers. However, on the whole one can understand why Kelley's version (a first draft, dated 28 April 2004) would have held so much appeal for Agatha Christie Ltd, since not only did it have the possibility of attracting star names, it is also a pacey take on a particularly strong story. Kelley even uses technology to a completely legitimate and interesting advantage, as he has Robarts receive an email from Christine while he is meeting the owner of a series of letters that would seem to incriminate her for perjury. As those familiar with the story will guess, this person—a cleaning lady called Tina—is Christine in disguise, making this an excellent way to provide an alibi, and eminently possible in the world of handheld technology.

Perhaps one reason why the use of mobile phones and computing is not always effective in modern takes on the stories is because even a casual member of the audience will know that Christie died long before the rise of the related technology, meaning that it always seems particularly incongruous. While only fans will notice the addition or removal of characters or changes in motive or even murderers, almost all of those watching will be reasonably sure that Christie's original story did not have characters using mobile phones, nor following events on rolling news channels. However, the success of programmes such as *Sherlock* (BBC, 2010–) and *Elementary* (CBS, 2012–) has shown that such updating can work, often to the delight of established and new fans alike, although both also feel like series with old-fashioned lead characters stuck in the modern day, which may have been a better stance than the full integration presented in most Christie adaptations that are moved to the present.

No one seems to be able to recall precisely why this *Witness for the Prosecution* project continued no further, since all parties seemed keen, but it was not the final attempt to 'update' Christie's works. *Destination Unknown* is a 1954 Christie mystery thriller that has the dubious distinction of being one of very few of her novels that have never been adapted for film or television.[9] As with many of her thrillers, the story involves international travel, a visually attractive if expensive attraction for screen adventures, and although it does not feature any of her recurring characters, it is nevertheless a solid story with a dark edge that may have made it particularly interesting for modern audiences, opening as it does with a woman on the brink of suicide, who then finds a reason to live through her journey. In this sense it has much in common with the more meditative and existential focuses of Christie's novels written under the pseudonym Mary Westmacott (often misattributed as romances), but the grounding of the thriller within then-contemporary politics (in this case, the Soviet Union's international position) is an unmistakably Christie trait for her books of this type. Work on the project was undertaken over the course of several years, following an initial script by Nicholas Osborne in 2002, with later rewrites and amendments coming from both Osborne and Rupert Walters.[10] The screenplay opens with the character of Hilary Craven walking along a busy Virginian road in a dressing gown, clearly having some sort of breakdown, before we cut to her in Washington, DC four months later, after she has been recruited into a taskforce to help fight an international menace. The idea of a Virginian woman being able to head off a terrorist attack in post–9/11 America is a good premise for a US movie, and it may simply be that audiences grew weary of so many on-screen discussions and depictions of terrorism by the time the project was ready to move into full production. However, it is still one of Christie's novels that could work well on screen if updated.

Asked about the attempts to move Christie into the present day during this period, Prichard points out that the situation has now changed. 'The interesting thing is nowadays, some of the projects we're looking at doing now, almost nobody wants to set it in the present day,' he says. 'There are quite a few people who don't want to do them in the time when they were written. But most people want a degree of period.'[11] Although adaptations of Agatha Christie that move to the present day have rarely met with critical or popular acclaim, it may be that the success of other updated properties means that we have not seen the last of them yet. However, soon after these attempts Agatha Christie Ltd did find a way to rework Christie's tales for a mainstream audience in a way that met with commercial success—even if it left many of her fans less than happy with the result.

AGATHA CHRISTIE: MARPLE

Perhaps no production is more difficult to discuss in this book than *Agatha Christie: Marple*, for which 23 television films were shown on ITV between 2004 and 2013. A lively and bold reworking of Christie's novels, the series has also been widely derided—even reviled—by long-term fans of her work. And yet it was a popular success for much of its run, and even achieved a degree of critical acclaim early in proceedings, despite the widespread changes from the original mysteries. Whatever the feelings of many fans regarding the series, there is no doubting the fact that Agatha Christie Ltd achieved its stated aim to introduce the author's mysteries to new audiences.

Even though the BBC's run of Miss Marple stories starring Joan Hickson had finished over a decade prior to *Marple*'s 2004 debut, the earlier series cast a long shadow over this production, and the immediate intention was to create a new programme that felt very different. This extended to the tone, now a little brasher and apparently keen to add some twenty-first-century drama to the 1950s setting, as well as a different type of supporting cast, made up of fashionable and recognisable faces, whatever their acting pedigree, in order to add to the publicity for a programme now operating in an increasingly congested television schedule. Perhaps most important was the casting of Miss Marple herself, but this presented its own problems—how could one follow Joan Hickson? The answer, it was decided, was by choosing someone who offered a different take on the character, even if she was not the preferred actress. 'The person who I always wanted was Gemma Jones', admits Mathew Prichard, referring to the BAFTA-winning actress whose career stretches from Shakespeare and Jane Austen to the Harry Potter films, as well as an appearance as Miss Williams in the *Poirot* adaptation of *Five Little Pigs*. 'Phil Clymer was very discreet and he always told me he thought Gemma was the best one we interviewed and did screen tests for us, but she was too much like Joan.'[12] For a series of adaptations that was attempting to differentiate itself from its predecessor, any notable similarity was to be avoided, even if it went against the instinct of producers. 'I'll bet you a small sum that if we'd actually got Gemma Jones to do it, it would have been comparable to the success that David had', claims Prichard.[13] In the end, it was Geraldine McEwan who was cast in the role, an actress of considerable repute who had been particularly successful on stage and was probably best known for her BAFTA-winning turn in the 1990 BBC adaptation of Jeanette Winterson's *Oranges Are Not the Only Fruit*.

However, the lead actress was the least of the programme's problems for critics of the show. At times, the approach of the production feels heavy-handed, occasionally even bordering on the distasteful. The supporting cast often perform as if play-acting in a parody of Agatha Christie, dredged from some vague cultural memory of what her mysteries must encompass; this is an issue so uniform that it must have been part of the house directorial style. This results in productions that often feel like a barely filtered pastiche, where the mise-en-scène and performances can completely lack of any sense of naturalism or realism. Plots and characters are generally sketched out in broad strokes, lacking in subtlety, which results in a series that is nowhere near as fun as the makers seem to assume it would be. There is an attempt to have the production evoke a sense of archness and camp but, as Susan Sontag once famously pointed out, pure camp must never be knowing—and this series tries too hard, making the attempts fall flat.[14] This sense that the programme can riff on a vague memory of what Agatha Christie stories must have been like, polluted by the likes of the Margaret Rutherford films and endless parodies, means that a talented group of people have somehow created an unsatisfying and meandering final product that does not really seem to know what it wants to say about either the period or Christie. As a result, the programme does her stories a disservice, perpetuating the idea that Christie was some generic and old-fashioned mystery writer whose work can only be read or adapted ironically. This is simply not the case.

Even if many fans may not enjoy the final product, it is easy to sympathise with the fact that the programme needed not only to be distinctive in terms of the Christie canon, but also to appeal to audiences for whom Christie held only a casual appeal—exactly the type of viewers who had enjoyed the Margaret Rutherford films. 'I very much take the view that in the same way that people don't bat an eyelid at there being a new production of *King Lear*, with a new person playing King Lear, we'd all be much the poorer if that didn't happen', explains Prichard, adding:

> The same applies, in my view, to Agatha Christie. So it seems to me to be rather a shame, for the public as well as for financial reasons, if we say—Joan Hickson, the BBC have done it, we'll never do it again. I think that is indefensible. But I think that if we're going to allow people to do it I think you have to reckon that they're going to do something a little different with some of the stories. The trick is to allow that without too many unacceptable things happening. I will be the first to admit that, on occasions, either we or the script writers, or a combination of both, or the producers or whoever have done things that I have later regretted. On the whole I don't think there have been too many.[15]

The series debuted on Sunday, 12 December 2004 with an adaptation of *The Body in the Library* by Kevin Elyot, who had written the *Death on the Nile* and *Five Little Pigs* screenplays for *Poirot*, and would eventually script the Belgian's final case, *Curtain*. Elyot supplies a fast-paced investigation that sensibly puts McEwan's inscrutable Miss Marple alongside the rather more vivacious Dolly Bantry, played by British icon Joanna Lumley. The pair hare around the countryside trying to piece together the truth behind the murder of a young woman whose body is found in the Bantrys' library before Simon Callow's rather slower detective can. It is all jolly high jinks for much of the time, with the mystery framed as a puzzle to be solved, and even if it may not be to the taste of many old-school Christie fans, a more general audience may find something to enjoy. However, it is with the story's resolution that the programme really created a divide in its viewers that set the scene for the reaction to many later productions, since the adaptation's denouement changes the culprits from a heterosexual couple to two women in a secret relationship with each other. 'I think that was a mistake', admits Prichard.[16]

The series deviates further from its source material when it indicates that spinster Miss Marple is still pining for a failed relationship with a married man that took place long in her past, as well as with the occasional use of bad language (the series has its first use of 'bastard' a mere seven minutes into the opener)—taken in conjunction with the addition of a homosexual relationship as motivation for murder, then we have a programme that has a rather juvenile sense of how to make itself relevant for a modern audience. Making such attention-grabbing changes merely alludes to depth of thought that is not actually present in the programme, making these additions little more than ill-placed devices that distract from rather than complement the mysteries. Furthermore, they show a lack of ambition and nuance when it comes to really working out how to make an effective and popular final product for the modern age. The greatest puzzle is that in order to feel entitled to make these changes, the writers must have considered that in their one-dimensional reworking of the stories and characters they had created stories that were somehow more sophisticated than Christie had managed, despite her exceptional grip on human nature and motivation. Any such arrogance is misplaced.

Nevertheless, the initial critical reaction to the production was warm, even from Nancy Banks-Smith of *The Guardian*, whose credentials as a bona fide Agatha Christie fan had long been asserted. 'It was quite beautifully done and exceptionally faithful to the original with one staggering deviation', she wrote, continuing:

> Geraldine McEwan is vivid [...] Her tiny face is screwed up like a withered apple, sharp and possibly a little tart. Talking of little tarts, her sidelong eyes are full of mischief, and one suspects that this Miss Marple has a racy past. [...] The film opens with a V2 falling on a birthday party and ends with a bit of a bomb-shell too. The ending has been changed. The murderers are now lesbian lovers. The solution of a murder mystery is supposed to take your breath away and this

certainly does that. I have to say, through slightly gritted teeth, that it actually strengthens the story.[17]

If nothing else, Banks-Smith's review demonstrates that even Christie fans may enjoy a new twist on an old story—especially one that has already been faithfully brought to the screen. Several reviewers commented on the changes from the source text, but few ventured an opinion on whether it was an improvement; instead, they explained that changes would likely infuriate many of her readers, although there was a general sense that such tinkering was inevitable. Several preview articles emphasised the revelation that this Miss Marple had a past relationship ('TV Tec's Sexy Side Will Stun Her Fans' claimed the *Daily Mirror* headline), while all noted that ITV had carefully constructed the series to garner maximum publicity in its casting of well-known celebrities designed to appeal to younger audiences as well as old. This included an early drama role for David Walliams, then flying high as one half of the *Little Britain* (BBC, 2003–06) team, and later to spearhead his own series based on Christie characters. Despite misgivings in some quarters, the programme was a popular success, averaging over 8 m viewers—if the remaining three films achieved similar success then ITV had a new hit on its hands.

Following *The Body in the Library* was another of the more iconic Miss Marple mysteries, with an adaptation of her debut novel, *The Murder at the Vicarage*. This film was the first of six to be written by Stephen Churchett, whose prior experience included the scripts for two episodes of legal drama *Kavanagh QC* (ITV, 1995–2001). Churchett is also a familiar face on television, especially for his recurring role of solicitor Marcus Christie in long-running soap opera *EastEnders* (BBC, 1985–) since 1990 (and occasional cameo appearances in *Marple* as a coroner). The adaptation opens with a flashback, which dramatises a portion of Miss Marple's relationship with a soldier in 1915; while the principle of the character having once loved and lost is perfectly reasonable, one wonders what function the scene offers. Perhaps it was felt that modern audiences would not believe that the character would know enough about the whole world, but whatever the rationale, the references soon disappear as the series progresses. The film continues in a similar vein to its predecessor, with a bright and brash approach to murder—played as a game, rather than a real event with emotional resonance. Miss Marple is laid up with an ankle injury, allowing salient plot points to be relayed to her, which keeps her as the focus of the action while not allowing her to solve the case too quickly.[18] The cast is even more exceptional than the opener, including such illustrious names as Derek Jacobi, Miriam Margolyes, Jane Asher, Robert Powell, Rachael Stirling and Tim McInnerny. Unlike *The Body in the Library*, there are no big surprises in terms of the way the story is adapted for the screen, with the identity of the murderer remaining as Christie intended. The ratings continued on a par with the opener, indicating that audiences had taken to this new incarnation of Agatha Christie, while one reviewer at least felt it to be superior to ITV's other Christie series. Simon Edge in the *Daily Express* claimed that the series showcased 'first-rate scripts and to-die-for casts show up those ropy *Poirot*s as the *Crossroads* of the whodunnit. Sometimes, though, Dame Agatha herself doesn't quite cut the mustard.'[19] Readers may decide for themselves if this questionable judgement on the programmes' relative merits should be taken seriously.

4.50 from Paddington, broadcast on 26 December 2004, was the third instalment of the series and Churchett's second script.[20] Fittingly, the action is set at Christmas time, and it is at this point that the series really starts to affirm its credentials as a 1950s pastiche. While its use of picture wipes to transition between screens is surely in homage to the lighter pictures from the classical Hollywood period, it is a shame that a small but charming touch such as this is then countered by the irritating addition of Noël Coward to the cast of characters. This is just one example of a change that can only distract rather than entertain, but the rest of the production is one of the stronger instalments of *Marple*, helped by an excellent cast including Pam Ferris, Jenny Agutter, Celia Imrie and David Warner. While there are many small changes they are all reasonable and the final result provides a reasonably enjoyable two hours of television.

The final adaptation from this first series of four tackled *A Murder Is Announced*, a novel that brims with sub-plots, and so it should be no surprise that it is simplified and reworked for 90 minutes of screen action.[21] Stewart Harcourt, who would later work on *Poirot*, supplied the script for this production, which perhaps lacks subtlety until its pleasingly under-stated finale. This is especially true in the characters of Murgatroyd and Hinch; the former is now simply stupid, emphasised by her misreading 'murder' as 'marriage', while Hinch wears a suit, in case anyone needed the implicit nature of the couple's relationship underlining. It is hard to imagine that Christie's Miss Marple, no lover of excess, would wander round a spa in a dressing gown, but here we have it. However, once more there is no doubting the calibre of the cast, including Keeley Hawes, Cherie Lunghi, Frances Barber, Matthew Goode and Catherine Tate, and the audience held firm once more, having dropped by only a million since the opening episode.

By the end of this first run, fans may have been interested to see in which direction the programme would go with its second series—would it deviate further from Christie's originals or move closer to them? When the list of titles to be adapted was announced, they had their answer.

McEwan Returns as Marple

The second run of *Marple* would once more star Geraldine McEwan as the sleuth in a series of four adaptations based on Agatha Christie novels, with all-star casts joining her for each mystery, as had been established in the first set of films. The first two titles, *Sleeping Murder* and *The Moving Finger*, are understandable choices—each is a solid Miss Marple mystery that would naturally be expected to appear in a new series of adaptations starring the spinster sleuth. However, the other two choices, *By the Pricking of My Thumbs* and *The Sittaford Mystery*, are more of a surprise, since neither novel included the character of Miss Marple at all. Instead, the former title had been written with husband and wife team Tommy and Tuppence heading the investigation, while the latter is a standalone novel with several characters as detectives, including Inspector Narracott of the Exeter police. Resultantly, it was obvious even before this second run was broadcast that *Marple* had made its position clear—it existed to fillet Christie's stories for material deemed to be worth reshaping as part of a rather more generic set of adaptations.

For the producers and broadcasters there are certainly advantages when it comes to placing disparate adaptations within an umbrella series, not least because this makes it easier to sell as a package internationally. Clearly the name Marple also had a cachet of its own, and so there is certainly a strong business case for this adaptation, no matter how much it may upset the relatively small band of purists who recoil at such changes. However, the series's take on the Miss Marple book *Sleeping Murder* indicated that sweeping changes were not reserved for novels that needed to be radically reworked in order to include the elderly sleuth. This adaptation, broadcast on 5 February 2006 and once more written by Stephen Churchett, makes considerable changes to the narrative, the characters and their relationships. The result is an adaptation that differs so much from the original that it can really only be considered to be based on a part of the premise and a handful of the original characters. At least by the second series the programme has the courage of its convictions and is not really pretending to be true to the original text nor improve on it—instead, this is a heavily reworked version of the story designed to be a bright and bold piece of entertainment for a general audience. Many Christie fans may dislike these changes, but by this point in the programme's history they would know what they were getting, and should have felt no compulsion to continue tuning in to a series that was clearly not aimed at them.

However, perhaps there is a danger that such swingeing changes do Christie a disservice, since casual audiences are not able to see the dividing line between the original work and any later (usually inferior) alterations. Nevertheless, this has always been the case for adaptations and Christie fans should not operate under the misapprehension that her works have been particularly mistreated—they have not. Indeed, these editions of *Marple* generally treat their lead characters and original author with more respect than the Basil Rathbone Sherlock Holmes films did with the consulting detective and Arthur Conan Doyle, but those films evoke a haze of nostalgia of their own that generally overrides such concerns, helped by the use of titles that are generally not the same as the stories on which they are broadly based, all of which allows them to evade in-depth criticism.

Kevin Elyot returned to bring *The Moving Finger* to the screen again in another highly stylised production that evokes the look of 1950s Hollywood with (one hopes) deliberately non-naturalistic back projection during driving scenes, for example. As with the novel, Miss Marple is kept on the periphery of the action, but the production itself is surprisingly dull and is a marked contrast to the opening, indicating that the programme was still finding its feet in terms of style, even if it does stick relatively closely to the plot. For the following film, *By the Pricking of My Thumbs*, the tone was lightened and the pace picked up as Miss Marple is accompanied by Tuppence Beresford (Tommy is sent abroad on business). The Tuppence of this adaptation, played by Greta Scacchi, is a cartoonish but entertaining extension of the original character, wishing to muscle in on any action of which Tommy may be a part and throwing herself into any mysteries that present themselves, with hip flask on standby to keep her nerves steady. This was to be the first time that this particular novel was adapted, with a screenplay by Stewart Harcourt, and it lends itself well to the screen. By this point McEwan is playing Miss Marple in a manner that is a little more theatrical, perhaps noting the extrovert performances around her. Despite the personnel changes the story opens and initially develops rather faithfully, with an investigation into what may be one or more murders; suspicion is stoked by the mutterings of a woman in an old people's home, who asks 'Was it your poor child? There behind the fireplace?', only to disappear shortly afterwards. Realism is not the order of the day, especially when the production climaxes with the murderer marauding around a tiny cottage in the woods that looks to have been rebuilt from the pages of a fairy tale, wearing a cape suitable for Red Riding Hood.

For *The Sittaford Mystery*, which was broadcast on 30 April 2006 after a two-month break, the changes by the script's writer Stephen Churchett went further still. The adaptation really only uses some of the iconography of the original novel—a murder in a snow-bound house—since it broadens out the action considerably, and goes so far as to change the identity of the murderer once more (although their name is retained, having been transplanted to a different character entirely). The final product is a hodgepodge of ideas and characters, failing to gel as a piece of drama and offering confusing developments that make it difficult to follow or care about proceedings. Once more a well-known figure from the period is unnecessarily inserted, as if this were a children's television drama, with Robert Hardy popping up as Winston Churchill. Unsurprisingly, Miss Marple is relegated to the background of a story in which she has no real place. There is actually great potential in using the series as a way to get some of Christie's individual mysteries to the screen, but if even the best elements of the story are then dispensed with, we have a series that is effectively making new mysteries using the Christie name—the type of production that Agatha Christie Ltd has long resisted.

When the series returned on 23 September 2007, the set of four adaptations once again mixed two Miss Marple stories with two novels that had not featured the character. Opening the run was an adaptation of *At Bertram's Hotel*, and every attempt is made to render this potentially claustrophobic setting more interesting for the audience, although the changes are not always to good effect. Christie's story has Miss Marple returning to an old-fashioned hotel before becoming embroiled in a murder, and this production does its best visually to reflect the grandeur and scale of the location, although it uses an overbearing amount of cacophonous music, which reaches headache-inducing heights as it serves to underscore every last moment at excessive volume. By this point we should not be surprised that the production makes many changes from the original story, including the removal of many characters from the novel and the addition of several more. The adaptation by Tom MacRae, whose most notable credit to this point was two episodes of *Doctor Who* (BBC, 1963–) in 2006, pushes the series even further towards farce and cliché, with a Nazi vicar and a tediously obvious sub-plot involving twins. A surprise but welcome highlight is the presence of former soap star Martine McCutcheon as maid Jane Cooper, a character that the audience can care about and is easily the most likeable aspect of the whole production.

With the choice to next adapt *Ordeal by Innocence,* the *Marple* production team was effectively making a statement that almost any of Christie's stories might be deemed suitable for inclusion in the series, since it is a novel that has a markedly different tone from the usual Miss Marple fare. The original story, previously adapted as a 1985 film, is a bleak tale of the unsettling legacy of an old murder. Once more the changes made were extensive, with Stewart Harcourt's script effectively using only basic elements of the original. Some of the new plotting feels illogical, and most of the characterisation is thin, but the performances are good and those who were still avidly watching the series no doubt found it as enjoyable as any other episode. Tonally it has the feel of a thriller rather than a mystery at some points, which means that Miss Marple's inclusion seems particularly incongruous (especially when she reveals an unconvincing talent for breaking into safes), but the fast pace helps to hold the attention of the audience; those unfamiliar with the original novel are likely to be swept along by the action.

Although the first two episodes of the series aired in consecutive weeks, there was to be something of a wait until the next adaptation, *Towards Zero,* which was finally screened on 3 August 2008—the time of year traditionally used as a dumping ground for projects in which broadcasters had less faith.[22] Perhaps this was because viewing figures had dropped to around 5.5 m, 3 m down on the first series, even though the opposition on other channels was no stronger than it had been. The adaptation itself, from Kevin Elyot, has a charming opening with Tom Baker and Eileen Atkins chatting like old friends so that Baker's character of Frederick Treves can outline the premise of the novel and the significance of its title. The addition of Miss Marple to the story is reasonably well integrated, as she effectively stays in the background and pipes up only when she has something to say about the investigation or events—this is not unlike her characterisation and role in several of the novels in which she stars. The final film perhaps best strikes the balance between a reworking of themes and ideas to fit within the series's expectations and exploiting the very best elements of Christie's original story, where a twisted family dynamic results in murder, which had previously been unsuccessfully adapted as 1995's *Innocent Lies.*

The last film, an adaptation by Stephen Churchett of the Miss Marple novel *Nemesis*, was broadcast on New Year's Day 2009, and has the unfortunate distinction of being the lowest-rated episode of the whole run, with fewer than 4.5 m viewers tuning in. It is once more a very loose adaptation, with considerable changes to characters and motivation, and yet another example of this era of adaptations' bizarre fixation with villainous religious figures.[23] This change is a further indication of the series as pastiche of a vague memory of Christie's mysteries that actually encompasses thrillers of the 1930s and 1940s such as *The Lady Vanishes*, rather than anything in Christie's own work. The production also saw the final performance of Geraldine McEwan as Miss Marple. McEwan had garnered a reputation among some of those on the production as being difficult to work with, and it may be that her decision to leave was to the satisfaction of all. The series itself would live on, however—the name Marple was bigger than any individual actress, although the next person to take on the role would offer a fresh approach on the character that deserves some appreciation, whatever one's views of the production itself.

Julia McKenzie as Marple

One month after the January 2008 announcement that McEwan was to leave the role of Miss Marple, it was revealed that Julia McKenzie was to take over for the next run of adaptations. McKenzie was probably best known for her appearances in the sitcom *Fresh Fields* (ITV, 1984–86), and was quoted as saying: 'Just about everybody in the world knows about Miss Marple and has an opinion of what she should be like, so I'm under no illusions about the size of the task ahead.'[24]

As soon as the audience sees this new Miss Marple in *A Pocket Full of Rye*, the first adaptation in this fourth run of four films, broadcast on 6 September 2009, it is clear that McKenzie is not offering an imitation of any of the previous actresses to play the part, least of all Geraldine McEwan. This Miss Marple is more thoughtful and less caricatured than McEwan's had been, in terms of mannerisms as well as her slightly formal but realistic costume. McKenzie's Marple feels more like a real person, having lost some of the character's excesses, although her first appearance as the sleuth is in a story that is little different from the previous adaptations in the series (it is written by Kevin Elyot), especially with the inclusion of a sex scene that is more explicit than one might normally expect from an Agatha Christie production. Yet the second McKenzie story, broadcast the following week, is an unwelcome peak of the series in terms of tastelessness. Although *Murder Is Easy* had not originally featured Miss Marple, it was a natural choice for an adaptation as its country village murder shares many of the traits that are usually associated with mysteries investigated by the sleuth, and so her inclusion is as well integrated as the series ever achieves. However, the resolution added to this production—in which it is revealed that the murderer Honoria has been raped by her brother—demonstrates a crass sensibility that would be difficult to stomach in the most sensitive of productions, and is certainly not appropriate here, as it is clearly inserted for impact rather than any plot reason. It is particularly unfortunate that this occurs because Shirley Henderson gives an excellent performance as Honoria (now a young woman, rather than the spinster of the novel), which is rather overshadowed by the unpalatable resolution to the story.

When *They Do It with Mirrors* had been previously adapted for the BBC's *Miss Marple* series, it had been acknowledged that it was one of the toughest novels to rework for the screen. This is not least because it relies on a convincing depiction of what is, in the end, revealed to be a trick played on a group of people located in a room close to the murder, which somehow goes unnoticed. Because the new series of *Marple* had never been worried about making changes to the original story, this actually enabled this adaptation to strengthen the original plot a little so as to make the events more credible. The film, written by Paul Rutman (who had previously worked on *Lewis*) and broadcast on New Year's Day 2010, makes the mystery work well for a 90-minute version for a general audience, providing a hint of how the series could be a success when the focus was on making changes for reasons beyond attention seeking, or the crowbarring in of Miss Marple herself. This served as a contrast to the adaptations that both preceded and followed it, since the final film of the fourth series saw Miss Marple dropped into a story quite unlike her normal mysteries— *Why Didn't They Ask Evans?* The novel had previously been the first of the prestige television adaptations when the LWT production was transmitted in 1980, but while the story of high-spirited young adventurers tearing around the country trying to follow the trail of a mystery hardly cries out for an old lady from St Mary Mead to be in on the action, she is added all the same. In fact, the film takes about as much as inspiration from the original novel as might be gleaned from a cursory reading of the book's back cover, so in the end it hardly matters. There is a fair amount of entertainment value to be had from the production, especially the relationship between Miss Marple and Georgia Moffett's vivacious Frankie, but the script from Patrick Barlow—best known as an actor, appearing in film and television shows including *Notting Hill* (d. Roger Mitchell, 1999) and *Absolutely Fabulous* (BBC, 1992–2012)—is really a story of its own, rather than an adaptation of anything written by Agatha Christie. The fact that the episode eventually aired on ITV on 15 June 2011, after the following season was shown and some two years after it was seen on American screens, may be an indication that the broadcaster did not feel particularly confident in the production.

The next two *Marple* films continued with the tradition of inserting the character into stories to which she did not seem terribly well suited, with *The Pale Horse*, an apparently supernatural tale that had previously been adapted for ITV in 1997, where it had its own fair share of plot changes and character alterations. Adapted by Russell Lewis, whose previous credits include crime dramas such as *Cadfael* (ITV, 1994–98), *Kavanagh QC* and *Taggart* (ITV, 1983–2010), the film was broadcast on 30 August 2010 and removes characters who also appear in Poirot stories (including crime writer Ariadne

Oliver), perhaps an indication that there was no wish for there to be any crossover between the series.[25] Miss Marple is firmly integrated into the story rather than simply being an observer as often happens; this includes becoming a victim of a poisoning. When she learns of the death of one character, she is genuinely upset, and McKenzie's subtle and effective performance shows us just how much potential there was with her in the part. Subtlety is not a strength of the next film, however, with *The Secret of Chimneys* adapted by Paul Rutman. Another story in a similar vein to *Evans?* (although, in the event, broadcast by ITV before it, on 27 December 2010), the film feels like a reversion to the caricatures and over-played performances that had started to die away a little. The production feels cheap and stagey, with an unusually weak cast, resulting in an amateurish adaptation that once more resembles a poorly executed parody rather than a genuine attempt to bring an Agatha Christie novel to the screen.

The third film of the fifth series of *Marple* opened an intriguing new area that some Christie fans may have wished had been explored further, as it brought to the screen a Miss Marple short story, rather than another novel. *The Blue Geranium* adapted a tale that had been published as part of *The Thirteen Problems* in 1932, which concerns an elderly invalid, Mrs Pritchard, who is found dead in bed one morning through unexplained causes; even more curiously, this event coincides with a geranium on her wallpaper turning blue. The original story is a short and not particularly complex one, but its use of visual elements as part of the mystery makes it an attractive choice for a television adaptation. Stewart Harcourt's script necessarily greatly expands it, and as with the original text it is told retrospectively, with Miss Marple explaining all. By the end, we see her on the witness stand testifying about the events to a presiding judge, and this perspective works well with McKenzie's portrayal of Miss Marple as an astute observer of society who does not draw attention to herself. Her performance when explaining developments and revelations to the police is a particularly entertaining piece of light comedy, and she infuriates those who either feel threatened by her or under-estimated the spinster's powers of deduction. It is a little more sedate as a production than some others in the series, perhaps because the main death does not occur until approximate two-thirds of the way through, but it remains an intriguing and interesting story. The adaptation was broadcast on 29 December 2010, only two days after *The Secret of Chimneys*, and a mere three days before the next, on 2 January 2011.

This next film adapted *The Mirror Crack'd from Side to Side*, one of the better candidates for screen adaptations of Miss Marple novels, as it is a tale of murder in the shadow of a glamorous film production (concerning Nefertiti, in this version) and a village fête that is visually striking, with a pleasing denouement that reveals one of Christie's more memorable motivations for murder. Another strong cast is headed by the return of Joanna Lumley as Dolly Bantry, while Kevin Elyot's script keeps the story moving along at a good pace, resulting in a production perfectly pitched at a slightly lethargic captive audience just after New Year celebrations.

THE END OF *MARPLE*

The final series of *Marple* saw just three stories brought to the screen, and the programme seemed to be running out of energy. 'Julia [McKenzie] loved it and I think was a bit sorry it didn't go on but we really were running out of stories by then', points out Mathew Prichard.[26] At the same time, an exclusive deal with the BBC to make the corporation the televisual home of Agatha Christie was in its early stages, so *Marple*'s days were numbered. In what served as a neat summary of the various approaches taken to the series of adaptations, these last three films encompass a Miss Marple novel and a short story, alongside a mystery that did not originally feature the character.

A Caribbean Mystery, broadcast on 16 June 2013, has Miss Marple solve a murder in the titular region, and had been twice adapted in the previous 30 years, making it one of the more familiar stories to audiences. This version follows a script by Charlie Higson, who by this time was probably best known as the author of a series of *Young James Bond* novels. This connection manifests itself in the production itself, with a bizarre and distracting sub-plot that has Ian Fleming (writer of the Bond books) meet the ornithologist James Bond.[27] According to Higson, the request to include real historical figures came from the production team, presumably with the intention of aiding the publicity drive, since the instruction cannot have been for the benefit of the film itself.

The second film, *Greenshaw's Folly*, adapts a short story that was published as part of *The Adventure of the Christmas Pudding* collection, in which a murder takes place while witnesses overlooking the scene are locked in their rooms, unable to escape in order to help or investigate. The cause of death—an arrow in the chest—is a pleasingly visual one, but the advantages of this are more than counterbalanced by the problems encountered with one traditional problem with bringing Christie on screen: that of convincing disguises. The story, which is adapted by Tim Whitnall, is understandably padded out, with new sub-plots added and even allusions to another Miss Marple short story, 'The Thumb Mark of St Peter', published in *The Thirteen Problems*.

After a gap of a few months, 29 December 2013 saw the transmission of the final *Marple* episode, with an adaptation of *Endless Night*. This is an unusual choice for Marple because the story does not really operate as a murder mystery, at least not in the traditional sense; instead, the novel is about a series of mysterious circumstances and is particularly striking in its original form as a psychological thriller.[28] However, in this screen adaptation the young couple at the centre of the mysterious events may reasonably be expected to point the finger of blame at the old woman who seems to be stalking them, even going as far as to popping up on their honeymoon—Miss Marple herself. This insertion of Miss Marple into the story stretches credulity, although she is often relegated to the background. This causes its own problems as the final film, written by Kevin Elyot, is so different in structure and emphasis to a normal Miss Marple that the audience may reasonably wonder precisely what they are watching.

The mystery with *Marple* is its tonal approach. Throughout the series the programme veers from comedy and parody, through to pastiche, occasional melancholy and some outright tastelessness. It wanted to assert itself as something wholly different to the earlier Miss Marple adaptations on the BBC, which are still regularly repeated, but the series falls between two stools, purporting to bring Christie's books to the screen while trying to do something that is not a simple adaptation. *Marple* may have been better served to follow the example set by French adaptations of the era, which do not pretend to be at all faithful, but take the spirit and basics of the stories and do something new and distinctive with them. Perhaps the appeal (and commercial allure) of the Miss Marple name was too strong, however, as there is also the inescapable fact that, regardless of the fact that many Christie fans dislike this particular series, it was a popular success, and ensured that Agatha Christie's name remained on television screens across the globe for nearly a decade.

NOTES

1. Interview with the author, August 2013.
2. Interview with the author, August 2013.
3. Following the American television movie two decades earlier.
4. In the original novel, it is Colonel Race (not Reece) who is the lead investigator.
5. *The Guardian*, 4 October 2003.
6. *The Times*, 4 October 2003.
7. *The Times*, 27 September 2003.
8. *The Times*, 30 August 2003.
9. Nor for any other medium, such as stage and radio, at the time of writing.
10. It is not clear which Nicholas Osborne working in the industry supplied the first draft, but it seems likely that this is the same Rupert Walters who wrote three episodes of the BBC espionage drama *Spooks* in 2004 and 2005.
11. Interview with the author, August 2013.
12. Interview with the author, August 2015.
13. Interview with the author, August 2015.
14. By contrast, the character of Poirot is much more fun as a camp figure, because he has no conception of the idea that his mannerisms and approach could be seen as such. In the stories and adaptations his camp moments are peripheral to the action and pass by briefly—perhaps even beyond the notice of Christie herself—increasing the pleasure for the attuned reader or viewer.
15. Interview with the author, August 2013.
16. Interview with the author, August 2013.
17. *The Guardian*, 13 December 2004.
18. There are shades of *The Mirror Crack'd from Side to Side* here, especially the 1980 film version.

19. *Daily Express,* 21 December 2004.
20. The film was called *What Mrs McGillicuddy Saw* in the United States, matching the novel's different title in that territory.
21. Excluding adverts.
22. The fact that the DVD release of the series offers the episodes in a different order to the broadcast may indicate that ITV was cherry picking stories for particular times of year (the DVD has the stories in the order *Towards Zero, Nemesis, Ordeal by Innocence* and finally *At Bertram's Hotel*).
23. Or apparent religious figures—see the Poirot adaptation of *Appointment with Death* for the most egregious example.
24. *BBC News,* 'Actress McKenzie to Play Marple,' 11 February 2008, accessed 1 October 2015, http://news.bbc.co.uk/1/hi/entertainment/7238884.stm.
25. The fact that there was a much shorter gap between this episode and the last than there had been between the previous two episodes— despite *The Pale Horse* ostensibly being the opener to a new series—is an example of how ITV generally regarded the programmes as independent films, rather than as individual seasons.
26. Interview with the author, August 2015.
27. This is an event that did occur in the real world (James Bond was indeed the name of a prominent American ornithologist) and provided Fleming with the inspiration for the name of his fictional spy.
28. However, the novel has much in common with the Miss Marple short story 'The Case of the Caretaker'; perhaps we may wish to consider the film to be an adaptation of this, rather than *Endless Night*!

Chapter 16: Looking to the Future

Spoilers: *And Then There Were None; N or M?*

For almost as long as there have been Agatha Christie adaptations, there have been pastiches and parodies that take some of the best-known elements of her stories and rework them for either humorous purposes or as an outright homage (whether credited or not). To list all such examples would be an impossible task, but the twenty-first century has seen a continuance of this tradition as some of the biggest names in film and television continue to present their own take on Christie's work.

And Then There Were None has long been one of the most frequently homaged Christie stories, having been the apparent inspiration for episodes of television series including *The Avengers* (ITV, 1961–69) and *Doctor Who* (BBC, 1963–) as well as such films as the 2003 thriller *Identity* (d. James Mangold), the 2014 Arnold Schwarzenegger action film *Sabotage* (d. David Ayer) and most recently Quentin Tarantino's *The Hateful Eight* (2015). Meanwhile, on American television the story has continued to inspire writers and producers working on shows in several genres. In 2009, the CBS network broadcast the 13-part series *Harper's Island*, which concerns members of a wedding party on the eponymous island being murdered one by one—Christie's influence here is obvious. The following year saw Fox's animated comedy *Family Guy* put its own spin on the story, merging the mystery with the underrated 1985 comedy film classic *Clue* (d. Jonathan Lynn), which was ostensibly based on the board game Cluedo but owed more than a little debt to the Christie oeuvre. The *Family Guy* episode, called 'And Then There Were Fewer', combined the show's typical mix of wit and crass humour with a smartly plotted mystery that had a genuinely surprising denouement. That a single work of Agatha Christie's could inspire such a methodical parody from one of the world's biggest shows some 70 years after publication demonstrates how engrained in the public's consciousness the story has become. More recently, the creators of Fox's 2015 teen horror series *Scream Queens*, a show in which characters on a university campus are killed off one by one by an unknown person, have

© The Author(s) 2016
M. Aldridge, *Agatha Christie on Screen*,
DOI 10.1057/978-1-137-37292-5_17

explicitly acknowledged Christie's influence. Co-creator Ryan Murphy told *Entertainment Weekly* that 'It's always somebody you least suspect or expect. The killer is on a reign of terror. It's very much like *Ten Little Indians*. There's a real tune-in factor because it's like, who's going to be picked off this week? And also who is the killer?'[1]

However, one programme that has not yet made it to television screens was the frequently mooted, but seemingly ill-fated series following the adventures of a young Miss Marple, which was originally planned to have starred Hollywood actress Jennifer Garner. News of the deal was revealed in March 2011, with Disney attached as producer of the series, although within two days the company clarified that it was no longer part of the project, and that Garner's own production company was now at the helm.[2] The very principle of the young adventures of Miss Marple was anathema to many fans, who unsurprisingly strongly denounced the idea of the series, but even those involved with the project do not seem to have had high confidence that this particular project would have been a success. A pilot script was written, which purportedly was set in the present day and used the basic premise of *A Murder Is Announced* as its opening, before ricocheting off into a more standard action and adventure mould, complete with chase sequence. The original idea for the series had come from Hollywood producer Sean Bailey at some point prior to 2010, when he was recruited by Disney and brought the project with him—with Garner attached. Bailey's previous projects included *Gone Baby Gone* (d. Ben Affleck, 2007), while his first major work at Disney was on successful sequel *TRON Legacy* (d. Joseph Kosinski, 2010), and Garner is probably best known for her leading role in spy thriller series *Alias* (ABC, 2001–06). Although Bailey brought the project with him to Disney, it soon became clear that it did not sit easily with the company's aims. Mathew Prichard remembers that 'Disney came to the conclusion that any serious way of representing Agatha Christie was not going to be in their image either', with one particular sticking point: 'They even tried to say, could we find a way of doing a film where we don't actually show a murder, as that's not very Disney.'[3] When it became clear that the project was losing traction, it seems that sighs of relief were emitted all round. 'I think we're all very relieved that it's over, as I really think it was going nowhere,' Prichard says. 'And it took so long that Jennifer Garner was starting to realise that she was getting too old to play young Miss Marple!'[4] However, while the Garner project may be dead, the basic concept of a series following a younger Miss Marple has since re-emerged, with October 2015 seeing the announcement that CBS was developing its own series, simply called *Marple*.[5] Industry news website *Deadline* claimed that the premise would see a young Miss Marple 'inheriting her grandmother's bookstore and realizing that things in this small California town aren't what they seem, [and so she] begins working as a private investigator to get to the bottom of the town's mysteries'.[6] With the continued interest in mystery series such as *Elementary* (CBS, 2012–) and the demise of stalwart titles such as the *CSI* franchise, perhaps it is no surprise that the major networks are looking for another recognisable name in the mystery genre to shore up their schedules.

Back in the UK, in 2008 one of the biggest programmes on television made a foray into the world of Agatha Christie—quite literally. 'I love *Doctor Who*!' declares Mathew Prichard when asked about the episode 'The Unicorn and the Wasp', which saw the Doctor (David Tennant) and his friend Donna Noble (Catherine Tate) join Agatha Christie (Fenella Woolgar) for a tea party in 1926, which eventually turns to murder with a twist, resulting in a sci-fi explanation for exactly where Agatha Christie was for the days when she went missing that year. This fourth season of the revived *Doctor Who* saw the programme at the peak of its strength, with the highest average figures for its twenty-first-century incarnation, and this episode plays to many of its strengths. The script by Gareth Roberts (himself a Christie fan) brings together comedy, action and mystery in a wholly satisfying 45 minutes of drama, which plays with the generic expectations of Christie (including the relocation of the events to summer—as befits a typical tea party—rather than the less nostalgically sun-drenched December of her actual disappearance) while frequently homaging her works.[7]

Prichard recalls that Agatha Christie Ltd was not involved early in the production, but confesses that this might have been for the best. 'If someone had asked us before they did the *Doctor Who* thing, we probably would have said no,' he says. 'I think we would have been wrong and I think, unintentionally, we may have garnered a new young audience who came to Christie from *Doctor Who*.'[8] The episode, which Prichard describes as 'brilliant and affectionate', looks at Christie the person and, more particularly, the legacy of her works.[9] In the final scene, the Doctor shows Donna a reprint of *Death in the Clouds* from the year Five Billion—showing how Christie's work would never be forgotten. This scene was a replacement for the originally filmed, but less effective, framing sequence that showed Christie on her deathbed, visited by the Doctor and Donna for one last time. Seeing a representation of the writer at this stage in her life is an uncomfortable experience, especially as the performances in the scene are uncharacteristically weak for the series, and so the decision to replace it with a more upbeat and simpler moment was a good one. Despite the episode's success, it has not inspired the Christie estate to bring other depictions of the novelist to the screen. 'I retain a nervousness bordering on distaste for portrayals of my grandmother', says Prichard, and indeed on-screen representations of the writer are relatively rare, although 2004 had seen the BBC's unexceptional docu-drama *Agatha Christie: A Life in Pictures*, written and directed by Richard Curson Smith, starring Olivia Williams, Anna Massey and Bonnie Wright as the author at various stages of her life. Prichard adds:

> We have had at least two actually quite serious and potentially well financed offers to do an *Agatha Christie Investigates* type series, where she actually investigates her own crimes and that sort of thing. I have always refused, and as long as I'm around, we always will refuse, particularly as my grandmother was a very private person and almost all the proposals inevitably feature my father, step-father,

grandfather, and I do not feel I am entitled to trespass on her life to that extent. So if you see one of those appearing I hope it won't have anything to do with me.[10]

PARTNERS IN CRIME

As both of ITV's flagship Agatha Christie series, *Poirot* and *Marple*, reached the end of their runs in 2013, it was clear that the time was right for thoughts to turn to the next era of adaptations. In February 2014 it was announced that the 125th anniversary of Christie's birth, in 2015, would see the BBC become the new home for television adaptations of her work.[11] The first production to be produced and televised, *Partners in Crime*, would comprise adaptations of a pair of Tommy and Tuppence novels. There were two key factors that led to this being the next television project, the first of which was simply the fact that Tommy and Tuppence are reasonably well-known characters who had not starred in an English-language series of their own for more than three decades.[12] 'After *Poirot*, we had to go somewhere,' points out Mathew Prichard. 'I think it's just a continuation of our policy of trying to make as many of the stories visually available, worldwide, as we can, and Tommy and Tuppence is the obvious way to go.'[13] The second factor was that David Walliams had expressed interest in bringing the series to the screen, and in playing the part of Tommy. By this time Walliams had been part of a string of successful projects, perhaps most famously the *Little Britain* comedy series that he wrote and performed in with Matt Lucas. However, in more recent years Walliams has turned his hand to writing, including highly successful children's books, as well as to some dramatic roles, including a part in the first edition of ITV's *Marple* series, *The Body in the Library*. As a well-known name he could bring a certain amount of publicity and audience interest with him, especially as since 2012 he has appeared as a judge on light entertainment show *Britain's Got Talent* (ITV, 2007–), one of the country's top-rated television programmes—and so his attachment to the project as both leading man and executive producer could only help the programme make an impact.

Perhaps unsurprisingly given his background in comedy, the casting of Walliams was poorly received by many fans, but his presence did bring the required publicity given that news of the deal and forthcoming production was widely reported. It took a few more months for the name of the actress playing Tuppence to be announced, but when it was revealed that Jessica Raine was to take on the part, the news was received more warmly. Raine had found fame through the acclaimed and hugely popular BBC drama *Call the Midwife* (2012–), itself set in the 1950s, just as this adaptation would be. However, for these characters the choice of period in which to set the stories was always going to be a difficult one. Tommy and Tuppence had appeared in stories set anywhere from the 1920s to the 1970s, and so had no natural home, especially as—unlike most Christie characters—they aged considerably as the years passed, moving from young adults to pensioners. The two novels to be adapted for this series were to be *The Secret Adversary* and *N or*

M?—the first of these had been published in 1922 and was clearly set in the political environment following the First World War, while *N or M?* had been published in 1941 and had the early years of the Second World War as its background. Practical realities meant that the series needed to be set in one particular period and the stories altered to match, and the 1950s was decided on; had the series continued then later books would have been more easily adapted to this setting.

The first episode, broadcast on 26 July 2015, clearly demonstrates the series's strengths and weaknesses to the audience. This adaptation of *The Secret Adversary*, by playwright Zinnie Harris, has an uneven tone that struggles to structure clearly what was already one of Christie's more convoluted stories. When we first meet Tommy and Tuppence they are boarding a train having recently purchased a queen bee for Tommy's new beekeeping business; it is on this train that they meet Jane Finn, a woman whose involvement with the world of espionage is the backbone for this thriller. The characters of Tommy and Tuppence move between over-played caricatures and under-played down-beat realists. Their faltering marriage and relationship dynamic are addressed in scenes including Tuppence comedically struggling with their bags while Tommy carefully holds the small package containing the bee, through to more low-key and melancholy bedside scenes implicitly addressing the apparent lack of excitement in their marriage. The Tommy of this version is a rather pathetic, child-like stick-in-the-mud, having been invalided out of the war after being run over by a catering truck, and now showing no interest at all in the exciting adventure laid at his door. The audience may retain a hope that Tuppence will eventually leave her husband at home, where he can tend to his bees off screen, while we follow her rather more promising solo adventures, but an unwilling Tommy is continually roped in nevertheless.

While the series generally looks good, as one would expect from a BBC period drama, the performances falter as the actors struggle to work out from the script if they are part of a thriller or a comedy; few scenes satisfactorily balance these elements, despite the undoubted talents of the leads and supporting cast. Some of the action-orientated sequences work well, courtesy of Edward Hall's direction, but their relevance is not always clear and there is a certain lack of energy to the proceedings at times—not helped by the insipid opening titles and dull theme music. Meanwhile, the running theme of Tommy being particularly unhappy with undertaking the case soon becomes a bore. Walliams's performance is especially variable—perhaps surprisingly he is at his strongest in the more low-key scenes, but any more comedic sequences show an uneasy balance between playing the part as both a believable real person and a rather unbelievably wet and blinkered comedy character. The scripting does not help him—we may sense real melancholy within the character when reflecting on his life (and disappointments) to date, but when he is then cast as an obsessive bee keeper and (later) wig seller, Walliams's dramatic aspirations are undermined.

Over the course of the three episodes some of the basic elements of the story are retained, and it is pleasing that the series uses a racially diverse cast, meaning it eschews the clichéd all-white depictions of a nostalgic British past, but there are major changes in plotting and incident (too numerous to outline here). Even key characters such as bellboy Albert are radically changed: he is now a science teacher in a school with a background in bomb disposal. By the time the first story reaches its climax in the third episode it is difficult to follow the plot—and even tougher to care about it. Some of the press gave the first episode a cautiously optimistic review, while still highlighting flaws, and with an audience of over 8.5 m it seemed that the BBC had a new Agatha Christie hit on their hands. However, by episode three this audience was only a little over 6 m—still a good figure for drama, but a considerable drop. 'I'm not convinced by *Partners in Crime* just yet, but it has lots of potential', wrote Gerard O'Donovan in his three-star *Daily Telegraph* review of the opening instalment.[14] However, by the time O'Donovan reviewed the fourth episode, he was less confident: 'Initial hopes that the series of *Partners in Crime* might start firing on all cylinders after a disappointing opening three weeks ago drifted away in a cloud of expensively filmed confusion,' he wrote. 'The sparkle of Agatha Christie's original was smothered by an austere Fifties setting, a tension-free script, and direction and acting that couldn't decide whether to go for comedy or suspense, and delivered neither.'[15]

For Christie fans, the second half of the *Partners in Crime* series was the most keenly anticipated since it would be the first ever adaptation of the thriller *N or M?*, in which Tommy and Tuppence stay at a seaside boarding house and try to work out which of the residents are spies. The adaptation may retain the basic premise, but is plotted entirely differently—and when the writer (Claire Wilson, in her first credited production) dispenses with the most interesting and memorable elements, there is a problem. Particularly missed is a sequence that echoes the judgment of Solomon (the biblical story where King Solomon must discover who is the true mother of a baby), which provided the novel with one of its most dramatic and important moments. As with earlier episodes in the series the style is strong, but the substance is weak and there is no peripheral pleasure to be gained from the relationship between Tommy and Tuppence because each of them seems to be permanently irritated with the other.

By the time the series drew to a close at the end of August 2015, the ratings had nearly halved, to 4.46 m viewers, having reduced each week. A month later, it was revealed that there would not be a second series of the programme—alluding to an explanation of the stars' busy schedules. The fact that the series will now not continue means that the final Tommy and Tuppence novel, *Postern of Fate*, will remain among the handful of Christie novels not to have been adapted for the screen—so far.[16] While it is unfortunate that the series failed to capitalise on the strengths of the source material, the fact that it had initially drawn high ratings showed that the general public was far from bored with Agatha Christie on the screen—and the next BBC adaptation would prove to be a rather more successful take on the writer's work.

AND THEN THERE WERE NONE

By the time filming commenced on the BBC's adaptation of *And Then There Were None* in summer 2015, more than a quarter of a century had passed since the last official screen adaptation—and this time, the production would offer a distinctive and largely faithful retelling of Christie's original novel, rather than her stage play. In conjunction with Agatha Christie Productions, Mammoth Screen was the company chosen to bring the story to the screen, following on from its successful adaptation of *Poldark* for the BBC earlier in the year, and a well-received adaptation of the M.C. Beaton murder mystery *Agatha Raisin and the Quiche of Death* for Sky One in 2014. The project had been commissioned by Controller of BBC One Charlotte Moore and the BBC's Head of Drama Ben Stephenson, who had initially considered undertaking an entirely different type of adaptation. 'Originally, Ben Stephenson had this idea about doing *And Then There Were None* on three evenings, and doing it live,' reveals Mathew Prichard. 'Unfortunately, people at the BBC tried very hard, and eventually succeeded in persuading him that he was stark staring mad. Where are you going to do it? What happens if it rains? Common or garden things.'[17]

Sarah Phelps was the writer selected to bring the novel to the screen, having most recently adapted J.K. Rowling's *The Casual Vacancy* for BBC One in 2015, following a career that included landmark episodes of the popular long-running soap opera *EastEnders* (BBC, 1985–). Phelps was an excellent choice, having consistently shown exceptional insight into the human psyche, and a clear sense of how well-drawn characters can lead a drama and hold the audience's attention. She had also made it clear that her job was to adapt the novel rather than any other version, so this became the first officially licensed screen adaptation of the story to use the original ending, in which all ten lead characters die. Director of this adaptation, Craig Viveiros, had previously worked on critically acclaimed episodes of forensic drama *Silent Witness* (BBC, 1996–), while the cast included such names as Sam Neill, Anna Maxwell Martin, Miranda Richardson and Toby Stephenson. Charles Dance was cast as Justice Wargrave, while Aidan Turner—who had created a tabloid stir following a shirtless scene in *Poldark* earlier in the year—would once more remove some of his clothes for this adaptation, in the role of Lombard. The original intention had been to cast a transatlantic star name as the character of Vera, but the actress concerned dropped out of the production at the last minute, resulting in the rapid casting of Australian actress Maeve Dermody in the part, just two days prior to the read-through; Dermody would prove herself to be a more than suitable replacement.

It had always been the intention to broadcast the production around Christmas and the New Year, and in the end it was decided that the three-part adaptation would be shown on consecutive nights from 26 December 2015. The miniseries immediately asserts its modern credentials, with an atmospheric title sequence showing off the ten model figures in a manner reminiscent of the way in which the geography of the world of *Game of Thrones* (HBO, 2011–) is displayed in that series's opening titles. The story itself then opens with a dream-like beach scene with Vera, where few details of the event's significance are revealed; readers of the novel will understand the relevance of this, while it sets up a mystery for those unfamiliar with the original. By opening with a pre-view of her story, this also establishes Vera as a lead character—but not in the same mould as previous adaptations, nor Christie's own play. Here, there are no heroes, and although the audience may reasonably assume that she will be revealed to be innocent of the murder of which she is accused, the final truth exposes the fact that she has a past as dark as any of her fellow islanders. For the journey to the island we see several hints of character traits to come—espe-cially for the character of speeding driver Anthony Marston (Douglas Booth), whose obnoxiousness commands much of the attention for the initial episode, before he becomes the first victim. Interspersed with depictions of characters' journeys to the island are other moments that establish what will come, includ-ing an effective sequence where we see the creation of the record that will later accuse the ten characters of past misdemeanours, with a jobbing actor asking an unseen person about its eventual use (in, he believes, a play).

Once on Soldier Island the mood turns darker still, with a balance between claustrophobia and bleakness, all underscored by an effective, rumbling musi-cal score that emphasises the gravity of the events. There is no rose-tinted past in this Agatha Christie adaptation. These characters exist in a harsh, blood-soaked reality: dead bodies are gruesomely displayed, while heavy drinking, swearing and drug use all feature—a breath of fresh air when compared with so many sanitised and naïve images of the past so often seen on screen. These are people who live in the real world. However, while there are horrific elements, this is not a horror series—it is an honest thriller, with the characterisation and mystery foregrounded throughout. When the adaptation kills off its characters while moving towards its grim but inevitable resolution, so the atmosphere becomes increasingly electric as desperate characters try to find out the truth; occasionally this leads to moments of comedy, including the admission from a terrified Blore (Burn Gorman) that he has been constipated during the mur-derous sequence of events. Such is the stress on character and atmosphere that elements that have been key to previous adaptations are not given the same emphasis here, especially the rhyme itself, which is frequently alluded to but rarely clearly seen or heard. This change means that the precise structure of the murderous game played by the killer remains something of a surprise to the casual viewer.

By the end, the unpalatable truth about all characters and their pasts has been comprehensively revealed, with Vera killing Lombard (for real this time, unlike in the play and most previous screen adaptations) before she prepares to hang herself from a hook in the ceiling that viewers may have noticed early in proceedings; those familiar with the story's final outcome may have guessed its eventual function. It is in this situation, with a noose around her neck, that Vera then has her surprising, and lengthy, discussion with Justice Wargrave regarding the truth behind the events on the island. There is no escaping the fact that this sequence stretches credulity, as Vera teeters on the edge of a chair for several minutes while the conversation continues, but it is difficult to see how else it could be done—and the adaptation has gained so much goodwill from the audience by this point for its brutal and bleak tone that it can be forgiven this indulgence.

Prior to transmission the adaptation was heavily publicised as a modern take on the world's bestselling mystery novel, and if there had been any fears that its natural audience might have been dissuaded from watching due to the poor reception of later episodes of *Partners in Crime*, then they were soon proven to be unfounded. On the night of the first episode 6 m viewers tuned in, but even more impressively this increased to some 9.56 m once those watching recordings or on demand within 28 days were included, a very high figure for any programme. The next two episodes were similarly well received, with interest in the programme growing by the day, resulting in a popular and critical hit. In the *Independent*, Sarah Hughes wrote:

> Christmas viewing wouldn't be complete without a piece of quality drama amid the soaps, movies and comforting specials. This year the honours fell to Sarah Phelps' smart, sharp adaptation of Agatha Christie's greatest novel [...] Yet, ingenious as the ultimate puzzle was (and it is one of Christie's best), *And Then There Were None* owes its reputation to the fact that it's not so much a whodunit as an examination of guilt and the possibly (or lack thereof) of redemption. Phelps [...] clearly understood this, placing Dermody's grief-haunted Vera centre stage to great effect and asking which is worse: to pretend to feel guilt for something you did as a way of living with yourself or to cheerfully admit that you are a killer and feel no guilt at all?[18]

In the *Daily Telegraph*, Tim Martin's view was that 'this was a stonker: classily photographed in low light, moonlight and candlelight, and with strong performances from the weighty ensemble cast throughout, it made a strong case for Phelps to be put on seasonal murder duty at the BBC every year'.[19] Here, Martin unwittingly echoed thoughts elsewhere, since it would later be revealed that Phelps would script an adaptation of *Witness for the Prosecution* for Christmas 2016, another of Christie's best mysteries. This principle of an annual, big adaptation had underpinned the BBC deal, and one can only hope that it will continue to maintain the quality seen in *And Then There Were None*, which can stand proudly as one of the very best screen adaptations of Christie's work.

THE FUTURE

What, then, does the future hold for Agatha Christie screen adaptations? In October 2015 Mathew Prichard stood down as chairman of the board of Agatha Christie Ltd, with his son James Prichard taking over. At the time of writing, it is too early to tell whether this will result in a notable change in the way in which Agatha Christie stories are brought to film and television, but one hint may be in the release of the *Mr Quin* app for mobile phones in November 2015, in which users can follow a Christie story through videos and messages rather than traditional text. Such a foray into new media may demonstrate that Agatha Christie Ltd is keen not to appear old-fashioned or to stick rigidly to tried-and-tested modes of adaptation.

Nevertheless, work continues on traditional film and television adaptations, including a big-screen take on *And Then There Were None*, in development from 20th Century Fox, which will have to work miracles to better the BBC's recent version.[20] Fox has also announced that it will be bringing a new version of *Murder on the Orient Express* to cinema screens, with Sir Kenneth Branagh directing as well as starring as Poirot, following years of discussions with the film's producer, Sir Ridley Scott.[21] When first in development there was an expectation that this adaptation would feature a younger Poirot than would normally be the case, but Branagh's attachment to the project is a coup that has moved the film in a slightly different direction. Current indications are that all involved would be keen for the film to herald a new era of regular big-screen versions of Poirot stories, but intriguingly the further titles under consideration are not necessarily ones that may seem to be natural candidates for more traditional adaptations, indicating that this will be a fresh take on the character and canon. In addition to this, the relationship between Agatha Christie Ltd and the BBC has been further cemented by the August 2016 announcement that the Corporation will adapt another seven Agatha Christie adaptations. Titles include a long anticipated production of Death Comes as the End, which is set in Ancient Egypt, and one of Poirot's best mysteries, The ABC Murders.

Throughout the last 90 years of Agatha Christie adaptations there have been many variables but few constants when it comes to the manner in which her stories are brought to the screen. What we have seen is that Christie adaptations tend to move in phases, often dictated by fashions or interests of the time, since they also indicate broad shifts in viewing patterns and interests, as well as different expectations of fidelity to the source and the stories' innate appeal. Some eras saw the mystery element emphasised, others wowed the audience with sumptuous locations and star casts—and all have had their successes alongside their failures. For decades, Christie's stories were usually filleted for the material of most interest to those adapting it, dispensing with everything else. It was only in the 1970s, following the success of *Murder on the Orient Express*, that it was realised that Christie's original works were more than capable of working as pieces of screen entertainment without excessive tinkering, or reworking into entirely different types of films. That is not to say that additions by screenwriters and directors were always a negative—great productions such as Billy Wilder's *Witness for the Prosecution* have shown that sympathetic handling of the original story, combined with the strengths of a screenwriter and director, can result in an adaptation that rivals the original. There is no strict formula that will guarantee a good Agatha Christie adaptation, but there is one golden rule—do not under-estimate the skill that underpins her stories. Agatha Christie will outwit any reader who thinks they can predict her solutions, and any producer who thinks they can easily replicate or even improve on her carefully crafted mysteries; they have stood the test of time for good reason.

NOTES

1. *Entertainment Weekly*, '*Scream Queens:* First Look,' 23 April 2015, accessed 21 November 2015, http://www.ew.com/article/2015/04/23/scream-queens-first-look.
2. *Deadline*, 'Disney Deal to Remake Miss Marple Not Closed,' 30 March 2011, accessed 15 August 2014 http://deadline.com/2011/03/disney-deal-to-remake-miss-maple-has-not-closed-says-agatha-christie-estate-118631/.
3. Interview with the author, August 2013.
4. Interview with the author, August 2015.
5. And so duplicating the name used for ITV's Miss Marple series.
6. *Deadline*, 'Young Miss Marple Series from MI-5 Creator in Works at CBS,' 6 October 2015, accessed 6 October 2015, http://deadline.com/2015/10/young-miss-marple-series-cbs-david-wolstencroft-1201568396/.
7. Indeed, despite being the seventh episode of the season, it was filmed first in order to catch the summer weather.
8. Interview with the author, August 2014.
9. Interview with the author, August 2014.
10. Interview with the author, August 2014.
11. *BBC Media Centre*, 'BBC One to Become New Home of Agatha Christie in UK,' 28 February 2014, accessed 1 September 2014 http://www.bbc.co.uk/mediacentre/latestnews/2014/agatha-christie.
12. That is not to say they had been entirely absent from the screens—with versions of the characters having appeared in both ITV's *Marple* series and in French film adaptations.
13. Interview with the author, August 2015.
14. *Daily Telegraph*, 'Jessica Raine and David Walliams in *Partners in Crime*: "watchable",' 27 July 2015, accessed 27 July 2015, http://www.telegraph.co.uk/culture/tvandradio/tv-and-radio-reviews/11761691/Partners-in-Crime-episode-1-review.html.
15. *Daily Telegraph*, '*Partners in Crime, N or M?*, part one: "tension free",' 16 August 2015, accessed 16 August 2015, http://www.telegraph.co.uk/culture/tvandradio/tv-and-radio-reviews/11803884/Partners-in-Crime-N-or-M-part-one-review.html.
16. Although given its generally poor critical reception, it is probably only completists clamouring for its adaptation.
17. Interview with the author, August 2014.

18. *The Independent*, 'Not so much a whodunit as an examination of guilt,' 28 December 2015, accessed 2 January 2016, http://www.independent.co.uk/arts-entertainment/tv/reviews/and-then-there-were-none-bbc1-tv-review-not-so-much-a-whodunit-as-an-examination-of-guilt-a6788641.html.

19. *Daily Telegraph*, '*And Then There Were None*, episode three, review: "a class act",' 28 December 2015, accessed 28 December 2015, http://www.telegraph.co.uk/culture/tvandradio/tv-and-radio-reviews/12071655/And-Then-There-Were-None-episode-three-review.html.

20. *The Wrap*, '*And Then There Were None* Movie: Who Should Star in Agatha Christie's Mystery Masterpiece?,' 25 September 2015, accessed 2 January 2016, http://www.thewrap.com/and-then-there-were-none-movie-who-should-star-in-agatha-christies-mystery-masterpiece/.

21. Official Agatha Christie website, 'Branagh to Direct and Star in *Murder on the Orient Express*,' 21 November 2015, accessed 23 November 2015, http://www.agathachristie.com/news/2015/kenneth-branagh-to-direct-and-star-in-murder-on-the-orient-express.

BIBLIOGRAPHY[1]

Adams, Tom, and John Curran. 2015. *The Art of Agatha Christie and Beyond*. London: HarperCollins.

Bargainnier, Earl F. 1980. *The Gentle Art of Murder*. Ohio: Bowling Green University Popular Press.

Barnard, Robert. 1980. *A Talent to Deceive*. New York: Dodd Mead.

Billips, Connie, and Arthur Pierce. 1995. *Lux Presents Hollywood*. London: McFarland and Company.

Chibnall, Steve. 2007. *Quota Quickies: The Birth of the British 'B' Film*. London: BFI.

Cooke, Lez. 2003. *British Television Drama: A History*. London: BFI.

Curran, John. 2010. *Agatha Christie's Secret Notebooks*. London: HarperCollins.

———. 2012. *Agatha Christie's Murder in the Making*. London: HarperCollins.

Edwards, Martin. 2015. *The Golden Age of Murder*. London: HarperCollins.

Flanders, Judith. 2011. *The Invention of Murder*. London: HarperPress.

Green, Julius. 2015. *Curtain Up: Agatha Christie: A Life in Theatre*. London: HarperCollins.

Gregg, Hubert. 1980. *Agatha Christie and All That Mousetrap*. London: W. Kimber.

Haining, Peter. 1990. *Agatha Christie: Murder in Four Acts*. London: Virgin Books.

———. 1995. *Agatha Christie's Poirot: A Celebration of the Great Detective*. London: Boxtree.

Harkup, Kathryn. 2015. *A is for Arsenic: The Poisons of Agatha Christie*. London: Bloomsbury Sigma.

Keating, H.R.F., ed. 1977. *Agatha Christie: First Lady of Crime*. London: Weidenfeld and Nicolson.

Low, Rachael. 1997a. *The History of the British Film: 1918–1929*. London: Routledge.

———. 1997b. *The History of the British Film: 1929–1939*. London: Routledge.

Lumet, Sidney. 1995. *Making Movies*. London: Bloomsbury.

Macaskill, Hilary. 2009. *Agatha Christie at Home*. London: Frances Lincoln.

Maida, Patricia D., and Nicholas B. Spornick. 1982. *Murder She Wrote: A Study of Agatha Christie's Detective Fiction*. Ohio: Bowling Green State University Press.

Makinen, Merja. 2006. *Agatha Christie: Investigating Femininity*. Basingstoke: Palgrave Macmillan.

© The Author(s) 2016
M. Aldridge, *Agatha Christie on Screen*,
DOI 10.1057/978-1-137-37292-5

Mallowan, Max. 2010. *Mallowan's Memoirs: Agatha and the Archaeologist*. London: HarperCollins.

McNally, Karen. 2011. *Billy Wilder: Movie Maker*. London: McFarland.

Merriman, Andy. 2010. *Margaret Rutherford: Dreadnought with Good Manners*. London: Aurum Press.

Morgan, Janet. 1997. *Agatha Christie: A Biography*. London: HarperCollins.

Nickerson, Catherine Ross. 2010. *The Cambridge Companion to American Crime Fiction*. Cambridge: Cambridge University Press.

Osborne, Charles. 1999. *The Life and Crimes of Agatha Christie*. London: HarperCollins.

Palmer, Scott. 1993. *The Films of Agatha Christie*. London: Batsford.

Prichard, Mathew, ed. 2013. *Agatha Christie: The Grand Tour*. London: HarperCollins.

Priestman, Martin, ed. 2003. *The Cambridge Companion to Crime Fiction*. Cambridge: Cambridge University Press.

Richards, Jeffrey. 1998. *The Unknown 1930s: An Alternative History of the British Cinema, 1929–1939*. London: I.B. Tauris.

Saunders, Peter. 1972. *The Mousetrap Man*. London: HarperCollins.

Shayne, Alan, and Norman Sunshine. 2011. *Double Life: A Love Story from Broadway to Hollywood*. New York: Magnus.

Simmons, Dawn Langley. 1985. *Margaret Rutherford: A Blithe Spirit*. London: Sphere.

Smith, Anthony, ed. 1998. *Television: An International History*. Oxford: Oxford University Press.

Street, Sarah. 2008. Heritage Crime: The Case of Agatha Christie. In *Seventies British Cinema*, ed. Robert Shail. Basingstoke: Palgrave Macmillan.

Suchet, David, and Geoffrey Wansell. 2013. *Poirot and Me*. London: Headline.

Symons, Julian. 1974. *Bloody Murder*. London: Penguin.

———. 1981. *Tom Adams' Agatha Christie Cover Story*. London: Paper Tiger.

Terrace, Vincent. 2013. *Encyclopedia of Television Pilots*. Jefferson: McFarland.

Thompson, Laura. 2008. *Agatha Christie: An English Mystery*. London: Headline.

Thumim, Janet, ed. 2002. *Small Screen, Big Ideas: Television in the 1950s*. London: I.B. Tauris.

Toye, Randall. 1980. *The Agatha Christie Who's Who*. London: Frederick Muller.

Vahimagi, Tise. 1996. *British Television*. Oxford: Oxford University Press.

Wood, Ean. 2002. *Marlene Dietrich: A Biography*. London: Sanctuary.

Worsley, Lucy. 2013. *A Very British Murder*. London: BBC.

York, R.A. 2007. *Agatha Christie: Power and Illusion*. Basingstoke: Palgrave Macmillan.

Notes

1. Readers should take it for granted that all of Agatha Christie's published work were read (and, in most cases, re-read) during the course of writing this book. For reasons of brevity Christie's works are not included here.
2. This bibliography lists some of the most useful titles consulted during the long gestation period of this book.

INDEX

Note: Page numbers followed by "n" refer notes.

© The Author(s) 2016
M. Aldridge, *Agatha Christie on Screen*,
DOI 10.1057/978-1-137-37292-5

CPI Antony Rowe
Eastbourne, UK
May 31, 2019

The statistics in Figure 1.1 refer to officially recorded cases rather than the full extent of maltreatment within the population. They may therefore not present an accurate picture of the absolute or relative incidence of maltreatment across different categories and age groups.

An important alternative source of evidence on this matter is a prevalence study of maltreatment and victimization recently conducted in the UK by the NSPCC (Radford *et al.* 2011). The study interviewed parents and guardians of children under the age of 11, young people aged 11 to 17 and their parents or guardians, and young adults aged 18 to 24 (in order to ask them retrospectively about their childhoods). It gathered data on lifetime occurrence, and occurrence in the past year, of maltreatment. Basing measurement on the official definitions in England (see Chapter 2), neglect was the most prevalent form of maltreatment within the family. Lifetime prevalence of neglect was estimated at 5 per cent for the under-11 age group and at 13 per cent for the 11- to 17-year-old age group. Sixteen per cent of the 18- to 24-year-olds also said they had experienced at least one type of neglect during childhood. These figures suggest a substantial prevalence of neglect experienced specifically between the ages of 11 and 17. The percentages of those affected by physical neglect in childhood were much lower. Overall 1 in 125 (0.8%) under 18-year-olds had experienced this in childhood and 0.2 per cent in the past year. The study repeated the same questions with 18 to 24 year olds about absence of parental care and supervision that were asked in the 1998 survey (Cawson *et al.* 2000) and found that the likely prevalence of parental neglect had remained stable over the intervening period.

The patterns described for the UK have also been found in other comparable countries. Neglect is the most common form of officially recorded maltreatment in the US (US Department of Health and Human Services *et al.* 2010) and in Canada (Public Health Agency of Canada 2010). A self-report study of a sample of just under 1500 young people aged 13 to 18 in the US (Arata *et al.* 2007) also found that neglect was the second most common form of (lifetime) maltreatment after emotional abuse.

All in all, then, there is substantial evidence indicating that neglect is a prevalent form of maltreatment among young people of secondary school age.

Current knowledge about the neglect of young people

Despite the statistical evidence outlined earlier, very little has been written about the neglect of young people in the UK, and the issue is also sparsely represented in international literature. A comprehensive search of English language literature covering the period from 1997 to 2006 inclusive, and a recent update of this search, yielded few references specifically focused on this topic. The reasons for this gap in the literature appear to be twofold.

First, despite its prevalence, the issue of child neglect has traditionally received relatively little research attention in comparison to other forms of maltreatment. This 'neglect of neglect' has been a well-recognized tendency in international literature reviews (Sullivan 2000; Wolock and Horowitz 1984) and there is a need for further exploration of the definition, nature and contextual factors related to neglect.

Second, the maltreatment of older young people has received relatively little specific attention within the child maltreatment literature. Literature on maltreatment in the UK has tended to treat all children up to the age of 18 as a homogeneous group. A review undertaken over a decade ago by two of the authors highlighted a dearth of literature on this topic (Rees and Stein 1999). A more recently updated search indicated little change in this situation (Rees *et al.* 2010). The issue has received more attention in other countries, particularly in the US and Canada, and this literature suggests that maltreatment of older young people should be viewed somewhat separately from that of children, owing to particular differences. These include differences in definitional issues; patterns of maltreatment for different age groups; consequences of maltreatment; and the kinds of interventions needed.

Despite this lack of literature, the neglect of older young people is a potentially distinctive and significant issue.

There is a lack of clarity and agreement about what exactly constitutes neglect, but definitions of neglect often focus on it as an act of omission rather than commission. It is clear that acts of omission on the part of parents and carers can be applied equally to adolescents and to younger children. As with other forms of maltreatment, some literature has focused on extreme cases of neglect experienced by very young children. However, as discussed in Chapter 2, there is a risk of a self-fulfilling pattern, based on attitudes and definitions as to what constitutes neglect, that may potentially exclude the experiences of adolescents.

The research on the neglect of children and young people in general has highlighted significant negative associations with well-being and outcomes for children. While we know little about the specific consequences of the neglect of older young people, there are reasons to be concerned about this issue. A longitudinal study in the US (Smith, Ireland and Thornberry 2005; Thornberry, Ireland and Smith 2001; Thornberry *et al.* 2010), reviewed in more detail later in the book, suggests that the repercussions of neglect during the teenage years may be at least as serious as neglect earlier in childhood.

Further to this, recent analysis of serious case reviews in England (Brandon *et al.* 2009) has shown that around a fifth of such cases related to children and young people aged 11 to 18 years at the time of the events that triggered the review, and that a history of neglect was identified in many of these cases (see Chapter 4 for further details).

Recent policy developments in child protection

Historically, policy developments in child protection have been shaped by many influences including inquiries into the deaths of individual children, public outrage, media scrutiny, the opinions of politicians, experts and senior staff, and research evidence (see Frost and Parton (2009) for an overview).

The recent phase of policy development on child protection in England can be traced back to the publication of a series of research studies on the workings of the child protection system in the early 1990s – summarized in the publication *Child Protection: Messages from Research* (Department of Health 1995). One of the key messages from these studies was that child protection practice at that time was too focused on investigations of immediate risk rather than the longer term context in which maltreatment might occur. The publication also drew attention to the negative impact of family environments with low warmth and high criticism – or, as relevant to our concerns, 'neglectful parenting' (see Chapter 2).

This set of studies led to what became known as the 'refocusing debate', which emphasized the importance of support to families with children in need, assessment and early intervention. As part of the response to this debate, in 2000 the Government published the *Framework for the Assessment of Children in Need* Department of Health, Department for Education and Employment and Home Office (2000), which is discussed in further detail later.

The Victoria Climbié Inquiry Report (Laming 2003) and the Government's Green Paper, *Every Child Matters* (HM Government 2004) provided the catalyst for further change, both in the organization and delivery of children's services and in the location of 'child protection' within a wider safeguarding agenda. The Climbié Report identified many issues that had been raised by earlier inquiries and research studies. These included poor inter-agency working and a failure to follow agreed protocols; a failure to 'share information', so nobody had an overall picture of the child and family; a failure to connect 'family support' with child protection; and insufficient awareness of child protection issues.

In *Every Child Matters*, the Government's aim for all children and young people, whatever their background or circumstances, was for them to have the support they needed to improve outcomes in five key areas: being healthy; staying safe; enjoying and achieving; making a positive contribution; and achieving economic well-being. It also set out four key themes: increasing the focus on supporting parents and carers; early intervention and effective protection; strengthening accountability and integration of services at all levels; and workforce reform.

Every Child Matters resulted in a major consultation exercise and review of children's services. This led to the publication of *Every Child Matters: The Next Steps* and the Children Act 2004, the latter strengthening the legal framework to protect and safeguard children from harm. This included setting out the *Every Child Matters* outcomes in statute; a requirement that local authorities combine their children's social care and education functions under a new Director of Children's Services; the replacement of Area Child Protection Committees by Local Safeguarding Children Boards (LSCBs) with membership drawn from all the agencies involved in improving outcomes for children and young people; the creation of Children's Trusts under the duty to co-operate; and the duty on all agencies to make arrangements to safeguard and promote the welfare of children.

In April 2006 the Government published its statutory guidance *Working Together to Safeguard Children* (HM Government 2006). This built upon the foundations and principles of its 1999 'working together' guidance, but was updated to take into account further developments including the 2003 Laming Report into the death of Victoria Climbié; joint inspectors reports; changes introduced by the *Every Child Matters: Change for Children* Programme; and the introduction of the Children Act 2004.

In December 2007, the then Department for Children, Schools and Families (DCSF) published *The Children's Plan: Building Brighter Futures*, setting out goals for improving the well-being and health, safety, education and careers of children and young people, by 2020. Also linked to the *Children's Plan* was the issuing of statutory guidance on Children's Trusts entrusted with responsibility for delivering the 'high ambitions' of *The Children's Plan* in placing the family 'at the centre of excellent integrated services' (see Chapter 6).

The Children's Plan included a commitment to a *Staying Safe: Action Plan*. Following a consultation document this was published by the DCSF in 2008, covering the full span of the *Every Child Matters* 'staying safe' outcome, with proposals organized to cover *universal* (all children and young people), *targeted* (vulnerable groups of children and young people) and *responsive* (children and young people who have been harmed) safety issues.

In November 2008, in response to the death of baby Peter Connelly, Lord Laming was asked by the Secretary of State for Children, Schools and Families to 'provide an urgent report of the progress being made across the country to implement effective arrangements for safeguarding children', (HM Government 2010, p.30). In March 2009, he published *The Protection of Children in England: A Progress Report*. His report concluded that 'robust legislative, structural and policy foundations are in place' but made 58 recommendations 'to ensure that services are as effective as possible at working together to achieve positive outcomes for children' (HM Government 2010, p.30).

Statutory guidance on safeguarding children

The Government accepted all Lord Laming's recommendations and in May 2009 published *The Protection of Children in England: Action Plan* detailing its response. In March 2010 the Government published *Working Together to Safeguard Children*, which revised and updated their 2006 guidance and addressed 23 of Lord Laming's recommendations (HM Government 2010).

The Government's statutory guidance for all agencies and professionals describes 'safeguarding and promoting the welfare of children' as:

- protecting children from maltreatment
- preventing impairment of children's health or development
- ensuring that children are growing up in circumstances consistent with the provision of safe and effective care, and
- undertaking that role so as to enable these children to have optimum life chances and to enter adulthood successfully. (HM Government 2010, p.34)

Working Together also details how 'child protection' relates to 'safeguarding':

> Child protection is a part of safeguarding and promoting welfare. This refers to the activity which is undertaken to protect specific children who are suffering or are at risk of suffering significant harm. (HM Government 2010, p.35)

The developments detailed have led to the current framework for organizations that work with children and young people. This consists of three connected levels: universal outcomes for all children; safeguarding children, including prevention and promotion; and child protection, focusing on the children most 'at risk' of harm. The latter group includes maltreated children and young people. They may:

> be abused in the family or in an institution or a community setting, by those known to them or, more rarely, by a stranger for example via the internet. They might be abused by an adult or adults, or another child or children. (HM Government 2010, p.38).

Local authorities have the responsibility for 'safeguarding and promoting the welfare of children, working in partnership with other public organizations, the voluntary sector, children and young people, parents and carers and the wider community' (HM Government 2010, p.9). As well as children's services, 'other functions of local authorities that make an important contribution to safeguarding are housing, sport, culture and leisure services, and youth service' (HM Government 2010, p.9). The implications for these and other statutory and third sector services intervening in the lives of neglected young people are explored in Chapter 7.

Children and young people who generate professional concern are regarded as having 'additional needs' – such as targeted or specialist support to progress towards the five universal outcomes. The Common Assessment Framework (CAF) is used to identify these additional needs and the involvement of agencies. If there are concerns about children's welfare then the processes outlined in *Working Together* are followed: assessment (by completing the CAF on children in need and their families); planning; intervention; and reviewing (see Chapter 7).

The main responses to individual children and young people when there are concerns about their welfare, as outlined in *Working Together*, include referral to a statutory organization; undertaking an initial assessment; taking urgent action, if necessary, to protect a child from harm; holding a strategy discussion or, where appropriate, convening a child protection conference; undertaking a core assessment as part of the section 47 enquiries to decide whether a child is at continuing risk of significant harm and, if so, putting a child protection plan in place; implementing the plan; and reviewing it at intervals.

In light of the Laming recommendations, the importance of being 'child centred' is emphasized. The child's 'welfare should be kept sharply in focus in all work with the child and family. The significance of seeing and observing the child cannot be overstated' (HM Government 2010, p.133).

In *Working Together* the importance of 'child development' is stressed: 'Each stage from infancy through middle years to adolescence, lays the foundation for more complex development…planned action should also be timely and appropriate for the child's age and stage of development' (HM Government 2010, p.134).

In Chapter 9 of *Working Together*, 'Lessons from research', 'the children's age' is recognized as important in considering the impact of neglect. This makes reference to the project upon which this book is based: *Neglected Adolescents: Literature Review Research Brief* (Stein *et al.* 2009). In the same chapter research evidence on the consequences of social exclusion, domestic violence and the mental illness of a parent or carer are explored in relation to 'four stages of childhood: the unborn child; babies and infants (under 5 years), middle childhood (5–10 years) and adolescence (11–16 plus years)'.

More focus on the protective needs of adolescents has also been prompted by the analysis of serious case reviews in England – reviews usually held in cases of death or serious injury to a child or young person – that has shown that over a fifth of these cases involve young people aged 11 and over (Brandon *et al.* 2009). Greater recognition of the needs of young people over 11 years of age is to be welcomed, especially in the wider context of the debates about child abuse and the child protection system that have, in the main, taken place in response to inquiries into the tragic deaths of younger children.

Munro review of child protection

The Coalition Government, which came to power in May 2010, set up the Munro review of child protection in response to a number of concerns raised by social workers and other staff involved in child protection work. These included the impact of bureaucratic processes, performance indicators and targets both on the professional judgement of social workers and the time they were able to spend in direct work with children, young people and their families; and the impact of the high media profile, including anger directed at social workers and other staff, on child protection practice.

The Review has adopted a 'systems approach' or a 'holistic approach to child protection' in identifying how the system can be improved and stay 'child-focused' (Munro, 2010). Its final report, published in May 2011, has made 15 recommendations which aim 'to reform the child protection system from being over-bureaucratised and concerned with compliance to one that keeps a focus on children' (Munro, 2011 p5). The main recommendations are applicable to children and young people of all ages. However of particular relevance to neglected adolescents, as discussed elsewhere in this book, is the importance attached to the views of young people, having time to carry out direct work with them, and intervening in their lives when problems first arise (Allen 2010).

The Review also identified adolescents as one of the groups it received evidence about, who 'were not receiving services adequately adapted to their needs' (p37) and noted that 'issues specific to adolescents and young people, such as self-harm, involvement with, or fear of gang related violence, and sexual exploitation require appropriate consideration and tailored interventions' (p37). At the time of writing the Coalition Government is considering the Review's recommendations.

An ecological framework

A key organizing concept that we have utilized at various points in the book is the ecological systems framework. This framework has its roots in Bronfenbrenner's ecological systems theory (Bronfenbrenner 1979). Bronfenbrenner conceptualized five different aspects of the environment or systems that affect children's development:

- The microsystem (the level closest to the child – e.g. parents and siblings).

- The mesosystem (the relationship between microsystems).

- The exosystem (people or places that the child may not connect with directly but which nevertheless have an effect, such as the local community).

- The macrosystem (more remote social and cultural factors).

- The chronosytem (the history of growth and development).

In the UK, ecological systems thinking informed the development of the *Framework for the Assessment of Children in Need and their Families* (Department of Health *et al.* 2000) (henceforth referred to as the 'Assessment Framework'), which describes the ecological approach as follows:

> An understanding of a child must be located within the context of the child's family (parents or caregivers and the wider family) and of the community and culture in which he or she is growing up. The significance of understanding the parent–child relationship has long been part of child welfare practice: less so the importance of the interface between environmental factors on parents' capacities to respond to their child's needs. (Department of Health *et al.* 2000, p.11)

The framework consists of three inter-related systems or domains, each being sub-divided into a number of dimensions:

1. Child's developmental needs.

2. Parenting capacity.

3. Family and environmental factors.

These are shown in Figure 1.2.

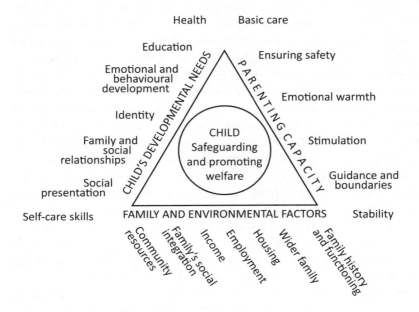

Figure 1.2: The Assessment Framework diagram
Source: HM Government (2006) *Working Together to Safeguard Children*, p.109.

The representation of the three systems as a triangle emphasizes the interplay between each system.

A key aspect both of Bronfenbrenner's theory and the Assessment Framework is a consideration of children's and young people's development. In thinking about the neglect of young people aged 11 to 17 years a developmental perspective helps to locate needs as they come to vary over time. It aids in thinking about how definitions of neglect may need to vary with age (see, for example, Scannapieco and Connell-Carrick 2005). Nevertheless, we recognize that there is a risk of conflating age and development and reaching normative conclusions that are not relevant to many children and young people.

We refer to the Assessment Framework at various points in the book and it is particularly helpful, for example, in thinking about the range of background and contextual factors that may be associated with the neglect of young people (see Chapter 3).

Scope and content of the book

The material in this book is drawn primarily from a project funded by the DCSF and the Department of Health (DoH) in England and undertaken jointly by the authors between 2007 and 2009. The project was one of a series of 11 studies commissioned as part of 'Safeguarding Children'. The project consisted of three components. First, a comprehensive search and review was undertaken of literature relevant to the neglect of young people (Stein *et al.* 2009). This component informed the development of the other two strands of the project – a series of focus groups with young people, and a series of multi-agency focus groups and consultations with professionals working with young people. These led to the publication of a young person's guide to neglect[3] and a guide for professionals working in multi-disciplinary teams (Hicks and Stein 2010). The book makes use of each of these aspects of the research overall as well as referring to related literature, some of which has been published since the initial searches were undertaken.

The book explores the issues raised by each of the components of the original research. A broad outline of the book is as follows.

First, we consider definitional issues regarding neglect and explore how these might vary according to the age of the child or young person concerned. Inevitably, such definitions are influenced by social and cultural factors, and these factors are likely to be particularly strong influences during a young person's developmental journey to adulthood. Chapter 2 therefore begins with a general overview of approaches to defining neglect. It draws on the literature on child neglect, and also related literature on child development and on parenting. It also considers policy documents that describe or define neglect.

Chapter 3 focuses on the causes of the neglect of young people. The chapter summarizes evidence about contextual factors from the child neglect literature and then goes on to consider the part that these may play in terms of the neglect of young people in particular. The discussion takes an ecological approach and is structured around the dimensions of the Assessment Framework. The chapter also consider issues of neglect in relation to some specific sub-groups of young people.

Chapter 4 discusses the potential consequences of the neglect of young people in terms of the impact on well-being and outcomes. The chapter includes the wide-ranging body of evidence that suggests links between neglect, or neglectful parenting, and negative outcomes for teenagers.

---

3   See www.nspcc.org.uk/neglectmatters

Chapter 5 examines key questions raised by earlier chapters from the perspectives of young people. Consideration is given to young people's definitions of neglect, their awareness of causes and consequences of neglect, how professionals might notice signs of neglect and their knowledge of whom and where to go for help.

Chapter 6 addresses the question 'Whose business is the neglect of young people?'. Young people have a variety of needs arising from neglect, which indicates that more than one agency is likely to be involved in helping to address these needs. The chapter investigates the context from which multi-agency work in England is delivered and considers what this implies for work with adolescents who are neglected. Drawing on our empirical research with professionals from multi-agency backgrounds, the chapter details some of the specific challenges encountered in practice. In particular, the chapter explores some of the issues involved in shifts in perceptions of where responsibility lies for young people, engagement, definitions and thresholds. The chapter highlights the implications for developing multi-agency work with adolescents who are neglected.

We then move on in Chapter 7 to a discussion of possible interventions to tackle the neglect of young people. Literature that focuses on interventions for adolescent neglect is sparse. This is not surprising in that neglect may be one of a whole range of issues being tackled by interventions rather than the specific focus. However, consideration of a broader range of child care literature points to a model of intervention using the concepts of primary, secondary and tertiary intervention, each of which raises issues for discussion in different practice-based settings. Each of these elements are discussed in this chapter under the following headings – primary prevention; secondary prevention; tertiary prevention; the implications of child neglect interventions.

The concluding chapter provides a discussion of the key themes raised throughout this book, and draws out the implications for future practice, policy and research in relation to the neglect of young people aged 11 to 17 years.

Finally, it should be noted that the scope of the book relates to neglect experienced by young people within the family. There is a range of additional issues to consider in relation to the concept of neglect for young people living in out-of-home settings such as residential care. Specific discussion of this topic is beyond the scope of this book but much of the material presented will be equally applicable to, or transferable to, young people not currently living with their family of origin.

2

Defining the Neglect of Young People

> Neglect is when parents ignore you…when parents leave you and you get hurt…if you are bullied at school and you have no one to turn to… Neglect is scary. (Young person)

> When is it that an adolescent is just not taking care of themselves because they can't be bothered, or when is it because they have been neglected and not been taught those basic skills at an early age? (Professional)

> Neglect is such a large, loosely defined category that almost anything that has been written about child development has implications for our understanding of neglect. (Stone 1998)

This chapter focuses on definitional issues by clarifying what the neglect of young people involves. We discuss some of the key debates and lines of thought in defining child neglect in general and consider the particular relevance of these debates to the neglect of young people aged 11 to 17. We also discuss some of the assessment tools that have been developed in relation to neglect, and their potential relevance.

In England, the official description – used by all professionals responsible for children's welfare and including children up to the age of 18 years – is set out in the Government's statutory guidance *Working Together to Safeguard Children*:

> Neglect is the persistent failure to meet a child's basic and/or psychological needs, likely to result in the serious impairment of the child's health or development. Neglect may occur during pregnancy as a result of maternal substance abuse. Once a child is born, neglect may involve a parent or carer failing to:

- provide adequate food, clothing and shelter (including exclusion from home or abandonment)
- protect a child from physical and emotional harm or danger
- ensure adequate supervision (including the use of inadequate caregivers)
- ensure access to appropriate medical care or treatment.

It may also include neglect of, or unresponsiveness to, a child's basic emotional needs. (HM Government 2010, p.39)

A key concept within the guidance is that of 'significant harm' as a basis for the state intervening in family life to safeguard the welfare of children. The guidance acknowledges that 'There are no absolute criteria on which to rely when judging what constitutes significant harm' (HM Government 2010, p.36). However, it clarifies that 'Neglect, as well as abuse, can result in a child suffering significant harm to the extent that urgent protective action is necessary' (HM Government 2010, p.151) and goes on to provide examples of potential consequences:

> Severe neglect of young children has adverse effects on children's ability to form attachments and is associated with major impairment of growth and intellectual development. Persistent neglect can lead to serious impairment of health and development, and long-term difficulties with social functioning, relationships and educational progress. Neglected children may also experience low self-esteem, feelings of being unloved and isolated. Neglect can also result, in extreme cases, in death. The impact of neglect varies depending on how long children have been neglected, the children's age, and the multiplicity of neglectful behaviours children have been experiencing. (HM Government 2010, pp.260–261)

This description highlights some of the key debates regarding definitions of neglect – including the focus on children's needs, the parental role in neglect and issues of persistence of neglect that we consider further in this chapter. It also highlights the necessity of an age-sensitive consideration of neglect, which is a key overarching consideration for this book as a whole.

The need for age-specific definitions

It seems clear that some detailed aspects of neglect – such as the definition of what constitutes supervisory neglect – must vary with the age of the young person concerned. Most people would probably agree that allowing a 1-year-old to leave the house without supervision would be neglectful, whereas to allow a 15-year-old to do so would, in most circumstances, not be – a point made by Cicchetti and Toth:

> ... a caregiver must be able to adapt to the changing needs of a child. Failure to do so could constitute an act of maltreatment, depending on the development level of the child. For example, whereas close monitoring and physical proximity are expected with a new-born, a similar parenting style with an adolescent would be inappropriate and, taken to extremes, emotionally abusive. (Cicchetti and Toth 1995, p.543)

Thus one theme in this chapter is to try to ascertain whether the definitions given have included the issue of age-specific aspects of neglect.

This is one of the areas where a developmental perspective has value. In particular, it is helpful to think about the nature of the developmental issues and tasks that, on average, a young person will be faced with at different ages. This issue is relevant in that it helps to clarify the nature of the support that adolescents might need from parents and carers and the ways in which this might differ from the support needed by younger children. During the period from 11 to 17 years of age, young people typically go through transitions involving changes that are physical, cognitive, social and psychodynamic (Scannapieco and Connell-Carrick 2005). Scannapieco and Connell-Carrick observe that one of the 'primary tasks of adolescence is the discovery of self'. They argue that neglect is still a highly relevant concept for this age group and that failure to support young people through these transitions can have a wide range of negative impacts in terms of cognitive-behavioural, socio-emotional and physical outcomes. We review some of the evidence on the outcomes of the neglect of young people in Chapter 4.

So a developmental perspective may be helpful in thinking about definitions of the neglect of young people. However, as already noted in the introductory chapter, some caution is needed in making generalizations about development at specific ages, because all children and young people develop at different rates. An over-emphasis on 'typical' development stages may in practice lead to failure to identify the specific needs of individual young people.

Our research review revealed that the literature that informs definitions of neglect comes from a wide range of sources, such as child neglect, adolescent maltreatment, parenting and parenting styles, as well as more general issues and problems faced by teenagers. Additionally, those looking to the literature to assist in informing practice will find that research that focuses on neglect seldom uses definitions that are consistent across research studies.[1]

In the next section we discuss some of the key definitional themes identified in the literature and the specific relevance of these themes to definitions of neglect of young people aged 11 to 17.

Key themes

Neglect as an 'act of omission'

There is considerable agreement in the research literature that neglect may be defined as an act of omission rather than an act of commission as for other forms of maltreatment. However, it may be difficult in practice to distinguish between an act of commission and an act of omission purely on the basis of a description of the act itself, devoid of context. For example, the case of parents ignoring or not talking to their child may be viewed differently depending on whether this is the result of illness or stress (act of omission) or a deliberate strategy (act of commission).

There are some drawbacks to restricting the definition of neglect to acts of omission in relation to adolescents. Around 2 per cent of young people experience being forced to leave home by their parents or carers before the age of 16 (Rees and Lee 2005). Young people in this situation have limited alternative living and survival options available to them and therefore face significant risks while away from home. It can be argued that this is both an act of commission and an act of neglect on the part of parents.

Neglect as a persistent state

There has also been considerable debate regarding whether neglect refers to specific instances and/or whether it is more relevant to think of neglect as an ongoing state. It has been argued (Glaser 2002) that while physical abuse and sexual abuse can be regarded as events, neglect characterizes 'the relationship between the carers and the child'.

This is a complex topic and one that poses considerable risks in terms of professional responses or the lack of these. On the one hand, De Panfilis (2006a) cites evidence in the US in the 1990s that suggested that cases of persistent neglect were not being picked up by child protection systems because no individual incident met the criteria for intervention. On the

---

1   A review of methodologies for defining neglect drawn from the journal *Child Abuse & Neglect* over a period of five years (Zuravin 1999) showed only two studies – out of only 25 that reported on child neglect – that had used the 'same operational definition'. Only one study had used measures that were tested for reliability and validity.

other hand, in a recent review of professional responses to child neglect in the UK, Gardner (2008) notes that the emphasis on persistent neglect also poses risks of inaction because the implication is that 'short of a potentially criminal incident, neglect does not constitute significant harm unless and until it endures over time'. Recent research on child protection work with young people in England (Rees *et al.* 2010) also suggests that professionals find instances of possible neglect and emotional abuse particularly problematic in terms of deciding whether and when to make a referral to child protection services.

In their work on chronic child neglect, Turney and Tanner (2001) also focus on neglect that is 'a process or a way of life', as distinct from a single event, and the effect that this has on social work responses. This is an important distinction to which we will return when thinking about useful frameworks for and approaches to adolescent neglect.

Thus a balanced approach is needed. In some cases, an act of omission viewed in isolation – for example, failure to ensure that a child receives urgent medical treatment – may be deemed sufficient to be categorized as neglect. In other cases, there is need to look at patterns of neglect over periods of time.

The relevance of these debates for young people aged 11 to 17 is twofold. First, by virtue of their age, these young people may have experienced persistent neglect for very long periods of time. Any view of current neglect must also therefore be mindful of the historical context and experiences that may stretch back into early childhood. On the other hand, there may be cases of acute neglect that emerge during the teenage years but may not have been preceded by other forms of neglect in the past.

The distinction between neglect as an act and neglect as an experience

Defining neglect as an 'act' (either of omission or commission) tends to put the focus on particular social actors – usually parents. Some authors have argued that there is an important distinction to be made between behaviours that may be neglectful and children's and young people's experiences of neglect. For example, Dubowitz (1999) argues that a particular situation can be defined as constituting 'neglect' when a child or young person's needs are not met, irrespective of whether this was intentional or unintentional and irrespective of whether the neglectful party was a parent or some other person or agency. This is another area where there is a lack of consensus. Glaser (2002) refers to earlier research that reached the opposite conclusion

– that is, 'for definitional purposes, evidence of the ill treatment rather than harm to the child should be sought'.

This issue has considerable relevance to the discussion in Chapter 4 about the context of neglect. An ecological approach will consider all aspects of a child's environment, rather than focusing narrowly on parental factors alone. As will be discussed later, this approach is consistent with the principles underpinning the Assessment Framework in England and Wales, which was also informed by ecological models of child development. It also may have enhanced relevance when the discussion of neglect relates to adolescents. This is because adolescents, arguably to a greater extent than younger children, may often have their own views on whether a particular situation constitutes neglect. If we define neglect in terms of the situation rather than the act(s) that created it, we are confronted by the dilemma of whose perspective we prioritize. We return to the issue of different perspectives about neglect later in this chapter.

Overlaps between different forms of maltreatment

A recurring theme in the child neglect literature is the difficulty in drawing a clear dividing line between emotional abuse and emotional neglect (Stevenson 2007). Some authors treat the two categories as a unified phenomenon – for example, Glaser (2002) who groups both terms under the heading 'psychological maltreatment'.

Taking a broader view of maltreatment, some analysts (e.g. McGee *et al.* 1995) raise questions regarding whether maltreatment should be dealt with as a whole entity rather than being broken up into constituent parts. Their contention is that the large majority of maltreated young people suffer more than one form of maltreatment and these feed into each other. Certainly this seems to hold true in relation to emotional neglect. For example, a recent US study (Arata *et al.* 2007) using a self-report survey of a community sample of adolescents found that emotional abuse was 'almost a universal correlate of every other type of reported abuse'. In this study, neglect was the second most commonly used category of maltreatment, accounting for around 18 per cent of the sample without the occurrence of physical and/or sexual abuse; and a further 28 per cent of the sample in combination with physical and/or sexual abuse. In the UK, Cawson *et al.* (2000) found evidence of a substantial overlap between physical abuse and lack of physical care, but less evidence of a link between the former and supervisory neglect. This indicates that, while there is a high degree of overlap between neglect and emotional abuse, there is mixed evidence of the overlap between neglect and other forms of abuse.

Neglect as a culturally specific phenomenon

As with any form of child maltreatment, a number of authors (e.g. Straus and Kantor 2005) make the point that the definition of neglect will vary from culture to culture and from time to time according to norms and expectations. Thus, if neglect is defined in terms of children's basic needs not being met, then the concept of neglect will vary according to the ideas of acceptable standards of care within any given culture at a given point in time. Garbarino and Collins (1999) give the example of changes in the permissibility of smoking and suggest that 'in the future, smoking in the presence of a child may be seen as neglect'. They conclude that definitions of neglect evolve.

The fact that definitions of neglect are closely connected with normative standards of care within a given society at a particular point in time poses a number of challenges for attempts to define child neglect.

First, it is necessary to gather evidence on normative standards of care. We have found little recent evidence of this nature for the UK and this is an area where there are clear drawbacks to utilizing evidence from other countries (see, for example, Claes *et al.* (2003) who found considerable evidence of variations in normative parenting practices in Canada, France and Italy).

Second, even within a given society, normative standards of care are likely to vary between sub-groups within the population – for example, on the basis of ethnicity, economic prosperity or geographical location.

Some writers also caution against placing too much emphasis on the significance of cultural factors – see, for example, Stevenson (2007) who argues that 'there is a very significant cross-cultural consensus about the basic needs for healthy child development'.

Nevertheless, there may be some pertinent factors to consider here in relation to the needs and neglect of young people aged 11 to 17, bearing in mind the considerable cultural diversity that exists within the UK. For example, there may be different expectations of self-care, roles in caring for others and levels of independence among young people in this age group linked to cultural differences regarding family roles and perceptions of the threshold between childhood and adulthood.

Neglect as a unified phenomenon and categories of neglect

A further major definitional issue is a question over whether neglect can be seen as a single unified category of maltreatment at all. For example, Stevenson (1998, p.14) argues that neglect is an 'administrative category' that encompasses behaviours that have at their core omissions of some form of care, as distinct from being a single concept.

The literature about child neglect provides various typologies and categorizations of neglect. One of the most commonly cited is Straus, Kinard and Williams' (1995) division into emotional, cognitive, supervisory and physical sub-categories. There has been debate about the specifics of the various categorizations and about whether the phenomenon can be sub-divided in this way. However, an approach that aims to break down neglect into constituent parts is a helpful step in beginning to explore the ways in which we might define neglect specifically in relation to adolescents, and in thinking about its potential consequences. We pursue this latter point in Chapter 4.

'Neglectful parenting'

Another source of definitions of neglect is the extensive research literature about parenting styles. This is a topic area where there has been a considerable amount of coherence in research enquiry and we focus here on the dominant conceptual framework of parenting styles that stems from the work of Baumrind (1968), developed further by MacCoby and Martin (1983). The central idea within this framework is the combined effect of two aspects of parenting – control/demandingness and responsiveness/acceptance/warmth. From these two dimensions, a typology of parenting was developed based on four broad categories, as shown in Table 2.1.

Table 2.1: Parenting styles

	High control	Low control
High warmth	Authoritative	Permissive
Low warmth	Authoritarian	Neglectful

We will discuss some of the evidence on the relationships between these different parenting styles and outcomes for children and young people in Chapter 4.

In terms of definition, this conceptualization of neglectful parenting is evidenced by a combination of:

- a low level of parental control of young people (this dimension is often taken to include parental knowledge and monitoring of young people's activities and whereabouts, and establishment of boundaries)

- a low level of warmth and acceptance by parents towards young people.

These factors have particular relevance to thinking about persistent neglect rather than the short-term neglect that can stem from crises such as the illness of a parent. This conceptualization is helpful in thinking about the neglect of young people in particular because it is possible to consider how the two dimensions of control/supervision and warmth/acceptance are relevant to this age group. For example, issues of establishing and reviewing appropriate boundaries for young people as they mature and make the transition to adulthood are a key challenge for parents and carers.

Viewpoints on neglect

Neglect may, of course, be defined from different viewpoints including those of young people themselves, parents and carers, practitioners and researchers. Inevitably there may be substantial differences in the definitions employed by different participants.

McGee *et al.* (1995) explored these differences by comparing the views of agency workers, researchers and the young people themselves on open cases in the caseload of a child protection agency in the US. There was substantial disagreement between groups of participants in terms of the occurrence and severity of maltreatment. Among the different sub-categories of maltreatment, agreement was lowest for neglect – 63 per cent of cases were defined as including neglect according to the young people, compared with 81 per cent according to agency workers and 88 per cent according to researchers examining the case files. Notably, as discussed later, the young people's judgements were found to be more strongly linked to outcomes than the assessments of agency workers and researchers.

This strand of the literature emphasizes the importance of definitions of neglect that incorporate the child's perspective and, as Harrington *et al.* (2002) argue, this may be particularly pertinent to young people.

Young people may under-estimate neglect

While the above findings suggest the importance of taking into account young people's own definitions and perceptions of their experiences, research also draws attention to some of the potential pitfalls to this approach. There are risks that rather than defining an experience as neglect, young people may blame themselves for their parents' behaviour.

McGee, Wolfe and Olson (2001) explored the issue of blaming attribution amongst adolescents in relation to outcomes of maltreatment. They found that most adolescents 'spontaneously attributed the major cause of the maltreating events to the perpetrator'. This included 88 per cent of the sample in relation to neglect. However, when probed further, a significant proportion of the sample also identified their own role in the neglect including 'failing to prevent it' (20%). Thus, as with other forms of maltreatment, young people's own perspectives on potential neglect may be affected by a complex set of considerations. In addition, an emphasis on young people's own definitions of neglect presupposes that young people are in a position to judge the standards of care and supervision that are appropriate for them.

Bearing these considerations in mind, it would seem fitting for definitions of adolescent neglect to incorporate multiple perspectives including the young people themselves and others who may have a broader and more external perspective on their environment and care.

Assessing neglect

In this final section of the chapter, we briefly consider how the definitional issues discussed earlier have been translated into practice guidelines for assessing the occurrence of neglect. We review the current Assessment Framework in operation in England and some of the assessment tools that have been developed for research and practice in this area.

The Assessment Framework

As well as supporting thinking about the issues discussed earlier in this chapter, in England the *Framework for the Assessment of Children in Need and their Families* (Department of Health *et al.* 2000) provides practitioners with a working model for conceptualizing parental neglect. The Framework identifies six key dimensions of how parents or carers are able to support their children's development and respond appropriately to any needs. They are:

- basic care
- ensuring safety
- emotional warmth
- stimulation
- guidance and boundaries
- stability.

As a starting point, it could be argued that neglect, or at least neglect by parents or caregivers, should be seen as being represented by the failure of parents or caregivers to provide one or more of these components of parental capacity.

The appropriate balance of independence and protection will clearly differ according to the age of the child or young person concerned.

Some of the potential differences to be considered when identifying neglect according to the age of the child or young person are illustrated in the Core Assessment Records produced to support the implementation of the Assessment Framework.

The records are set out in the following age bands: 0 to 2 years old (including background information on pre-birth influences); 3 to 4 years old; 5 to 9 years old; 10 to 14 years old; 15 years and over. Each record includes the seven dimensions of a child's developmental needs identified in the Assessment Framework (see Figure 1.2). Within each of these dimensions a number of statements relating to parenting capacity are identified under each dimension of parenting capacity in the Assessment Framework.

There are differences in how parents nurture and provide care for children in the 5- to 9-year-old and the 10- to 14-year-old age bands, with an emphasis on direct care for the younger age group and on facilitative parenting for the older age group. There are additional relevant differences between bringing up children and young people in the 10- to 14-year-old and the 15 years and over age bands – for example, parental support for young people in further education and employment; recognition of parental acceptance of a young person's sexual orientation and in providing information on the risks to health of unprotected sex; and a greater recognition of young people's independence, which for some young people may include living in their own accommodation and looking after their own children.

These distinctive elements of appropriate parenting for adolescents provide important information for practitioners to use when considering the ways that neglect may be identified in this age group.

Other means of assessing neglect

A wide variety of other ways of assessing neglect has been suggested, particularly in the research literature. We list a few examples of common measures below.

Parental Bonding Instrument

In the UK, Lancaster, Rollinson and Hill (2007) tested the use of a parental care scale within the Parental Bonding Instrument as a measure of childhood neglect. They found that a 7-item version of the scale (Kendler, Myers and

Prescott 2000) was as effective as the 12-item version originally developed by Parker, Tupling and Brown (1979) and concluded that this scale had potential for use in large-scale studies. Items refer to people's experience of their mothers or fathers between the ages of 0 and 16.

Neglectful Parenting Checklist

Stevenson (2007) reproduces a comprehensive checklist (over 100 items) on neglectful parenting (from Minty and Pattinson 1994) that was devised to assist practitioners' assessments. This incorporates six dimensions – food and eating habits; health and hygiene; warmth and clothing; safety and supervision; emotional neglect; and school. The scale was designed with children under 7 years of age in mind and would require some modification for use with adolescents.

Childhood Trauma Questionnaire

In the US, Bernstein et al. (2003) developed several versions of the Childhood Trauma Questionnaire. This is a self-report scale that can be used with adolescents. The brief version consists of 28 items containing five sub-scales that measure physical abuse, sexual abuse, emotional abuse, physical neglect and emotional neglect. This questionnaire has been used in several self-report surveys.

Neglect Scale

Also in the US, there has been an ongoing piece of work on the development of a Neglect Scale. Initial 40-item and 20-item scales were developed by Straus et al. (1995), aiming to reflect four dimensions of neglect. Further work was done on this scale by Harrington et al. (2002) who tested a revised 24-factor model. There is also a short form of the scale, cited in Straus and Kantor (2005). However, it is worth noting that this particular scale was administered to adults who answered retrospectively about their childhood as a whole.

US National Incidence Study definitions

The series of National Incidence Studies conducted periodically in the US has included the development of precise definitions for all forms of maltreatment to ensure consistent standards of measurement and reporting (Sedlak 2001). In terms of neglect, four categories are identified – physical neglect, educational neglect, emotional neglect and general or unspecified neglect, each with sub-categories.

Discussion

Key points

In this chapter we have reviewed some of the key issues in the literature regarding the definition of child neglect as a phenomenon. Child neglect is a relatively under-explored aspect of child maltreatment, in comparison particularly with the issues of physical abuse and sexual abuse. Moreover, the literature that does exist, very little of which relates to the UK, is disparate and there has been little consistency in the ways in which child neglect has been defined within academic research.

We have also identified the relative lack of discussion within this literature on child neglect of age-specific issues. These two aspects combined mean that there is almost no discussion in the literature that relates to definitions of adolescent neglect as a discrete phenomenon.

The first part of the chapter summarizes a number of key debates in the literature on child neglect in general, including the question of whether neglect can be defined solely as an act of omission, the distinction between behaviours and experiences, and the overlap between different forms of maltreatment. It also considers the ways in which the literature about child development and parenting styles might offer useful frameworks for developing age-specific definitions of neglect.

The second part of the chapter focuses on tools for the assessment of neglect. The Core Assessment Records produced to support the implementation of the Assessment Framework provide valuable indications of the kind of issues to be incorporated into an age-sensitive definition of neglect. We also review several research instruments that have been developed to measure neglect.

Implications

The key points have implications both for operational definitions of neglect for use in practice and also for developing a research agenda.

In terms of practice with adolescents, research in the US, reviewed earlier, has indicated that practitioners' assessments of neglect can be variable. In England and Wales, practitioners have access to a comprehensive set of age-specific indicators to support assessments of levels of care and meeting basic needs through the Core Assessment Records. These offer the potential for a consistent way of defining neglect in relation to individual cases.

In terms of the research agenda, the almost complete lack of UK research that contains definitions of adolescent neglect represents both a major gap and an opportunity. The opportunity is to avoid the pitfalls from the (primarily US-based) research literature to date – characterized by a high level of inconsistency in terms of definitions, categorizations and measures of child neglect that has hampered progress. There is a need for research development in this area that fits the UK context and adopts a consistent approach, preferably linked with practice frameworks.

In relation to both sets of definitions (practice and research) there is a need to pay specific attention to:

- the distinction between neglectful behaviours and experiences of neglect
- different viewpoints on neglect, including those of young people
- contextual and environmental aspects of definitions
- cultural diversity in terms of what is regarded as an appropriate level of care
- issues of persistent neglect and the relevance of isolated but serious incidents of neglect.

3

The Causes and Contexts of Young People's Neglect

> There are so many young people who are neglected and they have coped thus far...they are coping in a society that just recognizes they are neglected. (Professional's view)

> Young people might think it is their fault that they're being neglected, so they go along with it. (Young person's view)

In this chapter we consider the background and contextual factors associated with adolescent neglect.

This is one of the areas where our literature review unearthed very little material specifically about young people. Therefore in this chapter we attempt to do two main things – to briefly summarize the research findings on the background to child neglect in general and to draw attention to what the implications of these findings might be when thinking about the neglect of young people aged 11 to 17 in particular. We also consider other potential factors not covered in the literature on child neglect that may be particularly pertinent in relation to the neglect of young people in this age group.

There is a substantial amount of evidence on the contextual factors associated with child neglect in general (see, for example, reviews by Evans (2002) and Zielinski and Bradshaw (2006), and more recent studies such as Mayer *et al.* (2007) in relation to Canada). These factors can mostly be linked to the 'family and environmental factors' dimensions set out in the Assessment Framework – although some factors also overlap with the 'parenting capacity' domain (see Table 3.1).

Table 3.1: The Assessment Framework and child neglect research

Assessment Framework	Child neglect research
Family history and functioning	Lone parent families Mothers who have children at younger ages and have more unplanned pregnancies Larger family size Domestic violence Adult mental health problems Low parental self-esteem
Wider family	Low levels of social support from own family
Employment, housing and income	Low income Unemployment Lower parental educational attainment
Family's social integration	Less cohesive families Poor attachments of parents to their own parents
Community resources	Low levels of social support

Source: Adapted from Hicks and Stein 2010

In addition Evans (2002) notes that sudden onset of neglect may also be related to 'stress points or life changes, for example bereavement, redundancy, divorce or illness'. This points to the dynamic nature of neglect.

We now go on to summarize the evidence on associations between each of the key factors identified in Table 3.1 and child neglect, under headings from the Assessment Framework. At the end of each section, we also consider any specific issues regarding how these factors may take on a different complexion in relation to young people in comparison with younger children.

Family structure and gender
Mothers

Child neglect has often been associated with households headed by lone female parents, which in itself has prompted considerable attention. Coohey (1995) observes that the main focus of research and theory building on child neglect in the US had been on three main areas: the characteristics of neglectful mothers; the demographics of neglect cases; and the social networks of mothers. Swift (1995) notes that there are other characteristic components, such as poor housing and drug abuse, which are not attributed with responsibility for neglect in a similar manner to those associated with mothers. She suggests that focusing on maternal failures allows for individual as distinct from societal solutions to be sought, thereby avoiding responsibility at the level of the public purse. There are thus gender-based assumptions about care that tend to focus attention on mothers in particular (Daniel and Taylor 2006).

Fathers

Fathers have received less attention and historically there is relatively little research into their experiences and behaviours in relation to neglect. The role that fathers, and other male adults taking on parenting roles, may play in child neglect involves both risk and protective factors. Dufour *et al*. 2007 highlight the complexity of the issues relating to fathers and neglect. Clearly this is an area where more research is needed in the UK, as highlighted by Gardner (2008) and Daniel, Taylor and Scott (2009).

Family size

In terms of family structure, a link has also been found between neglect and a large number of children within the household (Bovarnick 2007).

Implications for young people

The specific role that these factors might play in relation to the neglect of young people aged 11 to 17 has not been fully explored. However, one important factor to consider here is that, necessarily, the older children or young people are, the more likely they are to have experienced family change, including the separation of birth parents and the introduction of new adults (parents' new partners) who may take on a parenting role. This means that, to the extent that lone parenting, absent parenting and step-parenting are associated with the incidence of neglect, then young people are more likely to experience these situations than younger children. While there seems to be very little literature specifically on the neglect of young people in this age group, other research on topics such as young runaways provides useful insights. This research has drawn attention to the potential for young people, particularly those who are closer to the transition to independence and adulthood, to feel emotionally neglected and ultimately 'pushed out' in some restructured families involving newly introduced step-parents (Rees and Rutherford 2001; Rees and Siakeu 2004). Research by ChildLine (NSPCC 2008) shows family relationship problems to be of huge concern to young people.

The role of parental issues and problems

Parental substance use

Neglect is known to be a key effect of parental problem alcohol and drug use (Advisory Council on the Misuse of Drugs 2003; Tunnard 2004). Tunnard cites statistics from NSPCC's helpline for children that indicate that almost 'a quarter (23%) of calls about suspected neglect mentioned drinking by parents'. The review also cites a local 'matching needs and services audit' that indicated substantially higher than average levels of neglect among families with problematic drinking.

Cleaver, Unell and Aldgate's (1999) study of the impact of parental problems (including substance use and mental health) on children's development provides a number of examples of the ways in which these problems increase the likelihood of neglect, and the consequences for young people as they grow up. This study is particularly helpful in that it distinguishes between issues faced by, and consequences for, children and young people at different ages and stages of development (see later). One repercussion is the necessity for children and young people to take on a self-caring role, and often also a caring role for others, at a much younger age than is typical (Bancroft et al. 2004). Other identified effects of children living with parental substance misuse include young people missing school to care for or watch over parents, which may in turn lead to failure in exams and poorer outcomes post-education; physical risks associated with used needles or drugs being left around; and young people themselves becoming drawn into crime and substance misuse (Gorin 2004).

It should also be noted that other contextual factors – such as strong social support networks; a strong positive relationship with a particular supportive adult; and good experiences at school – may protect children and young people, to a greater or less extent, from the impact of this range of parental problems.

Parental mental health problems

The existence of parental mental health problems may also be associated with neglect. Ethier et al. (2000) cite several studies that have found a link between child neglect and parental mental health problems (Browne and Saqi 1988) and depression and stress (Kotch et al. 1995). This was also a key focus of Cleaver et al.'s (1999) study in the UK. However, it is also important not to leap to assumptions, over-generalize here and stigmatize parents with these issues (Aldridge and Becker 2003; Olsen and Wates 2003). There is also evidence that, in cases of parental mental illness, the capacity to parent may fluctuate considerably over time and there is a great deal that can be done through professionals and other sources of support to minimize the extent of neglect during periods when it may be more likely to occur (Tunnard 2004).

Implications for young people

The key point to emerge from this discussion in relation to adolescent neglect is that a background of parental problems may lead to neglect in distinctive ways for children in different age groups. The evidence suggests that older children and adolescents living with parental substance use problems, and possibly also mental health problems, may be drawn into taking on caring roles rather than being cared for themselves. As a result, young people aged 11 to 17 living in these contexts may face additional risks. Young people may not receive support at key developmental stages, such as puberty, early and later adolescence. Moreover, lack of supervision and boundaries may result in young people being exposed to greater likelihood of harm both inside and outside the family home.

Wider family and support networks

Neglectful mothers have been found to have less social support both from extended family and from the community in general (see, for example, Coohey 1996). It might be tempting to move from this evidence of a shortfall in personal support to a conclusion that practice should aim to enhance these networks. However, it should not be assumed that this will necessarily be beneficial for the mothers and children concerned. For example, attempts to enhance social networks may also create a negative reaction from others that could exacerbate the sense of social isolation rather than diminish it (Stevenson 2007).

There is some evidence that this issue may be particularly pertinent to parents of young people aged 11 to 17. Hooper *et al.* (2007) found that parents who were living on a low income most wanted support about how to parent teenagers and manage their behaviour. This was a key source of frustration with lack of support from Children's Services. In some cases parents spoke of hitting a young person to get a service. Farmer and Lutman (2010), in their study of outcomes for neglected children returned to their parents, found that 'the parents of...older children received significantly less support than those with younger children, even though many were struggling with their adolescent children's serious emotional and behavioural problems'. The older children received more types of help than younger ones but were also more likely to receive insufficient support. A lack of specialist help for parents was linked to poor outcomes.

Implications for young people

The typically wider social networks of young people in comparison with younger children and their increased capacity to act independently of parents means that they may be more likely to establish their own networks of social support outside the immediate family through, for example, extended family networks, friendships and school networks. It is possible therefore that the links between social support and neglect might take on a different aspect for this older age group and that there is greater potential to bring protective factors into play to mitigate the effects of neglectful parenting.

Housing, employment and financial considerations

Much of the literature focusing on the aetiology of neglect centres around the relationship between neglect and socio-economic factors, although causality is not attributed. Without doubt, as for other forms of maltreatment, there is a strong association between neglect and poverty. However, as Stone (1998) observes, research in this area emanates mainly from the US and is troubled by a degree of circularity. Research from the US on neglect and poverty is likely to be based on assumptions that define neglect in terms of 'poor material conditions of life for children' (Stone 1998, p.17).

Research and its methods in respect of the aetiology of neglect suffer from a number of difficulties that are not easy to rectify, such as problems with sampling and lack of consensus about the nature of neglect. For example, as Sullivan (2000) notes, research samples are often drawn from families registered with child protection agencies and who are thus identified as 'neglectful or abusive'. Overall, despite the evidence of associations, it is not at all clear that poverty is a cause of neglect (Crittenden 1999, cited in Evans 2002; McSherry 2004 cited in Bovarnick 2007). This appears to be an under-explored area that would merit further research.

This is one of the few areas where the literature review has identified specific UK evidence in relation to adolescent neglect (at least in terms of parenting styles). Shucksmith, Hendry and Glendinning (1995) found only limited evidence of associations between different parenting styles and parental employment status, education and social class. Wight, Williamson and Henderson (2006) found that lower parental monitoring was associated with lower social class, a lower level of parental educational qualifications, living in rented housing and younger mothers. However, these findings are too limited and inconclusive to be given a great deal of weight. A recent study by Hooper *et al.* (2007) also looks at issues of neglect among families living in poverty.

Implications for young people

Again, given the limited evidence on this issue, it is only possible to suggest some plausible hypotheses regarding the distinctive nature of these contextual factors when considering the neglect of young people aged 11 to 17. One potential issue is that the importance of peer acceptance during the teenage years may generate particular problems for young people when their material needs are being neglected by parents and carers. A second potential issue is that economic strains within the family may heighten tensions between parents or carers and young people, particularly as they reach an age where they might be expected to earn money themselves. There is tentative evidence from UK research on runaways that these factors can lead to young people being forced to leave home at age 15 to 17 (Rees and Siakeu 2004).

Community elements and resources

As discussed, ecological approaches have made important contributions to current understanding of child maltreatment in general. This includes the multilevel influence on child maltreatment with special emphasis on the role of neighbourhood. There is a range of research findings that have established associations between 'rates of child maltreatment and neighborhood poverty, housing stress (e.g. residential instability, vacant housing), and drug and alcohol availability' (see review by Freisthler, Merrit and LaScala 2006).

Implications for young people

We have found relatively little discussion of the neglect of young people in the literature identified through our search strategy on ecological models. However, some of the material on parental substance use discussed earlier highlighted the fact that supervisory neglect of adolescents is likely to place young people at increased risk outside the home through, for example, involvement in drug use. It seems likely that this risk will be increased if young people are also living in an environment with higher than average rates of poverty, instability and drug and alcohol availability as indicated earlier. The typically greater autonomy and wider networks of young people in comparison with younger children may therefore mean that risk factors within the wider community are more pertinent when interacting with experiences of parental neglect within this older age group.

Disabled children and young people

Specific concerns have been raised by a number of writers about the rates of neglect (and other forms of maltreatment) among disabled children, for example, National Working Group on Child Protection and Disability (2003). Despite these concerns, there is relatively little firm evidence on this issue.

The study most often cited is Sullivan and Knutson (2000), which was based on a large sample of children's services case records in Nebraska. It found much higher than average rates of recorded neglect for disabled children than non-disabled children. To summarize some of the key relevant findings for this review, in comparison with non-disabled children, the risk of neglect was twice as high for deaf and hard-of-hearing children; five times as high for children with speech and language impairments; twice as high for children with learning disabilities; seven times as high for children with behaviour disorders; and three times as high for children with health-related disabilities. This is an important study, but it does have limitations. First, it was a study of officially recorded maltreatment and it therefore cannot estimate prevalence. Second, the associations identified do not imply a one-directional causal link. Sullivan and Knutson cite earlier research based on a US national incidence study (Westat Inc. 1993) that indicates that, based on professional assessments, disability can be both a risk factor for, and a consequence of, neglect. Third, Sullivan and Knutson found a greater over-representation of disabled children among maltreated children in younger age groups. Therefore the differences in rates of maltreatment may not be so pronounced for adolescents.

UK evidence of a link between neglect and disability is sparse. A report by the National Working Group on Child Protection and Disability (2003) cite some tentative evidence that suggests a link between disability, likelihood of child protection registration and likelihood of being subject to a care order. The report identifies some of the factors that may lead to disabled children being more vulnerable to abuse. These include attitudes and assumptions, inadequacies in service provision and factors associated with impairment such as communication difficulties.

Implications for young people

None of the above evidence directly relates to adolescent neglect.

A recent study of serious case reviews (Brandon *et al.* 2008b) provides a case study that illustrates some of the potential issues in relation to disability and neglect. It describes a 12-year-old disabled male who was removed from the care of his parents as a result of severe neglect – a decision that was delayed for a year despite the involvement of several agencies. One of the key conclusions that Brandon *et al.* draw from this case study is particularly relevant to the current review, and the discussion of definitions of neglect in Chapter 2: it is the need for training about recognizing neglect.

> There was clear evidence of neglect in this case yet agencies failed to follow these pointers consistently or effectively. The model of neglect used was based on defining the concern in relation to parental action or omission rather than viewing neglect as a set of needs for care and protection regardless of the efforts of those caring for the child concerned. (Brandon *et al.* 2008b, p.96)

It is also worth reiterating a point made earlier that, while a developmental perspective can be helpful in thinking about age-related features of neglect, children and young people develop at different rates and in different ways, and it is very important to not rely on normative assumptions of child development when considering whether a particular child or young person is experiencing neglect.

Discussion

Key points

Literature on the background to child neglect has identified a wide range of contextual factors that are associated with the likelihood of neglect. These include family structure, parental problems, economic factors, social support factors, and the characteristics of the local community and environment.

Analysis of this literature has identified, for example, the need to pay more attention to the role of fathers in child neglect; the role of parental problems such as substance misuse; and also the value of an ecological approach to understanding the background factors associated with child neglect.

However, our literature review has identified relatively little research discussion of the contextual factors that may be specifically associated with adolescent neglect.

Implications

The lack of knowledge about contextual factors represents a major research gap that hinders a full understanding of the phenomenon of the neglect of adolescents. To some extent, it might be argued that the contextual factors identified for child neglect in general will be equally applicable across the whole age range of children up to the age of 18. However, the discussion in this chapter has highlighted some potentially distinctive issues in relation to adolescent neglect, all of which might warrant further exploration.

These include the following:

- Problems that parents themselves are experiencing, such as substance misuse or mental ill-health, may diminish their parenting capacity irrespective of the age of the child. However as children grow older, the implications of this are likely to change. Young people may be more likely than younger children to take on caring roles in addition to not always being adequately cared for themselves; may lack support and supervision at critical phases in their development; and may be at increased risk of poor educational outcomes. This impact may be strengthened where environmental factors are not favourable.

- In terms of poverty, older young people (particularly those aged 15 and over) living in families experiencing severe hardship may be at increased risk of being forced to leave home, at least partly due to economic factors.

- Tensions in the relationships between birth parents, partners and young people may also be a factor that can lead to young people feeling emotionally neglected and to their running away or being forced to leave home.

- The child neglect literature has begun to highlight the important role that fathers can play. Again, the absence of adequate care from fathers might have specific consequences during the transitions that young people make through the course of their adolescence.

These areas support the point that it is possible that the precise background and context of neglect varies for children and young people of different ages.

The factors identified here for the background of child neglect will be identifiable by practitioners in their work with individual young people. However, the material reviewed in this chapter suggests the need for some specific research on the contextual factors associated with adolescent neglect.

4

The Consequences of the Neglect of Young People

In this chapter we summarize what is known about the consequences of neglect for young people's well-being and longer term outcomes. We cover three issues.

- First, we consider what might be the potential consequences of neglect for young people aged 11 to 17, taking into account their age and development.

- Second, we review the extent of social research evidence on the links between experiences of neglect, well-being and outcomes.

- Third, we consider the evidence on the relative consequences of neglect for young people in comparison with those for younger children.

The potential consequences of neglect for young people

Viewed from the perspective of the needs for support and care among young people aged 11 to 17, there are a number of ways in which experiences of neglect may lead to negative consequences and outcomes.

Thinking first about physical neglect, given the typically greater capacities and competencies of this age group, compared to younger children, it may be that this form of neglect is less detrimental. For example, it might be expected that most young people aged 11 to 17 would be able to care for themselves physically to a greater or lesser extent. However, particularly at the younger end of the age group, young people are likely to still need support and encouragement in a number of areas – for example, accessing medical and dental health care services; adopting a healthy lifestyle in terms of diet and exercise; and adapting to the changes experienced during puberty and later sexual development. There may be some distinctive issues to consider here for females and males in this age group. As discussed in Chapter 5, obesity has been raised by young people as a particular concern in relation to neglect. A lack of parental care in these areas may well have negative consequences for young people's present and future health. In addition, bearing in mind the importance of peer relationships to young people, neglect of their physical needs such as hygiene, clothing and so on may have negative implications for peer acceptance and friendships.

Educational neglect clearly may have highly significant and long-term consequences for young people aged 11 to 17. A lack of parental care, support and encouragement in this area is likely to pose a risk to young people's educational behaviour, commitment and attainment. Young people in our research (see Chapter 5) were very aware of the impact of parental neglect in terms of lack of support for them in seeking appropriate training and job opportunities. Lack of appropriate guidance on sexual health may also lead to unwanted teenage pregnancies and sexually transmitted diseases.

Supervisory neglect also remains a key issue for young people aged 11 to 17. Typically, young people's friendships and lifestyles will mean a gradual broadening of horizons over this age range. Parents face a key task in maintaining an appropriate level of monitoring and boundaries during this period. A lack of sufficient supervision may mean that young people are exposed to risks outside the home, and may be more likely to become involved in crime and antisocial behaviour, while very strict boundaries may also be detrimental in terms of young people's peer relationships and move towards independence.

Finally, young people in this age group are still in need of emotional warmth and support. A neglect of their needs in this respect is likely to be detrimental to their emotional well-being. A combination of low warmth and low control constitutes the 'neglectful' parenting style discussed in Chapter 2.

It is clear from this brief consideration of the relevant issues for young people aged 11 to 17 that various forms of neglect can plausibly have negative consequences for their well-being in the present and in the future. We now go on to review the social research evidence on this issue.

Research evidence on links between neglect, well-being and longer term outcomes

Compared with the previous chapter on contextual factors, there is much more research evidence on the *potential* consequences of neglect of adolescents. This includes evidence relating to physical health, mental health, emotional well-being, school experiences and educational attainment, risk-taking and antisocial behaviours. Before reviewing this evidence, a few points about the strengths and weaknesses of current knowledge in this field are necessary.

The evidence base is strong in terms of the range of outcomes considered and the consistency of findings across studies. Additionally, while much of the evidence is from the US and other English-speaking countries, there are some similar findings from other cultural contexts. However, there are also some potential weaknesses of the research to bear in mind.

Most notably, as is often the case in social research, most of the relevant studies involve cross-sectional rather than longitudinal designs. This means that all the information relates to the same point in time. This in turn means that statistical associations between neglect and poorer well-being do not prove that the first causes the second. There is now a growing recognition that there are potentially two-way relationships that have led to a move away from 'parenting' towards parent–child relationships. Indeed, some studies (e.g. Buist *et al.* 2004; Huh *et al.* 2006; Kerr and Stattin 2003; Reitz, Dekovic and Meijes 2006), which have utilized longitudinal data have suggested the existence of reciprocal relationships where problem behaviour by adolescents may affect parenting styles rather than, or in addition to, vice versa. It may well be that, to some extent, behaviours by young people that are perceived negatively by parents contribute to a deterioration in parent–child relationships and the incidence of neglect. These behaviours may have their roots in earlier childhood experiences within the family, or may be connected with other factors in the young people's ecological systems such as the impact of peer relationships and the local area within which they live. Thus there may be a negative reinforcing cycle between parent–child relationships and young people's behaviour that contributes to the incidence of neglect. The question of causality is therefore currently contested.

In addition, it should be noted that much of the literature stems from the research on parenting styles rather than from research on the maltreatment of children and young people. The scope of 'neglectful' parenting within this literature is much broader than the scope of 'neglect' within the latter context. However, it may be reasonable to infer that patterns observed in relation to neglectful parenting styles in a broad sense are likely to be at least as, if not more, pronounced in relation to young people experiencing forms of neglect.

Finally, most of the studies rely on self-reporting of parenting styles by young people. Some questions have recently been raised regarding whether this method reflects parenting styles per se or whether it reflects a more complex interaction (Soenens *et al.* 2006).

We consider the research evidence under seven broad categories relating to:

- physical health
- mental health and emotional well-being
- peer relationships
- risky behaviours
- educational outcomes
- antisocial behaviour and offending
- longer term outcomes.

Physical health

As discussed earlier, it would seem likely that aspects of physical neglect such as failure to secure appropriate medical attention and lack of provision of adequate food are likely to lead to negative health outcomes. Unfortunately there appears to be very little research evidence on the links between adolescent neglect and physical health, and there may be a case for further exploration of these links to reflect current concerns – for example, in relation to obesity.

An exception is the recent study of serious case reviews in England (Brandon *et al.* 2009). Around two-thirds of these reviews related to the death of a child and the remaining third to a serious injury. Of a total sample of 189 cases in this study, 41 (22%) related to children and young people aged 11 to 17 at the time of the events that triggered the review. This compares with 86 (46%) in the under 1 age group and 62 (33%) in the 1-year-old to 10-year-old age group. Brandon *et al.*'s earlier (2008a) report provides an illustrative case study of a 16-year-old male who had experienced long-term neglect, rejection and serious abuse with clear consequences for his physical and mental health, as well as other risky behaviours such as running away.

Mental health and emotional well-being

There is stronger evidence of links between neglectful parenting and various aspects of young people's mental and emotional well-being. This includes links between parenting styles and internalizing problems such as depression (Thornberry *et al.* 2001 in the US; Vazsonyi, Hibbert and Snider 2003 in a study of family and parenting processes in Hungary, the Netherlands, Switzerland and the US). In fact, neglect may have a stronger impact on mental health than some other forms of maltreatment (Arata *et al.* 2007).

Peer relationships

Peer relationships are an important developmental issue in relation to adolescence, when image and peer acceptance are very important to young people (Scannapieco and Connell-Carrick (2005). There appears to be limited evidence on links between neglect and peer relationships for this age group. Consideration needs to be given to the peer problems that might arise for adolescents living with parents who are neglectful as a result of their own mental illness and substance misuse (Cleaver *et al.* 1999; Gorin 2004). It would also seem relevant to consider the issue of bullying linked to neglect in that physical neglect at home may well lead to children and young people being stigmatized and bullied by their peers. Young people who have been neglected may be socially withdrawn and more likely to be bullied (Cullingford and Morrison 1997, quoted in Moran 2009).

Risky behaviours

There is strong evidence of a relationship between parenting styles and risky behaviours that are likely to affect young people's health and well-being. This includes a link with drug and alcohol use (Barnes *et al.* 2000; Claes *et al.* 2005; Cleveland *et al.* 2005; Thornberry *et al.* 2001; Vazsonyi *et al.* 2003). Low parental monitoring also appears to be a factor associated with early sexual activity for females and males (see, reviews by DeVore and Ginsburg 2005; Miller, Benson and Galbraith 2001 and a study by Wight *et al.* 2006 in the UK).

Furthermore, experiences of emotionally neglectful parenting (e.g. young people not feeling cared about by parents and carers) have been linked with increased likelihood of running away in UK research (Rees and Lee 2005; Safe on the Streets Research Team 1999). This research highlights the risks faced by young people under the age of 16.

Educational outcomes

There is a range of evidence on links between neglectful parenting and educational issues. First, various dimensions of adolescent-reported parenting processes have been found to be associated with behavioural issues at school (Vazsnoyi *et al.* 2003; Williams and Kelly 2005). These dimensions included closeness, support, monitoring and communication, father-adolescent involvement and attachment. Second, young people who reported neglectful parenting have also been found to display poor academic achievement strategies characterized by 'high levels of task-irrelevant behaviour' (Aunola, Stattin and Nurmi 2000, in Sweden). Finally, there is evidence of links between parenting styles and school achievement, although these findings may vary according to culture and economic factors (Paulson, Marchant and Rothlisberg 1998 and a review by Spera 2005).

Antisocial behaviour and offending

In general, maltreatment during adolescence increases the chances of arrest, violent offending and drug use (Smith *et al.* 2005; Thornberry *et al.* 2001). The former study found that neglect had a stronger association than did physical and sexual abuse with the likelihood of late adolescent offending, violent behaviour and arrest, although the impact dissipated somewhat in early adulthood. There is also substantial evidence from the parenting styles literature that low parental warmth, involvement and control are linked with higher incidence of antisocial behaviour, offending and 'delinquency'. For example, Reitz *et al.* (2006) found a two-way connection between aspects of parental involvement and granting of autonomy, and externalizing problem behaviour.

Longer term outcomes

We have identified little direct evidence of links between experience of adolescent neglect and longer term outcomes for adults. However, the implications of the evidence discussed – for example, poor educational achievement, increased risk of offending – suggest that experiences of neglect during adolescence are likely to decrease the likelihood of achieving economic well-being as an adult. A policy review published by HM Treasury (2007) highlights the way in which multiple risk factors, including those linked to parenting and deprivation, can act together to significantly lower young people's chances later in life. The report estimates that adults who have experienced four of a range of risk factors (such as poor parental mental health, living in a deprived neighbourhood) during childhood have a 70 per cent chance of multiple deprivation at the age of 30, compared with a 5 per cent chance for those who experienced no risk factors.

The relative consequences of neglect at different ages

Finally, we turn to the issue of the relative consequences of neglect experienced at different ages during childhood and adolescence. The topic of age-specific consequences of maltreatment in general has been a matter of some theoretical debate (summarized in Kaplow and Widom 2007). One perspective holds that maltreatment is particularly damaging for younger children because of its impact on the achievement of key developmental milestones in early childhood, which can have an amplified effect later in childhood and adolescence (Schore 2002).

An alternative perspective argues that, because of their increased understanding, older children may be more distressed by experiences of maltreatment than younger children. Maltreatment can be viewed as an abuse of power and this may have greater impact as children develop a greater sense of autonomy and self-determination. There are also other suggestions that neglect during adolescence may have a particularly strong impact on brain development (De Bellis 2005, cited in Horwath 2007a).

There is relatively little conclusive research on this debate. However, there is some evidence (including the Thornberry study cited several times already and a study by Sternberg *et al.* 2005) that more recent experiences of maltreatment (including neglect) amongst adolescents were more strongly related to negative outcomes than were experiences earlier in childhood. As Thornberry *et al.* (2001) note, this may be at least in part because some of those children who were only maltreated earlier in childhood may have received social work interventions that successfully protected against negative longer term outcomes.

It would be unwise to place too much store on the findings of a body of research that is limited in terms of our focus. Nevertheless the study by Thornberry and colleagues poses some interesting questions regarding the impact of maltreatment at different stages of childhood and adolescence, and suggests the need for further research on this topic.

Discussion

Key points

In this chapter we have reviewed and summarized some of the substantial body of evidence that has identified associations between neglect or neglectful parenting and various negative indicators. This evidence shows that neglect has potential links with a broad range of negative outcomes. Neglect and/or neglectful parenting is/are associated with poorer physical health, mental health, risky health behaviours, risks to safety including running away, poorer conduct and achievement at school, and negative behaviours such as offending and antisocial behaviour.

Some research studies have also attempted to disentangle the effects of different forms of maltreatment and there are tentative indications that the negative impact of neglect is at least as significant, if not more significant, than other forms of maltreatment.

Additionally, several studies have explored the relative consequences of neglect experienced at different ages during childhood and adolescence. The limited evidence that exists from these studies suggests that, in terms of well-being, the neglect of young people may be at least as damaging across a range of areas as is the case for younger children.

Some caution is needed in interpreting these findings for the purposes of the current review – first, because not all the findings are specific to adolescent neglect, and, second, because there are some questions about the direction of causality between neglectful parenting and adolescent behaviour.

Implications

While bearing in mind the caveats about causality highlighted here, the substantial body of evidence indicating the possible negative outcomes of neglect and neglectful parenting, including specifically during adolescence, highlights the potential significance of adolescent neglect as an issue.

The findings reviewed here are connected with the issues of lack of attention both to neglect (in relation to other forms of maltreatment) and to maltreatment of young people (as distinct from younger children). Some of the evidence suggests a stronger association between neglect and negative outcomes than for other forms of maltreatment. Additionally, the evidence suggests a substantial association between neglect specifically during adolescence and negative outcomes. These points support the argument made throughout this book for stronger attention to the neglect of young people within research, policy and practice.

5

Young People's Views about Neglect

Neglect is... 'Getting blamed for everyone's arguments.' (Young person)

Neglect is... 'When parents leave you and you get hurt; if they don't do anything when something bad happens.' (Young person)

Even though neglect happens to children and young people, their experiences and views about it have rarely been explored in research or taken into account when developing policy and practice. In this chapter, we will briefly review the research that has been directly undertaken with young people about neglect. We will then discuss findings of our project with young people about neglect that provides the basis for this chapter. The project with young people set out to explore their definitions of neglect, their understandings of the causes and impact of neglect, and their awareness of ways they can seek help, and it gained their advice about ways to raise professional awareness and reach neglected young people. The main aim was to develop an output for young people that would provide them with information about neglect and how to access help.[1] A young people's advisory group was actively involved throughout the research process and focus groups were held with a range of young people aged 12 to 24, some of whom had experienced neglect themselves. The research involved 51 young people (31 boys and 20 girls) from a range of different ethnic backgrounds (the most prevalent being young people from Black and White ethnic groups). Young people in the focus groups were recruited via a school

---

1   For an online version of the leaflet and further information about the methodology (*Neglect matters: The Story of the guide*), see www.nspcc.org.uk/neglectmatters

for young people with learning difficulties, a young offenders' institution, a care leavers' team, a team supporting young people whose parents misuse substances and a young people's centre. All the names of young people quoted in the research have been changed to protect their identities. We will conclude the chapter with a discussion of the key findings and implications of young people's perspectives for practice, policy and future research.

Previous research with young people about neglect

Searches of literature about young people's views and experiences of neglect have found very little that directly addresses this area. In a systematic review of the recognition of neglect and early responses to it (Daniel, Taylor and Scott 2010), the authors state that the biggest gap in evidence they identified 'related to the views of parents and, even more, of children'. They go on to say that 'attempts to develop a swifter response to neglect must be informed by the views of parents and children about what would help' (p.255).

A recent poll of 3000 8-to 12-year-olds by Action for Children suggests that children and young people are aware of neglect happening to children around them. They found that almost two thirds (61%) of children had seen suspected signs of neglect (such as a child looking dirty, smelly or being hungry or lonely) and children as young as 8 years old were able to recognize signs of neglect in their peers. They identified the effects of neglect as including being bullied, ignored and laughed at, and said they saw signs of neglect in the classroom or playground (80%), neighbourhood (47%) and club or group (23%) (Action for Children 2010).

Much like neglect itself, information about young people's views and experiences is difficult to identify immediately, but can be found within broader studies of child maltreatment. It is also touched upon in some studies of neglect that largely focus on other perspectives or methods of data collection (such as case record analysis or interviews with professionals); and, as has been discussed in Chapter 3, information can be found in studies that focus on other issues, such as parental substance misuse.

Within broader studies about maltreatment, the largest scale study in the UK to have asked young people (aged 11 to 17) about prevalence of neglect is the child safety and victimization survey (see Chapter 2 for details) (Radford *et al.* 2011). A linked retrospective study undertook in-depth interviews with over 60 young people aged 18 to 24 who had experienced maltreatment (Radford *et al.* forthcoming). This latter study found that neglect was often hidden behind other problems. It was rarely identified by participants as the main reason for taking part in the research; instead, most young people initially cited experiencing physical or sexual abuse, but during the course of the interviews it became clear that some had also experienced varying degrees of neglect, particularly emotional neglect. Studies that have been undertaken with young people via ChildLine samples confirm that neglect may be present but is frequently not raised as a primary issue when young people seek external help (see Wales *et al.* 2009).

A study by Farmer and Lutman (2010) interviewed a small sample of children as part of a longitudinal examination of case management and predictors of outcomes for neglected children returned to their parents over a five-year follow-up period. They found that outcomes for younger children were much better than for older children and that, if children were older than six at the time of reunification with parents or guardians, actions taken to safeguard them and plan for their future reduced in effectiveness.

Most of the findings about children and young people's experiences of neglect can be found in studies that have focused on other safeguarding risks to children and young people. This includes research about the child protection system and looked after children (Rees *et al.* 2010); poverty (Hooper *et al.* 2007); parental substance misuse (e.g. Bancroft *et al.* 2004; Barnard and Barlow 2003; Gorin 2004; Kroll 2004; Liverpool Drug and Alcohol Action Team 2001; Mariathasan and Hutchinson 2010; Velleman *et al.* 2003); running away and homelessness (Macaskill 2006; Rees and Lee 2005; Smith and Ravenhill 2006); suicide (Brookes and Flower 2009) and young people vulnerable to sexual exploitation through prostitution (Coy 2009). A study by Smith and Ravenhill (2006) interviewed 24 young homeless people about their situation and their reasons for running away, and found that over half had experienced assault and/or extreme neglect by addicted parents. Hutchinson and Woods (2010), whose report examined loneliness among children who speak to ChildLine, report how neglect can make children feel uncared for and alone. Carla, aged 12, who experienced neglect told ChildLine:

> I get left alone when my mum goes to work. My mum leaves at 6.30a.m. and sometimes only comes home around 7.30p.m. Sometimes, I am also left on my own at weekends. Mum says she has to work to be able to get what we need. We argue a lot. (p.18)

Across all the research undertaken directly with young people, various themes can be drawn out, many of which echo findings discussed in earlier chapters.

- Neglect is often one part of a broader picture of deprivation and problems at home and may not be the *most* immediately concerning issue for young people. It may emerge when young people talk about other forms of abuse; wider family relationship problems at home; experiences, such as being bullied, depression, self-harming or suicide; and feelings such as loneliness and social isolation.

- Neglect can be experienced by young people in combination with parental problems such as substance misuse, mental health problems or learning difficulties and, as such, neglect may be episodic. Young people often talk about also having strong loyalty towards and positive experiences of care from parents.

- Physical neglect and absence of supervision is particularly reported in research on substance misuse if parents are physically absent from home acquiring drugs, drinking or undertaking criminal activity. It may also occur in cases in which parents have mental health problems and are unable to prioritize their children's needs. Children report worrying about parents' whereabouts if they are absent, and when or whether they will return. They often also have grave concerns about the health of parents and worry about parents dying.

- Young people may be particularly vulnerable to emotional neglect if parents are suffering from depression or withdrawing from drugs or alcohol. Children's accounts often talk about feeling as if parents are emotionally absent even when they are physically present – in other words, they are not 'there for them'.

- Young people who are neglected may also have to undertake inappropriate caring tasks for their age, such as looking after siblings or undertaking domestic chores, and they may be exposed to physical risks associated with parental substance misuse.

- Young people, especially boys, find it hard to talk to anyone when they experience problems at home, and they are most likely to speak to friends first. They are unlikely to approach a professional initially, unless it is someone they trust, and when they do they may be encouraged or supported by a friend.

- For a number of reasons many young people do not talk to anyone about experiencing neglect. One reason is a fear of upsetting parents, siblings and wider family members. A second is a fear of the consequences of talking to someone, especially worry about being taken into care, breaking up the family and what will happen to their parents. Fear and stigma surrounding disclosure of neglect may be more pronounced for some minority ethnic young people who may be concerned about preserving family honour.

- When young people do want to access help, they often do not know where to get it.

- If young people do talk to someone about problems at home, they may not be believed or concerns may not be acted upon. This can mean that young people do not talk about their problems again.

- Neglect is likely to lead to feelings such as fear, isolation, sadness and lack of confidence.

- Neglect may lead to problems at school with friendships and lack of concentration or poor attendance, health issues, difficulty sleeping, bullying, self-harm and suicide. It may also cause young people to run away from home and it can lead to a range of associated problems such as substance misuse, sexual exploitation, violence and crime.

- Young people want a constant person in their lives whom they can trust and talk to when they experience problems.

There is very little research about neglect that includes the perspectives of young people with disabilities, whom neglect may affect disproportionately (see Chapter 3). It is also worth remembering that neglect, like other forms of abuse, occurs across classes and cultures, yet much of our existing knowledge comes from research with young people whose parents misuse substances and this tends to be drawn from samples with deprived and predominantly white families.

Research findings with young people
Young people's definitions of neglect
Like much other research with young people on a range of subjects (Aldgate and Statham 2001; Gorin 2004), the young people we spoke to about neglect often had very different definitions and perceptions from those of adults. When asked what neglect was, one group of older care leavers (aged 19 to 24) immediately identified neglect as a culturally specific entity – that is, they talked about concepts of neglect being different in other countries and cultures – although this recognition was not widespread. It was also highlighted within the care leavers' groups that neglect may not just be perpetrated by parents; that for looked after young people neglect may also happen in foster and residential homes; and that young people could be neglected by social workers.

One young person felt that children may not know what neglect is:

> Children don't necessarily know what neglect is, they just think parents hate them.

This raises questions about whether children and young people who are neglected are able to recognize it at the time it is happening to them. Informal discussions with practitioners suggest that some believe recognition to be difficult for young people who have grown up within a neglectful home and have never known anything different. In our focus groups, most of the young people we spoke to were able to provide descriptions of what they thought neglect was. However, some of the focus groups we held included young people who had already been in contact with children's social care services. It is likely that, while young people may have been unaware of what neglect was before intervention, they were likely to be more aware than a general population sample of the term 'neglect' and its meaning once interventions had been put in place in their lives (see previous research such as Fuller *et al.* 2000).

Each of the groups of young people who took part in the research provided descriptions of aspects of neglect that might be anticipated, such as failure to provide adequate food or water, baths, clean or suitable clothes, shelter, a safe environment and protection. The following two young people who had experienced neglect themselves said:

> When you don't get fed properly. Like me, I'm always looking for food.

> *Young person:* 'I couldn't get a bath every day – I had to go stay with my aunty for a couple of weeks. I was underweight, the school was very concerned, 'cos my skin was dead pale.'

> *Interviewer:* 'Do you think that was neglect then Sian?'

> *Young person:* 'Yeah, it was a huge neglect, because the school was... I was putting myself at risk by picking needles up. They was only about 2 inches away from me, actually near me...so I couldn't do anything... but I thought I'd like pick it up and show my mum. And that's why I know that she was on heroin.'

Several groups also mentioned, in their definitions of neglect, the importance of parents' ensuring young people attended school, that they were involved in young people's education, through parents' evenings or awards evenings and that they ensured young people received medical care if they needed it:

> Basically if you had a burn and if they didn't do anything; if they didn't pay attention something bad could happen. That is serious neglect.

> Like if you don't take them to school for example, if they don't take them to the doctor. Something like that.

Interestingly, many young people did not see neglect as being distinct from other forms of abuse, and included all aspects of maltreatment in their definitions. In our discussions with young people, it was unclear whether they described physical, emotional and sexual abuse within the category of neglect because they saw different forms of harm as likely to be co-occurring or because all forms of abuse and neglect were just seen as forms of harm (or lack of caring parenting) and they therefore did not draw distinctions.

One young person said neglect was:

> Normally where you're either hurting the kids...that's the biggest neglect...or not feeding the kids.

Several young people talked of neglect including 'physical abuse'. One young man described neglect as being 'abused, beaten up, things put down to them'. Sian, aged 16, openly talked within a group about her experiences of being sexually abused and equated this with a form of physical neglect on the part of her mother's boyfriend:

> When your mum's boyfriend comes on to you that is a physical neglect.

Many young people spoke about neglect as including aspects of emotional harm. As has been discussed in Chapter 2, drawing a distinction between emotional 'abuse' and emotional 'neglect' is problematic and much debated and was not reflected in young people's understandings. They talked of neglect including 'mental abuse'; 'bullying'; 'lack of emotional security'; 'no love and affection'; 'no appreciation'; 'torment'; 'blamed for break-up in relationships'; 'singled out by parents, emotional focus'. One young person said that neglect was 'being unaware of your child's feelings, for example depression'.

Young people's descriptions of neglect incorporated an absence of caring parental responsibility. Their definitions included issues around ensuring that young people have a healthy diet and preventing obesity. Young people also felt that it was neglectful if parents did not teach their children basic social skills, morals (teaching right from wrong), manners and how to look after themselves. Some of the young people we spoke to, who were care leavers or who had parents with substance misuse problems, felt that they had not been taught independence skills by parents and that this was neglectful because they were ill-equipped to take care of themselves. Examples of the life skills they felt were important, and they did not necessarily have, included being able to cook; using a washing machine; and knowing how to search for jobs. This was raised by care leavers who were moving onto independent living and by young people with substance-misusing parents.

Some examples of their comments included the following:

> Neglect is…'parents not raising them properly, not cooking for them such as always giving them fast food.'

> When they're older they'll be sitting down, 'Oh I don't know how to do that, I'm going to get someone else to do it'; 'I can't do cooking 'cos my mum didn't teach me.' It's like a neglect because they're not shown the basics of life.

Parents leaving out children, favouring siblings or prioritizing new partners over their children was mentioned in several groups as being neglectful. One young person said:

> Say if you have a new baby coming along, the baby gets more credit than you.

Favouring siblings is an issue that has been raised by children and young people contacting ChildLine and it is clearly distressing for a number of young people (ChildLine 2008).

Another interesting issue that one young person described as 'neglect' was lack of support from an absent parent when children live in single-parent households. Research with families living in poverty has highlighted the emotional impact that absence, or unreliable experiences, of care from an absent parent can have on children and has described this as being akin to a form of emotional abuse (Hooper *et al.* 2007).

As has been covered in Chapter 2, much of the literature about definitions of neglect discuss whether the category of neglect should only include acts of omission or acts of commission too. Interestingly, young people's definitions included deliberate acts of commission such as 'having to do every single chore', 'disallowing a kid to play or free time', 'constant babysitting' and parents 'prioritizing new partners'. These were phrased by young people in terms of deliberate strategies on the part of parents, but could equally be viewed differently as acts of omission – for example, 'a young person having to do every single chore' could also be viewed as a parent failing to do physical caring tasks around the house, and having to do 'constant babysitting' could be seen as a parent failing to care for children as they should do. Within their definitions of neglect, young people also described parents 'spending all the money on drugs' and 'go(ing) out and get(ting) drunk'. By just seeing neglect as acts of omission is failing to recognize that definitions may vary depending on the individual viewpoint and may not take into account young people's perspectives.

Discerning poor parenting from neglect

As Chapter 2 discusses, neglect cases are often characterized by a long-term continuum of chronic issues or a 'way of life' (Turney and Tanner 2001), rather than a one-off event. This means that discerning the boundary between poor parenting and neglect can be difficult and this was illustrated in young people's responses. While most parents would expect young people to contribute to chores, or do occasional babysitting for siblings, at what point does this become neglectful and to what extent are these behaviours likely to be picked up by professionals? Smith and Ravenhill (2006) highlight a case in which a 15-year-old ran away from home, was placed in foster care but returned home to a neglectful mother; the alarm was only raised when the foster carer raised concerns that the young person had spent two months looking after siblings while her mother went away.

In the focus groups we undertook with young people, we tried to find out about their views by using a range of scenarios to explore their perceptions of neglectful parenting for children of different ages. The scenarios included having to do your own washing or cooking, being left unsupervised during the day for three hours, being left unsupervised overnight and being fed a diet of takeaways and fast food. The young people were asked whether they thought this would be neglectful for a 2-year-old, a 9-year-old, a 12-year-old and a 15-year-old. While there tended to be a broad consensus of opinion that all these behaviours would be neglectful for children under 10, the discussions about teenagers became more complex and there was some disagreement in groups, particularly around the age at which it became acceptable to leave children unsupervised either in the day or at night, and around the responsibility or indeed the ability of parents to ensure their children eat a healthy diet once they reach the teenage years.

All the groups concluded that it was not possible to provide a specific age at which these actions were neglectful but that it would depend on the individual ability and confidence of the young person:

> I was going to say, you can't really like put an age to you know the time where the parent kind of backs away. You have to kind of see potential in your child and say is she responsible,

is he responsible enough to handle this... I think what some people do yeah is 'Oh you're 16 now, you should be able to cook, clean' dadadada... What if there are people that can't even boil rice because they find it so difficult. My friend burns it every time...seriously, my friends, some of them can't actually do stuff. So they might feel neglected if their parents put it all on them – do this, do that. If you can handle it and if you're capable of doing the things that your parents are expecting you to do, then it's okay.

(There) shouldn't be a specific age, depends on the child, family and mum and dad. There shouldn't be a limit for someone to know how to wash up, it is something you grow with and you grow up learning to do, skills you should have to learn should be something taught, a gradual thing.

Within the research there were some young people who felt they would feel safe if they were left alone, while others had anxieties, particularly in relation to being left alone at night. One young person said:

No but like if I'm 12 and if I got left on my own for like 2 hours, 3 hours, it wouldn't matter, but if it was like overnight, yeah I suppose it would matter. But like if it was just for 2 hours in the daytime... 'cos you'd have all neighbours near you, no one would like burgle you in the middle of the day with everyone walking down the street.

The following conversation was between six young people who were discussing whether they felt it was appropriate to leave a 12-year-old at home for three hours on their own during the day:

Lee: It depends on the situation – if it is urgent like they need to go to the hospital or if a parent does it [to pursue own leisure].

Rubin: It is neglect.

Chris, Robin and Michelle agreed they thought it was neglect.

Robin: You are still young and not that sensible, you might do something silly.

Rubin: It is neglect.

Once a young person is 15 years old there was still disagreement about whether they thought it was neglect:

Lee: Not neglect, at 15 they are old enough to take care of themselves – need instructions and not to go out...not to open the door.

Jack: I told my mum the only way I am staying in the house is if I have a dog [doesn't like being at home by himself] in case someone breaks in.

The complexities for young people in identifying neglectful behaviours mirror those experienced by professionals, but, while young people were divided about whether lack of supervision was neglectful for teenagers, most felt that it was not desirable. There was a sense from the young people whom we spoke to that having an adult who was available and supportive of them was valued. All the young people were able to think about the situations we presented them with and say whether they would feel unhappy if they happened to them. The lack of agreement illustrates that parental behaviours (or omission of behaviours) have different impacts on young people whose capacities and needs are varied, so what is neglectful depends on how that behaviour feels and affects each individual young person.

Young people's awareness of the causes of neglect

Young people found it hard to think about reasons why neglect may happen, but all the groups were collectively able to come up with some ideas as to why parents may neglect their children. Reasons were given, such as not wanting your children, post-natal depression, other mental health problems, alcoholism and drugs. One young person who had a parent with a substance misuse problem said:

Because some houses that you go and see they're like dead horrible – the stench in the house and you see kids running about in just underwear, you're like 'Why don't you put some clothes on your kid?' 'Oh, I ain't got a washer yet'. So you go out and buy some clothes for that kid. If you just see it running about in a T-shirt you would say 'Oh that mother is a bad mother.' Well you can't really say that, because some parents can't cope – it depends if they've got depression or they're on loads of medication and plus they're getting away from their depressions by going on drink or heroin because they can't cope with it. Because when they take heroin it's like it's taking them away from...it's a dream world to them, sort of thing. So they think 'Oh everything's all right, it's all right, my kid's all right so...' But when they're on the drink or

> the heroin, they don't see that, they don't see the kids getting in danger with needles about and bottles being smashed.

Several groups mentioned that neglect may not be the fault of the parent because they may not know how to look after children properly or they may have been neglected themselves:

> Because they could be mentally ill or, they just don't know how to. 'Cos I know a case, that a boy in, what's it called, in primary school, his clothes was not washed and the teachers had, what's it called, they had, they were worried about it, so when they upfronted the mother it turned out that she didn't know how to, she wasn't very clever.

> It's not the parent's fault, 'cos the parent could have had a hard time as a kid.

> Maybe because they didn't get love and affection what they wanted from their parents.

Noticing signs of neglect

Young people were asked to think about how professionals may be able to tell if a child is being neglected. These were some of their ideas:

Physical signs by the young person

- They hide themselves.
- Withdrawn, shy and shaky.
- Dirty clothes or unkempt.
- They could be really scrawny.
- Too fat.
- Self-harm.

Emotional signs by the young person

- Young person might not trust adults.
- They may be lonely or isolated.
- Not feeling confident.
- Can't talk about their home life – speak openly.
- Might not want parents to come into school.

Interaction of the young person with others

- Might not have any friends.
- Never have friends home.
- Obvious lying.

Parent or home factors

- If parents are not involved in school or if the young person does not want them involved in school.
- Parents ensuring the child does not get too close (to other adults or children).
- Children have too many chores.

When we asked young people about how professionals could help young people talk to them about neglect, they listed the following ideas as advice to give professionals.

- Don't jump to conclusions.
- Be understanding – not judgemental.
- Talk to other young people who have been neglected.
- Don't be too intimidating.
- Don't make them feel isolated – let them know they can talk to them.

One young person simply said:

> Talk to the young people – make the young people feel they can trust you and communication.

Other ideas for identifying neglect included providing more opportunities for young people to talk to professionals by having questionnaires that could be completed with doctors, teachers and counsellors, and having more social gatherings for young people where professionals are also present so they have more chance to gain young people's trust.

Young people identified very similar characteristics in someone they might choose to talk to, as has been found in previous research. Characteristics included someone who is understanding, friendly, nice, funny and respectful and, importantly, they said they would talk to someone they could rely on (see Featherstone and Evans 2004; Willow 2009).

Young people's awareness of the impact of neglect

Within the focus groups, young people were asked to think about the impact of neglect and all were able to think of some likely effects on young people. Some young people described how it might make them feel – for example, sad, lonely, scared, angry, unconfident, embarrassed and insecure. Other young people described short-term effects such as not being able to look after yourself, not going to the dentist, missing school, not wanting to go out, not making friends easily, not being able to talk to people, doing badly in school, eating junk food and selling stuff to get food. One young person said:

> You could feel alone, it could cause you to self-harm, you could think it's your fault.

Several of the groups, with older young people, identified a range of long-term effects:

> *Raina:* Some people even when they grow up into their 40–50s remember their childhood and it makes them sad and depressed, people carry things with them, feel the effect for a long time. (They may) do things to their children – neglect their own children, not consciously repeat the same pattern.

> *Kelly:* Lack of self-esteem.

> *Raina:* Bullying at school they may have problems at home, transfer aggression, make others feel bad – bullied or bullying. Other people can hurt themselves. Self-harm – not happy, neglecting yourself.

> *Elisha:* Putting yourself down, feeling devalued and low self-worth.

> *Kelly:* Boozing, allowing yourself to be abused.

> *Elisha:* Allow yourselves to be used by the other sex.

> *Raina:* Anorexia.

> *Kelly:* Obesity.

The responses of the young offenders' group suggested that they were well aware of the impact of neglect. The following were some of the responses they gave when asked about how neglect might affect young people physically and emotionally:

Anger – taking it out on people.

If you are in jail, no visits.

Makes you think why am I still around.

If no love, no one to trust.

In the end leads to suicide.

Depression, self-harm and suicide were mentioned by four out of six of the groups, all of whom had older young people or those with direct experience of neglect. Bullying and being bullied was also seen as likely to be a common problem:

> We've got, they might self-harm. We have smelly, therefore they'll have no friends. Other problems they'll be stressed out, so then they'll do bad in school and misbehave. They'll be attention seeking because they get no attention from home. They may bully others... They're likely to be bullied so they'll get in with bullies to protect themselves.

While most of the young people thought of negative effects of neglect, one care leaver highlighted the resilience of young people:

> Depends on person, can make you stronger, it might not always have a negative impact. It could lead to positive achievements.

Young people's awareness of help available

As discussed earlier, previous research suggests that young people rarely seek help from professionals first if they have problems at home (Featherstone and Evans 2004; Gorin 2004). When asked about what they would advise young people to do if they were neglected, most young people we spoke to said to talk to someone and most thought about informal sources of support first, such as friends, grandparents, siblings and wider family. A few did mention approaching social workers, teachers and youth offending team workers, but awareness of these professionals was greater amongst the young people who had contact with children's social care services or youth offending services. This supports findings of previous research (Fuller *et al.* 2000).

Awareness of the professionals who may be able to help, and especially the roles of helping professionals, did not seem to be clear to many young people, especially those who had not previously had contact with them.

One group wanted the researchers to explain to them the difference between the roles of people such as social workers, Connexions workers and youth workers. The distinctions between who would deal with young people in which circumstances was not something that was familiar to them.

We also asked young people about what support services they were aware of for young people who were being neglected. Levels of awareness of services to support young people were varied but many of the young people struggled to think of any and not all thought about options such as ChildLine. No one talked about using new media options for support purposes, such as online counselling support. The need for better information about services for young people and signposting to helping services for young people and their families is a common finding of research projects with young people (Allard 2003; Gorin 2004; Hooper *et al.* 2007; Rees *et al.* 2010).

In discussions with young people, we talked about the best way to communicate messages to other young people about neglect. Overwhelmingly, young people thought that the most effective means of communicating messages about neglect were by the use of a hard copy leaflet that they could pick up and take with them. Views about use of websites and social networking websites such as Facebook and MySpace were varied, with some young people being more keen to access information on them than others. Most groups took the view that small, discreet hard copy information for young people was most likely to be read and kept, but that web-based information would also be a useful addition. However, they were clear that information on the internet needed to be engaging and specifically designed for their age group, and the preference was for material that was conveyed via short films or had interactive elements to it.

Previous research with young people by Smith and Ravenhill (2006) has found that there are many problems for young people who have run away from home when they try to access information about help via search engines. They describe there being a 'huge stumbling block' for young people actively seeking information through the internet and in interviews they undertook with school groups they found that many young people do not know of services in their area, either because the services do not exist or because the services are difficult to find.

During our focus groups with young people on neglect, several groups aligned the discussions with storylines they had seen on television soaps like *Eastenders*, talk shows such as *The Jeremy Kyle Show* and documentaries:

For example in *Eastenders* is a person that's in trouble, and she gets bullied by her mum, by her mum saying that you're fat, you're not going to get a job, no one loves you. So that's neglect as well. She laughs at her, she laughs about her child, behind her back and to her friends as well.

Television seemed to be the most influential form of media mentioned by young people and seemed to have provided them with an understanding of possible scenarios within which neglect could occur, which they could identify with. This was supported by the research by Smith and Ravenhill (2006) that found that 14- to 16-year-olds wanted more television programmes they could watch in private that were supported by helplines.

Discussion
Key points
This chapter has highlighted that there is a lot to learn from speaking directly to young people about neglect and that the way young people see things is often very different from the perceptions of adults. In terms of definitions, the young people we spoke to conceptualized neglect as part of a wider spectrum of harm that can occur to children, and they saw neglect as a lack of appropriate parental responsibility and care. They defined 'neglect' in broader terms than the definitions used for child protection purposes and their responses suggest that they may attach different significance to particular behaviours – for example, teaching of self-care skills and prevention of obesity – than may be attached to such events by adults. Their discussions highlighted that 'what is neglectful' varies depending on how that behaviour (or omission of behaviour) makes a young person feel and how it impacts upon them. Young people highlighted the links between neglect and mental health problems, such as depression, self-harm and suicide, and between neglect and bullying. These views are consistent with wider research evidence.

This research confirms the findings of previous studies about help seeking. Most young people suggested approaching friends or family members first, or someone with whom they have a trusting relationship. Many young people we spoke to, who had not been in contact with children's social care services, were not aware of where they would be able to get information about neglect. They also lacked knowledge about how to go about seeking help from professionals and what roles different professionals play in protecting children.

Implications

There is a dearth of research on young people's views and experiences of neglect, particularly the views of disabled young people and those from Black and minority ethnic groups. More research is urgently needed to address these gaps so we have more knowledge about the impact of neglect on young people and how to improve both short- and long-term outcomes. This project sought to explore young people's perspectives and provide some basis for discussion, but much more in-depth research needs to be undertaken.

Understanding what neglect means to young people and how it affects them should be central to any discussion among professionals about defining and addressing it. The way in which young people conceptualize neglect as part of the wider spectrum of abuse raises questions about whether we should, as some commentators such as McGee *et al.* (1995) suggest, treat maltreatment of young people as an entire entity rather than seeing it in standalone categories. It also suggests that we need to think carefully about the way we communicate with young people about neglect and abuse, especially with younger children and those with learning difficulties.

Previous literature has also suggested that, rather than just focusing on parenting behaviour as the means to defining neglect, definitions should be concerned with the impact of the behaviour on the individual young person. Our research with young people supports this approach, because what was important to young people was not necessarily the same as professional definitions of neglect and much of what young people discussed would not have reached thresholds for child protection. However, the inability of parents to undertake specific tasks may hold particular emotional significance for some young people. Discussions with young people about thresholds for neglect highlighted the differences that exist among young people in terms of their capabilities and confidence, and the differences in how certain parental behaviours (or omissions) would make them feel. It is important that social workers pay special attention to talking directly with young people about neglect and discuss which particular parental behaviours, or absence of behaviours, have the most impact on that particular young person, and that these feelings and perspectives are used to make fully informed assessments. Professionals also need to be made more aware of the potential links between neglect and mental health problems, suicide and bullying, in order to aid identification of neglect cases. More research that focused on these potential links would also be helpful.

Awareness needs to be raised among young people about neglect and ways in which they can seek help. Information needs to be tailored to engage young people, and to be provided through a range of different media such as television, online video clips, hard copy and web-based information. Information needs to be concise and convey key messages about what neglect is and routes to seek help. This would not only help young people to recognize if it is happening to them, but also to identify if friends are experiencing neglect and support them to gain help. Universal delivery of information through schools is central to improving young people's understanding and improving early identification. Young people also need to be provided with more ways in which they can develop trusting relationships with peers and professionals, through peer mentoring schemes in schools and counselling or advocacy routes.

6

Whose Business is the Neglect of Young People?

I think it's a really very scary place to be if you're 13 to 18 and actually nobody cares about you or loves you and out there you're perceived to be old enough to take responsibility for yourself. (Professional)

We don't get the category 'neglected teenagers', it doesn't come as a category... There's not even a teenager's service, they're all mainly neglected and you can argue a case for that, but they become 'drug users' or it's the 'behaviour' which presents when they're that age. (Professional)

Introduction

As the earlier chapters of this book show, teenage neglect is multi-faceted in its origins and in the way its consequences are experienced by young people. Work that addresses the inherent complexities associated with neglect is likely to merit the involvement of several different agencies in order to meet the range of young people's needs. A multi-agency approach to adolescent neglect inevitably will require agencies to work alongside each other and, ideally, to work together to achieve common goals for and with young people.

Throughout this book we emphasize the importance of an ecological perspective when trying to understand and work with neglect. Interventions in relation to adolescent neglect are the focus of Chapter 7. For our purposes in the present chapter, where multi-agency working is highlighted, we suggest that effective interventions depend on professionals developing working relationships that are sympathetic to each others' environments and priorities. This apparently simple claim involves complex dynamics that require a considerable skills base on the part of those staff involved. These dynamic inter-relationships underpin this chapter, which investigates some of the particular challenges involved when different agencies are working for and on behalf of neglected young people.

The material in this chapter is based on focus group discussions with professionals from a range of agencies, undertaken as part of the *Neglected Adolescents* research project that forms the basis of this book (Stein *et al*. 2009; see Chapter 1). This strand of our research renders as problematic in empirical terms the gap in our understanding of multi-agency working with older children who are neglected. The approach takes the perspectives of professionals from different agencies as a starting point. In association with the literature review that formed the first stage of our research, this part of the project worked with LSCBs in two local authorities as the organizational basis from which to recruit multi-disciplinary focus groups. An LSCB functions as a statutory mechanism that brings together organizations in each locality so that they can co-operate in safeguarding and promoting the welfare of children, and ensure effective action (HM Government 2010).

Staff drawn from a range of agencies, such as children's services, health, Child and Adolescent Mental Health Services (CAMHS), police, Connexions, youth offending teams (YOTs) and housing were identified with the help of LSCBs and invited to participate in a series of discussions. The main purpose of forming these groups was to concentrate on adolescent neglect and in particular to share information from the research review, to explore the identification of common definitions and the thresholds of concern, and to assist in the preparation of a practice guide (Hicks and Stein 2010) for multi-disciplinary teams. In total, 28 staff took part in a series of group discussions, held on several occasions. In addition, group members commented on progressive drafts of the literature review and the practice guide.

The enthusiasm of group members in relation to this area was unequivocal and this is accounted for primarily in terms of the relatively unusual opportunity that the research presented. Recently, many LSCBs have set up neglect working groups and have produced various documents for local use that support practice in relation to neglect – for example, neglect protocols and guidance, frameworks of good practice and assessment toolkits. While these documents are robust and essential to practice, rarely do they make detailed or direct address to either the needs of adolescents or to multi-agency working. Practitioners taking part in this study were aware that, as an aspect of practice, 'neglected adolescents' claim little focused attention as a category, despite representing a large proportion of the work that takes place. Group members were keen to address this apparent gap. As one participant noted about work with adolescents, 'neglect is the former lack of care and we work with that all the time'. This pervasiveness may be taken as indicative of one of the ways in which neglect comes to be seen as part of routine practice and, in a sense, to be normalized.

The chapter considers briefly the context surrounding multi-agency working in England and what this implies for work with adolescents who are neglected, before focusing on our empirical research about challenges encountered in practice – specifically, responsibility and engagement; and definitions and thresholds. The chapter ends by thinking about the implications for developing multi-agency work with adolescents who are neglected.

Multi-agency working in England: the context

Moving into the 21st century, England experienced something of a sea-change in terms of what was considered to be essential in children's social care practice. Prior to the Children Act 1989, the terms 'interagency', 'multi-disciplinary', 'multi-agency' and 'collaborative working' were loosely defined and somewhat hazily discerned on the horizon. Since then, these terms have come to describe particular modes of operation that are now considered to be central to the delivery of effective social care practice (Anning *et al.* 2006; Whittington 2003b). Although this shift has occurred over a relatively short period of time, much has been experienced and much has been learned. Regrettably, sometimes this has been at a serious cost to many young people, their families and friends and associated professionals. Enquiries into child deaths and poor practice have been well documented (Reder and Duncan 2004; Sinclair and Bullock 2002) and have identified shortcomings in communication between agencies, in seeking the advice or perspective of others and in sharing crucial information (Brandon *et al.* 2008a; Parton 2004). These, along with broader political, economic and legal factors, have contributed to driving changes in policy and practice (Parrott 2005). Multi-agency collaboration is regarded now as essential to good practice (Barrett and Keeping 2005), the assumption being that better outcomes should be achieved by means of a holistic approach to needs. The Children Act 1989 began the shift towards working across disciplines. The Children Act 2004 placed a duty of co-operation on local authorities and agencies to 'work together to safeguard children's welfare'. The Act required that collaboration should be developed to bring together services to strengthen multi-agency working in relation to the welfare of children.

The *Working Together to Safeguard Children* guidance, first published in 2006 and revised in 2010, explicitly details this expectation. At a policy level, the drive towards multi-agency working is consolidated in *Every Child Matters* (HM Government 2004), where all professionals in contact with children and families are seen to have a duty to safeguard children, promote their well-being and work together in offering a consistent response to needs. This agenda is supported extensively – for example, by freely available multi-agency toolkits, guidance on information sharing and the CAF and training materials geared towards supporting integrated working.

Corresponding with these movements in direction, the landscape of practice has altered to enable changes in functioning. Multi-agency hubs, which operate at varying levels, are now fundamental to practice. These include statutory mechanisms such as LSCBs, partnerships such as Children's Trusts and service nexus such as Sure Start and Connexions. Each of these has a major role to play in facilitating and strengthening multi-agency working. Again, the nature and success of such hubs are continuing to be explored and it is not the intention here to give a full investigation of this area. However, for the contextual purposes of this chapter, it is important to establish that apparent advantages are well documented, emphasizing the ways in which crucial areas of practice have the potential to be enhanced by structured approaches to multi-agency working. These areas include the benefits of co-location (Anning *et al.* 2006; Frost and Robinson 2007), awareness of the importance of confidentiality and sharing (Loxley 1997; Richardson and Asthana 2006), together with a willingness to take risks, a 'can do' culture and one that retains user needs as central to activity (Stewart, Petch and Curtice 2003).

In parallel, challenges to multi-agency working are identified in literature, not least in terms of the relative absence of meaningful debates around differences in professional identities, ethics and values (Parrott 2008), integrated delivery systems as distinct from merely integration at a structural level (Johnson *et al.* 2003), the difficulties involved in achieving open dialogue and effective communication (Atkinson *et al.* 2002; Biggs 1997; Moreland *et al.* 2004) and what it takes to establish positive and functional relationships (Brandon *et al.* 2006; Leiba and Weinstein 2003). Factors to consider in collaborative ways of working are described extensively by McCray (2007) and these include agencies' language, not making assumptions about shared beliefs and views, establishing clarity on resources, being confident in own role, delivering as agreed, and establishing consensus on leadership and accountability. The value of interprofessional education (Carpenter and Dickinson 2008), shared governance (Glasby and Dickinson 2008), and common assessment and delivery systems (Stein 2009) are all promoted as supporting successful multi-agency working.

As will be seen from the increasing knowledge base surrounding multi-agency working, the most developed understanding of this arena lies in work with younger children, known in England as 'early years' provision (Gasper 2009; Moran *et al.* 2007). Multi-agency working is a key part of the Early Years Foundation Stage (EYFS) framework for setting the standards for learning, development and care for children from 0 to 5 years (H.M. Government 2008). Along with the legislative, policy and practice emphasis on the protection of younger children, the concentration of attention on this age group is not surprising. In consequence, however, the gap is accentuated in our understanding of multi-agency working with older children, and specifically with those who are neglected.

Responsibility and engagement

As this chapter will indicate, much multi-agency work that takes place in relation to young people is dependent on a reliable starting point in terms of defining neglect and assessing it. There are particular challenges involved in making judgements in these areas and these need to be thought through and addressed by those practising in this arena before embarking on work that takes place across different agencies. Working with adolescents brings into play dimensions associated with the shift in responsibility for action and behaviour. This is a complex area of human development, compounded by distinctions in age-based legislation. There is variation in the ages at which young people legally may act in specific ways. Examples of this include the age of criminal responsibility and variation in the right to vote, drive, marry, have sex, drink alcohol, buy a firearm, buy a pet, borrow money from a bank and smoke. These differences take on a distinctive hue in relation to service provision, where varying approaches to responsible age may prove to limit the extent of support provided:

> My 13-year-old could give his own consent for medical treatment but now that he's 17½ I still have to sign a slip for him to go on a school trip. He can make his own decisions about whether he wants to go and see a GP because he's feeling depressed or anxious and that referral could be made because he'd been to see a GP at 15, and I don't have a right to know that as a mother. However, if that referral has been picked up because he was very depressed, they can't work with him if I don't engage. That's really, really confused, isn't it? For them as young people, it's all very blurred.

In this quote from a professional speaking from a parental perspective, parental engagement is raised in this example as important in relation to intervention, a point to which this chapter will return. For younger children, the boundaries of responsibility for action are clearly drawn because neglect is usually more apparent as an act of omission by a parent or carer. For adolescents, there is assumed to be an element of choice that comes into play alongside progress towards greater independence. The possibility is raised of teenagers starting to neglect themselves. A likely turning point is that of entering secondary education, where more responsibility is placed on children for their behaviour. Again, establishing norms in terms of responsibility for adolescent behaviour is not a simple matter:

> Sexual exploitation becomes self-neglect to some extent and that's insofar as they [young people] are beyond the control of their parents and their parents aren't able to implement any strategies to control their behaviour. And the children will often say it's the choice that they have made... And that's where we then struggle with 'Are we going to put this kid in secure or are we going to do nothing?' And sometimes it almost feels as polarized as that, where the kid is essentially telling us to get lost, basically.

At an age when autonomy and responsibility are being established, willingness on the part of some young people to accept or engage with professional involvement may be difficult for practitioners to secure:

> For practitioners with a non-statutory responsibility in, say, the youth service or youth workers, it's very difficult to actually identify and have a longer term relationship because of that lifestyle and therefore in terms of addressing areas of need with somebody that's not engaging in education, not engaging in training, is 15, 15½ years old, statutory services reticent to get involved in terms of coming close to 16 years old, etc., etc., and for that person to have a very sort of disjointed lifestyle, it's very difficult, and even if you do have concerns about that sort of young person at that age or stage of their life to actually have a level of intervention in terms of a longer term relationship is really difficult.

Levels of concern and offers of support are often rejected by young people as a matter of choice. The issues of volition and permission – choice and consent – are important concerns. There are clear tensions here, where on the one hand adolescents may prefer to have greater autonomy and responsibility for themselves and, on the other, professionals may see that young people are vulnerable and in need of support. Vocabulary is important and many practitioners, while recognizing the relative maturity of adolescents, see the term 'young person' as implying a level of responsibility for oneself that is not always positive. 'Falling through the net', a frequently used phrase in relation to those suffering disjunctures in service delivery, becomes particularly important here, not least because consequences may prove to be severe, as in the example given by this practitioner, from a serious case review:

> That issue about social care, child protection intervention, [a young person] becomes an adolescent, gets into offending behaviour, over to youth offending services, which has obviously got a very different focus to their intervention and a far more specific focus; then the case gets closed and some of the welfare issues, which are probably still there, do not get addressed because he's an adolescent. Parental non-engagement is effectively not picked up.

The issue of engagement is, of course, very relevant both to adolescents and/or to their parents or carers. In effect, lack of parental engagement may mean that it is only possible to work with the symptoms of neglect, as distinct from the causes of it:

> You end up dealing with, almost solely with the child's behaviour, because you cannot get, because the parents aren't bothered enough to keep that kid and you don't engage with parents because as far as the parents are concerned they've done their job.

The longer term consequences of working in a piecemeal, 'quick fix' fashion over short periods of time are glaringly apparent to practitioners:

> We have very arbitrary timescales. If you're going to try and understand the complexity of the family with the kind of problems, you're not going to give help within 35 days, it's going to take longer. You need a skilled work force who understand the complexities and the subtleties of those issues in order to understand the question, the issues, and unless we understand the issues we're not ever going to bring about any lasting change; all we're going to do is change some of the external elements, or we might get the kid into school, but we're not necessarily addressing what it was that led to the child not going to school in the first place.

It is helpful here to remind ourselves that neglect is often experienced as an accumulation over time of experiences and behaviours. Earlier chapters in this book indicate that neglect, or a history of neglect, is a prominent aspect in serious case reviews related to children and young people aged 11 to 18 years (Brandon *et al.* 2008a). Brandon and colleagues identify the 'start again syndrome', where history, past behaviour patterns and poor parenting are not taken into account by practitioners, who frequently are concerned with the present and helping parents to make a new start. Incorporating the past so that it may inform present potential is vital when working with neglected young people:

> It's difficult to get a definitive view of what's going on – persistent but not necessarily consistent – parental input comes and goes, inconsistency in itself is quite damaging. It's not necessarily a consistent lack of parenting or providing the basics.

Something of a conflict arises when the resource implications of fuller engagement are considered:

> You end up trying to compromise the short-term pieces of work which – even putting plasters over it sometimes. A colleague of mine this week dealing with a case...an adolescent who's been very neglected but is kicking off big time at her school and was harangued in a multi-agency meeting because we hadn't provided family therapy... The tension arises in these things because there aren't enough people very often to do the long-term pieces of work in supporting these young people and indeed their families.

Professionals are acutely aware of the cycles of abuse and neglect that exist in families. These are intrinsically difficult to influence and staff may feel themselves to be reinforcing these cycles by being unable to bring about change, particularly when families cannot be engaged. Many parents and carers are felt to be doing the best for their children and are generally striving to make improvements:

> Neglect is different, because you are very often working with parents who are really struggling to care for their children and that is a long-term process to change. That comes back to what resources you can put in to that family for 6 months or for 10–15 years. Kids who are on the register stay on the list for longer than those under other categories. That's an enormous thing for practitioners – what is success?

Standards of parenting differ widely and professionals encounter degrees of parental complacency in relation to adolescents:

> The risk that we all are presented with is parents are less committed to teenagers than they are to younger children and so frequently the referrals into our service [social care] are actually from the parents themselves, they're not from the schools who should be referring them in.

The recognition that work with young people and their parents or carers is likely to be most useful if carried out in combination is seen as a high ambition that frequently may not be fulfilled:

> They get to years 4 or 5 and schools are concerned to focus on practical skills, self-care. I've worked with young people who are showered before we let them go into the classroom because they smelled so bad and didn't get parental permission because the parents hadn't been engaged for the last seven years so why should they now?

Acting to assist young people without parental engagement is not always thought to be either possible or worthwhile:

> CAMHS is often quite reluctant to work with children without their families because they often think with things like anxiety if parents aren't on board then what's the point? It's a cycle of neglect; it feels like we sometimes reinforce it.

Again, increased awareness is essential. Reder and Duncan (2004) emphasize the value of regular and meaningful supervision. Reviewing levels of engagement needs to form a regular part of supervisory processes so that intra- and inter-agency co-operation that recognizes the consequences of non-engagement for young people takes place.

Clearly, a mutual understanding of issues related to responsibility, choice and consent, together with the engagement of young people and their parents and carers, are aspects that are crucial to establishing good multi-agency practice.

Definitions and thresholds

Defining adolescent neglect underpins the potential for good practice, because this represents the starting point from which work ensues. The range of services available to children and young people is dependent on levels of need, the identification of which requires professional judgements to be made. Multi-agency responses are not always appropriate. The continuum of services covers the spectrum of need, from universal through to acute. 'Universal' services are those that are available to all young people. An individual agency might be involved with disadvantaged young people who would benefit from support from public agencies in order to make the best of their life chances. Such young people would be identified as 'vulnerable'.

A co-ordinated multi-agency response, led by multi-agency partners such as CAMHS or YOT, as distinct from children's social care services, would be appropriate in cases of 'complex' need. This would include those young people whose health or development would be likely to be significantly impaired without provision of services. At the furthest end of the need continuum, services for those young people who have suffered, or are likely to suffer, significant harm would be led by children's social care services as a specialist integrated or individual service response under care proceedings, or as a child protection case. Identification of this highest level of need would appear to be most clear-cut. Lower level neglect, despite its pervasiveness and long-term deleterious consequences, is less easy to determine:

> Neglect is a bit amorphous and therefore it's difficult to decide when to intervene; it's more straightforward in extreme or acute cases.

While examples of the range of needs act to support practice in relation to these distinctions, the boundaries between needs levels remain open to interpretation and a matter of professional judgement and practice experience. Such judgements are a contested area of practice and continue as a matter of post-modernist debate, where the struggle with contradictions is seen as an essential part of ethical conduct (Hugman 2003). At a practice level, the worker must make on-the-ground decisions from within a set of agreed contextual norms. This form of agreement is rarely a matter for open debate. Assumptions that are implicitly held frequently underpin professional judgements in relation to neglect:

> In terms of emotional and social neglect it's the absence of care in earlier years. There is no commonly held definition within the [YOS] team, but there is an implicit understanding.

These implicit assumptions may create difficulties within a team and across teams. Making explicit the driving assumptions is an essential foundation from which to build effective multi-agency practice. A useful starting point lies in raising awareness of the assumptions being made by means of discussion and considering the differences in viewpoints – for example, between health care providers, social workers and young people – so that a working consensus can be established. This consensus needs to be set within the context of professional duty and the *Every Child Matters* agenda, while being grounded in reality in terms of service users' everyday lives:

> For standards of care it's very difficult [to judge], because what you might say isn't suitable to live in, 50 per cent of the estate lives in.

Awareness of the relatively difficult circumstances in which many young people live guides the approach used:

> So many young people are neglected and they have coped thus far. Schools concentrate on self-care skills, giving information so they can make choices. They're coping in a society that just recognizes that they are neglected. High schools would only make a referral in the most serious cases of neglect, [such as] abandonment or failure to seek medical care.

Here the consequences for a young person's health and development are taken as important factors in distinguishing between neglect that is generally prevalent – and that, although not preferable, to some extent has to be treated as acceptable – and neglect that is acute and likely to have extreme consequences for the young person. The challenges that young people with multiple needs experience and the influence that these have on their life chances may remain out of reach of service provision. Again, a normalization of adolescent neglect is seen to operate, albeit reluctantly on the part of the practitioner. Organizational considerations sometimes outweigh the central concerns of the service:

> All agencies have a way of self-regulating the work they do, and try to direct their resources where they think they will have the most impact – thresholds, etc. are all constrained by that. It can be uncomfortable – sometimes they don't see or hear because they can't.

As may be anticipated, the description of neglect taken from *Working Together* (see Chapter 1) is most commonly used in practice as a definition. Although the description is thought to be clear and helpful, in relation to adolescents there remains ambiguity insofar as it applies to all ages, from babies to teenagers:

...if we're talking about a 5-year-old and the child isn't getting to school, that easily comes into the field of neglect because we see it as being very much the parental responsibility to ensure that the child does get the appropriate education. But if we're talking about a 14- or a 15-year-old, we're clearly not conferencing every 14- and 15-year-old in [city] who isn't getting education. So, the definition does fluctuate according to age, without there being a real sort of acknowledgement of that. It's implicit.

As noted in previous chapters, the Core Assessment Records, published in relation to the *Framework for Assessment of Children in Need and their Families*, offer distinctions in terms of age and these are pertinent to the assessment of adolescent neglect. In terms of defining neglect, our findings show that age-related interpretation is thought to be required and this is seen to vary within and between agencies, meaning that there are grey areas in this respect. Crucial to multi-agency working is arriving at consistency in the agreement of definitions, their interpretation and their application:

...the difficulty is in how the definition is applied in a practical situation. For some of us in the city there is consistency because of a professional network...

The robust nature of these essential professional networks relies on good communication, close working relationships, keeping pace with changes in the circumstances of young people and the agreement of common goals.

Linked to variation in defining neglect is the sensitive issue of clarity in interpreting the thresholds that govern the provision of services geared towards best meeting the needs of young people:

It's very difficult to establish thresholds and criteria, e.g. in relation to common assessment; one of the biggest problems is deciding on a threshold or a level at which lead practitioners [from children's social care services] will be involved in relation to undertaking a common assessment, in other words at what point does this become something above the 25–30 per cent of the adolescent population being in need? At what point does that individual young person become a young person that is being neglected?

Multi-agency work requires a thorough awareness of the contexts from which each professional offers services. Included here are legal responsibilities, thresholds, agency purposes and procedures, role boundaries and agency capacities. Providing services in combination with other agencies is often thought to be in the interests of young people, although in practice this may be difficult to achieve. Thresholds may be regarded differently by partner agencies and this presents difficulties at times, especially when making referrals to other agencies, as this CAMHS worker suggests:

> ...one case in particular, where we made the referral and we thought there was a really serious longstanding issue of neglect that we were all really concerned about and we made that referral and then the assessment was done and it was felt that it wasn't at a level where social care services would intervene and the case was passed back to us, which made it really difficult for us then because we couldn't, or we felt like it was difficult for us to work with those issues because we're primarily involved with the mental health of young people, and we kind of felt like we needed to be working alongside social services to do that adequately really. So it felt like we were left holding something that we couldn't intervene with really.

Boundaries between agencies in this and other instances serve to leave observable needs without agency support. Awareness of all agencies involved with particular families and/or young people and the approaches that are being used, is vital. Arriving at a shared awareness of the value of good communication and all that this entails is a great help:

> I actually don't see criminal prosecution for neglect as a way to benefit anyone in any way at all and fines make family relationships worse. Is it in the interest of us [police] to prosecute when social care is trying to work with them? We need to know they are doing that.

Brandon and her colleagues (2008a) make a case for a 'shared commitment to children and young people and clear, well-coordinated multi-agency involvement' as distinct from arguing about whether or not thresholds for intervention are met. Close liaison and information sharing serve to facilitate clarity about contexts, thresholds and roles.

Discussion
Key points
In this chapter, we have considered the context surrounding multi-agency working in England and what this implies for work with young people who

are neglected. We have described briefly some findings from our research with multi-agency groups. We have considered also some of the challenges encountered in practice and in particular those associated with age-related shifts in where responsibility is thought to lie for young people and their engagement with services.

Elements of choice come into play when developing towards independence and this is crucial when young people are establishing levels of autonomy and responsibility. These arenas require judgements to be made by professionals, particularly in terms of identifying whether or not a young person is being neglected. Such judgements may vary considerably at an individual level, and between and within different services. Effective supervision, which allows for the careful consideration of inconsistencies in the way neglect is approached, is essential.

Defining adolescent neglect is complex. Distinguishing between generally prevalent neglect – which to some extent may become normalized – and neglect that is likely to have extensive consequences presents difficulties in practice. This is compounded by differences in age-related interpretations of what constitutes neglect. Consistency in agreement of definitions, their interpretation and application is vital at the level of practice.

Robust professional networks are essential to multi-agency practice, along with clarity in interpreting thresholds for delivery between agencies. An awareness of the context from which each professional provides services, together with a shared awareness of the value of effective communication, is at the heart of good practice for and on behalf of neglected young people.

Implications

What are the key elements that need to be taken into account in multi-agency work with adolescent neglect? We have indicated the importance of good communication, close working relationships and developing a mutual understanding of the language being used within and between the different agencies that are involved with neglected young people and their families. Additionally, we have pointed towards the value of sharing the responsibility for the work that takes place, and being mindful of the goals each party is working towards. These areas represent abiding challenges in multi-agency work. In order to develop multi-agency practice with adolescent neglect, it is essential to understand the assumptions being made by different parties, including those made within and between agencies involved and those made by young people and families. This forms a necessary preliminary to establishing a working consensus that takes account of the approaches being used and the expectations of all concerned.

Each professional context needs to be understood by the respective agencies – for example, agency purposes and procedures, role boundaries and agency capacities. Professionals' definitions of what neglect entails need to be consistent so that their interpretation across agencies is applied reliably. Clarity in interpreting thresholds within and between agencies is needed. This will facilitate the setting of appropriate and realizable multi-agency goals. These need to be meaningful to the everyday lives of young people while taking account of the duty to promote well-being and provide a consistent response to needs.

A series of tensions emerges from our multi-agency groups in relation to work with developing adolescents. Neglect occurs within or as a result of the nature of a relationship – between young people and their parents or carers. Where changes take place in expectations surrounding responsibility and autonomy, young people may be thought to hold responsibility for themselves; therefore, adult responsibility for neglect may be seen as debatable. Neglect also occurs within a broad context, where standards of care may differ and neglect itself may be pervasive. In this sense, neglect occurring in teenage years may be seen as relatively normal and not amenable to change. Neglect may be longstanding for adolescents and assessments must show awareness of what has taken place previously in order to understand what is occurring currently. Each of these elements will involve professional judgements.

The value of robust supervision that is alert to these intractable aspects of practice cannot be underestimated. Supervision is a means towards establishing confidence and consistency in practice within agencies. It also offers practitioners a channel to keep managers up-to-date with emergent difficulties, so that these may be communicated at both practice and strategic level between agencies. These elements contribute to sharing an enhanced understanding of young people, their situations and transitions, and they mean that practitioners will be better placed to work together towards shared goals.

Our next chapter takes a close look at interventions on behalf of neglected young people.

7

Interventions with Neglected Young People

Introduction

'What can I do about young people who are neglected?' This is a question that practitioners and their managers seek an answer to on many occasions in their workplaces. Our earlier chapters have shown that it is not an easy question to answer. As one practitioner put it, commenting on her work with adolescents, 'all of my work is about trying to rectify neglect of some sort' (Hicks and Stein 2010, p.27). Neglect, then, may just be one of a whole range of issues being tackled by practitioners, especially given what our earlier chapters have shown about its wide-ranging causes and consequences. To the busy practitioner, a neglected young person may appear in many guises: being sad and miserable, missing school, running away from home, getting into trouble, having alcohol and drug problems, or displaying serious mental health problems. So, where do practitioners begin?

This chapter draws upon the issues identified in our earlier chapters in exploring what interventions may assist neglected young people. These will be organized and discussed within a preventive framework and will draw upon research evidence of evaluated interventions, policy and practice literature, as well as our ideas about what should be done to improve the lives of neglected young people.

A preventive framework

As already mentioned, in considering the different types of intervention, we will adopt a preventive framework, using the concepts of primary, secondary and tertiary prevention. In the context of neglect, primary interventions are those that aim to prevent neglect from occurring by promoting the well-being of young people and families; secondary interventions aim to assist young people and their families when problems first arise – they are early interventions to prevent more serious problems arising from neglect; and tertiary interventions are those that aim to prevent neglect from recurring, or causing longer term harm to young people, whose problems have persisted beyond, or not responded to, early interventions.

Our preventive framework is underpinned by an ecological perspective: the neglect of young people should be studied in a multi-dimensional context, drawing on different disciplines – including sociology and psychology – in understanding causation and recognizing the connections between individual, family, community, cultural and structural dimensions, and their implications for interventions. The breadth of this preventive framework is reflected in the current safeguarding policy agenda that includes the promotion of universal outcomes for all children, the prevention of maltreatment, and the protection of children and young people most 'at risk' of harm (HM Government 2010). Also, central to this preventive framework, as detailed in an earlier chapter, is the involvement of young people themselves.

Primary prevention

Primary prevention is about preventing neglect before it occurs, and it can be universal or targeted. At the most general level, it includes the provision of a range of universal services, such as education, income support, health care, housing, youth and recreation facilities – in fact, all services that have an important role to play in engaging and promoting the health and well-being of young people and their families. Conversely, variations in the range and quality of these services, as well as barriers to their accessibility, may have a harmful effect on young people, including their neglect.

Schools and colleges

In schools, consideration of issues relating to neglect in the personal, social, health and economic education (PSHE) curriculum, the promotion of education for citizenship and a commitment to promoting the well-being of young people have the potential to contribute to primary prevention. A positive school or college environment and culture, generating respect between young people themselves, and between young people and staff, can enhance young people's worth and self-esteem and help them to maximize their educational and social potential.

Youth services

Involvement in youth and leisure services may also benefit young people and provide them with new opportunities and potential turning points. Since 2007, youth agencies have been providing 'integrated youth support', which includes both universal services and targeted youth support (see later discussion of secondary prevention). The universal agenda is about providing 'positive activities' accessible to all young people, and there is evidence of local authorities providing a wide range of services, from information about 'things to do and places to go' at weekends, to youth centres offering sport, music, opportunities to develop personal, vocational and social skills, and a place to meet friends. An evaluation of these projects showed that they 'often had long-standing relationships with young people, knew about any individual's situation, including any risk-taking behaviour, and were able to encourage young people to assume new responsibilities, and learn from them' (Ofsted 2010, p.23–24).

Families

Within families, primary preventive strategies to reduce poverty, through, for example, employment opportunities, income support and progressive taxation, will benefit young people, given the adverse impact of poverty on young people's lives including the increased risk of neglect.

As discussed in Chapter 4, research on the outcomes of parenting for children and, in particular, the work on *parenting styles*, identifies the contribution of an 'authoritative' parenting approach in preventing the neglect of young people. The evidence shows that combining love, emotional warmth, basic physical care, safety, stability, guidance and boundaries as well as stimulation is most likely to contribute to young people's all-round well-being. Neglectful parenting can be seen as being evidenced by a combination of a low level of parental control of young people (including parental knowledge and supervision of young people's activities and whereabouts) and inadequate establishment of boundaries; and a low level of warmth and acceptance by parents towards young people.

The promotion of 'authoritative parenting', as a primary prevention strategy, has been concerned in the main with improving 'early years' outcomes. This has included the Healthy Child Promotion Programme, Sure Start Local Programmes (targeted at neighbourhoods considered to be at higher than average risk of poor outcomes), and Children's Centres (Department of Health 2008; Frost and Parton 2009). However, in terms of evaluation, what we don't know about is the longer term impact of these 'early years' programmes in preventing the neglect of teenagers, or the impact of primary prevention programmes aimed at the parents of teenagers.

These issues could also be organized within a resilience framework. Resilience can be defined as the quality that enables some young people to find fulfilment in their lives despite their disadvantaged backgrounds, the problems or adversity they may have undergone or the pressures they may experience. Resilience is about overcoming the odds, coping and recovery. But it is only relative to different risk experiences – relative resistance as distinct from invulnerability – as well as age and cultural contexts, and it is likely to develop over time (Masten 2006; Rutter 1999; Schofield 2001).

There has been increased recognition of the contribution of *resilience* to an understanding of vulnerable children, young people and families. It appeals in a number of ways: first, in its optimism – the evidence of young people doing well in adversity – against all the odds; second, in offering a working framework of 'risk' and 'protective' factors that can provide a clear focus for policy and practice interventions; and third, in giving expression to a 'strength based' practice in children's services, which also provides the platform for participatory and rights-based approaches (Stein 2009). As Hicks and Stein (2010) comment, 'recent research on resilience (Schoon and Bartley 2008) has reinforced the importance of an ecological perspective, recognizing the interaction between individual development and context, including social and economic factors such as poverty and deprivation, family environment and community resources' (p.24).

However, it is also important to recognize that resilience can be seen as an individual protective quality to justify non-intervention, especially with this age group. Research exploring how the age of young people affects professionals' perceptions of risk found that older young people were perceived by some professionals as more 'resilient' – meaning more able to cope with the experiences of maltreatment – than younger children (Rees *et al.* 2010).

Masten (2006, p.7) summarizes the 'short list of resilience correlates' as shown in Table 7.1.

Secondary prevention

The focus of secondary intervention is when problems first arise – or early intervention in the history of a difficulty through informal or more formal responses.

Table 7.1: Factors associated with behavioural resilience in children and youth

Relationships and parenting
• Strong connections with one or more effective parents • Parenting quality (providing affection, rules, monitoring, expectations, socialization) • Bonds with other prosocial adults (kinship networks, mentors, elders, teachers) • Connections to prosocial and competent peers.
Individual differences
• Learning and problem-solving skills. • Self-regulation skills (self-control of attention, emotion and arousal, impulses). • Positive views of the self and one's capabilities (self-efficacy and self-worth). • Positive outlook on life (beliefs that life has meaning, faith, hopefulness). • Appealing qualities (social academic, athletic, attractive: engaging personality, talents).
Community context
• Effective schools. • Opportunity to develop valued skills and talents. • Community quality (safety, collective supervision, positive organizations). • Connections to prosocial organizations (clubs, faith groups). • Socio-economic advantages (in contrast to impact of 'poverty' as a risk factor, see Masten (2006) p.5).

Empowering young people

As discussed earlier, schools and colleges have an important role to play in primary prevention – in promoting the well-being of young people. Young people who are experiencing neglect may often talk to their friends before anybody else about their problems (Rees *et al.* 2010). Also, as mentioned in Chapter 5, raising the awareness of young people about neglect by young people's guides, accessible information in different formats, and having a clearly identified person to talk to, will all contribute to early intervention.

Obstacles to young people seeking help

A complementary study on responding to issues of maltreatment of young people aged 11 to 17, which three of the authors contributed to, found that in practice there were a number of obstacles to young people seeking help (Rees *et al.* 2010). One of these – lack of awareness of services – has already been discussed in this chapter and in Chapter 5. Another important obstacle for young people was a concern about the potential impact of a disclosure of maltreatment on themselves and for their family. Additionally, young people identified trust and confidentiality as key issues. The *Safeguarding Young People* project (Rees *et al.* 2010) highlighted the challenges to professional practice in these respects – including the capacity of agencies to provide consistency of contact for young people that can foster trust, and the dilemmas inherent in balancing a respect for young people's confidentiality with the need to safeguard their welfare. This latter point raises particular issues for information sharing within multi-agency working, which we discuss later in this chapter. A lack of ability to provide young people with sufficient guarantees of confidentiality means that they are less likely to disclose and engage. Without the assurance of confidentiality, young people are aware that decisions may be taken out of their hands and they may lose control of the process. They may therefore reject or avoid support services as a means of maintaining a sense of control over their lives (Coy 2009). Finally, young people's previous negative experiences of helping agencies could be a barrier to help seeking.

Perceptions of risk

Whether young people are referred for help in the first place will, in part, depend upon the professionals' perceptions of risk, dependent on the age of the child or young person. A number of research studies – primarily not from the UK (Back and Lips 1998; Collings and Payne 1991; Maynard and Wiederman 1997; Webster *et al.* 2005; Zellman 1992) have found that, in response to hypothetical vignettes of cases of potential maltreatment, professionals may be more likely to attribute blame to older young people. There is also a tendency to perceive older young people as less at risk, and to be less likely to refer them to child protection agencies.

Some of these findings were also reflected in the *Safeguarding Young People* research project (Rees *et al.* 2010). In particular, professionals' perceptions of long-term risk in a range of scenarios of potential maltreatment (including neglect) were affected by the age of the child or young person. Older young people tended to be seen as at less long-term risk and this finding was strongest for scenarios involving supervisory neglect and emotional abuse.

The survey and interviews with professionals shed light on some of the age-related factors at play here. Some professionals expressed the view that older young people were more 'resilient' to the effects of maltreatment – a view that is not supported by the evidence presented in Chapter 4. In addition, young people aged 11 to 15 (compared with younger children) were seen as more competent to deal with maltreatment – either through removing themselves from risky situations and/or through being able to seek support. Professionals felt that in some cases young people's own behaviour contributed to or exacerbated situations of maltreatment – for example, young people may themselves be violent or may fight back in response to abuse. Finally, there was an increased focus, with older age groups, on the risks that young people might experience outside the home, including 'putting themselves at risk'.

Obstacles to professionals making referrals

In addition to the issues just discussed, professionals (including teachers, police, voluntary sector workers and youth justice workers) in the *Safeguarding Young People* study identified a number of obstacles to making a referral to children's social care services (Rees *et al.* 2010). These obstacles included:

- a perception of high thresholds for social care intervention
- complex ethical decisions – for example, if young people did not want to be referred
- the potential negative impact on young people and families of making a referral – particularly if the referring professional did not believe that significant action would be taken as a result of the referral
- pressure on resources within referring agencies.

Many of these issues have also been identified in the wider literature on child neglect (Horwath 2007a). However, some of the issues have particular relevance for young people aged 11 to 17. For example, the debate about thresholds was seen as more important as young people got older. In the *Safeguarding Young People* research, there was a perception among referring professionals that children's social care services were increasingly unlikely to view a referral as warranting a child protection intervention once young people reached 14 years of age and older.

The Common Assessment Framework

It is important that the causes and consequences of neglect are identified and assessed at an early point. For example, a teacher may notice a sudden deterioration in the appearance or cleanliness of a young person that may be very much out of character. If this cannot be addressed by informal measures, such as discussions with the young person and parents, offers of assistance are declined and the concerns persist, then it is important that an early assessment takes place to determine the appropriate level and type of intervention. The purpose of the CAF (Department for Education and Skills 2006) is to:

- help practitioners from different agencies to assess young people's 'additional needs' for services at an early stage
- develop a common understanding of those needs between different agencies
- agree a process of working together
- identify, if appropriate, a lead professional to assist the family and young person.

This may lead to interventions, at this early stage, to tackle the causes of neglect and its impact upon the young person, by assisting the parents to overcome their difficulties: for example, helping parents to reduce their alcohol abuse may lead to improvements in household income and more money available for the young person to improve their appearance or for the parents to provide better financial support for their child's education.

What is also important, and is illustrated by this example, is that the young people do not see themselves as the cause of the problem, and blame themselves for being neglected. Interventions, through the involvement of the young people, informally, or by the use of the CAF, may contribute to what Parton and O'Byrne in their principles of 'constructive social work' call the 'externalization' of the problem, providing young people with opportunities to consider different solutions to the neglect they are experiencing (Parton and O'Byrne 2000). One way of achieving this is illustrated by our guide for young people (see Chapter 5).

Targeted youth support

As detailed earlier, targeted youth support is a key component of integrated youth services. It 'aims to ensure that the needs of vulnerable teenagers are identified early and met by agencies working together effectively' (Department for Education and Skills 2007, p.4). As our previous discussion of the diverse consequences of neglect has shown, many neglected young people are likely to be 'vulnerable teenagers' and could be assisted by targeted youth support services.

A recent evaluation of targeted youth support showed that delivery at an area level was, in the main, through multi-agency teams that included members from youth services, youth offending, the Connexions service, the voluntary sector, the police, housing, children's social care, education, the substance misuse team and the voluntary sector (Ofsted 2010). The evaluation found that the CAF was being used to identify young people's individual needs and make plans for their integrated support. At a more local level, there were practitioner groups such as 'the team around the child', 'the team around the school' or 'the team around the family'. Their roles included carrying out a common assessment and the designation of a lead professional to work with a young person (Ofsted 2010; Rees *et al.* 2010). The evaluation of youth support in 11 local authority areas showed that targeted support was successful in increasing speedier access and services for vulnerable young people through agencies working together and sharing resources. It also found that young people were being involved in developing services and decision making. This included structures such as youth forums and councils that gave young people 'regular access to officers and elected council members, and the opportunity to campaign on their own issues and to act as advocates for their peers' (Ofsted 2010, p.24).

However, the evaluation also found that services for young people over 16 years of age were less developed than for young people under 16. It also showed that there was confusion over who should take responsibility for initiating the CAF, and how this related to established forms of assessment, such as those used by Connexions and youth offending teams, and sometimes leading to duplication of assessment. There was also evidence that practitioners were reluctant in some local areas to take on the 'lead professional' role, in order to provide a link between a young person and other agencies, to ensure support is co-ordinated well (Ofsted 2010).

Tertiary prevention

Tertiary intervention aims to prevent the recurrence of problems that have already come to light, and have usually persisted beyond, or have not responded to, early interventions. Tertiary prevention also aims to prevent longer term harm to young people, such as the continuation of mental health problems into adulthood.

There is very little research on evaluated interventions in relation to adolescent neglect. For example, Biehal (2005) comments 'Few studies in either the UK or the USA have focused on the issue of support services for adolescents considered to be on the brink of admission to substitute care' (Biehal 2005, p.47–48). She notes that, whereas family support and preservation in relation to young children have been concerned with the prevention of neglect and abuse, the focus of work with adolescents has been on their behavioural and emotional problems rather than on abuse and neglect.

However, this does not mean that work is not being carried out with neglected young people. It was evident from our discussions with staff from different agencies in the preparation of our multi-agency guide that a lot of individual work is being undertaken to assist vulnerable teenagers and support their families, including those who have been neglected (Hicks and Stein 2010). What this does suggest is the need for an evaluative culture to be built into the organizations that are carrying out such difficult work – not least to reflect on existing practice and to guide effective interventions. In this context, we will draw on other research and literature that has implications for tertiary interventions with young people. This includes evaluated interventions on child (as distinct from adolescent) neglect, and interventions, either evaluated or descriptive, for the wider group of maltreated and troubled young people that may have implications for practice where adolescent neglect has been identified.

The Assessment Framework

Depending on the extent and severity of a young person's neglect, a referral to children's social care may be appropriate, in which case the *Framework for the Assessment of Children in Need and their Families* (Department of Health *et al.* 2000) would be used (which may build upon the CAF), or a referral may be made at a later stage, if a young person's needs persist or deteriorate. The ecological perspective of this Assessment Framework furthers an understanding of both the causes and consequences of adolescent neglect and not only provides a framework for assessment but also for planning, interventions and review (see Chapter 1).

Other tools developed to assist practitioners in understanding and linking the range of influences on a young person's life and experience include Smith's ecological map and Thompson's Personal, Cultural and Structural (PCS) model (Smith 2008; Thompson 2006). The former tool (the ecological map) is helpful in distinguishing between both 'levels' of experience and 'types' of influencing factors, and the latter (the PCS model) is particularly useful in the analysis of different forms of oppression that young people may have experienced.

A thorough and holistic assessment is critical to planning interventions and there is evidence from an overview of research studies that good quality assessments can contribute to positive outcomes for children and families (Stein 2009). What we know about the causes and consequences of neglect discussed in earlier chapters, and the diversity of needs within families and young people, indicates that a range of individual interventions is likely to be required.

There is some literature on assessment in relation to child neglect, although this makes relatively little direct reference to issues of assessment of adolescent neglect. However, two key points emerge from the literature that are of relevance here.

The first issue is whether existing frameworks for assessment are constructed in a way that is helpful to the assessment of child neglect. Horwath (2002) and others such as Jones and Gupta (1998) have pointed to the way that, where systems are designed with protection against acute risk in mind, the chronic nature of neglect itself may be overlooked. Thoburn, Wilding and Watson (2000) indicate the pivotal role of appropriate assessments in ensuring effective interventions that prevent re-referrals. The authors indicate the need for long-term interventions that include multi-dimensional work, which, in turn, requires co-ordinated approaches. An evaluation of the use of the Assessment Framework by Horwath (2002) showed that practitioners found difficulties in giving equal attention to the three domains of the framework (child development, parenting capacity and family or environmental factors). There was also a tendency at times to overlook the needs of minority groups; to ignore the multi-disciplinary nature of the assessment; to use recording forms inappropriately; and to fulfil some assessments according to expected timescales rather than in line with the needs of the child. The problem of excessive workloads was also noted. Clearly many of these issues relate to the implementation of the Framework rather than the value of the Framework per se.

The second issue of relevance is the way in which factors extraneous to assessment frameworks may influence practitioners' assessments. In a study in the Republic of Ireland, Horwath (2005) showed that practices varied in the way that assessments were approached, and that teams influenced the ways that workers defined neglect. This raises questions about the influence of workers' own perceptions on assessment practice. The adequacy of support offered on the basis of inconsistent assessments is a matter for concern and there is no evidence to suggest that this applies less to adolescents than to younger children.

Horwarth (2007b) expands on this work and makes the distinction between two aspects of assessment activity – technical-rational and practice-moral. The former aspect relates to professional toolkits, assessment frameworks and so on. The latter aspect refers to a range of other factors that may influence professionals' decision-making, including their perceptions of child neglect; their interpretation of their professional role; their perception of social work services; their personal feelings; and their feelings or expectations about their colleagues, or the wider community. Horwarth argues that this cluster of issues could be viewed as constituting a missing 'practitioner domain' within assessment frameworks.

This suggests that, in connection with the subject matter of this book, more attention might be given to two key questions. First, to what extent do existing assessment frameworks work effectively in relation to assessments of adolescent neglect? Second, to what extent do professional attitudes and other extraneous factors influence assessments in relation to cases of potential adolescent neglect?

The implications of child neglect interventions

Evaluations of programmes that aim to reduce the effects of neglect on very young children propose the adoption of a wide range of interventions. De Panfilis (2006b), for example, categorizes interventions in terms of ecological (concrete – improving material resources); ecological (improving social support networks to reduce isolation); developmental (improving role achievements); cognitive-behavioural (improving parenting); individual (tackling problems such as alcohol abuse); and family systems (using family therapy). The author also emphasizes the importance of collaboration across welfare systems and communities both to prevent and to reduce the effect of neglect.

The breadth of this approach reflects the ecological approach represented by the 'Child's Developmental Needs', 'Parenting Capacity' and 'Family and Environmental Factors' domains of the Assessment Framework (see Figure 1.2 on p. 18). De Panfilis concluded that the most positive benefits for all those with whom direct work took place were associated with cognitive-behavioural interventions. This finding is consistent with Barlow and Schrader Macmillan's (2010) research review of what works to prevent the recurrence of parental emotional abuse. The authors do, however, offer a note of caution by indicating that the characteristics that defined parents who responded well to cognitive-behavioural therapy were not clear and that the successful treatment of severely abusive parents remained unproven.

The implications of other work on evaluated interventions on child neglect include the importance of addressing parent–child interaction with parents to prevent longer term attachment deficits that become hard to redress once entrenched (Iwaniec and McSherry 2002). The same authors in their review of preventative projects dating back to the early 1980s, conclude that given the complexity of neglect and its 'intergenerational pervasiveness' there is a need for a 'multi-faceted approach'. The authors recommend four main ways of enhancing understanding of neglect: a clear and concise definition of neglect; prioritization within social services; 'a critical time scale for cases of child neglect to be established'; and a clarification of the relationship between neglect and poverty (Iwaniec and McSherry 2002).

Young children and teenagers: different needs and responses?

As discussed earlier in respect of secondary prevention, it is important to recognize how parental behaviour has an impact upon teenagers, as well as young children. Although the underpinning ecological principles and breadth of approach identified in the evaluations and reviews are helpful, the programme content aimed at parents and children will need to be adapted to take into account the developmental issues related to adolescence and emerging adulthood. These will include the different ways the consequences of neglect may manifest themselves in young people – for example, getting into trouble, emotional and behavioural problems, running away from home – and the impact of young people's behaviour on their relationships with their parents and others. The involvement of young people themselves will be critical to any intervention.

There is evidence from a study of maltreated young people that they are often *perceived by practitioners* as more resilient, more able to cope with the effects of abuse, more able to remove themselves from abusive situations, and more likely to disclose abuse than younger children. However this perception was not borne out by the findings of the study. Young people were also seen as a lower priority and a greater challenge to engage and work with by practitioners. These perceptions could affect practitioner responses (Rees *et al.* 2010).

The same study found that, as young people who are maltreated become older, they are less likely to receive a child protection response from children's social care services and more likely to be responded to through the 'child in need' pathway, leading to multi-agency responses including the use of the CAF and 'team around' approaches, as described earlier (see p.97) (Rees *et al.* 2010).

Work with adolescents: specialist support teams

Evaluations of tertiary interventions with maltreated and troubled adolescents are also important to consider – as suggested earlier, the consequences of different forms of maltreatment may be very similar to the consequences of neglect.

In the UK, Biehal (2005) evaluated the effectiveness of local authority specialist support teams in preventing young people 'at risk' from being taken into care. All the teams offered a short-term, task-centred service and worked in partnership with parents and young people. The focus was on helping the parents to improve their 'authoritative parenting skills' (see earlier discussion of primary prevention) and for young people to change their behaviour. Most of the teams offered a similar method of working, which is as follows:

Intensive family support work by the Met West team

- Systematic assessment of family functioning (may use genograms).

- Problems identified, goals set, work planned, clear agreements drawn up.

- Work reviewed every 4–6 weeks.

- Identification of deficits in parenting skills and provision of support to parents in developing coping skills, taking responsibility and regaining control.

- Work with parents: emphasis on appropriate parenting including behaviour management through positive reinforcement, boundary setting, developing routines.

- Work with young people, exploring views, identifying triggers to conflict and behaviours that are dangerous, being alert to any evidence of abuse.

- Use of sessional staff to befriend young people, build self-esteem and engage them in positive local activities.

- Assessing, repairing and enlarging support networks.

- Providing information and advice (e.g. on health or personal safety).

- Partnership work with parents. (Biehal 2005, pp. 65–66)

The evaluation compared the young people referred to the local authority specialist teams with others receiving a service from mainstream area social workers. Overall it was found that outcomes for both the support teams and mainstream services were similar but, importantly, the support teams achieved change with more young people with longer term and severe difficulties.

Biehal's study found that successful outcomes were those where:

- interventions were multi-faceted, including individual work with young people – though building positive relationships

- support and advice were given to parents – with a focus on their strengths and a greater sense of perceived control

- mediation took place between parents and young people, including help with reframing patterns of communication

- workers addressed multiple difficulties, including risk factors in the lives of young people and their parents

- young people and their parents were motivated, or became motivated, to work towards change. (Biehal 2005, p.197)

Poorer outcomes were where parents and young people could not be engaged, or showed no motivation to change; involvement in antisocial peer groups persisted; young people's mental health difficulties or parents' marital conflict were chronic or severe; and short-term interventions were the main response to chronic or severe difficulties.

Kids Company

Another example of a tertiary intervention is Kids Company, set up in 1996 in London by Camila Batmanghelidjh (Batmanghelidjh 2006). It provides practical, emotional and educational support to many highly vulnerable teenagers whose needs have not been met by local authority children's services (possibly including the group of young people not meeting the threshold for services identified in Rees *et al.* 2010). The participation of young people is entirely voluntary – they are not required to attend or take part. Its first premises were two converted railway arches and in a short time it attracted over a hundred chronically neglected children and young people.

These early project experiences contributed to Kids Company's approach of providing young people with consistent, long-term loving care, grounded in attachment theory – attempting to promote their emotional well-being by compensating them for their damaged family lives. This is achieved by a 'wraparound' model of care for each young person, so that all personal issues are addressed by one team in one place, without the need for professional referrals or waiting periods.

Kids Company's methods include providing stability by first of all meeting young people's practical needs; second, helping young people to address their emotional and behavioural difficulties; and, finally, helping them to identify talents, interests and aspirations. The interventions aim to strengthen, supplement or substitute the young people's parenting experiences. The team approach combines a wide range of resources to assist them, including health, housing, emotional well-being, mental health, arts, sport, youth justice, education and employment.

Kids Company's current programme includes two street-level centres, a therapy house, a drop-in centre and therapeutic services in over 30 schools, and work with 400 highly disturbed young people over the age of 14. Its services are provided by both paid staff and volunteers.

An evaluation of this service based on 240 young people (randomly chosen from 749 street-level centre users) carried out in 2008 highlighted the high level of young people's problems (over 80% had emotional and mental health difficulties; sustained trauma; substance abuse; and homelessness) as well as how the support assisted them (for nine out of ten young people it contributed to reduced criminal involvement; reduced substance abuse; reintegration in education; improved employability; improved relationships with family members; improved accommodation; and improved anger management). The great majority of young people (97%) found Kids Company effective in supporting their needs (Gaskell 2008).

Evaluated work in the US

In the US, the findings from Cameron and Karabanow's (2003) study of the effectiveness of programme models for adolescents at risk of entering the formal child protection system are consistent with the findings from Biehal's research. Cameron and Karabanow review five categories of intervention: adolescent competence and skill development; family-focused interventions; social integration projects; multiple-component interventions; and neighbourhood transformation projects. The authors identify a number of interventions that demonstrate positive outcomes with respect to parent–child relationships, young people's social skills, parental support, and connections between young people, parents and community. However, they identify obstacles to success in relation to ecological problems within communities and argue for a holistic approach that tackles the various dimensions and domains that affect young people's lives, rather than focusing narrowly on issues within the family environment.

Jonson-Reid (2002) looks at the reporting and processing of child protection cases in the US, with a specific focus on early adolescence. The study used secondary analysis of child protection records. This analysis indicated that cases involving early adolescents were less likely to be investigated than those relating to younger children, but that where an investigation took place the former cases were more likely to be opened than the latter. Jonson-Reid also draws attention once again to the incidence and chronic nature of neglect during adolescence and the potential negative outcomes for young people.

UK and US literature about the use of Multi-systemic Therapy (MST) views individuals as nested within a network of interconnected systems that encompass individual, family and community (peer, school and neighbourhood) – again, emphasizing the importance of the Assessment Framework and a multi-disciplinary approach. To date, MST has been used primarily to work with young offenders and a small-scale study that focused on child abuse and neglect reported positive results (Brunk, Henlegger and Whelan 1987). MST is being piloted in England as part of the *Care Matters* White Paper implementation plan and may well be applicable to neglected and maltreated teenagers (Biehal 2005; HM Government 2008).

Summary points

We propose that interventions with neglected young people should be organized within a preventive framework that includes primary, secondary and tertiary prevention, and is underpinned by an ecological perspective.

Primary prevention includes both universal and targeted services that aim to promote the well-being of young people and their families – preventing neglect before it arises.

- The culture and curriculum of schools and colleges, youth services promoting positive leisure activities, and policies that have an impact upon families, including the promotion of 'authoritative parenting', can all make an important contribution.

- Another way of considering these issues is about promoting the resilience of neglected young people, focusing interventions on relationships and parenting, individual qualities and the wider community context.

Secondary prevention aims to address problems when they first come to light. It may focus on:

- raising young people's awareness about neglect by providing accessible information and guides

- challenging professional perceptions of risk and overcoming obstacles to professionals making referrals

- informal responses by those working with young people, the use of the CAF by practitioners from different agencies and targeted youth support, which may include a 'team around' the young person approach.

Tertiary interventions may come into play when problems persist, despite earlier interventions. They aim to prevent problems continuing into adulthood.

- For tertiary interventions, good quality assessment represents the starting point.

- The consistent message from the evaluations of services to assist neglected younger children and a larger group of vulnerable teenagers is the need for a wide range of interventions, including individual and sustained work with young people by a trusted practitioner; where possible, work with their families; and the involvement of other key agencies.

- A specialist team approach or 'wraparound' model is the most likely to reach the most vulnerable young people.

8

Conclusions

In this concluding chapter, we summarize the key messages contained within the book regarding the neglect of young people aged 11 to 17, highlighting both what is currently known and also the gaps in current knowledge. We then conclude with a set of implications, drawn from this material, for policy makers, practitioners and researchers.

Knowledge and gaps
Putting the neglect of young people into context
A substantial number of young people aged 11 to 17 experience neglect. We can be fairly confident in this assertion because it is a consistent picture from official statistics, from contemporaneous and retrospective self-report studies of childhood maltreatment, and from research on parenting styles.

Yet relatively little is currently known about the neglect of young people aged 11 to 17 – what might be the key causes and contextual factors associated with neglect of this age group; what might be its consequences for young people's well-being and longer term outcomes; and what might be the most effective interventions to prevent the neglect of young people and to support those who have experienced it. This is partly to do with the relative 'neglect of neglect' in a general sense within the research literature on child maltreatment, and partly to do with the relative lack of attention to age-specific questions within this same literature.

Nevertheless, it is possible to piece together a broad picture of many of the key issues to consider when thinking about neglect of young people in particular. This is what we have attempted to do in this book with the aims of informing policy and practice development in this area, and highlighting the need for further research to fill the many gaps in knowledge that currently exist.

In the first chapter, we introduced a key conceptual framework that is useful in thinking about this issue and that we have borne in mind at various stages throughout the book. This is an 'ecological' framework that proves valuable in thinking about the different dimensions of young people's needs.

Defining the neglect of young people

Definitions of what constitutes neglect are inextricably linked to notions of the needs of children and young people. A developmental perspective offers clarity that, as these needs vary as children develop, so must definitions of what constitutes neglect. Supervisory neglect of a 'typical' 1-year-old cannot be defined in the same way as for a 'typical' 15-year-old, except in the broadest possible terms.

There is surprisingly little discussion of age-specific definitional issues within the research and policy literature on the maltreatment of children and young people. In Chapter 2, we provide several examples of ways in which this might be problematic. For example, neglect has been defined very broadly as an 'act of *omission*'. However, we know that many young people in the UK (particularly in the 15- to 17-years-old age range) are forced to leave home by their parents and carers – thus finding themselves in a situation where their basic needs for shelter, food and care are not being met. This 'act of *commission*' would appear to fit broadly within a definition of 'maltreatment', and more specifically to fit within concepts of supervisory, physical and emotional neglect.

The key message from the discussion on definitions is the need to re-examine current definitions, viewing issues specifically from the perspective of age-related differences. In this respect, it is interesting to note the research that has explored definitions of neglect from the perspectives of young people and professionals. Several research studies have found that young people's assessments of the occurrence and severity of neglect (and other forms of maltreatment) can both differ from those of professionals and also be good predictors of outcomes. In one study cited in Chapter 2, young people's assessments were more accurate predictors of outcomes than were those of professionals. This highlights a recurring theme in the book about the importance of taking into account young people's own perspectives on the issue of neglect, which is our main focus in Chapter 5.

There have been some welcome developments in terms of age-sensitive descriptions of neglect in the UK. The Core Assessment Records, which support the Assessment Framework, are helpful tools in considering neglect in an age-sensitive way. There appears to have been less attention to age-specific considerations in operational definitions of neglect used for research purposes.

Finally, on the matter of definitions of the neglect of young people, we note that it is more common for two or more forms of maltreatment to co-occur than it is for one form to occur in isolation. Children and young people who experience neglect are also likely to experience various forms of abuse. There seems a particularly strong overlap between emotional abuse and neglect. These connections and overlaps need to be borne in mind when considering definitional issues for particular categories of maltreatment.

What are the causes of young people's neglect?

There is a reasonably strong evidence base on the background factors that may be associated with the neglect of children and young people in general. This includes evidence of links with family history, family structure and functioning, economic factors, levels of social support within the extended family and the community, and broader factors related to the local community and environment. This evidence points to the value of an ecological approach, which takes into account proximal and distal factors in a child's environment, in understanding the contexts associated with child neglect.

Despite the extent of this general evidence, there is relatively little research that considers the contextual factors that may be specifically associated with adolescent neglect. The small amount of evidence that does exist suggests that there may be key differences in terms of some of the specific backgrounds and histories underlying neglect in different age groups. Here also, given the lack of substantial evidence, a developmental perspective and a consideration of the particular circumstances of young people's lives can be helpful in thinking about some of these possible differences.

A first point to consider is the typically increased competence of young people in the 11- to 17-year-old age group, compared with younger children. It seems likely that in situations where parents themselves are struggling to care for their children (for example, because of problems related to substance use, mental health and so on), this increased competence may lead to young people in this age group taking on a caring role within the family, both for younger siblings and for parents. This in turn may lead to their own needs being neglected.

Second, young people in this age group are more likely than younger children to be living in families that have undergone or are undergoing significant structural change. While young people can thrive within a wide variety of family forms, there are indications in the research literature of an increased risk of emotional neglect within families that have recently restructured. This, of course, applies to all age groups of children and young people. However, the issue may have distinctive relevance for young people close to independence where the commitment of new step-parents or carers, and of young people themselves, to forge relationships may be less strong and the young person may feel emotionally excluded from new family forms.

These are just examples of possible distinctive contextual factors associated with the neglect of young people aged 11 to 17. There is a need for research evidence to explore these and other potential issues in order to develop a fuller understanding of the particular needs of young people in this age group who are experiencing neglect.

In addition to these general points, there is a lack of in-depth knowledge about the context and nature of neglect for particular sub-groups of young people who may be at particular risk. We have already drawn attention to the issue of young carers. A second group that warrants additional consideration is disabled children. There is a paucity of literature about the maltreatment of disabled children in general, and this includes a lack of exploration regarding what may be the distinctive features of neglect for disabled young people.

What are the consequences of the neglect of young people?

This is a topic for which a reasonable number of research findings exist in relation to young people aged 11 to 17. Some of this evidence specifically relates to child maltreatment and some is from the broader literature on parenting styles, which includes consideration of 'neglectful' parenting.

There is sufficient evidence to suggest that neglect and/or neglectful parenting of young people is/are associated with poor mental health and emotional well-being; risky health behaviours; risks to safety, including running away; poor conduct and achievement at school; and the likelihood of involvement in offending and antisocial behaviour.

There have been some studies about the relative effects of different forms of maltreatment of young people in this age group. These suggest that the negative impact of neglect may be at least as significant, if not more significant, than other forms of maltreatment.

Additionally, there is some evidence on the relative impacts of neglect experienced by children and young people at different ages. This is a contested area and no clear picture emerges. However, the research findings are sufficient to caution against any assumptions that neglect is necessarily less damaging for young people than it is for younger children.

The increased likelihood of offending among young people experiencing neglect also draws attention to potential 'boundary' issues between different services for young people. Neglected young people who commit criminal offences may be channelled through the youth justice system as a response to the 'presenting issue' (i.e. offending) when the underlying context of neglect would suggest a more comprehensive approach to meeting the needs of the young person.

Although there is a reasonable amount of existing research literature on this topic, there remain gaps – for example, regarding the links between neglect of young people and issues such as physical health, peer relationships and bullying, and the implications of neglect specifically experienced in the 11 to 17 age range for longer term outcomes into adulthood. There are also some limitations of the evidence in terms of establishing causality between neglect and outcomes – including, for example, some important questions to explore further in relation to the direction of causality between neglectful parenting and young people's behaviour.

Young people's views about neglect

We have already highlighted research evidence on the potential importance of considering young people's own definitions of neglect. In a more general sense, there is clearly a great deal we can learn from speaking directly to young people about their views on, and experiences of, neglect. In Chapter 5, we presented some learning from focus group work with young people on this topic. This work was undertaken to inform the development of a young person's guide to neglect. It generated important messages about defining the neglect of young people, about potential causes and consequences of neglect, and about issues of awareness, help seeking and intervention for this age group.

In terms of definitions, the discussions with young people suggested that they conceptualize neglect as part of a wider spectrum of harm that may happen to children. This conceptualization went well beyond the boundaries of what professionals might consider to constitute 'maltreatment'. For example, in thinking about neglect, young people gave consideration to issues such as the development of self-care skills and the prevention of obesity.

Young people's views also highlighted another definitional issue raised earlier in this chapter on the difficulties of disentangling neglect from other forms of maltreatment. This has important implications for considering how best to communicate with young people specifically about neglect, and indeed whether it is helpful to make distinctions between different forms of maltreatment when all maltreatment may be viewed by young people as a neglect of caring, parental responsibility.

Discussions with young people can also help to develop an understanding of the particular contextual factors that may be associated with young people in this age group experiencing neglect. For example, young people spoke about the emotional significance of whether parents were able to fulfil particular aspects of what might normatively be considered to be a parenting role. These perspectives can aid our understanding of the way in which particular family factors and problems can contribute to feelings of neglect among young people. The impact of these factors may vary from one young person to another and this draws attention to the importance of considering individual young people's feelings as part of a holistic assessment of neglect.

In terms of consequences of neglect, young people highlighted links between neglect and mental health, which are already fairly well established through research. They also discussed the links between neglect and bullying, which we have highlighted as a possible research gap. More qualitative research of this kind with young people could be valuable in generating hypotheses for research on the consequences of neglect and in informing professionals' assessments of neglect within this age group.

Because of their typically increased competence, young people aged 11 to 17 may be more able than younger children to seek help when experiencing neglect. Our focus group work aimed to explore the means of most effectively raising awareness of neglect among young people in order to facilitate help seeking. It highlighted the potential to achieve this goal through the use of a variety of communication strategies, and also drew attention to the important role that schools might play due to their status as an almost universal service for young people, at least up to the age of 16.

The focus groups also echoed previous UK research with young people in identifying a number of barriers to help seeking that need to be overcome in order to maximize the likelihood of young people being able to 'self-refer' in instances of neglect. These include a lack of awareness and understanding of the range and functions of helping services available; and significant concerns about trust and confidentiality. The latter are a key issue for professionals engaging with this age group.

Whose business is the neglect of young people?

Chapter 6 explores issues relating to practice and multi-agency working in relation to the neglect of young people aged 11 to 17. As with Chapter 5 on young people's views, it is based primarily on new work that we have undertaken to explore such issues through discussions with relevant stakeholders – in this case, through multi-disciplinary focus groups of professionals. These focus groups have highlighted some key distinctive challenges in working with young people who are experiencing neglect.

One key area of concern for professionals is the increased capacity for, and expectation of, independence and autonomy as young people grow older. This poses a number of challenges for professionals working to protect young people who may be experiencing neglect. These challenges include the importance of engaging young people actively in processes and procedures in a way that might not be so relevant when working with younger children. Recent research suggests that the current child protection system in the UK may not be particularly well suited to working with young people in this way.

A second issue identified through the discussions with professionals is that of the relative 'responsibilities' of young people and parents or carers in relation to neglect. Research on maltreatment in general suggests that professionals are more likely to attribute blame to young people, in comparison with younger children, when maltreatment occurs. In addition, recent UK research on safeguarding young people identified a professional focus on young people 'putting themselves at risk' outside the home. These tendencies may cloud the issue and divert attention away from tackling the continuing responsibilities of parents to provide an environment that meets young people's needs and gives them the best chance of making a positive transition to adulthood.

The issue of young people's autonomy and choice also raises important issues for professionals in terms of information sharing and taking action. On the one hand, professionals may feel that they need to share information or act in the 'best interests' of a young person. On the other hand, there is an awareness that, if professionals act without young people's agreement or consent, then they may alienate young people who are quite capable of 'voting with their feet'. Thus, working with neglected young people can involve a particularly difficult balancing act between protection and participation. Establishing trust with young people is therefore crucial to good practice in this area. The focus groups highlighted the importance of effective professional supervision to support practitioners in managing this balance.

The discussions with professionals also raised some key definitional issues relevant to working with neglect within this age group. First, there is a risk of persistent neglect becoming 'normalized' and having an ongoing corrosive effect on young people's well-being while never quite reaching accepted thresholds for intervention. This risk may be heightened because of differences in professionals' conceptualizations of neglect for different age groups of children and young people. The focus groups highlighted inconsistencies and ambiguities in this respect that support our earlier points about the importance of clear age-specific guidance to support consistent assessment of neglect by professionals across a range of agencies.

In relation to multi-agency practice, the discussions highlighted the importance of establishing frameworks and processes that aid communication and collaboration between professionals from different disciplines. Neglected young people may initially come to the attention of professionals working within a wide range of systems including education, health and youth justice as well as social care. Successful multi-agency working is a pre-requisite for effectively meeting the needs of such young people.

Interventions with neglected young people

The final topic addressed in the book relates to the nature of interventions in relation to young people who experience, or may be at risk of experiencing, neglect. This is another topic area where the current evidence base is quite limited.

While there are some examples of evaluations of interventions targeted at neglect of children and young people as a whole group, there are relatively few studies on interventions specifically targeted at young people aged 11 to 17. There are, however, some key messages from the small number of studies that have been undertaken. In general, these studies tend to support an ecological or multi-systemic approach to interventions, which fits well with the approach of the Assessment Framework and also the evidence on background factors of child neglect discussed earlier.

Given this limited amount of evidence, we focus in Chapter 7 on working from first principles in terms of constructing a picture of what effective interventions with neglected young people might look like. We make use of a three-part framework relating to primary, secondary and tertiary intervention.

Primary prevention can be divided into universal and targeted approaches. Universal or whole population interventions might include a role for schools (e.g. the inclusion of discussion of neglect in the school curriculum) and for youth services (e.g. integrated youth support). There may also be a link with broader social policies such as measures to tackle child poverty, which is a known correlate with likelihood of neglect. Targeted early intervention might include parenting skills courses focusing on models of 'authoritative' parenting – either specifically for parents of young people aged 11 to 17, or at an earlier stage.

Secondary prevention focuses on early intervention to tackle emerging issues. We suggest that an important aspect of this level of prevention is to ensure that young people are aware of the meaning of neglect; are also aware of the potential role of helping services; and feel that such services are directly accessible to them. Achieving these goals would significantly increase the potential for early intervention. In terms of approaches and models of intervention, we identify a number of positive developments in the UK that may play a part in an effective early response to the neglect of young people aged 11 to 17 including the use of the Common Assessment Framework and the creation of a multi-disciplinary 'team around' the young person.

Turning to tertiary interventions with young people with persistent or acute experiences of neglect, there is certainly a need for systematic evaluation of possible responses such as the multi-systemic therapy model that has been developed in the US. In the current absence of such evaluations, based on evidence from other related areas such as evaluations of services for 'vulnerable' teenagers in general, we suggest that a specialist team approach is one that is likely to be effective in working with neglected young people.

Implications for practice, policy and research

We conclude by drawing out what we feel are the key implications of the materials presented in the book for practitioners and practice managers, policy makers and other key stakeholders, and researchers.

Implications for practice

Our review of research, and focus group work with young people and professionals, has identified a wide range of messages in relation to professionals' understandings of, and responses to, the neglect of young people aged 11 to 17. Some of the key points are as follows.

- It is important for professionals working with neglected young people to be aware of the evidence that does exist on the potential impact of neglect for this age group. Recent UK research suggests that some professionals may have a tendency to consider young people to be more 'resilient' than younger children to the impacts of maltreatment. The limited evidence on this issue does not support this view. Young people who experience maltreatment, including neglect, in comparison with younger children, may be particularly likely to 'externalize' their problems and this may manifest itself in, for example, antisocial behaviour and offending. Professionals should be aware of the potential underpinning role that neglect can play in these behaviours. This will help to avoid circumstances where the needs of neglected young people are not effectively met – for example, if there is solely a 'youth justice' response.

- A second topic from research that warrants particular consideration relates to the evidence on young people's own assessments of neglect (and other forms of maltreatment). Several studies in the US have suggested that young people's assessments can be helpful in identifying the existence and severity of neglect and in predicting longer term outcomes. Young people's own feelings are also an important factor to consider, because the same parental behaviours and family contexts may have different impacts on different young people. Hence, there is a critical potential role for young people to play in professional assessment processes. However, it is important also for practitioners to be aware of the evidence that suggests that young people are less likely to categorize acts or situations as neglect than are professionals. This may be to do with acceptance of experienced standards of parenting by young people. The implication of this evidence is that it is important to take into account young people's views but there is also a value in the experience and external perspective that professionals are able to bring to the assessment process.

- US research also suggests that practitioners' own assessments of neglect can be variable. In England and Wales, practitioners have access to a comprehensive set of age-specific indicators to support assessments of levels of care and meeting basic needs through the Core Assessment Records. These offer the potential for a consistent way of defining neglect in relation to individual cases.

- A recurring theme in the general literature on child neglect is the distinction between persistent neglect and isolated but serious incidents of neglect. This is an issue that needs careful consideration for all age groups but there are some specific issues to consider in relation to young people aged 11 to 17. At the other end of the continuum, neglect may be longstanding for young people in this age group and assessments must show awareness of what has taken place previously in order to understand what is occurring currently. Each of these elements will involve professional judgements.

- In their assessments, practitioners might also need to consider the potentially distinctive contextual factors leading to neglect of young people. These might include being a young carer, economic strains within the family and family dynamics during periods of restructuring, such as the introduction of a step-parent, which might have particular impacts on older young people.

- Assessments also need to be quite broad. For young people in the 11 to 17 age group, issues such as bullying or running away may be important indicators of potential neglect.

- There needs to be more awareness of the long-term impact of neglect on young people in terms of mental health problems. Recent UK research indicates that neglect may be linked with self-harming or suicidal behaviour.

- In several parts of the book, we have discussed the potential for young people to self-refer to helping agencies. This could substantially increase the likelihood of early intervention and the advantages that this might bring in terms of preventing problems becoming engrained. However, for this potential to be a reality, a number of obstacles need to be overcome. First, young people need a good understanding of what neglect is and when they might be experiencing it. Second, they also need a good understanding of the help that might exist and how they can access this help. Third, they need to have confidence in agencies and perceive them to be accessible.

- Issues of trust and confidentiality are particularly important to young people and this may require a flexibility of working approach in terms of boundaries of confidentiality that is not so common when working with younger children. This could involve finding ways of facilitating young people's active involvement in professional working processes, and generally recognizing the importance of control and autonomy for young people in this age group.

- Recent UK research has also highlighted the importance that young people attach to having one consistent person with whom they can build a relationship of trust and then work with. The Common Assessment Framework is a good example of how young people can keep the same professional as their key worker.

- Professionals working with young people who are neglected should be aware of the risk of shifting the focus from parents' behaviour (or lack of) to young people's behaviour, as discussed earlier.

- Turning to multi-agency working, a number of the issues we have identified – such as the importance of good communication, close working relationships, sharing of responsibility and developing a mutual understanding of language and definitions – are common to many types of collaborative working between people from different backgrounds or disciplines. In addition, in order to develop multi-agency practice with adolescent neglect, it is essential to understand the assumptions being made by different parties, including those made within and between the agencies involved and those made by young people and families. Clarity of definitions and thresholds may be a particular challenge here.

- Finally, given the extent of the challenges faced by practitioners in responding effectively to the neglect of young people, the availability and use of professional supervision is an important ingredient of good practice.

Implications for policy

Following on from these implications for practitioners and practice managers, there are a number of key messages for policy makers at both local and national levels and other key decision makers in terms of an effective strategic response to the needs of young people aged 11 to 17 who experience neglect.

- Definitions of neglect need to vary according to the age of the young person. The Core Assessment Records materials contained within the Assessment Framework offer an excellent starting point for age-sensitive definitions of neglect. There may be a case for further documentation that pulls together some of this material and draws attention to some of the age-specific assessment issues contained within the materials in relation to older young people.

- Neglect makes up a large proportion of child protection cases in all age groups. However, there is a wide variation in proportions between areas and more guidance on definitions may be helpful in terms of producing more consistent and reliable statistics.

- There are a number of major gaps in UK research in this area identified through the review, and this suggests the case for policy makers and funding bodies to support research that explores definitions, prevalence, aetiology and outcomes of adolescent neglect.

- There is also a major gap in knowledge about interventions with neglected adolescents. Internationally, there is very little empirical evidence of the effectiveness of interventions with this target group, and there is virtually no UK-based evaluative research. There are, however, examples of potentially promising interventions from the US literature. There is, therefore, a need for research funding for pilot projects in this area with a strong commitment to evaluating outcomes.

- Policy guidance for professionals needs to include a focus on young people in relation to their particular experiences of neglect.

- Finally, the age categories within the official child protection statistics are not particularly helpful for exploring issues in relation to adolescents. The 10- to 15-year-old age band spans late primary school and early to mid-adolescence. For more detailed future analysis, it may be helpful if more precise age reporting was available.

Implications for research

In terms of the research agenda, the almost complete lack of UK research that contains definitions of adolescent neglect represents both a major gap and an opportunity. The opportunity is to avoid the pitfalls from the primarily US-based research literature to date − characterized by a high level of inconsistency in terms of definitions, categorizations and measures of child neglect that has hampered progress. There is a need for research development in this area that fits the UK context and adopts a consistent approach, preferably linked with frameworks and definitions commonly used in policy and practice.

The key research gaps we have highlighted span the whole range of topics covered in this book − prevalence and incidence of neglect of young people, cause and consequences, and evaluations of interventions. In summary:

- There is a shortage of research that explores normative parenting of young people and the prevalence of different parenting styles in the UK.

- Research is needed on the contextual factors associated with neglect of young people and how these may vary compared with younger children. This is a gap in the research internationally rather than just within the UK. Research on contextual factors needs to include consideration of the issues faced by specific groups including young carers and disabled children.

- There is a need for UK research on the association between neglect and outcomes. However, there is more evidence from the international literature on this area than on contextual factors and, given a number of competing priorities, it may not make sense to replicate this work.

Therefore, particular attention might be given to some of the gaps we have identified in the research from other countries. These include work on some specific outcomes – for example, physical health and bullying. However, more critically, any work on links between experiences of neglect and outcomes should pay attention to the need to address issues of causality, as discussed in Chapter 4. This indicates a particularly pressing need for longitudinal studies.

- There is a dearth of research on young people's views and experiences of neglect, particularly the views of disabled young people and those from Black and minority ethnic groups. More research needs to be undertaken with general population samples and more specifically with young people who have experienced neglect. Also little is known about parents' views and experiences of seeking and experiencing help in neglect cases. More research is certainly needed to address these gaps so we have more knowledge about the impact of neglect on young people and how to improve both short- and long-term outcomes. We have begun to explore young people's perspectives through the focus group work described in Chapter 5, and this provides a starting point for discussion; but much more in-depth research needs to be undertaken.

- There is little understanding of multi-agency working in response to neglect and older young people. In particular, more needs to be understood about the differing nature of approaches and expectations of practitioners in this area. Greater understanding is needed in terms of the operation and interaction of thresholds and financial responsibilities between agencies, together with the underpinning assumptions. Additionally, clarity is urgently needed about practitioners' perceptions of case history, autonomy and responsibility in relation to neglected adolescents, so that this may inform ways of achieving consistency in practice. There is a considerable gap in knowledge about the form and nature of supervision that may enable best practice in multi-agency contexts, particularly in relation to neglect and adolescence.

- There is also a major gap in research on interventions with neglected adolescents, with only a very small number of identified peer-reviewed studies, mostly from the US. Filling this gap in knowledge would constitute a major evaluative research programme. As a first step, it would certainly be helpful to have robustly evaluated piloting of a range of possible models of intervention, prior to more extensive implementation of any particular model.

- Finally, we note the extent of overlap between different forms of maltreatment. This raises risks that studies of one category of maltreatment in isolation may, for example, erroneously attribute outcomes to this category in particular, when the situation may in reality be more complex. So, while we have advocated for substantial new research on neglect in particular, we would also argue that researchers need to take into account the interaction between various forms of maltreatment. Thus researchers undertaking studies of other forms of maltreatment should ensure that information is also gathered about neglect.

References

Action for Children (2010) *Seen and Now Heard: Taking Action on Child Neglect*. London: Action for Children. Available at www.actionforchildren.org.uk/content/179/Publications, accessed on 25 February 2011.

Advisory Council on the Misuse of Drugs (ACMD) (2003) *Hidden Harm – Responding to the Needs of Children of Problem Drug Users*. London: ACMD.

Aldgate, J. and Statham, J. (2001) *The Children Act Now: Messages from Research. Studies in Evaluating the Children Act 1989*. London: Department of Health.

Aldridge, J. and Becker, S. (2003) *Children Caring for Parents with Mental Illness*. Bristol: Policy Press.

Allard, A. (2003) '*The End of My Tether': The Unmet Support Needs of Families with Teenagers – A Scandalous Gap in Provision*. London: Action for Children. Available at www. actionforchildren.org.uk/uploads/media/36/1586.pdf, accessed on 25 February 2011.

Allen, G. (2011) *Early Intervention: The Next Steps*. Available at http://media.education.gov. uk/assets/files/pdf/g/graham%20allens%20review%20of%20early%20intervention. pdf

Anning, A., Cottrell, D., Frost, N., Green, J. and Robinson, M. (2006) *Developing Multiprofessional Teamwork for Integrated Children's Services*. Maidenhead: Open University Press.

Arata, C., Langhinrichsen-Rolling. J., Bowers, D. and O'Brien, N. (2007) 'Differential correlates of multi-type maltreatment among urban youth.' *Child Abuse & Neglect 31*, 393–415.

Atkinson, M., Wilkin, A., Stott, A., Doherty, P. and Kinder, K. (2002) *Multi-Agency Working: A Detailed Study*. Slough: NFER.

Aunola, K., Stattin. H. and Nurmi, J.E. (2000) 'Parenting styles and adolescents' achievement strategies.' *Journal of Adolescence 23*, 2, 205–222.

Back, S. and Lips, H.M. (1998) 'Child sexual abuse: Victim age, victim gender, and observer gender as factors contributing to attributions of responsibility.' *Child Abuse & Neglect 22*, 12, 1239–1252.

Bancroft, A., Wilson, S., Cunningham-Burley, S., Backett-Milburn, K. and Masters, H. (2004) *Parental Drug and Alcohol Misuse: Resilience and Transition Among Young People*. York: Joseph Rowntree Foundation.

Barlow, J. and Schrader MacMillan, A. (2010) *Safeguarding Children from Emotional Maltreatment: What Works*. London: Jessica Kingsley Publishers.

Barnard, M. and Barlow, J. (2003) 'Discovering parental drug dependence: Silence and disclosure.' *Children and Society 17*, 1, January, 45–56.

Barnes, G.M., Reifman, A.S., Farrell, M.P. and Dintcheff, B.A. (2000) 'The effects of parenting on the development of adolescent alcohol misuse: A six-wave latent growth model.' *Journal of Marriage and The Family 62*, 1, 175–186.

Barrett, G. and Keeping, C. (2005) 'The Processes Required for Effective Interprofessional Working.' In G. Barrett, D. Sellman and J. Thomas (eds) *Interprofessional Working in Health and Social Care: Professional Perspectives.* Basingstoke: Palgrave Macmillan.

Batmanghelidjh, C. (2006) *Shattered Lives.* London: Jessica Kingsley Publishers.

Baumrind, D. (1968) 'Authoritarian vs. authoritative parental control.' *Adolescence 3*, 11, 255–272.

Bernstein, D.P., Stein, J.A., Newcomb, M.D., Walker, E. *et al.* (2003) 'Development and validation of a brief screening version of the Childhood Trauma Questionnaire.' *Child Abuse & Neglect 27*, 2, 169–190.

Biehal, N. (2005) *Working with Adolescents: Supporting Families, Preventing Breakdown.* London: British Association for Adoption and Fostering.

Biggs, S. (1997) 'Interprofessional Collaboration: Problems and Prospects.' In J. Øvretveit, P. Mathias and T. Thompson (eds) *Interprofessional Working for Health and Social Care.* Basingstoke: Palgrave Macmillan.

Bovarnick, S. (2007) *Child Neglect.* Child protection research briefing. London: NSPCC.

Brandon, M., Bailey, S., Belderson, P., Gardner, R. *et al.* (2009) *Understanding Serious Case Reviews and Their Impact: A Biennial Analysis of Serious Case Reviews 2005–2007.* DCSF Research Report, RR129. London: Department for Children, Schools and Families.

Brandon, M., Howe, A., Dagley, V., Salter, C. and Warren, C. (2006) 'What appears to be helping or hindering practitioners in implementing the common assessment framework and lead professional working?' *Child Abuse Review 15*, 396–413.

Brandon, M., Belderson, P., Warren, C., Gardner, R. *et al.* (2008a) 'The preoccupation with thresholds in cases of child death or serious injury through abuse and neglect.' *Child Abuse Review 17*, 5, 313–330.

Brandon, M., Belderson, P., Warren, C., Howe, D. *et al.* (2008b) *Analysing Child Death and Serious Injury Through Abuse and Neglect: What can we Learn? A Biennial Analysis of Serious Case Reviews 2003–2005, Research Report RR023.* Nottingham: Department for Children, Schools and Families.

Bronfenbrenner, U. (1979) *The Ecology of Human Development.* Cambridge, MA: Harvard University Press.

Brookes, H. and Flower, C. (ed) (2009) *Children Talking to ChildLine About Suicide,* ChildLine casenotes. London: NSPCC.

Browne, K., and Falshaw, L. (1998) 'Street children and crime in the UK: A case of abuse and neglect.' *Child Abuse Review 7*, 4, 241–253.

Browne, K. and Saqi, S. (1988) 'Approaches to screening for child abuse and neglect.' In K. Browne, C. Davies and P. Stratton (eds) *Early Prediction and Prevention of Child Abuse,* Chichester: Wiley.

Brunk, M., Henlegger, S.W. and Whelan, J.P. (1987) 'Comparison of multisystemic therapy and parent training in the brief treatment of child abuse and neglect.' *Journal of Consulting and Clinical Psychology 55,* 171–178.

Buist, K.L., Dekovic, M., Meeus, W. and Aken, M.A.G. (2004) 'The reciprocal relationship between early adolescent attachment and internalizing and externalizing problem behaviour.' *Journal of Adolescence 27,* 251–266.

Cameron, G. and Karabanow, J. (2003) 'The nature and effectiveness of program models for adolescents at risk of entering the formal child protection system.' *Child Welfare 82,* 4, 443–74.

Carpenter, J. and Dickinson, H. (2008) *Interprofessional Education and Training.* Bristol: Policy Press.

Cawson, P., Wattam, C., Brooker, S. and Kelly, G. (2000) *Child maltreatment in the United Kingdom: A Study of the Prevalence of Child Abuse and Neglect.* London: NSPCC.

ChildLine (2008) *Children Talking to ChildLine About Family Relationship Problems.* London: ChildLine.

Cicchetti, D. and Toth, S. (1995) 'A developmental psychopathology perspective on child abuse and neglect.' *Journal of the American Academy of Child and Adolescent Psychiatry 34,* 5, 541–565.

Claes, M., Lacourse, E., Bouchard, C. and Perucchini, P. (2003) 'Parental practices in late adolescence, a comparison of three countries: Canada, France and Italy.' *Journal of Adolescence 26,* 387–399.

Claes, M., Lacourse, E., Ercolani, A-P., Pierro, A., Leone, L. and Presaghi, F. (2005) 'Parenting, peer orientation: A cross-national study.' *Journal of Youth and Adolescence, 34* (15), 40–411.

Cleaver, H., Unell, I. and Aldgate, J. (1999) *Children's Needs – Parenting Capacity: The Impact of Parental Mental Illness, Problem Alcohol and Drug Use, and Domestic Violence on Children's Development.* London: The Stationery Office.

Cleveland, M.J., Gibbons, F.X., Gerrard, M., Pomery, E.A. and Brody, G.H. (2005) 'The impact of parenting on risk cognitions and risk behavior: A study of mediation and moderation in a panel of African American adolescents.' *Child Development 76,* 4, 900–916.

Collings, S.J. and Payne, M.F. (1991) 'Attribution of causal and moral responsibility to victims of father-daughter incest: An exploratory examination of five factors.' *Child Abuse & Neglect 15,* 513–521.

Coohey, C. (1995) 'Neglectful mothers, their mothers, and partners – the significance of mutual aid.' *Child Abuse & Neglect 19,* 8, 885–895.

Coohey, C. (1996) 'Child maltreatment: Testing the social isolation hypothesis.' *Child Abuse & Neglect 20,* 3, 241–254.

Coy, M. (2009) 'Moved around like bags of rubbish nobody wants': How multiple placement moves can make young women vulnerable to sexual exploitation.' *Child Abuse Review 18*, 254–266.

Crittenden, P.M. (1999) 'Child Neglect: Causes and Contributors.' In H. Dubowitz (ed.) *Neglected Children: Research, Practice and Policy.* Thousand Oaks, CA: Sage.

Daniel, B.M. and Taylor, J. (2006) 'Gender and child neglect, theory, research and policy.' *Critical Social Policy 26*, 2, 426–439.

Daniel, B., Taylor, J. and Scott, J. (2009) *Noticing and Helping the Neglected Child: Literature Review. Research Report RBX-09-03.* London, Department for Children, Schools and Families. Available at www.education.gov.uk/rsgateway/DB/RRP/u015015/index. shtml, accessed on 26 February 2011.

Daniel, B., Taylor, J. and Scott, J. (2010) 'Recognition of neglect and early response: Overview of a systematic review of the literature.' *Child and Family Social Work 1*, 2, May, 248–257.

De Panfilis, D. (2006a) *Child Neglect: A Guide for Prevention, Assessment, and Intervention.* Washington, DC: US Department of Health and Human Services, Administration for Children and Families, Administration on Children, Youth and Families, Children's Bureau, Office on Child Abuse and Neglect.

De Panfilis, D. (2006b) 'Interventions for Children and Families who have Experienced Neglect in the US.' In C. McAuley, P.J. Pecora and W. Rose. (eds) *Enhancing the Well-being of Children and Families through Effective Interventions: International Evidence for Practice.* London: Jessica Kingsley Publishers.

Department for Children, Schools and Families (DCSF) (2007) *The Children's Plan: Building Brighter Futures.* London: Stationery Office.

Department for Children, Schools and Families (2008) *Staying Safe: Action Plan.* Nottingham: DCSF.

Department for Children, Schools and Families (DCSF) (2009) *Referrals, Assessment and Children and Young People who are the Subject of a Child Protection Plan, England – Year ending 31 March 2009.* London: DCSF.

Department for Education and Skills (2006) *The Common Assessment Framework for Children and Young People: Practitioners' Guide.* London: HM Government.

Department for Education and Skills (2007) *Targeted Youth Support: A Guide.* London: The Stationery Office.

Department of Health (1995) *Child Protection: Messages from Research.* London: HMSO.

Department of Health (DH) (2008) *UK Child Health Promotion Programme.* London: DH.

Department of Health, Department for Education and Employment, and Home Office (2000) *Framework for the Assessment of Children in Need and their Families.* London: The Stationery Office.

DeVore, E.R. and Ginsburg, K.R. (2005) 'The protective effects of good parenting on adolescents.' *Current Opinion In Pediatrics 17*, 4, 460–465.

Dubowitz, H. (1999) *Neglected Children: Research, Practice, and Policy.* Thousand Oaks, CA: Sage.

Dufour, S., Lavergne, C., Larrivée, M-C. and Trocmé, N. (2007) 'Who are these parents involved in child neglect? A differential analysis by parent gender and family structure.' *Children and Youth Services Review 30*, 141–156.

Ethier, L.S., Couture, G., Lacharite, C. and Gagnier, J-P. (2000) 'Impact of a multidimensional intervention programme applied to families at risk for child neglect.' *Child Abuse Review 9*, 1, 19–36.

Evans, H. (2002) *Child Neglect.* Research briefing. London: NSPCC.

Farmer, E. and Lutman, E. (2010) *Case Management and Outcomes for Neglected Children Returned to their Parents: A Five Year Follow-up Study.* Research briefing RB214. London: Department for Children, Schools and Families.

Featherstone, B. and Evans, H. (2004) *Children Experiencing Maltreatment: Who do They Turn To?* London, NSPCC.

Freisthler, B., Merrit, D.H. and LaScala, E.A. (2006) 'Understanding the ecology of child maltreatment: A review of the literature and directions for future research.' *Child Maltreatment 11*, 3, 263–280.

Frost, N. and Parton, N. (2009) *Understanding Children's Social Care, Politics, Policy and Practice.* London: Sage.

Frost, N. and Robinson, M. (2007) 'Joining up children's services: Safeguarding children in multidisciplinary teams.' *Child Abuse Review 16*, 184–199.

Fuller, R., Hallett, C., Murray, C. and Punch, S. (2000) *Young People and Welfare: Negotiating Pathways.* University of Stirling: ESRC.

Garbarino, J. and Collins, C. (1999) 'Child Neglect: The Family with a Hole in the Middle.' In H. Dubowitz (ed.) *Neglected Children: Research, Practice and Policy.* Thousand Oaks, CA: Sage Publications.

Gardner, R. (2008) *Developing an Effective Response to Neglect and Emotional Harm to Children.* Norwich and London: University of East Anglia and NSPCC.

Gaskell, C. (2008) *Kids Company Help with the Whole Problem.* Kids Company Research and Evaluation Programme. London: Queen Mary University of London.

Gasper, M. (2009) *Multi-agency Working in the Early Years: Challenges and Opportunities.* London: Sage Publications.

Glasby, J. and Dickinson, H. (2008) *Partnership Working in Health and Social Care.* Bristol: Policy Press.

Glaser, D. (2002) 'Emotional abuse and neglect (psychological maltreatment): A Conceptual Framework.' *Child Abuse & Neglect 26*, 6/7, 697–714.

Gorin, S. (2004) *Understanding What Children Say: Children's Experiences of Domestic Violence, Parental Substance Misuse and Parental Health Problems.* London: National Children's Bureau.

Harrington, D., Zuravin, S., De Panfilis, D., Ting, L. and Dubowitz, H. (2002) 'The neglect scale: Confirmatory factor analyses in a low-income sample.' *Child Maltreatment 7*, 4, 359–368.

Hicks, L. and Stein, M. (2010) *Neglect Matters: A Multi-agency Guide for Professionals Working Together on Behalf of Teenagers.* London: Department for Children, Schools and Families.

HM Government (2004) *Every Child Matters: Change for Children.* Nottingham: Department for Children, Schools and Families.

HM Government (2006) *Working Together to Safeguard Children: A Guide to Inter-agency Working to Safeguard and Promote the Welfare of Children.* London: The Stationery Office.

HM Government (2008) *Statutory Framework for the Early Years Foundation Stage, Setting the Standards for Learning, Development, and Care for Children from Birth to Five.* Nottingham: Department for Children, Schools and Families.

HM Government (2009) *The Protection of Children in England: Action Plan, The Government's Response to Lord Laming, CM 7589.* London: The Stationary Office.

HM Government (2010) *Working Together to Safeguard Children: A Guide to Inter-agency Working to Safeguard and Promote the Welfare of Children.* London: Department for Children, Schools and Families.

HM Treasury (2007) *Policy Review of Children and Young People: A Discussion Paper.* Norwich: HMSO.

Hooper, C-A., Gorin, S., Cabral, C. and Dyson, C. (2007) *Living with Hardship 24/7: The Diverse Experiences of Families in Poverty in England.* London, Frank Buttle Trust.

Horwath, J. (2002) 'Maintaining a focus on the child?' *Child Abuse Review 11*, 4, 195–213.

Horwath, J. (2005) 'Identifying and assessing cases of child neglect: Learning from the Irish experience.' *Child and Family Social Work 10*, 2, 99–110.

Horwath, J. (2007a) *Child Neglect: Identification and Assessment.* Basingstoke and New York: Palgrave Macmillan.

Horwath, J. (2007b) 'The missing assessment domain: Personal, professional and organisational factors influencing professional judgements when identifying and referring child neglect.' *British Journal of Social Work 37*, 1285–1303.

Hugman, R. (2003) 'Professional values and ethics in social work: Reconsidering postmodernism?' *British Journal of Social Work 33*, 8, 1025–1041.

Huh, D., Tristan, J., Wade, E. and Stice, E. (2006) 'Does problem behavior elicit poor parenting? A prospective study of adolescent girls. *Journal of Adolescent Research 21*, 2, 185–204.

Hutchinson, D. and Woods, R. (2010) *Children Talking to ChildLine about Loneliness.* Available at www.nspcc.org.uk/inform/publications/casenotes/clcasenotes_loneliness_wdf74260. pdfaccessed on 25 February 2011.

Iwaniec, D. and McSherry, D. (2002) *Understanding Child Neglect – Contemporary Issues and Dilemmas.* Belfast: Institute of Child Care Research, Queen's University of Belfast.

Johnson, P., Wistow, G., Schulz, R. and Hardy, B. (2003) 'Interagency and interprofessional collaboration in community care: The interdependence of structures and values.' *Journal of Interprofessional Care 17*, 1, 69–83.

Jones, J. and Gupta, A. (1998) 'The context of decision-making in cases of child neglect.' *Child Abuse Review* 7, 2, 97–110.

Jonson-Reid, M. (2002) After a child abuse report: Early adolescents and the child welfare system.' *Journal of Early Adolescence 22*, 1, 24–48.

Kaplow, J.B. and Widom, C.S. (2007) 'Age of onset of child maltreatment predicts long-term mental health outcomes.' *Journal of Abnormal Psychology 116*, 1, 176–187.

Kendler, S.K., Myers, J. and Prescott, C.A. (2000) 'Parenting and adult mood, anxiety and substance use disorders in female twins: An epidemiological, multi-informant, retrospective study.' *Psychological Medicine 30*, 281–294.

Kerr, M. and Stattin, H. (2003) 'Parenting of Adolescents: Action or Reaction?' In A.C. Crouter and A. Booth (eds) *Children's Influence on Family Dynamics. The Neglected Side of Family Relationships* (pp.121–152). Mahwah, NJ: Lawrence Erlbaum Associates.

Kotch, J.B., Browne, D.C., Ringwalt, C.L. and Stewart, P.W. (1995) 'Risk of child abuse and neglect in a cohort of low-income children.' *Child Abuse & Neglect 19*, 1115–1130.

Kroll, B. (2004) 'Living with an elephant: Growing up with parental substance misuse.' *Child and Family Social Work 9*, 2, May, 129–140.

Laming, W.H.L. (2003) The Victoria Climbié Inquiry: Report of an Inquiry by Lord Laming. London: The Stationery Office.

Lancaster, G., Rollinson, L. and Hill, J. (2007) 'The measurement of a major childhood risk for depression: Comparison of the Parental Bonding Instrument (PBI) "Parental Care" and the Childhood Experience of Care and Abuse (CECA) "Parental Neglect".' *Journal of Affective Disorders 101*, 263–267.

Leiba, A. and Weinstein, J. (2003) 'Who are the Participants in the Collaborative Process and What Makes Collaboration Succeed or Fail?' In J. Weinstein, C. Whittington and T. Leiba (eds) *Collaboration in Social Work Practice*. London: Jessica Kingsley Publishers.

Liverpool Drug and Alcohol Action Team (2001) *In a Different World*. Liverpool: Liverpool Drug and Alcohol Action Team and Barnardo's.

Loxley, A. (1997) *Collaboration in Health and Welfare: Working with Difference*. London: Jessica Kingsley Publishers.

Macaskill, C. (2006) *Beyond Refuge: Supporting Young Runaways*. London: NSPCC.

MacCoby, E.E. and Martin, J.A. (1983) 'Socialization in the Context of the Family: Parent-child Interaction.' In P.H. Mussen and E.M. Hetherington (eds) *Handbook of Child Psychology: Vol. 4. Socialization, Personality, and Social Development*. New York: Wiley.

Mariathasan, J. and Hutchinson, D. (2010) *Children talking to ChildLine about Parental Alcohol and Drug Misuse*. ChildLine casenotes. London: NSPCC.

Masten, A. (2006) 'Promoting Residence in Development: A General Framework for Systems of Care.' In R. Flynn, P. Dudding and J. Barber (eds) *Promoting Resilience in Child Welfare*. Ottawa: University of Ottawa Press.

Mayer, M., Lavergne, C., Tourigny, M. and Wright, J. (2007) 'Characteristics differentiating neglected children from other reported children.' *Journal of Family Violence 22*, 721–732.

Maynard, C. and Wiederman, M. (1997) 'Undergraduate students' perceptions of child sexual abuse: Effects of age, sex, and gender-role attitudes.' *Child Abuse & Neglect 21*, 9, 833–844.

McCray, J. (2007) 'Reflective Practice for Collaborative Working.' In C. Knott and T. Scragg (eds) (2007) *Reflective Practice in Social Work*. Exeter: Learning Matters.

McGee, R., Wolfe, D. and Olson, J. (2001) 'Multiple maltreatment, attribution of blame, and adjustment among adolescents.' *Development and Psychopathology 13*, 4, 827–846.

McGee, R.A., Wolfe, D.A., Yuen, S.A., Wilson, S.K. and Carnochan, J. (1995) 'The measurement of maltreatment: A comparison of approaches.' *Child Abuse & Neglect 19*, 2, 233–249.

Miller, B.C., Benson, B. and Galbraith, K.A. (2001) 'Family relationships and adolescent pregnancy risk: A research synthesis.' *Developmental Review 21*, 1, 1–38.

Minty, B. and Pattinson, G. (1994) 'The nature of child neglect.' *British Journal of Social Work 24*, 6, 733–747.

Moran, P. (2009) *Neglect: Research Evidence to Inform Practice*. London: Action for Children.

Moran, P., Jacobs, C., Bunn, A. and Bifulco, A. (2007) 'Multi-agency working: Implications for an early intervention social work team.' *Child and Family Social Work 12*, 2, 143–151.

Moreland, N., Read, K., Jolley, D. and Clark, M. (2004) 'Partnership Working in Service Provision for Ethnic Minority People with Dementia.' In R. Carnwell and J. Buchanan (eds) *Effective Practice in Health and Social Care: A Collaborative Approach*. Buckingham: Open University Press.

Munro, E. (2010) *The Munro Review of Child Protection – Part One: A System's Analysis*. London: Department for Education. Available at www.education.gov.uk/munroreview, accessed 28 June 2011.

Munro, E. (2011) *The Munro Review of Child Protection, Interim Report: The Child's Journey*. Available at www.education.gov.uk/munroreview/downloads/Munrointerimreport.pdf, accessed on 21 May 2011.

National Working Group on Child Protection and Disability (2003) *'It Doesn't Happen to Disabled Children': Child Protection and Disabled Children*. London: NSPCC.

NSPCC (2008) *ChildLine Casenotes: Children talking to ChildLine about Family Relationships Problems*. London: NSPCC.

Ofsted (2010) *Supporting Young People: An Evaluation of Recent Reforms to Youth Support Services in 11 Local Areas*. London: Ofsted.

Olsen, R. and Wates, M. (2003) *Disabled Parents – Examining Research Assumptions*. Dartington: Research in Practice.

Parker, G., Tupling, H. and Brown, L.B. (1979) 'A Parental Bonding Instrument.' *British Journal of Medical Psychology 52*, 1–10.

Parrott, L. (2005) 'The Political Drivers of Working in Partnership.' In R. Carnwell and J. Buchanan (eds) *Effective Practice in Health and Social Care*. Maidenhead: Open University Press.

Parrott, L. (2008) 'The ethics of partnership.' *Ethics and Social Welfare 2*, 1, 24–37.

Parton, N. (2004) 'From Maria Colwell to Victoria Climbié: Reflections on public inquiries into child abuse a generation apart.' *Child Abuse Review 13*, 2, 80–94.

Parton, N. and O'Byrne, P. (2000) *Constructive Social Work: Towards a New Practice.* Basingstoke, Palgrave.

Paulson, S.E., Marchant, G.J. and Rothlisberg, B.A. (1998) 'Early adolescents' perceptions of patterns of parenting, teaching, and school atmosphere: Implications for achievement.' *Journal of Early Adolescence 18*, 1, 5–26.

Public Health Agency of Canada (2010) *Canadian Incidence Study of Reported Child Abuse and Neglect – 2008: Major Findings.* Ottawa: Public Health Agency of Canada.

Radford, L., Allnock, D., Corral, S., Bradley, C. and Thompson, S. (forthcoming). *Who Do You Turn To?* London: NSPCC.

Radford, L., Corral, S., Bradley, C., Fisher, H. *et al.* (2011) *Child Abuse and Neglect in the UK Today.* London: NSPCC.

Reder P. and Duncan S. (2004) 'From Colwell to Climbié: Inquiring into Fatal Child Abuse.' In N. Stanley and G. Manthorpe (eds) *The Age of the Inquiry: Learning and Blaming in Health and Social Care.* London: Routledge.

Rees, G. and Lee, J. (2005) *Still Running II: Findings from the Second National Survey of Young Runaways.* London: Children's Society.

Rees, G. and Rutherford, C. (2001) *Home Run – Families and Young Runaways.* London: The Children's Society.

Rees, G. and Siakeu, J. (2004) *Thrown Away: The Experiences of Children Forced to Leave Home.* London: The Children's Society.

Rees, G. and Stein, M. (1999) *The Abuse of Adolescents Within the Family.* London: NSPCC.

Rees, G., Gorin, S., Jobe, A., Stein, M., Medforth, R. and Goswami. H. (2010) *Safeguarding Young People: Responding to Young People Aged 11–17 who are Maltreated.* Executive summary. London: The Children's Society.

Reitz, E., Dekovic, M. and Meijer, A.M. (2006) 'Relations between parenting and externalizing and internalizing problem behaviour in early adolescence: Child behaviour as moderator and predictor.' *Journal of Adolescence 29*, 3, 419–436.

Richardson, S. and Asthana, S. (2006) 'Inter-agency information sharing in health and social care services: The role of professional culture.' *British Journal of Social Work 36*, 4, 657–669.

Rutter, M. (1999) 'Resilience concepts and findings: Implications for family therapy.' *Journal of Family Therapy 21*, 119–144.

Safe on the Streets Research Team (1999) *Still Running – Children on the Streets in the UK.* London: The Children's Society.

Scannapieco, M. and Connell-Carrick, K. (2005) *Understanding Child Maltreatment: An Ecological and Developmental Perspective.* Oxford: Oxford University Press.

Schofield, G. (2001) 'Resilience and family placement: A lifespan perspective.' *Adoption and Fostering 25*, 3, 6–19.

Schoon, I. and Bartley, M. (2008) 'The role of human capability and resilience.' *The Psychologist 21*, 124–127.

Schore, A.N. (2002) 'Dysregulation of the right brain: A fundamental mechanism of traumatic attachment and the psychopathogenesis of posttraumatic stress disorder.' *Australian & New Zealand Journal of Psychiatry 36*, 9–30.

Sedlak, A. (2001) *A History of the National Incidence Study of Child Abuse and Neglect.* Rockville, MD: Westat Inc.

Shucksmith, J., Hendry, L.B. and Glendinning, A. (1995) 'Models of parenting – implications for adolescent well-being within different types of family contexts.' *Journal of Adolescence 18*, 3, 253–270.

Sinclair, R. and Bullock, R. (2002) *Learning from Past Experience: A Review of Serious Case Reviews.* London: Department of Health.

Smith, C.A., Ireland, T.O. and Thornberry, T.P. (2005) 'Adolescent maltreatment and its impact on young adult antisocial behavior.' *Child Abuse & Neglect 29*, 10, 1099–1119.

Smith, J. and Ravenhill, M. (2006) *What is Homelessness? A Report on the Attitudes of Young People and Parents on Risks of Running Away and Homelessness in London.* London: Centrepoint. Available at www.centrepoint.org.uk/assets/documents/publications/research-reports/what-is-homelessness-full-%20report.pdf, accessed on 25 March 2011.

Smith, R. (2008) *Social Work with Young People.* Cambridge: Polity.

Soenens, B., Vansteenkiste, M., Luyckx, K. and Goossens, L. (2006) 'Parenting and adolescent problem behavior: An integrated model with adolescent self-disclosure and perceived parental knowledge as intervening variables.' *Developmental Psychology 42*, 2, 305–318.

Spera, C. (2005) 'A review of the relationship among parenting practices, parenting styles, and adolescent school achievement.' *Educational Psychology Review 17*, 2, 120–146.

Stein, M. (2009) *Quality Matters in Children's Services: Messages from Research.* London: Jessica Kingsley Publishers.

Stein, M., Rees, G., Hicks, L. and Gorin, S. (2009) *Neglected Adolescents: Literature Review Research Brief.* London: DSCF.

Sternberg, K.J., Lamb, M.E., Guterman, E., Abbott, C.B and Dawud-Noursi, S. (2005) 'Adolescents' perceptions of attachments to their mothers and fathers in families with histories of domestic violence: A longitudinal perspective.' *Child Abuse & Neglect 29*, 853–869.

Stevenson, O. (1998) *Neglected Children: Issues and Dilemmas.* Oxford: Blackwell.

Stevenson, O. (2007) *Neglected Children and Their Families.* Oxford: Blackwell.

Stewart, A., Petch, A. and Curtice, L. (2003) 'Moving towards integrated working in health and social care in Scotland: From maze to matrix.' *Journal of Interprofessional Practice 17*, 4, 335–350.

Stone, B. (1998) 'Child neglect: Practitioners' perspectives.' *Child Abuse Review 7*, 2, 87–96.

Straus, M.A. and Kantor, G.K. (2005) 'Definition and measurement of neglectful behavior: Some principles and guidelines.' *Child Abuse & Neglect 29*, 1, 19–29.

Straus, M.A., Kinard, E.M. and Williams, L.M. (1995) *The Multidimensional Neglectful Behavior Scale, Form A: Adolescent and Adult-Recall Version.* Durham, NH: Family Research Laboratory.

Sullivan, S. (2000) *Child Neglect: Current Definitions and Models – A Review of Child Neglect Research, 1993–1998.* National Clearinghouse on Family Violence.

Sullivan, P.M. and Knutson, J.F. (2000) 'Maltreatment and disabilities: A population based epidemiological study.' *Child Abuse & Neglect 24*, 1257–1273.

Swift, K.J. (1995) 'An outrage to common decency: Historical perspectives on child neglect.' *Child Welfare 74*, 1, 71–91.

Thoburn, J., Wilding, J. and Watson, J. (2000) *Family Support in Cases of Emotional Maltreatment and Neglect.* London: Stationery Office.

Thompson, N. (2006) *Anti-discriminatory Practice.* Basingstoke: Palgrave.

Thornberry, T.P., Ireland, T.O. and Smith, C.A. (2001) 'The importance of timing: The varying impact of childhood and adolescent maltreatment on multiple problem outcomes.' *Development and Psychopathology 13*, 4, 957–979.

Thornberry, T.P., Henry, K.L., Ireland, T.O. and Smith, C.A. (2010) 'The causal impact of childhood-limited maltreatment and adolescent maltreatment on early adult adjustment.' *Journal of Adolescent Health 46*, 4, 359–365.

Tunnard, J. (2004) *Parental Mental Health Problems: Messages from Research, Policy and Practice.* Dartington: Research in Practice.

Turney, D. and Tanner, K. (2001) 'Working with neglected children and their families.' *Journal of Social Work Practice 15*, 2, November, 193–204.

US Department of Health and Human Services (USDHHS), Administration for Children and Families, Administration on Children, Youth and Families, Children's Bureau (2010) *Child Maltreatment 2009.* Washington, DC: USDHHS.

Vazsonyi, A.T., Hibbert, J.R. and Snider, J.B. (2003) 'Exotic enterprise no more? Adolescent reports of family and parenting processes from youth in four countries.' *Journal of Research on Adolescence 13*, 2, 129–160.

Velleman, R., Templeton, L., Taylor, A. and Toner, P. (2003) *The Family Alcohol Service: Evaluation of a Pilot.* Bath: University of Bath.

Wales, A., Gillan, E., Hill, L. and Robertson, F. (2009) *Untold Damage: Children's Accounts of Living with Harmful Parental Drinking.* Edinburgh: Scottish Health Action on Alcohol Problems (SHAAP).

Webster, S.W., O'Toole, R., O'Toole, A.W. and Lucal, B. (2005) 'Overreporting and underreporting of child abuse: Teachers' use of professional discretion.' *Child Abuse & Neglect 29*, 1281–1296.

Westat Inc. (1993) *A Report on the Maltreatment of Children with Disabilities.* Washington DC: National Center on Child Abuse and Neglect.

Whittington, C. (2003a) 'A Model of Collaboration.' In J. Weinstein, C. Whittington and T. Leiba (eds) *Collaboration in Social Work Practice*. London: Jessica Kingsley Publishers.

Whittington, C. (2003b) 'Collaboration and Partnership in Context.' In J. Weinstein, C. Whittington and T. Leiba (eds) *Collaboration in Social Work Practice*. London: Jessica Kingsley Publishers.

Wight, D., Williamson, L. and Henderson, M. (2006) 'Parental influences on young people's sexual behaviour: A longitudinal analysis. *Journal of Adolescence 29*, 4, 473–494.

Williams, S.K. and Kelly, F.D. (2005) 'Relationships among involvement, attachment, and behavioral problems in adolescence: Examining father's influence.' *Journal of Early Adolescence 25*, 2, 168–196.

Willow, C. (2009) 'Putting Children and their Rights at the Heart of the Safeguarding Process.' In H. Cleaver, P. Cawson, S. Gorin and S. Walker (eds) *Safeguarding Children: A Shared Responsibility*. NSPCC Wiley series in 'Safeguarding children: the multi-professional approach'. Chichester: Wiley.

Wolock, I. and Horowitz, B. (1984) 'Child maltreatment as a social problem.' *American Journal of Orthopsychiatry 54*, 530–543.

Zellman, G.L. (1992) 'The impact of case characteristics on child abuse reporting decisions.' *Child Abuse & Neglect 16*, 57–74.

Zielinski, D.S. and Bradshaw, C.P. (2006) 'Ecological influences on the sequelae of child maltreatment: A review of the literature.' *Child Maltreatment 11*, 49–62.

Zuravin, S.J. (1999) 'Child Neglect: A Review of Definitions and Measurement Research.' In H. Dubowitz (ed.) *Neglected Children: Research, Practice and Policy* (pp.24–46). Thousand Oaks, CA: Sage Publications.

Subject Index

Author Index